AMY KIM KIBUISHI

THE REMA CHRONICLES

BOOK ONE

REALM OF THE BLUE MIST

graphix

AN IMPRINT OF

■SCHOLASTIC

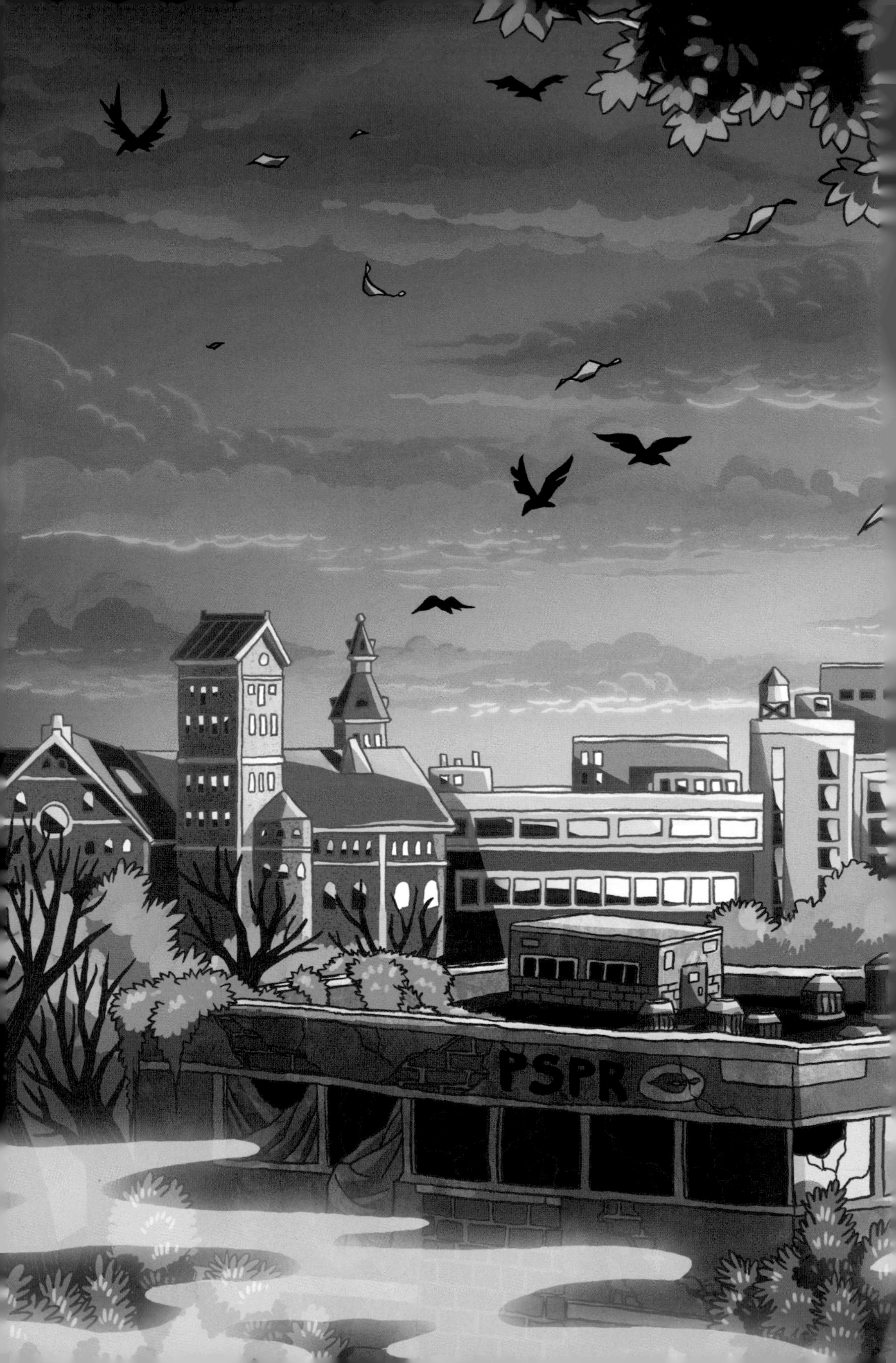
PSPR

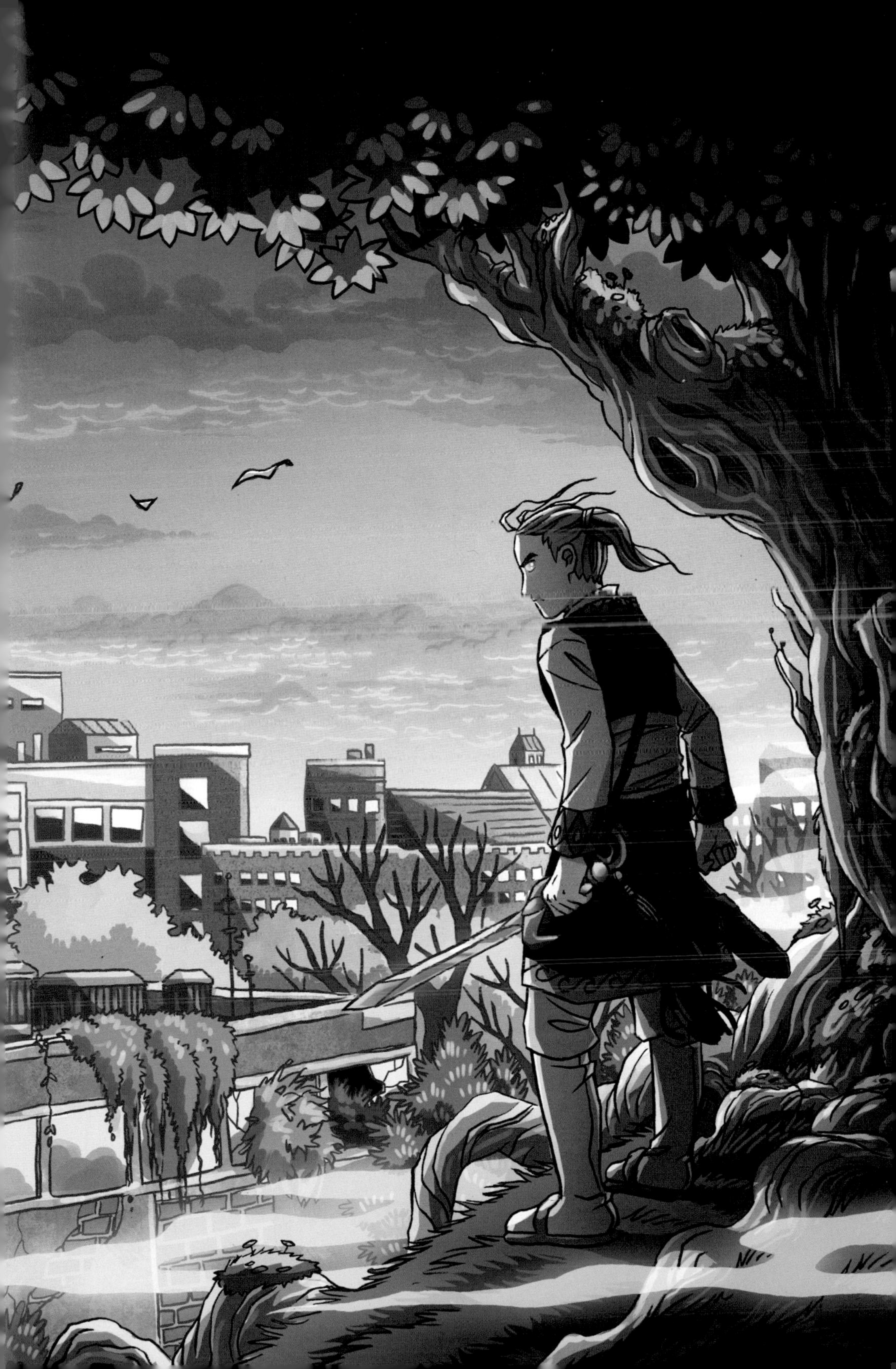

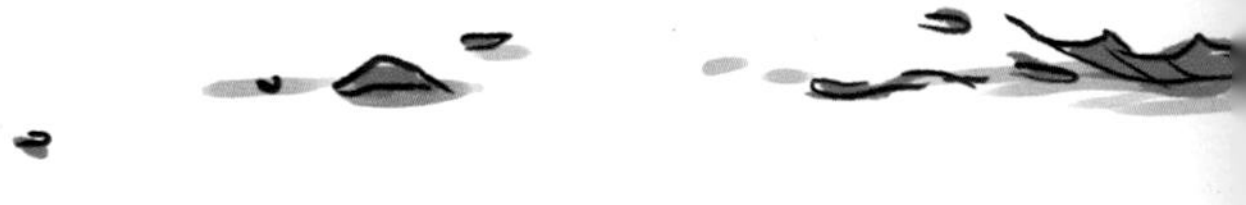

PART I

HAUNTED

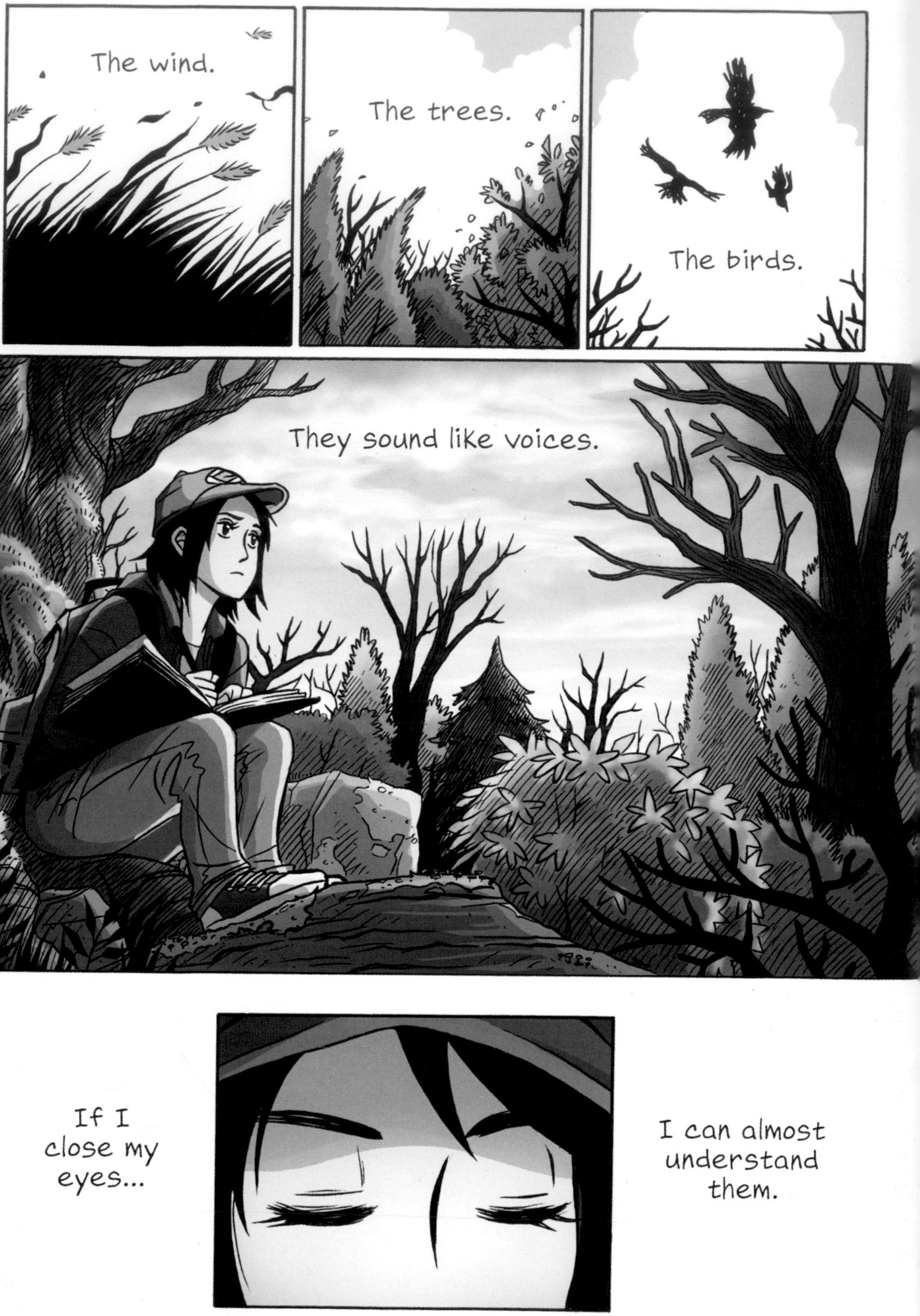
The wind.
The trees.
The birds.
They sound like voices.
If I close my eyes...
I can almost understand them.

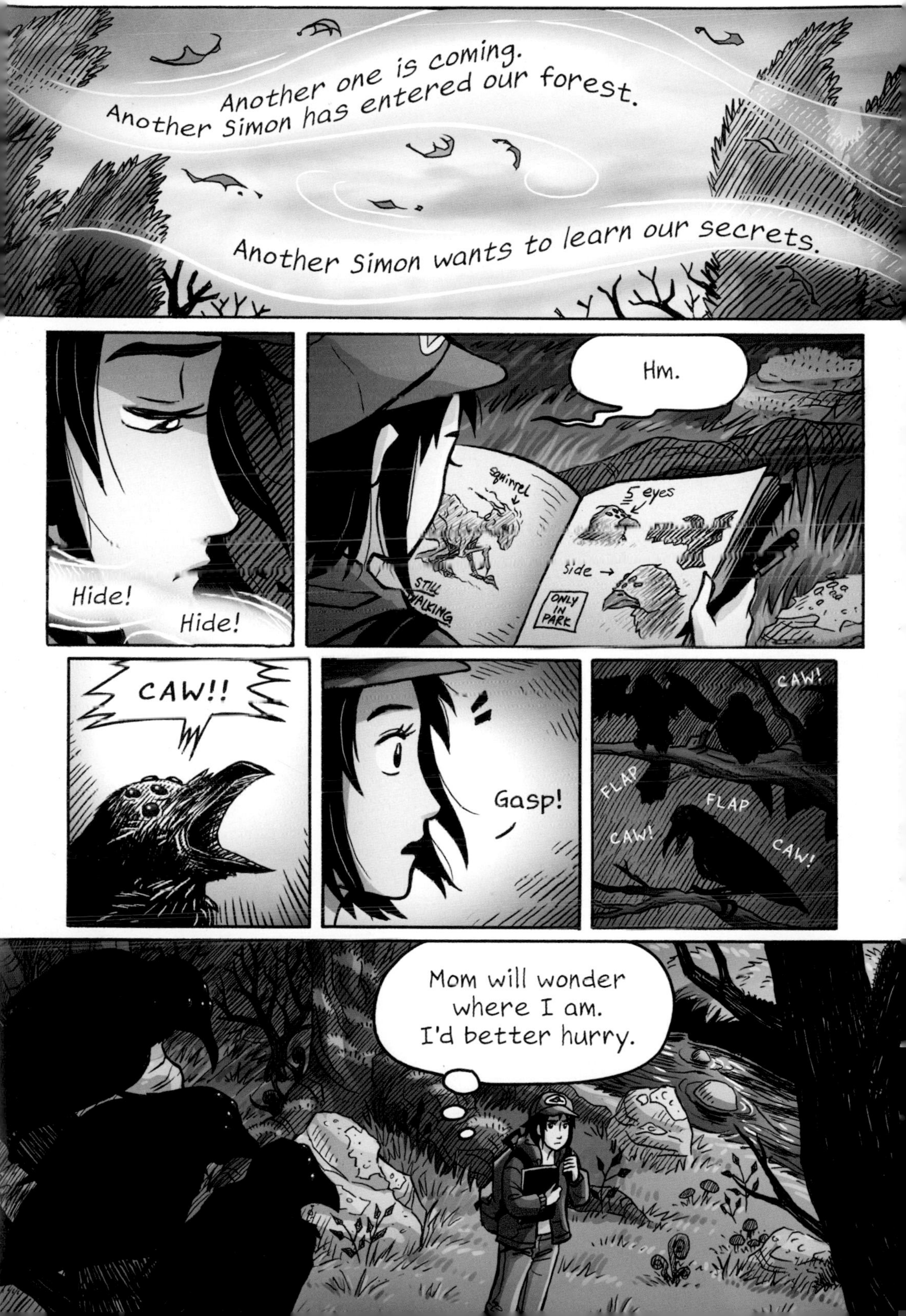
Another one is coming.
Another Simon has entered our forest.
Another Simon wants to learn our secrets.
Hide!
Hide!
Hm.
squirrel
STILL WALKING
5 eyes
side →
ONLY IN PARK
CAW!!
Gasp!
CAW!
FLAP
FLAP
CAW!
CAW!
Mom will wonder where I am. I'd better hurry.

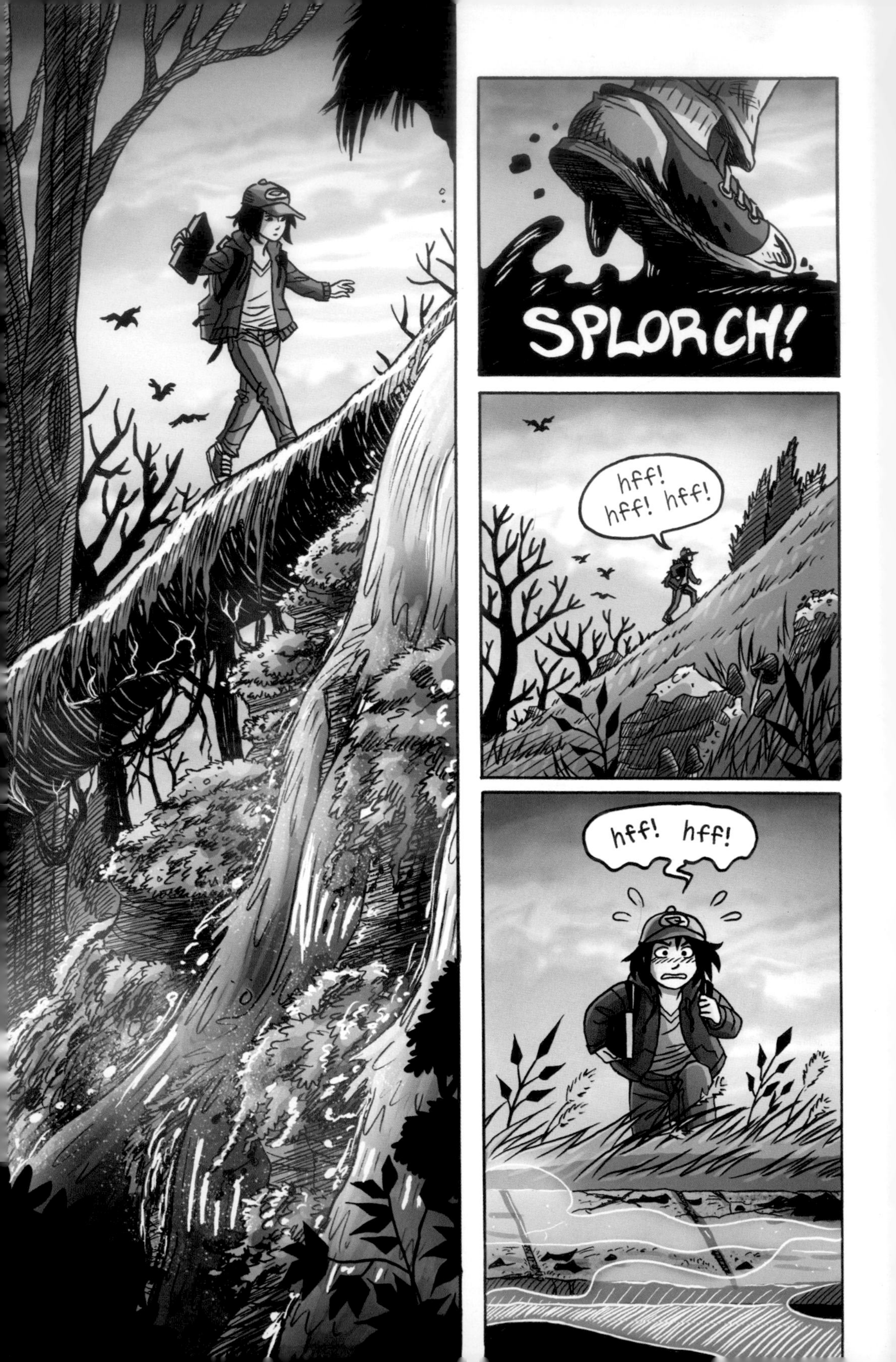
SPLORCH!
hff! hff! hff!
hff! hff!

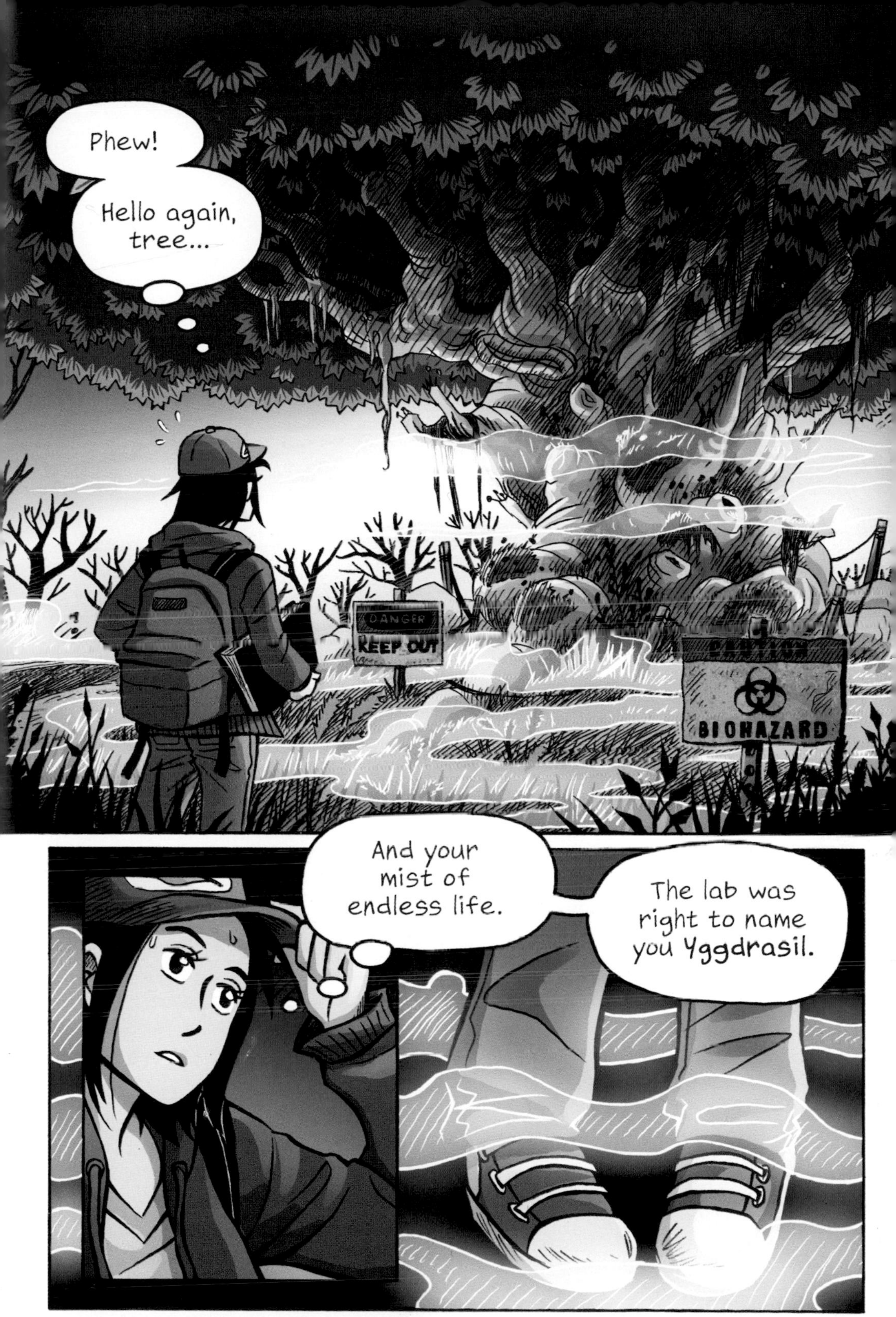

Phew!
Hello again, tree...
DANGER
KEEP OUT
BIOHAZARD
And your mist of endless life.
The lab was right to name you Yggdrasil.

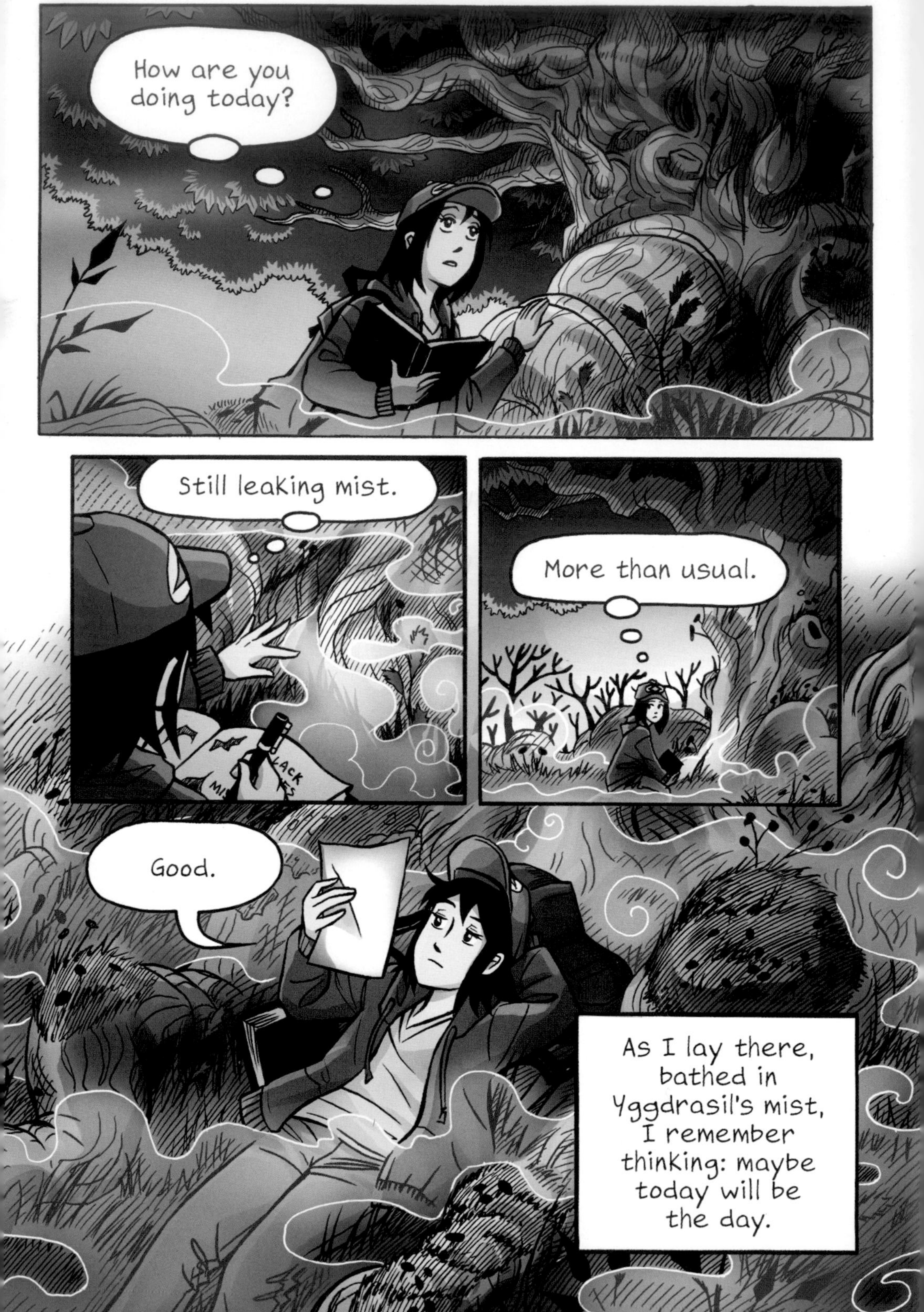
How are you doing today?
Still leaking mist.
More than usual.
Good.
As I lay there, bathed in Yggdrasil's mist, I remember thinking: maybe today will be the day.

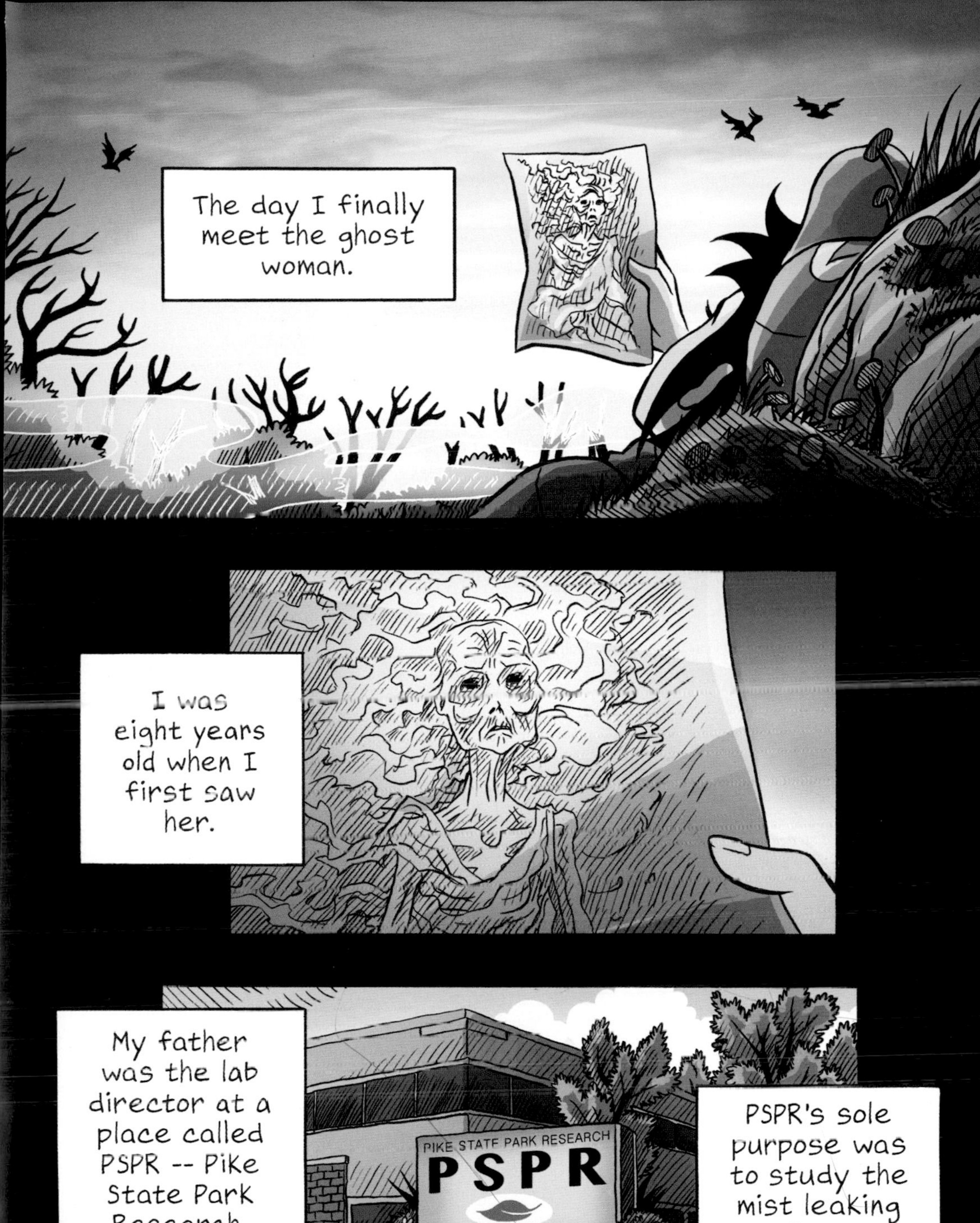
The day I finally meet the ghost woman.
I was eight years old when I first saw her.
My father was the lab director at a place called PSPR -- Pike State Park Research.
PIKE STATE PARK RESEARCH
PSPR
LABORATORIES
PSPR's sole purpose was to study the mist leaking from Yggdrasil.

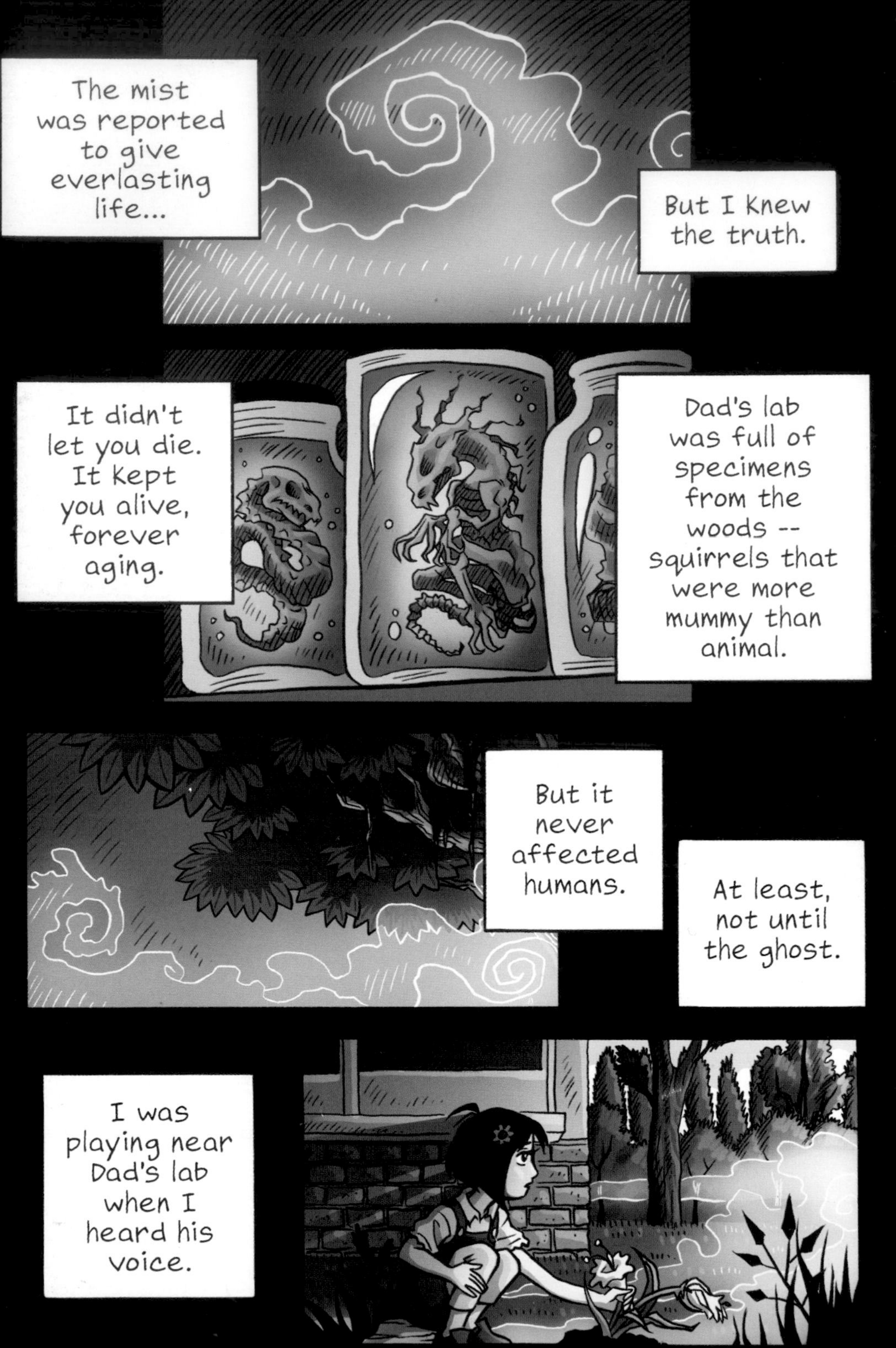

The mist was reported to give everlasting life...
But I knew the truth.
It didn't let you die. It kept you alive, forever aging.
Dad's lab was full of specimens from the woods -- squirrels that were more mummy than animal.
But it never affected humans.
At least, not until the ghost.
I was playing near Dad's lab when I heard his voice.

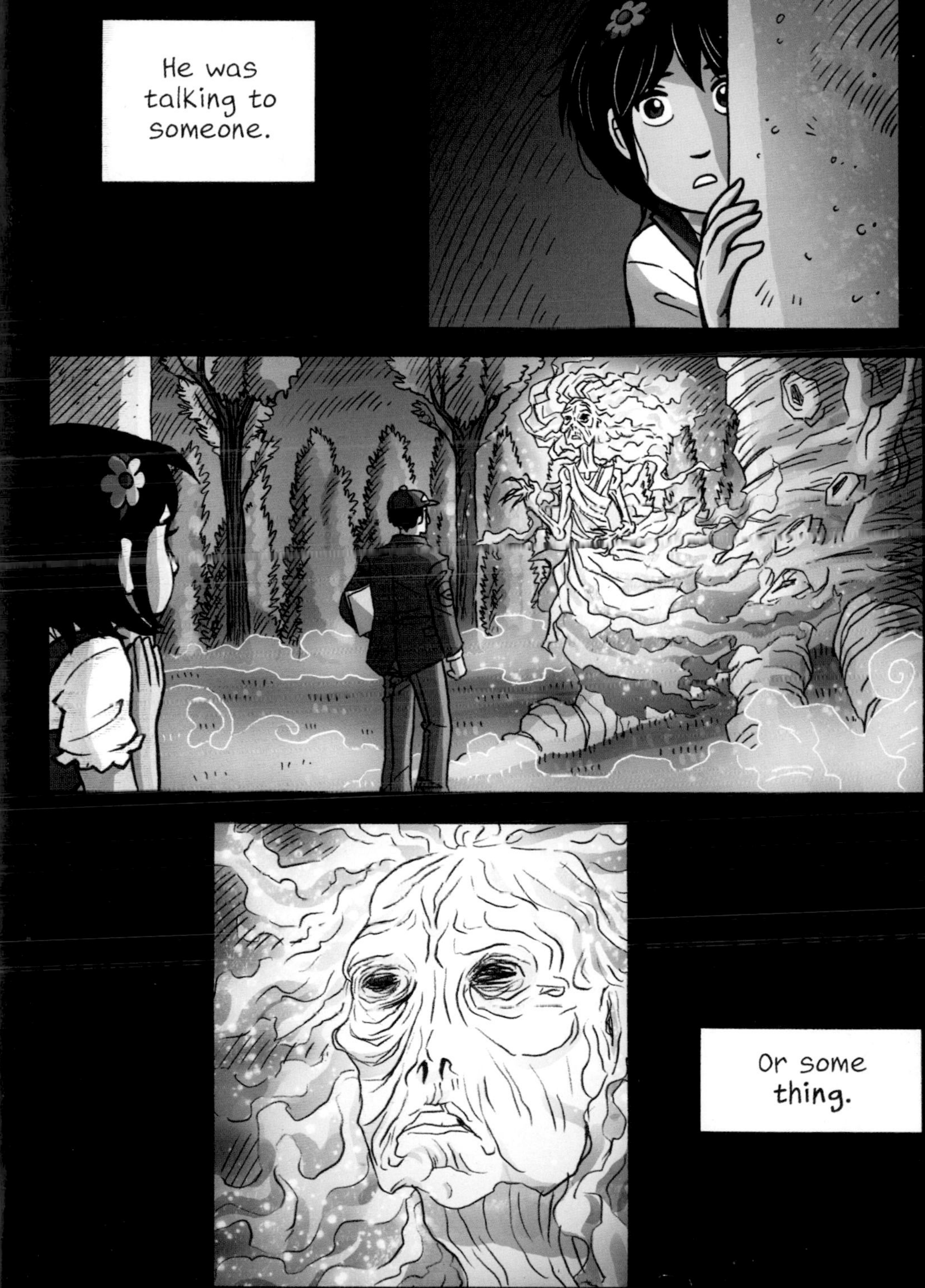
He was talking to someone.
Or some thing.

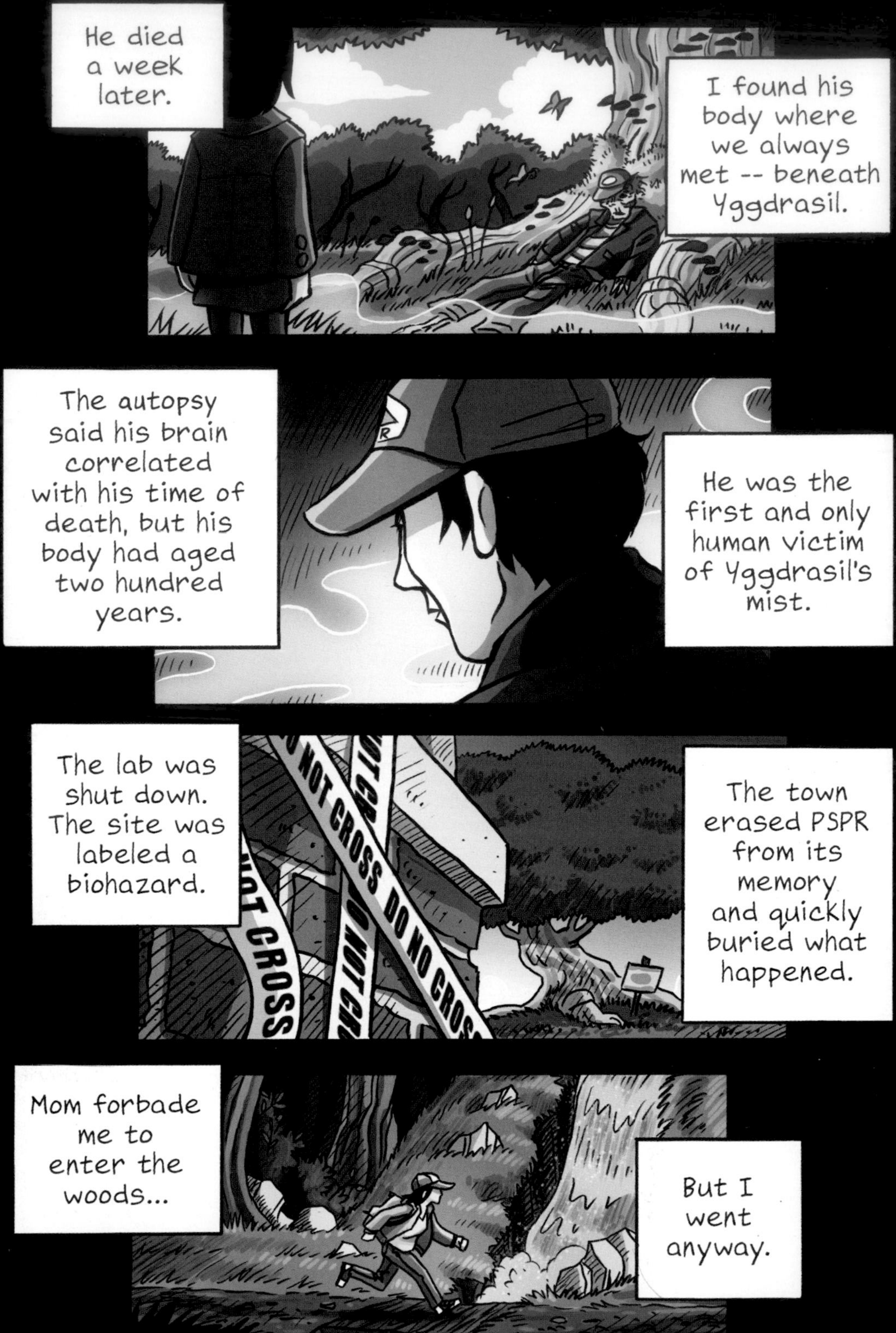
He died a week later.
I found his body where we always met -- beneath Yggdrasil.
The autopsy said his brain correlated with his time of death, but his body had aged two hundred years.
He was the first and only human victim of Yggdrasil's mist.
The lab was shut down. The site was labeled a biohazard.
DO NOT CROSS
The town erased PSPR from its memory and quickly buried what happened.
Mom forbade me to enter the woods...
But I went anyway.

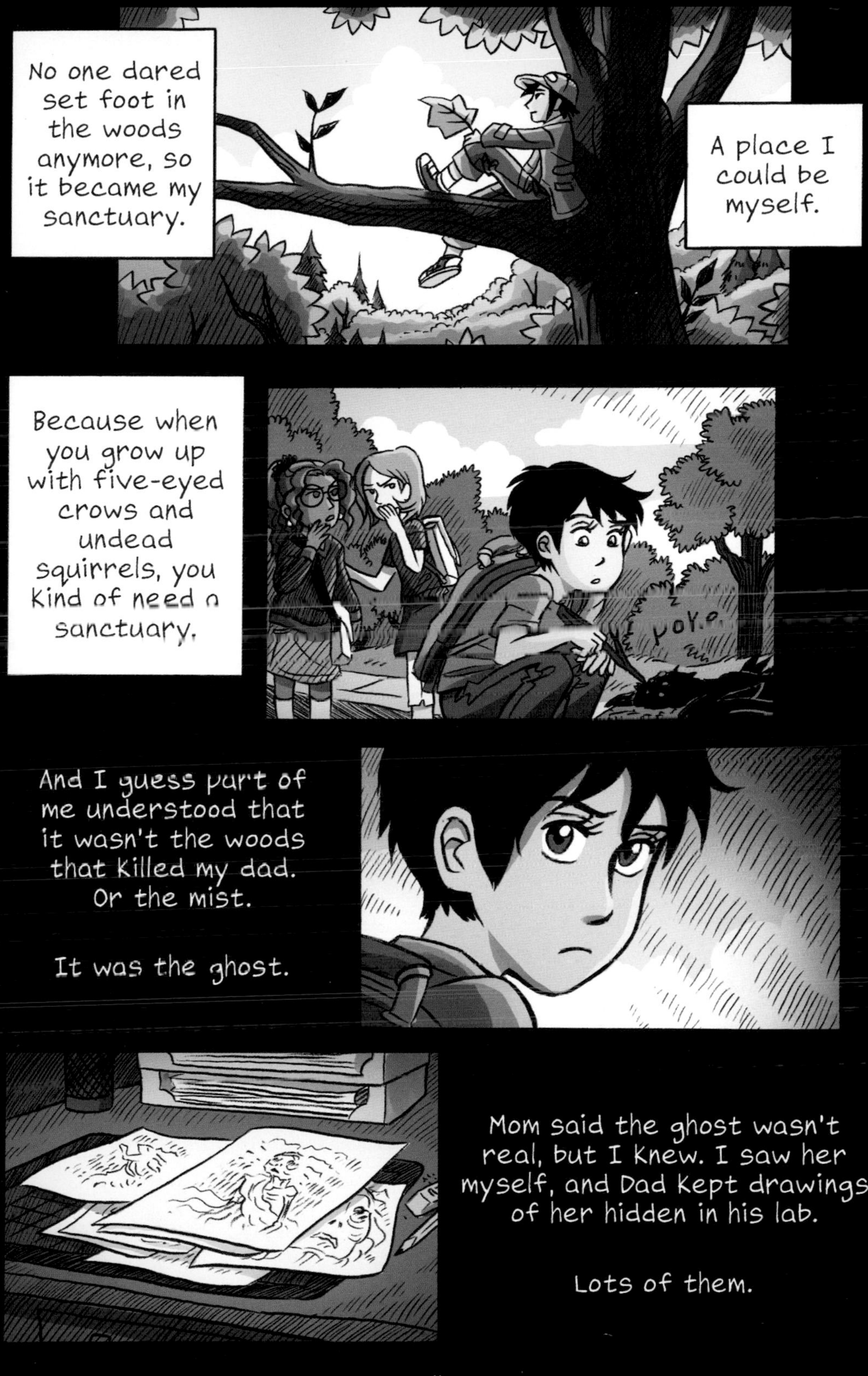
No one dared set foot in the woods anymore, so it became my sanctuary.
A place I could be myself.
Because when you grow up with five-eyed crows and undead squirrels, you kind of need a sanctuary.
And I guess part of me understood that it wasn't the woods that killed my dad. Or the mist.
It was the ghost.
Mom said the ghost wasn't real, but I knew. I saw her myself, and Dad kept drawings of her hidden in his lab.
Lots of them.

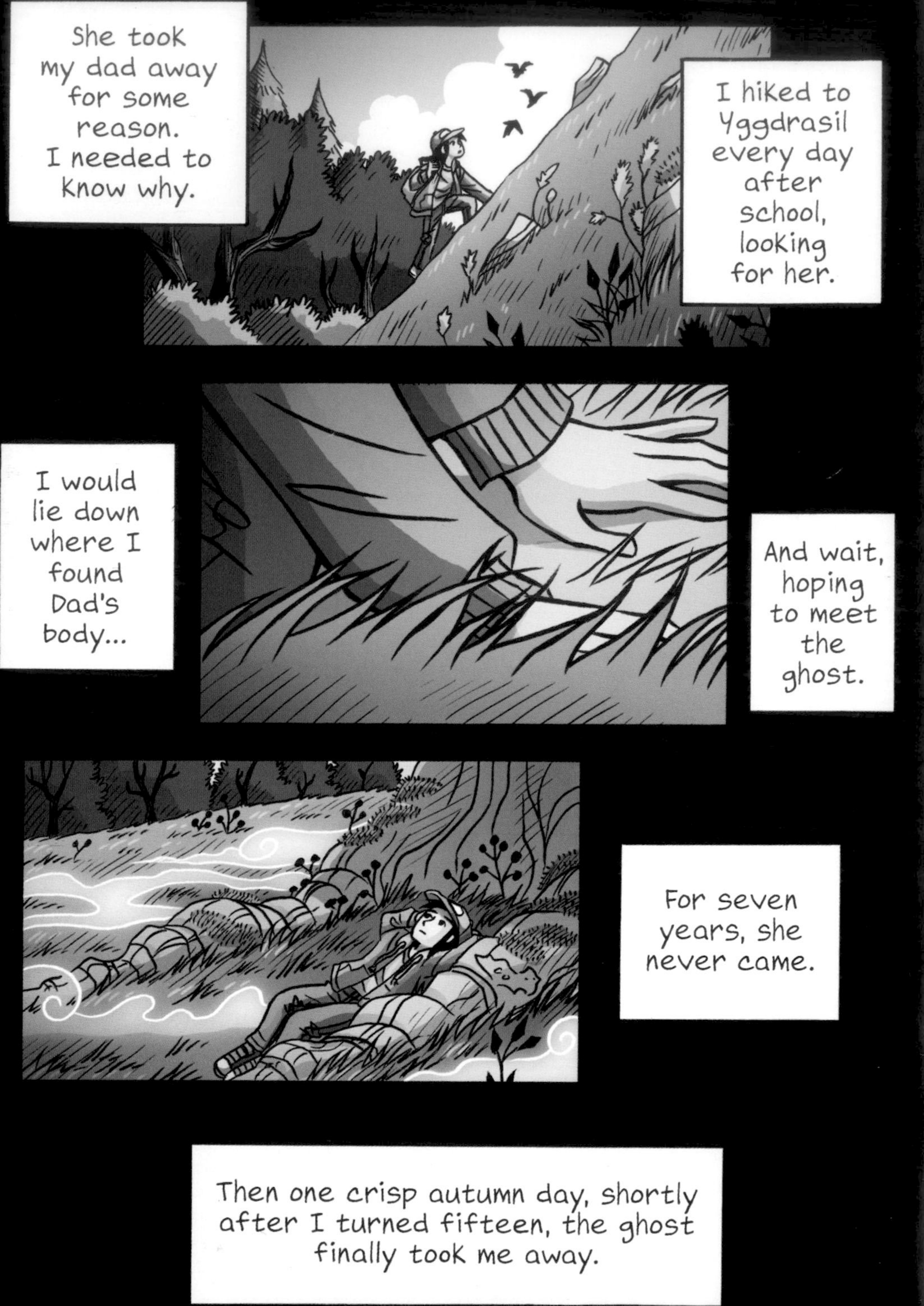
She took my dad away for some reason. I needed to know why.
I hiked to Yggdrasil every day after school, looking for her.
I would lie down where I found Dad's body...
And wait, hoping to meet the ghost.
For seven years, she never came.
Then one crisp autumn day, shortly after I turned fifteen, the ghost finally took me away.

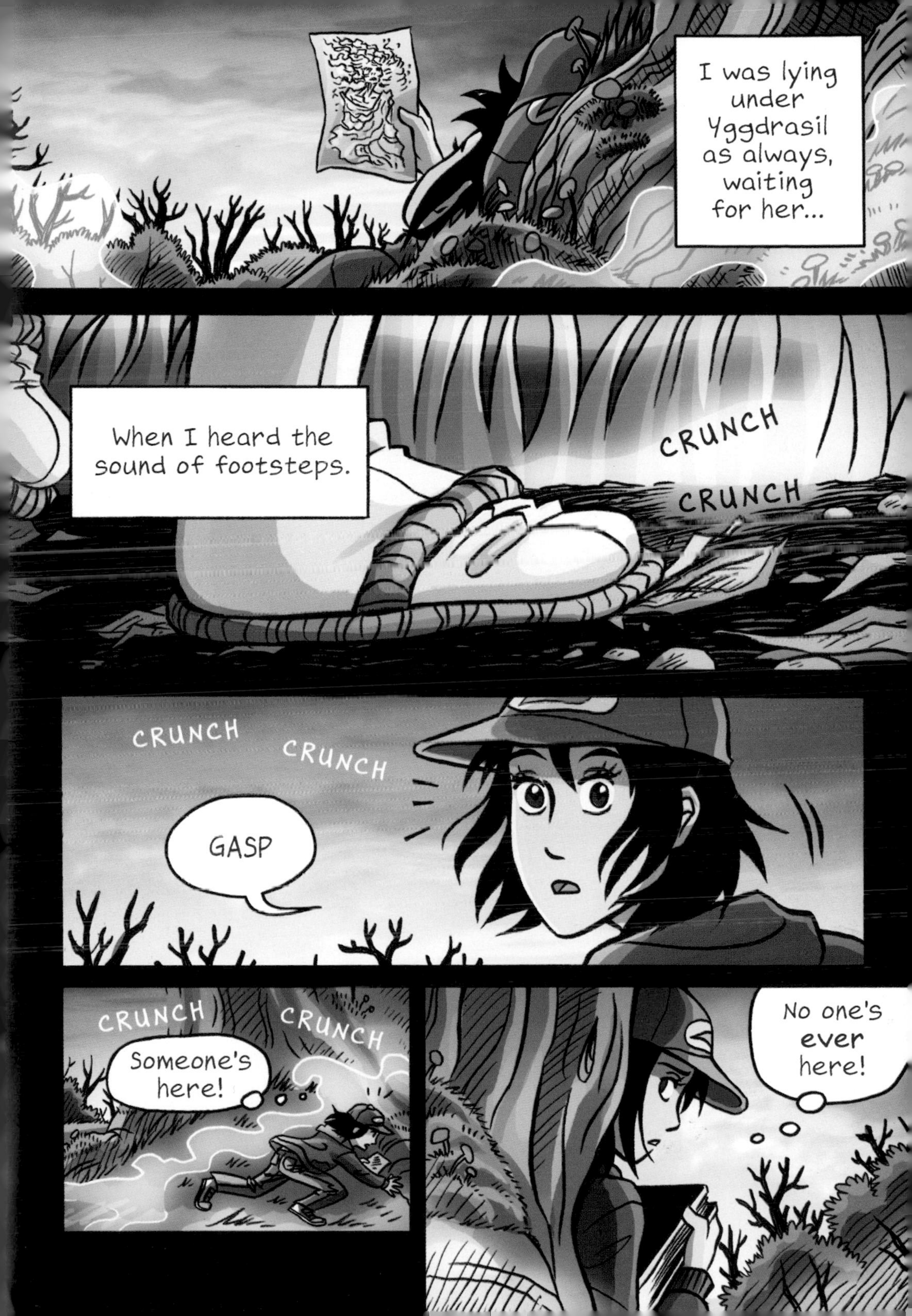
I was lying under Yggdrasil as always, waiting for her...
When I heard the sound of footsteps.
CRUNCH
CRUNCH
CRUNCH
CRUNCH
GASP
CRUNCH
CRUNCH
Someone's here!
No one's **ever** here!

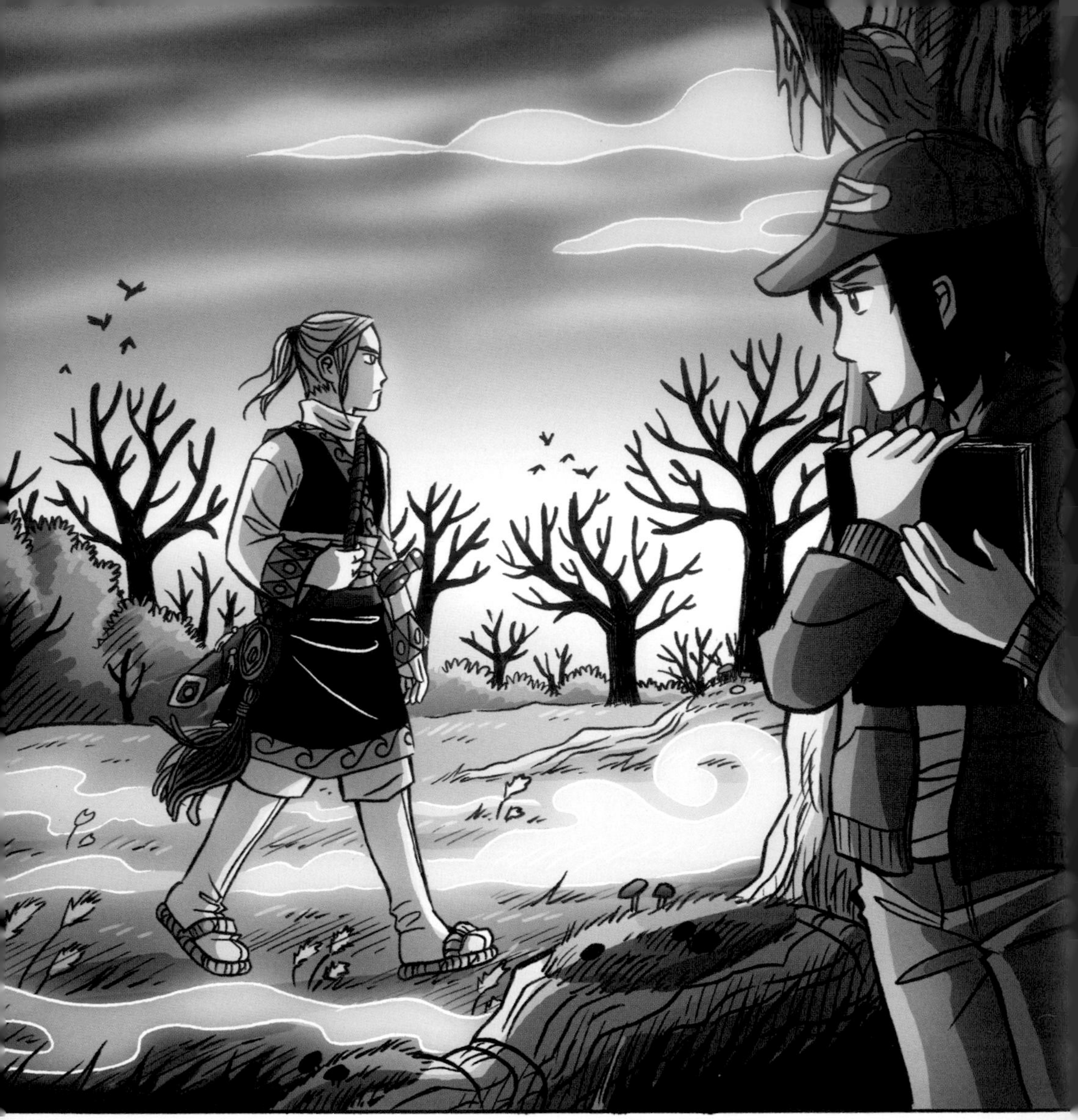

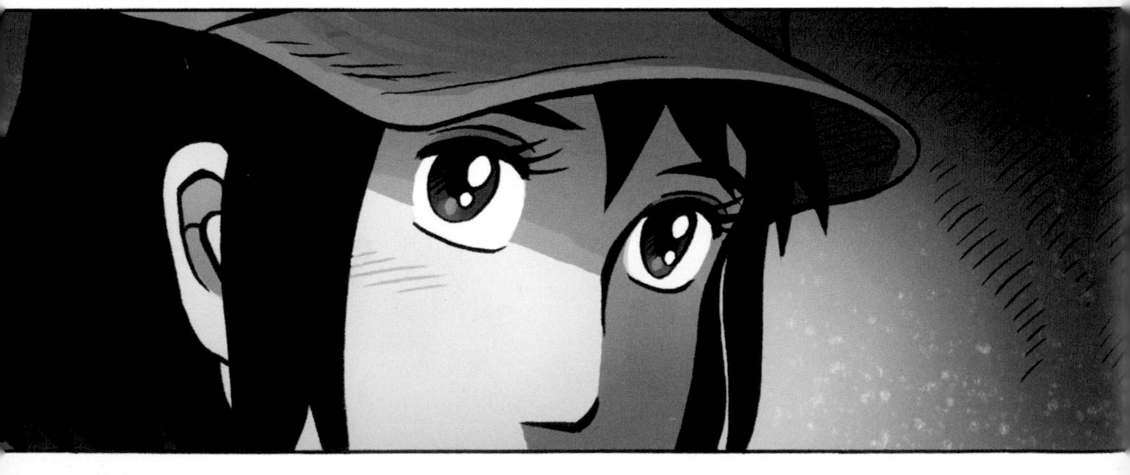

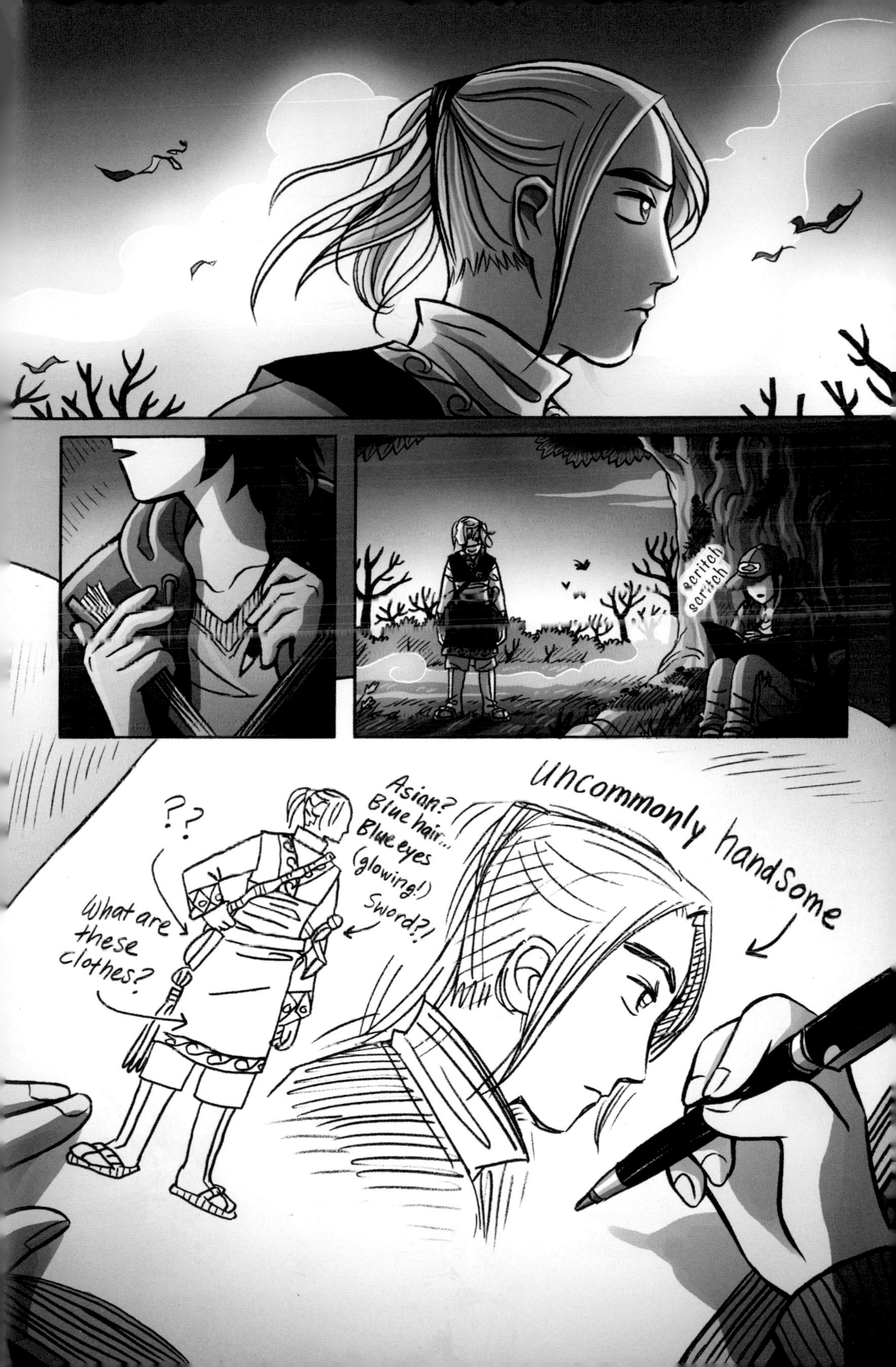
scritch
scritch
Asian?
Blue hair...
Blue eyes
(glowing!)
Sword?!
??
What are these clothes?
Uncommonly handsome

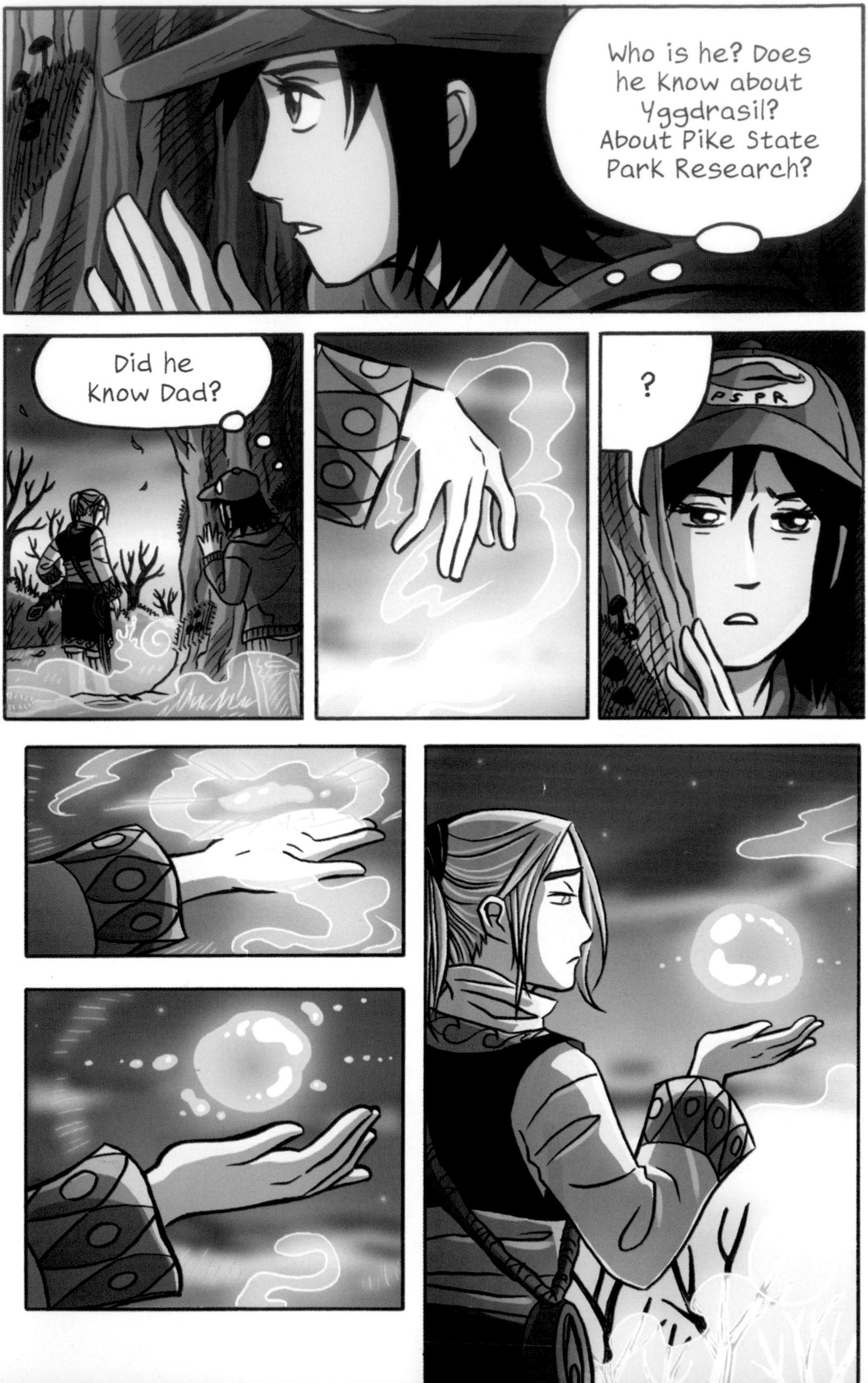
Who is he? Does he know about Yggdrasil? About Pike State Park Research?
Did he know Dad?
?
PSPR

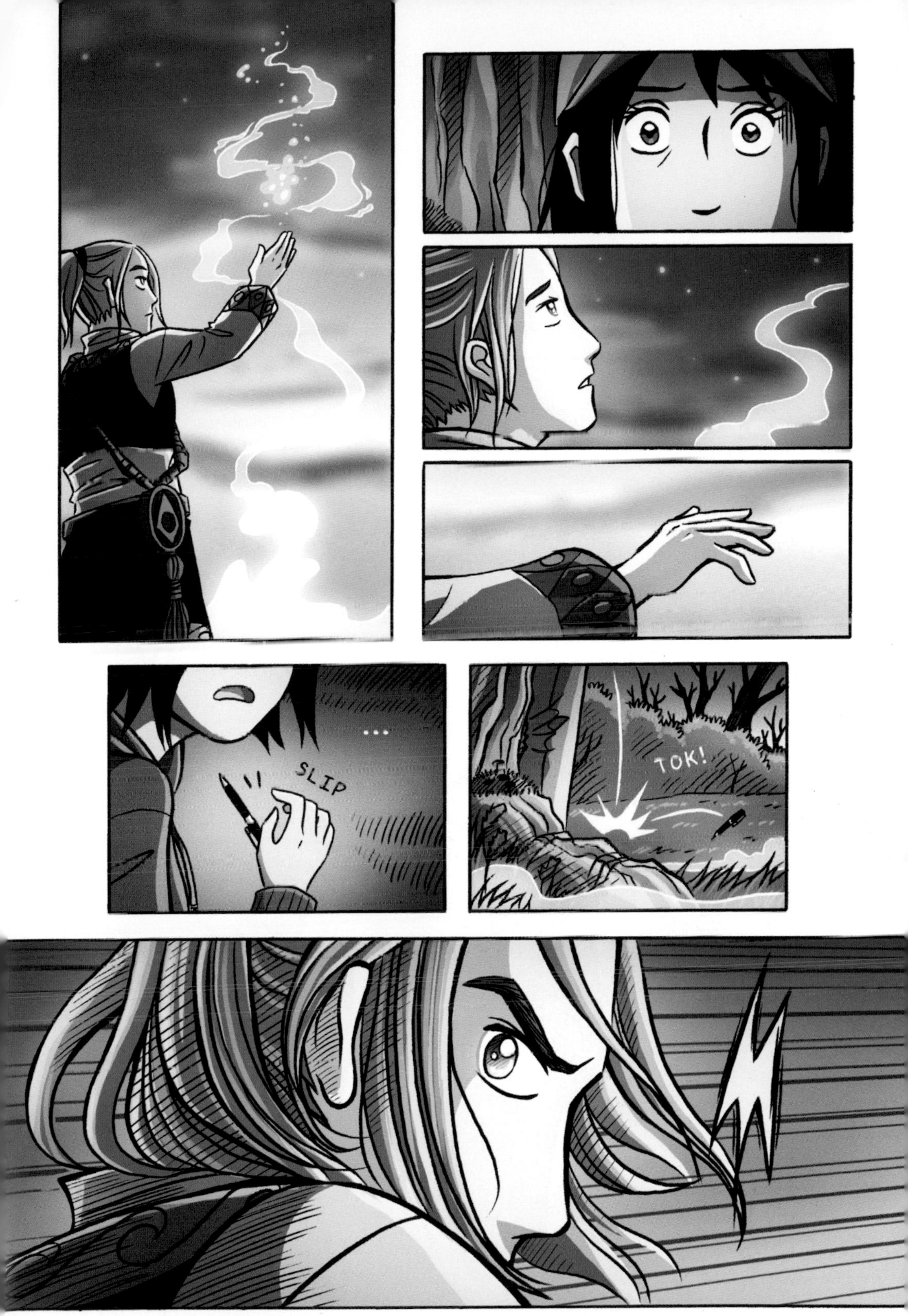
...
SLIP
TOK!

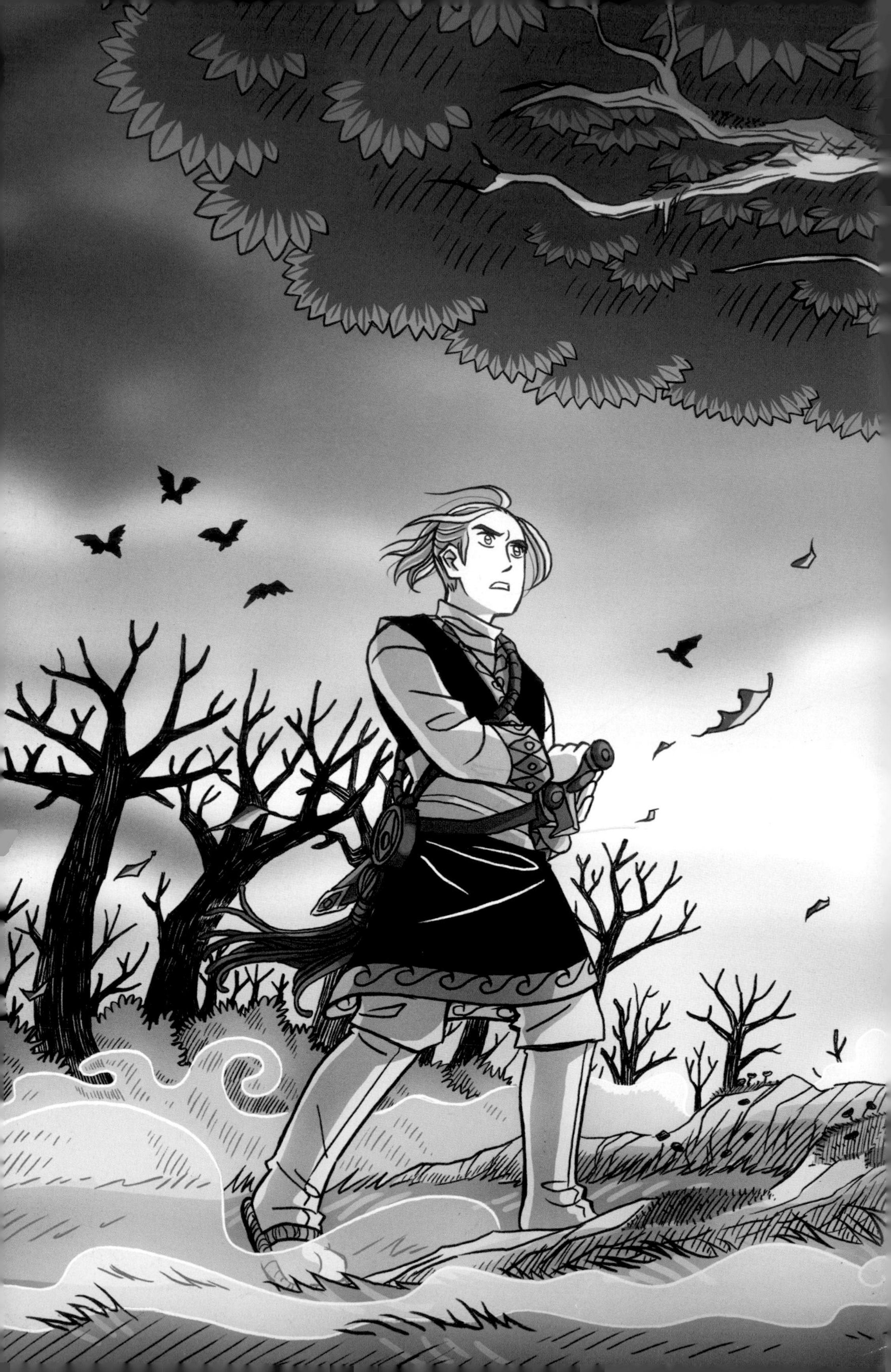

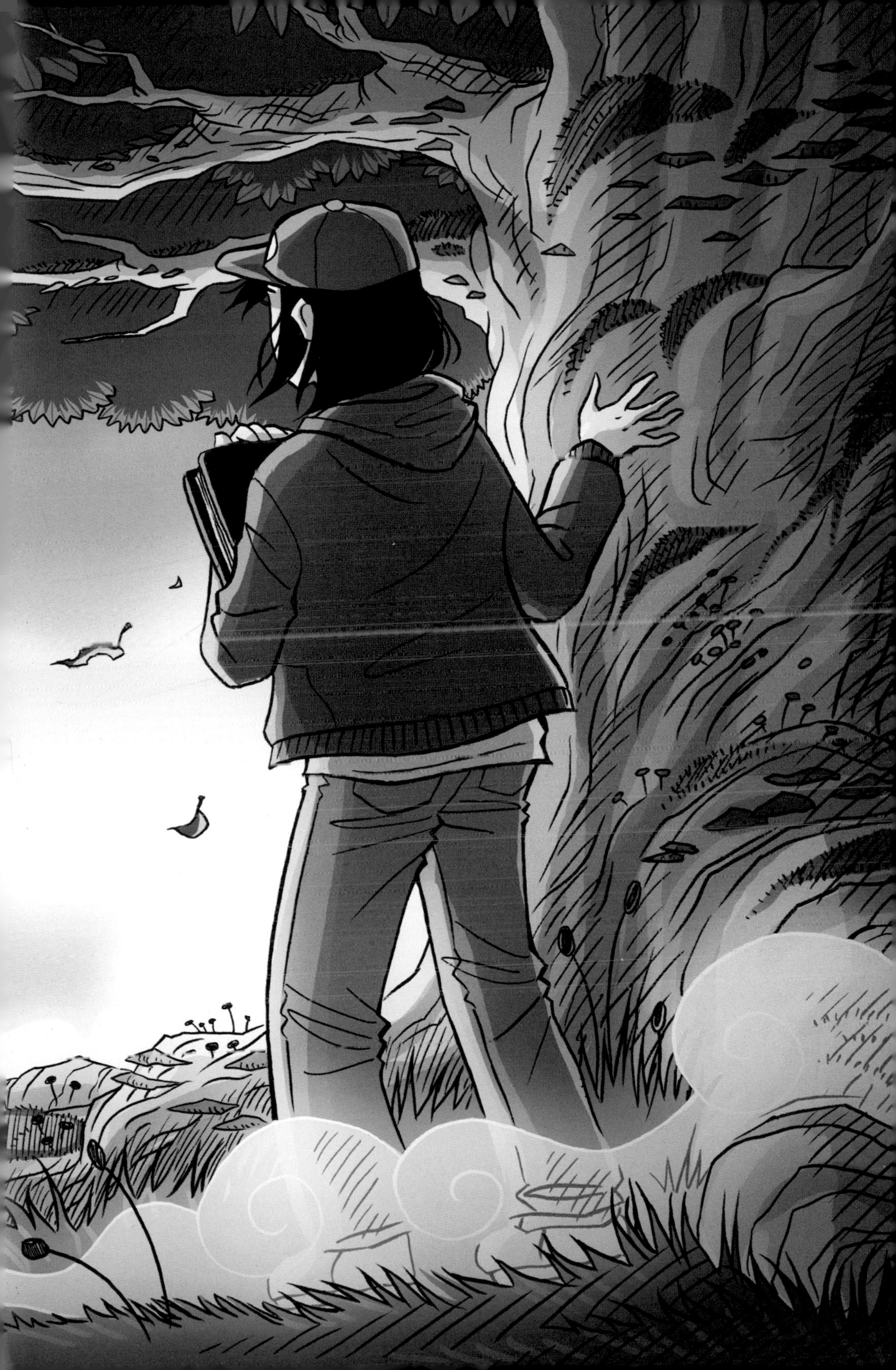

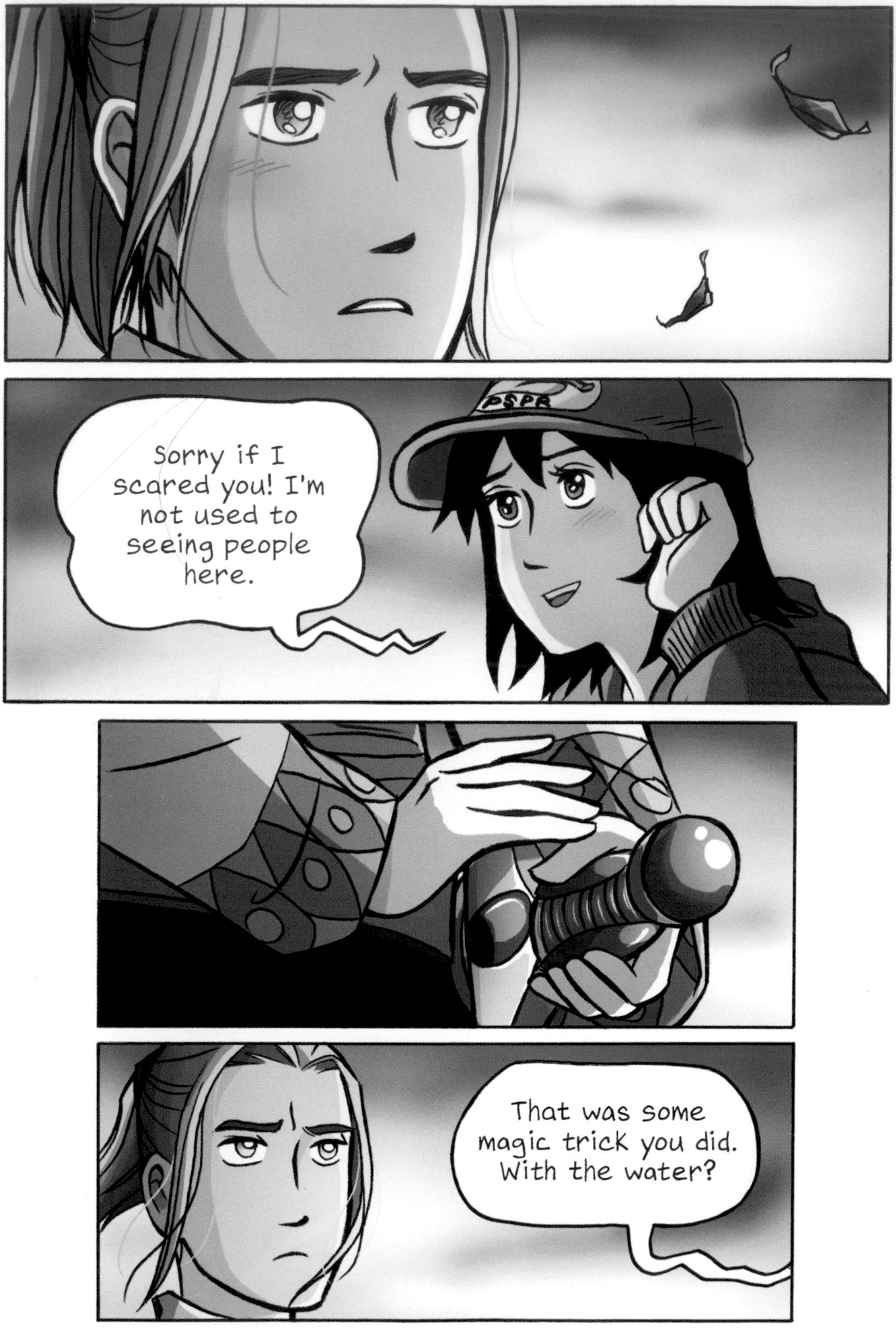
PSPR
Sorry if I scared you! I'm not used to seeing people here.
That was some magic trick you did. With the water?

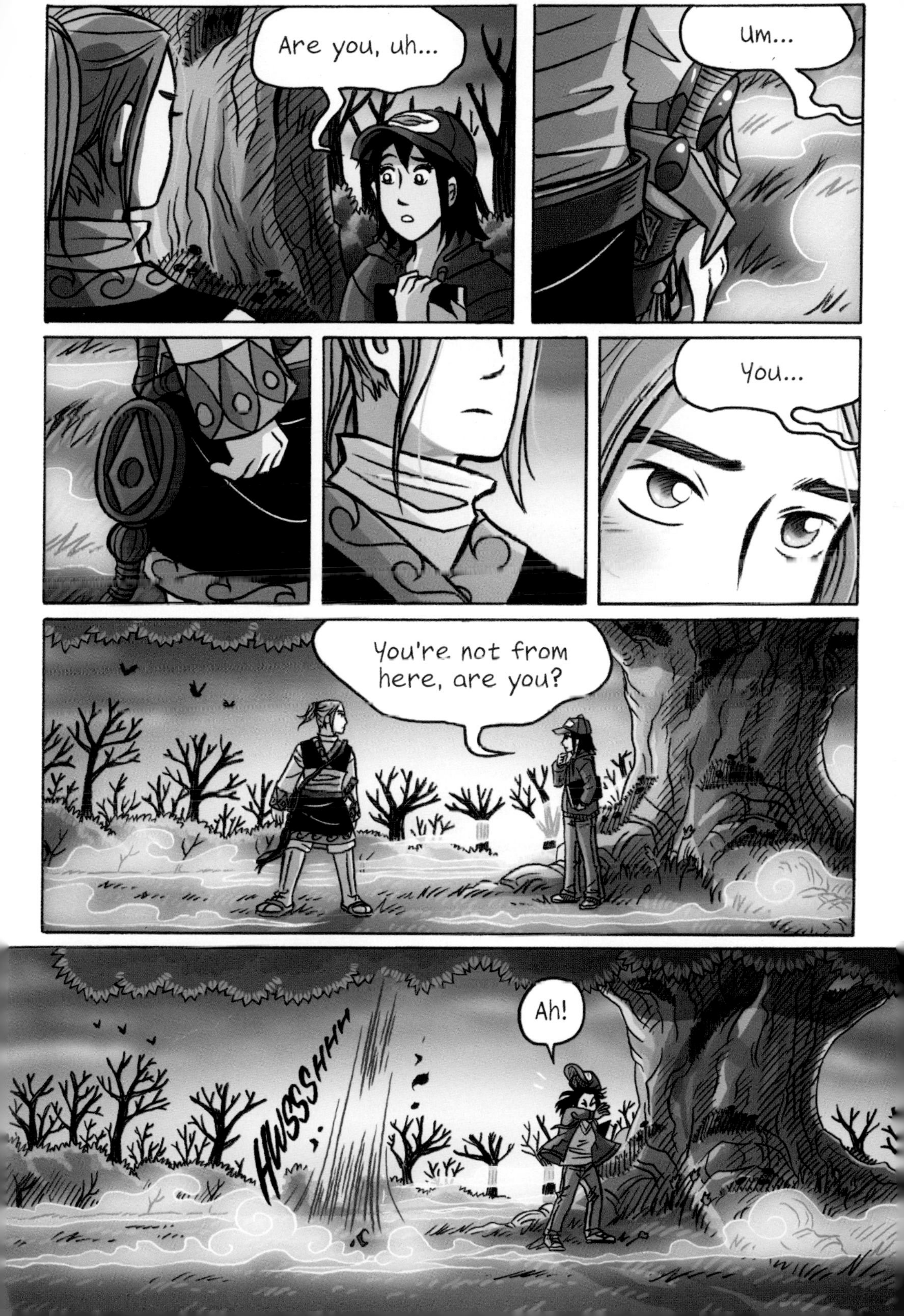
Are you, uh...
Um...
You...
You're not from here, are you?
HUSSSHHH
Ah!

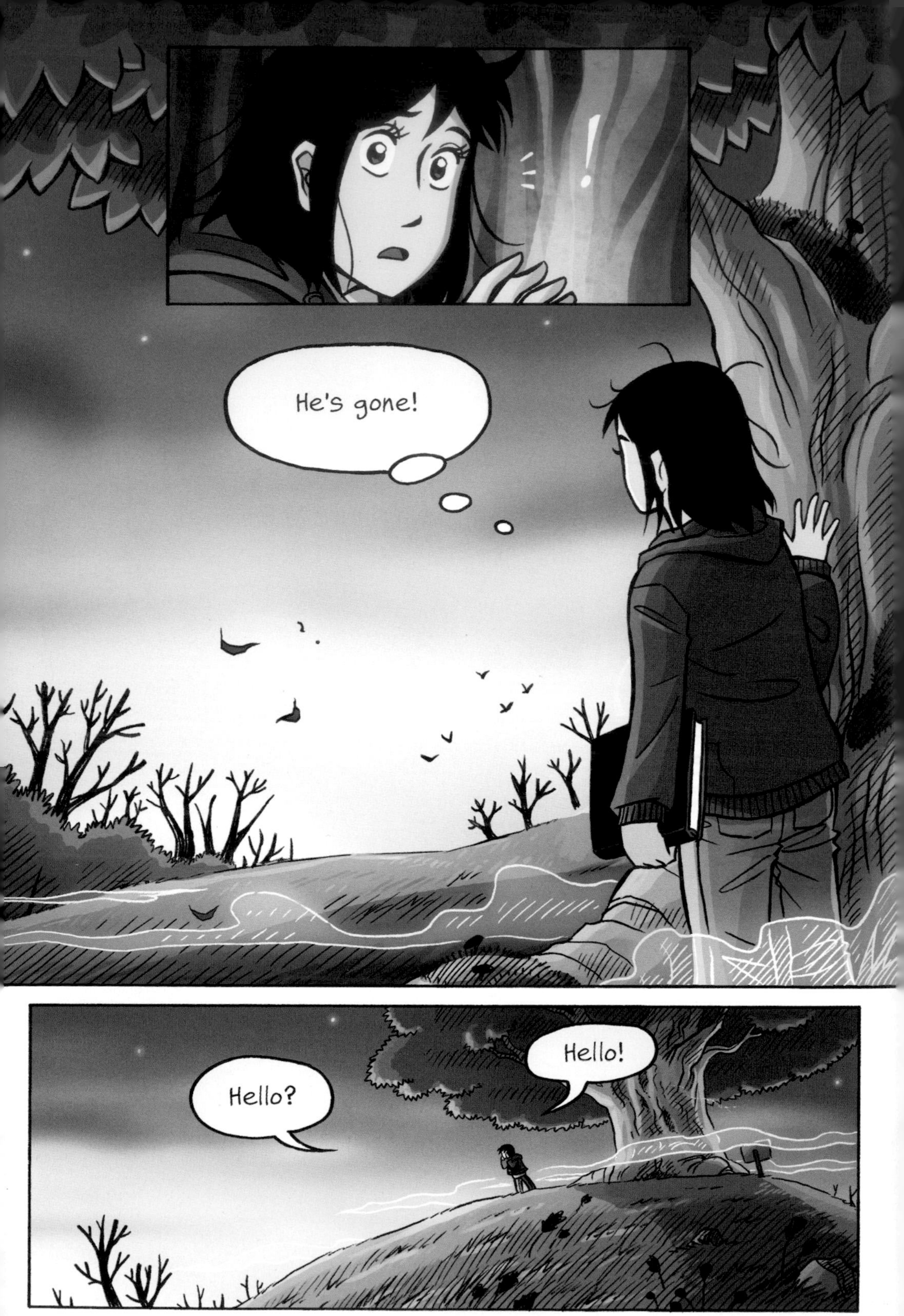
!
He's gone!
Hello?
Hello!

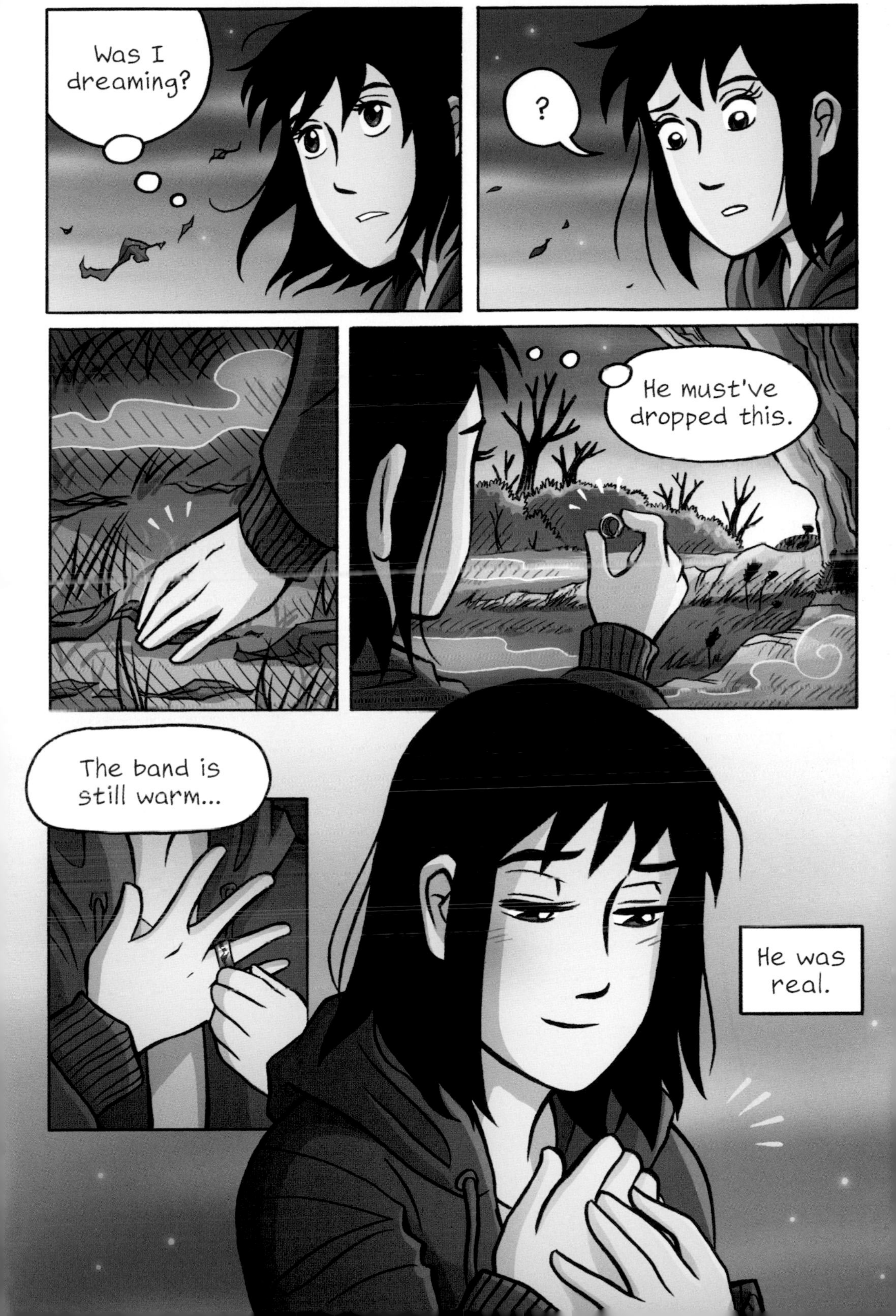
Was I dreaming?
?
He must've dropped this.
The band is still warm...
He was real.

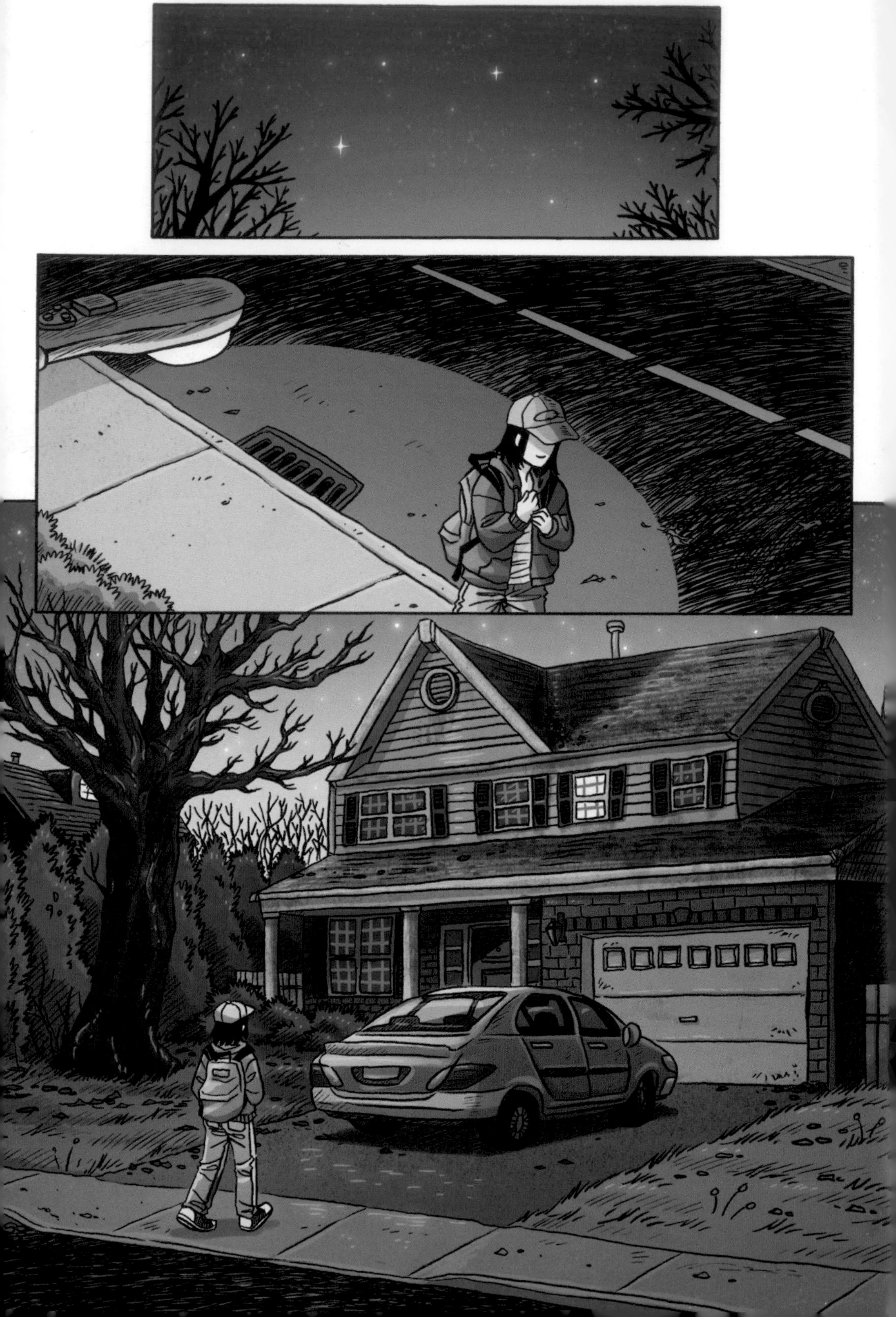

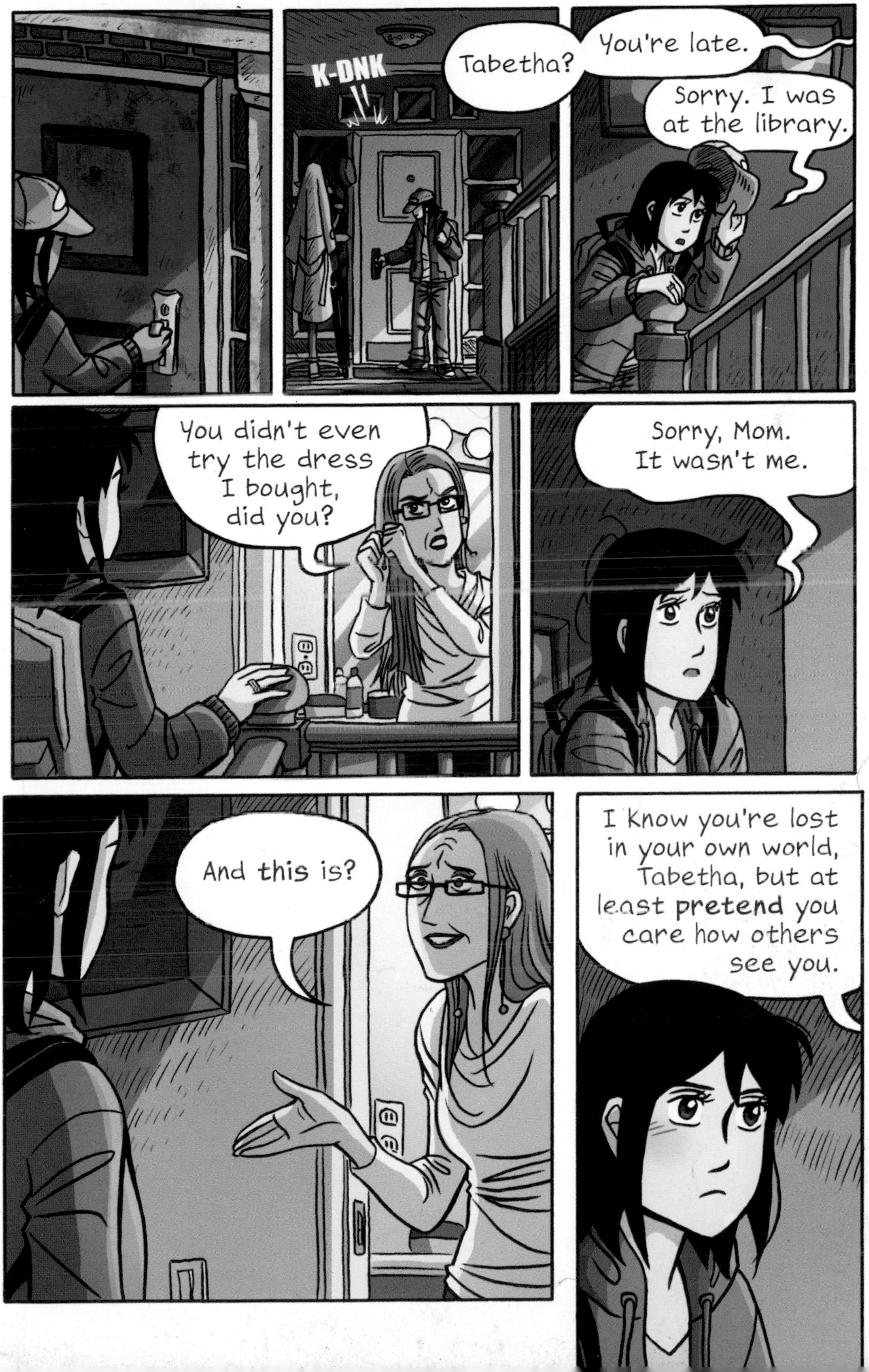
K-DNK
Tabetha?
You're late.
Sorry. I was at the library.
You didn't even try the dress I bought, did you?
Sorry, Mom. It wasn't me.
And this is?
I know you're lost in your own world, Tabetha, but at least pretend you care how others see you.

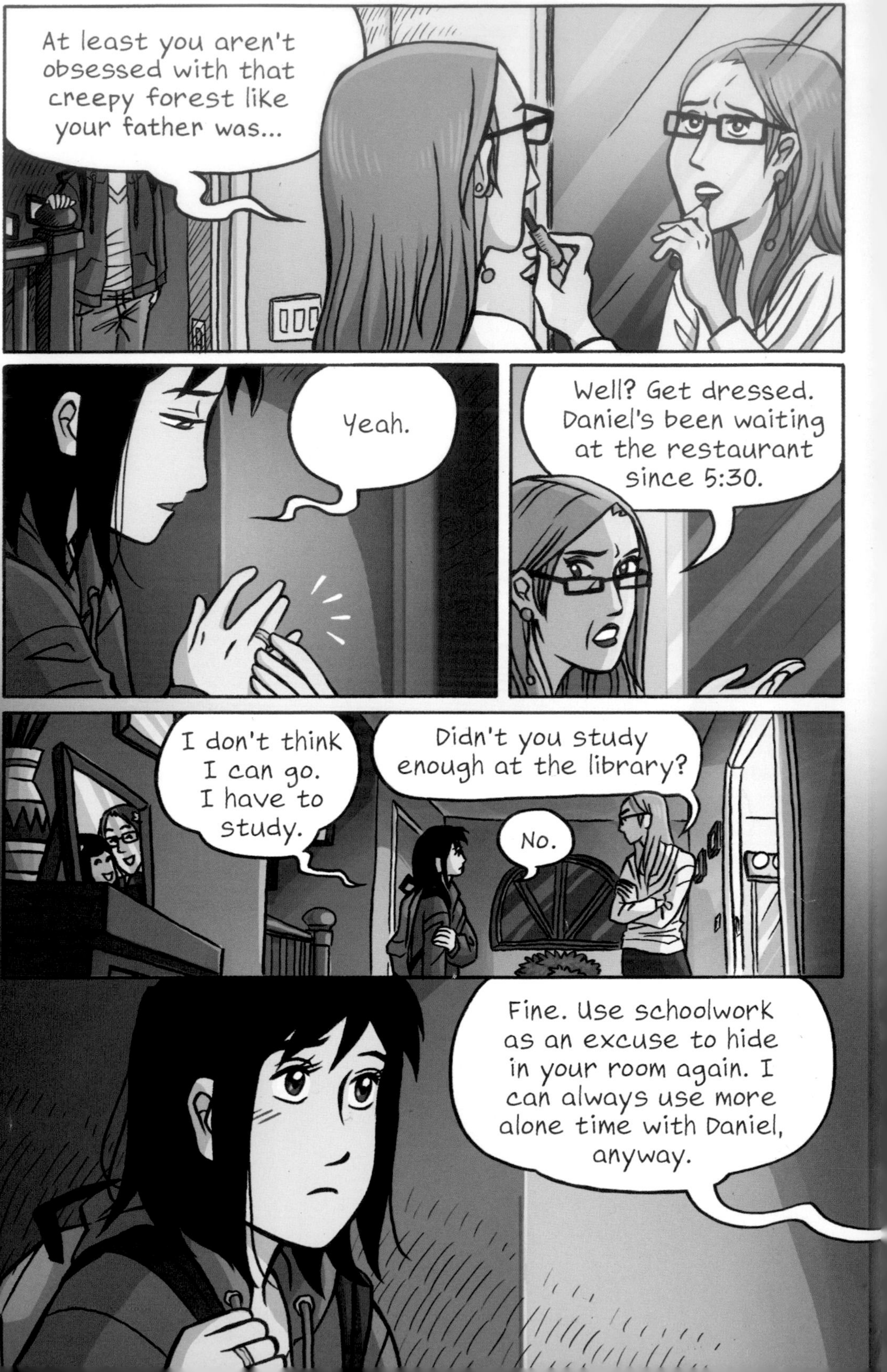
At least you aren't obsessed with that creepy forest like your father was...
Yeah.
Well? Get dressed. Daniel's been waiting at the restaurant since 5:30.
I don't think I can go. I have to study.
Didn't you study enough at the library?
No.
Fine. Use schoolwork as an excuse to hide in your room again. I can always use more alone time with Daniel, anyway.

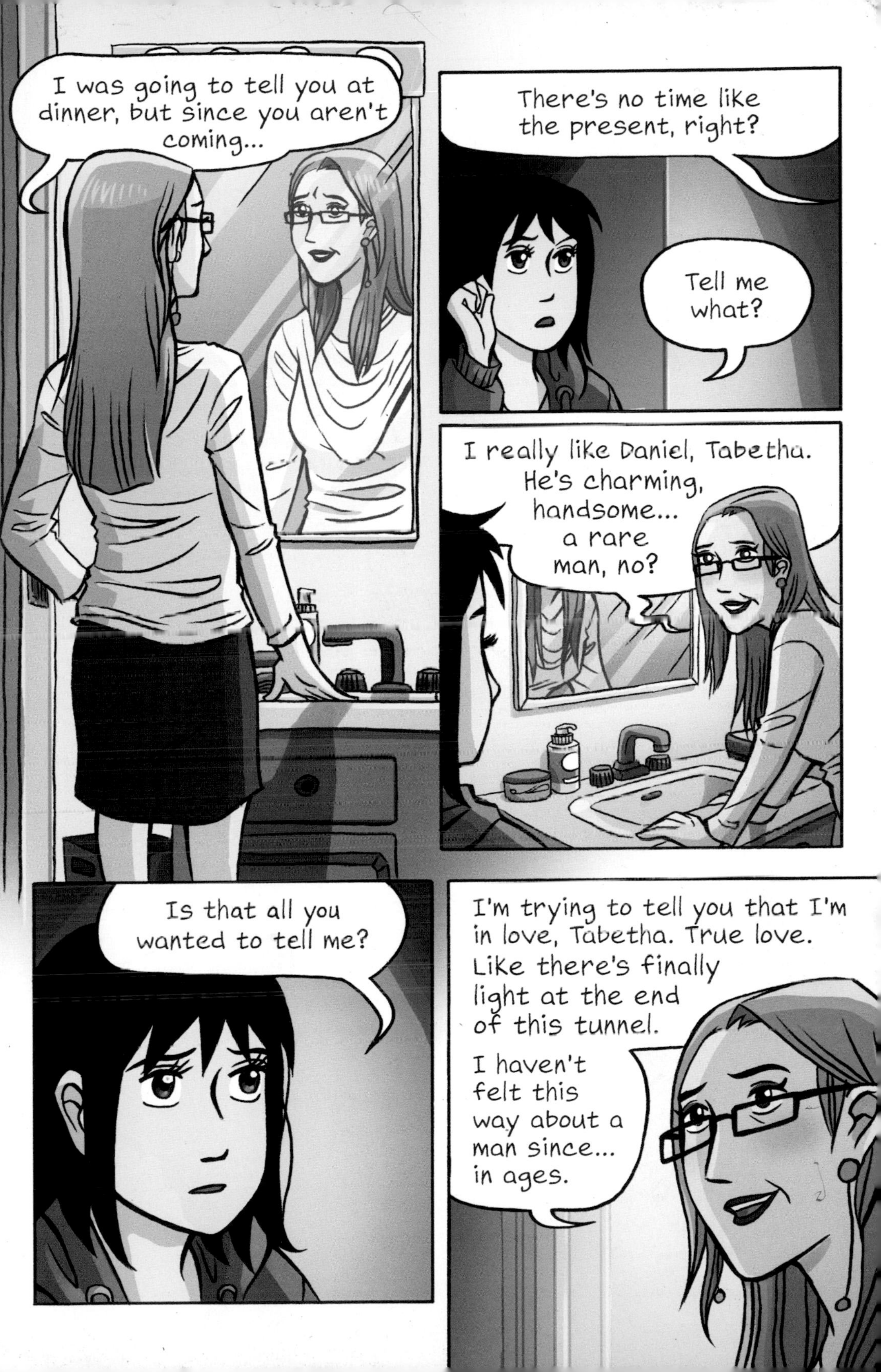

I was going to tell you at dinner, but since you aren't coming...
There's no time like the present, right?
Tell me what?
I really like Daniel, Tabetha. He's charming, handsome... a rare man, no?
Is that all you wanted to tell me?
I'm trying to tell you that I'm in love, Tabetha. True love. Like there's finally light at the end of this tunnel.
I haven't felt this way about a man since... in ages.

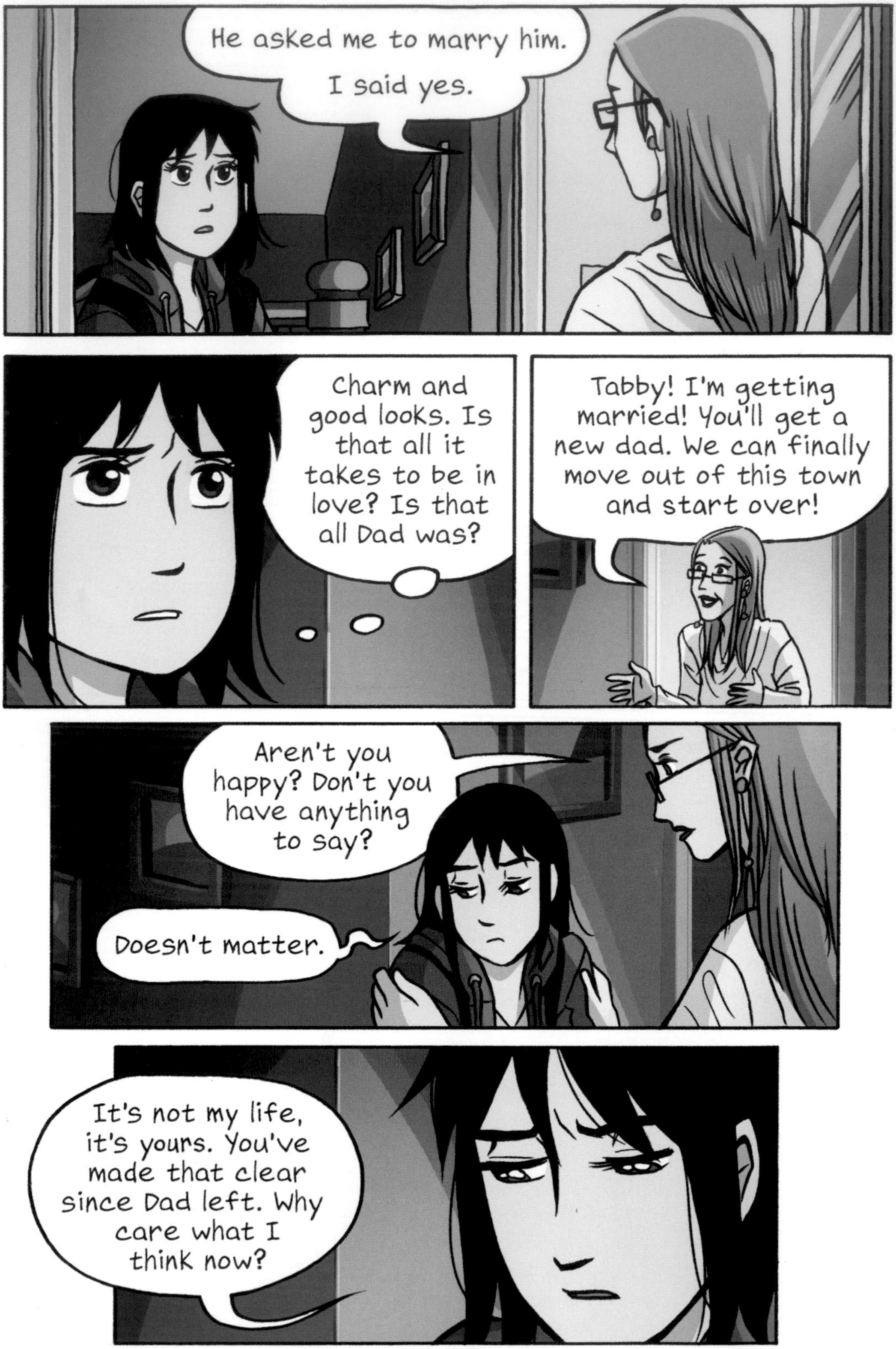
He asked me to marry him.
I said yes.
Charm and good looks. Is that all it takes to be in love? Is that all Dad was?
Tabby! I'm getting married! You'll get a new dad. We can finally move out of this town and start over!
Aren't you happy? Don't you have anything to say?
Doesn't matter.
It's not my life, it's yours. You've made that clear since Dad left. Why care what I think now?

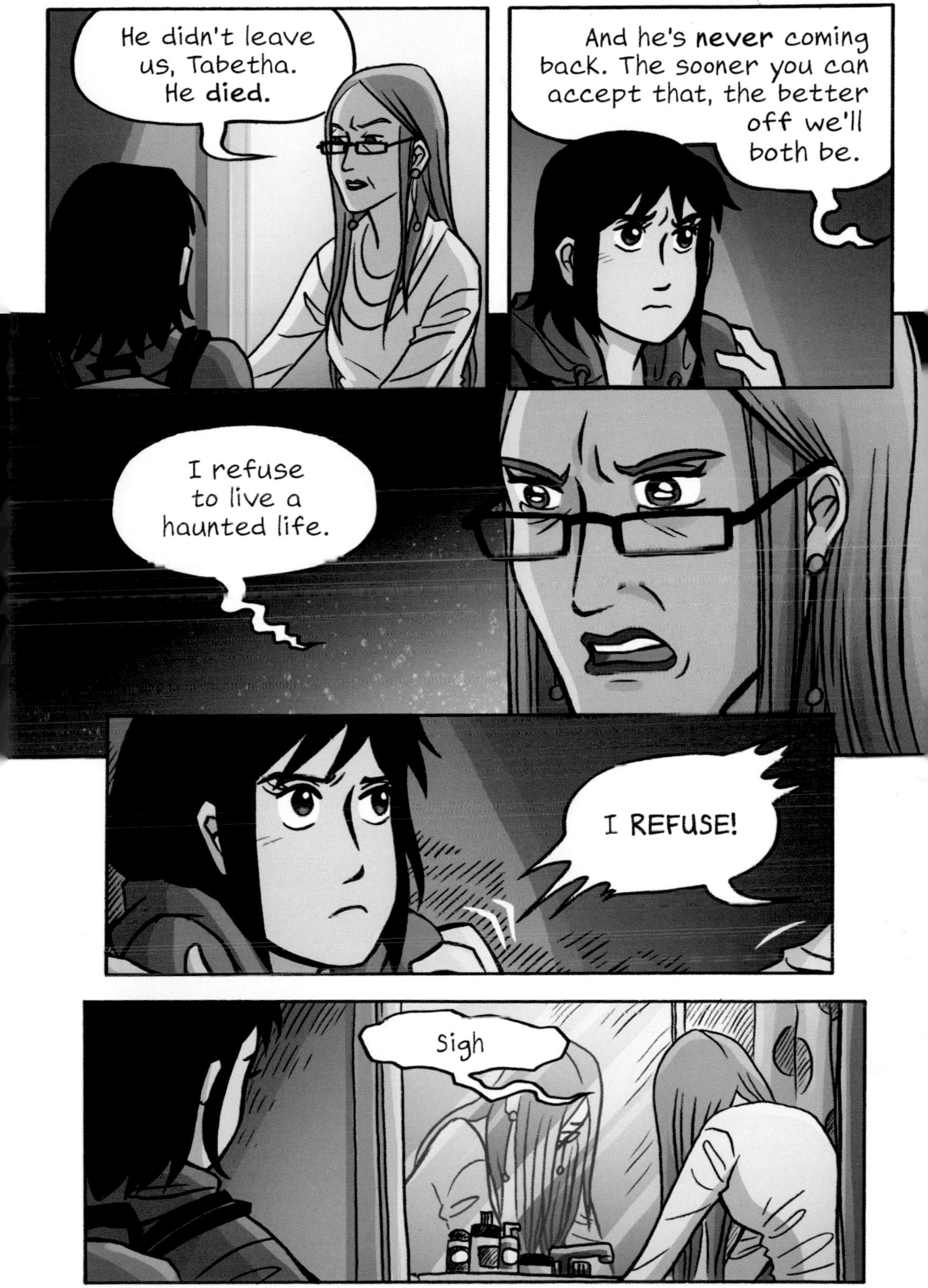
He didn't leave us, Tabetha. He died.
And he's never coming back. The sooner you can accept that, the better off we'll both be.
I refuse to live a haunted life.
I REFUSE!
Sigh

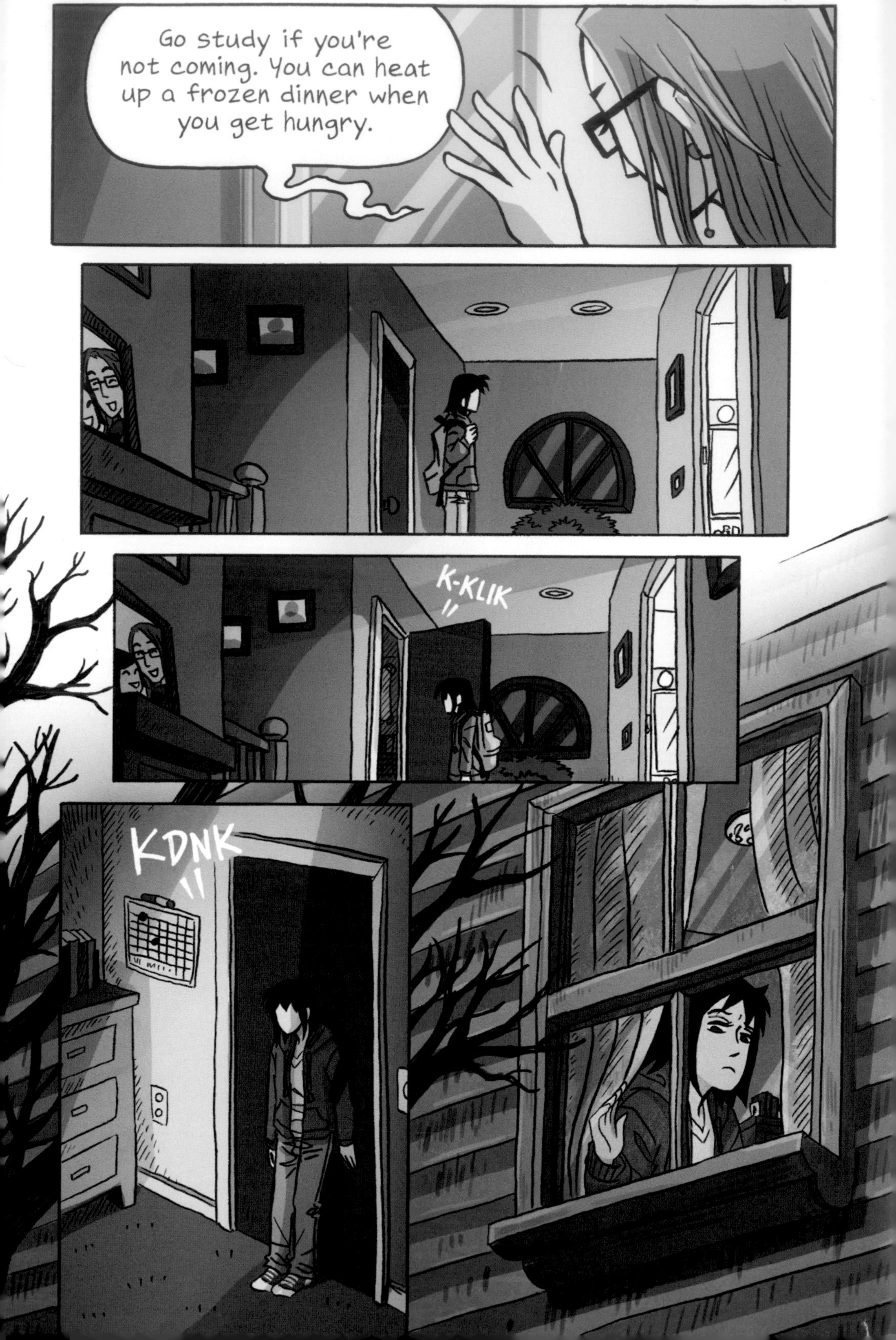
Go study if you're not coming. You can heat up a frozen dinner when you get hungry.
K-KLIK
KDNK

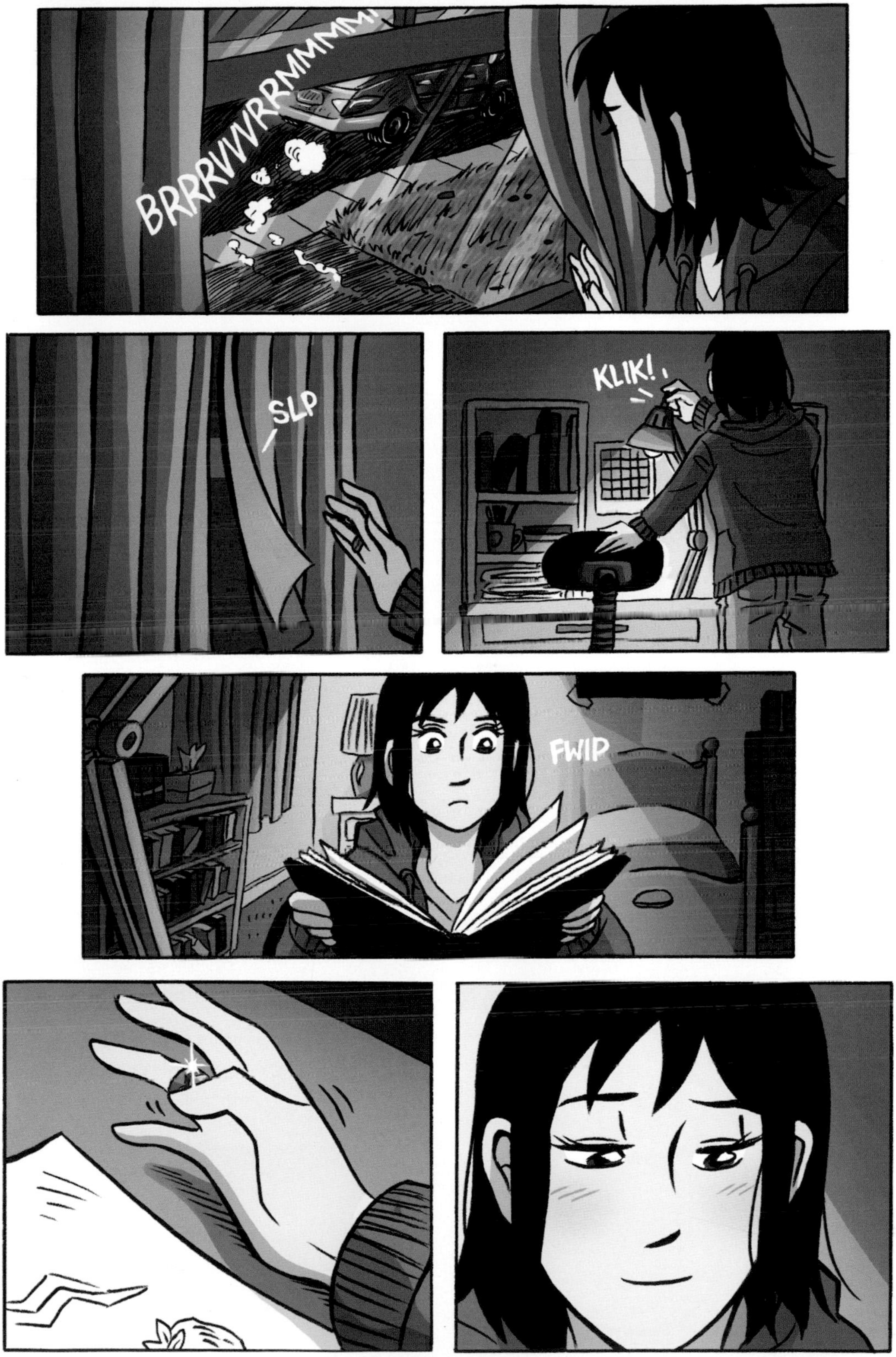
BRRRVVVRRMMMM!
SLP
KLIK!
FWIP

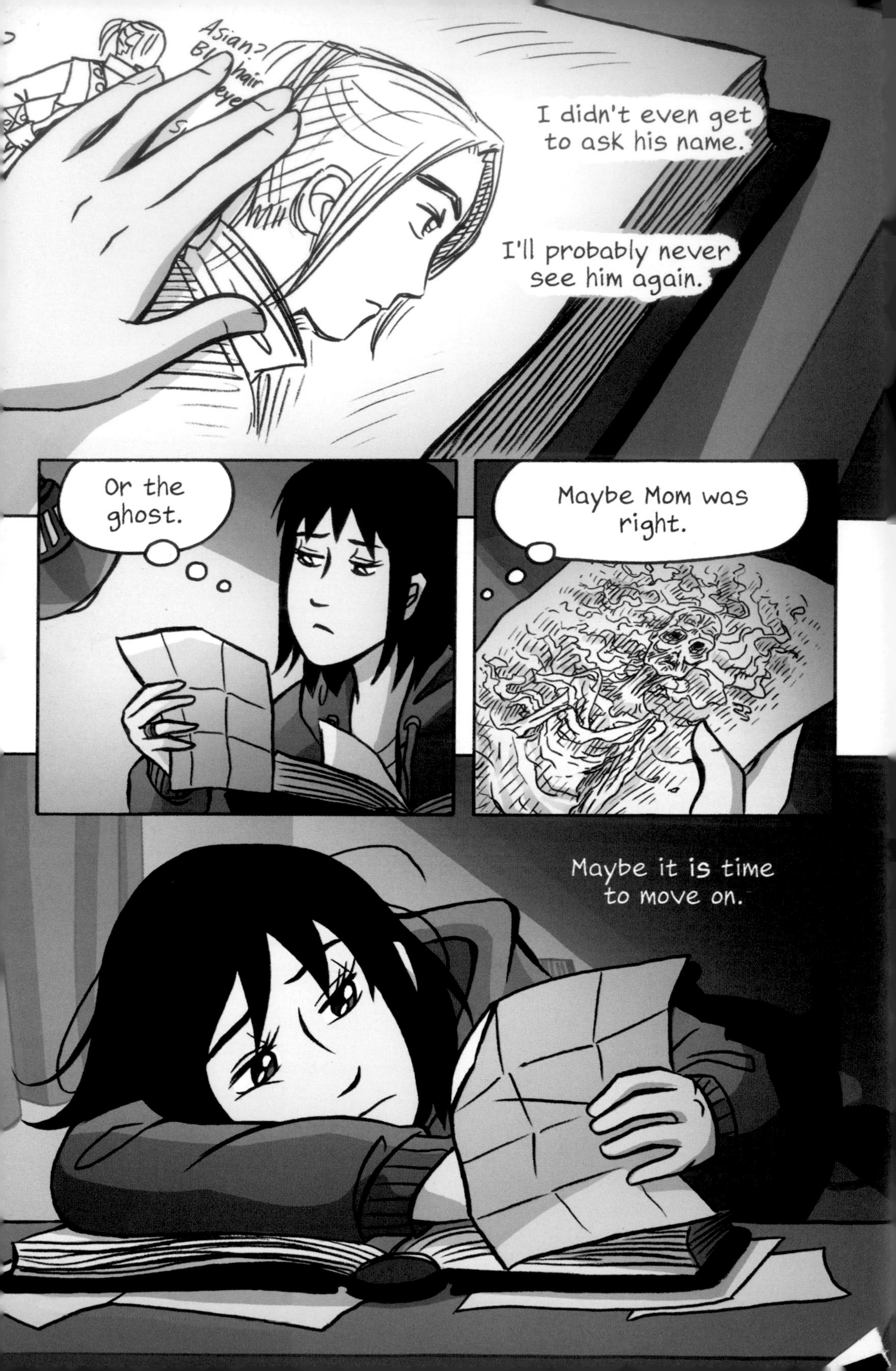
Asian?
Bl. hair
eyes
I didn't even get to ask his name.
I'll probably never see him again.
Or the ghost.
Maybe Mom was right.
Maybe it is time to move on.

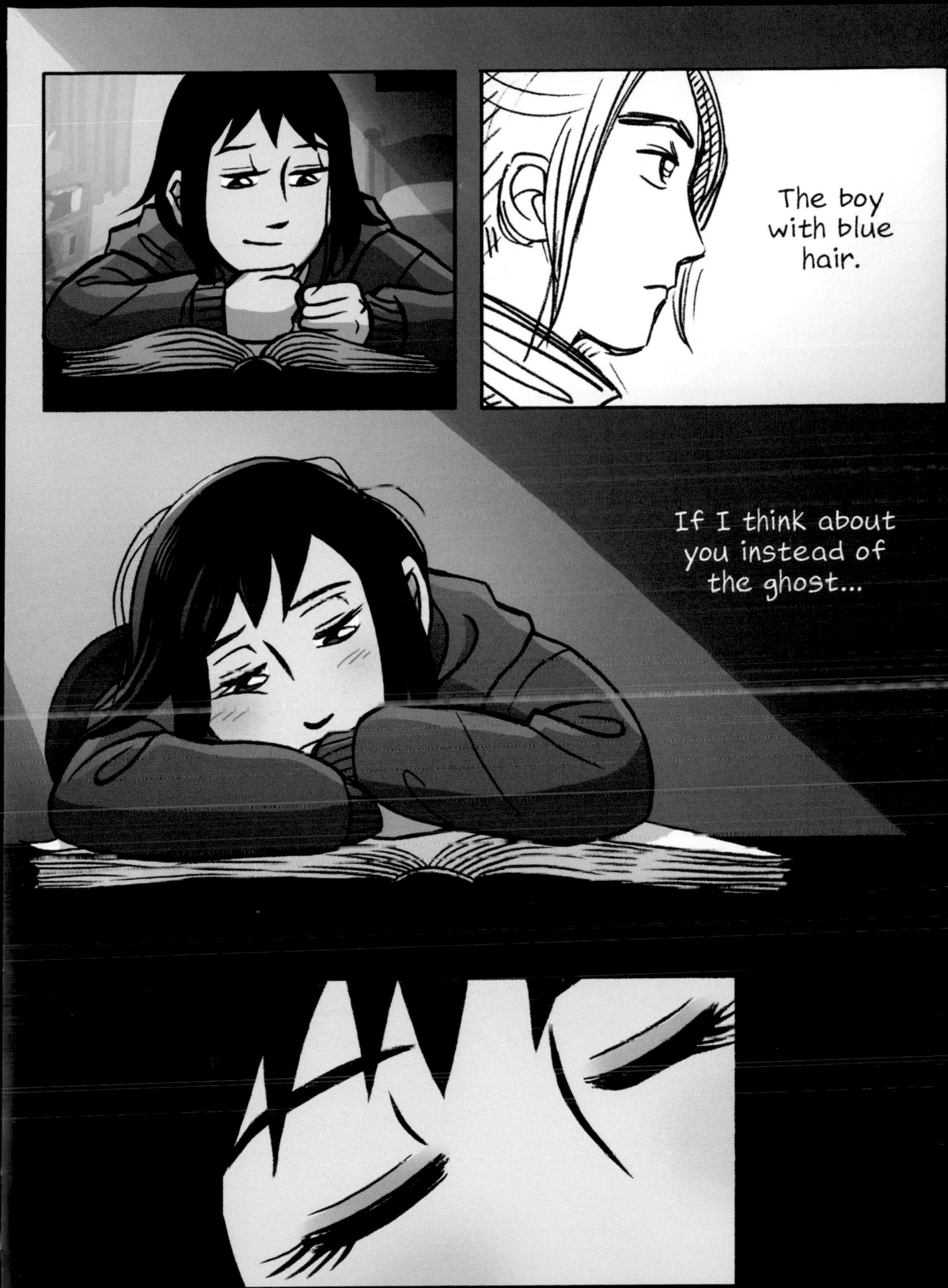
The boy
with blue
hair.
If I think about
you instead of
the ghost...

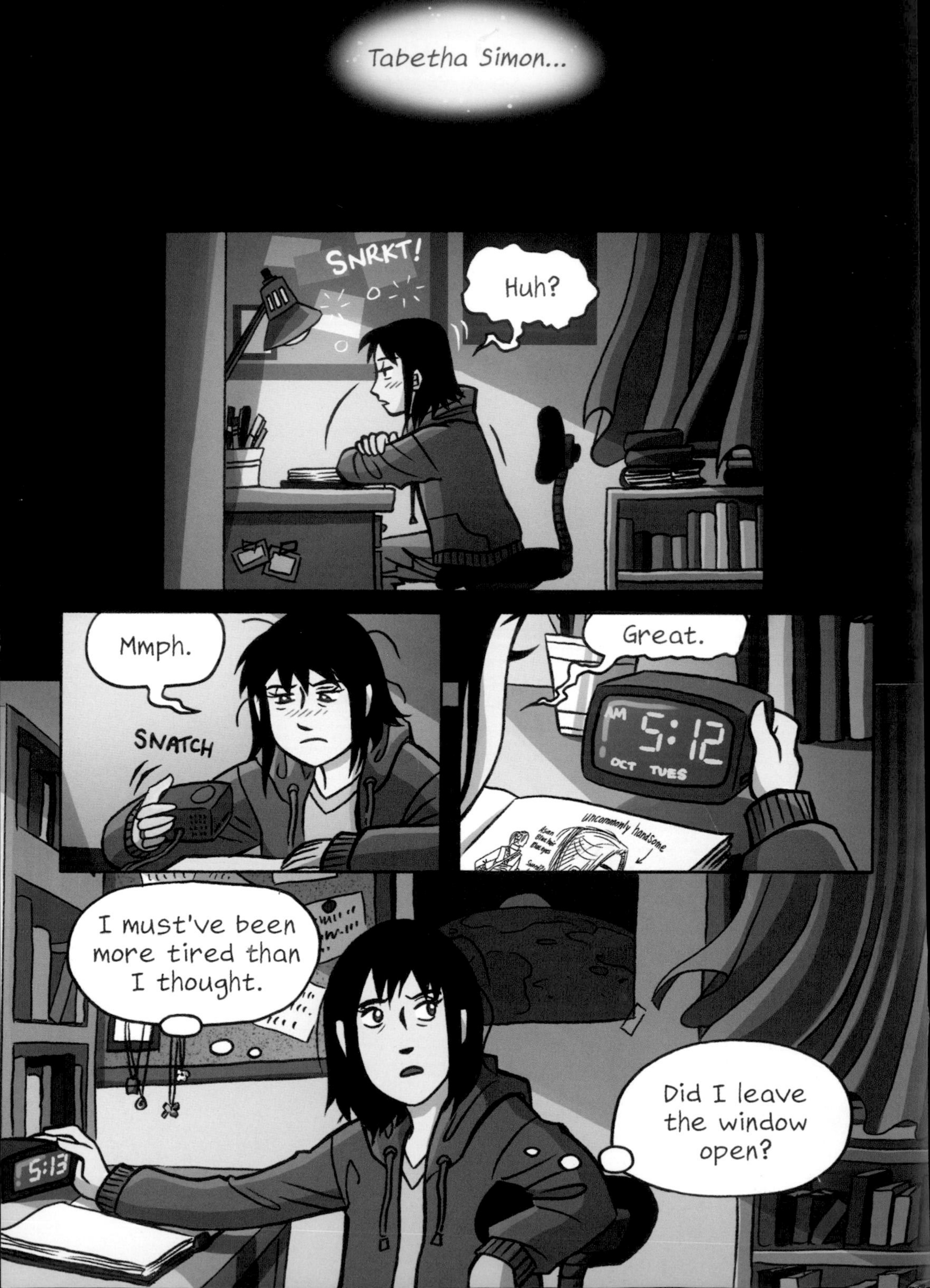
Tabetha Simon...
SNRKT!
Huh?
Mmph.
SNATCH
Great.
AM 5:12
OCT TUES
Uncommonly handsome
I must've been more tired than I thought.
5:13
Did I leave the window open?

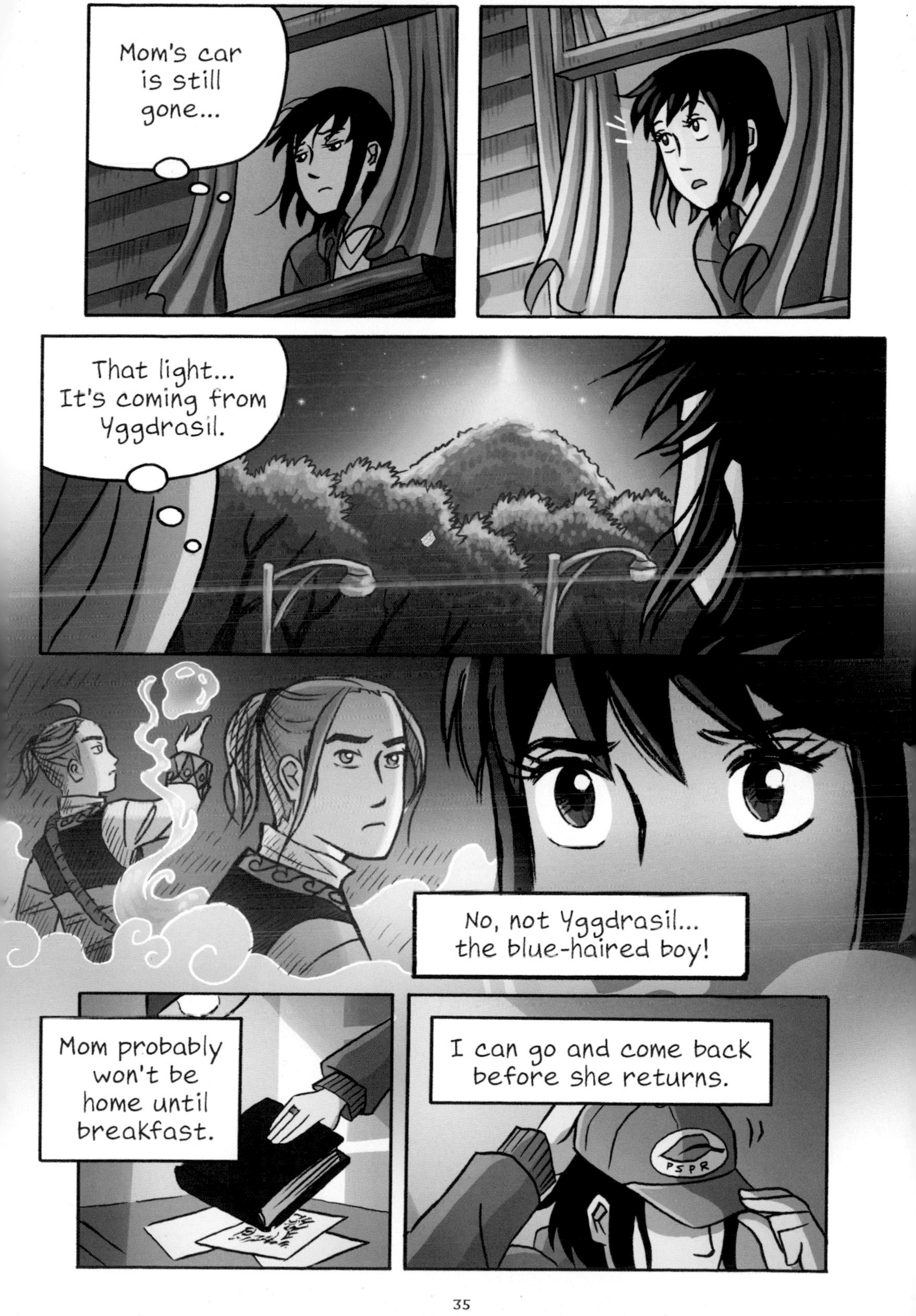
Mom's car is still gone...
That light... It's coming from Yggdrasil.
No, not Yggdrasil... the blue-haired boy!
Mom probably won't be home until breakfast.
I can go and come back before she returns.
PSPR

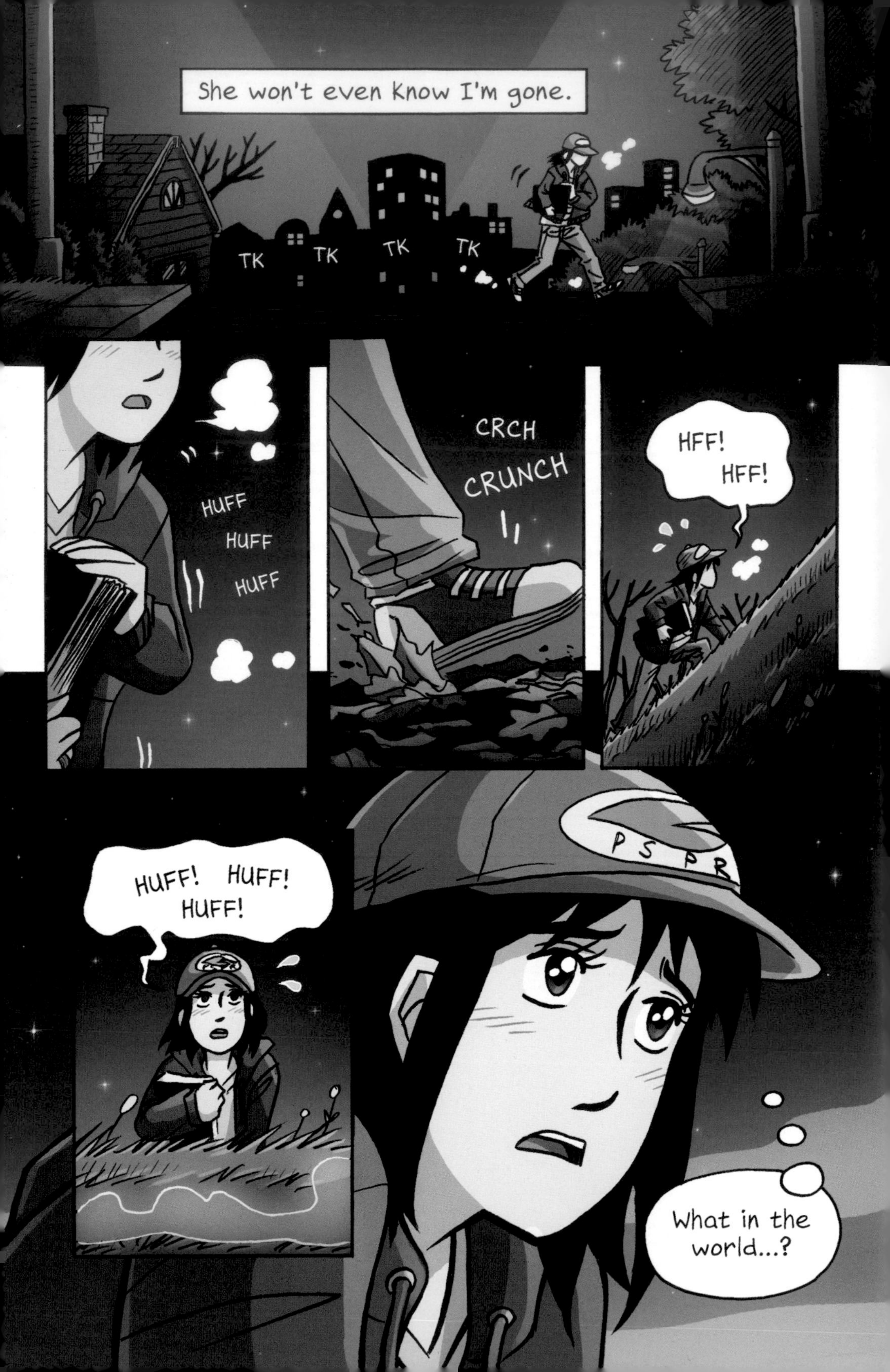
She won't even know I'm gone.
TK TK TK TK
HUFF
HUFF
HUFF
CRCH
CRUNCH
HFF! HFF!
HUFF! HUFF! HUFF!
PSPR
What in the world...?

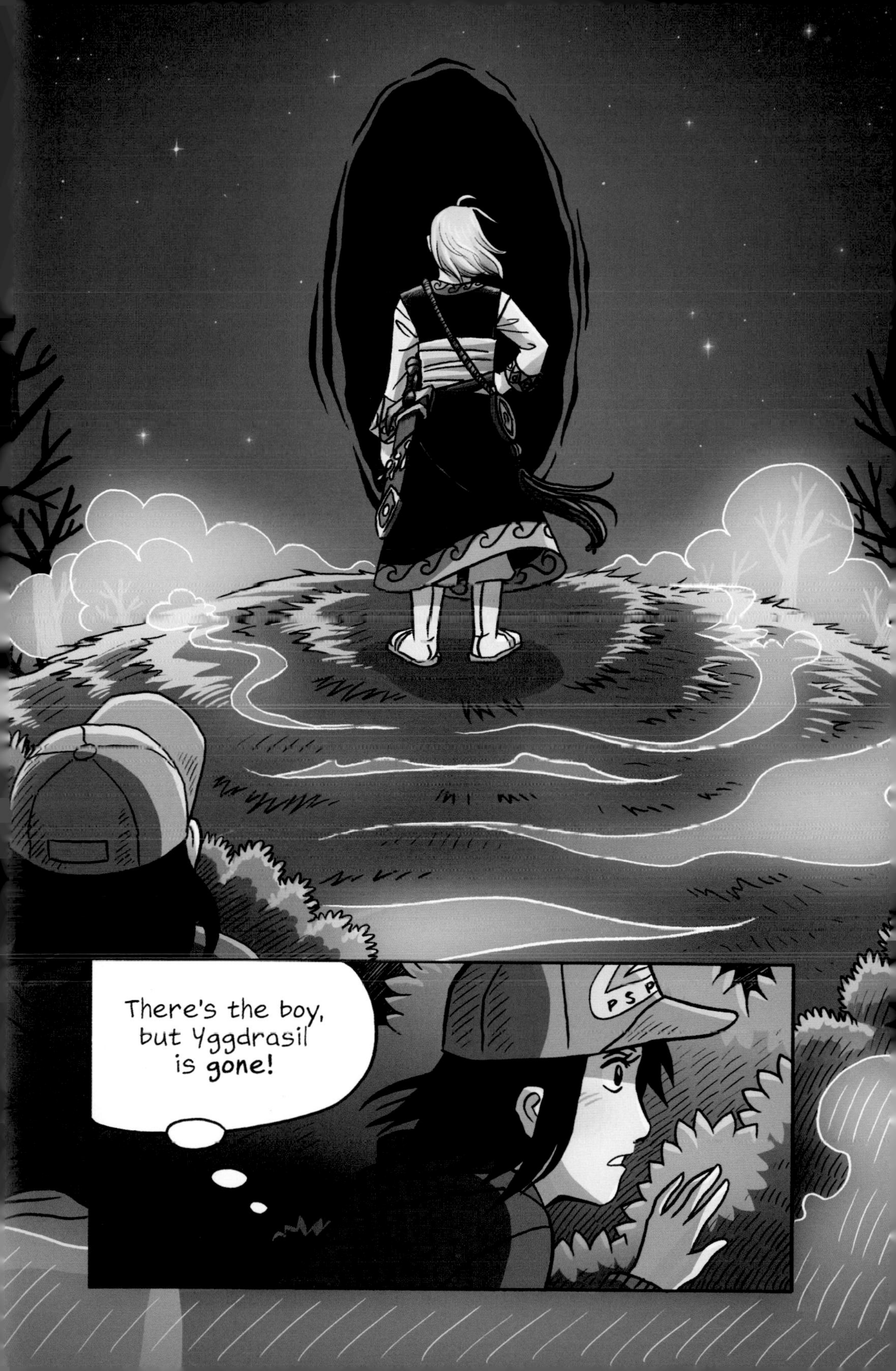
There's the boy, but Yggdrasil is gone!
PSP

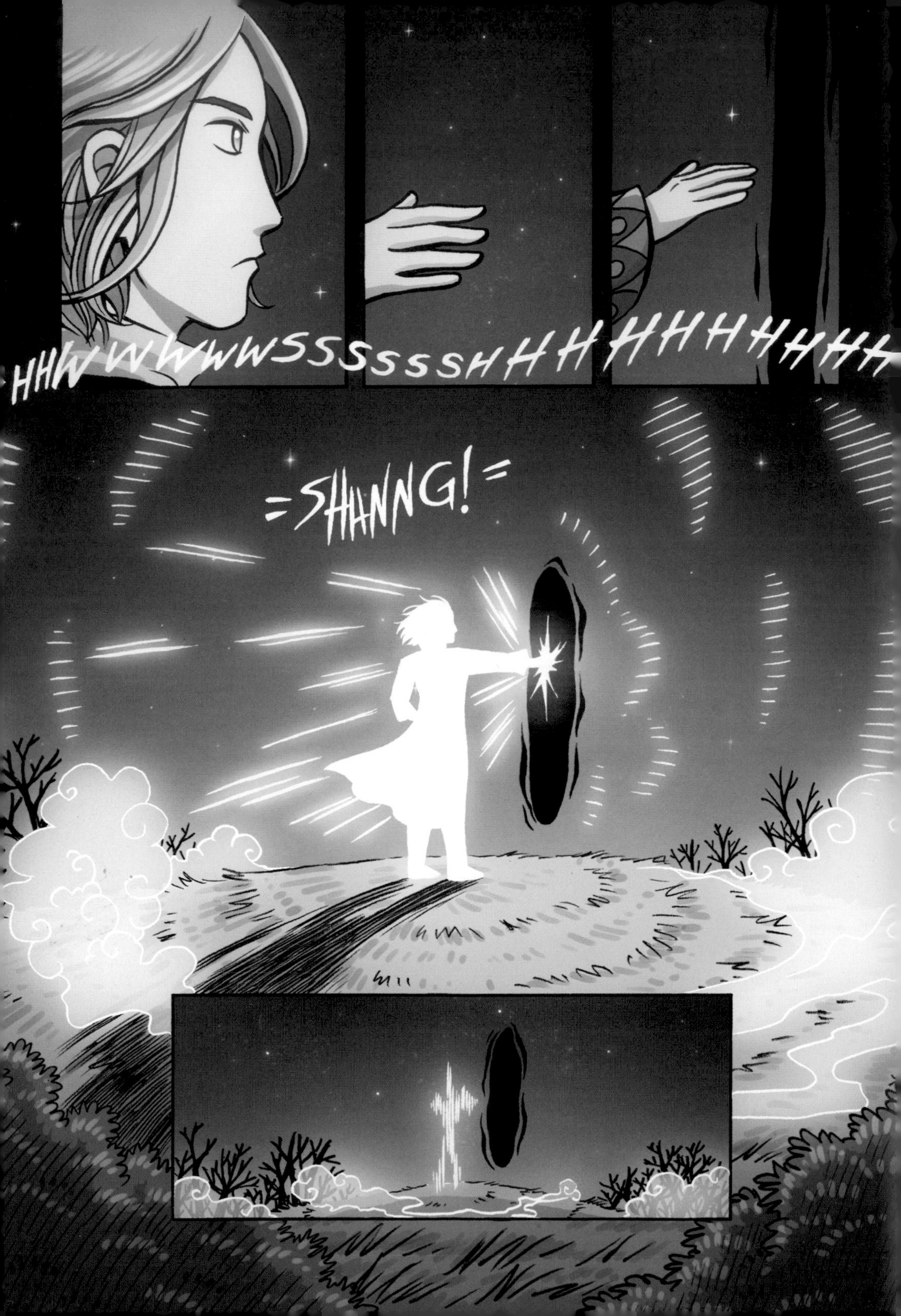
HHWWWWWWSSSSSSHHHHHHHHH
SHHNNG!

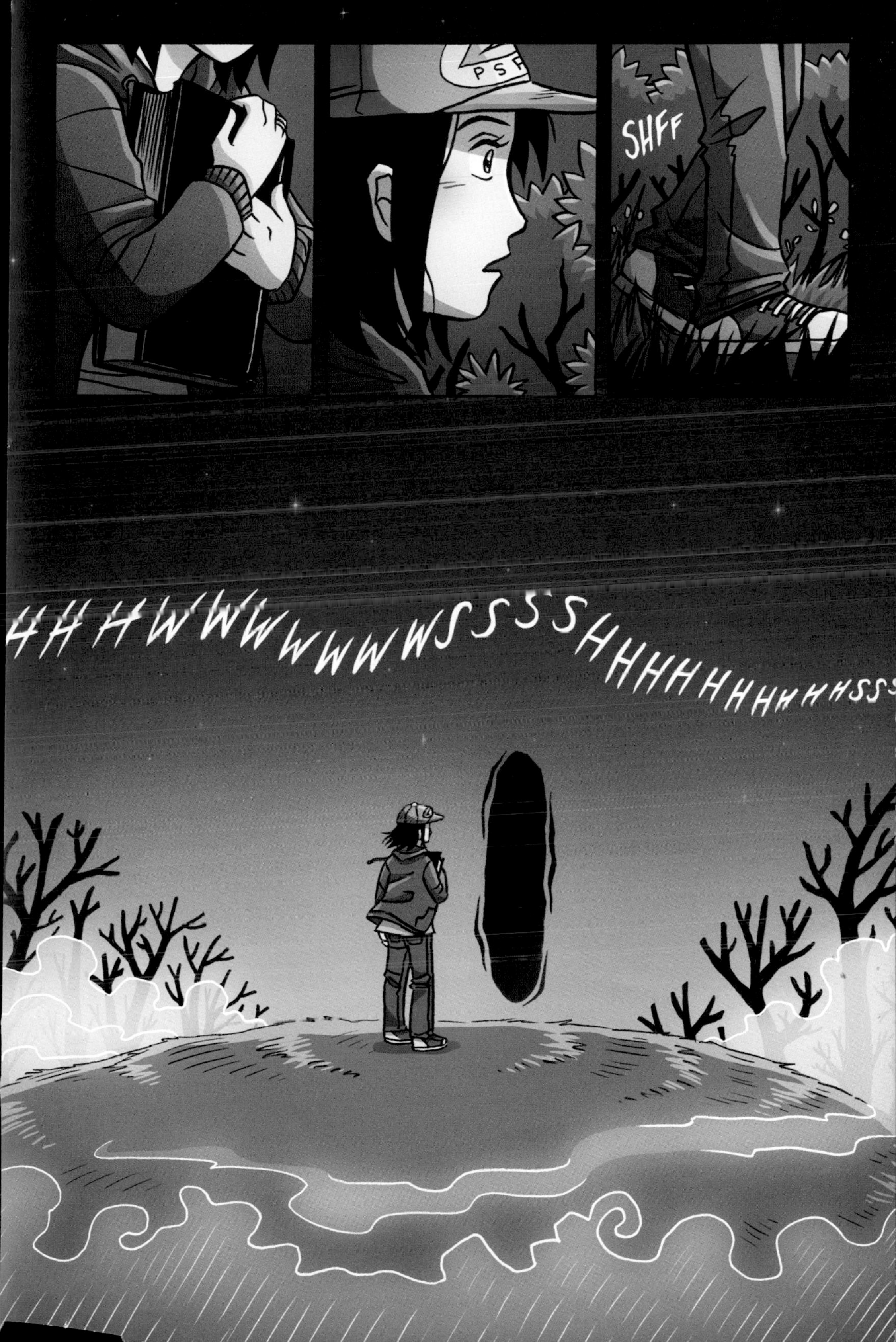
PSF
SHFF
HHHWWWWWWWSSSSHHHHHHHHHHSSS

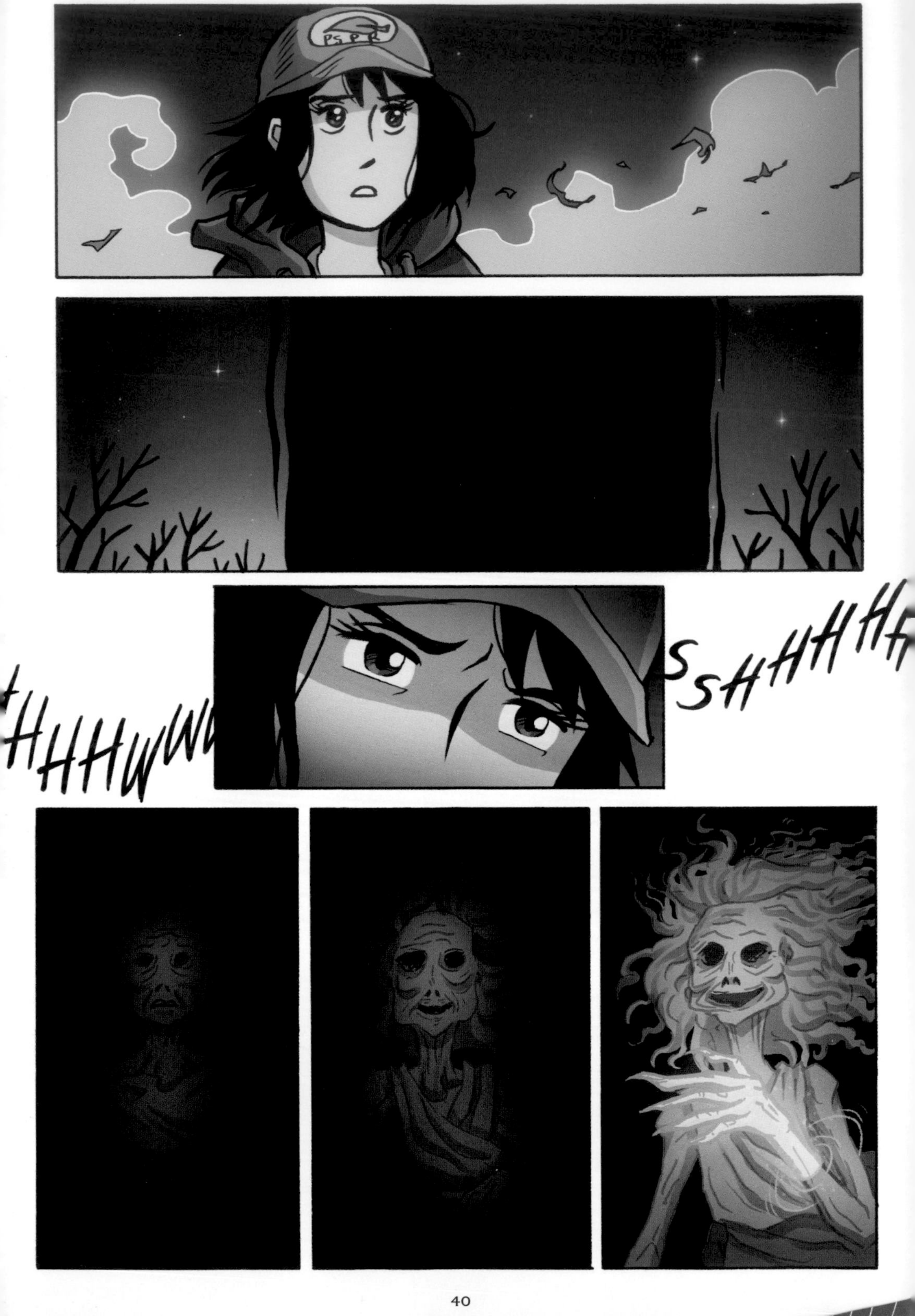
HHHWW
SSHHHH

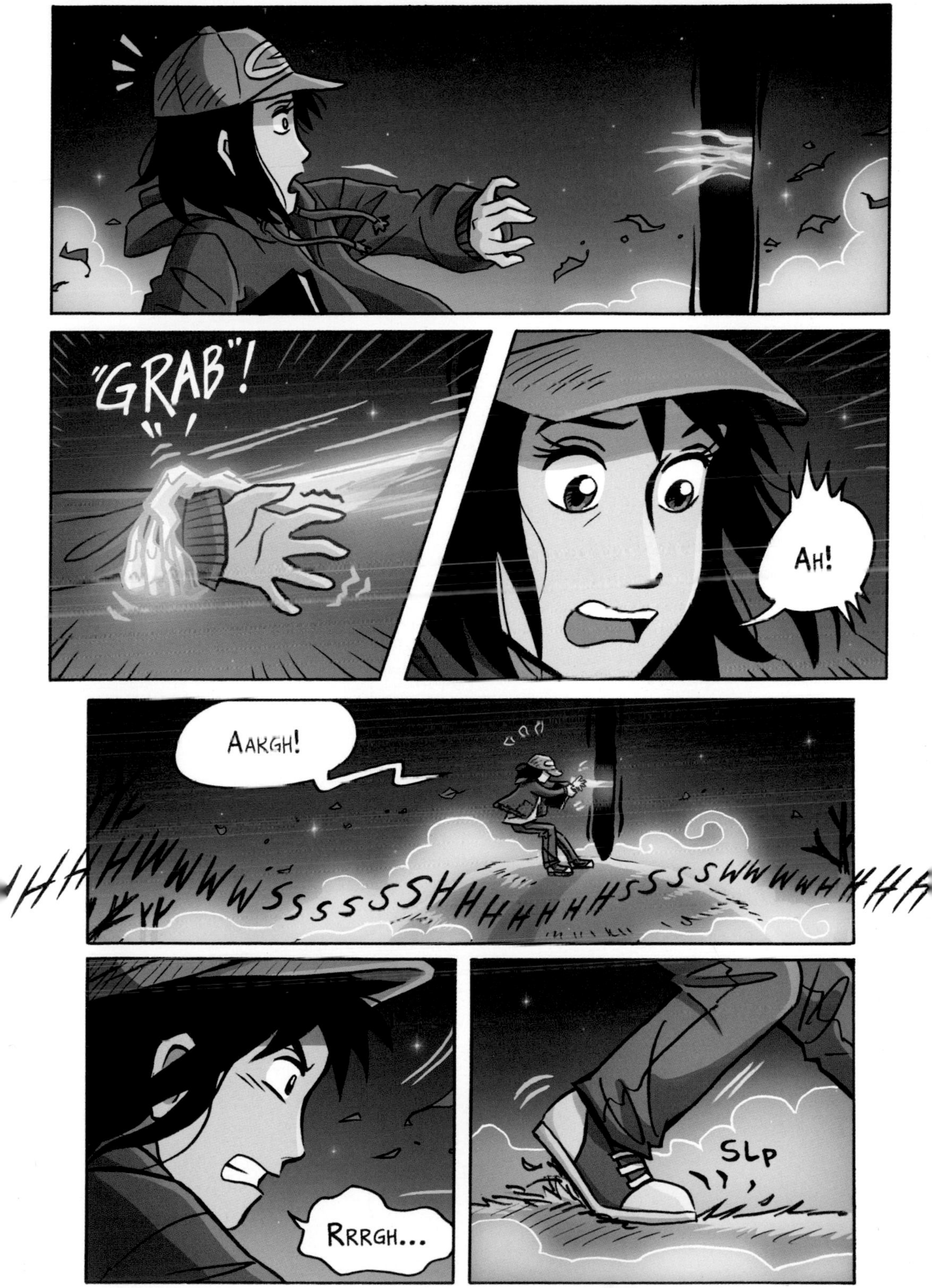
"GRAB"!
AH!
AARGH!
HHHWWWWSSSSSSHHHHHHHSSSSWWWWHHHH
RRRGH...
SLP

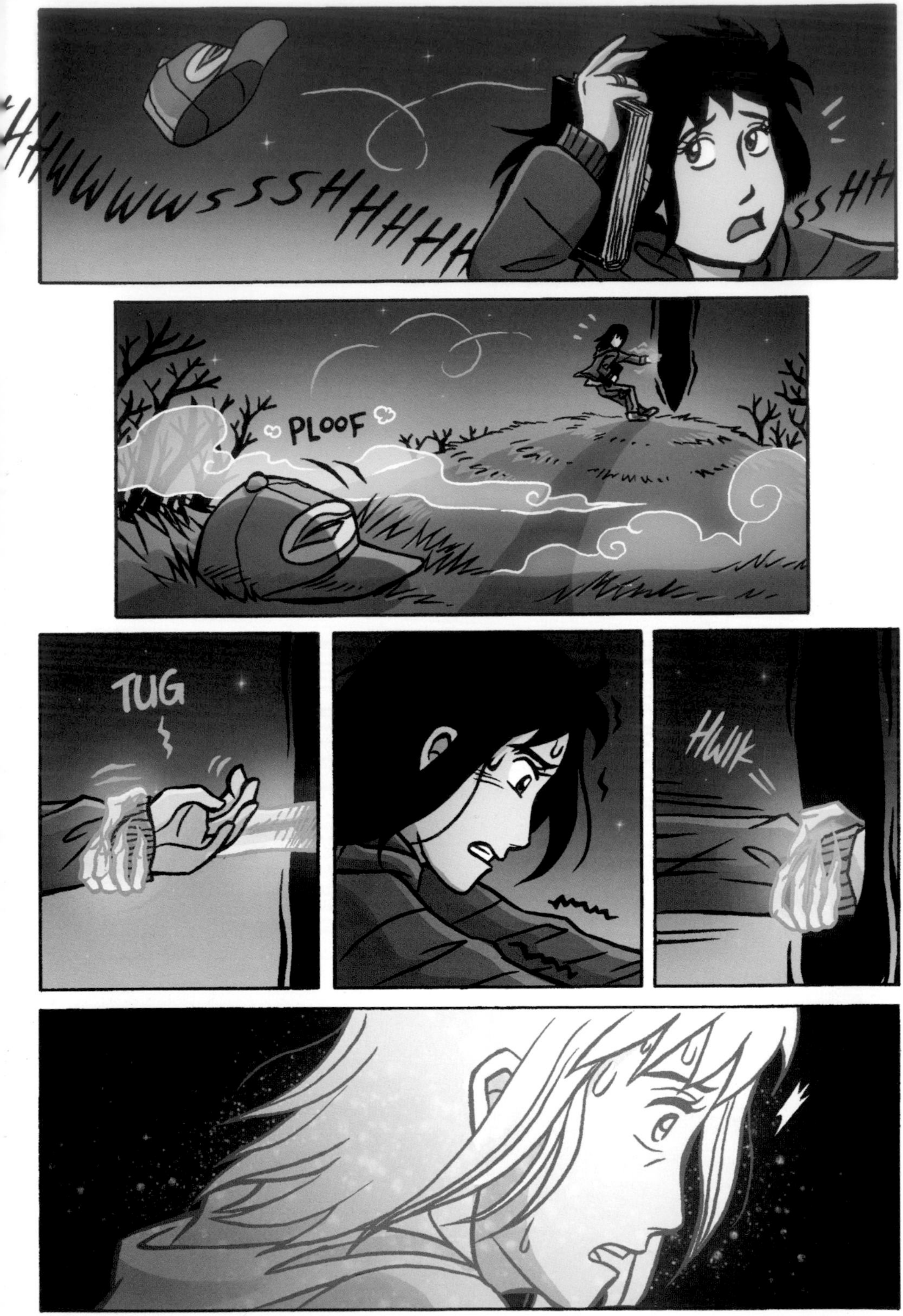

HWWWWWSSSHHHHHH
SSHH
PLOOF
TUG
HWIK

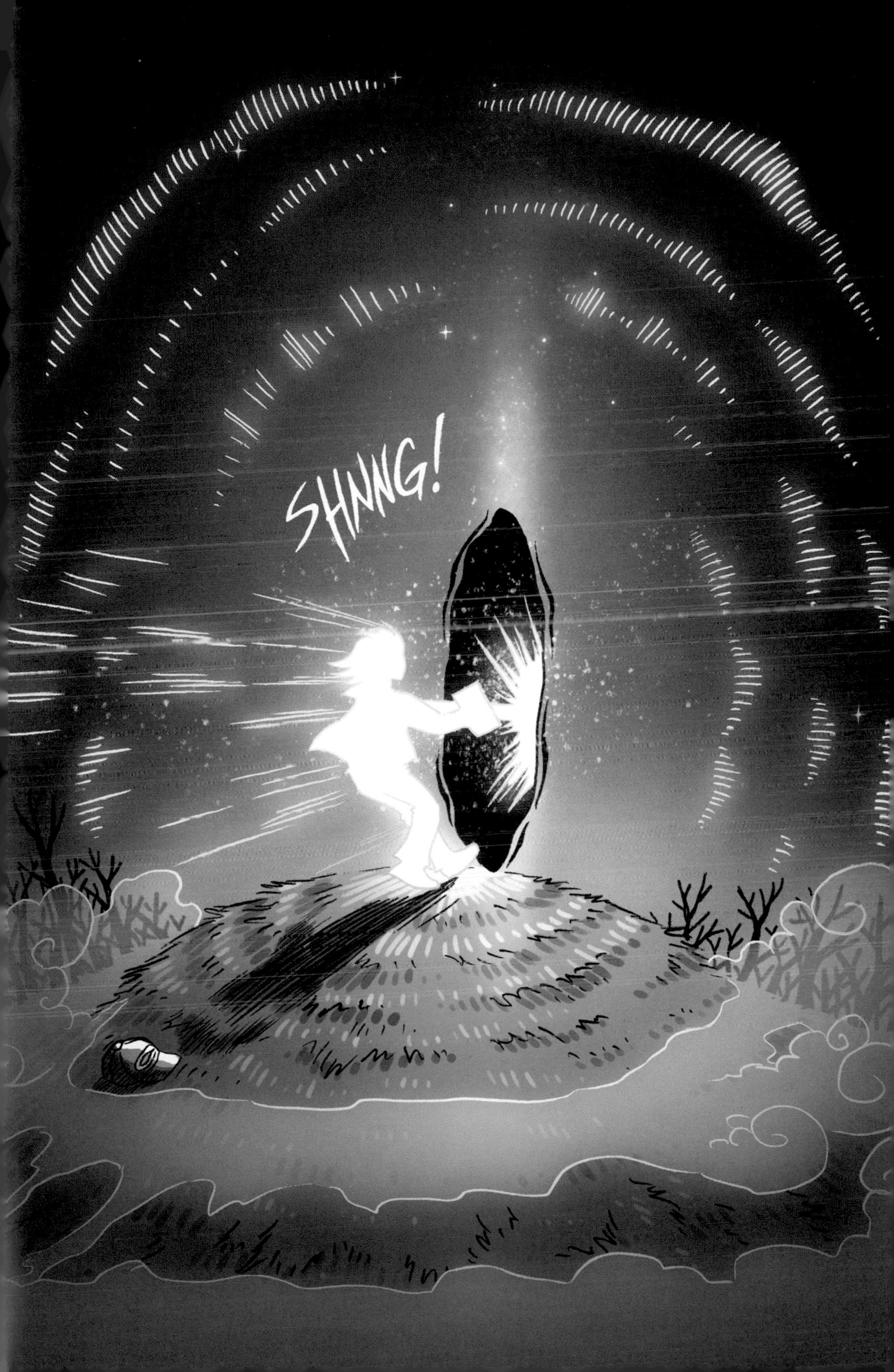
SHNNG!

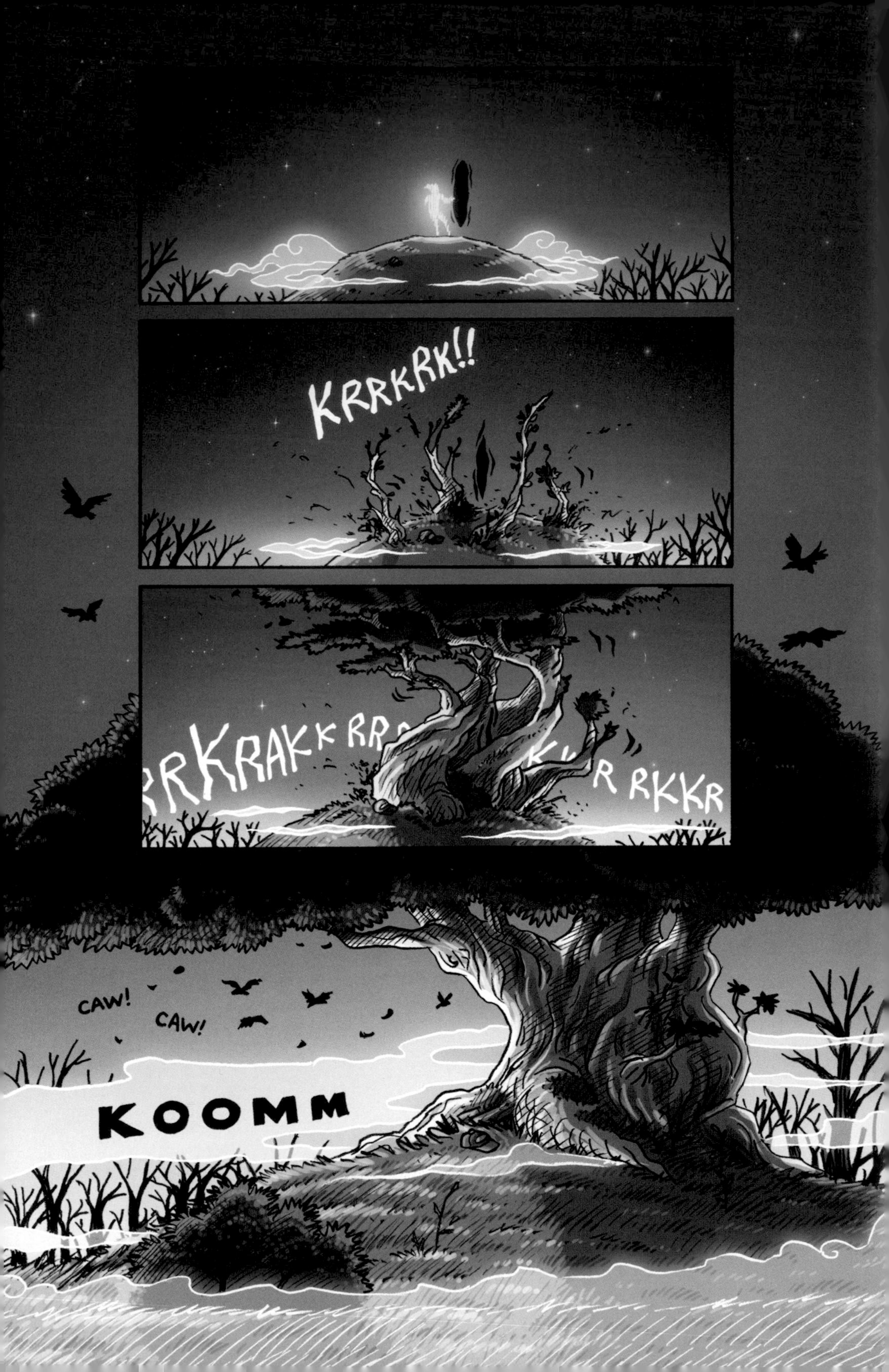
KRRKRK!!
RRKRAKKRR
K K R RKKR
CAW!
CAW!
KOOMM

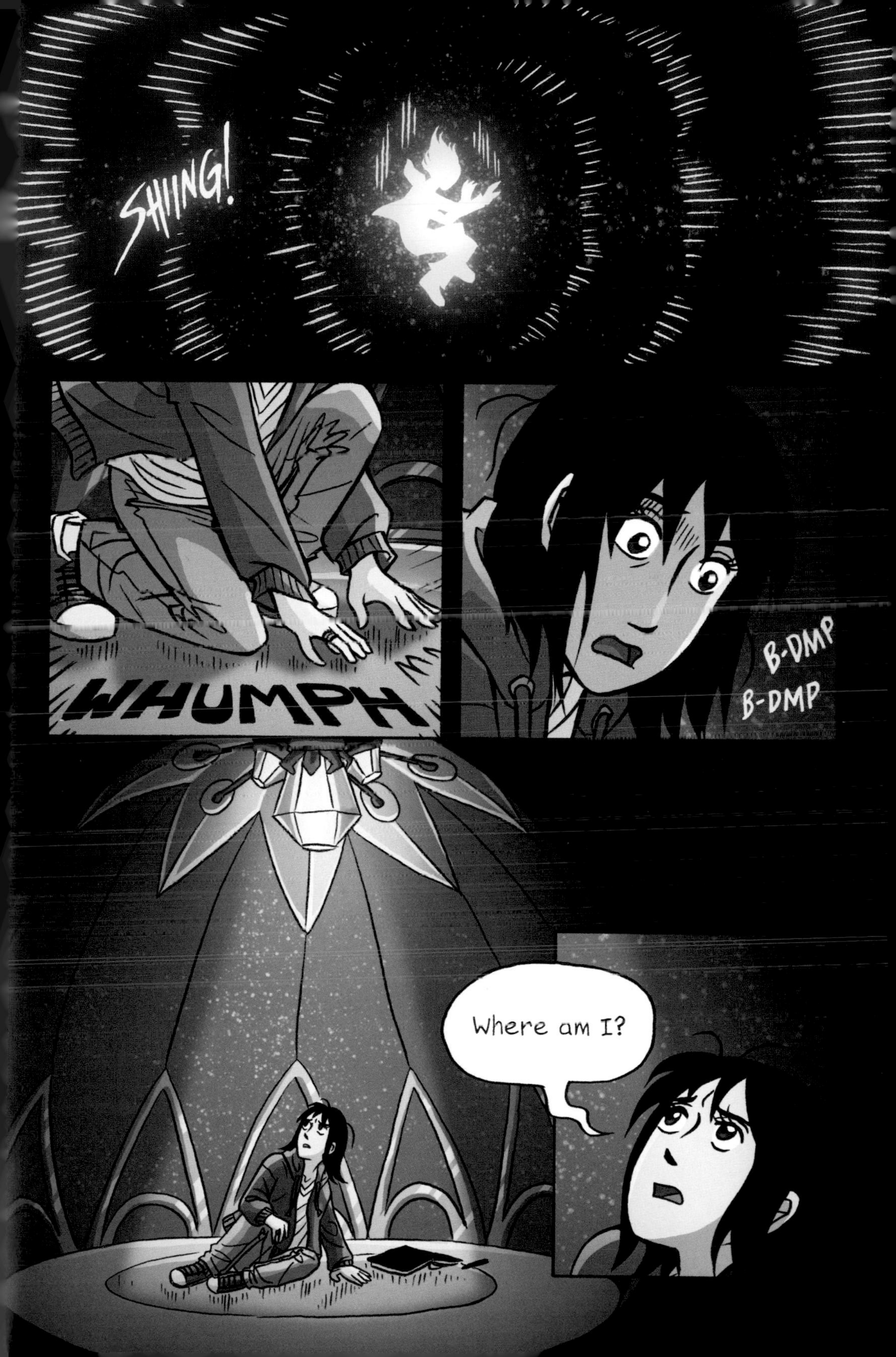
SHIING!
WHUMPH
B-DMP
B-DMP
Where am I?

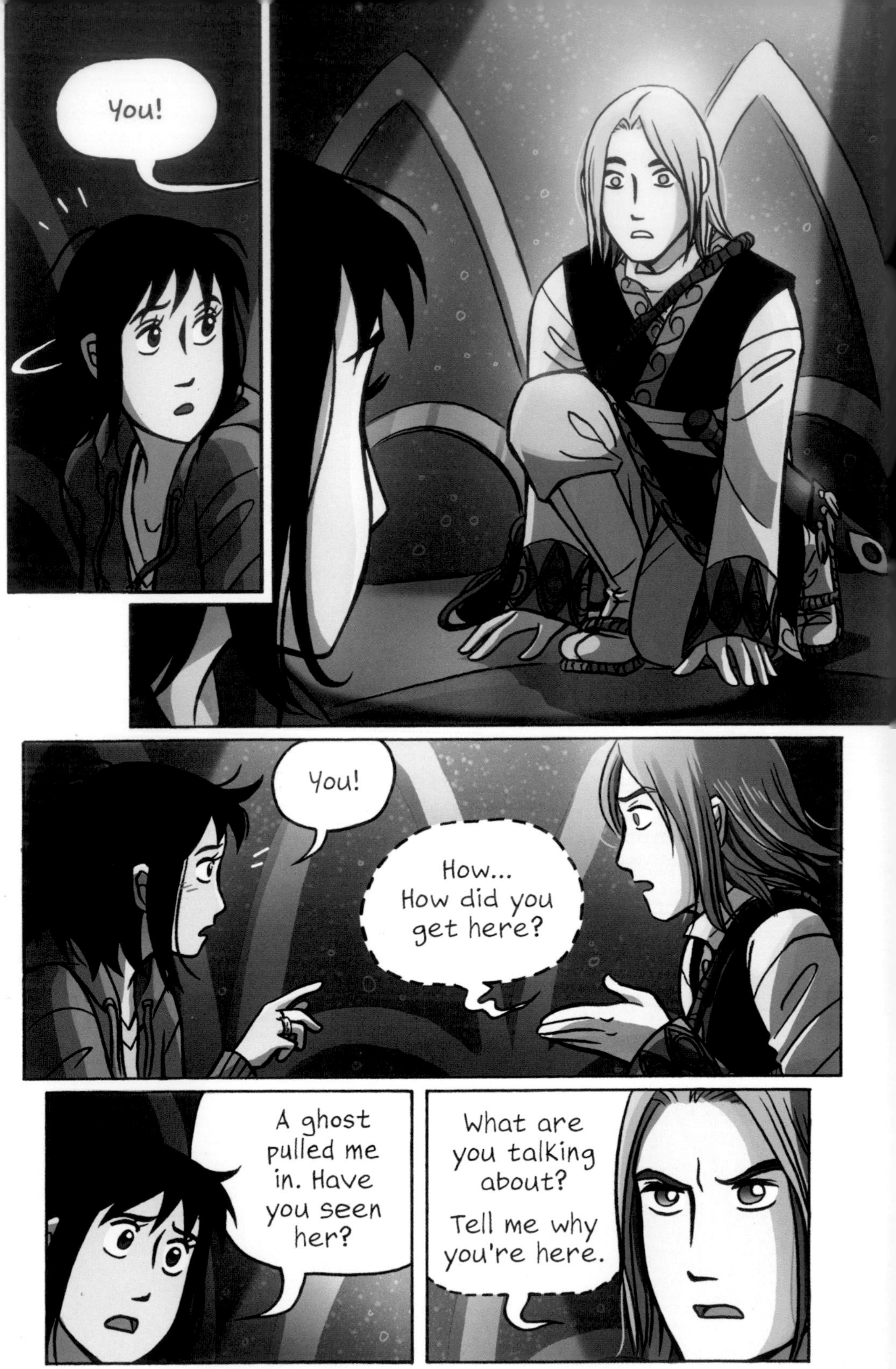
You!
You!
How... How did you get here?
A ghost pulled me in. Have you seen her?
What are you talking about?
Tell me why you're here.

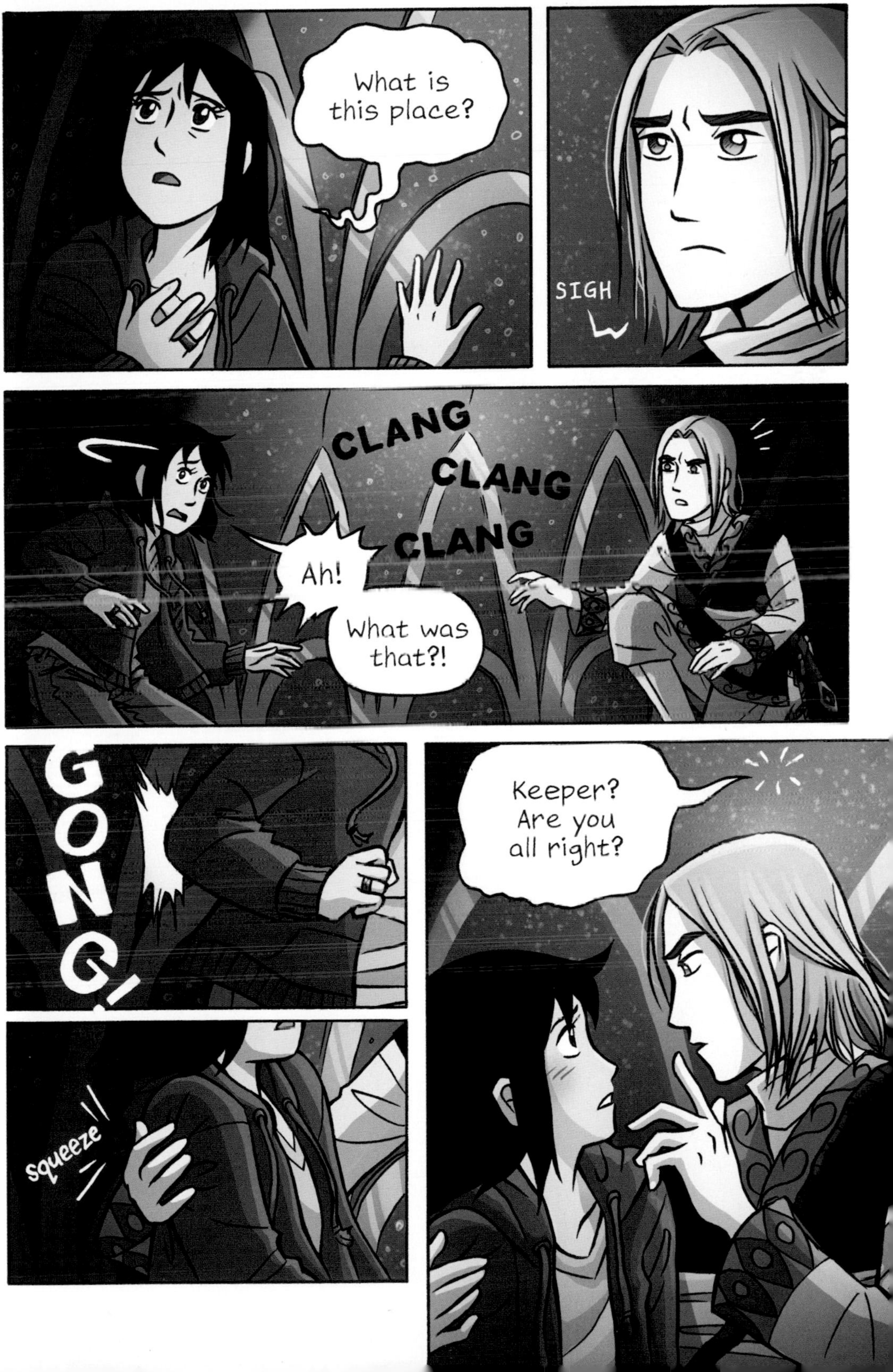
What is this place?
SIGH
CLANG
CLANG
CLANG
Ah!
What was that?!
GONG!
squeeze
Keeper? Are you all right?

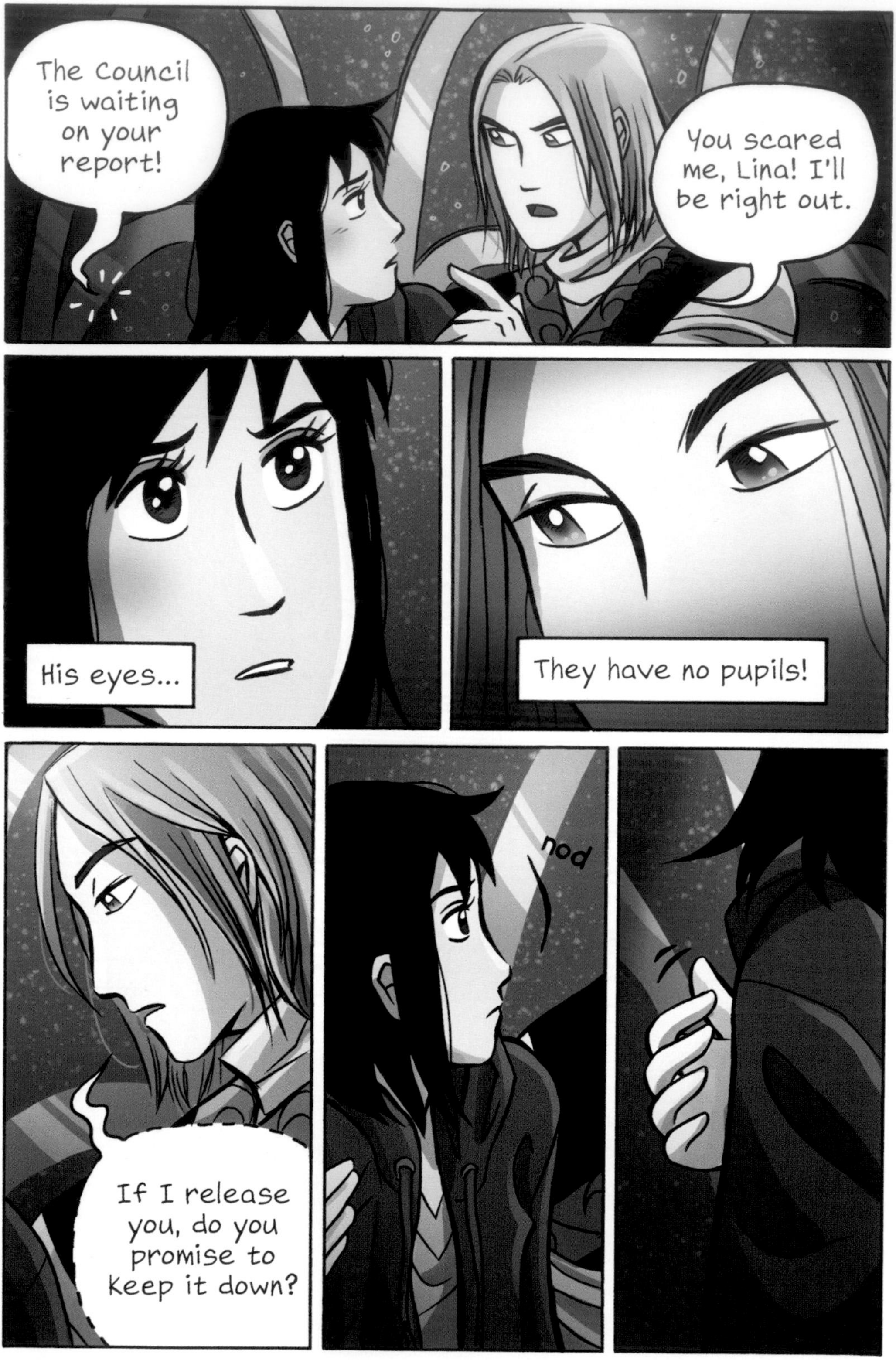

The Council is waiting on your report!
You scared me, Lina! I'll be right out.
His eyes...
They have no pupils!
If I release you, do you promise to keep it down?
nod

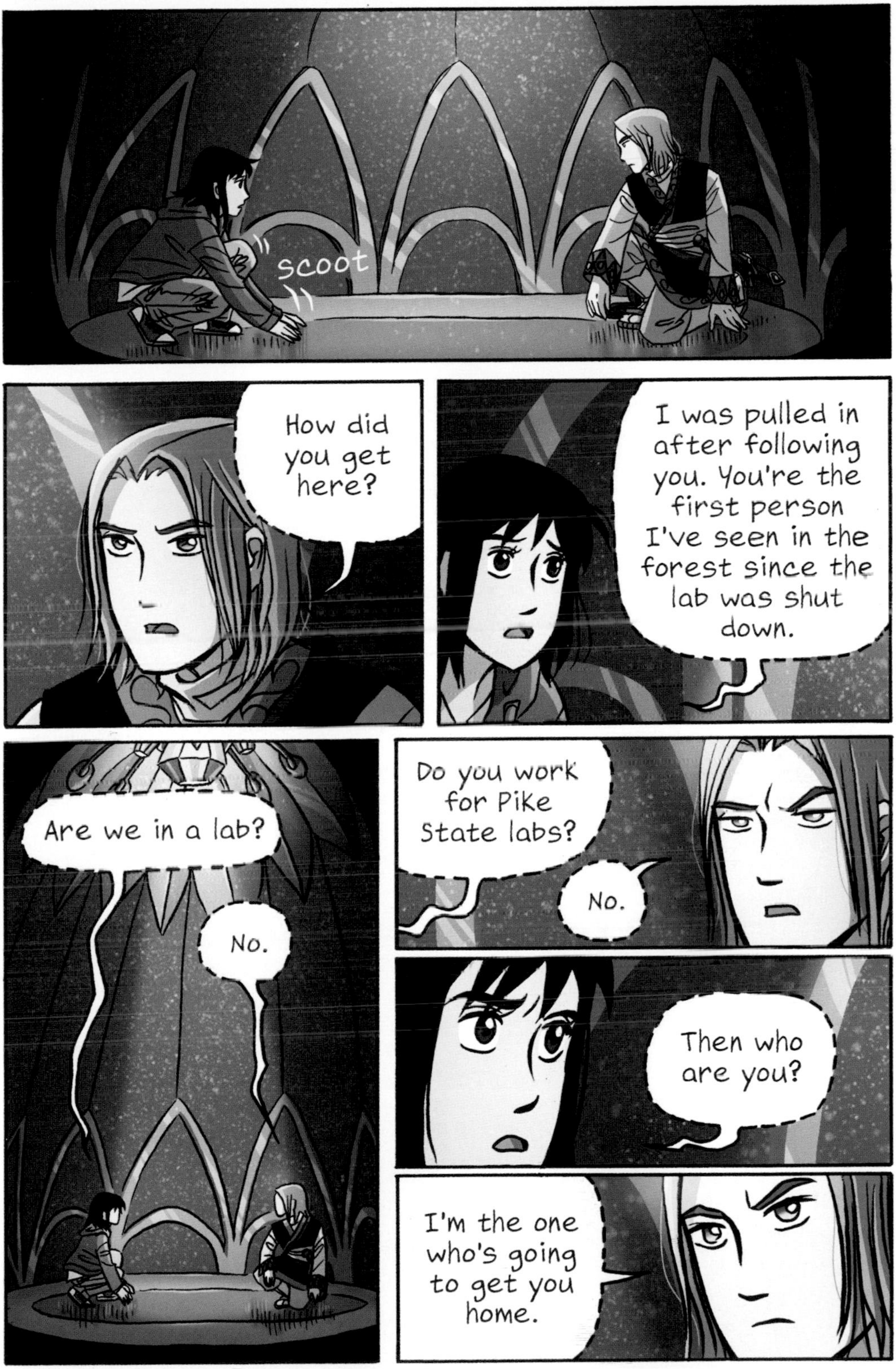
scoot
How did you get here?
I was pulled in after following you. You're the first person I've seen in the forest since the lab was shut down.
Are we in a lab?
No.
Do you work for Pike State labs?
No.
Then who are you?
I'm the one who's going to get you home.

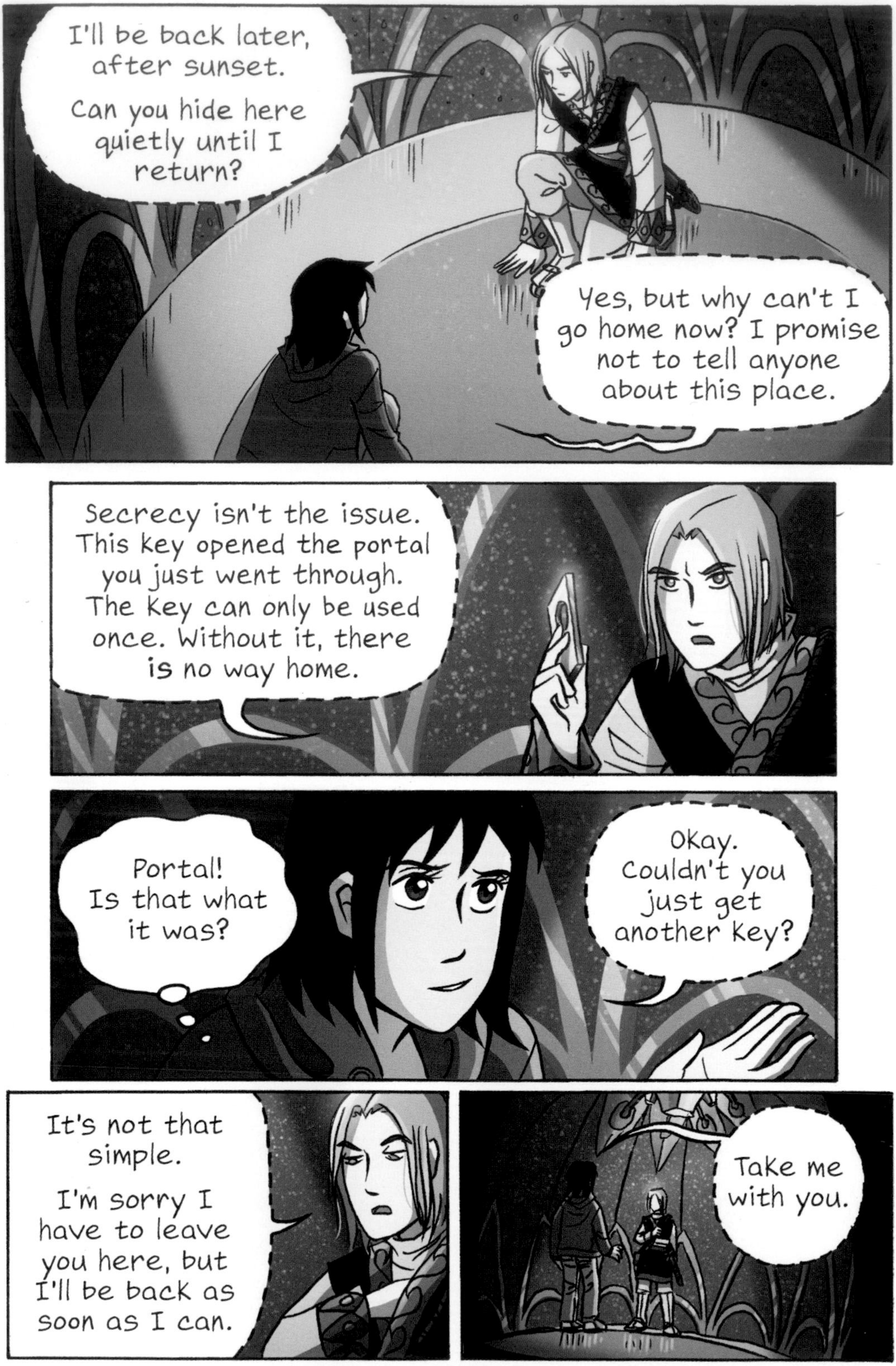

I'll be back later, after sunset.
Can you hide here quietly until I return?
Yes, but why can't I go home now? I promise not to tell anyone about this place.
Secrecy isn't the issue. This key opened the portal you just went through. The key can only be used once. Without it, there is no way home.
Portal! Is that what it was?
Okay. Couldn't you just get another key?
It's not that simple.
I'm sorry I have to leave you here, but I'll be back as soon as I can.
Take me with you.

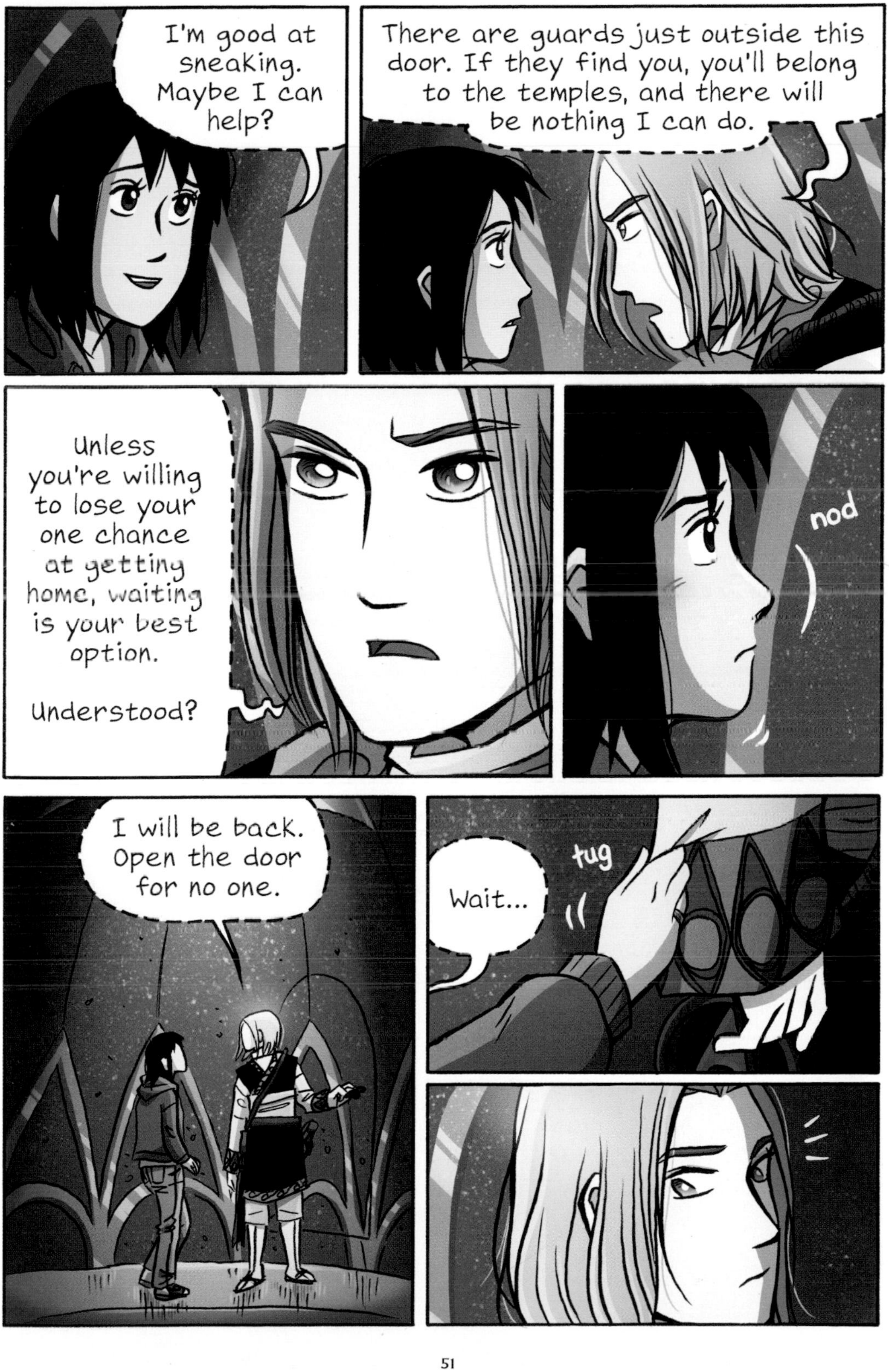

I'm good at sneaking. Maybe I can help?
There are guards just outside this door. If they find you, you'll belong to the temples, and there will be nothing I can do.
Unless you're willing to lose your one chance at getting home, waiting is your best option.
Understood?
nod
I will be back. Open the door for no one.
tug
Wait...

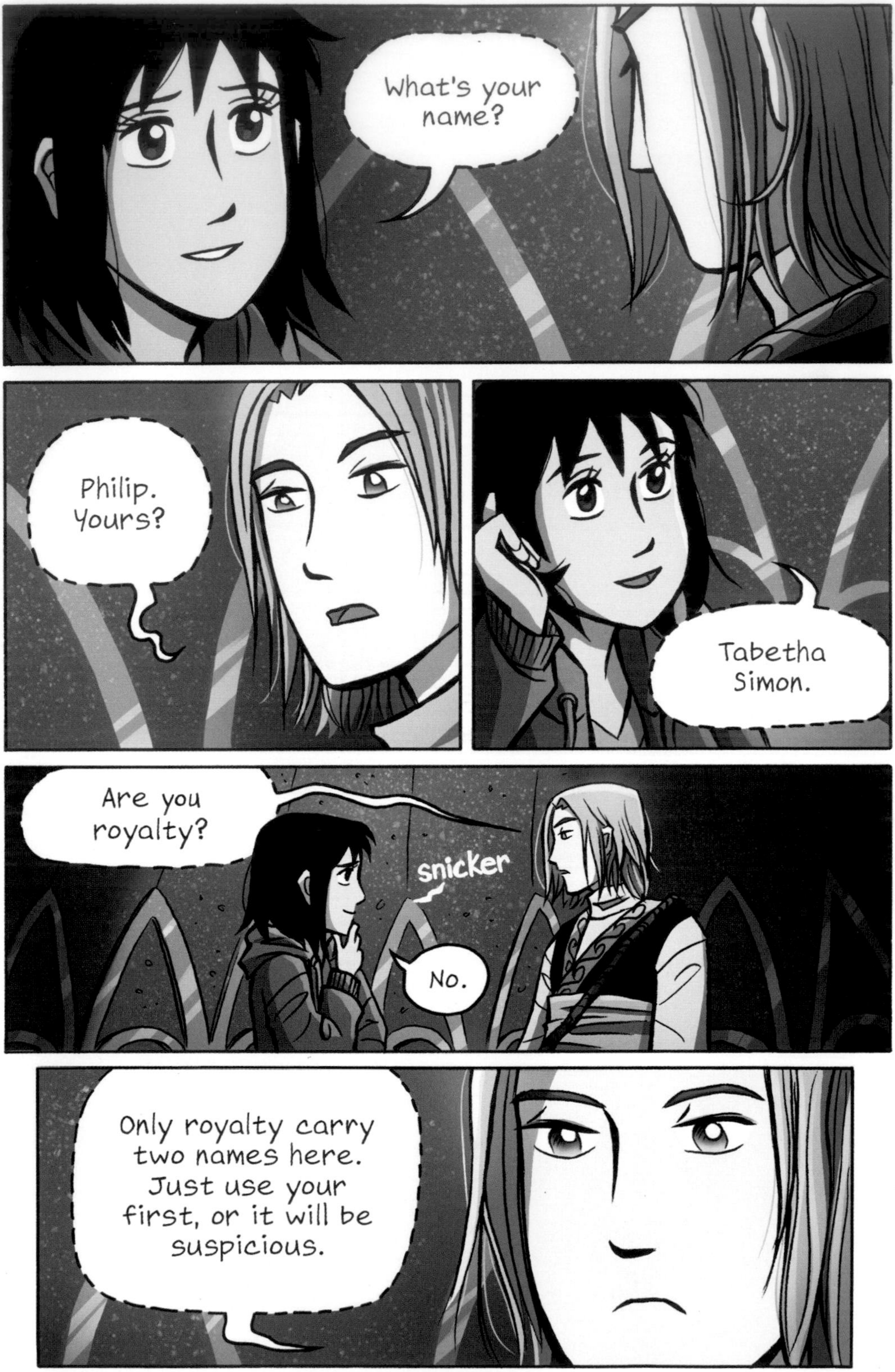
What's your name?
Philip. Yours?
Tabetha Simon.
Are you royalty?
snicker
No.
Only royalty carry two names here. Just use your first, or it will be suspicious.

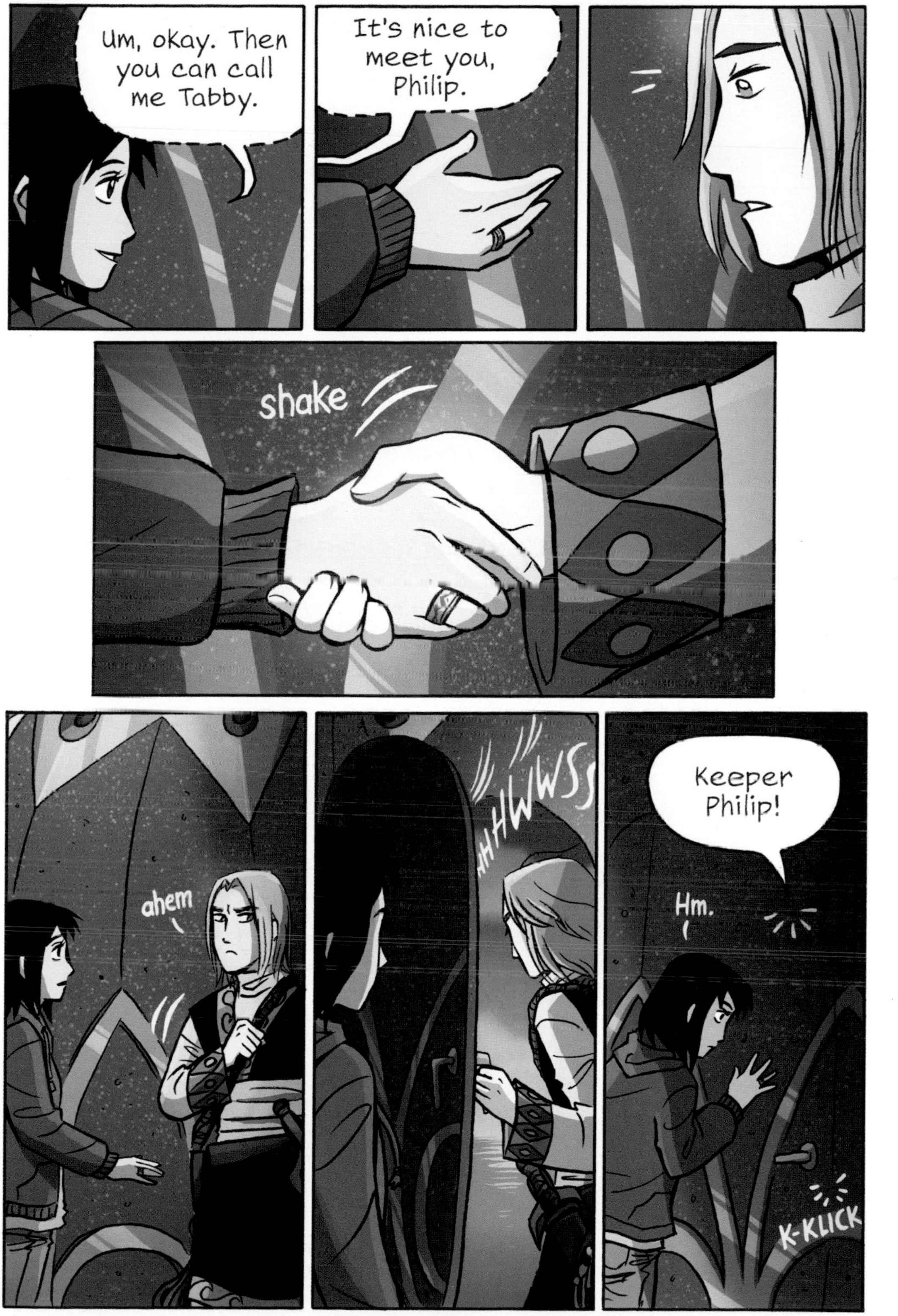
Um, okay. Then you can call me Tabby.
It's nice to meet you, Philip.
shake
ahem
HHHWWSS
Keeper Philip!
Hm.
K-KLICK

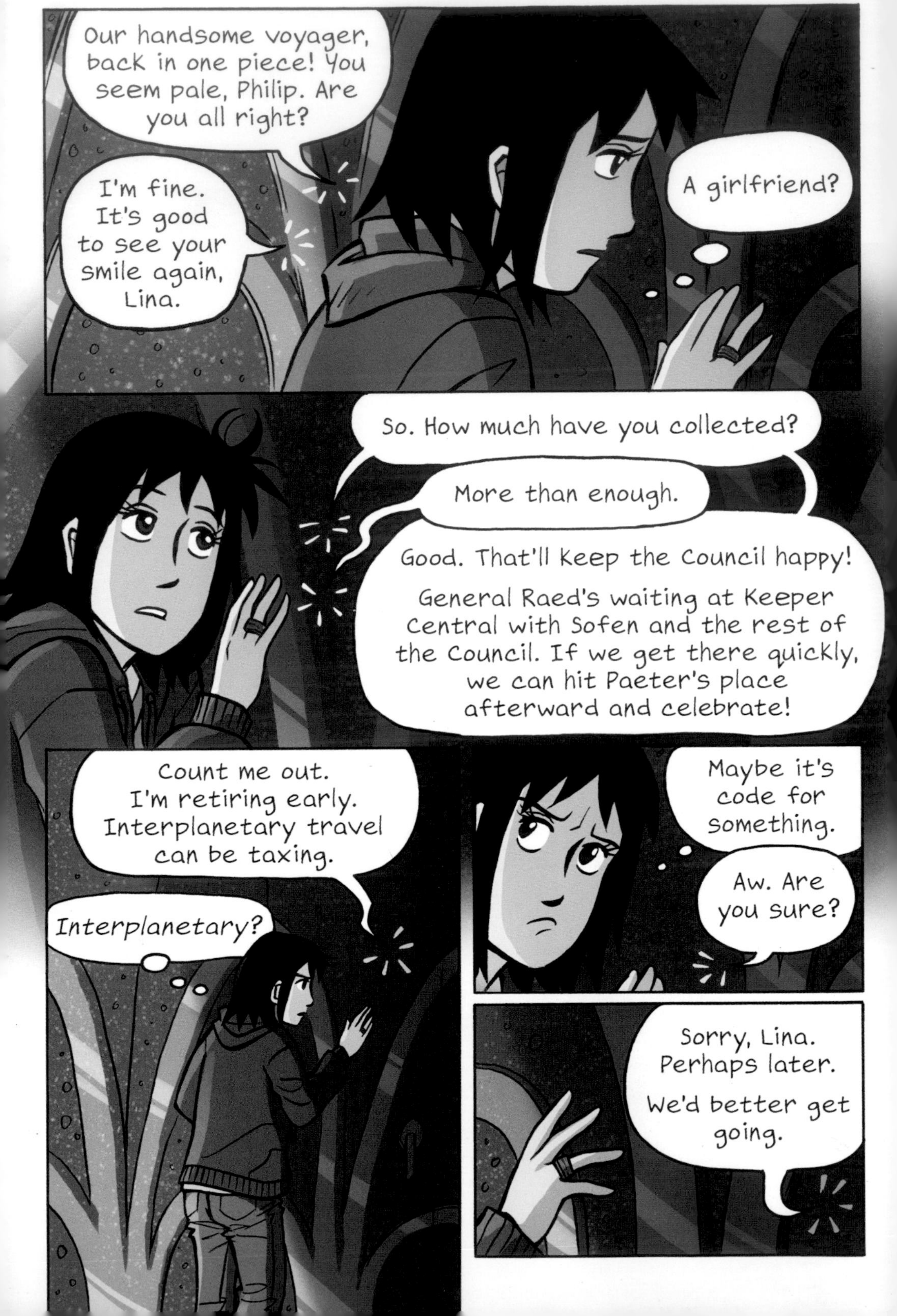
Our handsome voyager, back in one piece! You seem pale, Philip. Are you all right?
I'm fine. It's good to see your smile again, Lina.
A girlfriend?
So. How much have you collected?
More than enough.
Good. That'll keep the Council happy!
General Raed's waiting at Keeper Central with Sofen and the rest of the Council. If we get there quickly, we can hit Paeter's place afterward and celebrate!
Count me out. I'm retiring early. Interplanetary travel can be taxing.
Interplanetary?
Maybe it's code for something.
Aw. Are you sure?
Sorry, Lina. Perhaps later.
We'd better get going.

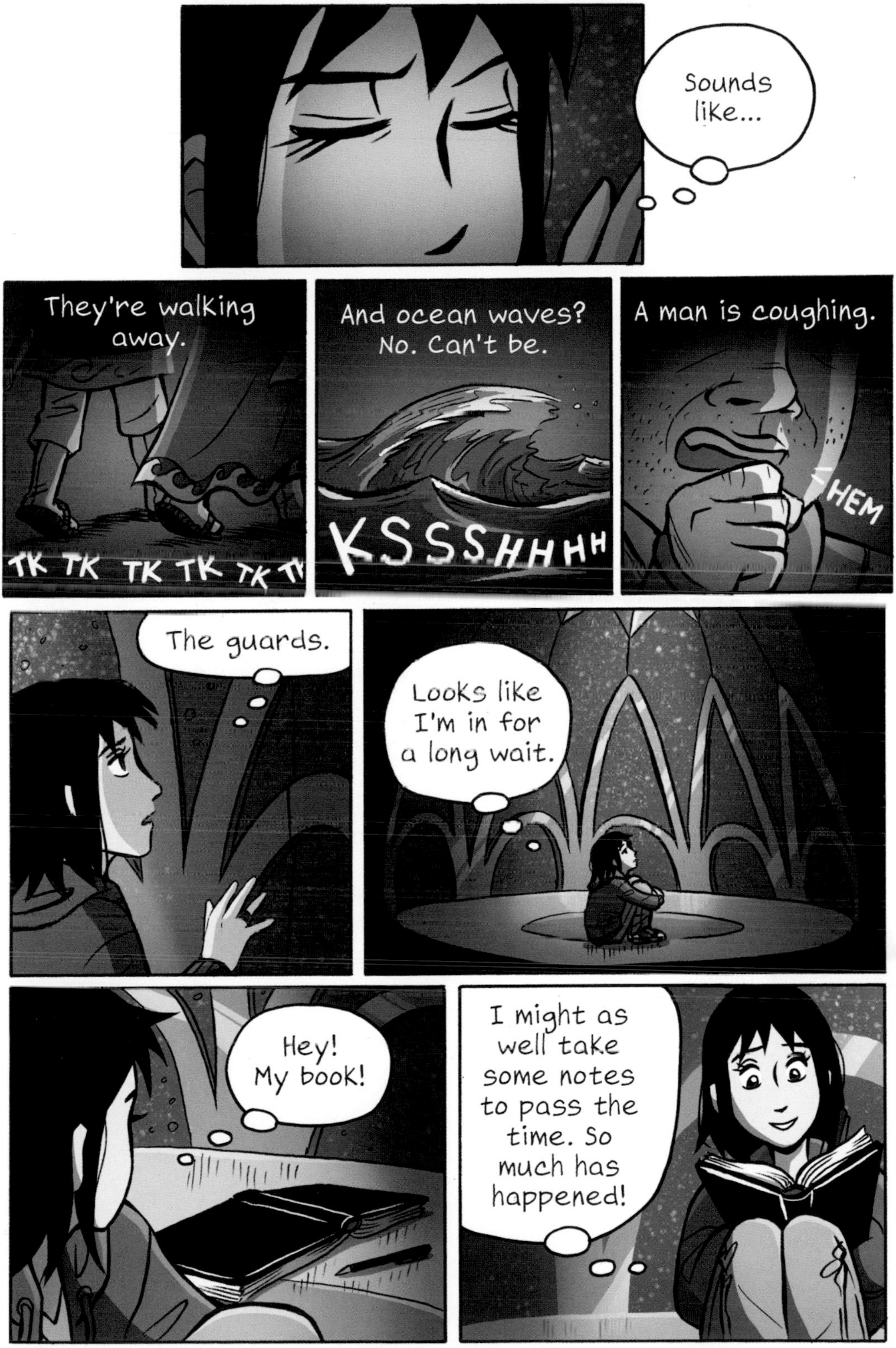
Sounds like...
They're walking away.
TK TK TK TK TK TK
And ocean waves? No. Can't be.
KSSSHHHH
A man is coughing.
HEM
The guards.
Looks like I'm in for a long wait.
Hey! My book!
I might as well take some notes to pass the time. So much has happened!

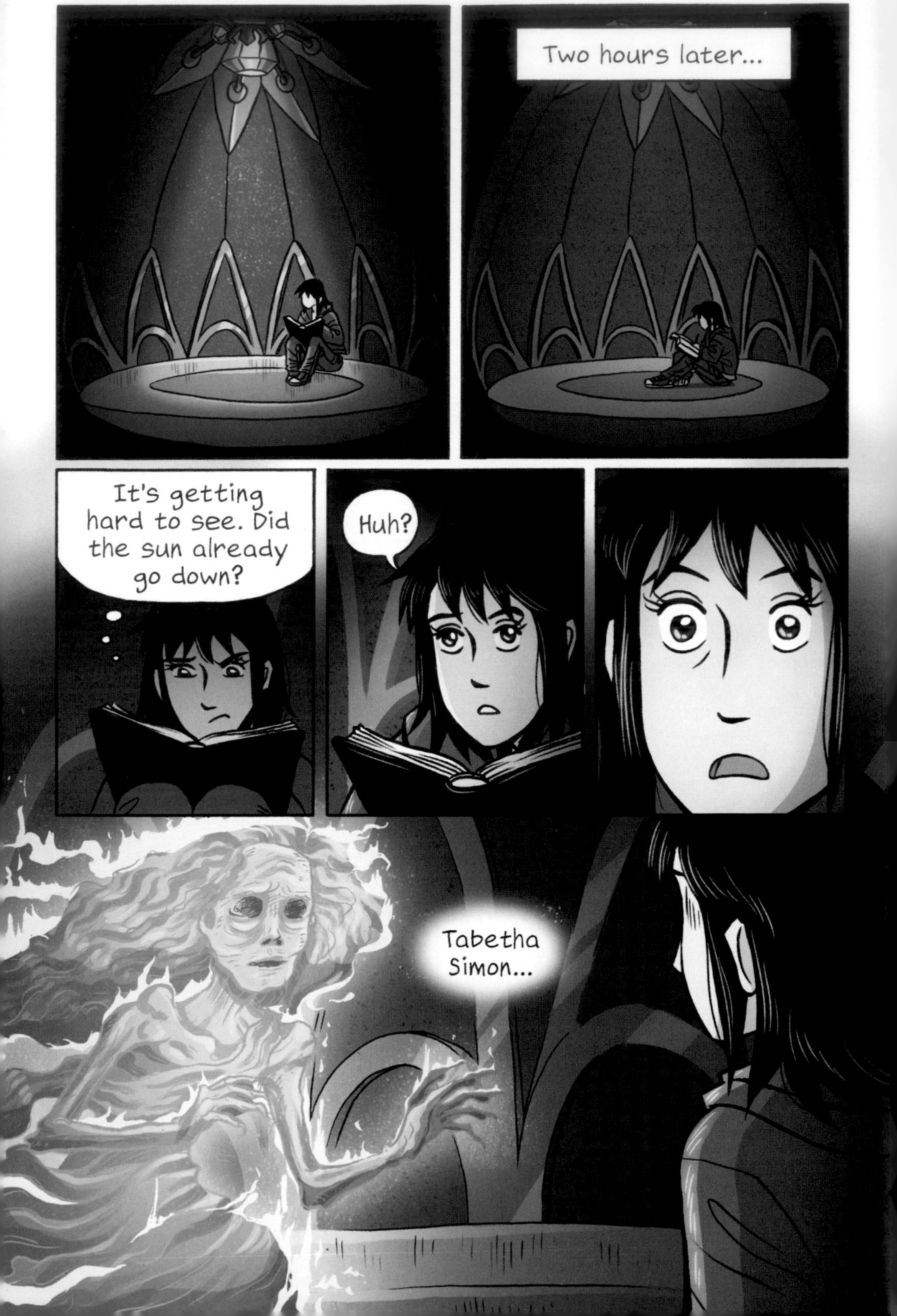
Two hours later...
It's getting hard to see. Did the sun already go down?
Huh?
Tabetha Simon...

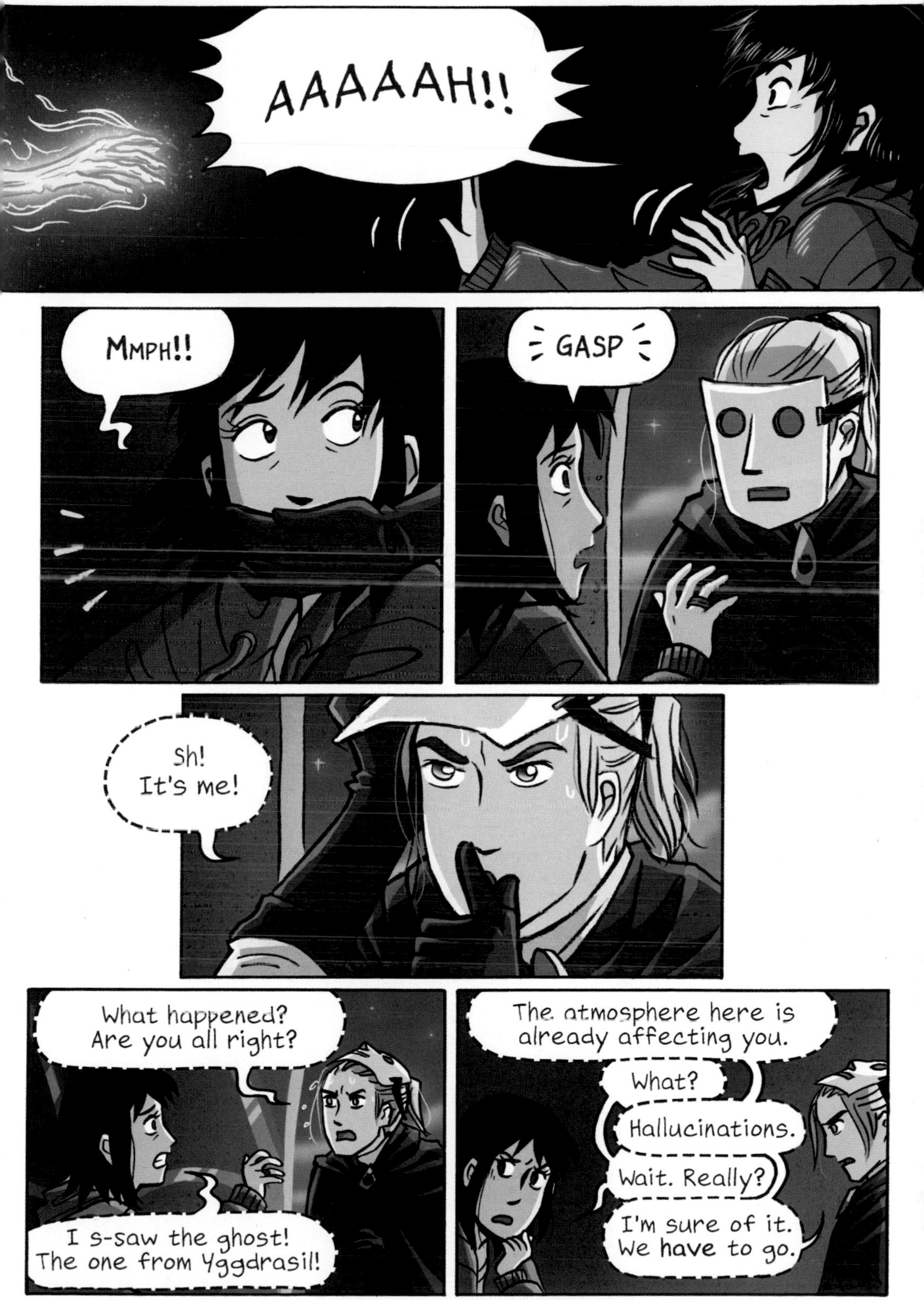
AAAAAH!!
MMPH!!
GASP
Sh!
It's me!
What happened?
Are you all right?
I s-saw the ghost!
The one from Yggdrasil!
The atmosphere here is already affecting you.
What?
Hallucinations.
Wait. Really?
I'm sure of it.
We have to go.

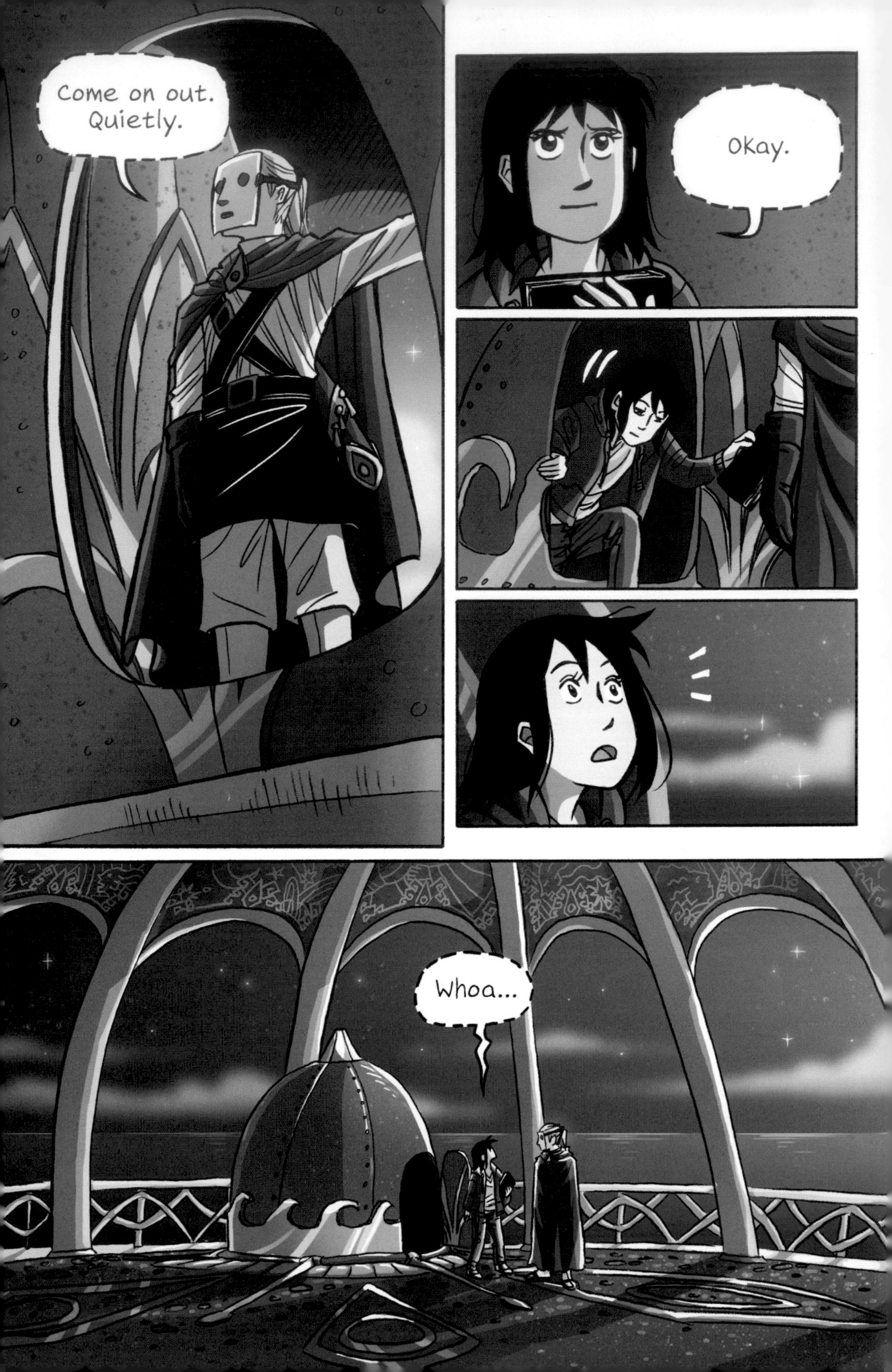
Come on out. Quietly.
Okay.
Whoa...

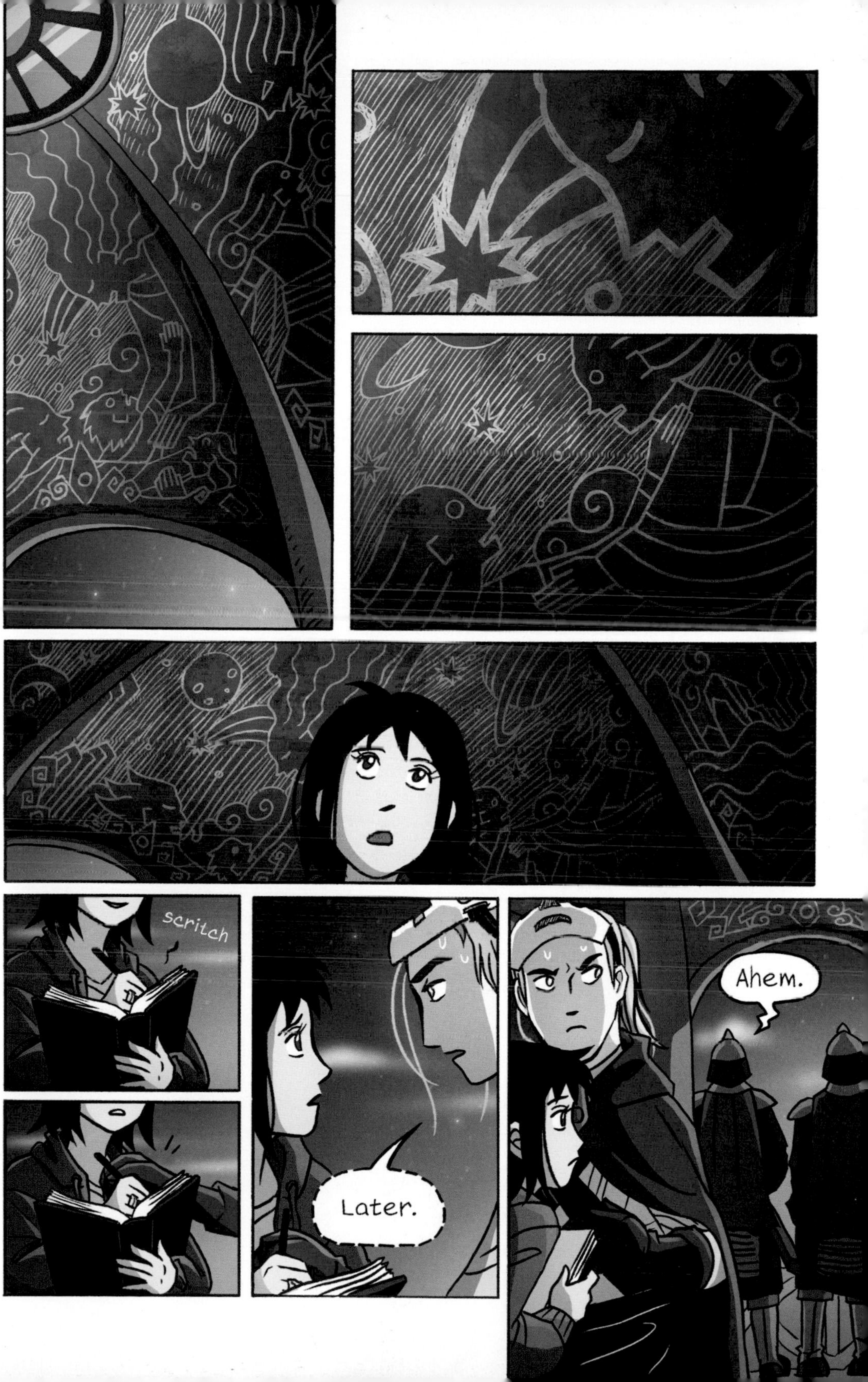
scritch
Later.
Ahem.

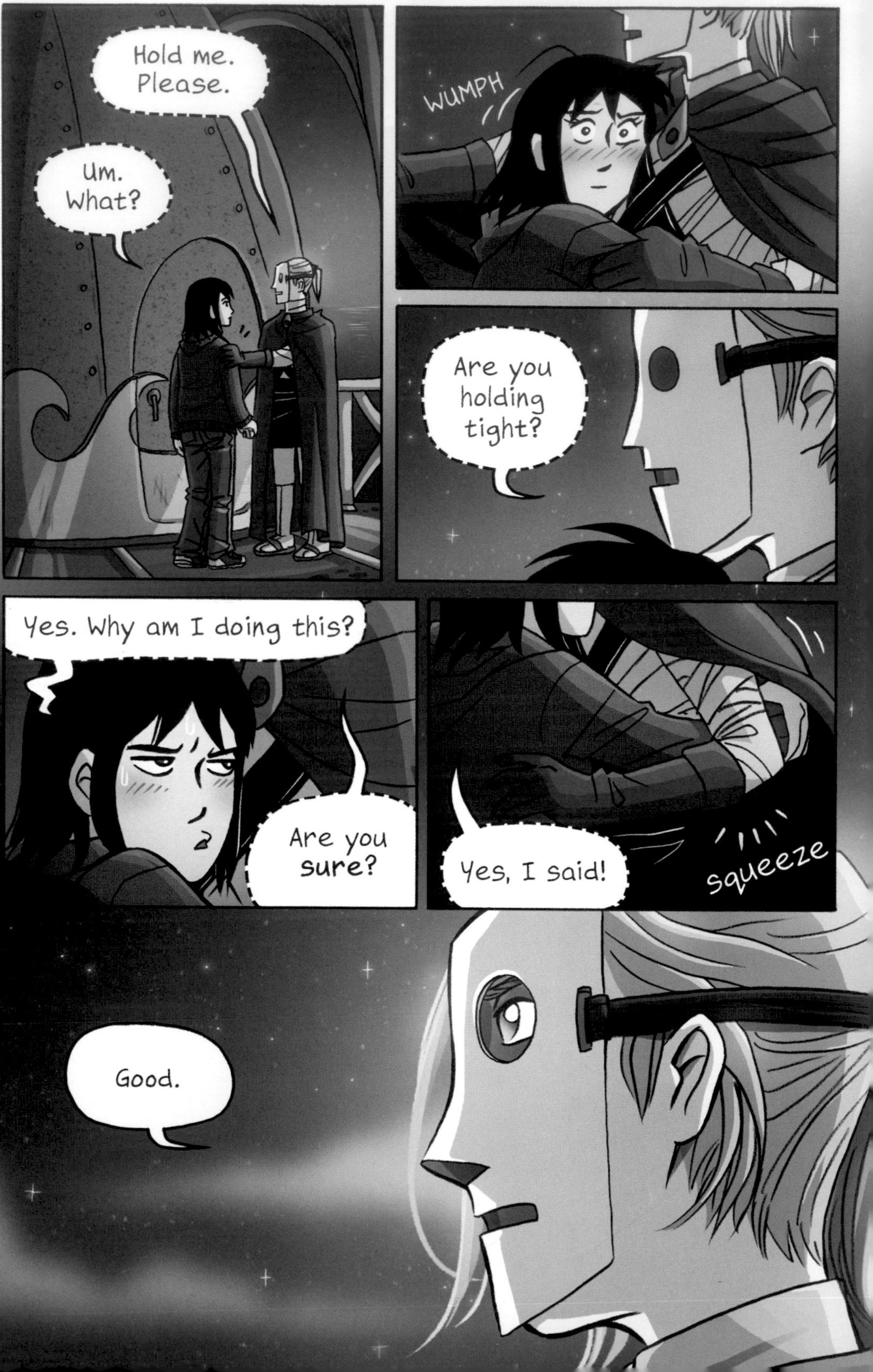
Hold me. Please.
Um. What?
WUMPH
Are you holding tight?
Yes. Why am I doing this?
Are you sure?
Yes, I said!
squeeze
Good.

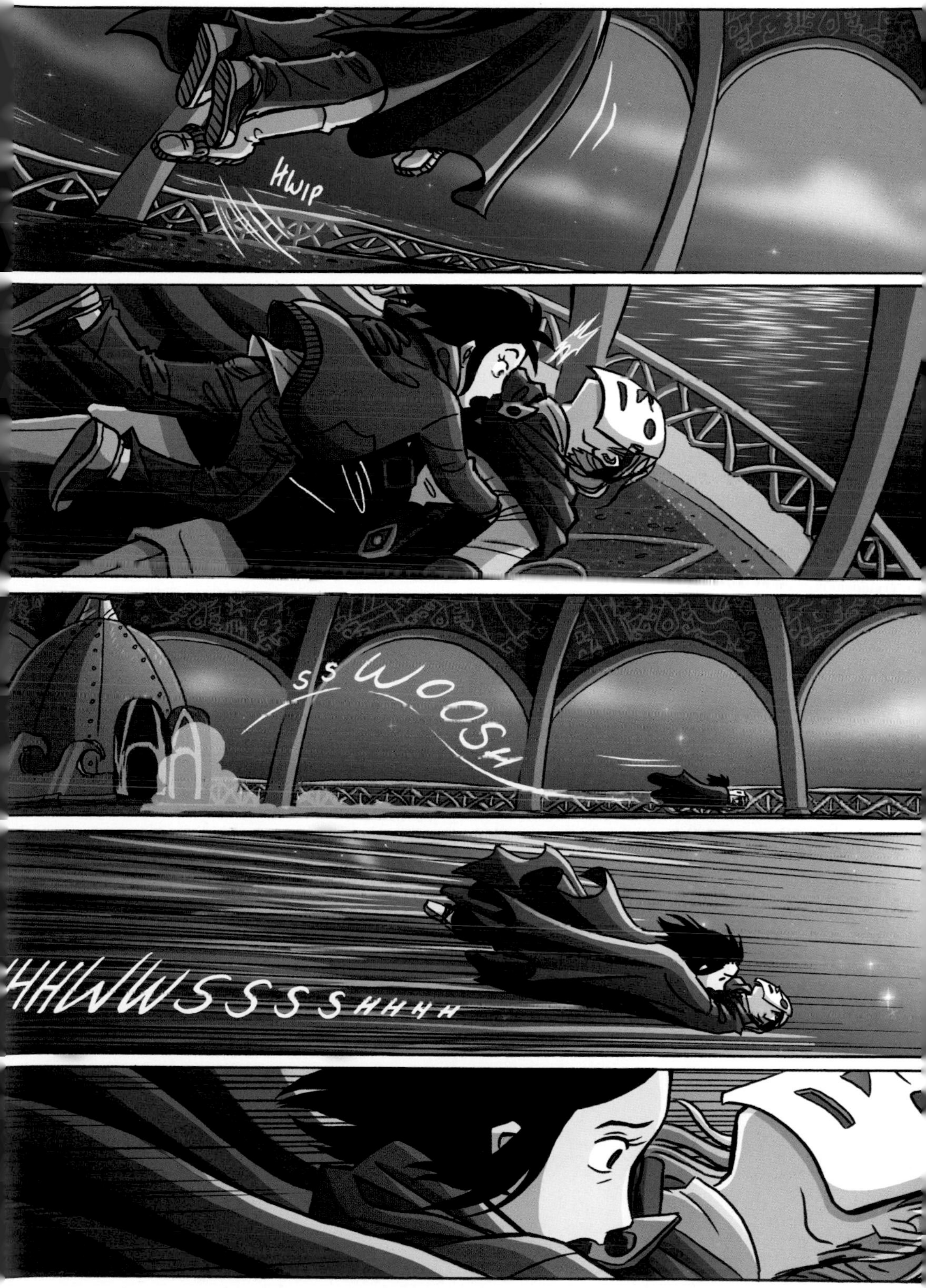
HWIP
SSWOOSH
HHWWWSSSSSHHHH

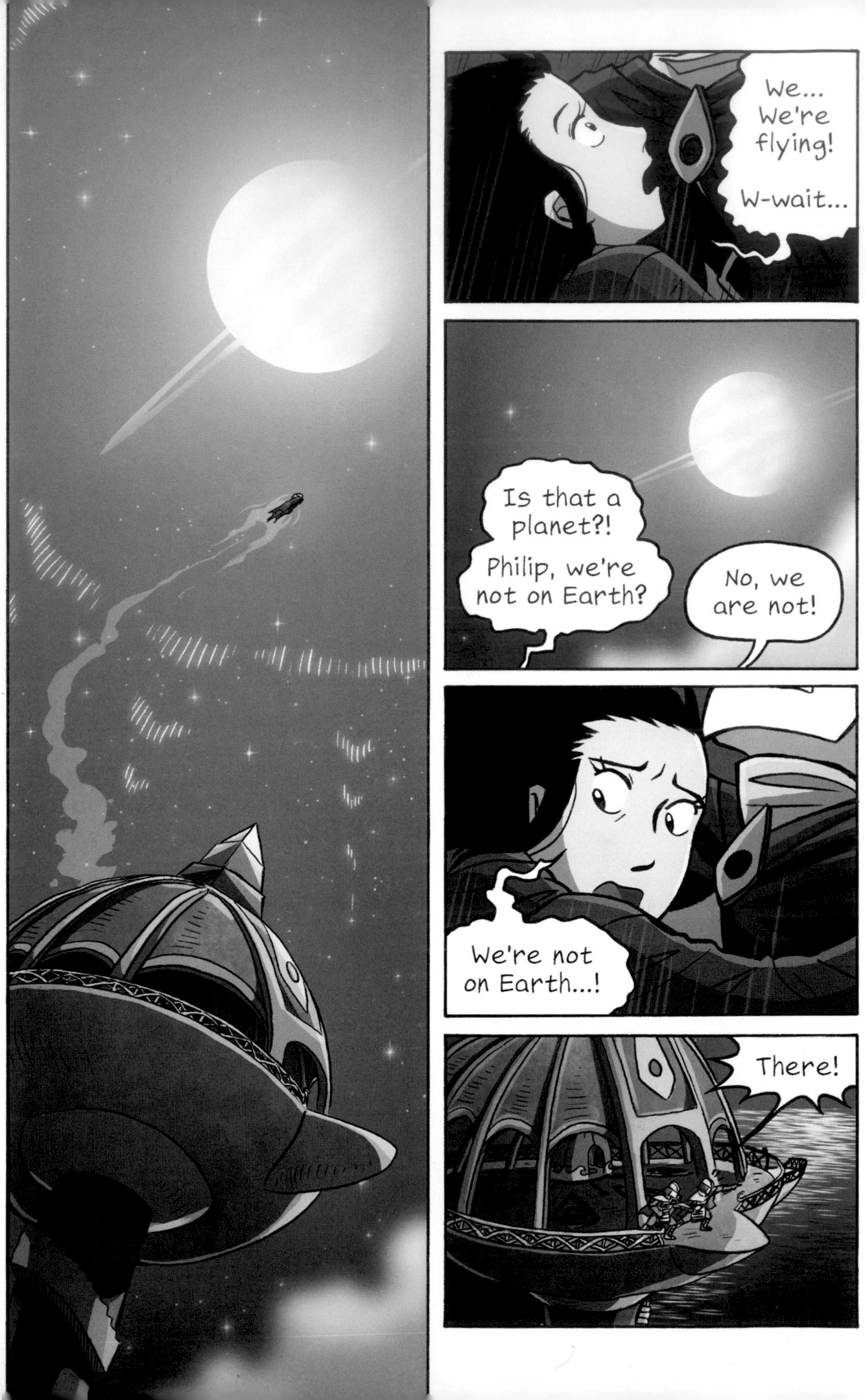
We... We're flying!
W-wait...
Is that a planet?!
Philip, we're not on Earth?
No, we are not!
We're not on Earth...!
There!

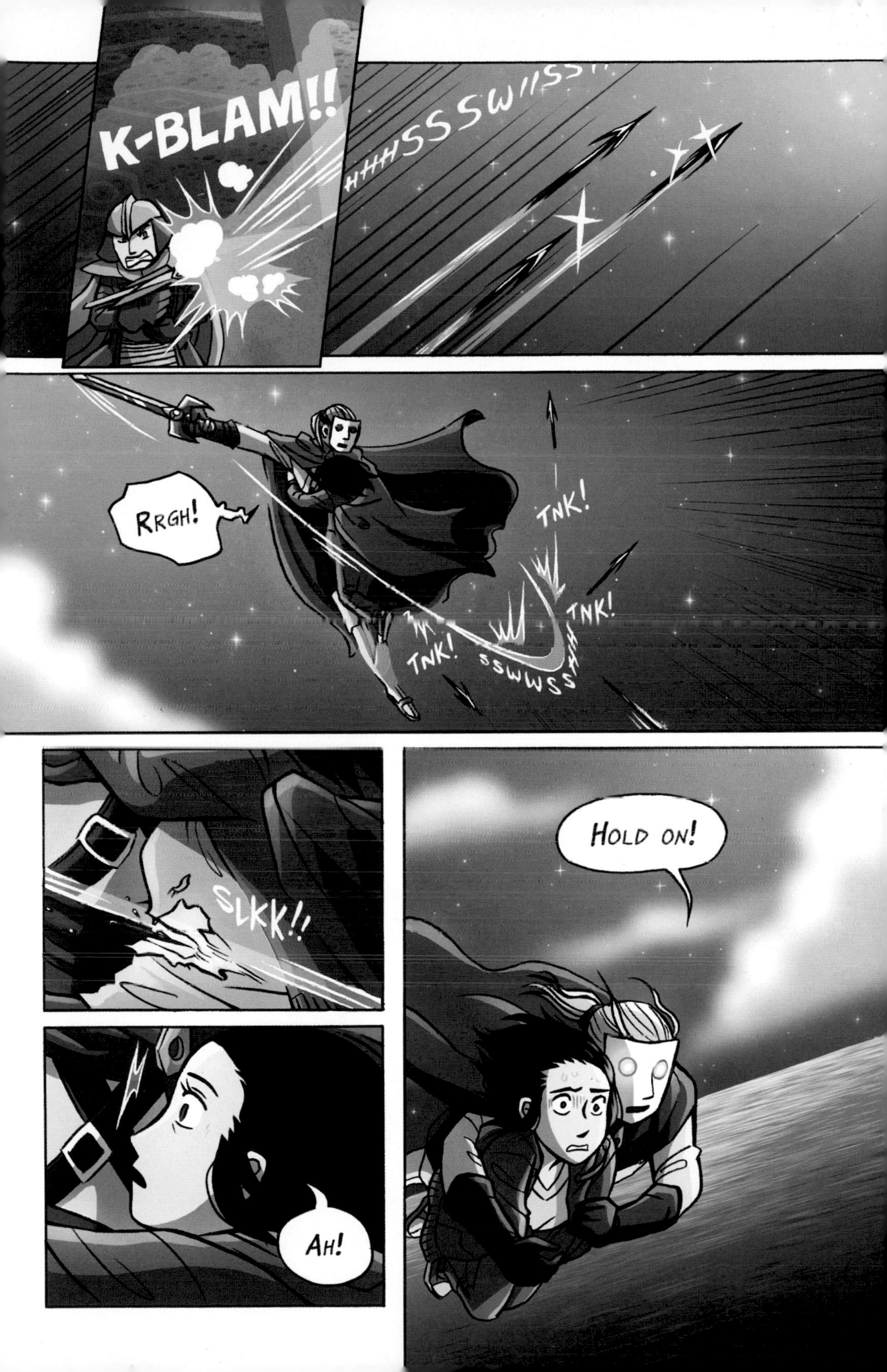
K-BLAM!!
HHHSSSW!!SS!!
RRGH!
TNK!
TNK!
TNK!
SSWWSSHH
SLKK!!
AH!
HOLD ON!

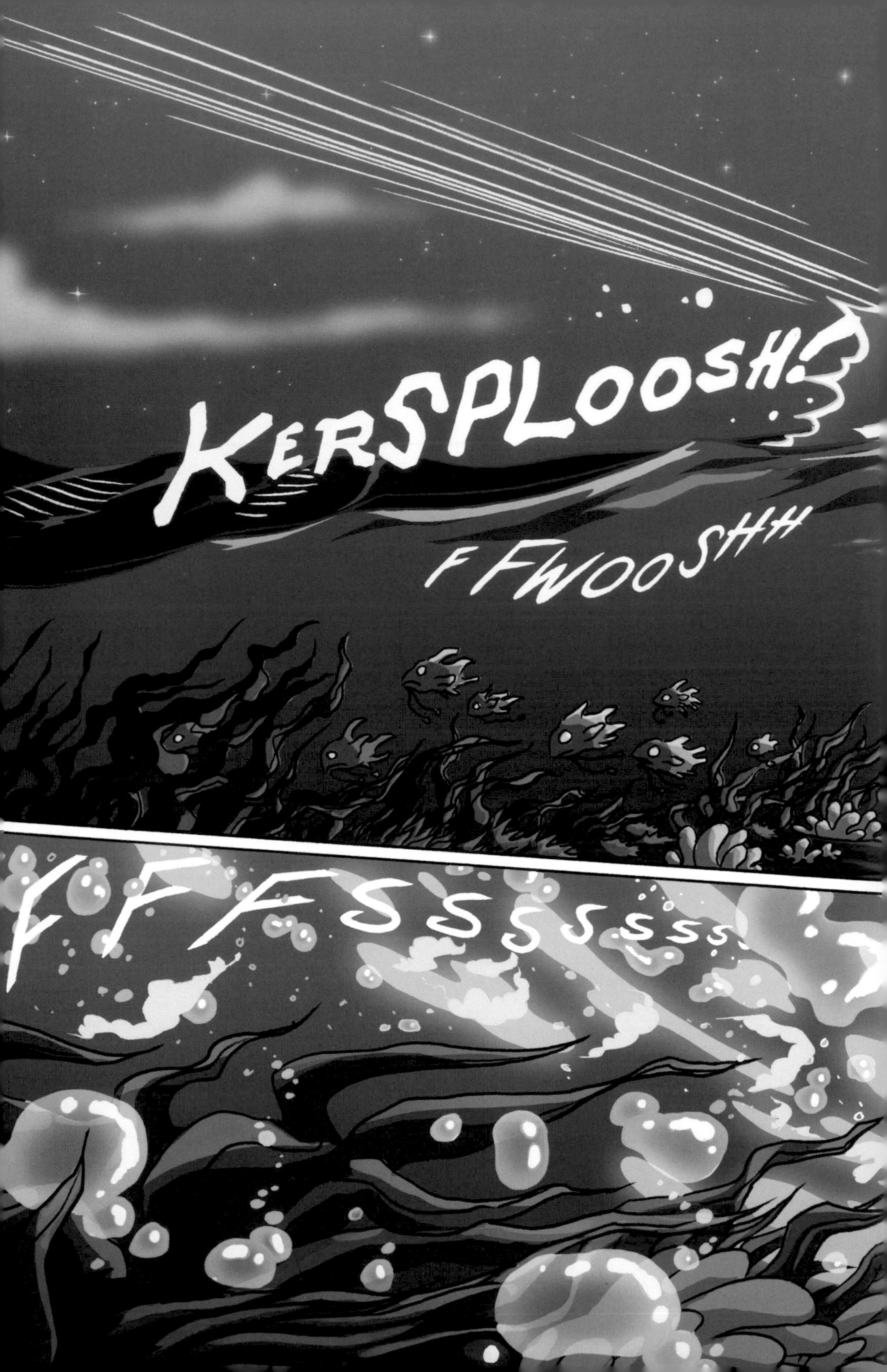
KERSPLOOSH!
FFWOOSHH
FFFSSSSSS

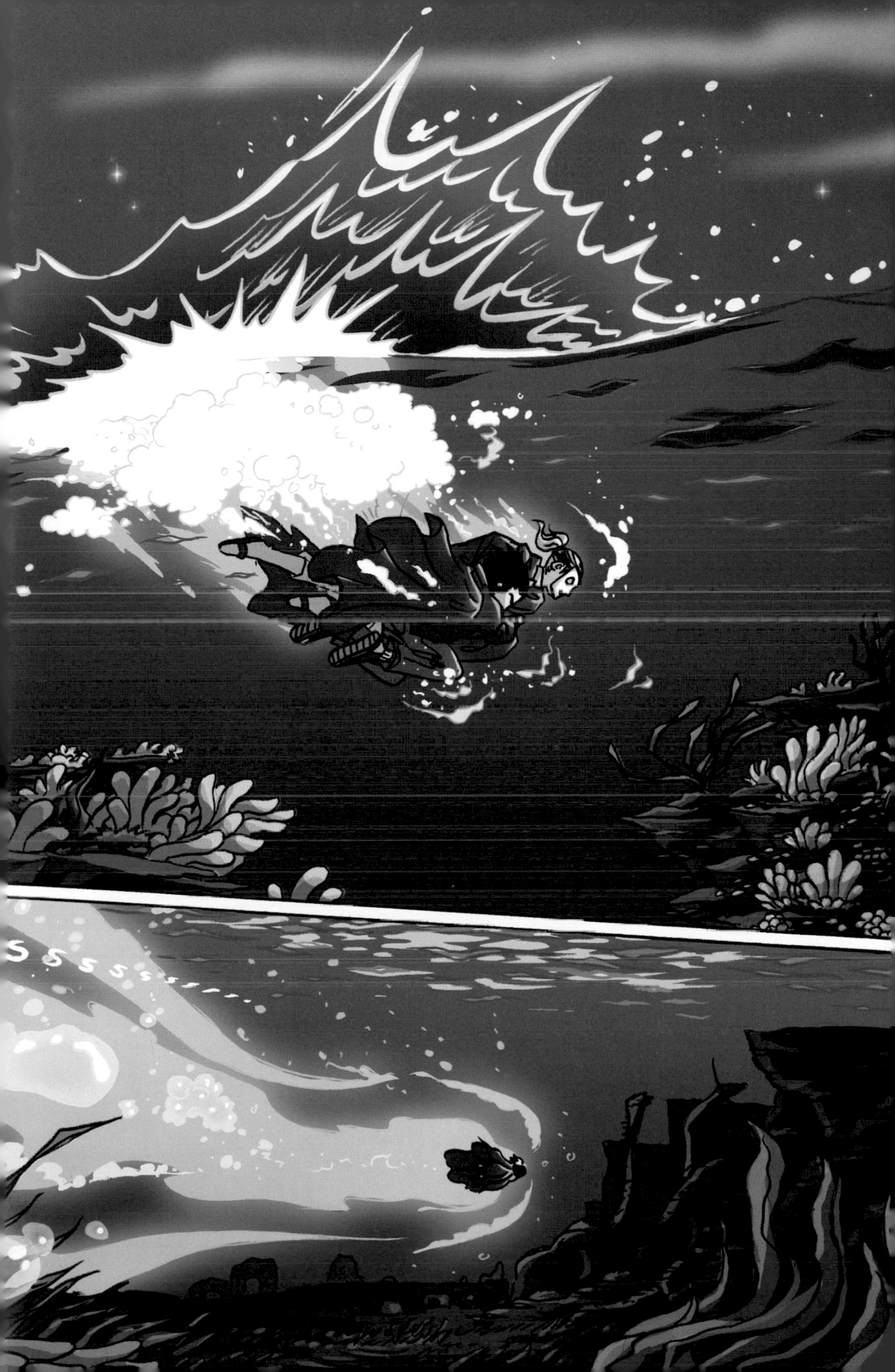
SSSSSS

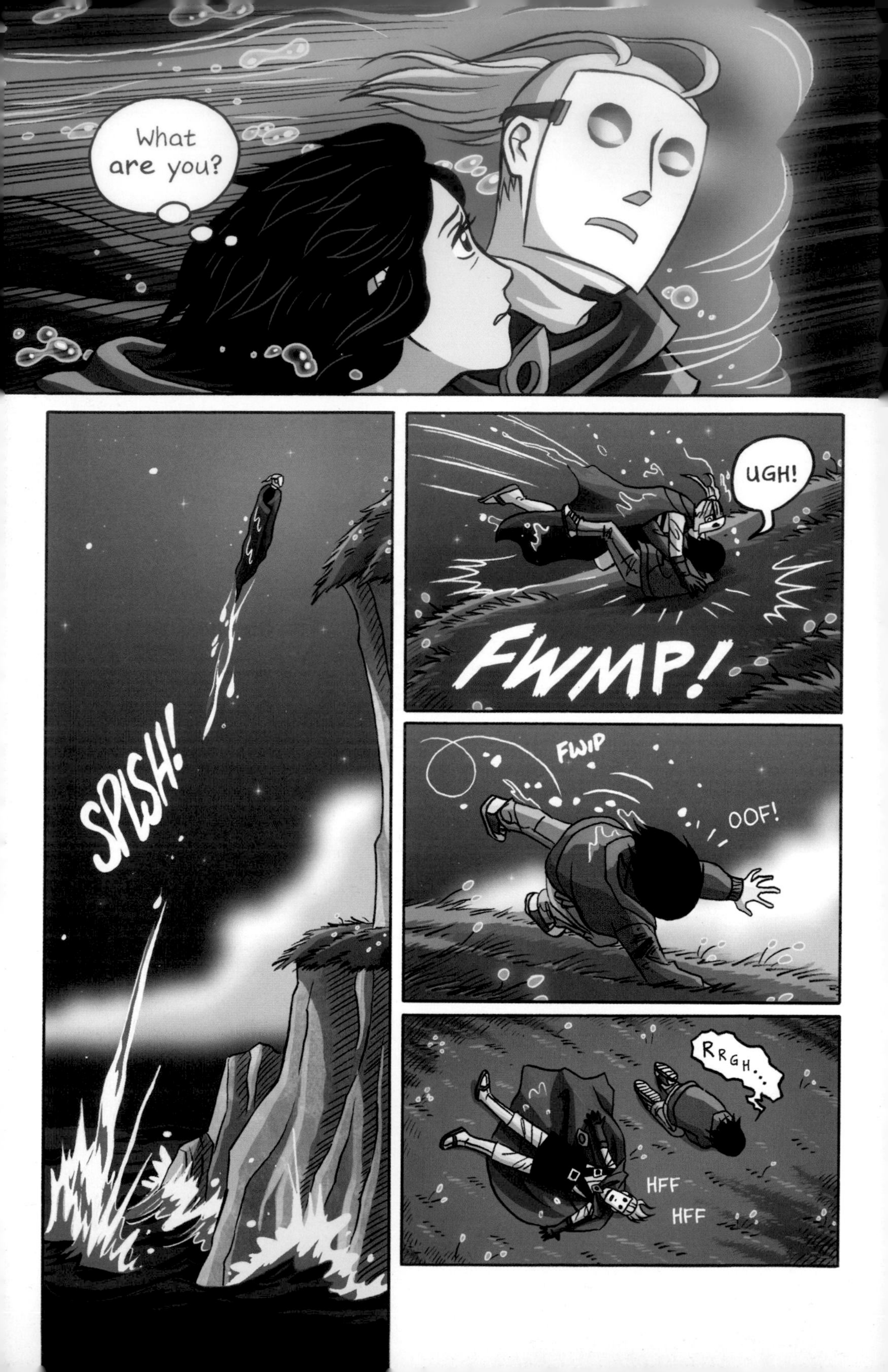
What are you?
SPLSH!
UGH!
FWMP!
FWIP
OOF!
RRGH...
HFF
HFF

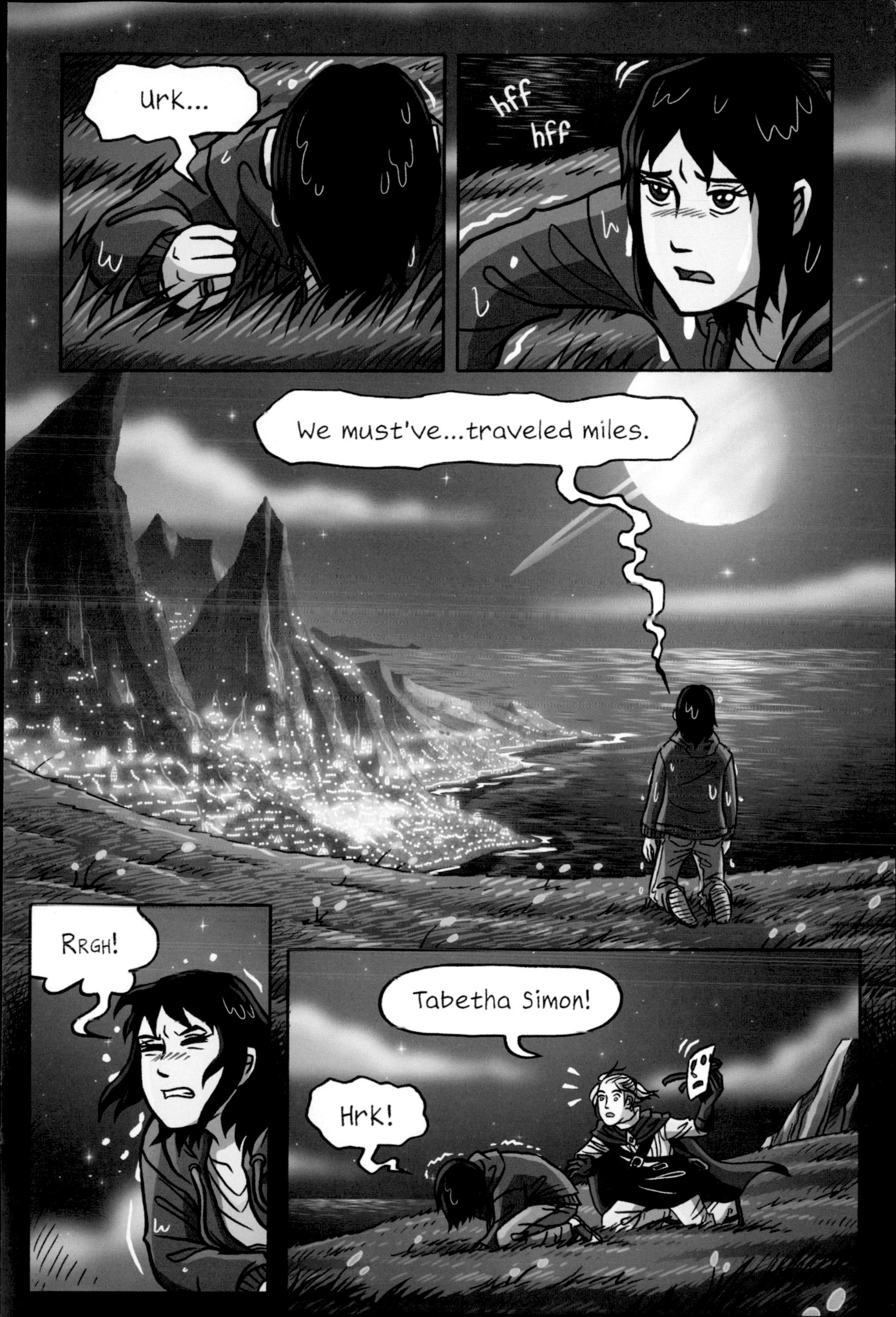
Urk...
hff
hff
We must've...traveled miles.
RRGH!
Tabetha Simon!
Hrk!

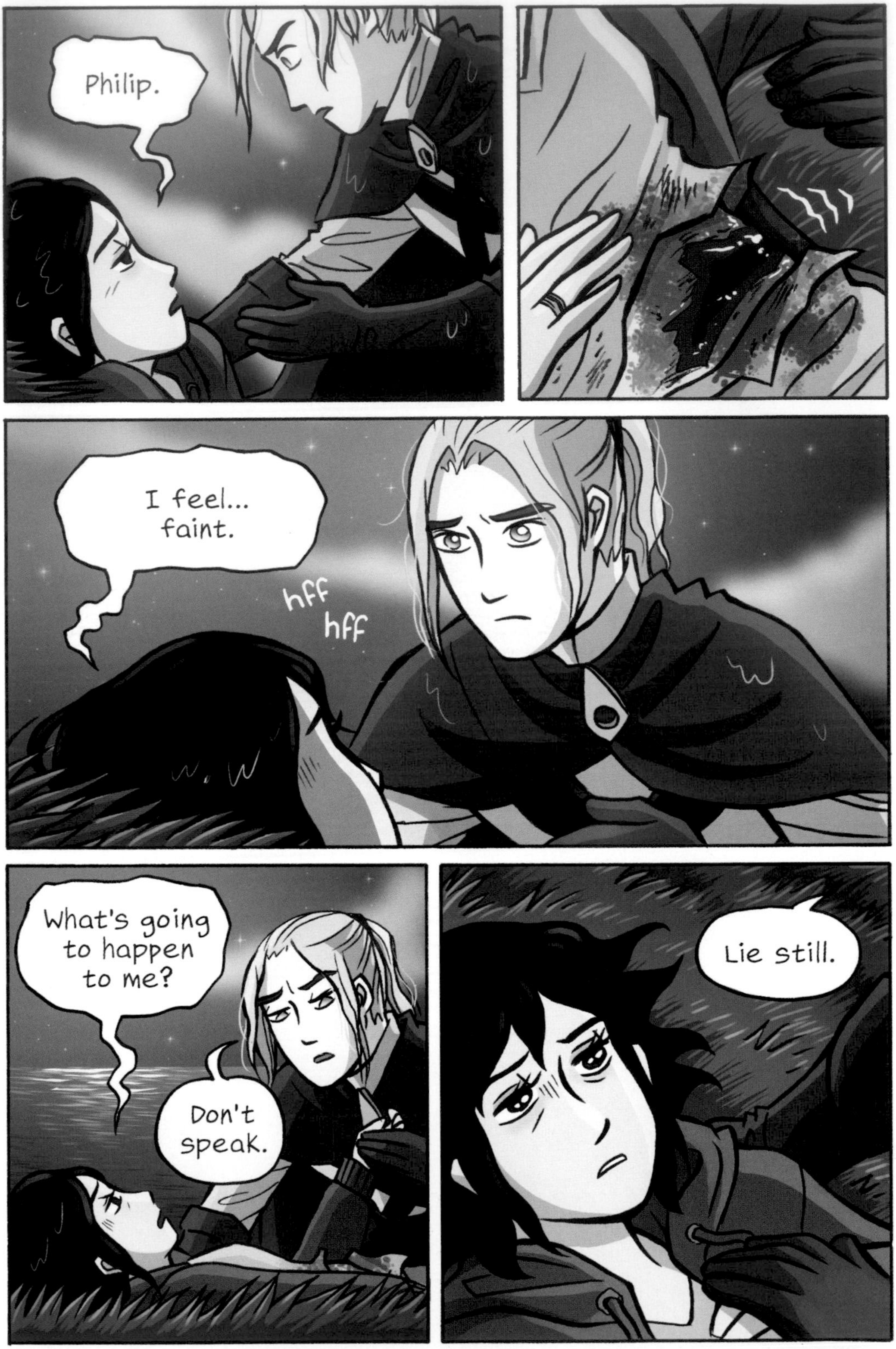

Philip.
I feel... faint.
hff
hff
What's going to happen to me?
Don't speak.
Lie still.

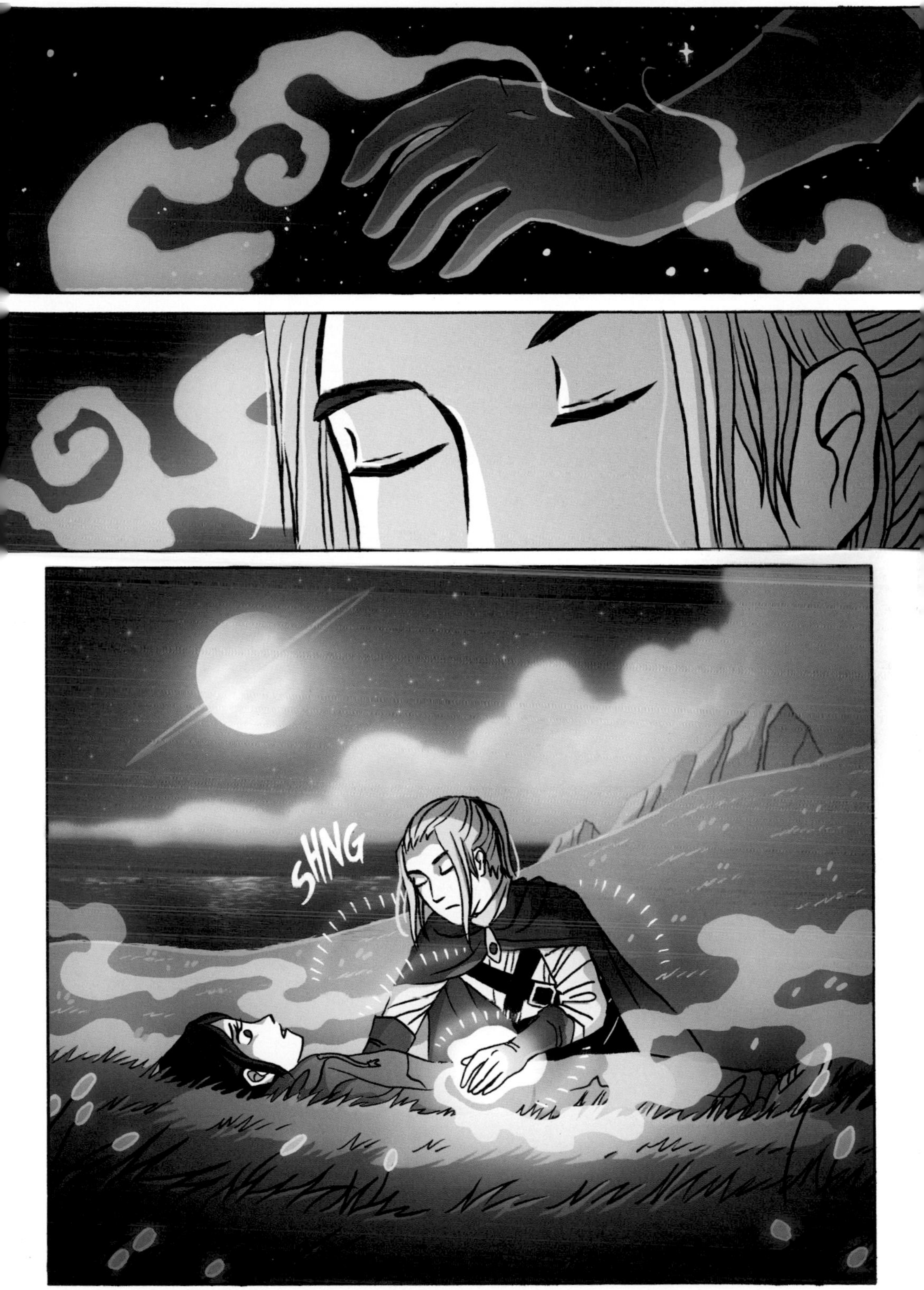
SHNG

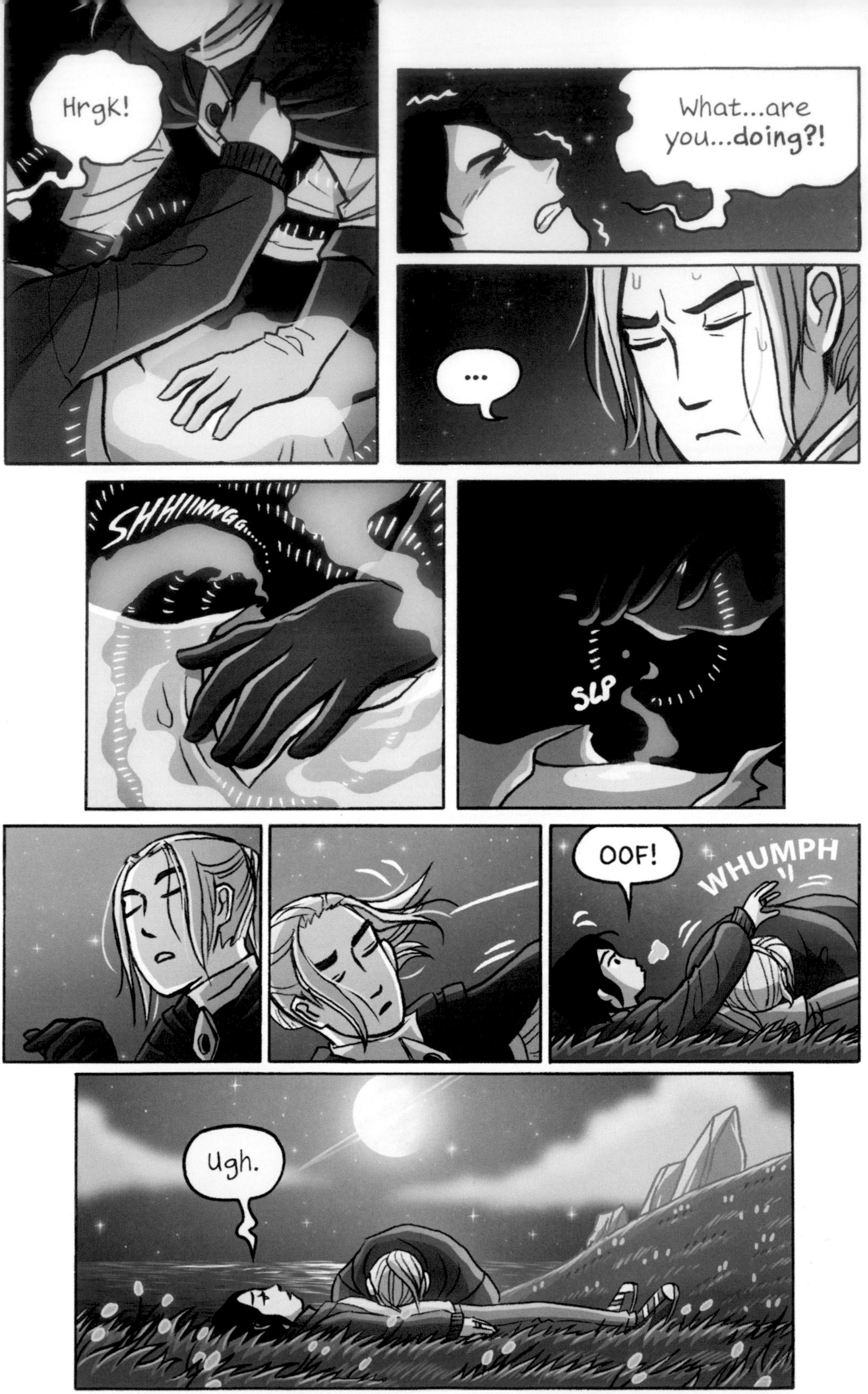
Hrgk!
What...are you...doing?!
...
SHHIINNGG......
SLP
OOF!
WHUMPH
Ugh.

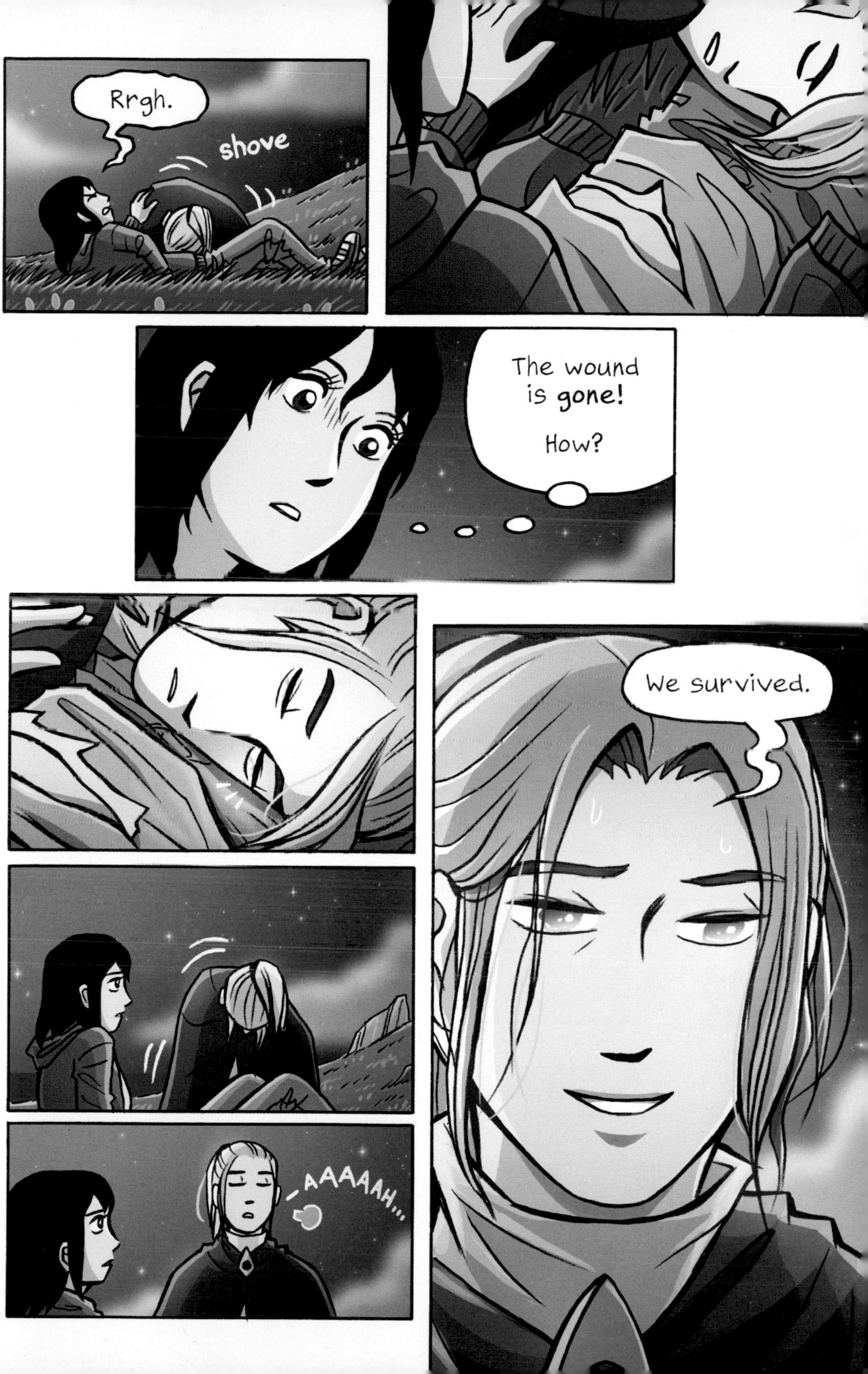
Rrgh.
shove
The wound is gone!
How?
We survived.
-AAAAAH...

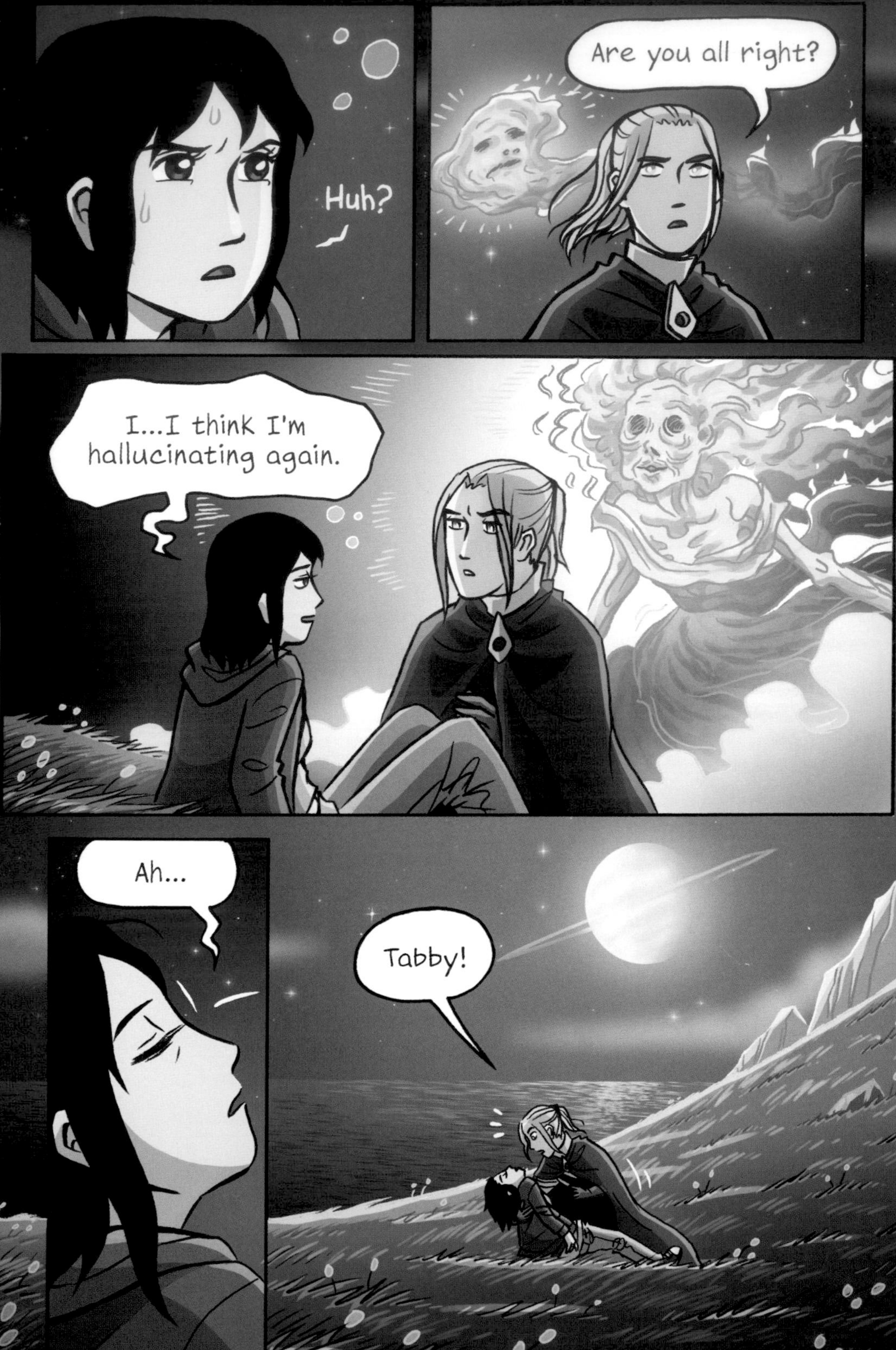
Huh?
Are you all right?
I...I think I'm hallucinating again.
Ah...
Tabby!

PART II
GEIST

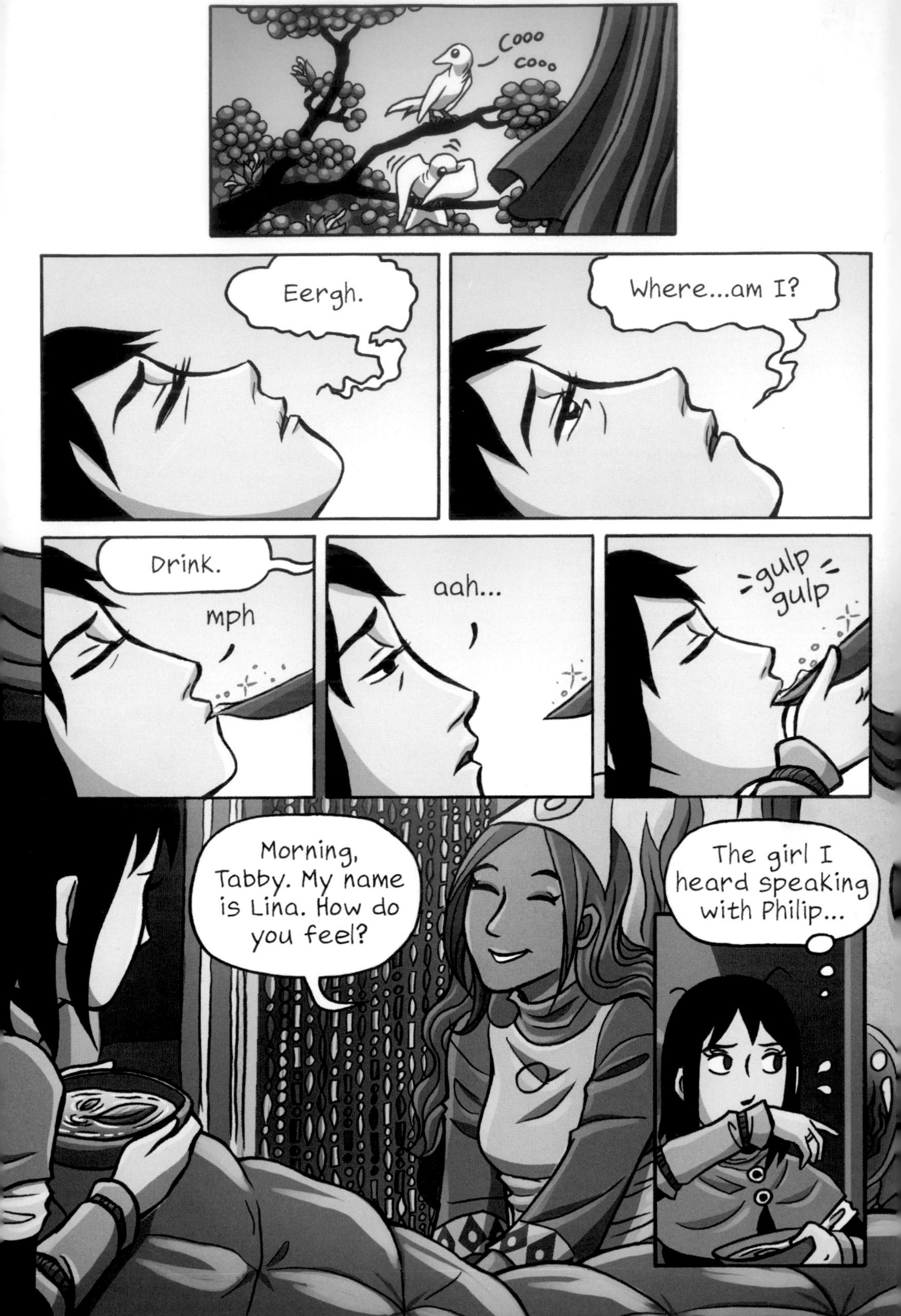
Cooo
cooo
Eergh.
Where...am I?
Drink.
mph
aah...
gulp
gulp
Morning, Tabby. My name is Lina. How do you feel?
The girl I heard speaking with Philip...

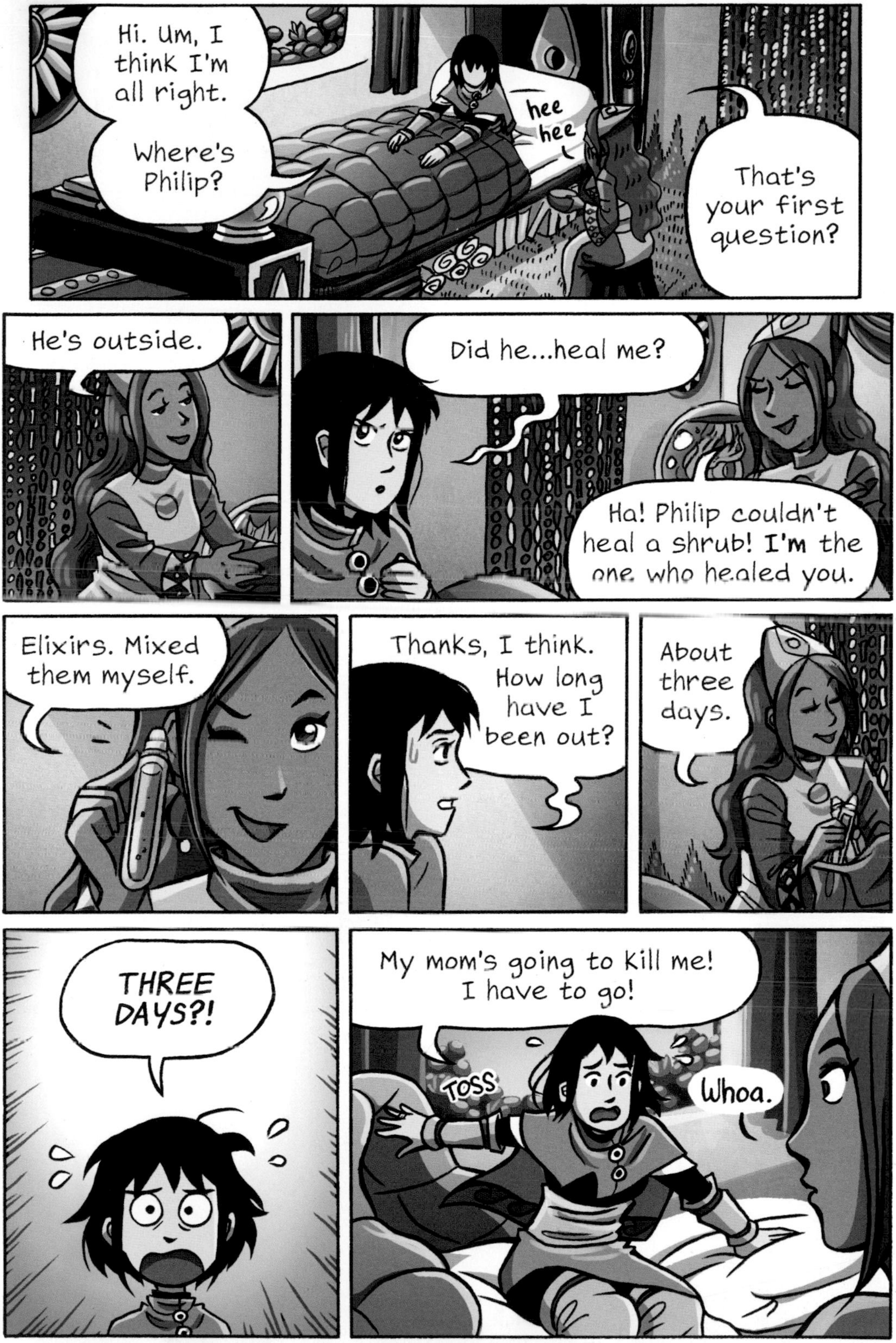
Hi. Um, I think I'm all right.
Where's Philip?
hee hee
That's your first question?
He's outside.
Did he...heal me?
Ha! Philip couldn't heal a shrub! **I'm** the one who healed you.
Elixirs. Mixed them myself.
Thanks, I think.
How long have I been out?
About three days.
THREE DAYS?!
My mom's going to kill me! I have to go!
TOSS
Whoa.

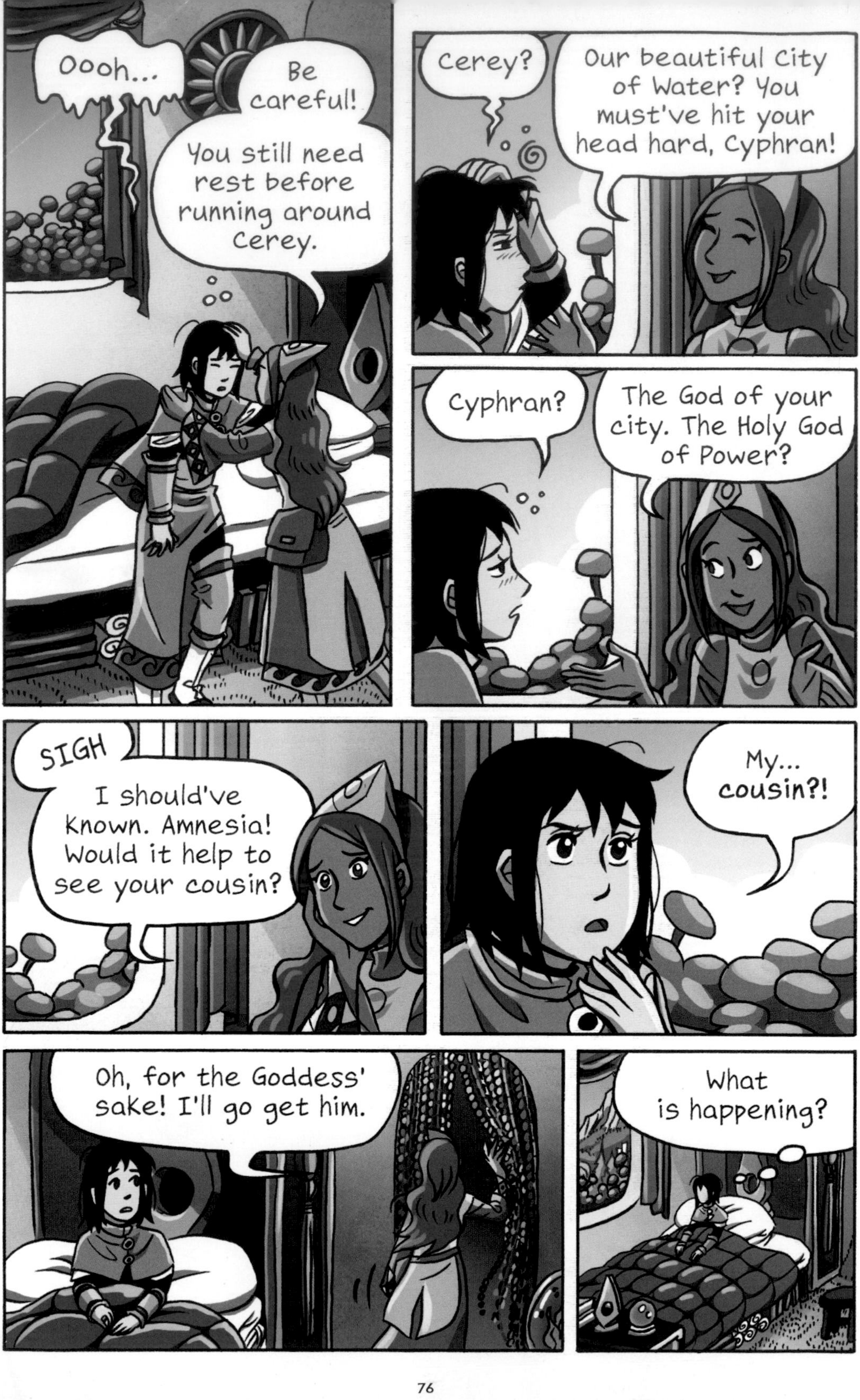
Oooh...
Be careful!
You still need rest before running around Cerey.
Cerey?
Our beautiful City of Water? You must've hit your head hard, Cyphran!
Cyphran?
The God of your city. The Holy God of Power?
SIGH
I should've known. Amnesia! Would it help to see your cousin?
My... cousin?!
Oh, for the Goddess' sake! I'll go get him.
What is happening?

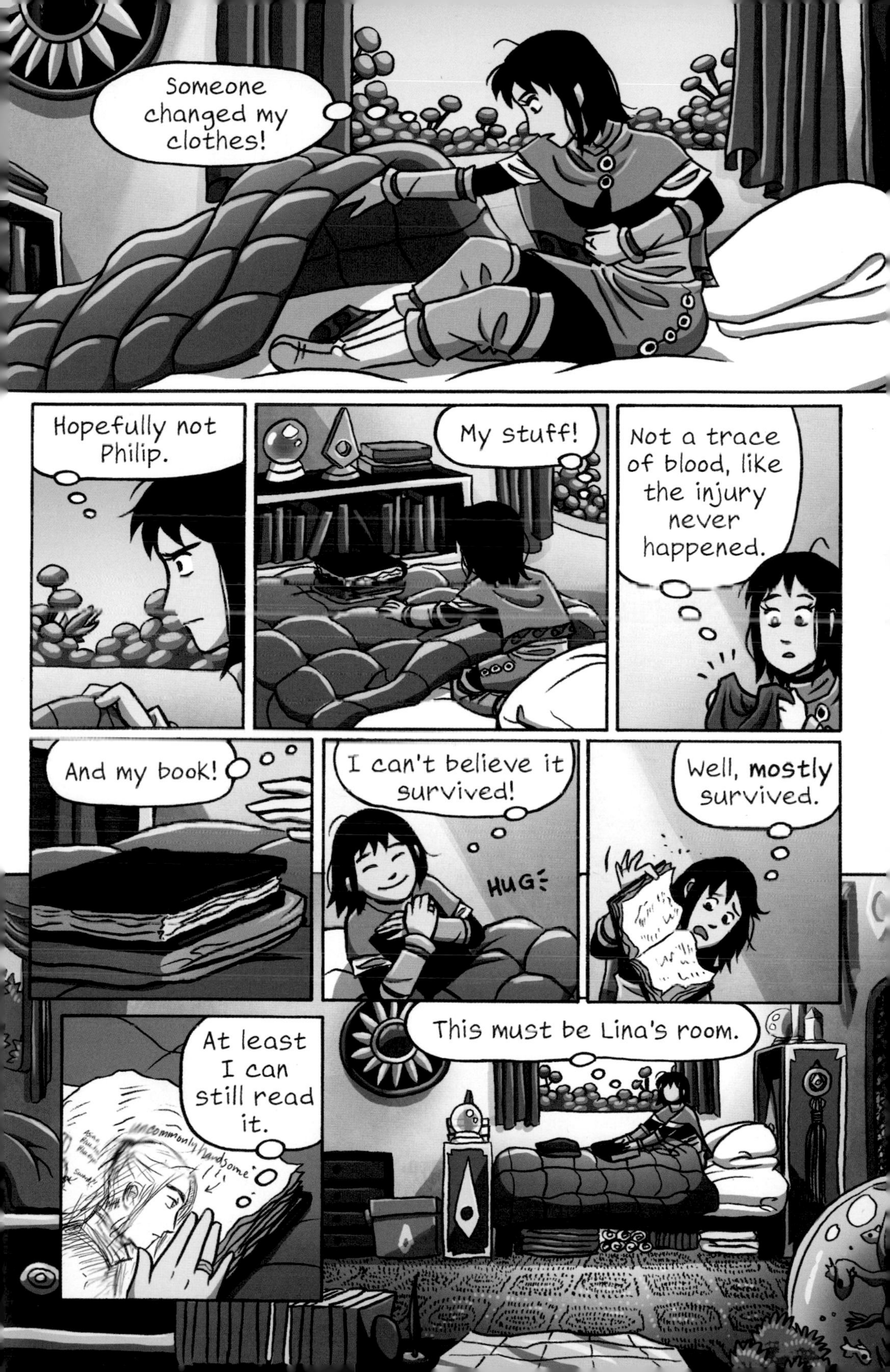
Someone changed my clothes!
Hopefully not Philip.
My stuff!
Not a trace of blood, like the injury never happened.
And my book!
I can't believe it survived!
HUG
Well, **mostly** survived.
At least I can still read it.
commonly handsome
This must be Lina's room.

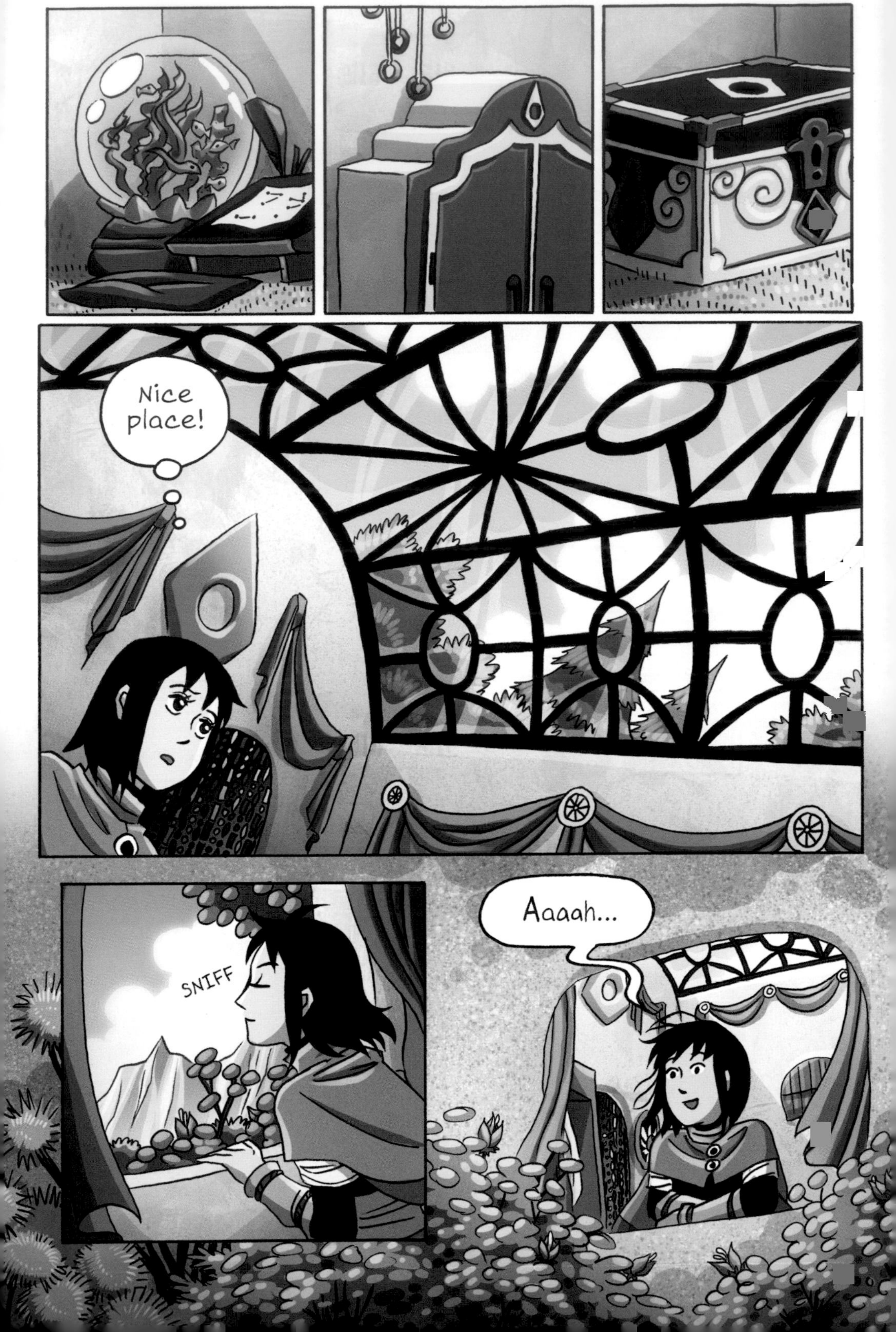
Nice place!
SNIFF
Aaaah...

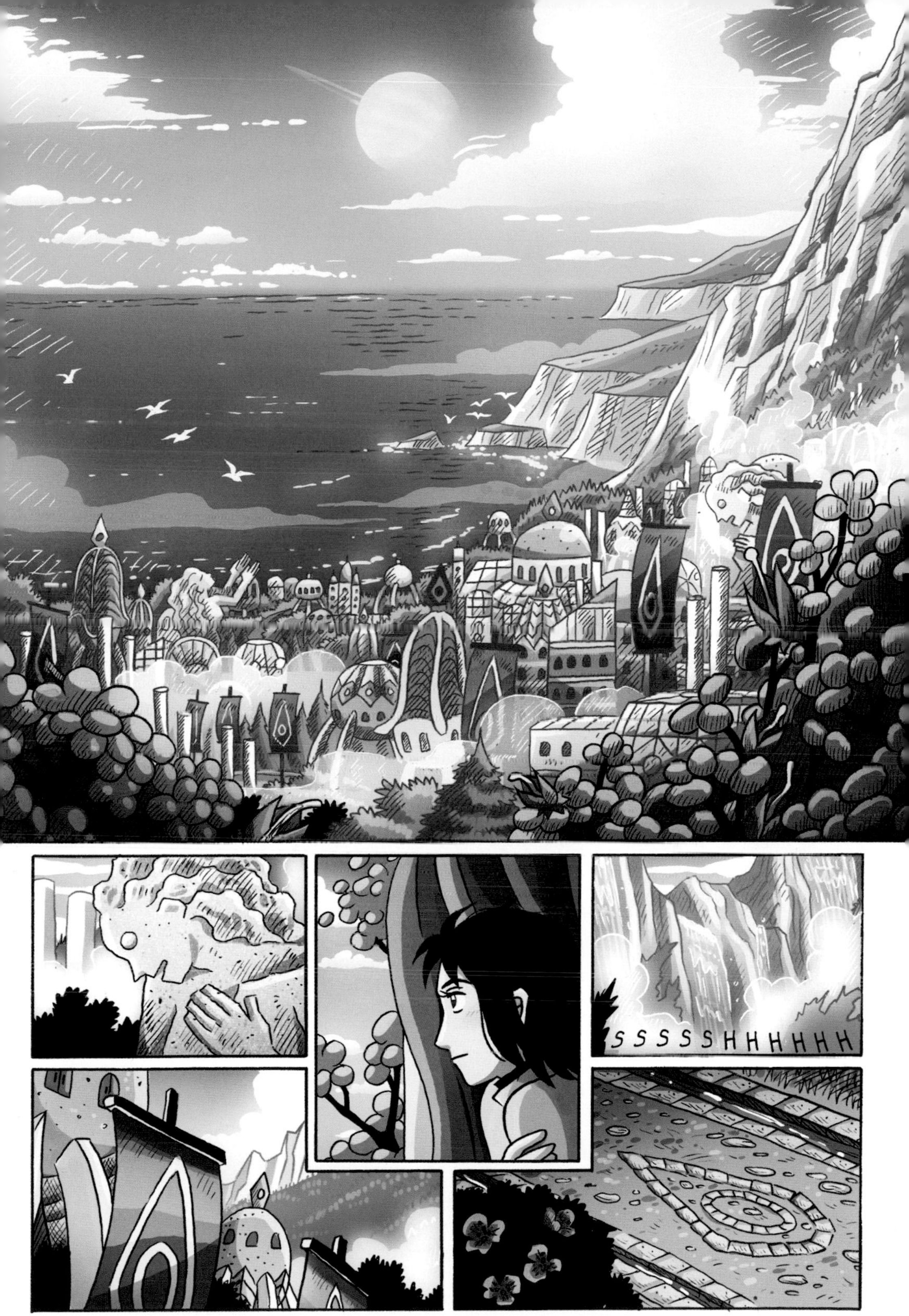
SSSSSHHHHHH

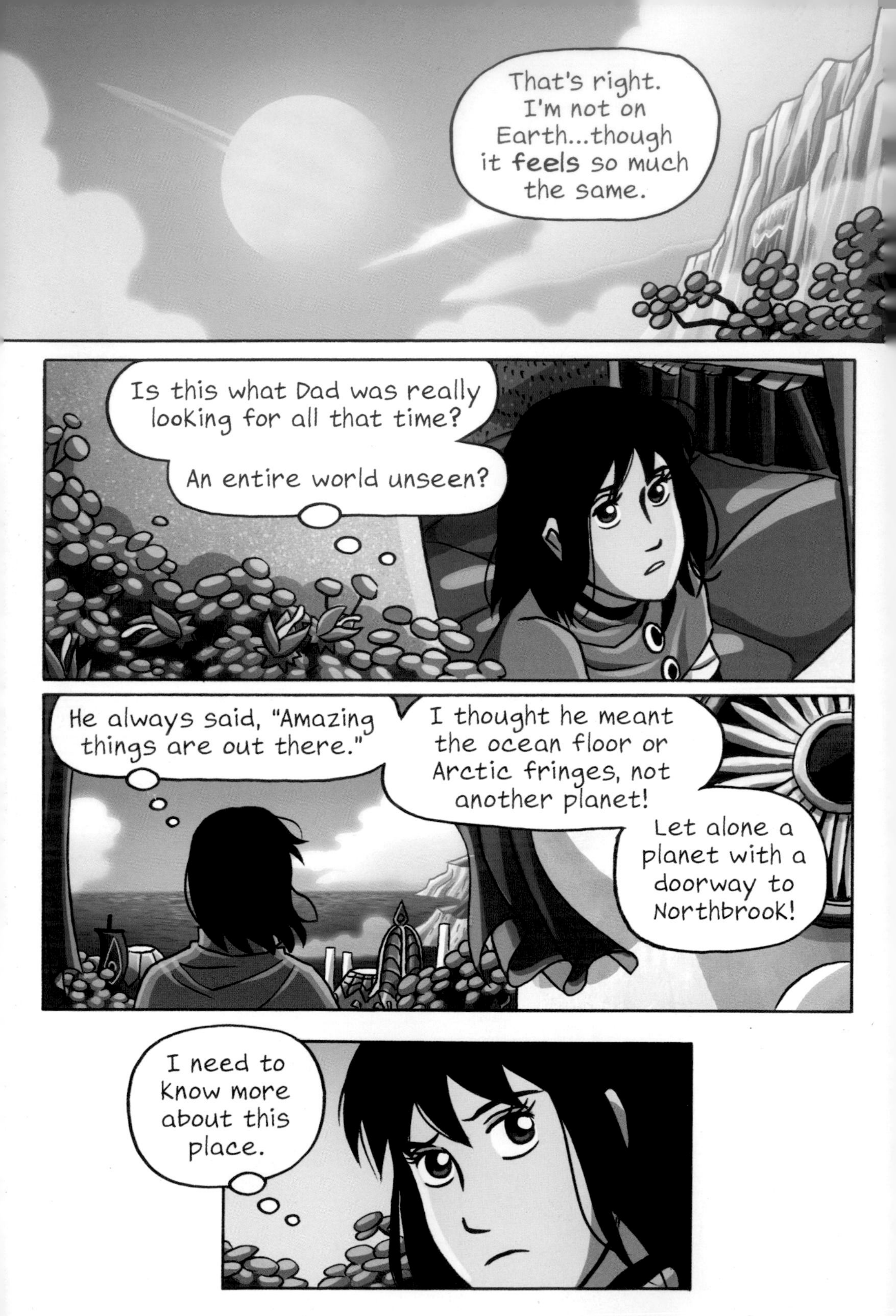
That's right. I'm not on Earth...though it **feels** so much the same.
Is this what Dad was really looking for all that time?
An entire world unseen?
He always said, "Amazing things are out there."
I thought he meant the ocean floor or Arctic fringes, not another planet!
Let alone a planet with a doorway to Northbrook!
I need to know more about this place.

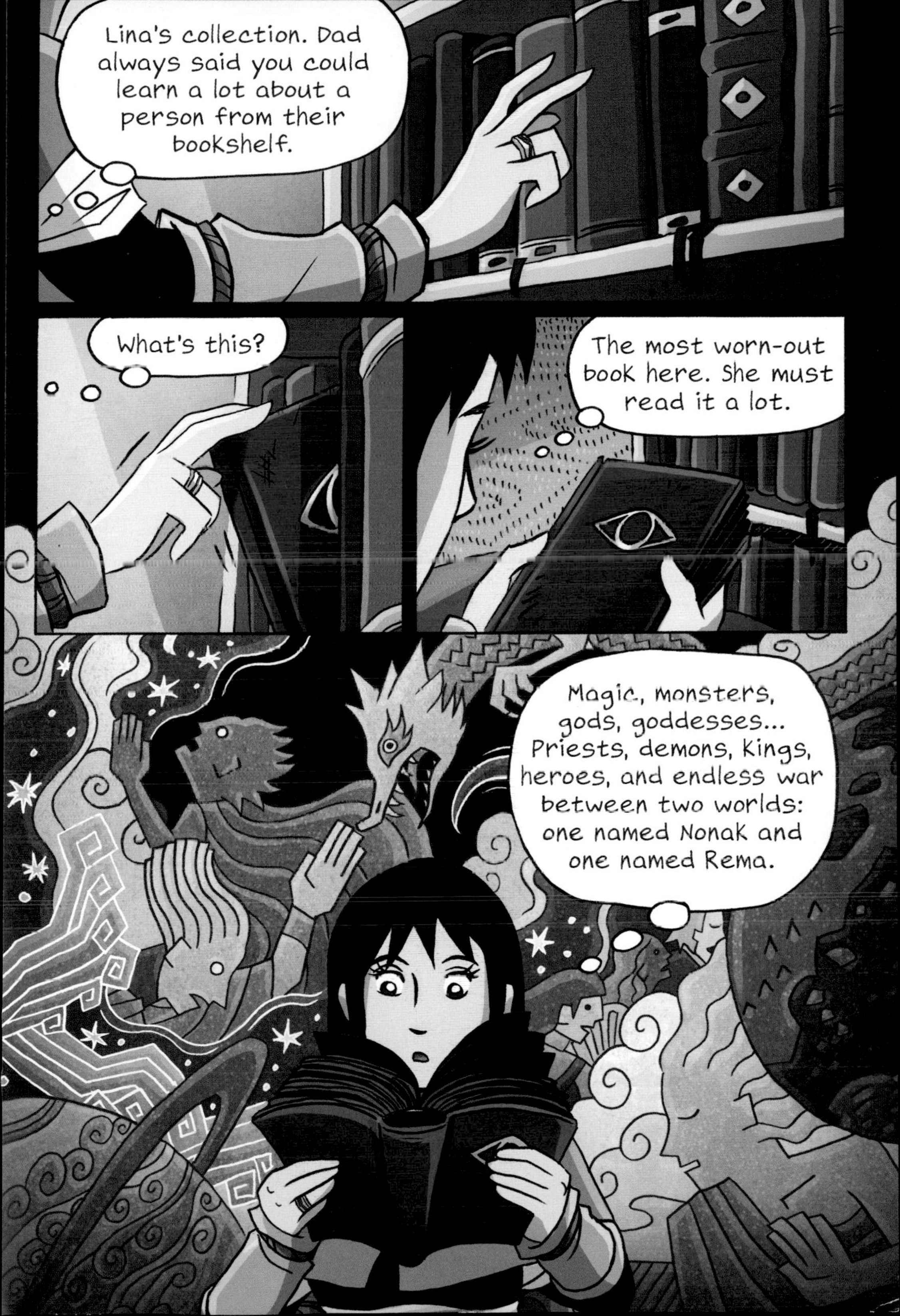

Lina's collection. Dad always said you could learn a lot about a person from their bookshelf.
What's this?
The most worn-out book here. She must read it a lot.
Magic, monsters, gods, goddesses... Priests, demons, kings, heroes, and endless war between two worlds: one named Nonak and one named Rema.

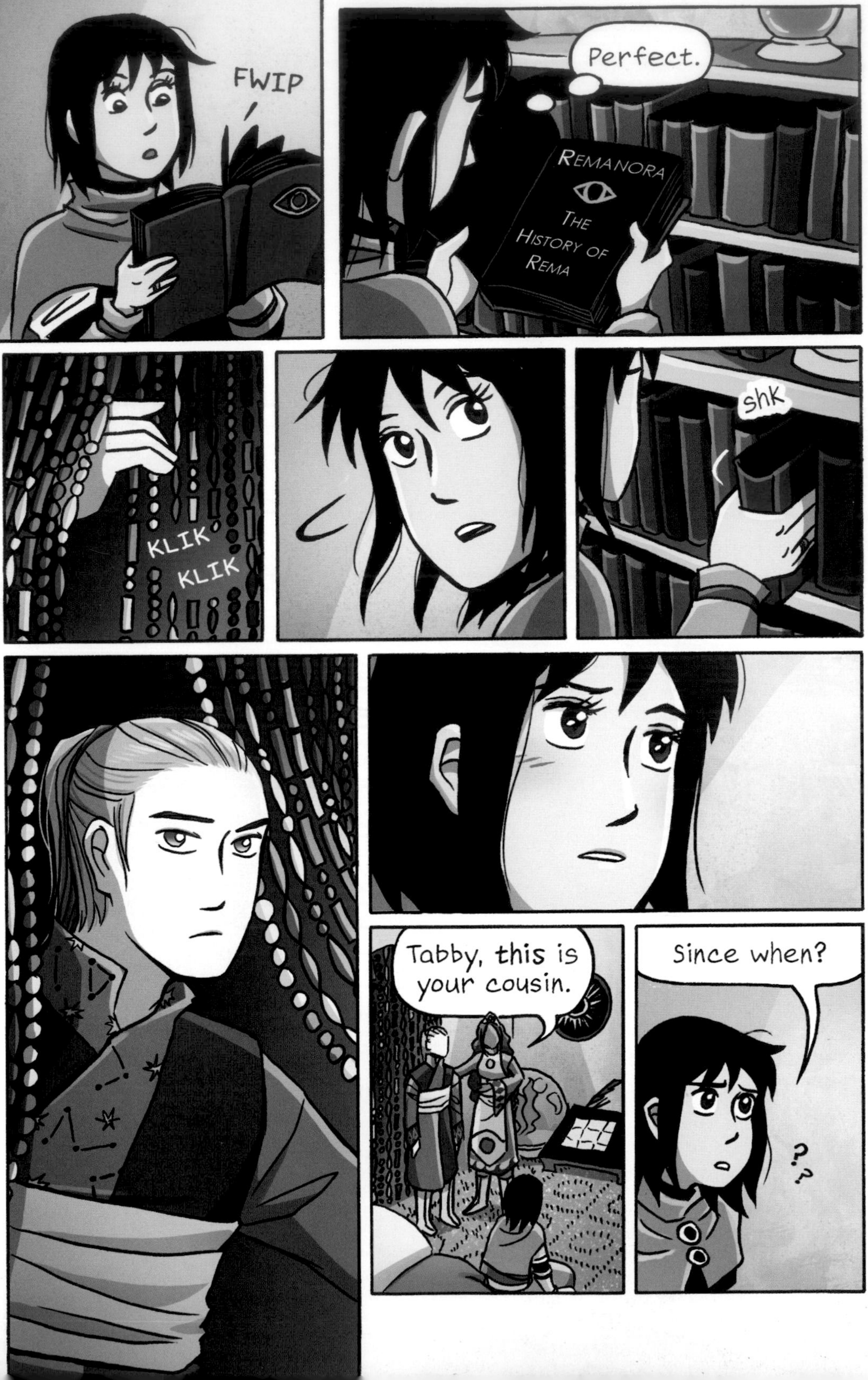
FWIP
Perfect.
REMANORA
THE HISTORY OF REMA
KLIK
KLIK
shK
Tabby, this is your cousin.
Since when?
??

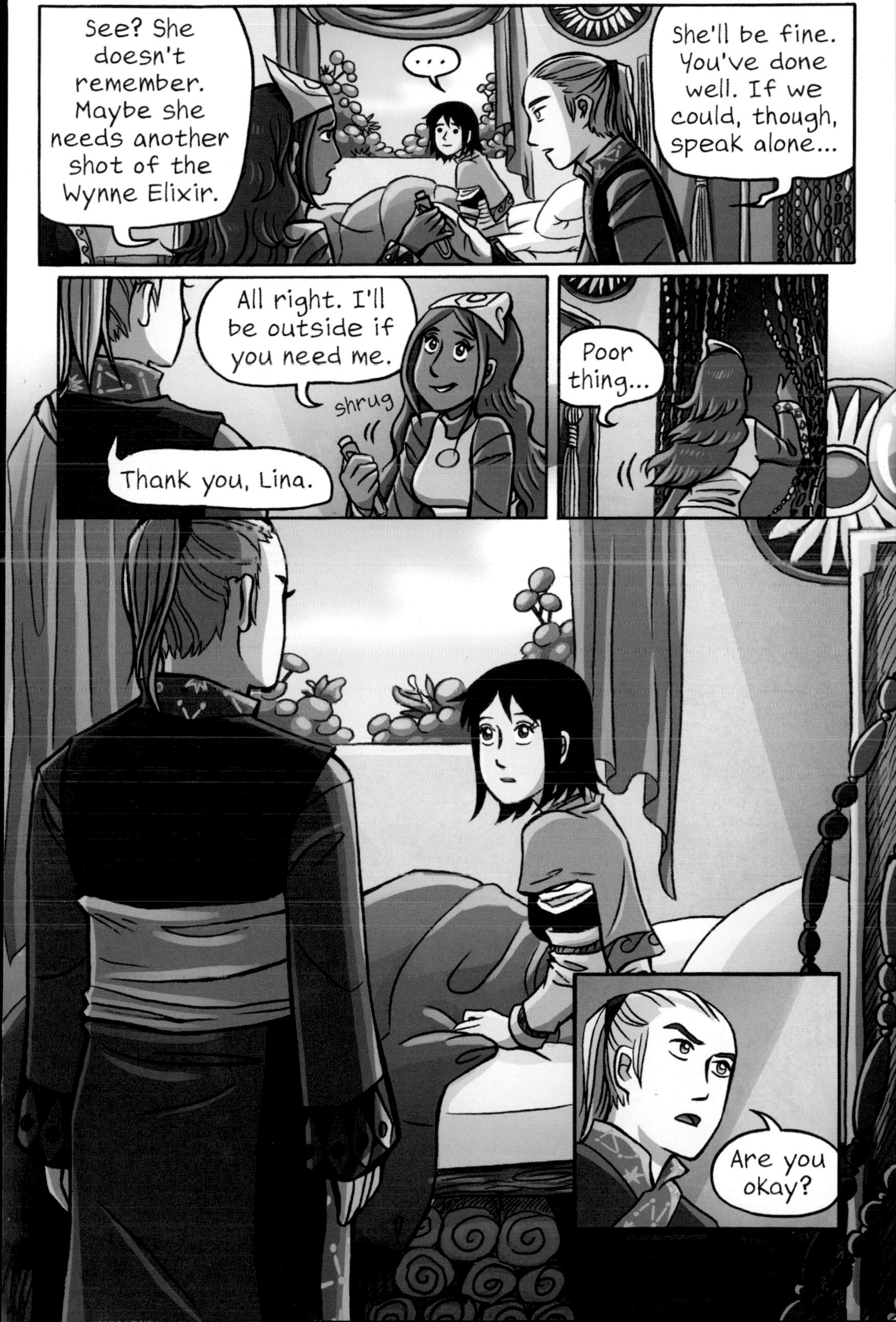
See? She doesn't remember. Maybe she needs another shot of the Wynne Elixir.
...
She'll be fine. You've done well. If we could, though, speak alone...
All right. I'll be outside if you need me.
shrug
Thank you, Lina.
Poor thing...
Are you okay?

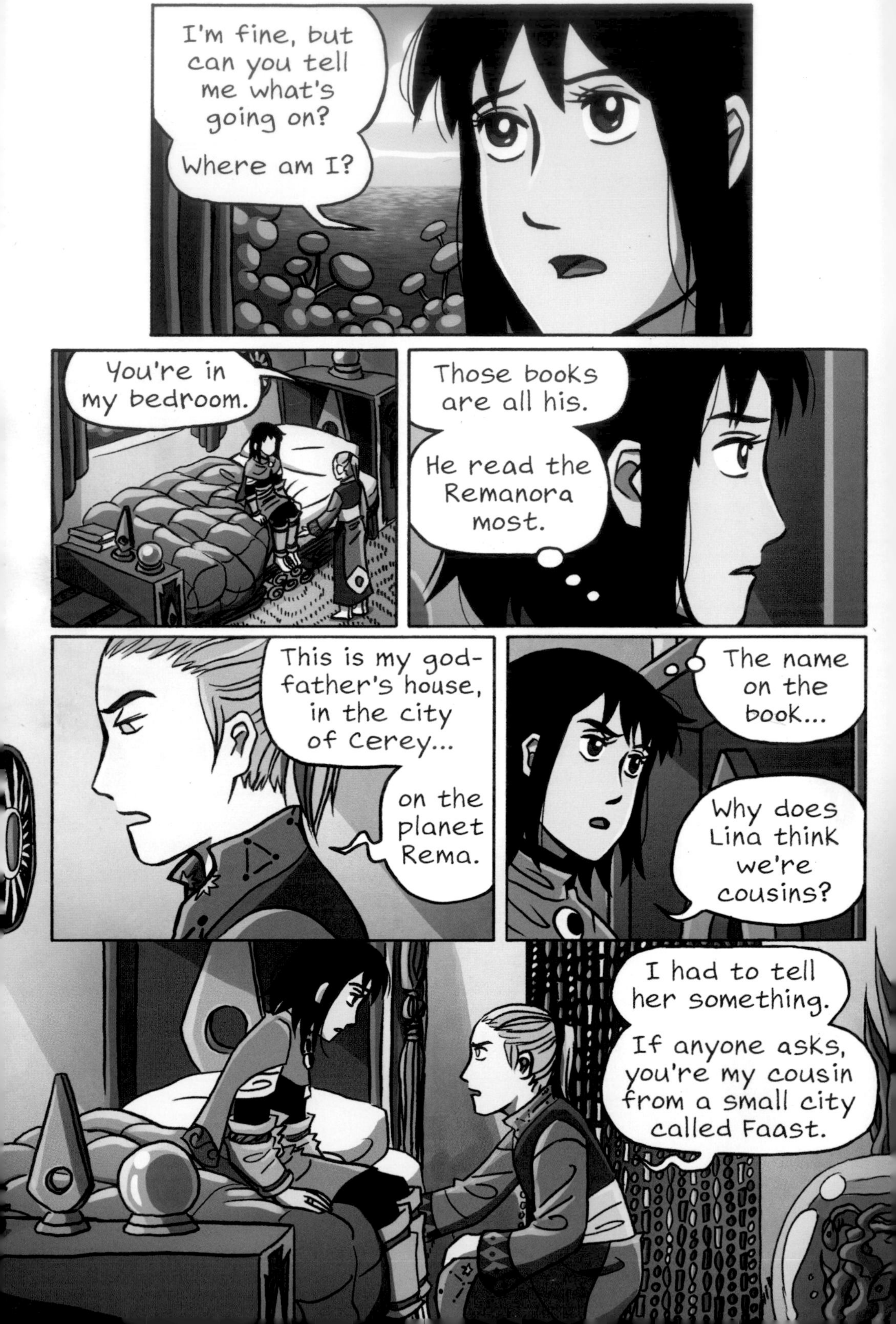
I'm fine, but can you tell me what's going on?
Where am I?
You're in my bedroom.
Those books are all his.
He read the Remanora most.
This is my god-father's house, in the city of Cerey...
on the planet Rema.
The name on the book...
Why does Lina think we're cousins?
I had to tell her something.
If anyone asks, you're my cousin from a small city called Faast.

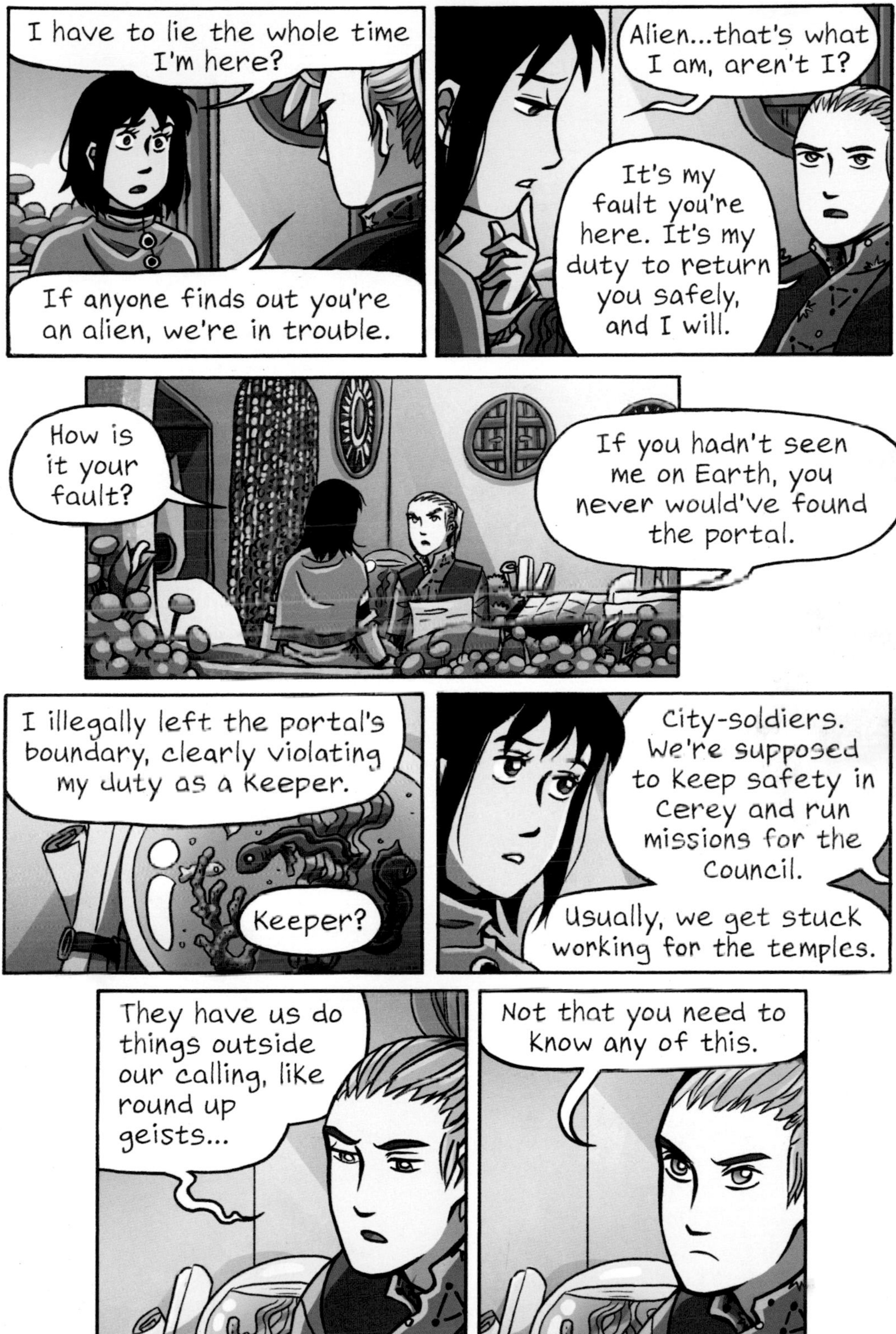
I have to lie the whole time I'm here?
If anyone finds out you're an alien, we're in trouble.
Alien...that's what I am, aren't I?
It's my fault you're here. It's my duty to return you safely, and I will.
How is it your fault?
If you hadn't seen me on Earth, you never would've found the portal.
I illegally left the portal's boundary, clearly violating my duty as a Keeper.
Keeper?
City-soldiers. We're supposed to keep safety in Cerey and run missions for the Council.
Usually, we get stuck working for the temples.
They have us do things outside our calling, like round up geists...
Not that you need to know any of this.

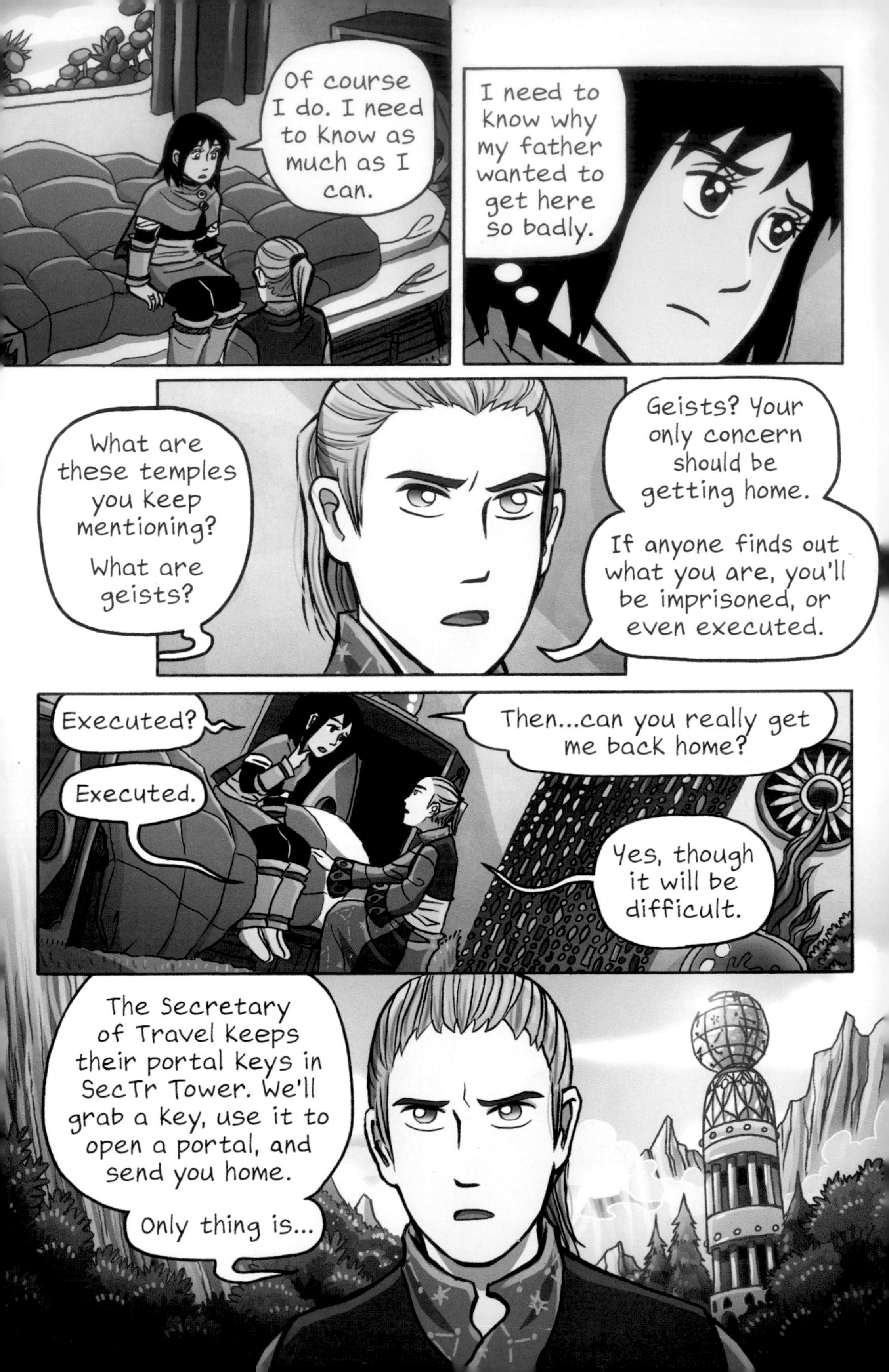
Of course I do. I need to know as much as I can.
I need to know why my father wanted to get here so badly.
What are these temples you keep mentioning?
What are geists?
Geists? Your only concern should be getting home.
If anyone finds out what you are, you'll be imprisoned, or even executed.
Executed?
Executed.
Then...can you really get me back home?
Yes, though it will be difficult.
The Secretary of Travel keeps their portal keys in SecTr Tower. We'll grab a key, use it to open a portal, and send you home.
Only thing is...

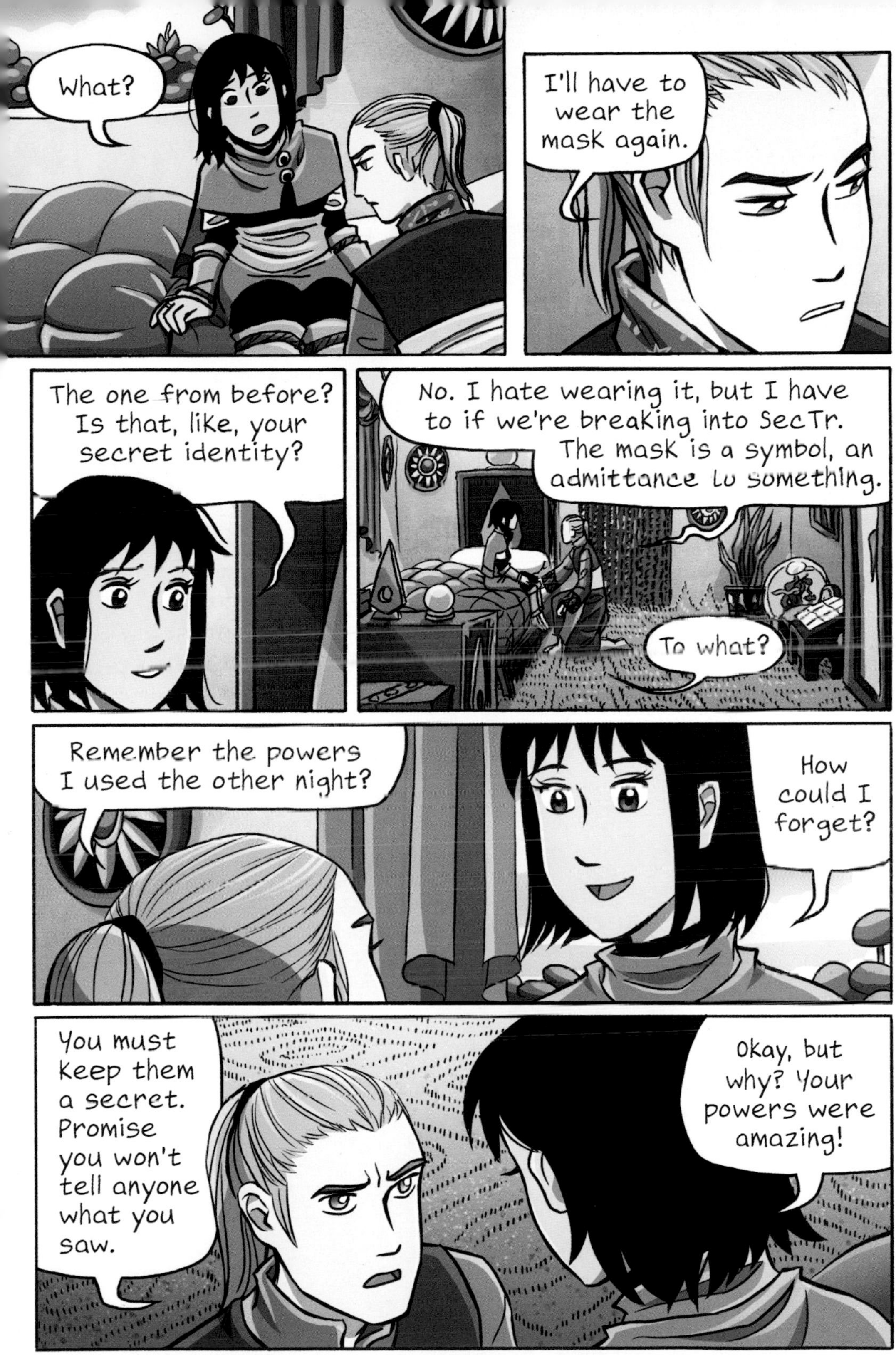

What?
I'll have to wear the mask again.
The one from before? Is that, like, your secret identity?
No. I hate wearing it, but I have to if we're breaking into SecTr.
The mask is a symbol, an admittance to something.
To what?
Remember the powers I used the other night?
How could I forget?
You must keep them a secret. Promise you won't tell anyone what you saw.
Okay, but why? Your powers were amazing!

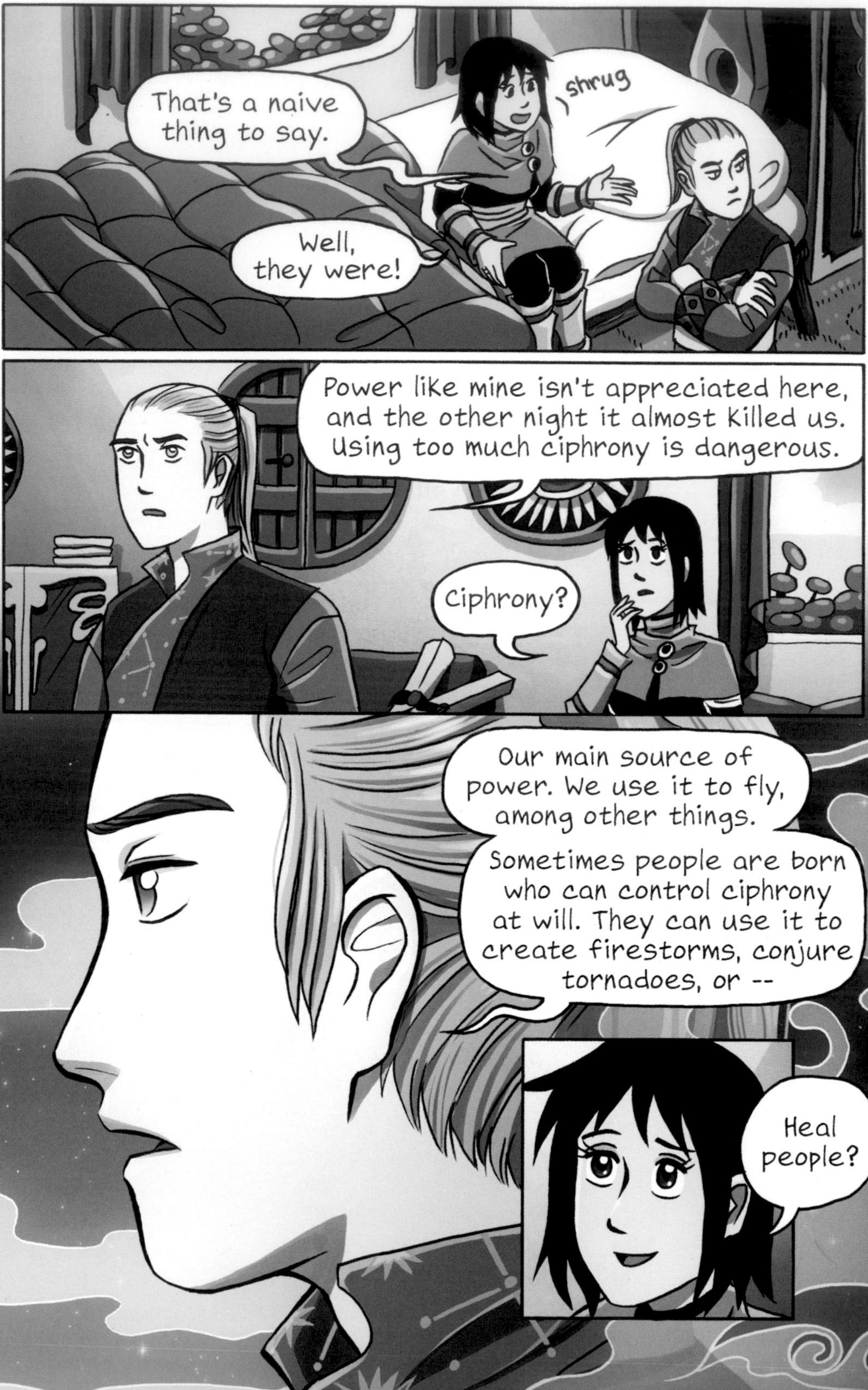
That's a naive thing to say.
shrug
Well, they were!
Power like mine isn't appreciated here, and the other night it almost killed us. Using too much ciphrony is dangerous.
Ciphrony?
Our main source of power. We use it to fly, among other things.
Sometimes people are born who can control ciphrony at will. They can use it to create firestorms, conjure tornadoes, or --
Heal people?

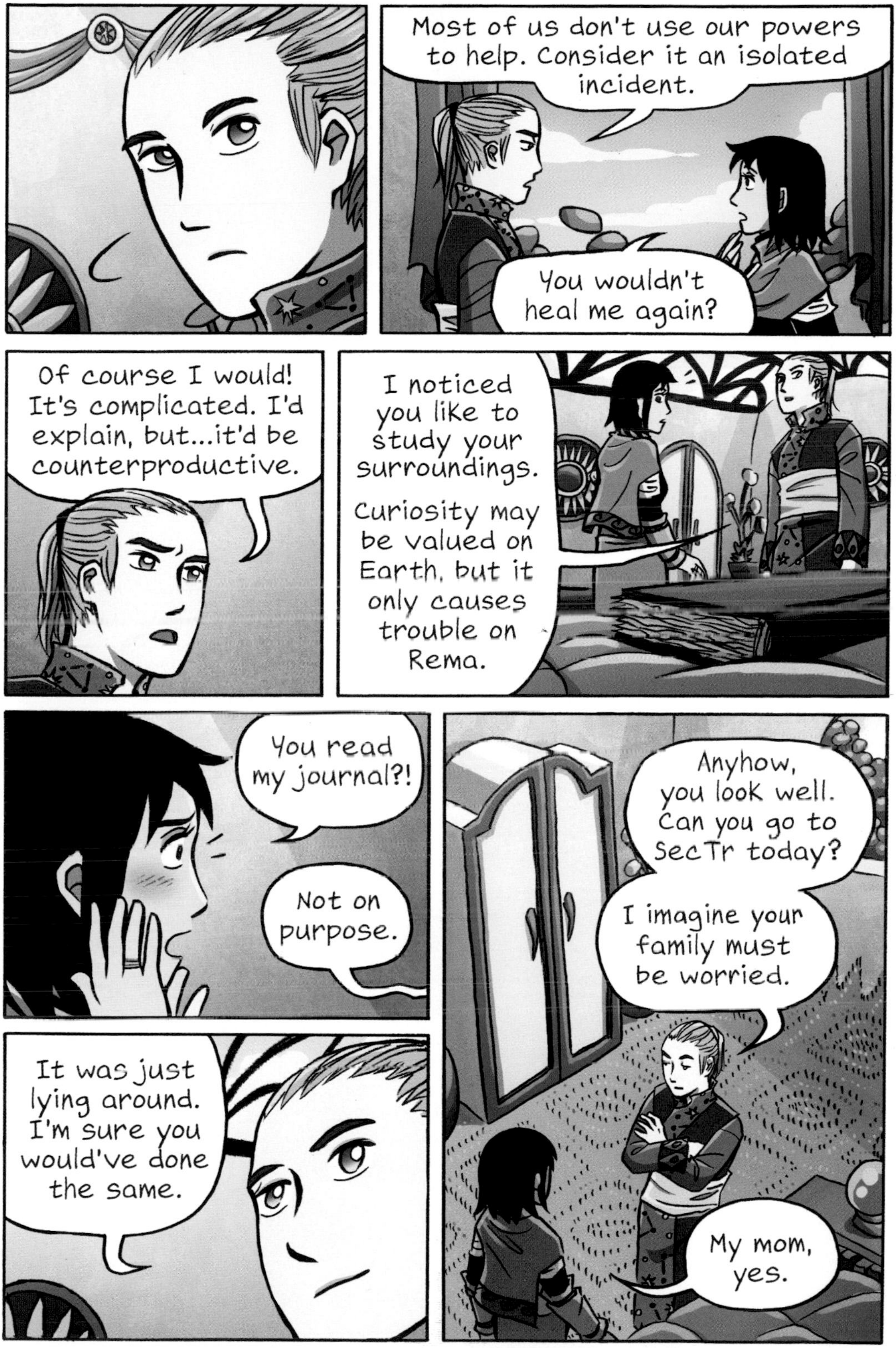
Most of us don't use our powers to help. Consider it an isolated incident.
You wouldn't heal me again?
Of course I would! It's complicated. I'd explain, but...it'd be counterproductive.
I noticed you like to study your surroundings.
Curiosity may be valued on Earth, but it only causes trouble on Rema.
You read my journal?!
Not on purpose.
It was just lying around. I'm sure you would've done the same.
Anyhow, you look well. Can you go to SecTr today?
I imagine your family must be worried.
My mom, yes.

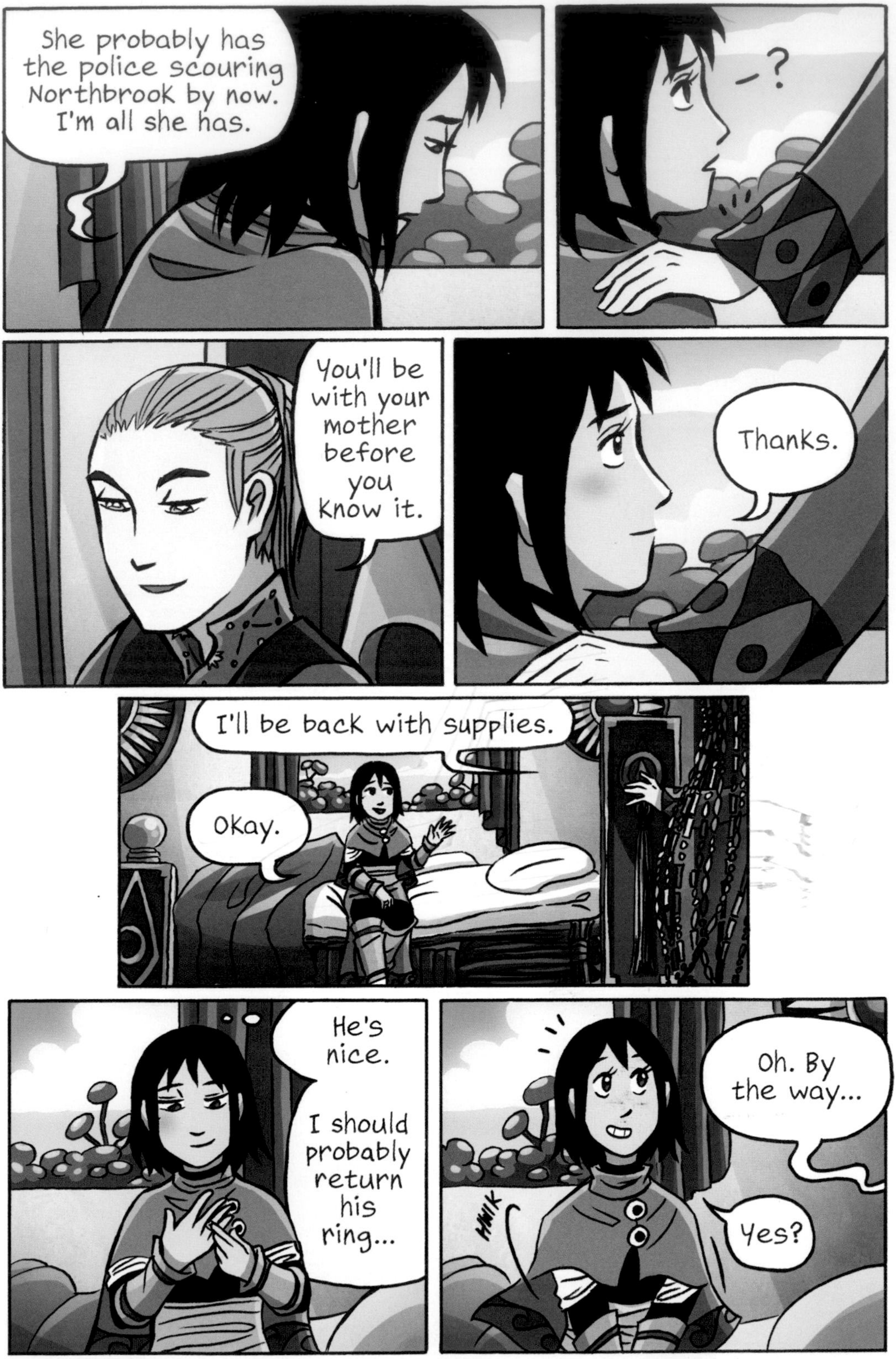
She probably has the police scouring Northbrook by now. I'm all she has.
–?
You'll be with your mother before you know it.
Thanks.
I'll be back with supplies.
Okay.
He's nice.
I should probably return his ring...
Oh. By the way...
Yes?

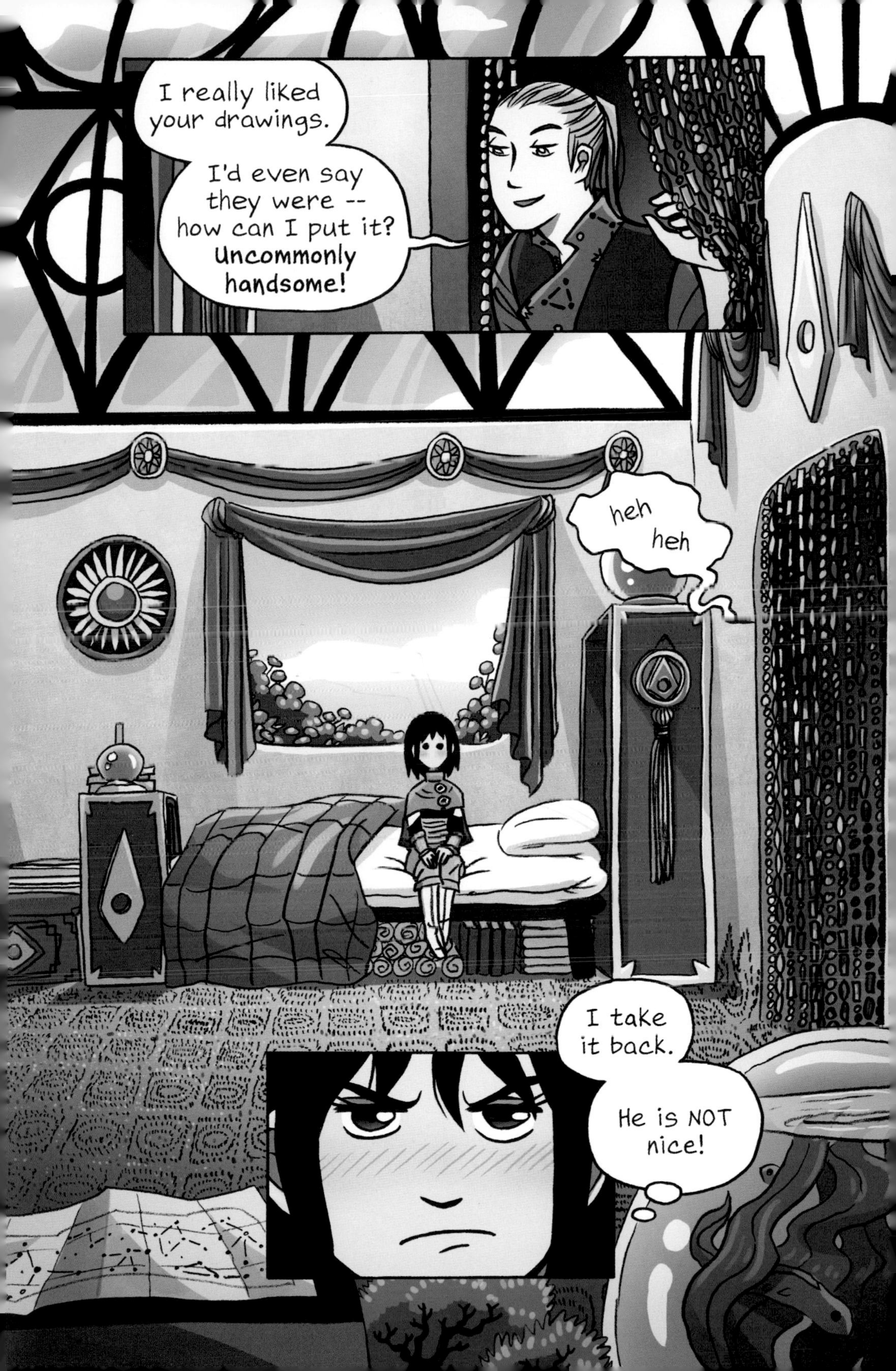
I really liked your drawings.
I'd even say they were -- how can I put it? **Uncommonly handsome!**
heh heh
I take it back.
He is NOT nice!

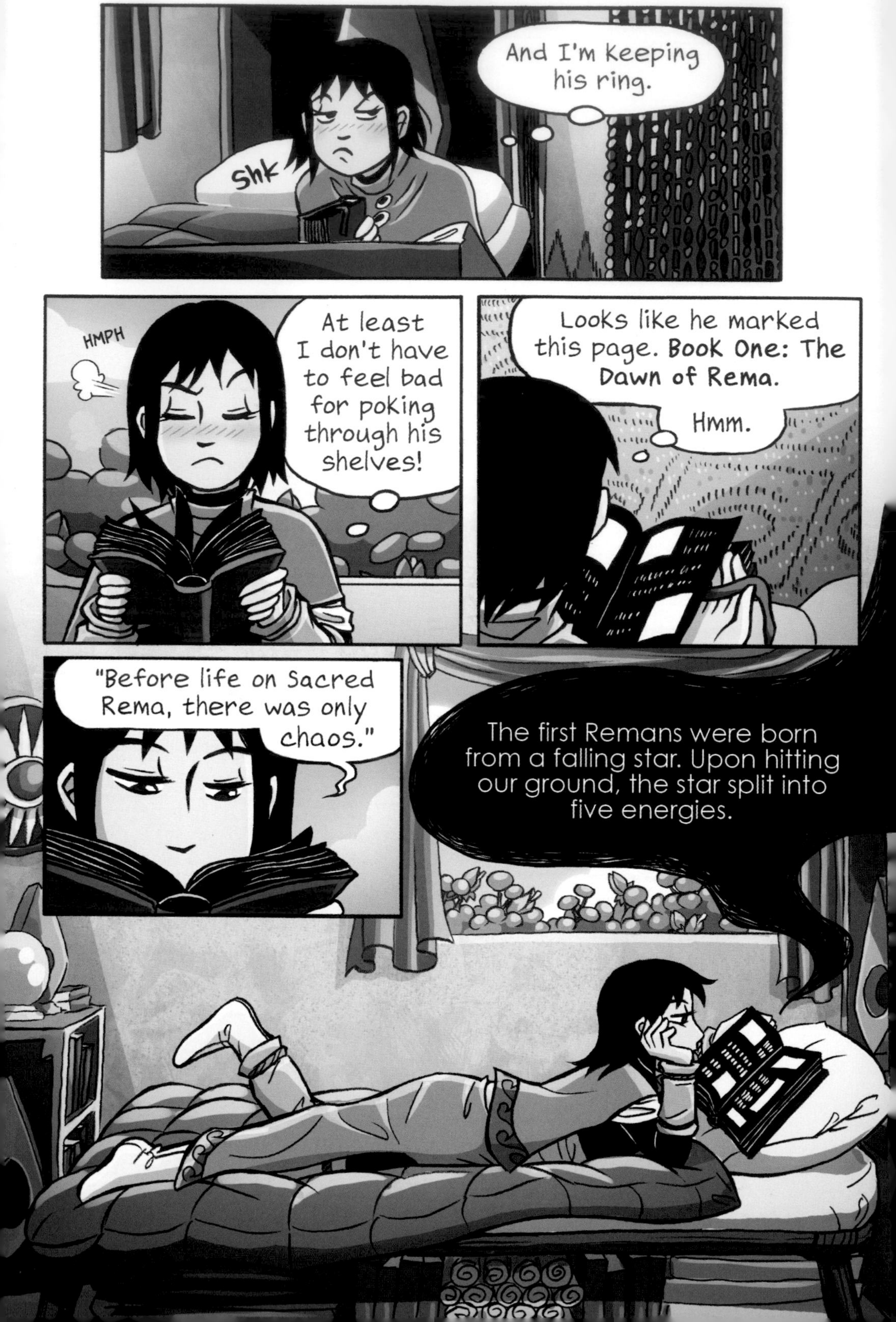
And I'm keeping his ring.
Shk
HMPH
At least I don't have to feel bad for poking through his shelves!
Looks like he marked this page. Book One: The Dawn of Rema.
Hmm.
"Before life on Sacred Rema, there was only chaos."
The first Remans were born from a falling star. Upon hitting our ground, the star split into five energies.

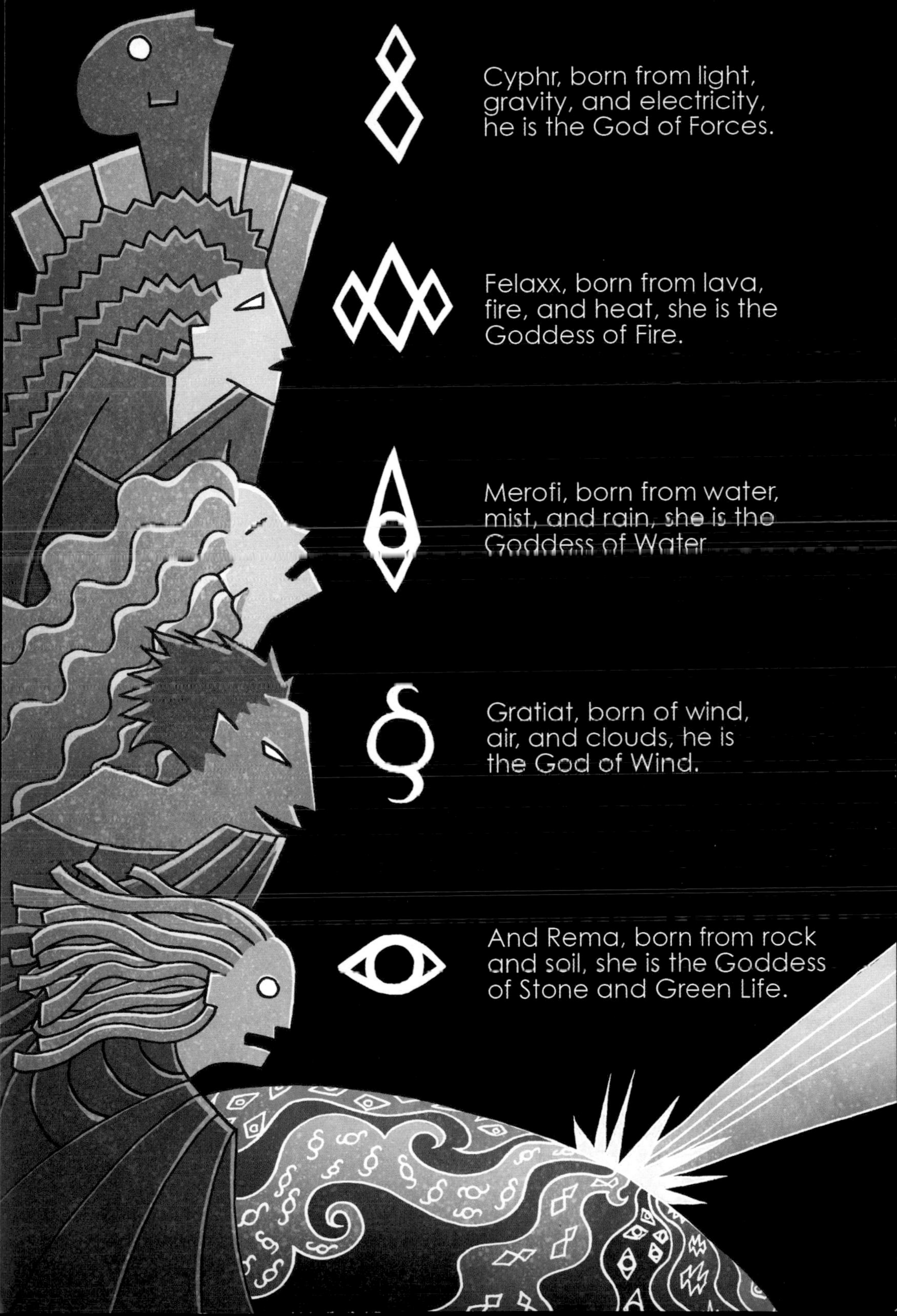
Cyphr, born from light, gravity, and electricity, he is the God of Forces.
Felaxx, born from lava, fire, and heat, she is the Goddess of Fire.
Merofi, born from water, mist, and rain, she is the Goddess of Water.
Gratiat, born of wind, air, and clouds, he is the God of Wind.
And Rema, born from rock and soil, she is the Goddess of Stone and Green Life.

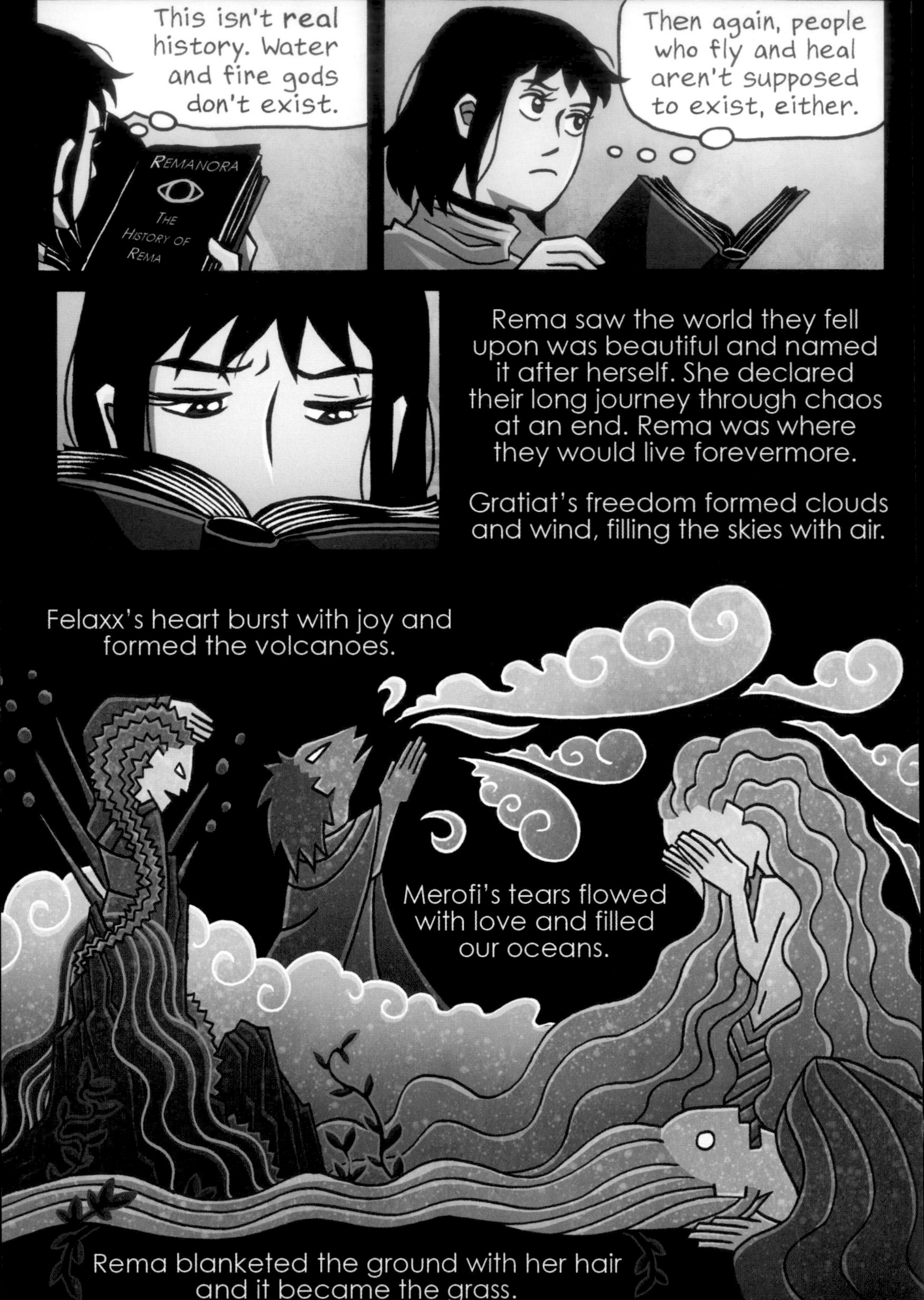
This isn't real history. Water and fire gods don't exist.
REMANORA
THE HISTORY OF REMA
Then again, people who fly and heal aren't supposed to exist, either.
Rema saw the world they fell upon was beautiful and named it after herself. She declared their long journey through chaos at an end. Rema was where they would live forevermore.
Gratiat's freedom formed clouds and wind, filling the skies with air.
Felaxx's heart burst with joy and formed the volcanoes.
Merofi's tears flowed with love and filled our oceans.
Rema blanketed the ground with her hair and it became the grass.

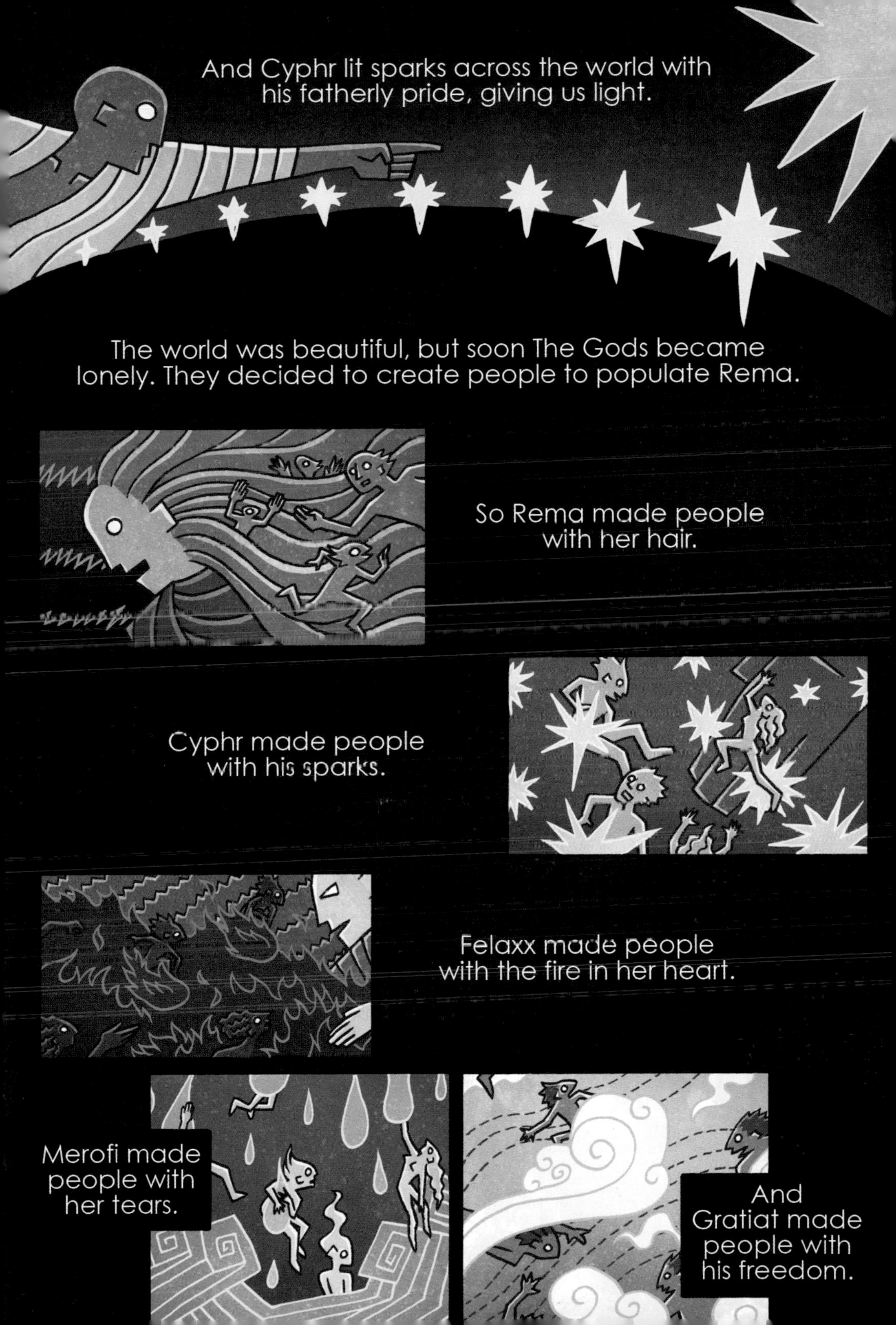
And Cyphr lit sparks across the world with his fatherly pride, giving us light.
The world was beautiful, but soon The Gods became lonely. They decided to create people to populate Rema.
So Rema made people with her hair.
Cyphr made people with his sparks.
Felaxx made people with the fire in her heart.
Merofi made people with her tears.
And Gratiat made people with his freedom.

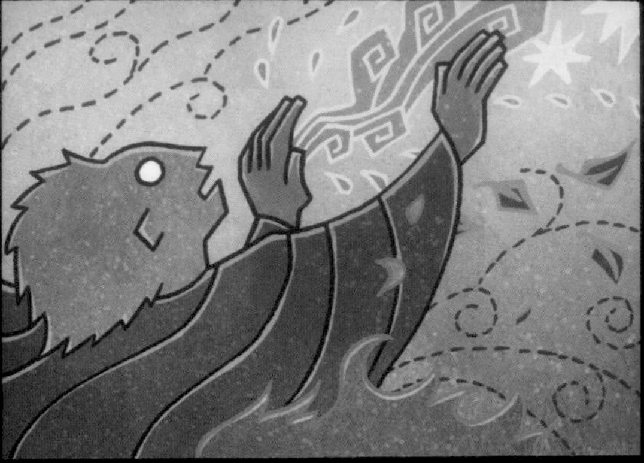

The people had godlike powers, able to sum[redacted]on water, fire, wind, ligh[redacted]nd rock at their bidd[redacted]g. They were beautiful bu[redacted]orrupt. They hungered [redacted]be as powerful as The Gods who created them.

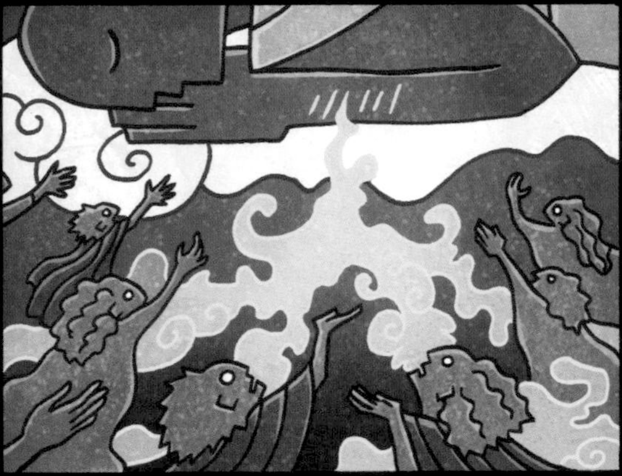

While The Gods slept, the people tapped int[redacted]heir veins and harvested the[redacted]r blood, spilling it over the land until it became part of th[redacted]round. The people drew the blood of The Gods at their whim and shaped the world as they pleased. They[redacted]named this power "ciphron[redacted]after Cyphr, the most pow[redacted]ul of The Gods.

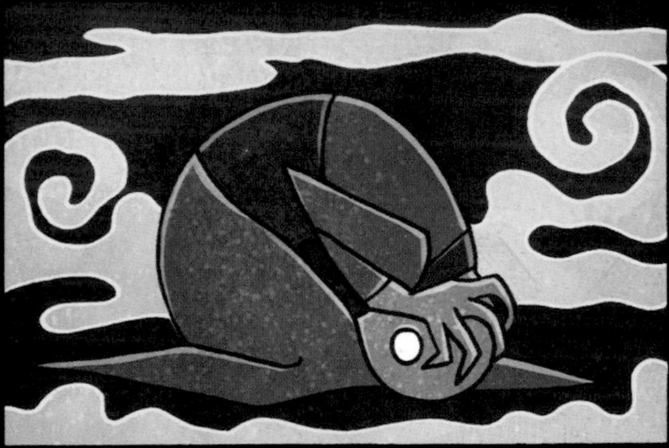

The Gods did not take this lightly. Enraged, Cyphr set a curse on all who dared to use their blood fo[redacted]power. From then on, ci[redacted]hrony corrupted the sou[redacted] the people, until they became possessed by it.

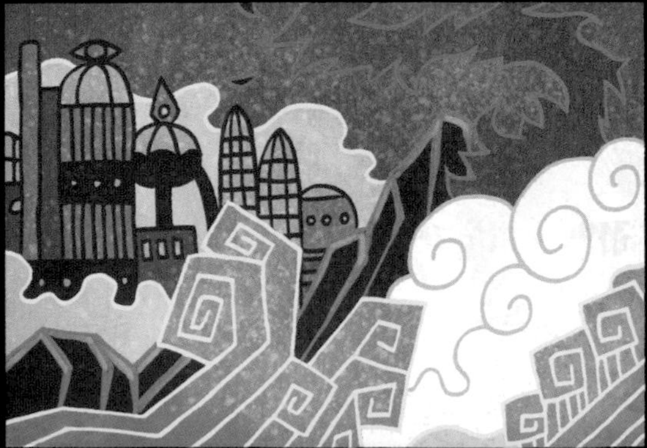

The more ciphrony they used, the more they craved, until entire nations destroyed themselves to obtain it. The people became mindless vessels that wandered the world like ghosts, flooding and burning everything in their paths. Thus, The Gods named them "geists."

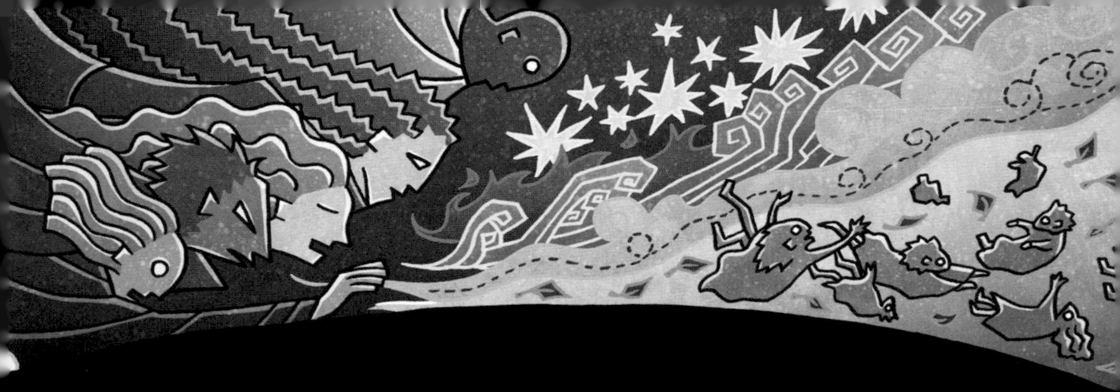

Fearing complete destruction of all they had built, The Five Holy Gods banded together and destroyed every geist they could find. All trace of the people was wiped from Rema's surface. The land was quiet for many eons after.

As the silent ages passed, The Gods became lonely once more.

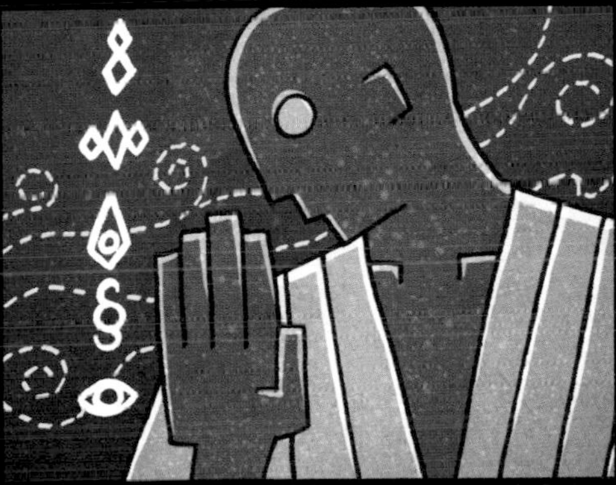

Meroti wanted to make new people. Cyphr, in his wisdom, reminded the others of the geists. They could not let pride get in the way of their creations. If they were to make new people, they must use their hair, sparks, heart, tears, and freedom all together, as one.

The other Gods agreed and they created a harmonious people -- good, humble, and harmless. The balanced people were kind and spent their days worshipping The Gods in peace. Finally, The Five Holy Gods had created a world they could share without fear, greed, or spite.

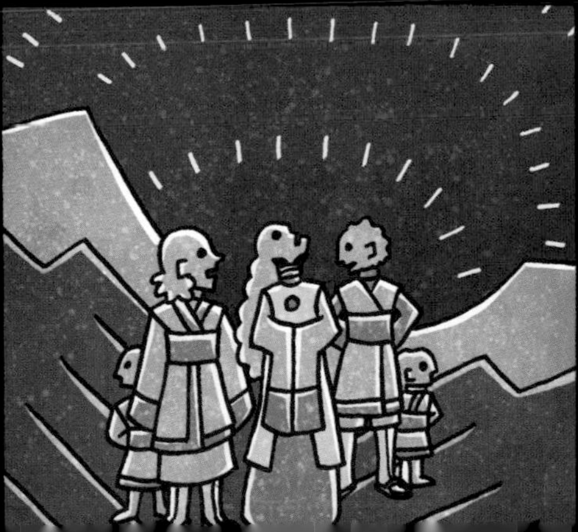

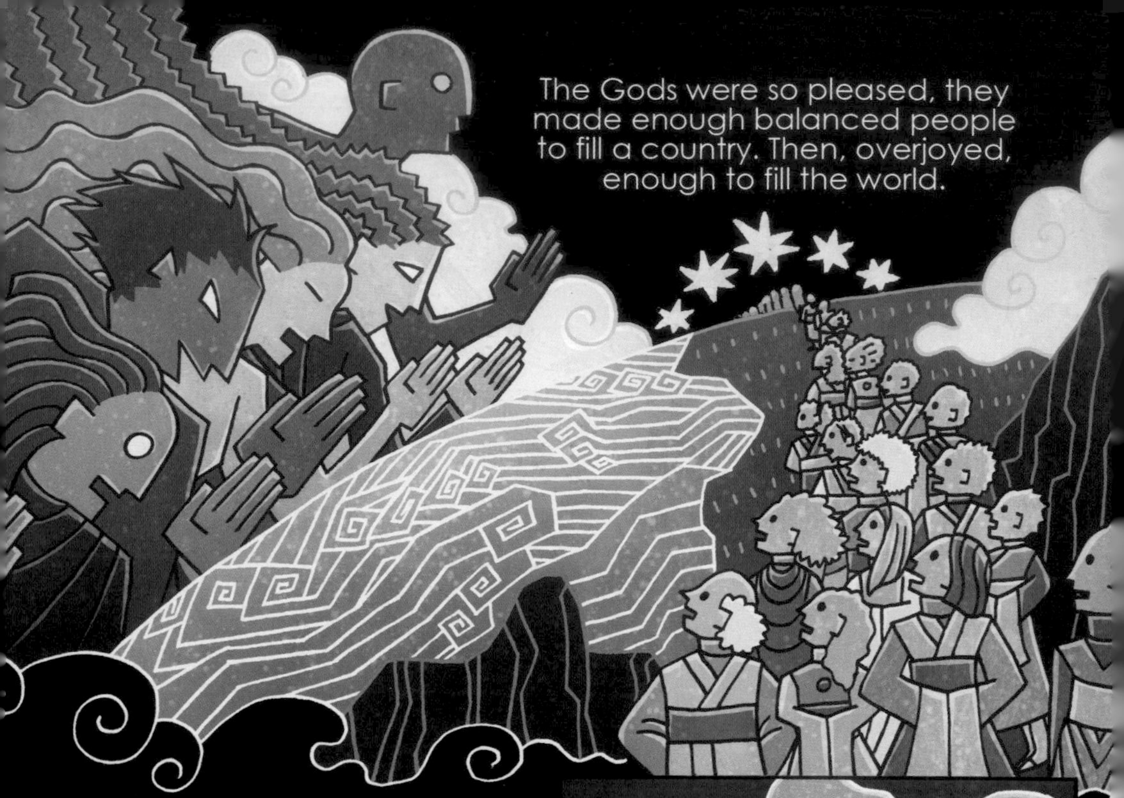
The Gods were so pleased, they made enough balanced people to fill a country. Then, overjoyed, enough to fill the world.

As they made more and more balanced people, filling the world with life and laughter, they unwittingly conjured an occasional geist. These geists were identical to the corrupt spirits from ages past. They were powerful, beautiful, and helplessly addicted to ciphrony, the blood of The Gods.

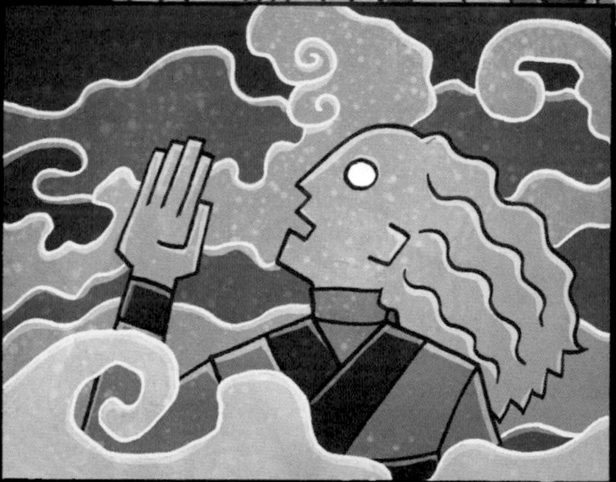

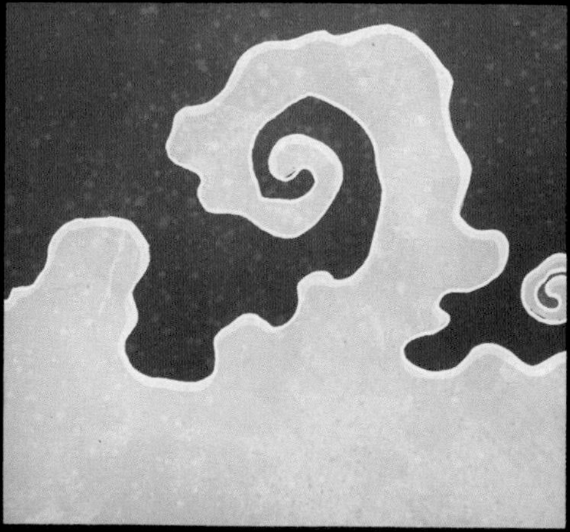

Ciphrony gave them memories that reached through Time. The geists remembered how The Gods gave them life. More than this, they remembered how The Gods took it away. They wanted to destroy The Gods and their people. They wanted to make them feel the pain they suffered so long ago.

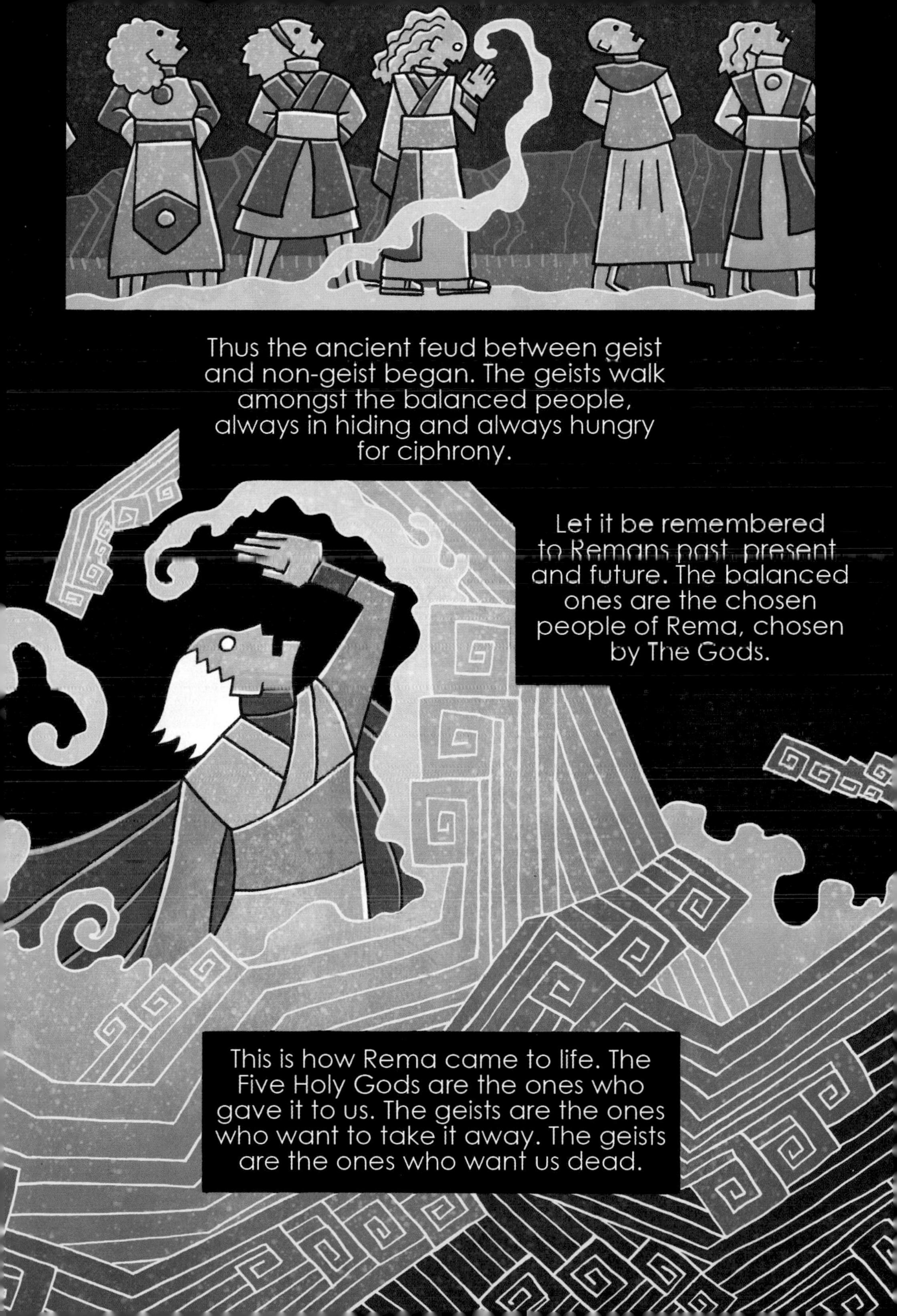
Thus the ancient feud between geist and non-geist began. The geists walk amongst the balanced people, always in hiding and always hungry for ciphrony.
Let it be remembered to Remans past, present and future. The balanced ones are the chosen people of Rema, chosen by The Gods.
This is how Rema came to life. The Five Holy Gods are the ones who gave it to us. The geists are the ones who want to take it away. The geists are the ones who want us dead.

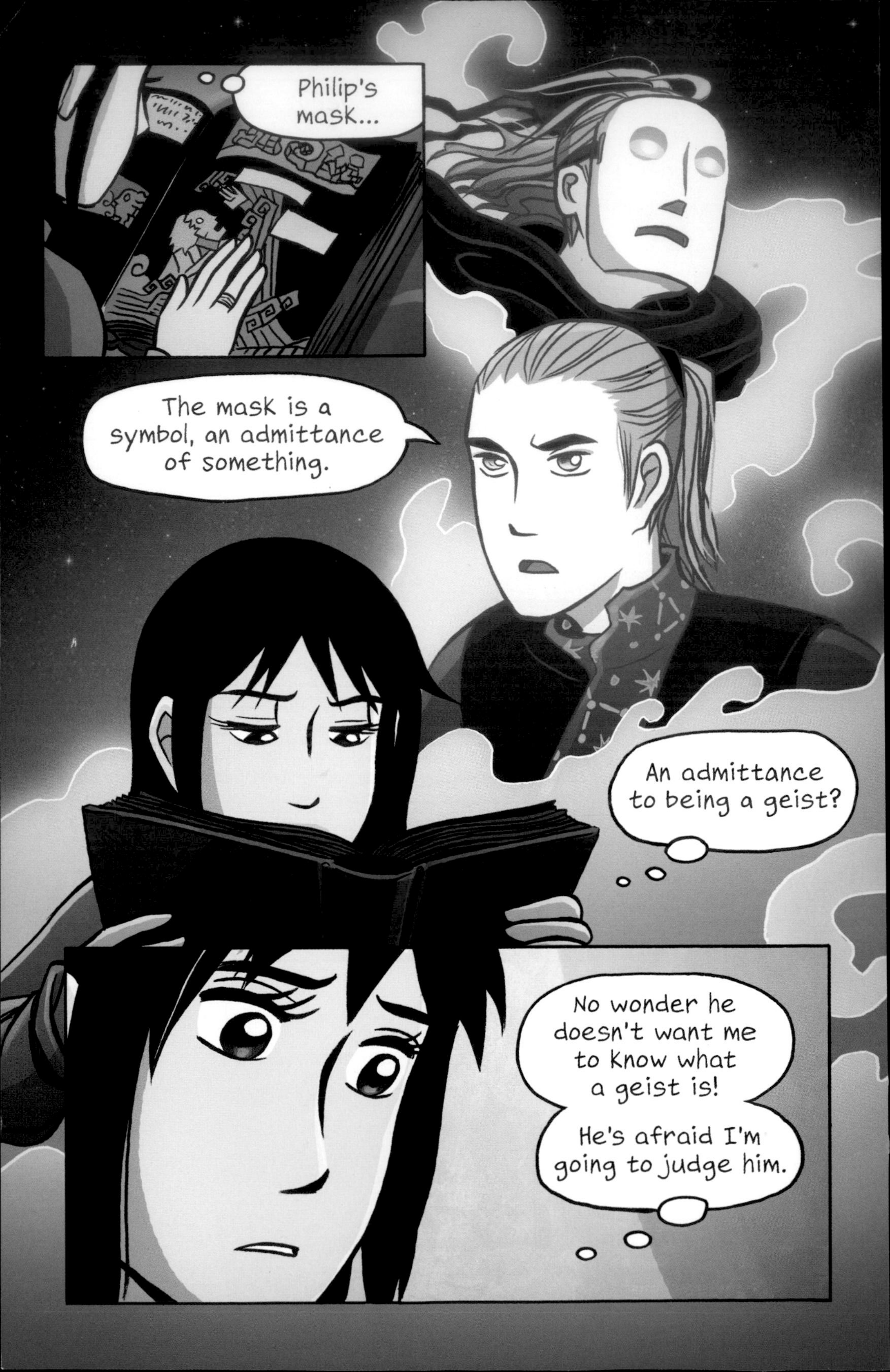
Philip's mask...
The mask is a symbol, an admittance of something.
An admittance to being a geist?
No wonder he doesn't want me to know what a geist is!
He's afraid I'm going to judge him.

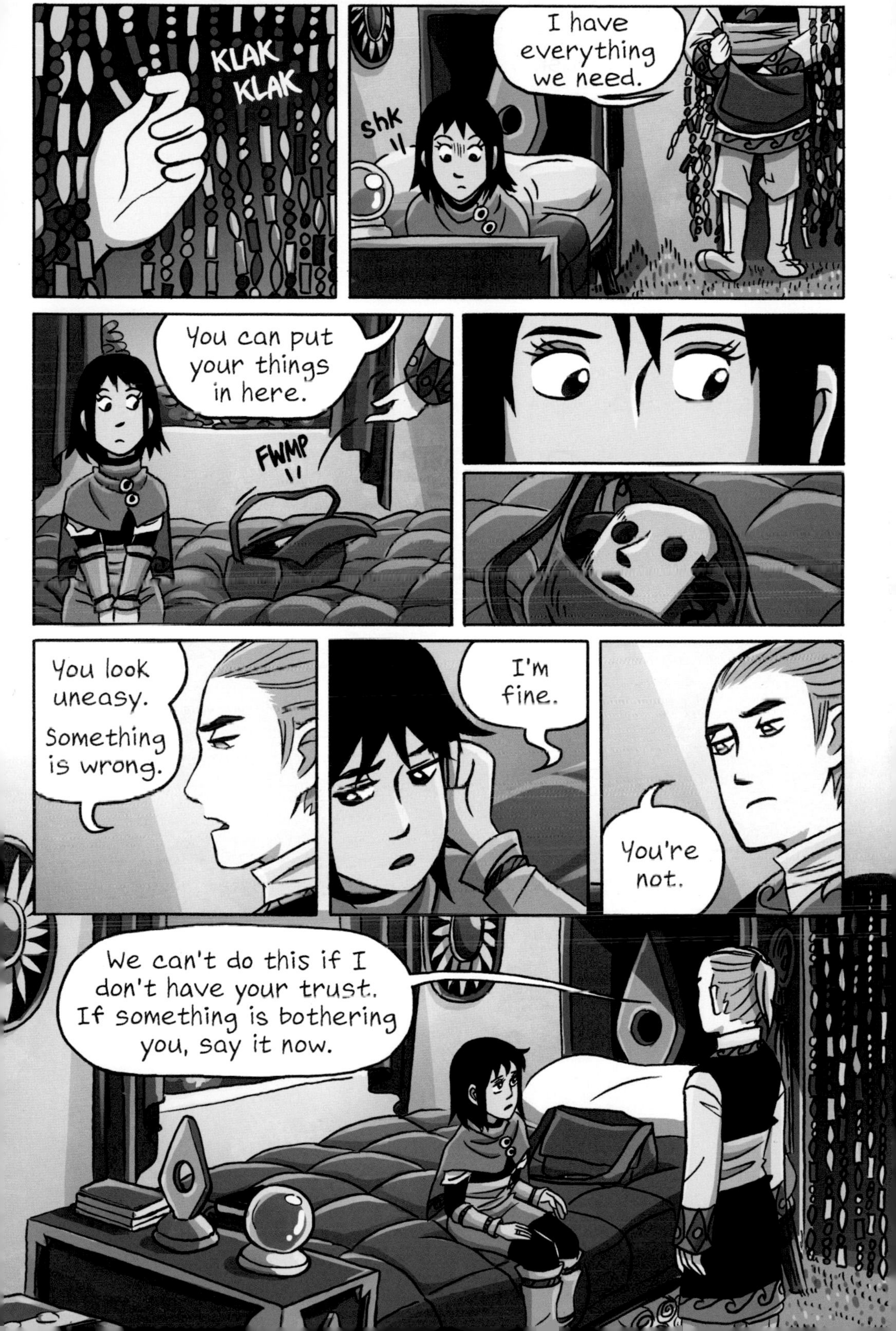
KLAK
KLAK
I have everything we need.
shk
You can put your things in here.
FWMP
You look uneasy.
Something is wrong.
I'm fine.
You're not.
We can't do this if I don't have your trust. If something is bothering you, say it now.

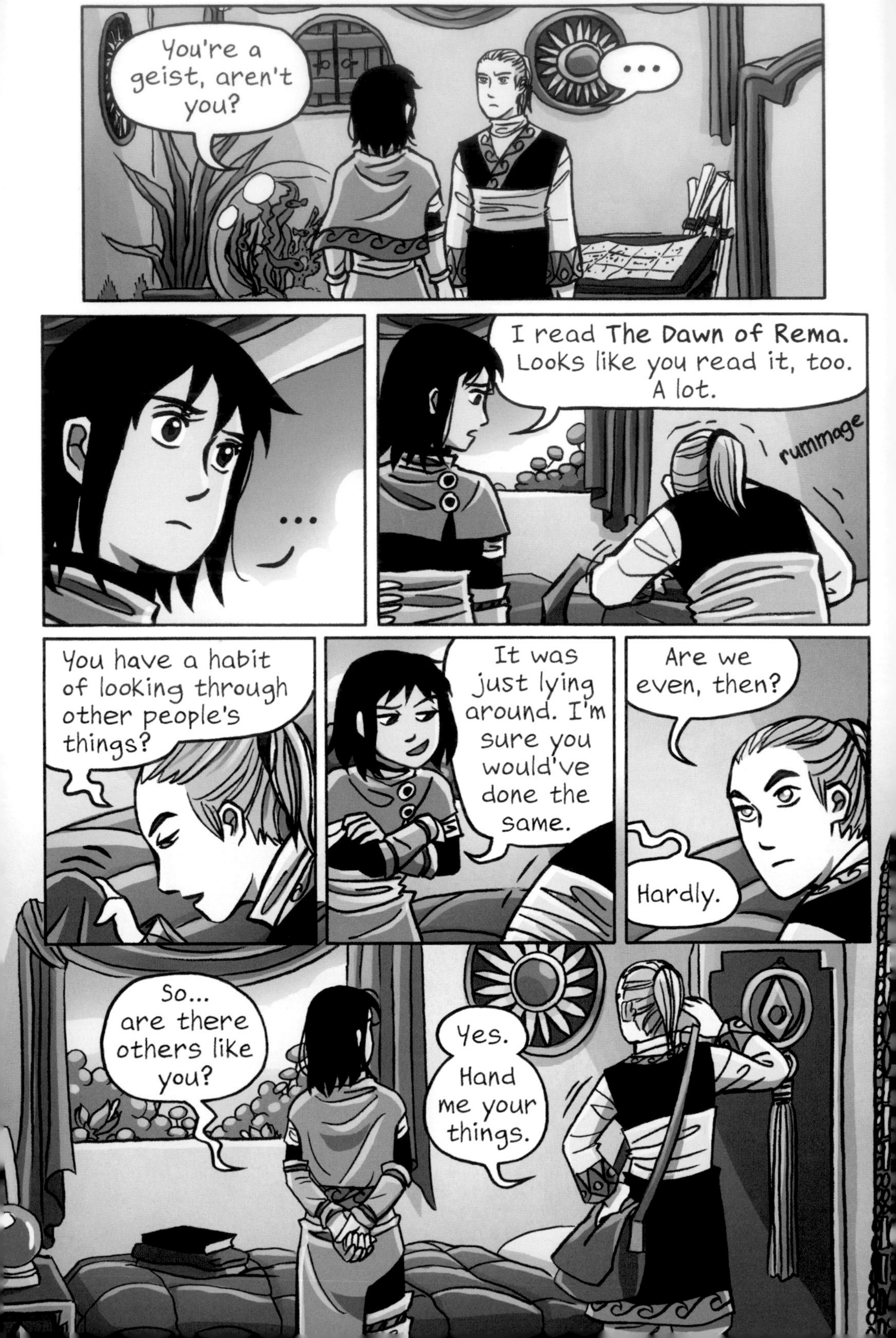
You're a geist, aren't you?
...
...
I read The Dawn of Rema. Looks like you read it, too. A lot.
rummage
You have a habit of looking through other people's things?
It was just lying around. I'm sure you would've done the same.
Are we even, then?
Hardly.
So... are there others like you?
Yes.
Hand me your things.

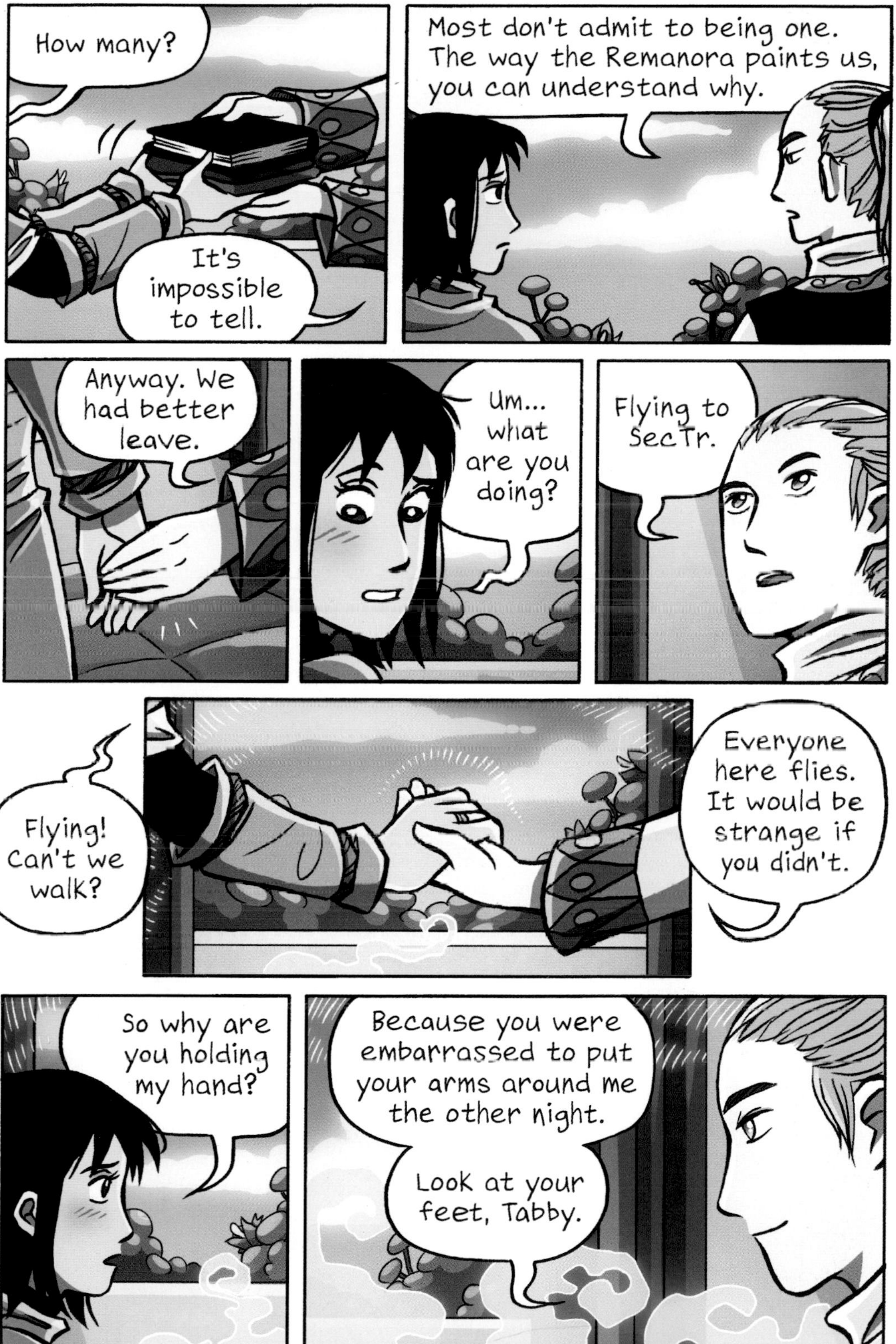
How many?
It's impossible to tell.
Most don't admit to being one. The way the Remanora paints us, you can understand why.
Anyway. We had better leave.
Um... what are you doing?
Flying to SecTr.
Flying! Can't we walk?
Everyone here flies. It would be strange if you didn't.
So why are you holding my hand?
Because you were embarrassed to put your arms around me the other night.
Look at your feet, Tabby.

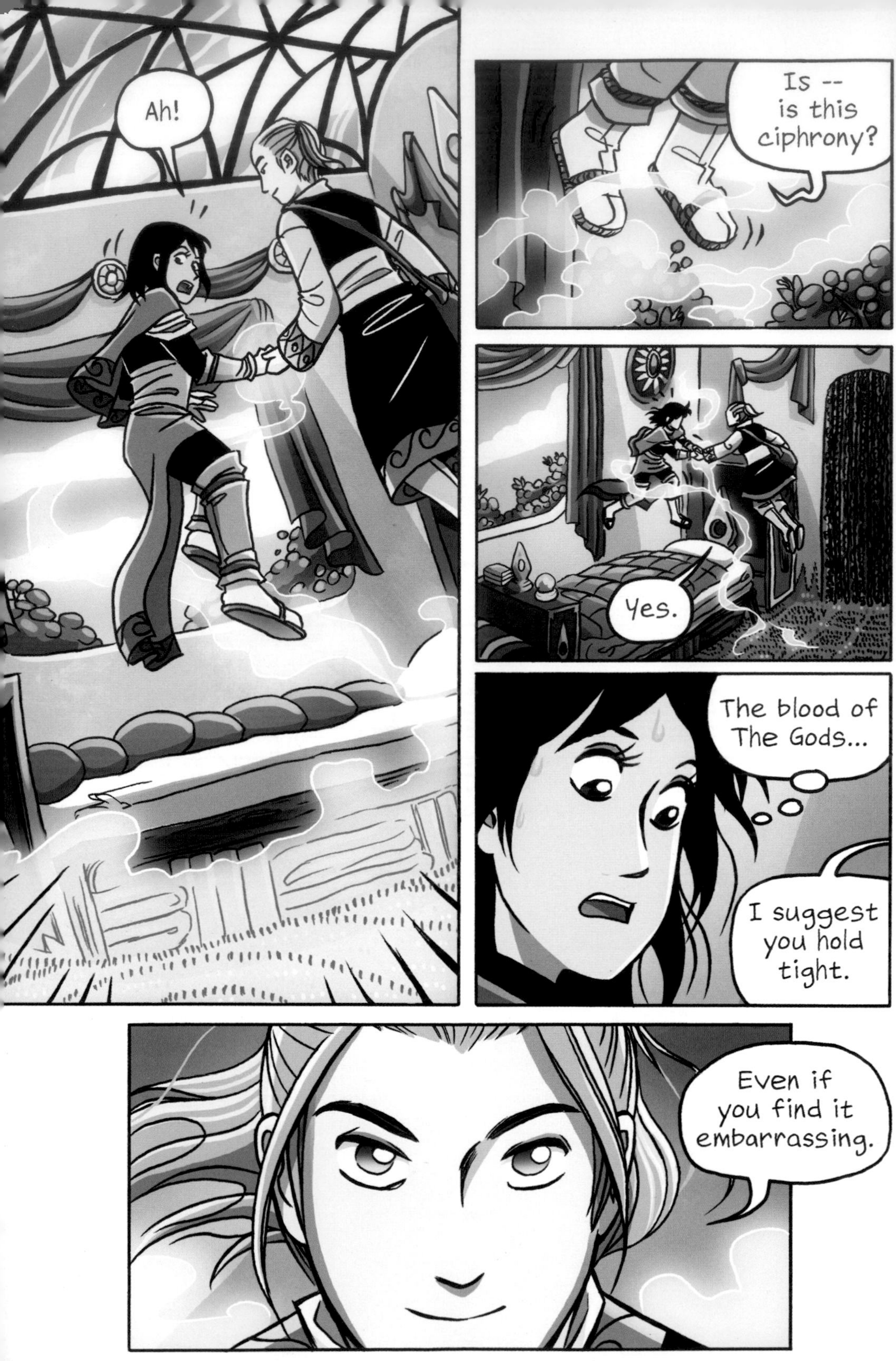
Ah!
Is -- is this ciphrony?
Yes.
The blood of The Gods...
I suggest you hold tight.
Even if you find it embarrassing.

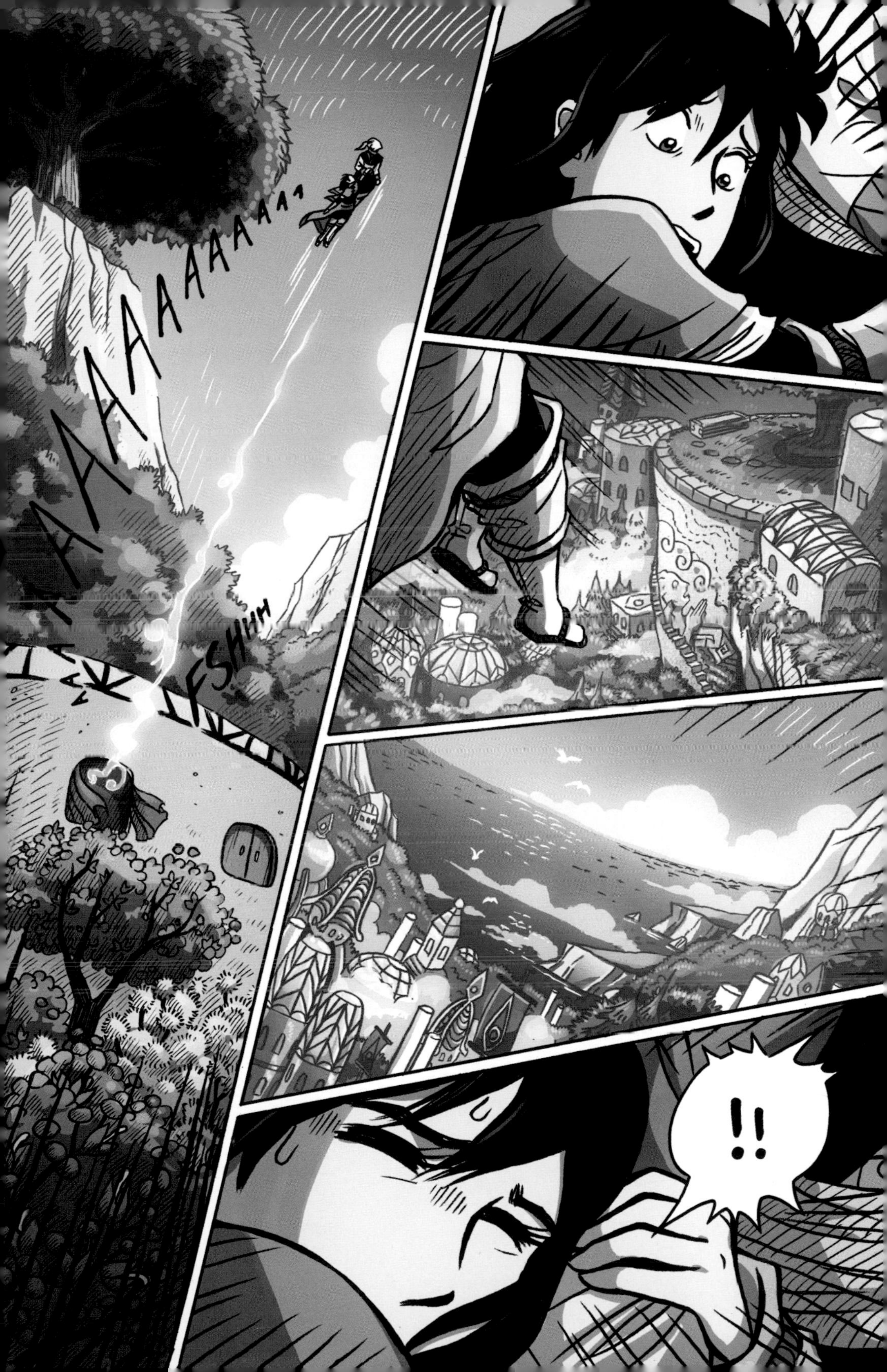
FSHHH
!!

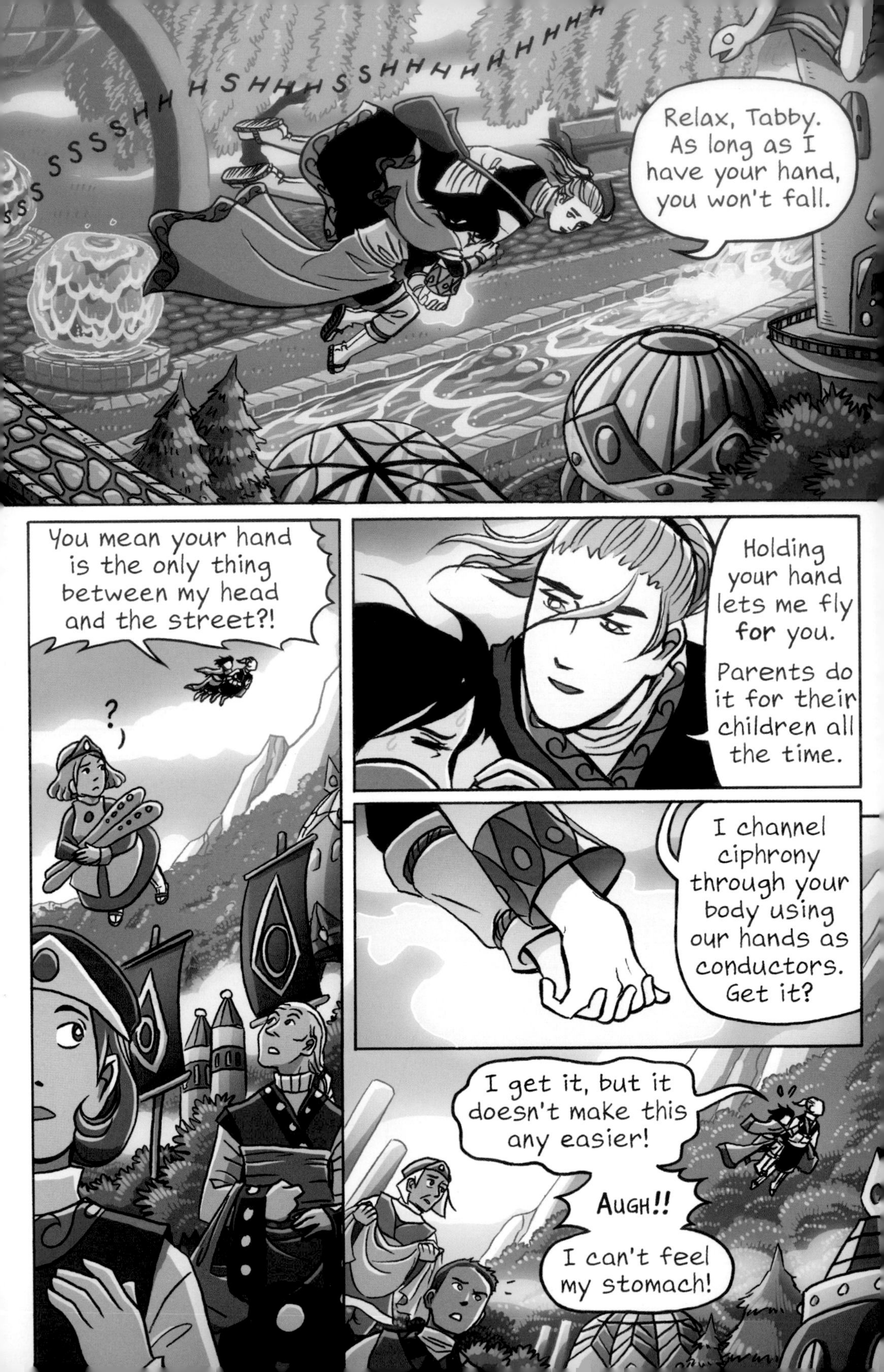
SSSSSSSHHHHSHHHHSSHHHHHHHHHH
Relax, Tabby. As long as I have your hand, you won't fall.
You mean your hand is the only thing between my head and the street?!
?
Holding your hand lets me fly for you.
Parents do it for their children all the time.
I channel ciphrony through your body using our hands as conductors. Get it?
I get it, but it doesn't make this any easier!
AUGH!!
I can't feel my stomach!

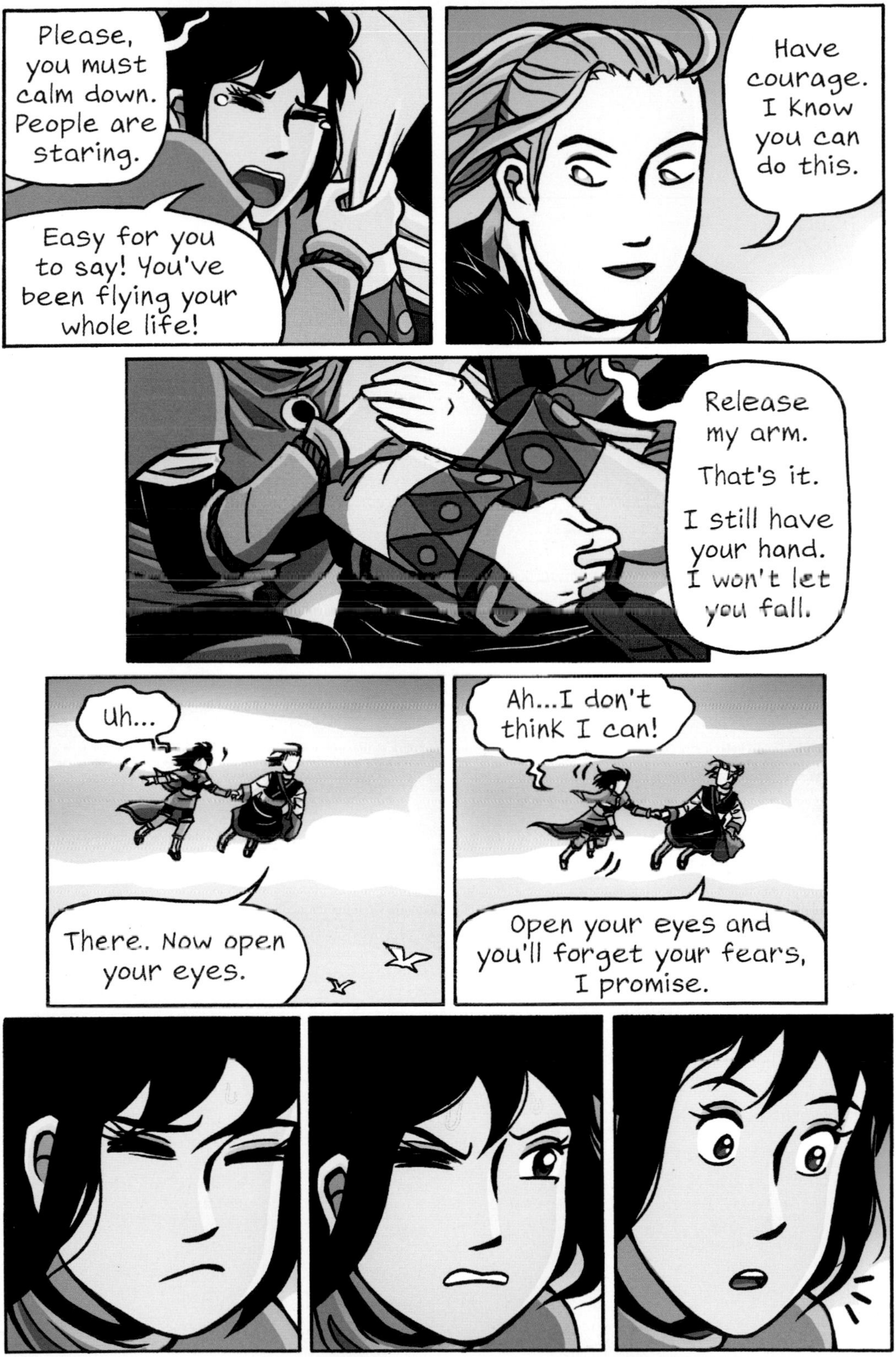
Please, you must calm down. People are staring.
Easy for you to say! You've been flying your whole life!
Have courage. I know you can do this.
Release my arm.
That's it.
I still have your hand. I won't let you fall.
Uh...
There. Now open your eyes.
Ah...I don't think I can!
Open your eyes and you'll forget your fears, I promise.

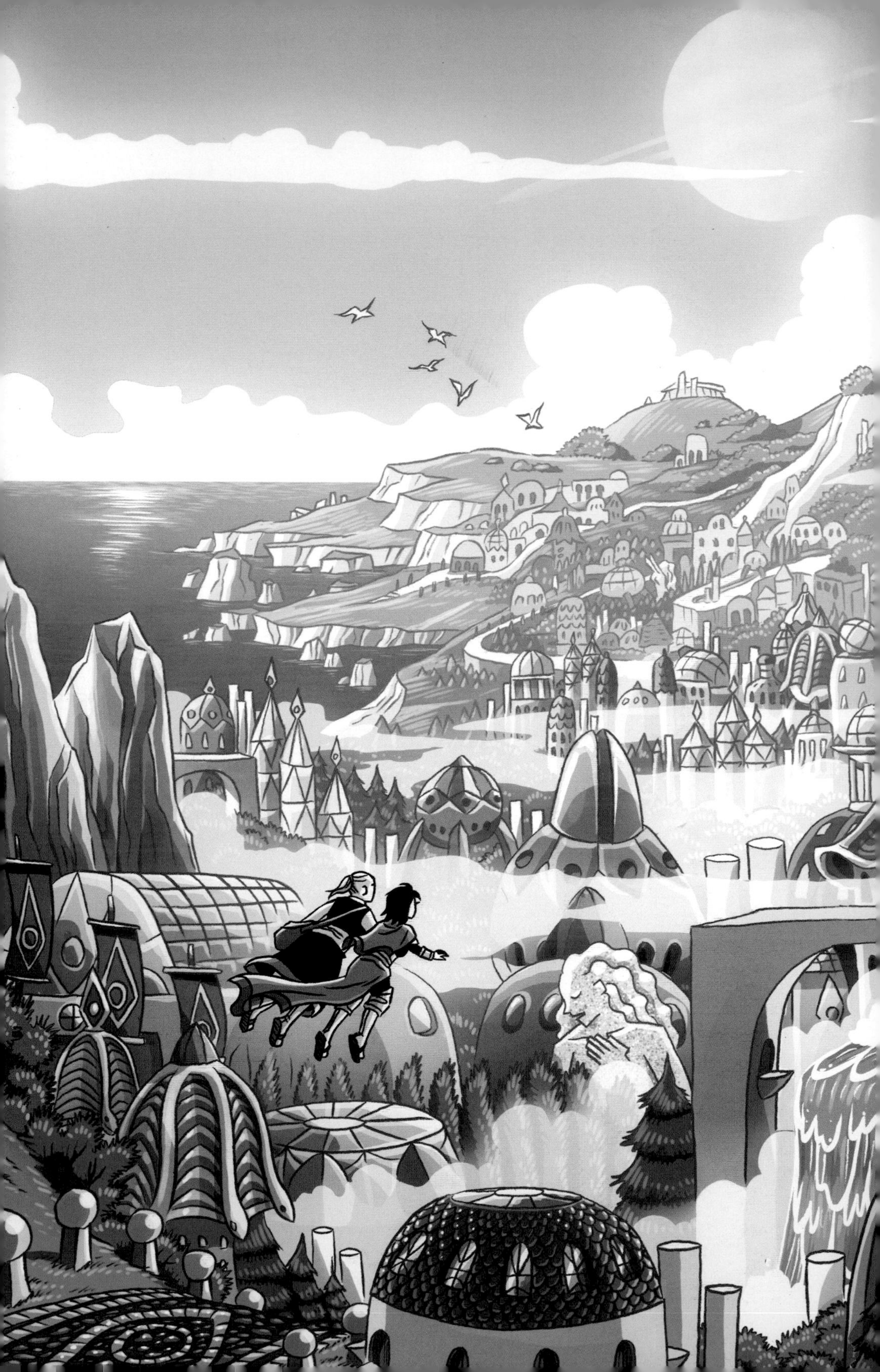

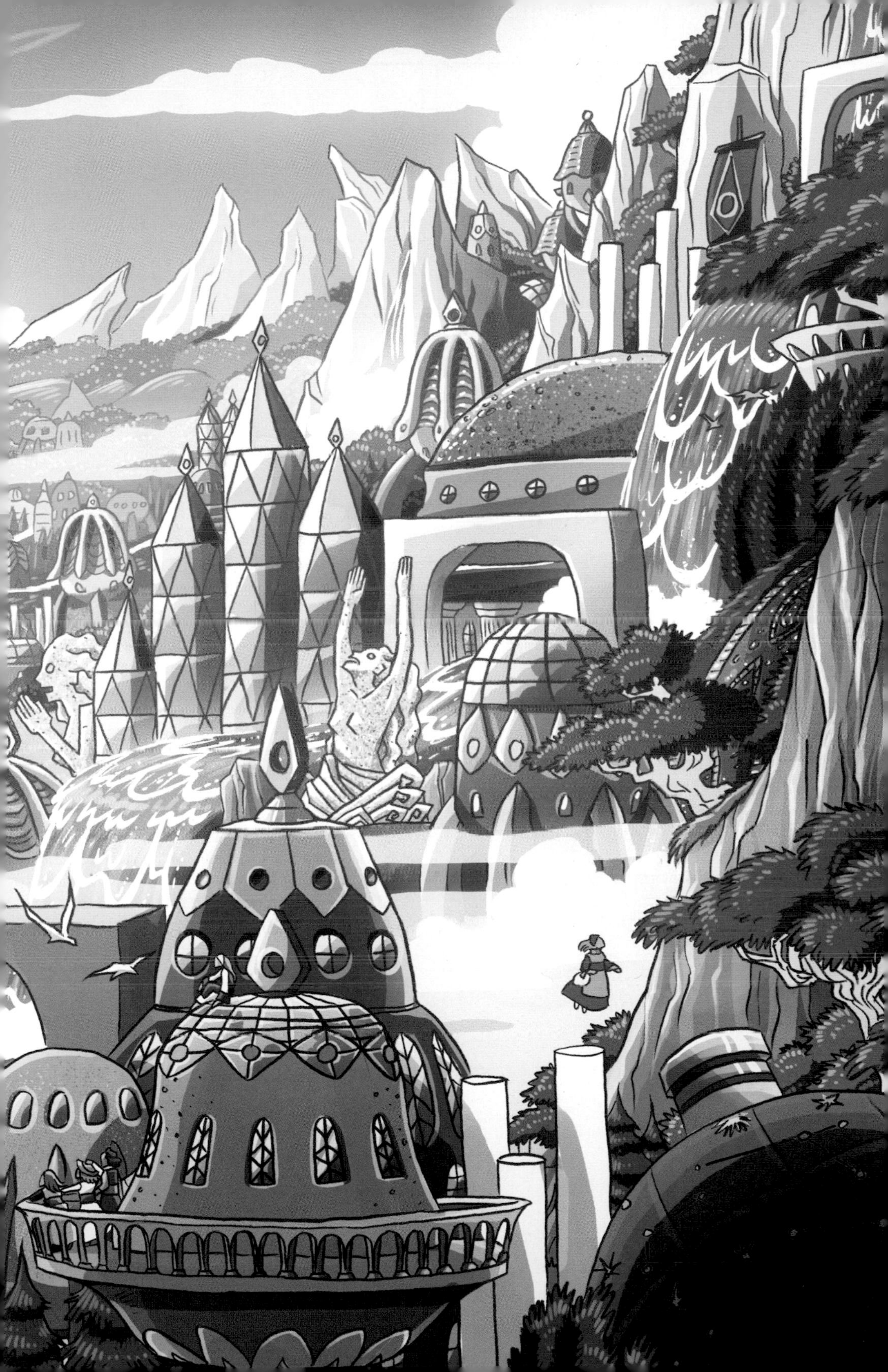

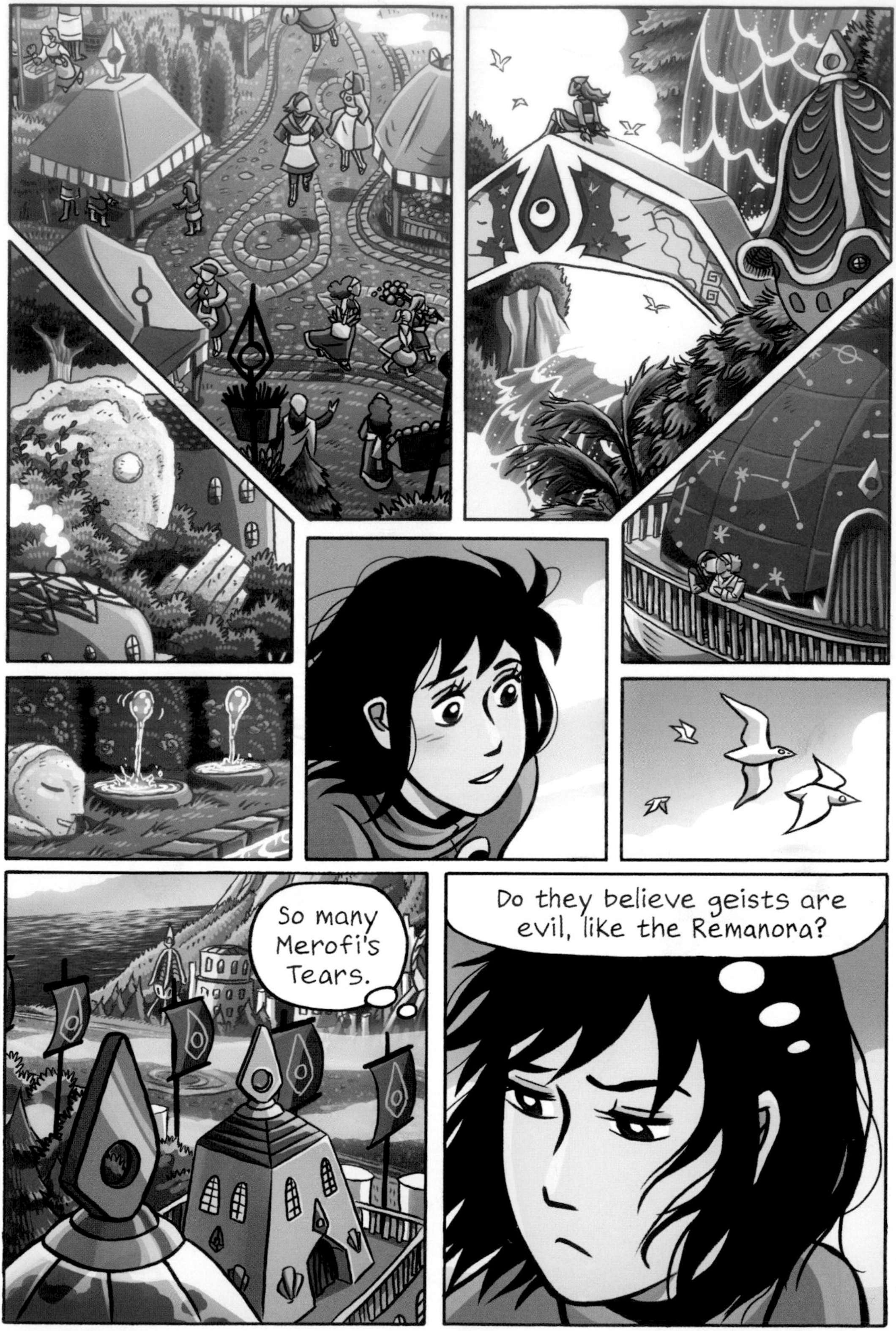
So many Merofi's Tears.
Do they believe geists are evil, like the Remanora?

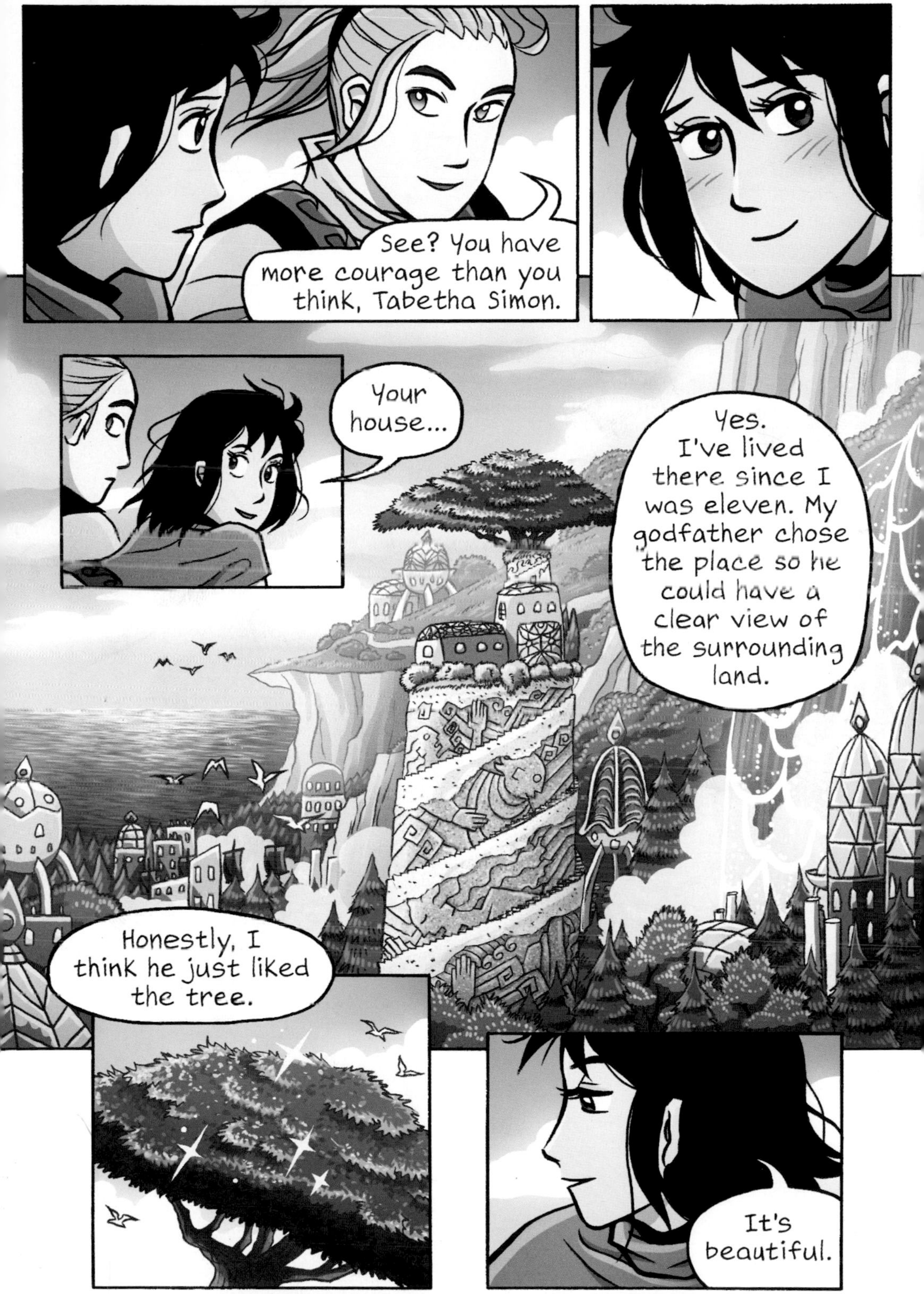
See? You have more courage than you think, Tabetha Simon.
Your house...
Yes. I've lived there since I was eleven. My godfather chose the place so he could have a clear view of the surrounding land.
Honestly, I think he just liked the tree.
It's beautiful.

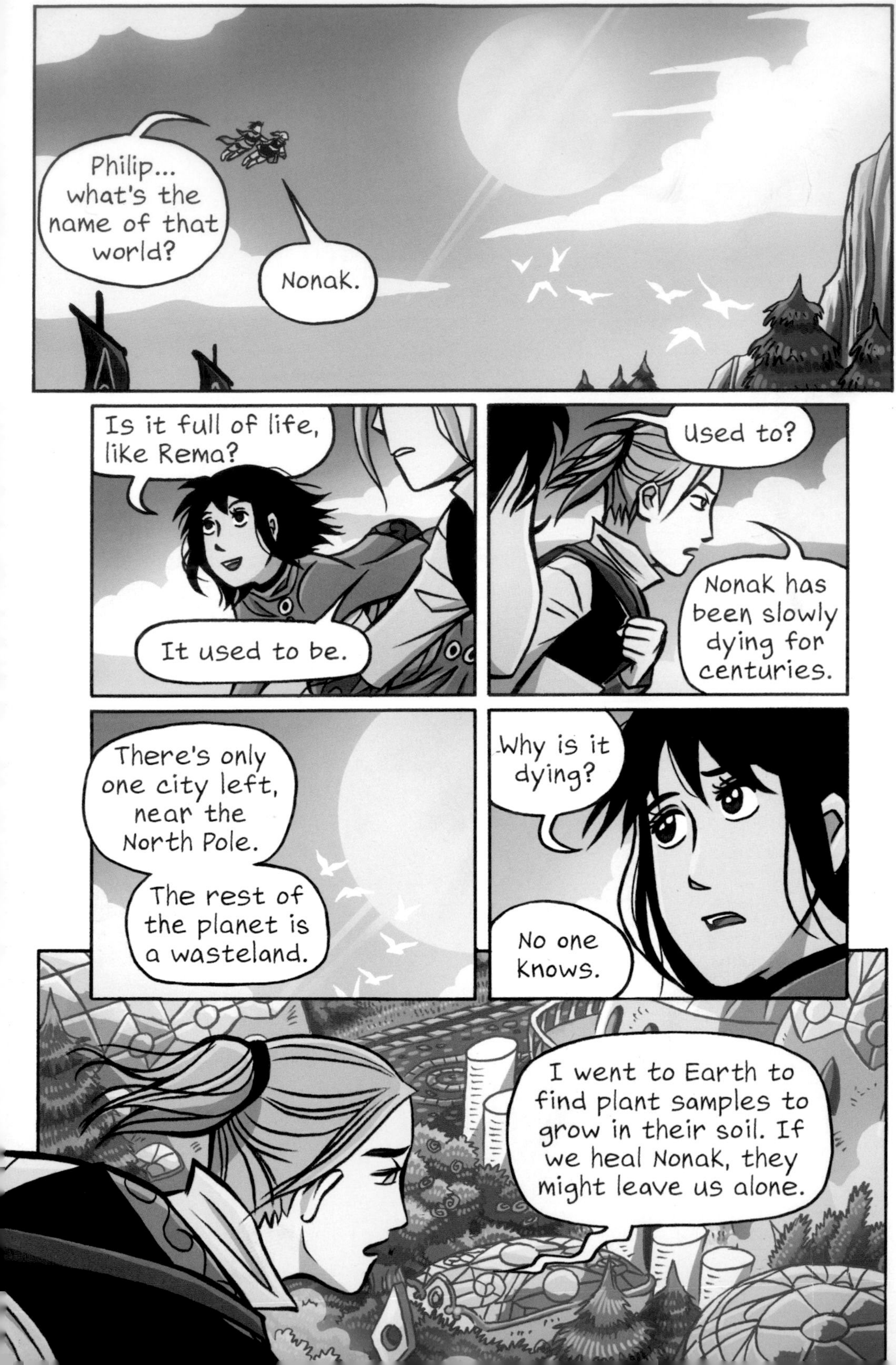
Philip... what's the name of that world?
Nonak.
Is it full of life, like Rema?
It used to be.
Used to?
Nonak has been slowly dying for centuries.
There's only one city left, near the North Pole.
The rest of the planet is a wasteland.
Why is it dying?
No one knows.
I went to Earth to find plant samples to grow in their soil. If we heal Nonak, they might leave us alone.

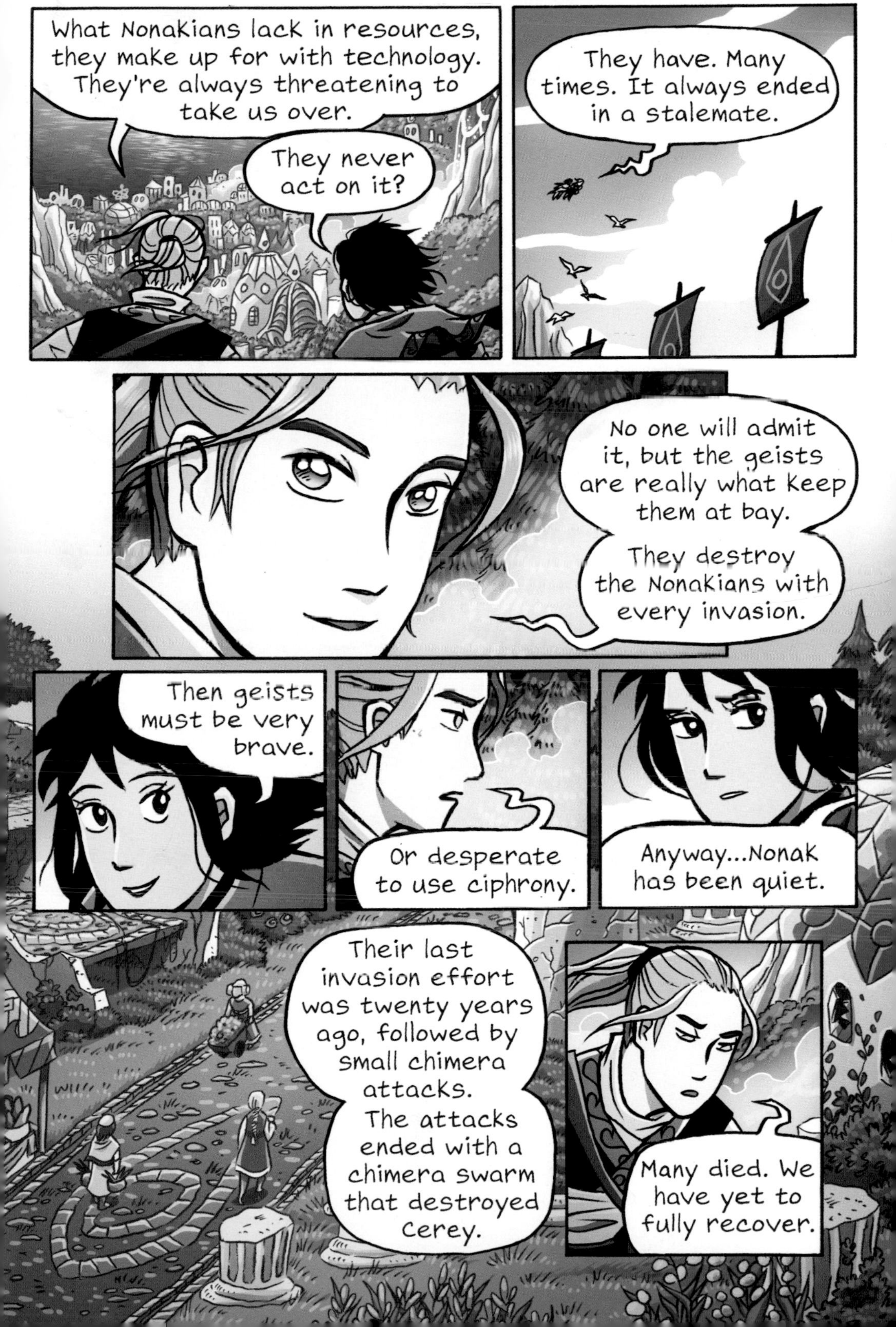
What Nonakians lack in resources, they make up for with technology. They're always threatening to take us over.
They never act on it?
They have. Many times. It always ended in a stalemate.
No one will admit it, but the geists are really what keep them at bay.
They destroy the Nonakians with every invasion.
Then geists must be very brave.
Or desperate to use ciphrony.
Anyway...Nonak has been quiet.
Their last invasion effort was twenty years ago, followed by small chimera attacks.
The attacks ended with a chimera swarm that destroyed Cerey.
Many died. We have yet to fully recover.

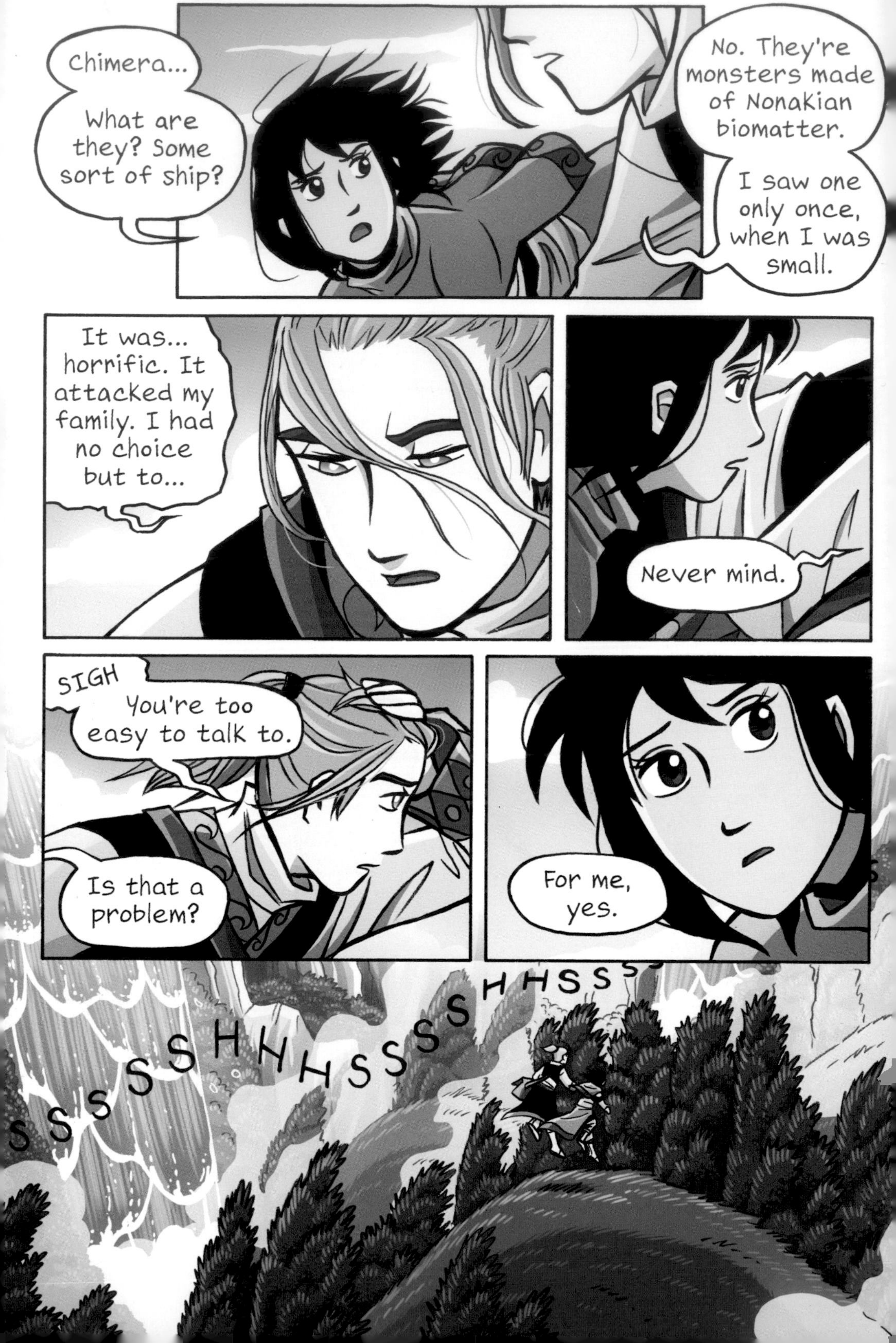

Chimera...
What are they? Some sort of ship?
No. They're monsters made of Nonakian biomatter.
I saw one only once, when I was small.
It was... horrific. It attacked my family. I had no choice but to...
Never mind.
SIGH
You're too easy to talk to.
Is that a problem?
For me, yes.
SSSSSHHHSSSSHHSSS

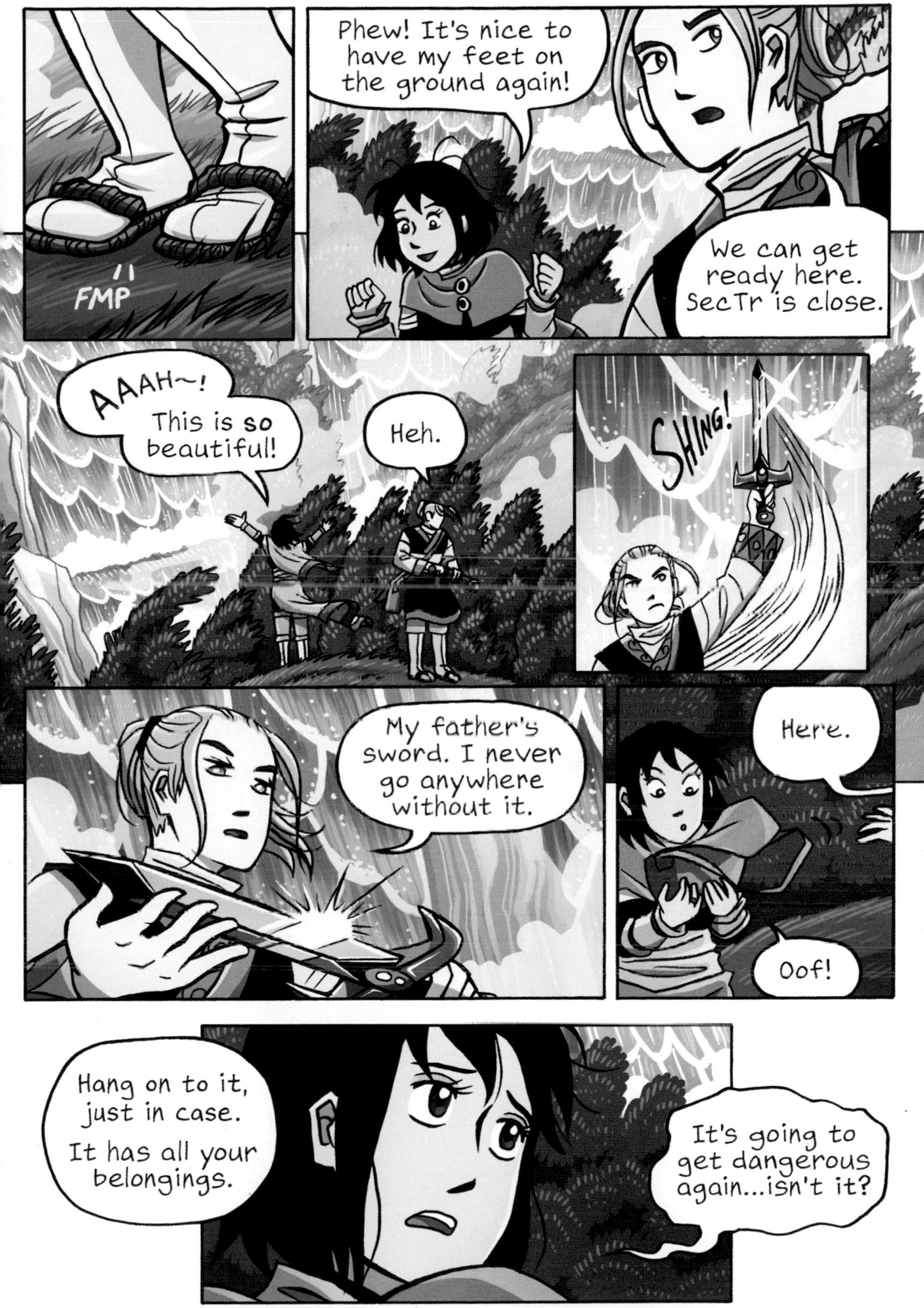
FMP
Phew! It's nice to have my feet on the ground again!
We can get ready here. SecTr is close.
AAAH~! This is so beautiful!
Heh.
SHING!
My father's sword. I never go anywhere without it.
Here.
Oof!
Hang on to it, just in case.
It has all your belongings.
It's going to get dangerous again...isn't it?

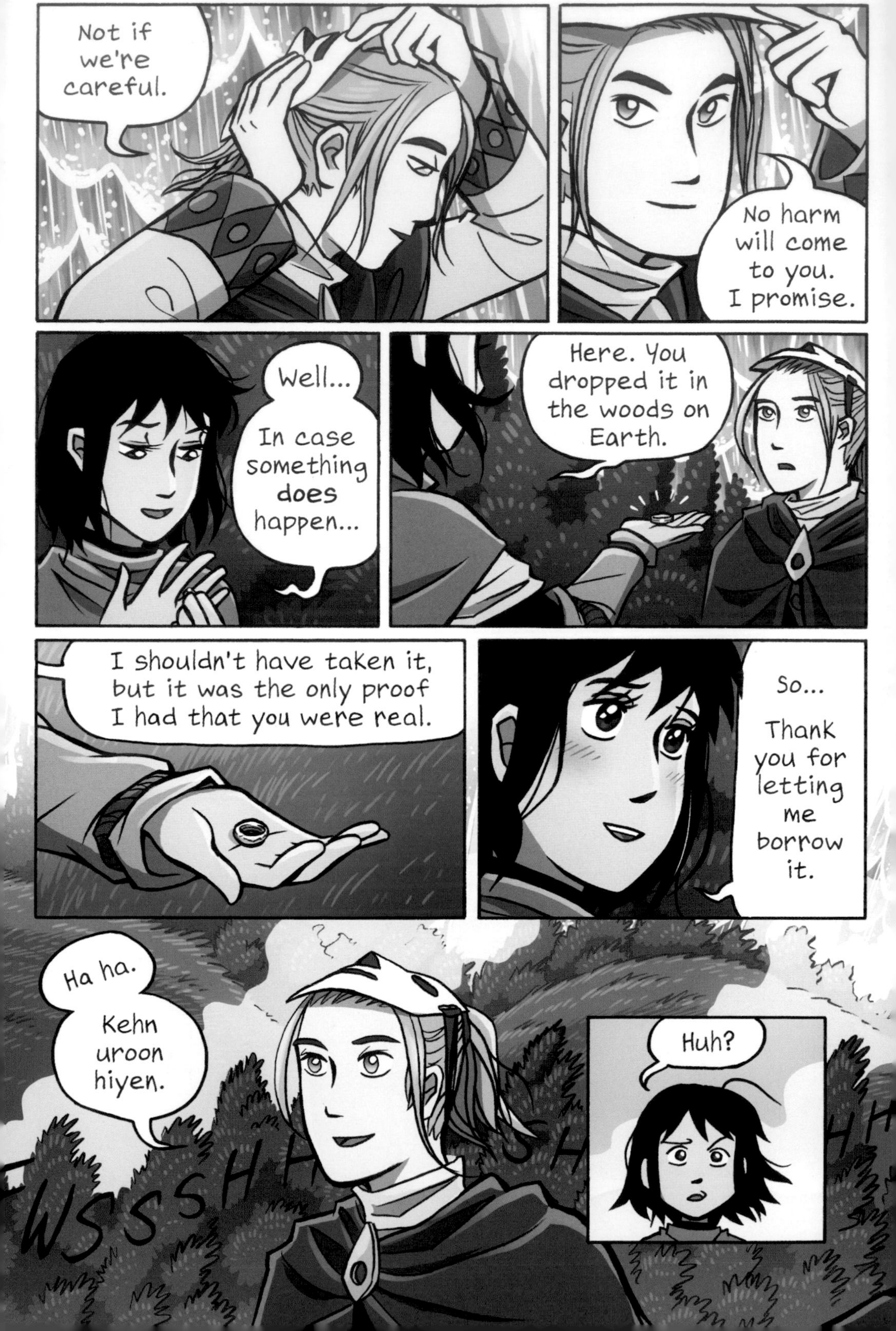
Not if we're careful.
No harm will come to you. I promise.
Well...
In case something **does** happen...
Here. You dropped it in the woods on Earth.
I shouldn't have taken it, but it was the only proof I had that you were real.
So...
Thank you for letting me borrow it.
Ha ha.
Kehn uroon hiyen.
Huh?
FWSSSHHHH

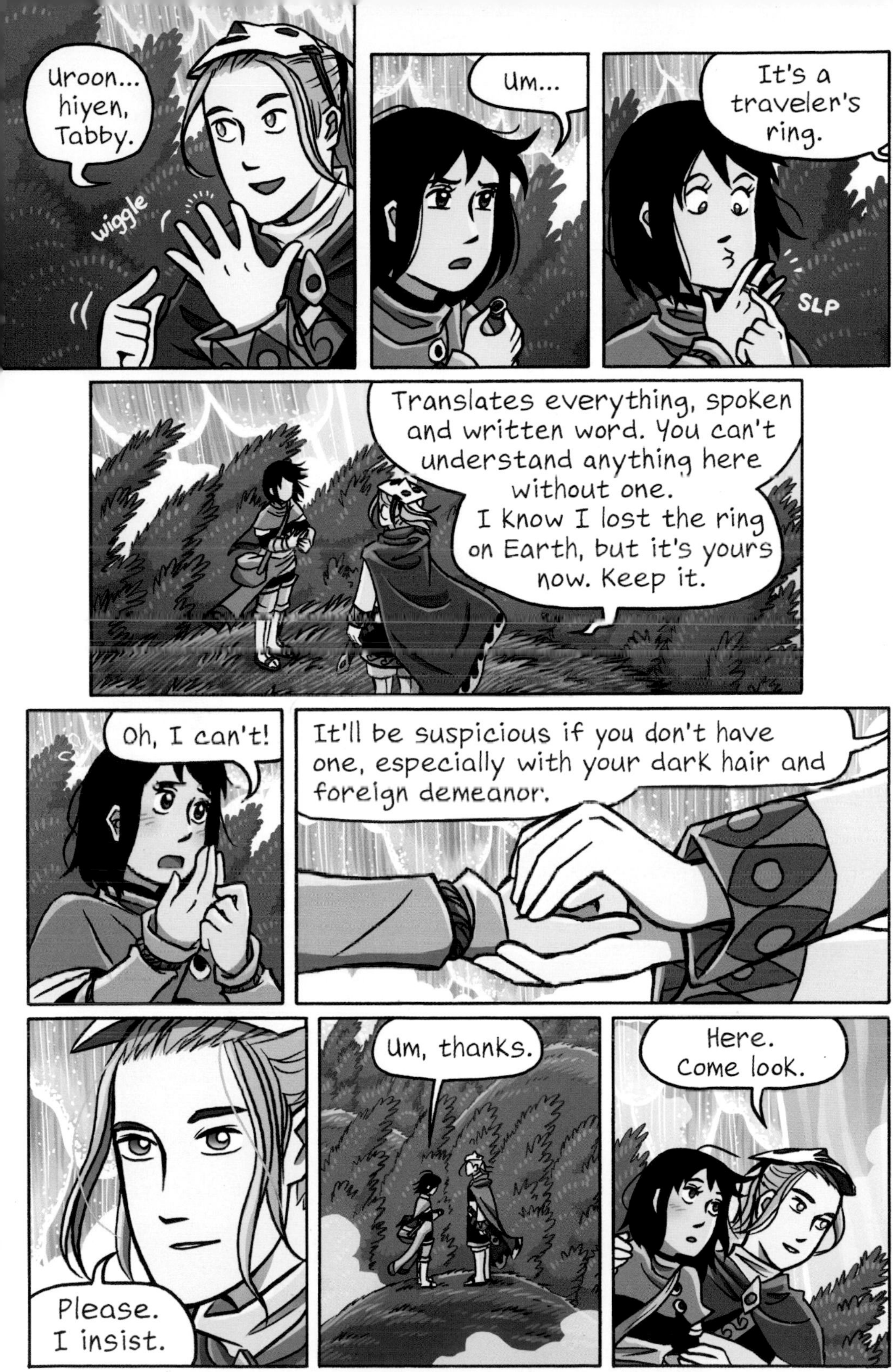
Uroon... hiyen, Tabby.
wiggle
Um...
It's a traveler's ring.
SLP
Translates everything, spoken and written word. You can't understand anything here without one.
I know I lost the ring on Earth, but it's yours now. Keep it.
Oh, I can't!
It'll be suspicious if you don't have one, especially with your dark hair and foreign demeanor.
Please. I insist.
Um, thanks.
Here. Come look.

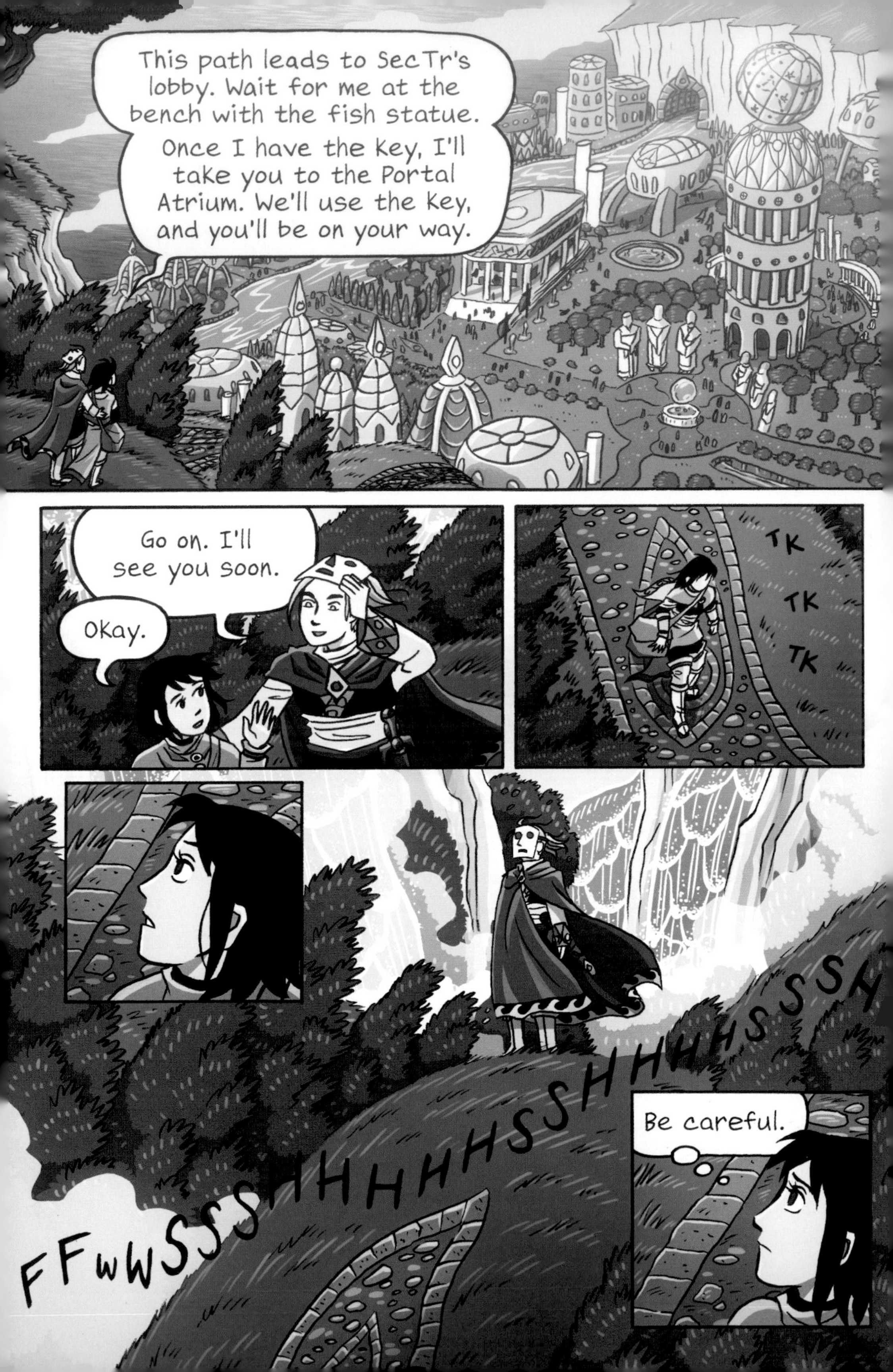
This path leads to SecTr's lobby. Wait for me at the bench with the fish statue.
Once I have the key, I'll take you to the Portal Atrium. We'll use the key, and you'll be on your way.
Go on. I'll see you soon.
Okay.
TK
TK
TK
FFWWSSSSHHHHHHSSHHHHHSSSSH
Be careful.

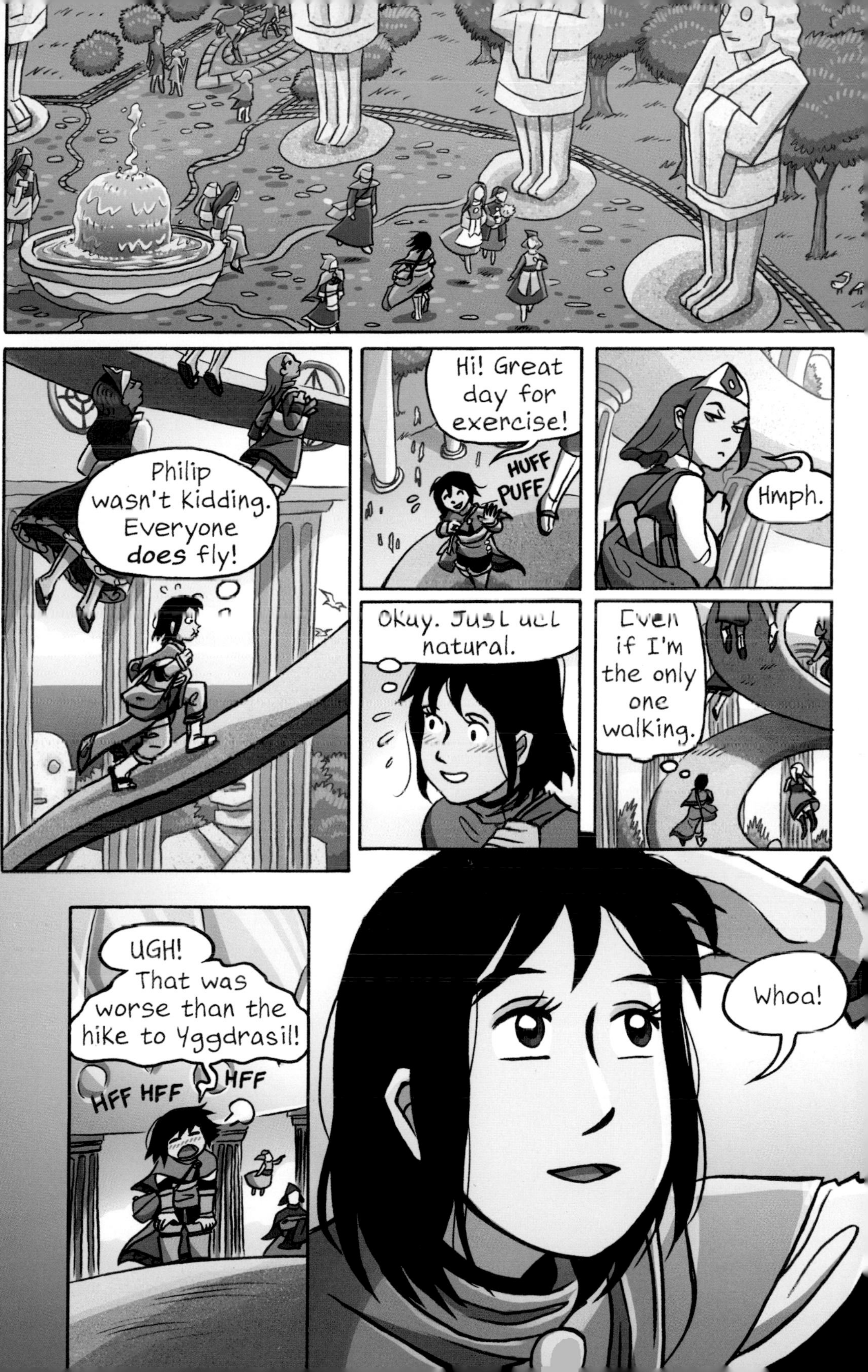
Philip wasn't kidding. Everyone does fly!
Hi! Great day for exercise!
HUFF
PUFF
Hmph.
Okay. Just act natural.
Even if I'm the only one walking.
UGH! That was worse than the hike to Yggdrasil!
HFF HFF
HFF
Whoa!

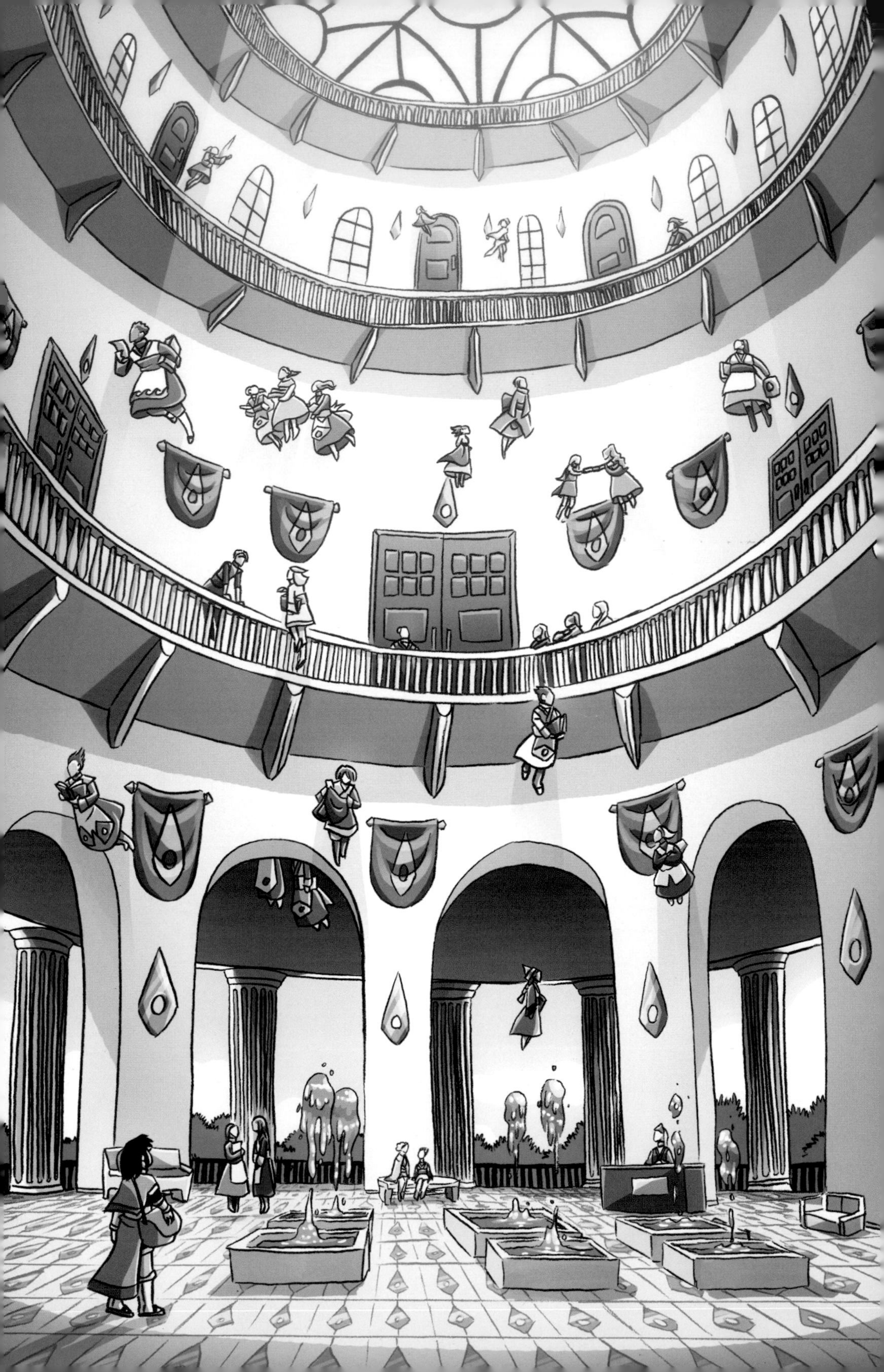

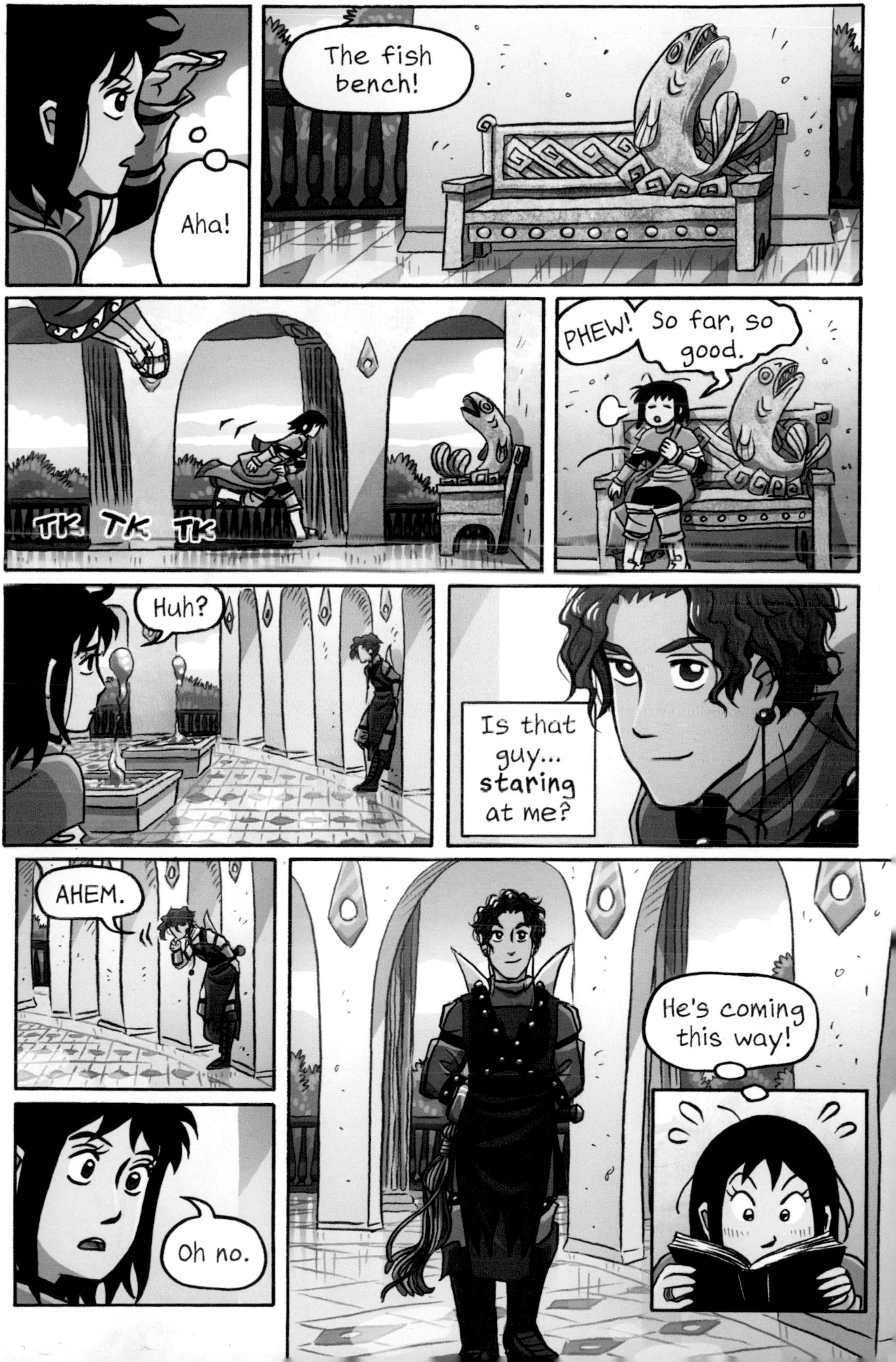
Aha!
The fish bench!
TK TK TK
PHEW!
So far, so good.
Huh?
Is that guy... **staring** at me?
AHEM.
Oh no.
He's coming this way!

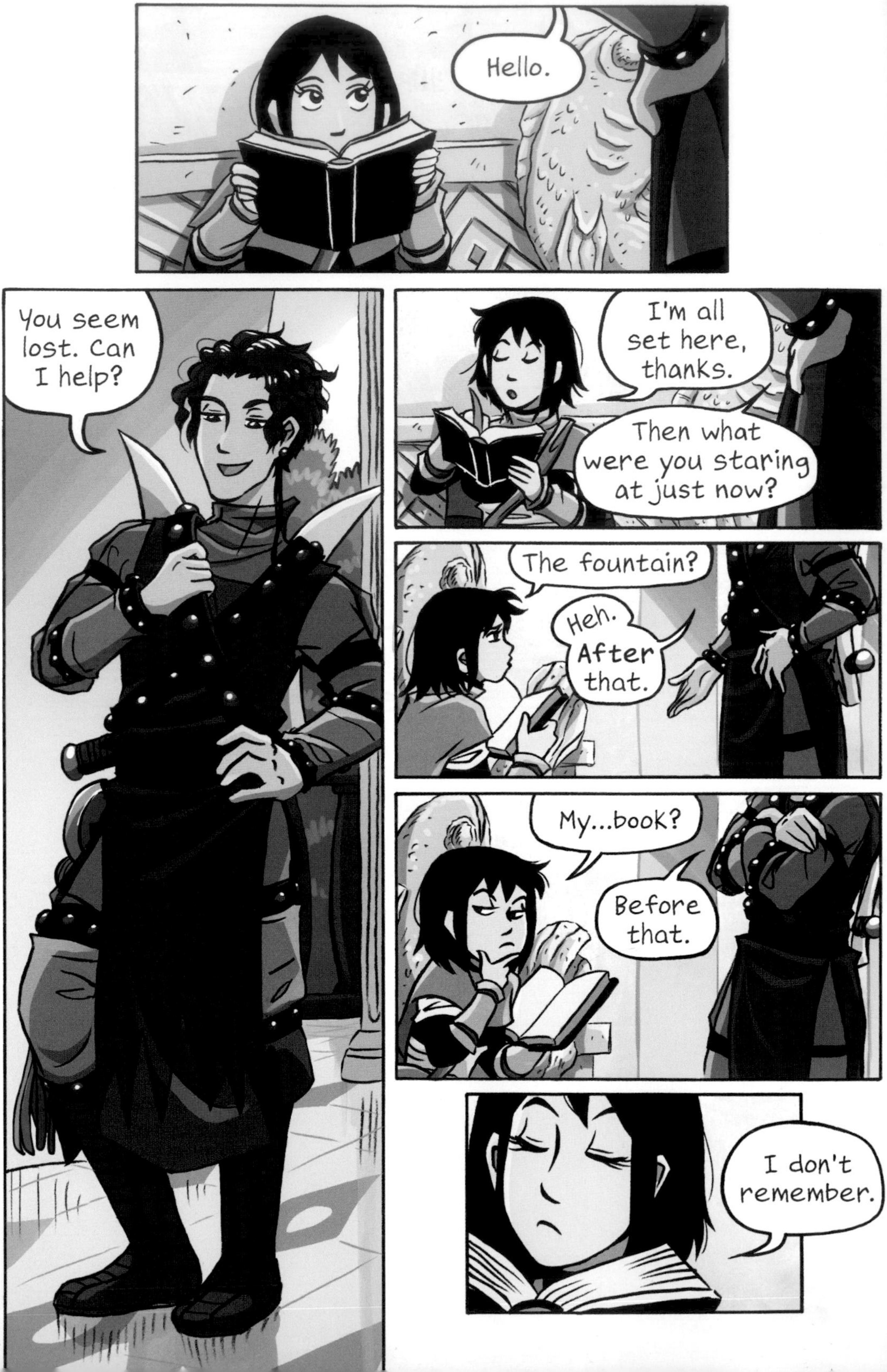
Hello.
You seem lost. Can I help?
I'm all set here, thanks.
Then what were you staring at just now?
The fountain?
Heh. After that.
My...book?
Before that.
I don't remember.

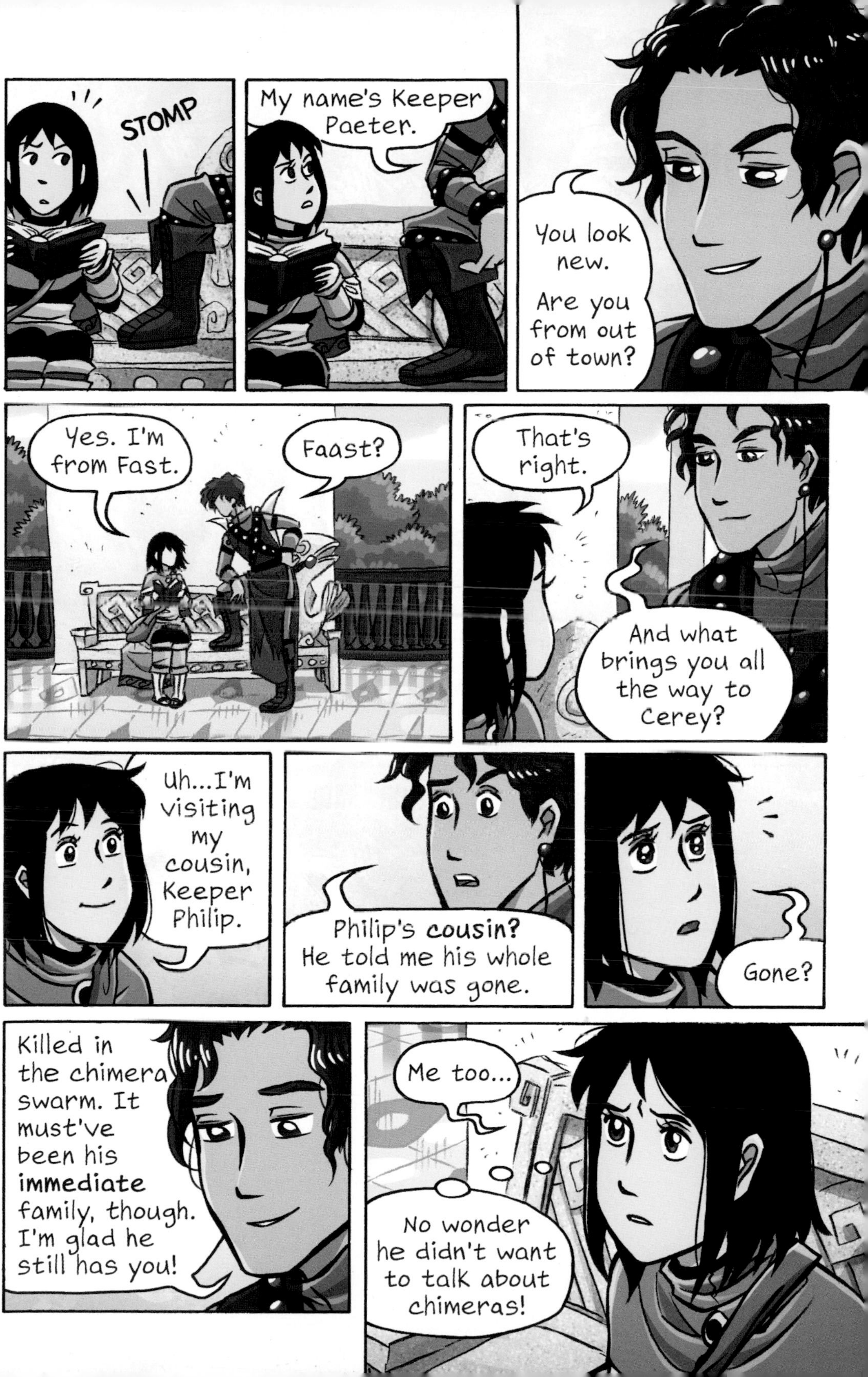
STOMP
My name's Keeper Paeter.
You look new.
Are you from out of town?
Yes. I'm from Fast.
Faast?
That's right.
And what brings you all the way to Cerey?
Uh...I'm visiting my cousin, Keeper Philip.
Philip's **cousin?** He told me his whole family was gone.
Gone?
Killed in the chimera swarm. It must've been his **immediate** family, though. I'm glad he still has you!
Me too...
No wonder he didn't want to talk about chimeras!

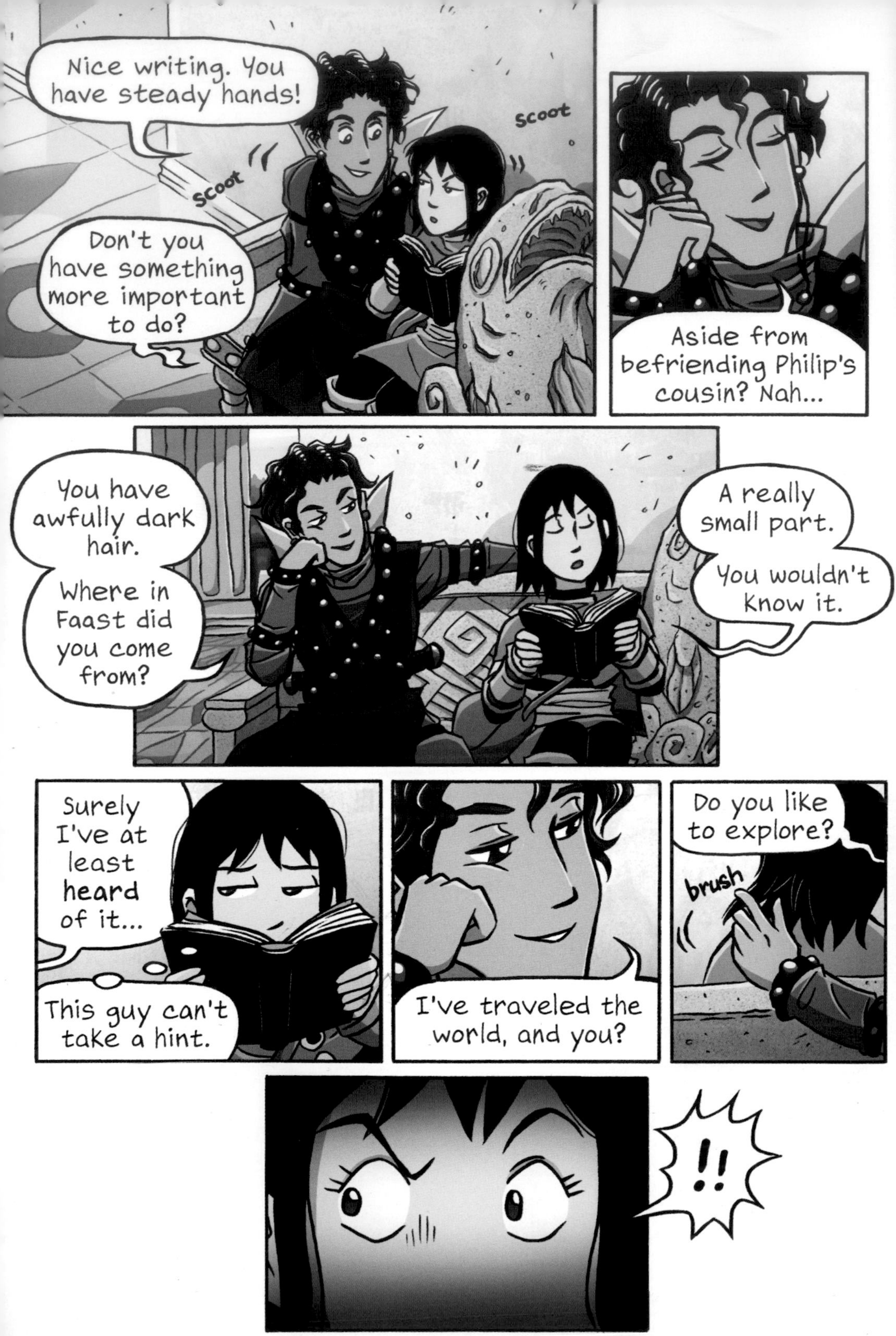
Nice writing. You have steady hands!
Scoot
Scoot
Don't you have something more important to do?
Aside from befriending Philip's cousin? Nah...
You have awfully dark hair.
Where in Faast did you come from?
A really small part.
You wouldn't know it.
Surely I've at least **heard** of it...
This guy can't take a hint.
I've traveled the world, and you?
Do you like to explore?
brush
!!

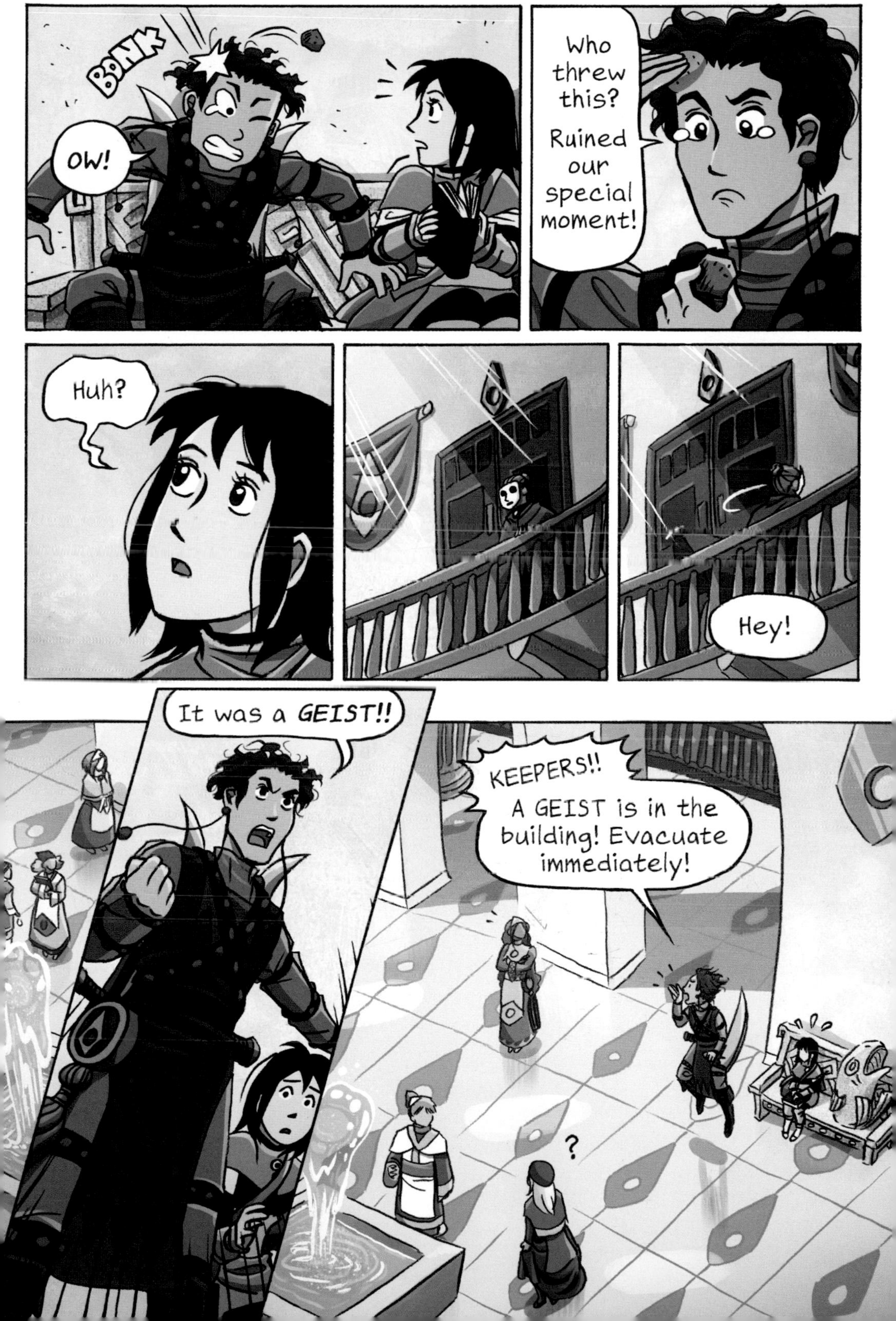
BONK
OW!
Who threw this?
Ruined our special moment!
Huh?
Hey!
It was a GEIST!!
KEEPERS!!
A GEIST is in the building! Evacuate immediately!
?

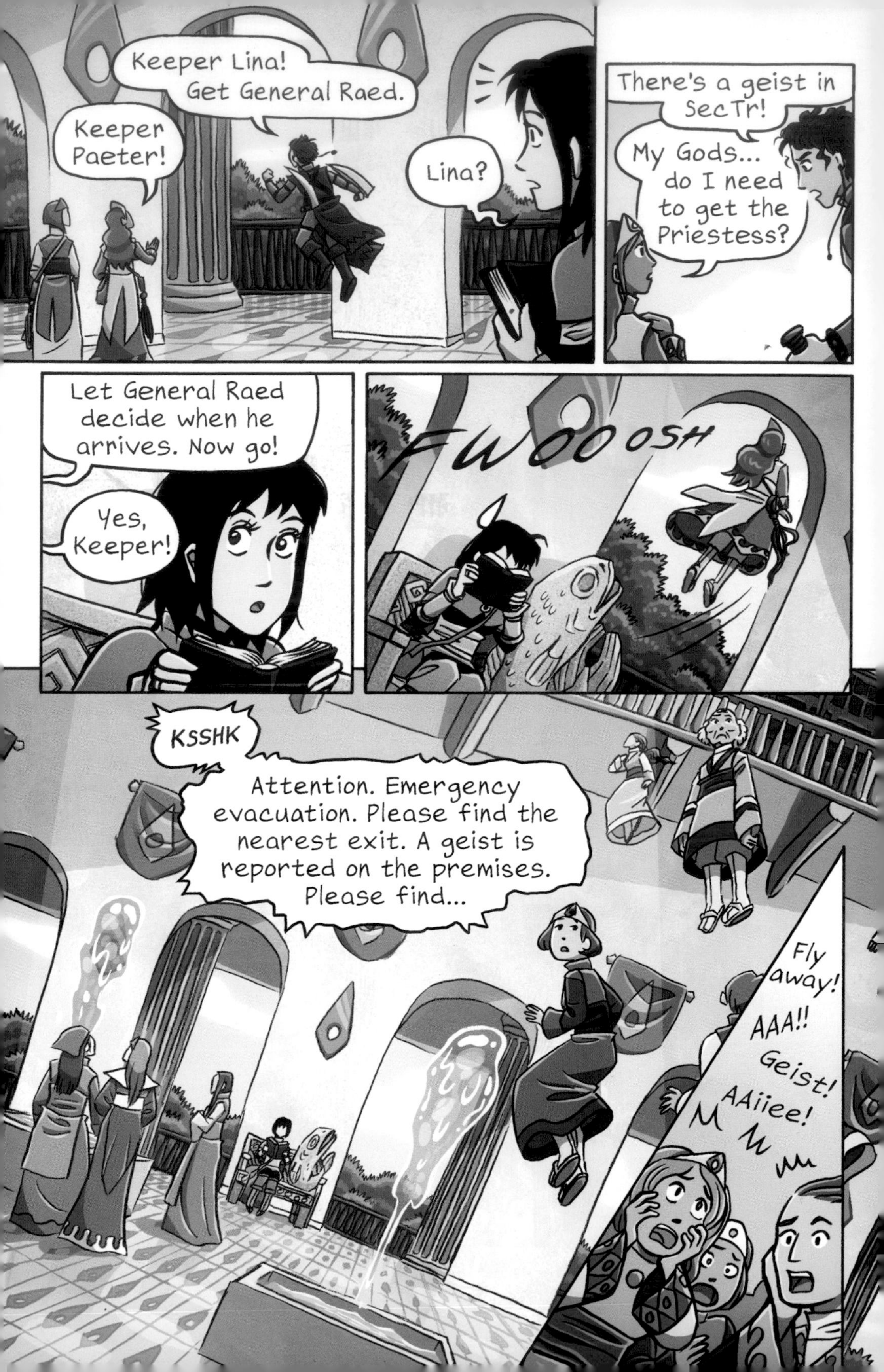
Keeper Paeter!
Keeper Lina! Get General Raed.
Lina?
There's a geist in SecTr!
My Gods... do I need to get the Priestess?
Let General Raed decide when he arrives. Now go!
Yes, Keeper!
FWOOOSH
KSSHK
Attention. Emergency evacuation. Please find the nearest exit. A geist is reported on the premises. Please find...
Fly away!
AAA!!
Geist!
AAiiee!

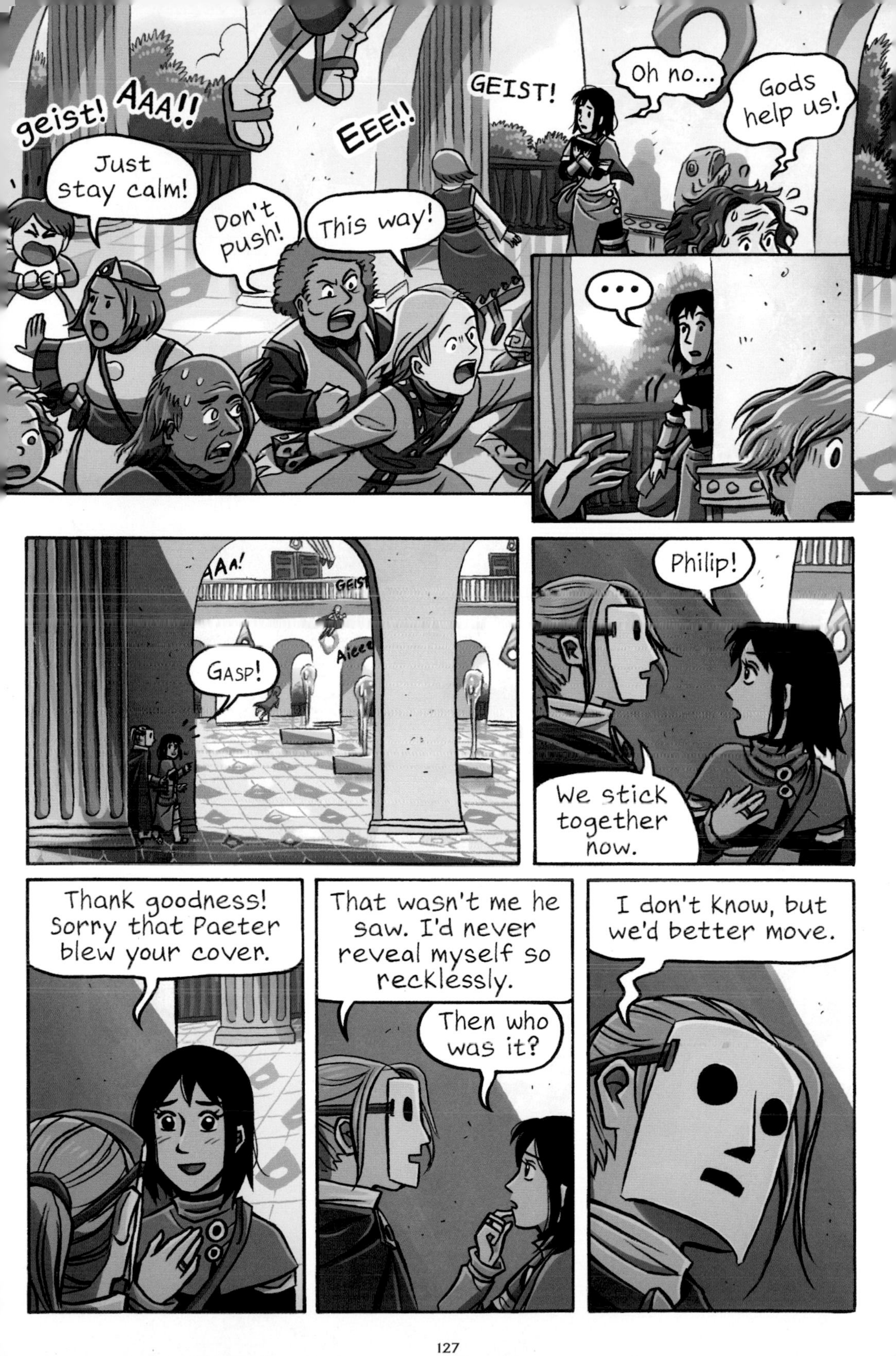
geist! AAA!!
EEE!!
GEIST!
Oh no...
Gods help us!
Just stay calm!
Don't push!
This way!
...
AAA!
GEIST
Aieee
GASP!
Philip!
We stick together now.
Thank goodness! Sorry that Paeter blew your cover.
That wasn't me he saw. I'd never reveal myself so recklessly.
Then who was it?
I don't know, but we'd better move.

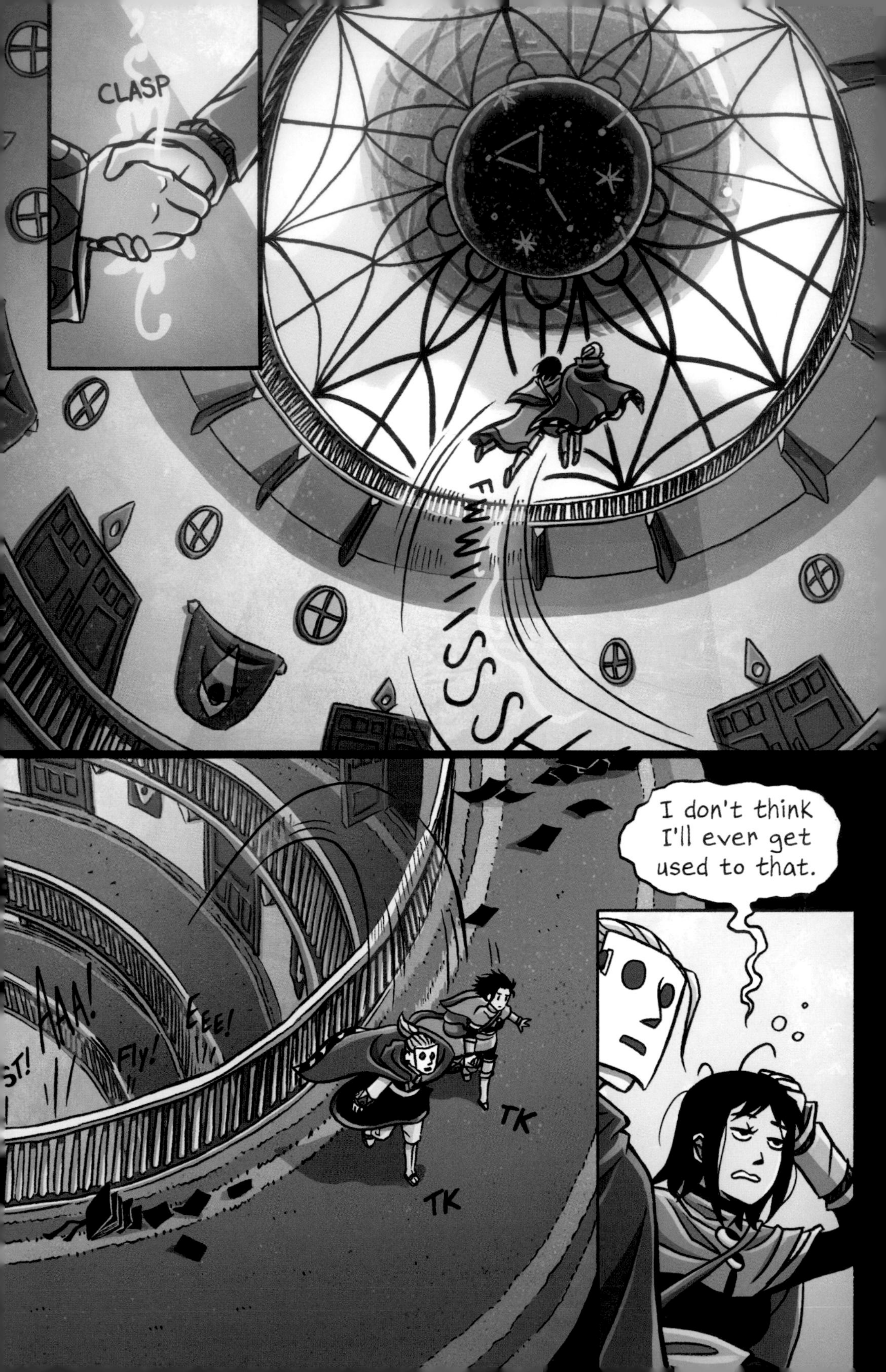
CLASP
FWWIIISSSH
AAA!
EEE!
FLY!
TK
TK
I don't think I'll ever get used to that.

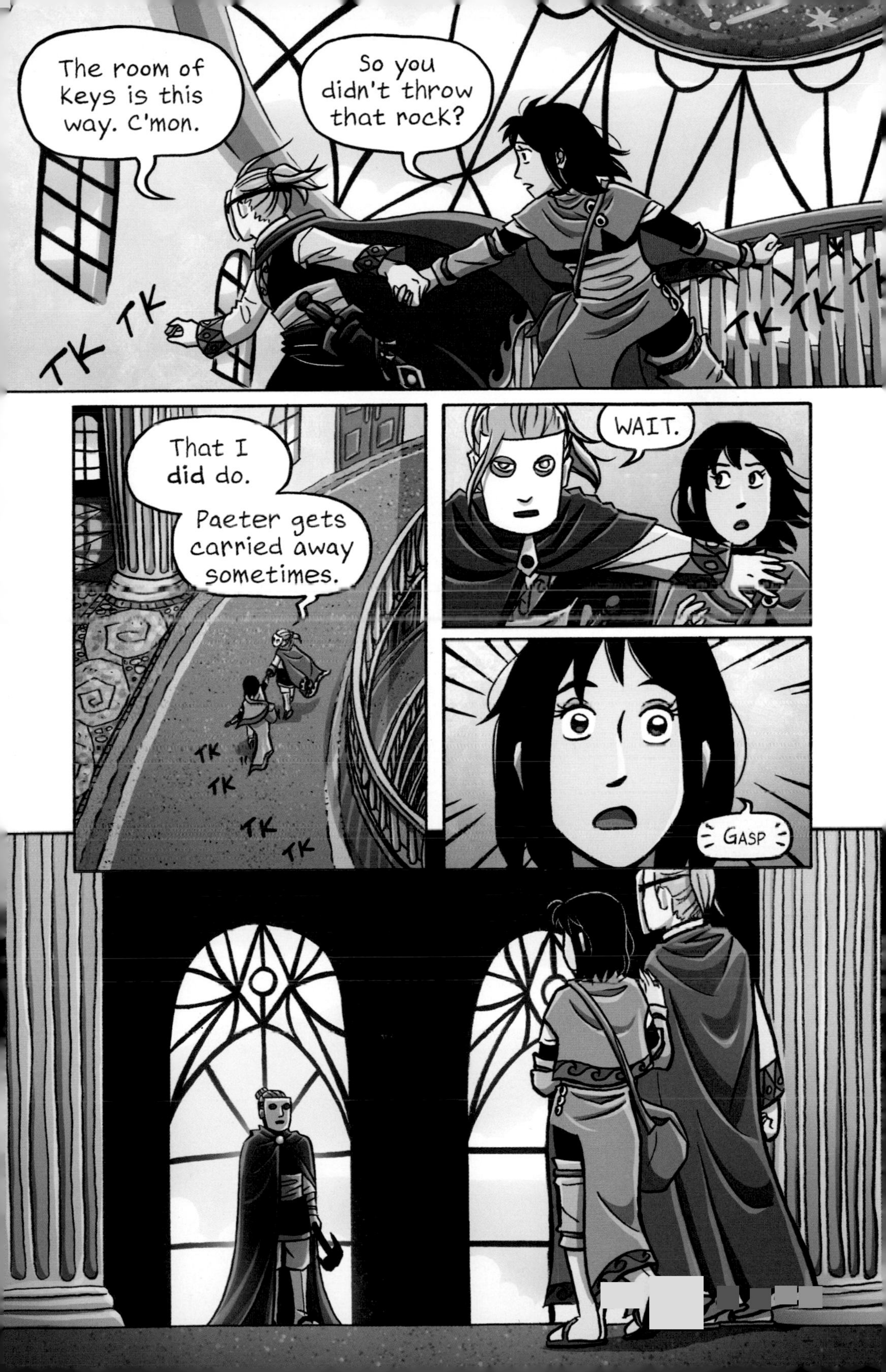
The room of Keys is this way. C'mon.
So you didn't throw that rock?
TK TK
TK TK TK
That I did do.
Paeter gets carried away sometimes.
TK
TK
TK
TK
WAIT.
GASP

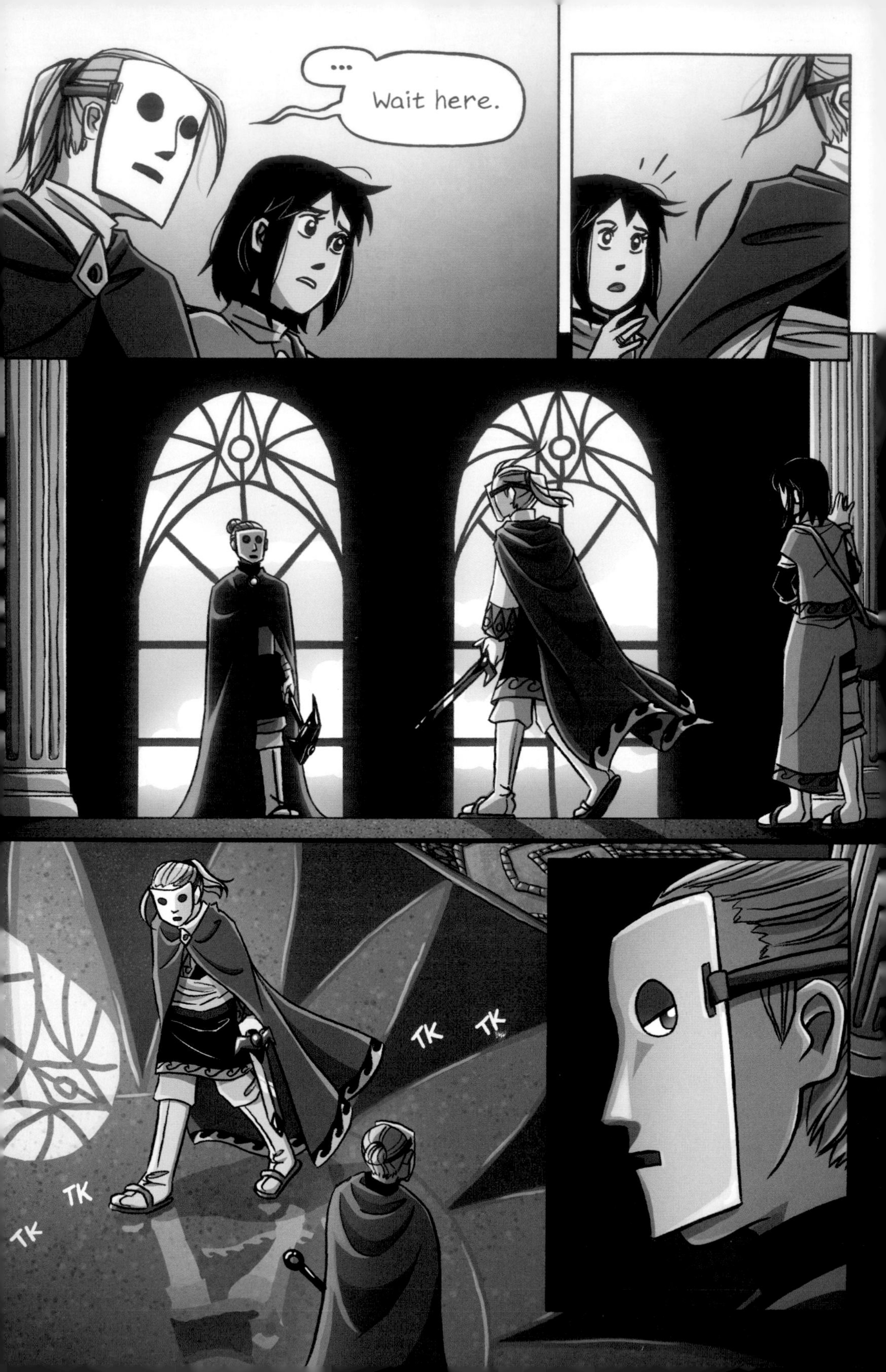
...
Wait here.
TK TK
TK TK

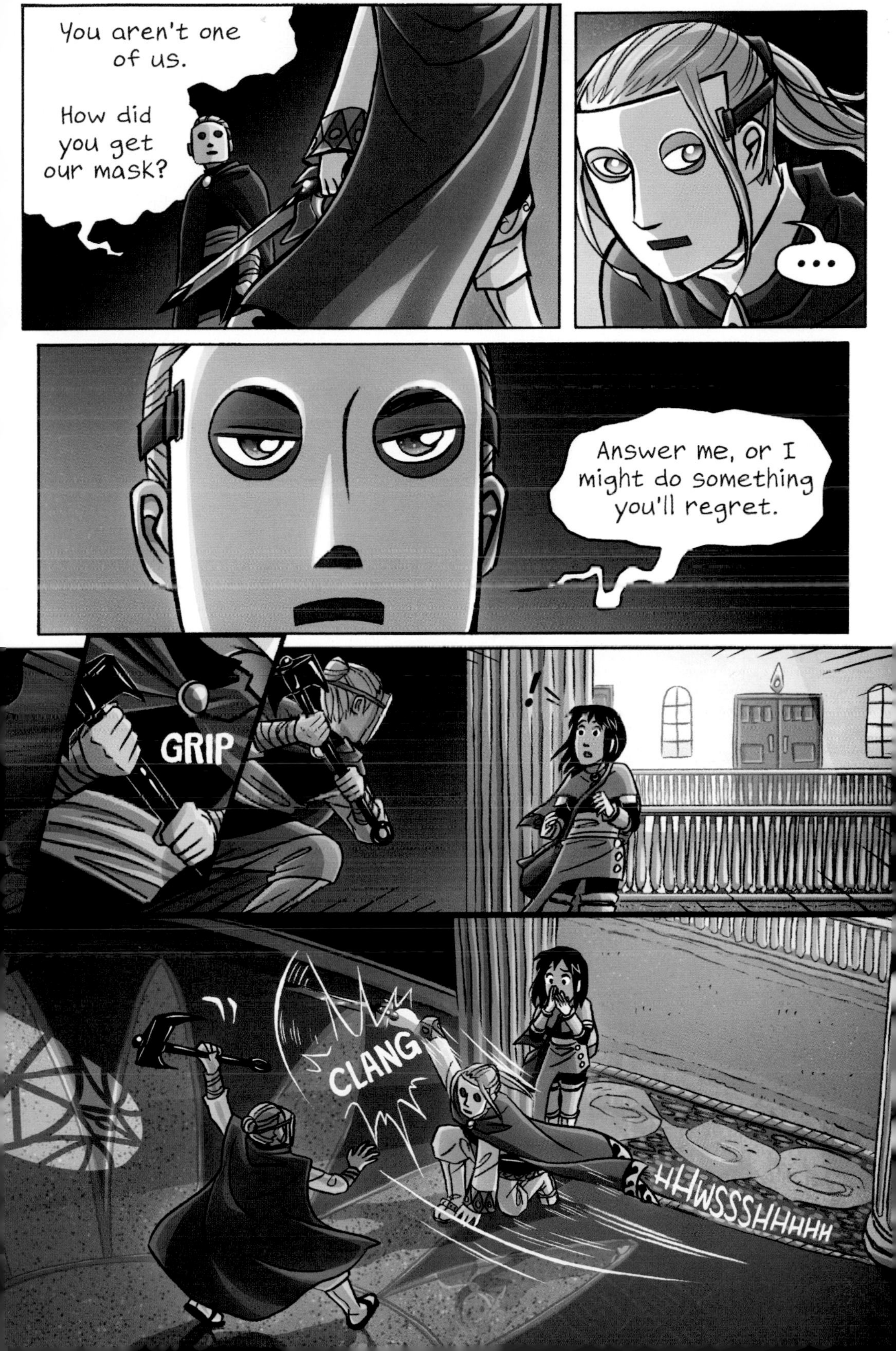

You aren't one of us.
How did you get our mask?
...
Answer me, or I might do something you'll regret.
GRIP
!
CLANG
HHWSSSHHHHH

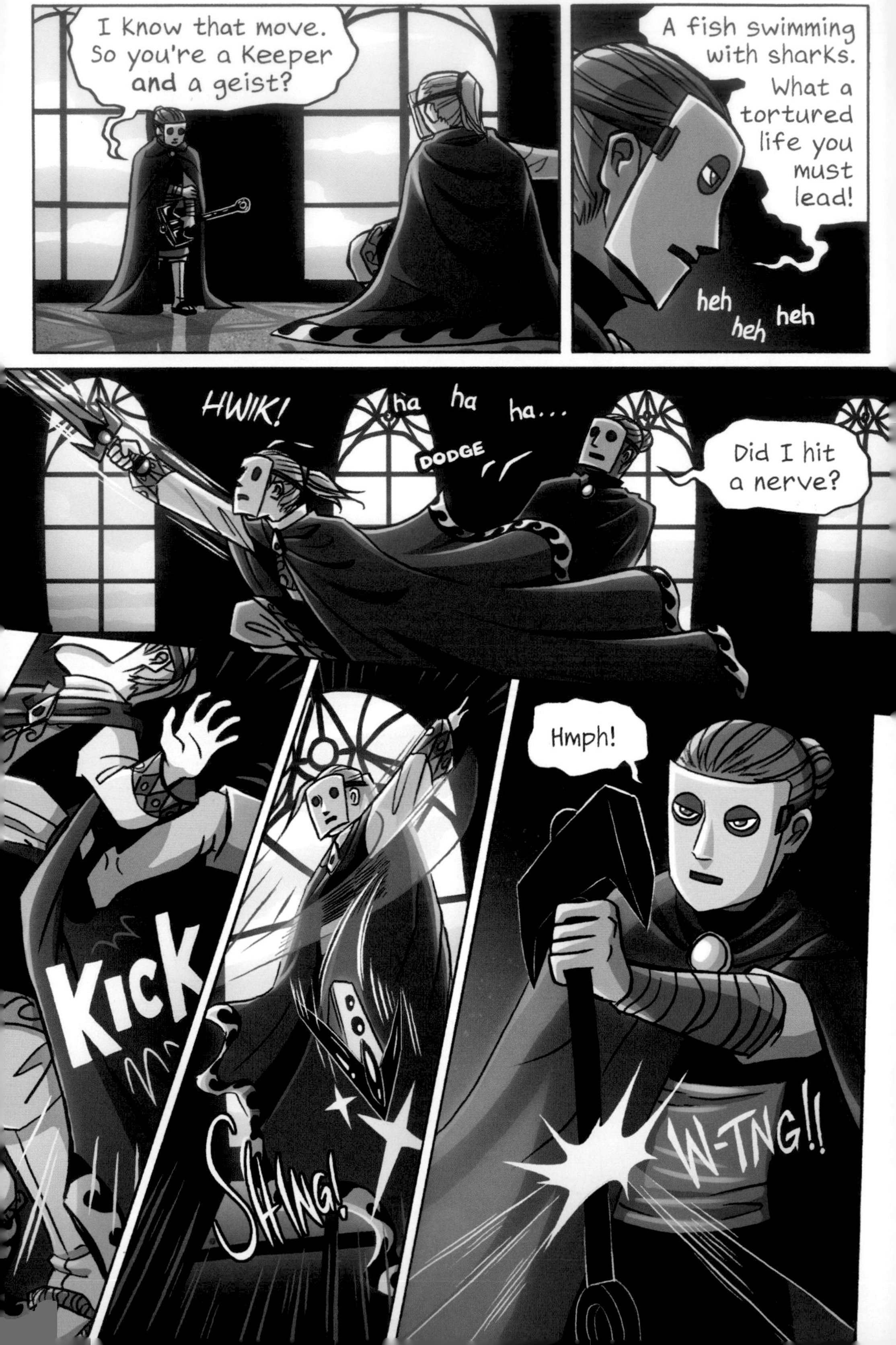
I know that move. So you're a Keeper and a geist?
A fish swimming with sharks.
What a tortured life you must lead!
heh heh heh
HWIK!
ha ha ha...
DODGE
Did I hit a nerve?
KICK
SHING!
Hmph!
W-TNG!!

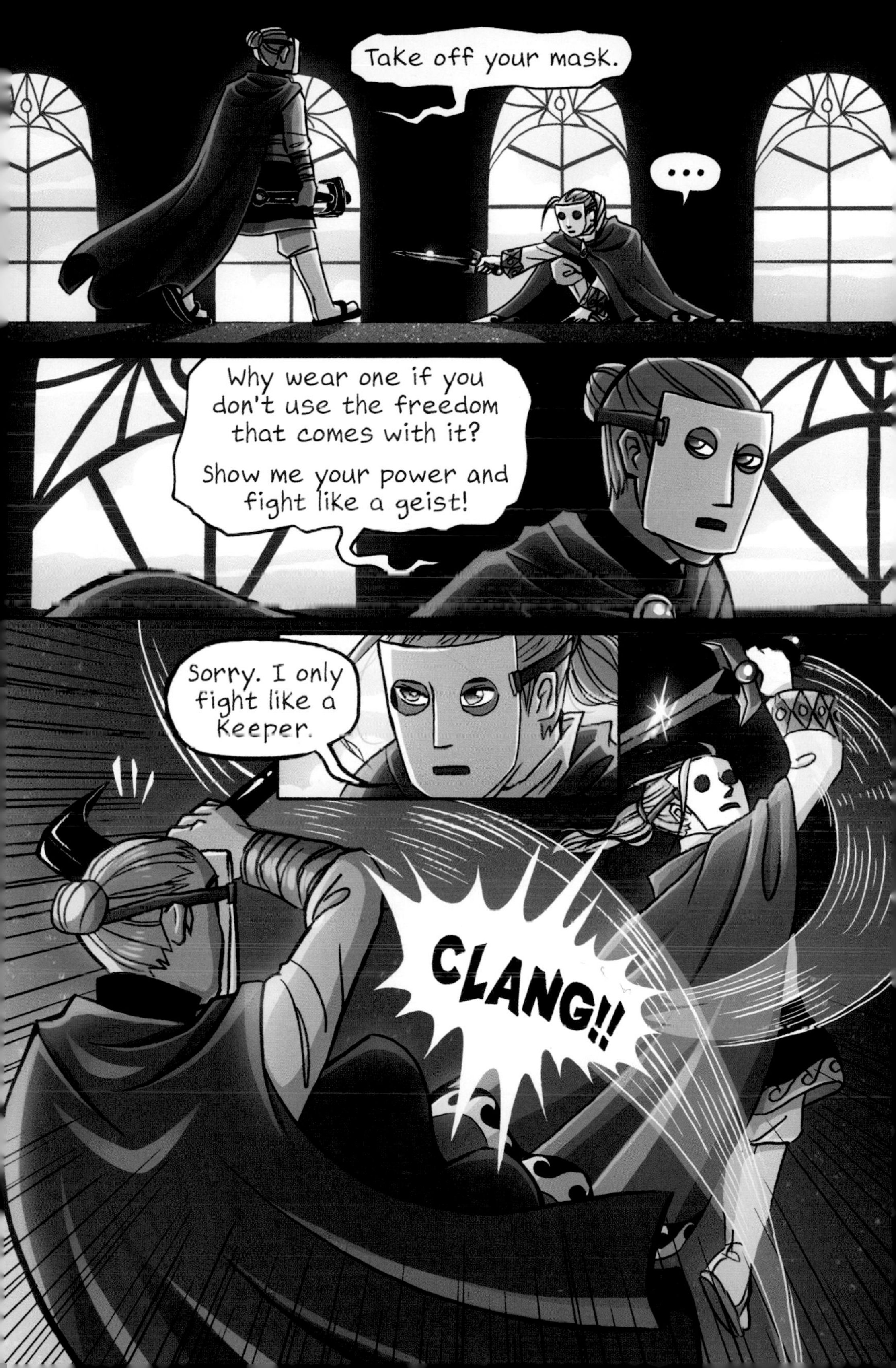
Take off your mask.
...
Why wear one if you don't use the freedom that comes with it?
Show me your power and fight like a geist!
Sorry. I only fight like a Keeper.
CLANG!!

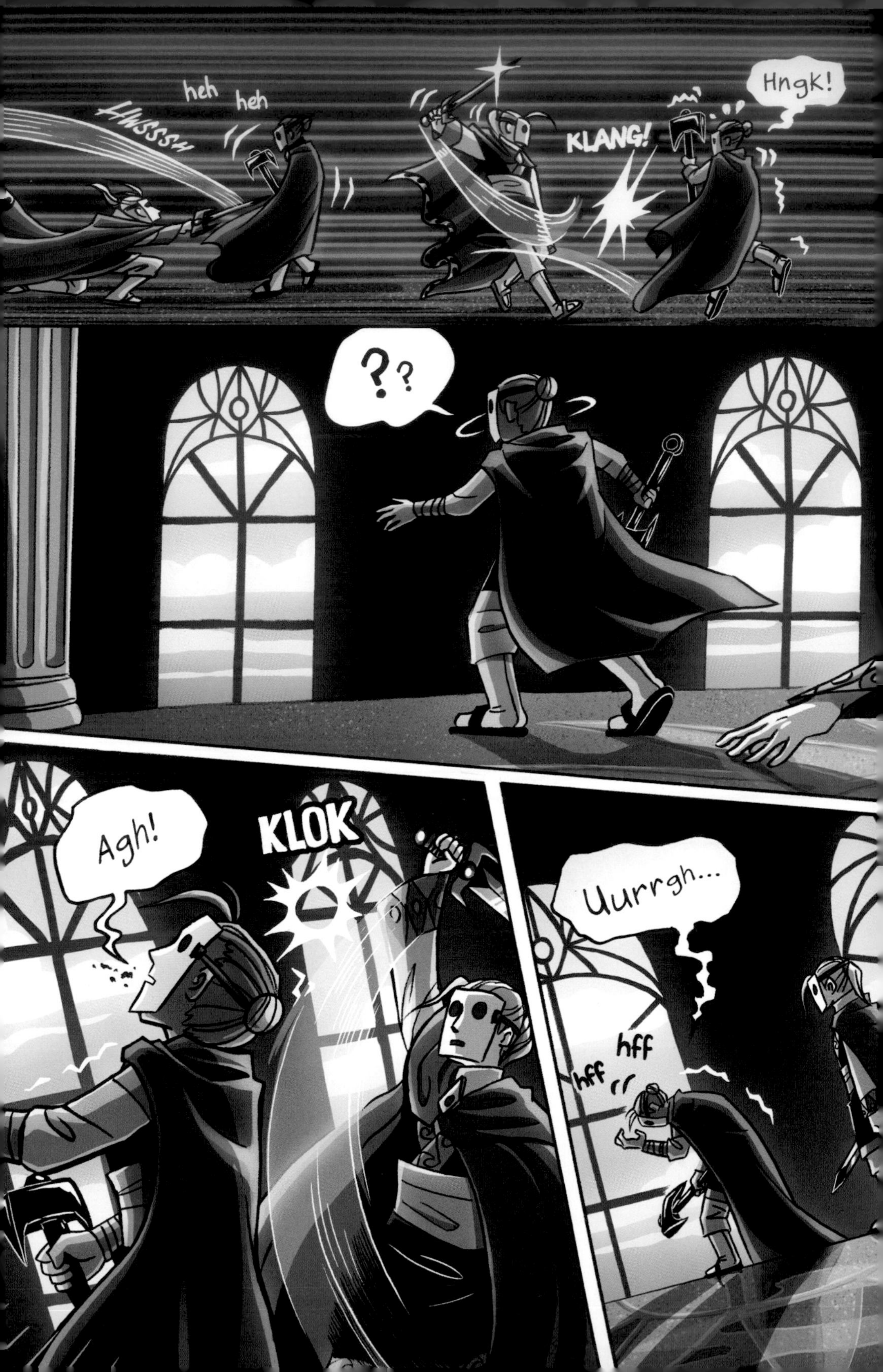
HWSSSH
heh
heh
KLANG!
Hngk!
??
Agh!
KLOK
Uurrgh...
hff
hff

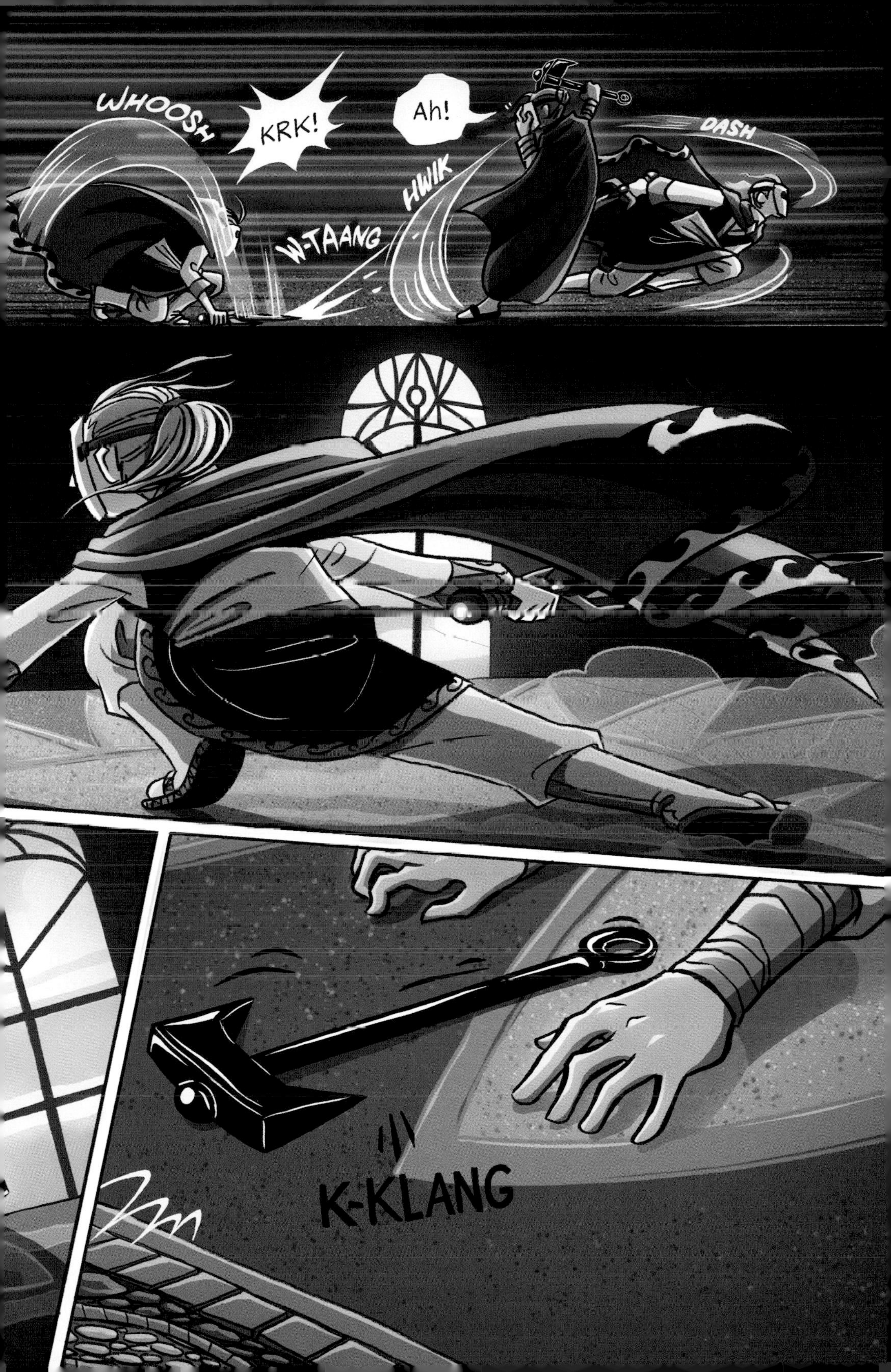
WHOOSH
KRK!
Ah!
DASH
HWIK
W-TAANG
K-KLANG

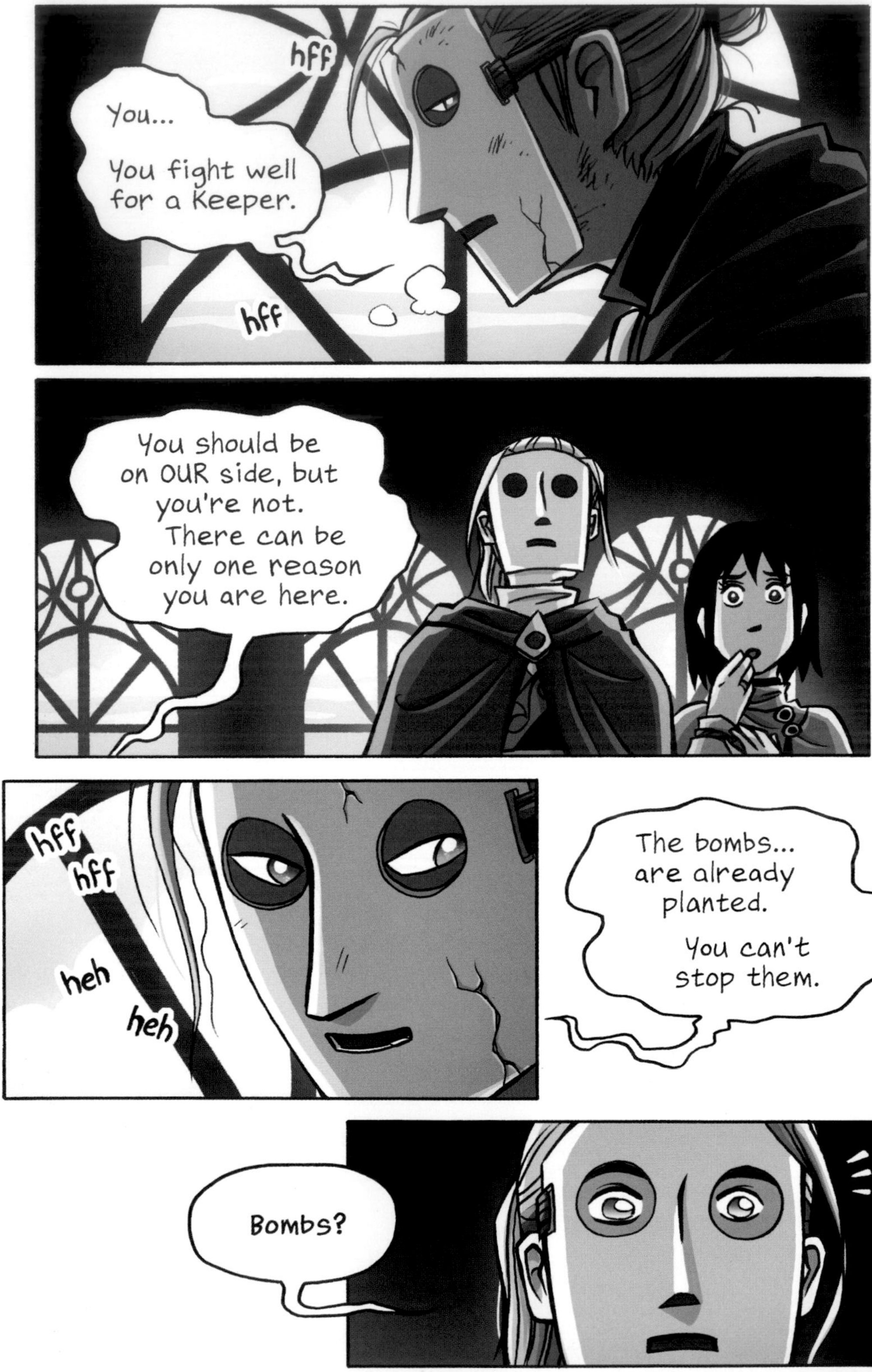
hff
You...
You fight well for a Keeper.
hff
You should be on OUR side, but you're not. There can be only one reason you are here.
hff
hff
heh
heh
The bombs... are already planted.
You can't stop them.
Bombs?

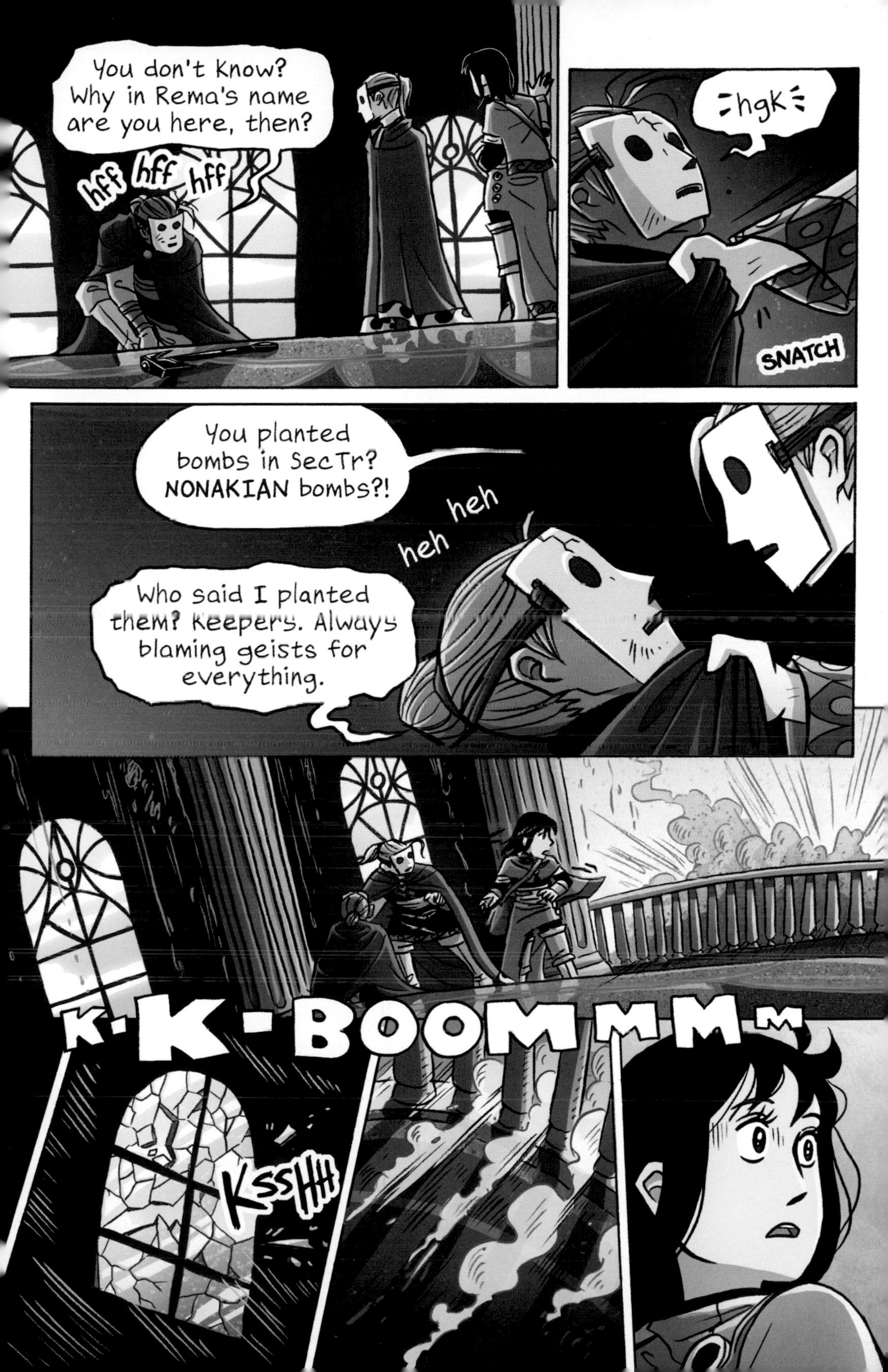
You don't know? Why in Rema's name are you here, then?
hff hff hff
hgk
SNATCH
You planted bombs in SecTr? NONAKIAN bombs?!
heh heh
Who said I planted them? Keepers. Always blaming geists for everything.
K-K-BOOMMMm
KSSHH

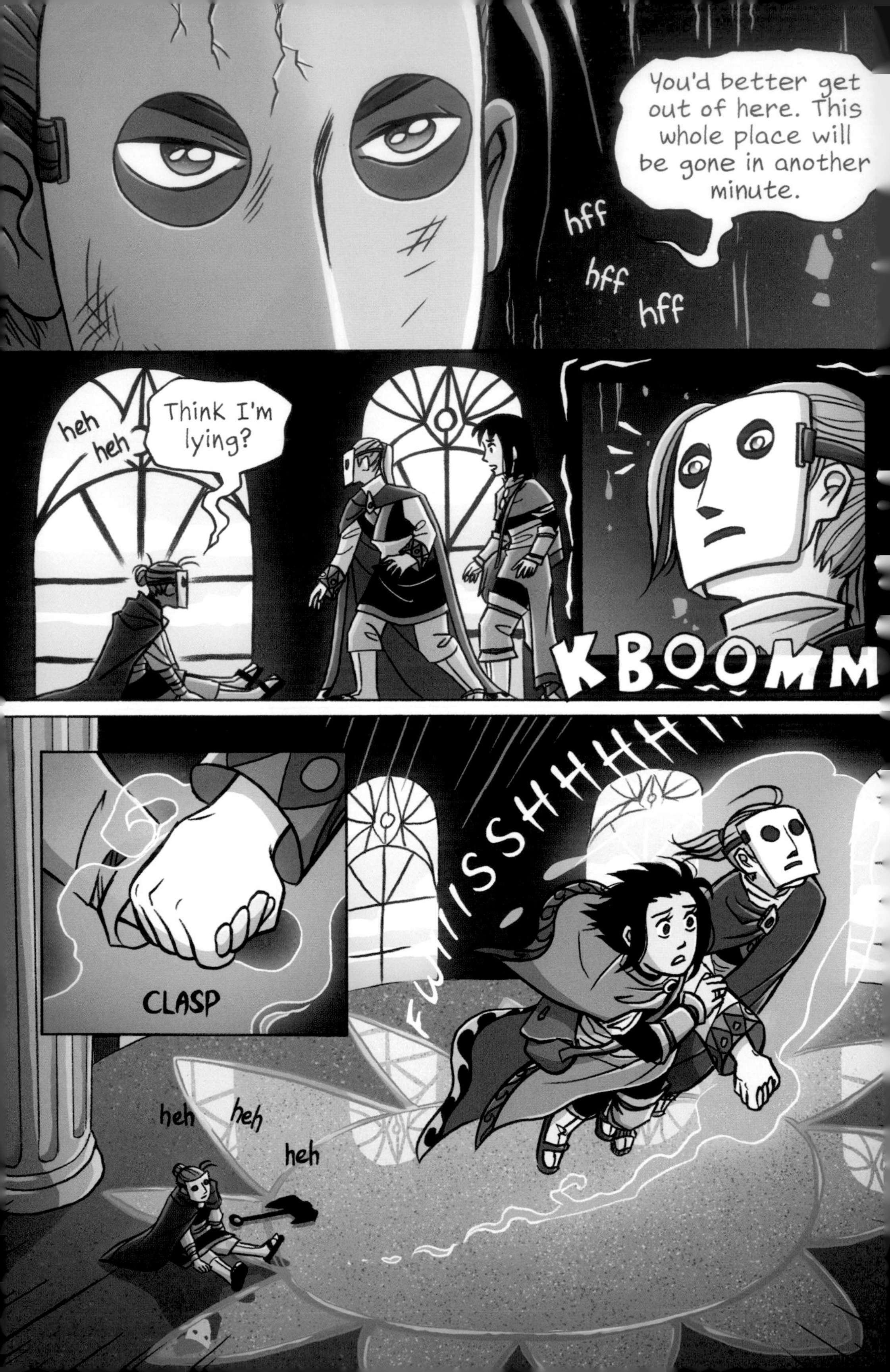
You'd better get out of here. This whole place will be gone in another minute.
hff hff hff
heh heh
Think I'm lying?
KBOOMM
CLASP
FWISSHHHH
heh heh heh

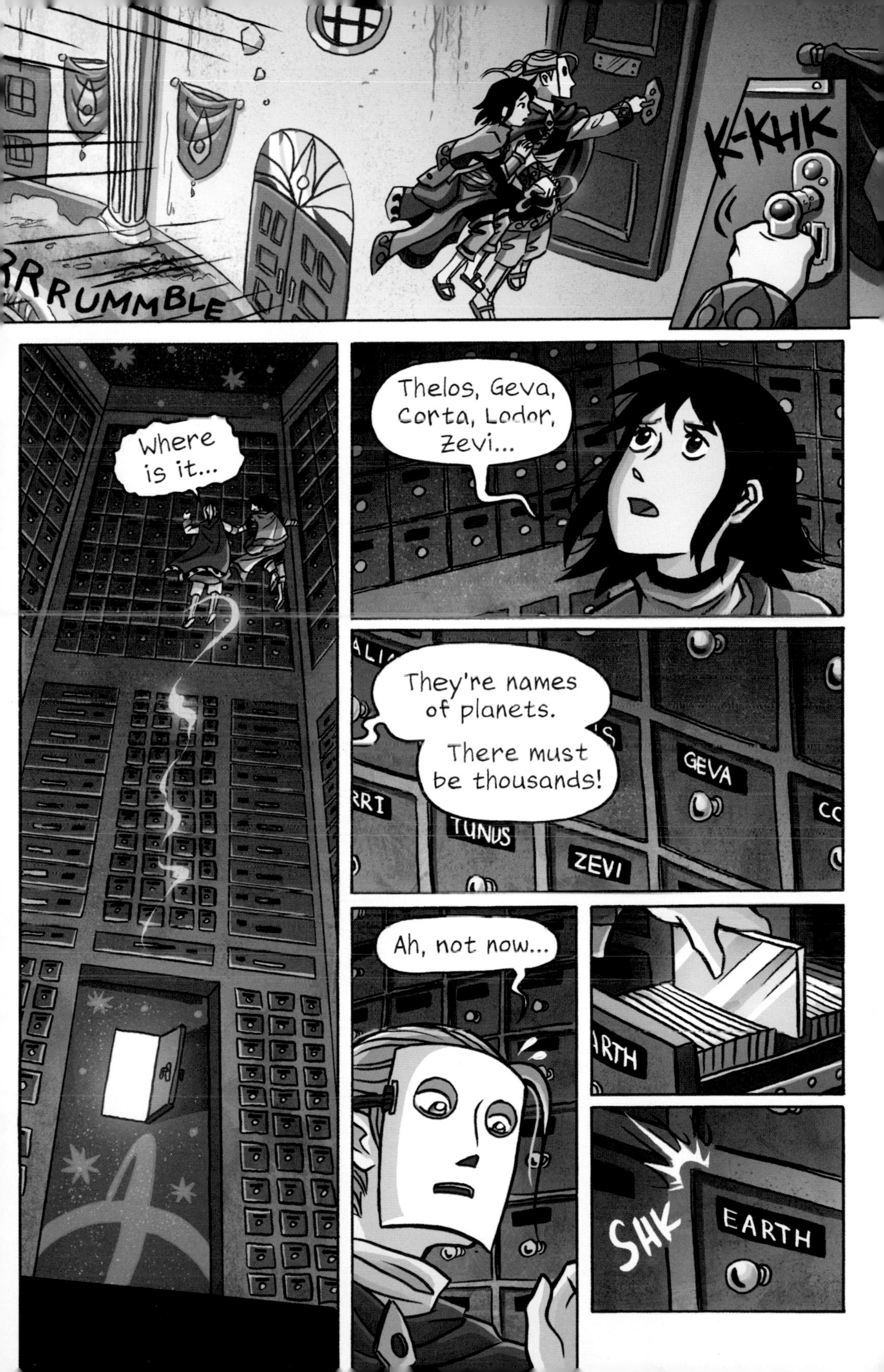
RRRUMMBLE
K-KHK
Where is it...
Thelos, Geva, Corta, Lodor, Zevi...
They're names of planets.
There must be thousands!
GEVA
TUNUS
ZEVI
Ah, not now...
SHK
EARTH

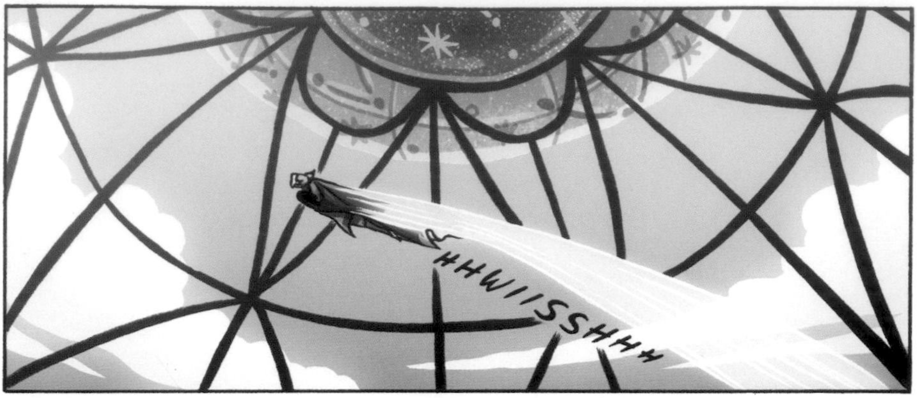
HHWIISSHHHH

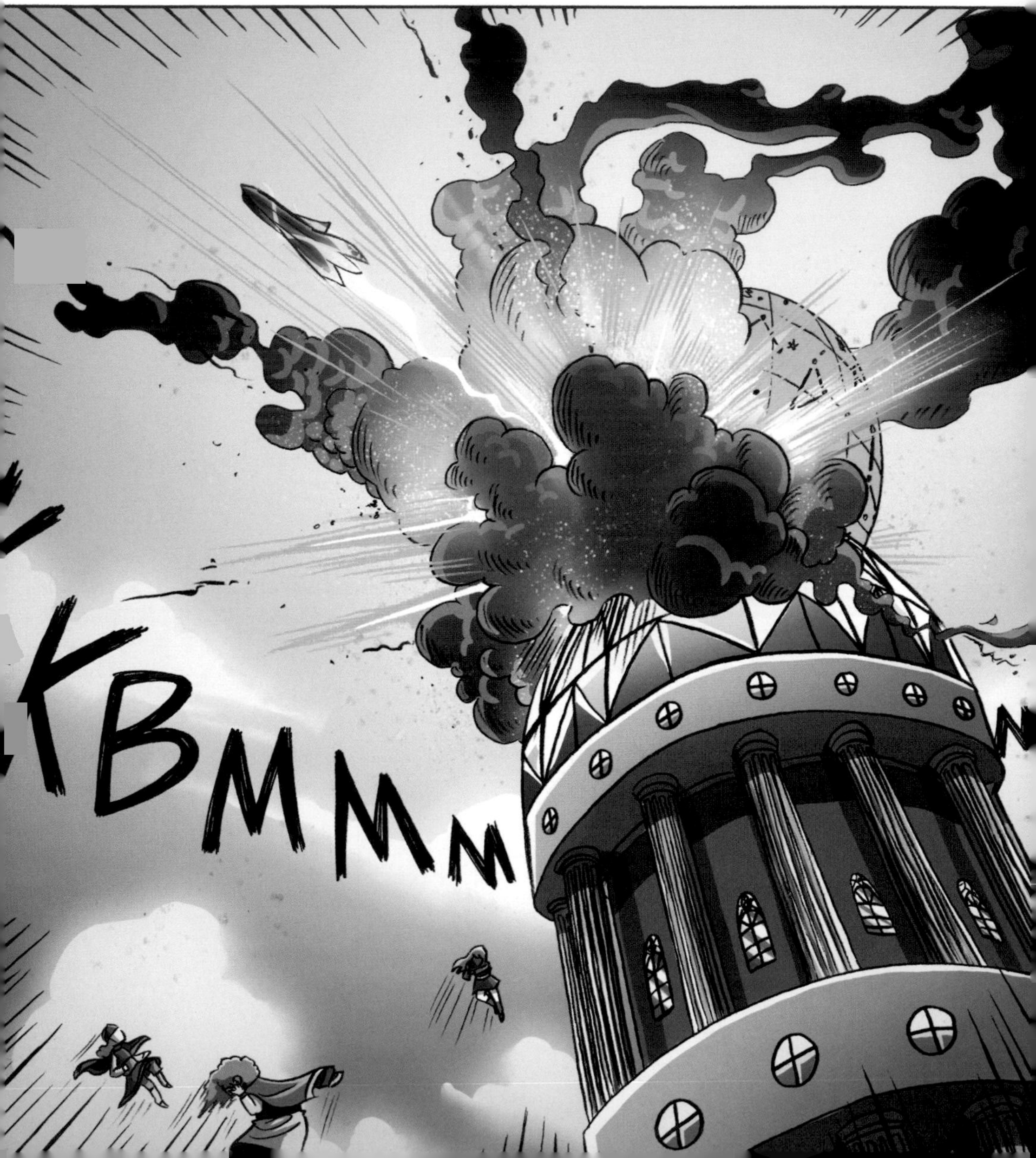
KBMMm

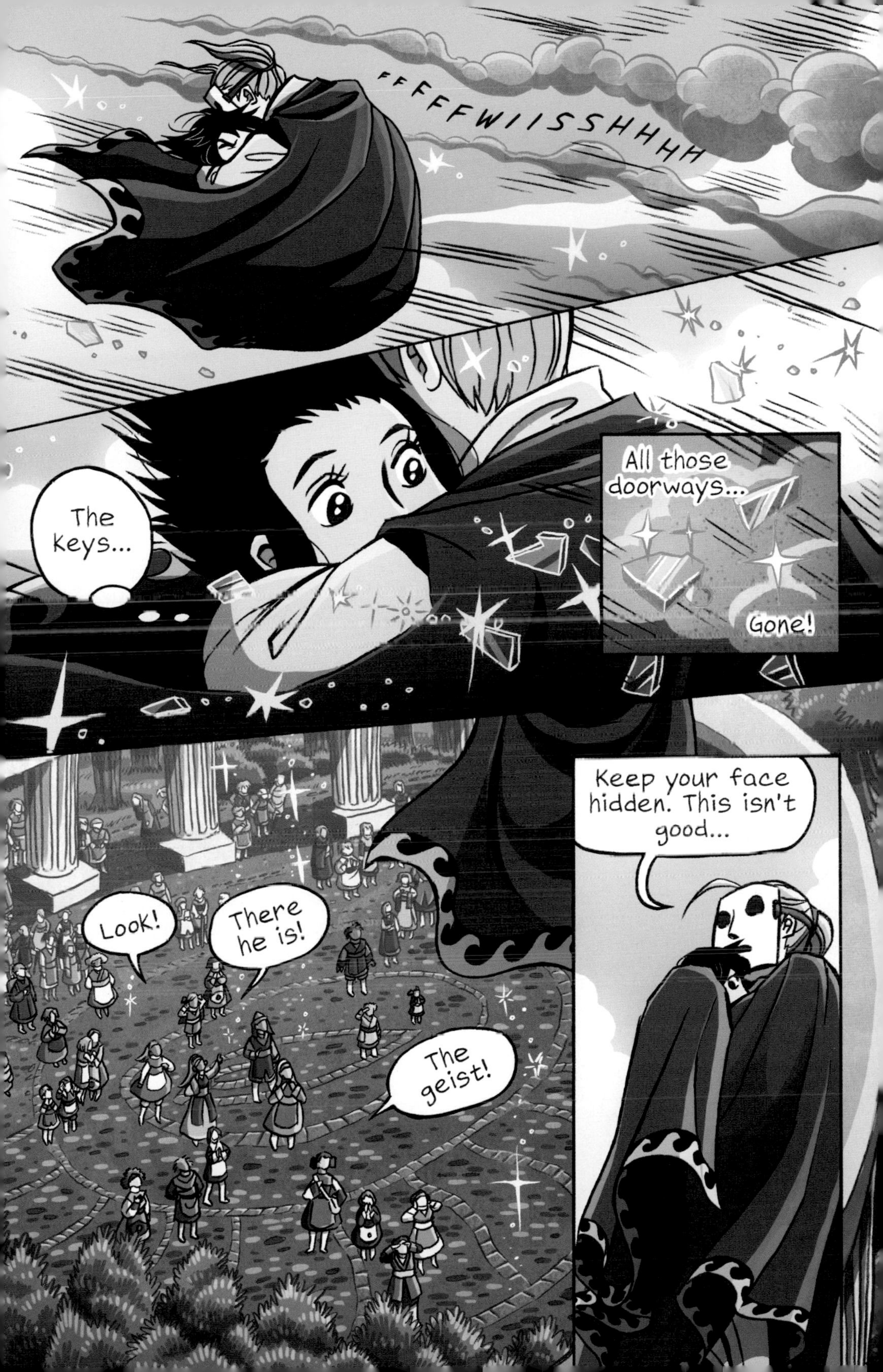
FFFFFWIISSHHHHH
The keys...
All those doorways...
Gone!
Keep your face hidden. This isn't good...
Look!
There he is!
The geist!

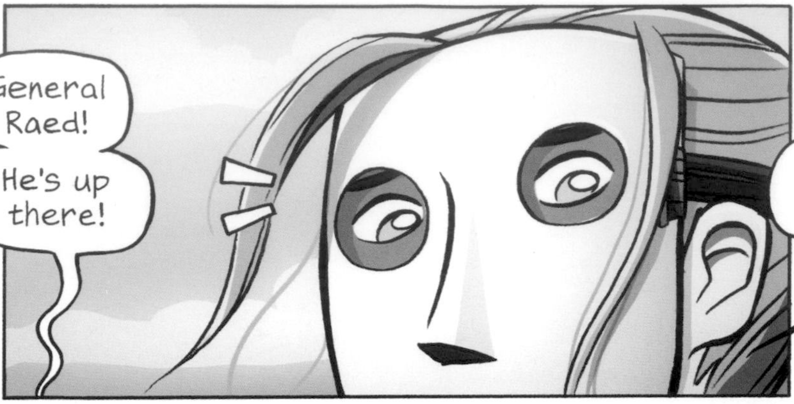
General Raed!
He's up there!
Raed?

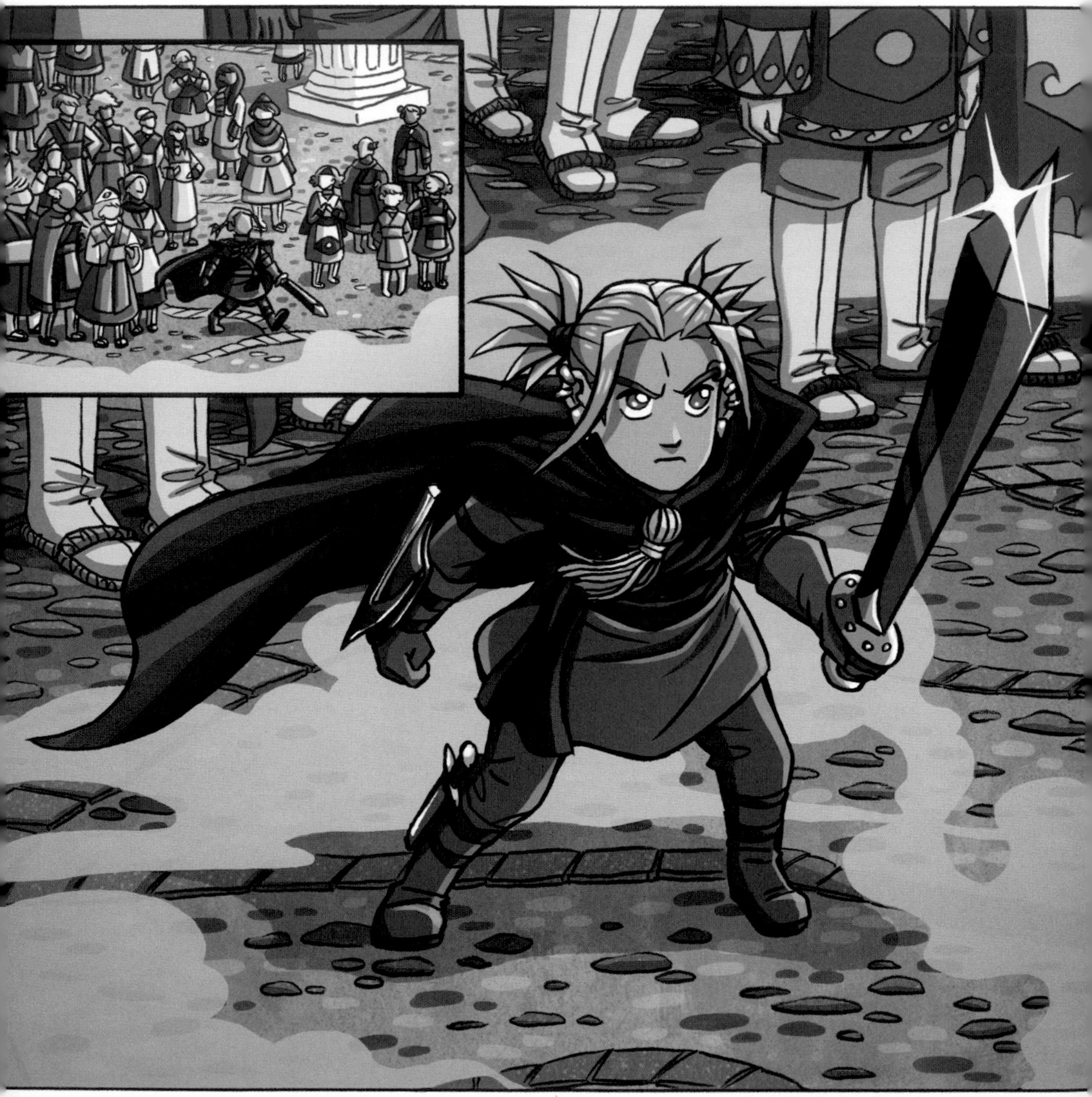

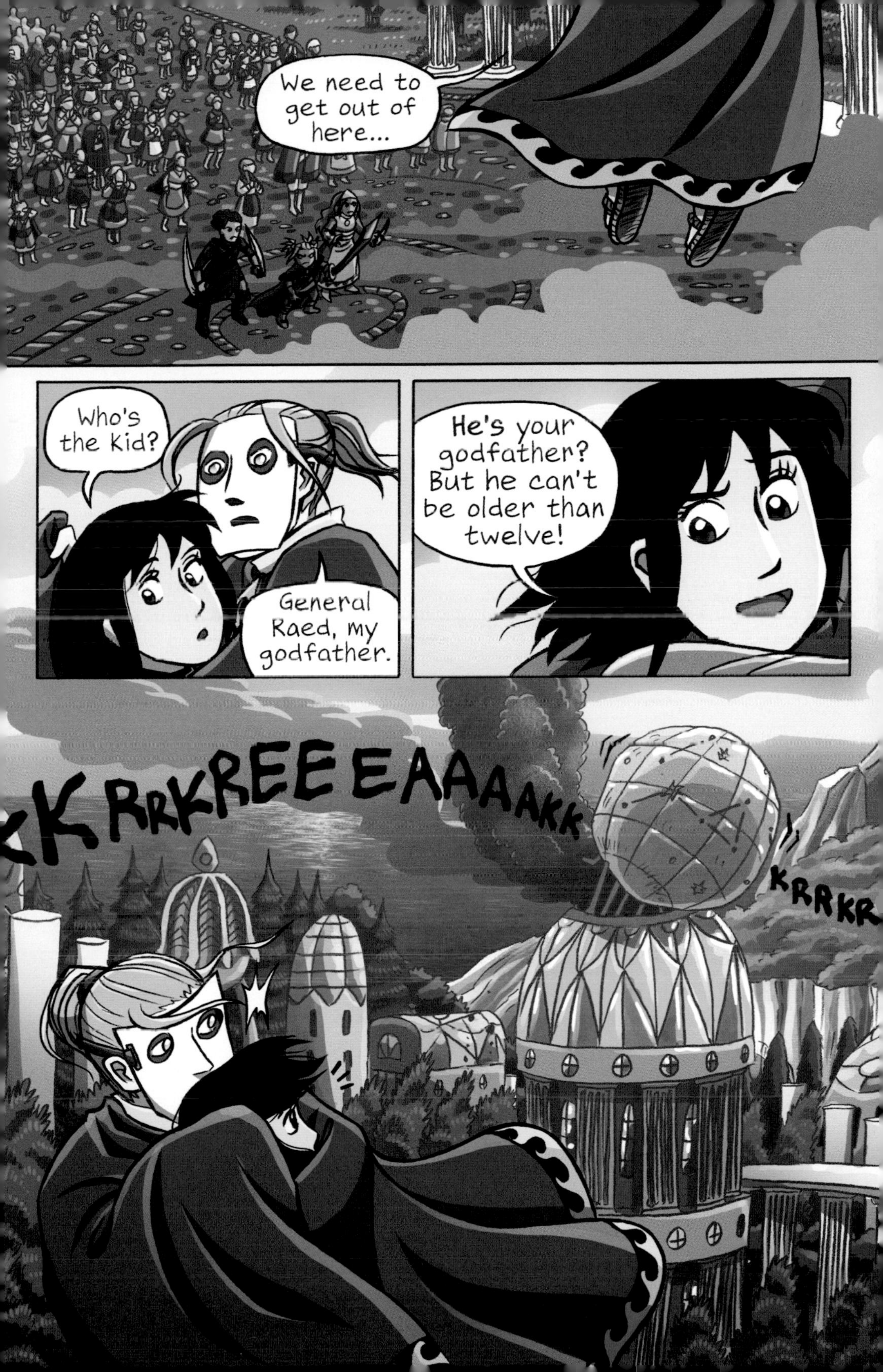
We need to get out of here...
Who's the kid?
General Raed, my godfather.
He's your godfather? But he can't be older than twelve!
KKRRKREEEAAAAKK
KRRKR

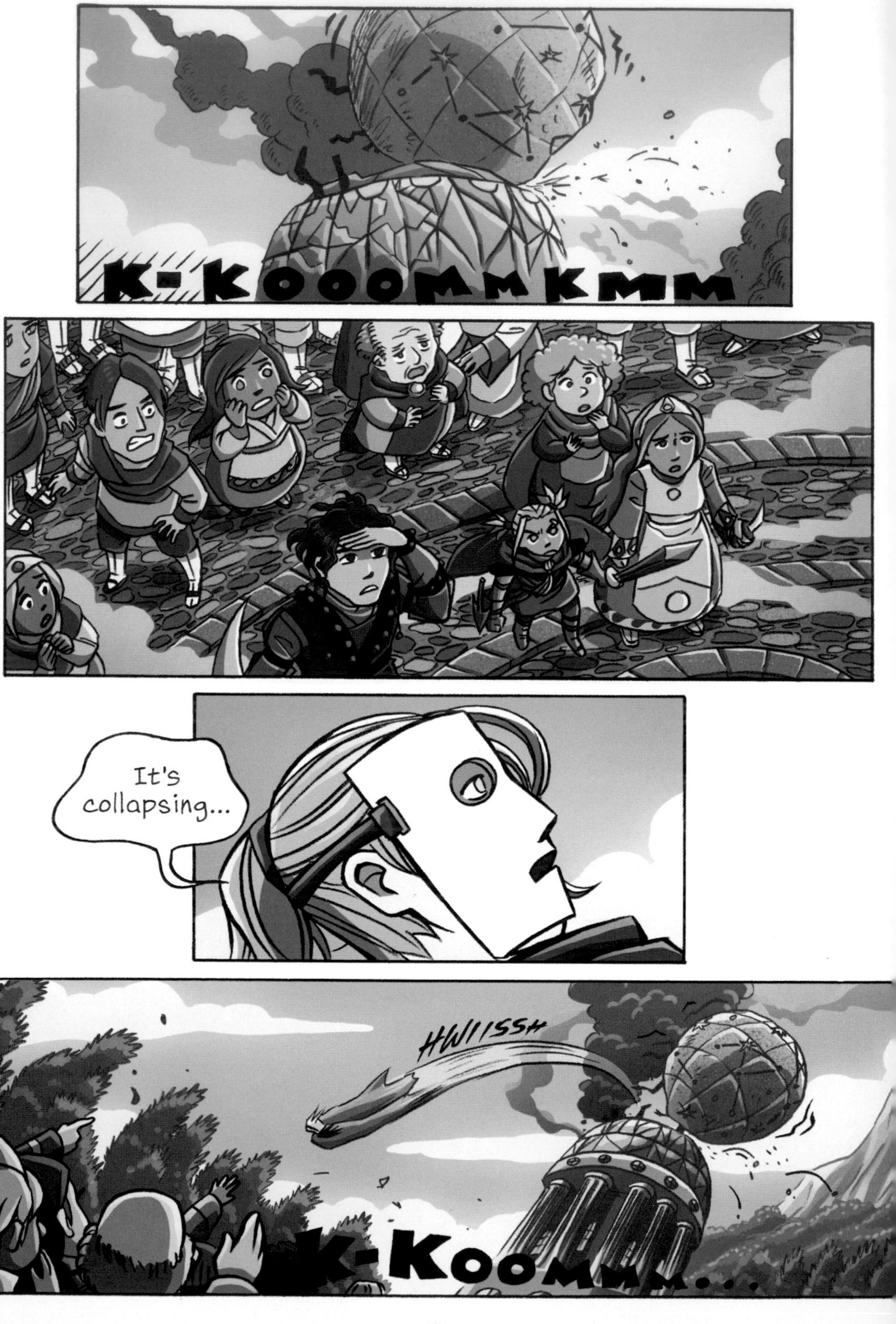
K-KOOOMMKMM
It's collapsing...
HWIISSH
K-KOOMM...

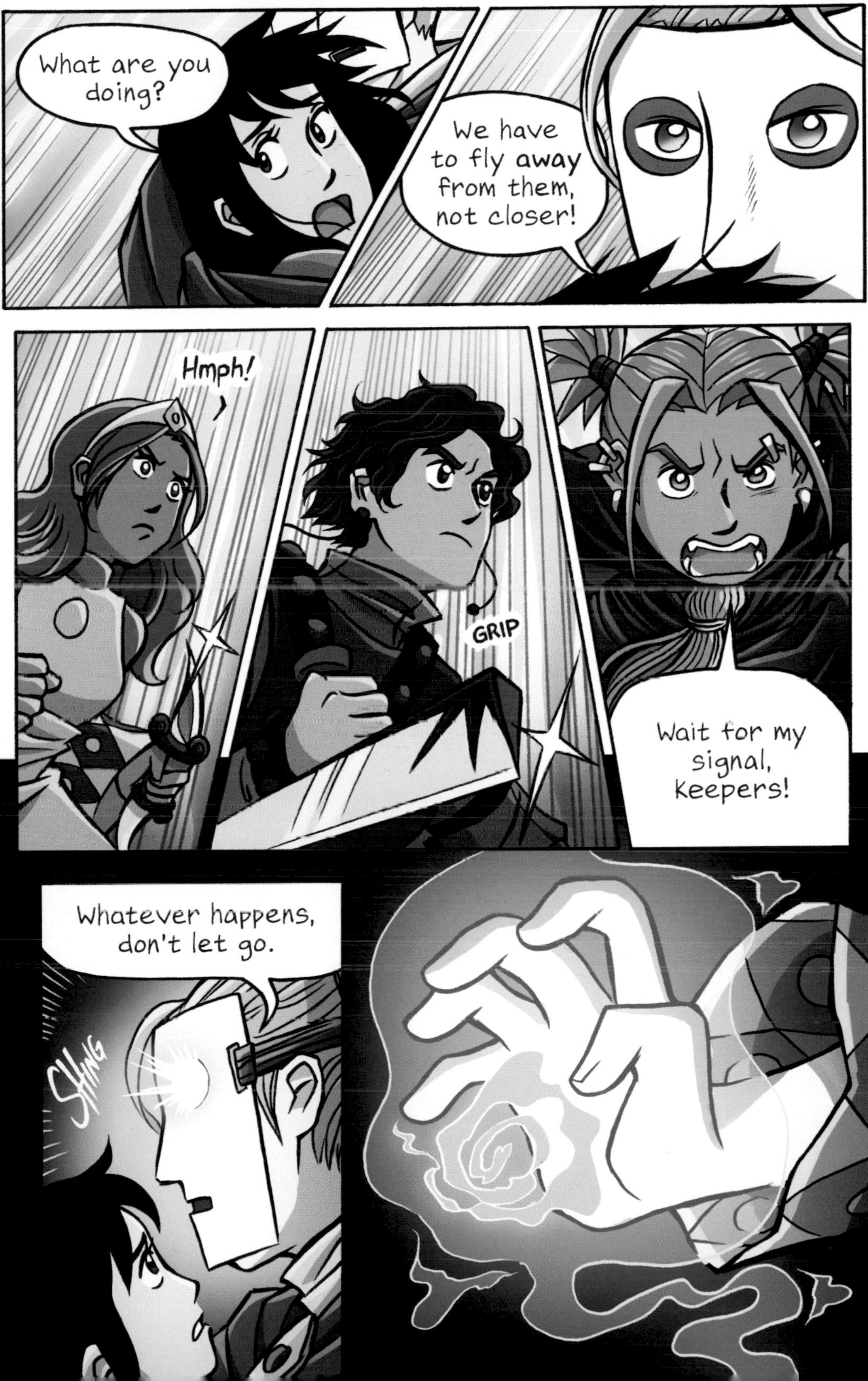
What are you doing?
We have to fly away from them, not closer!
Hmph!
GRIP
Wait for my signal, Keepers!
Whatever happens, don't let go.
SHING

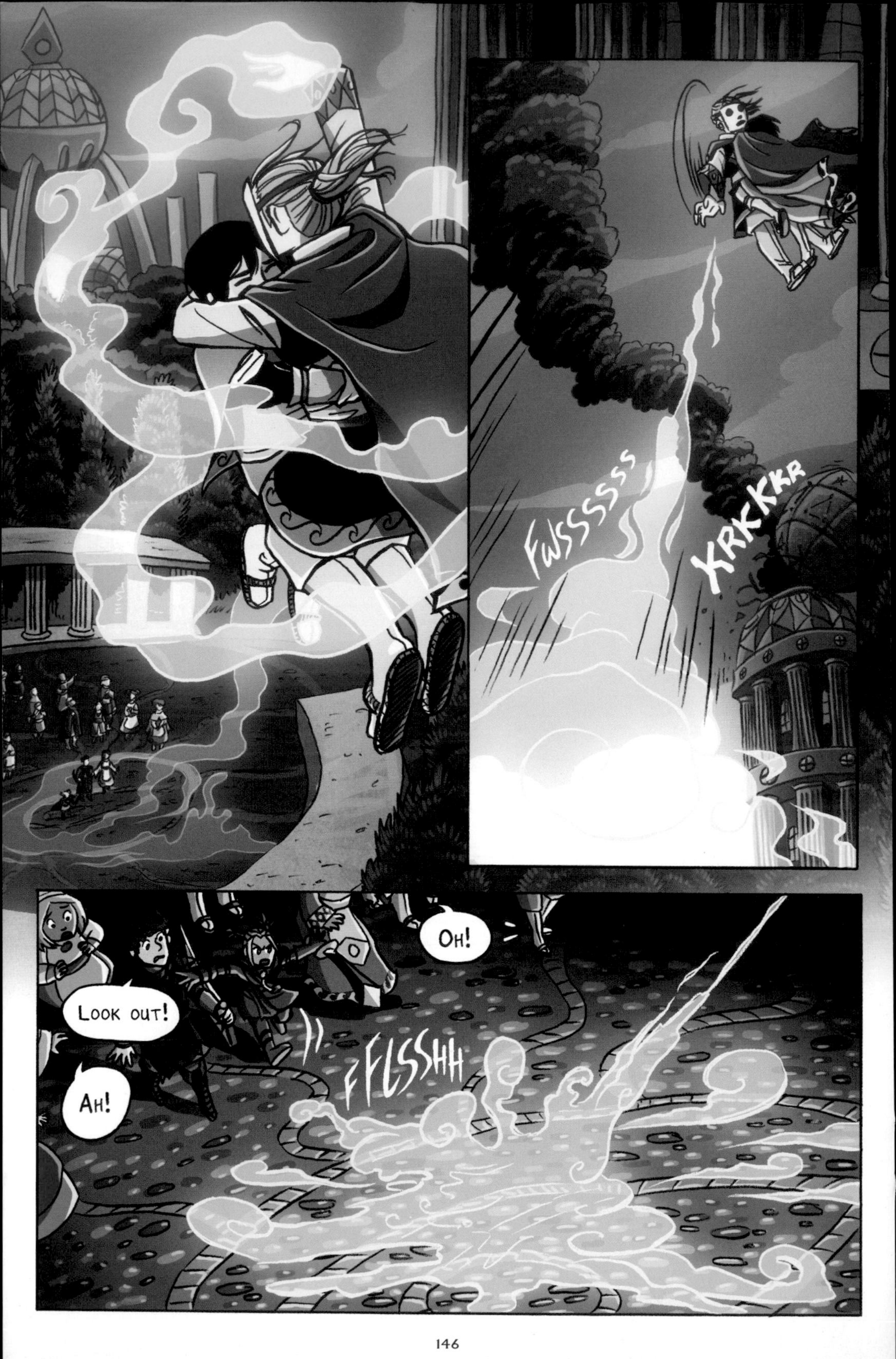
FWSSSSSS
KRKKKR
OH!
LOOK OUT!
AH!
FFLSSHH

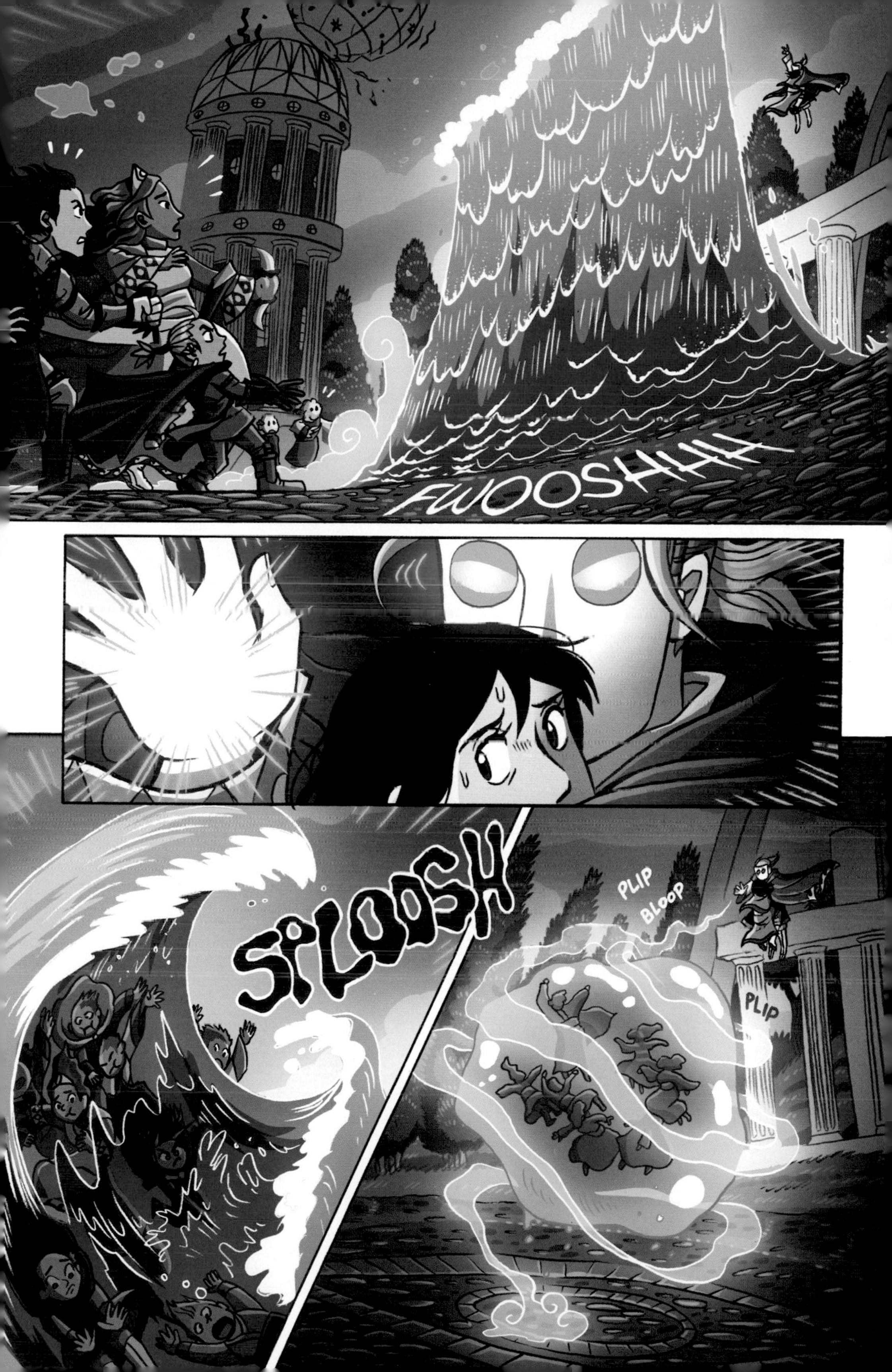
FWOOSHHH
SPLOOSH
PLIP
BLOOP
PLIP

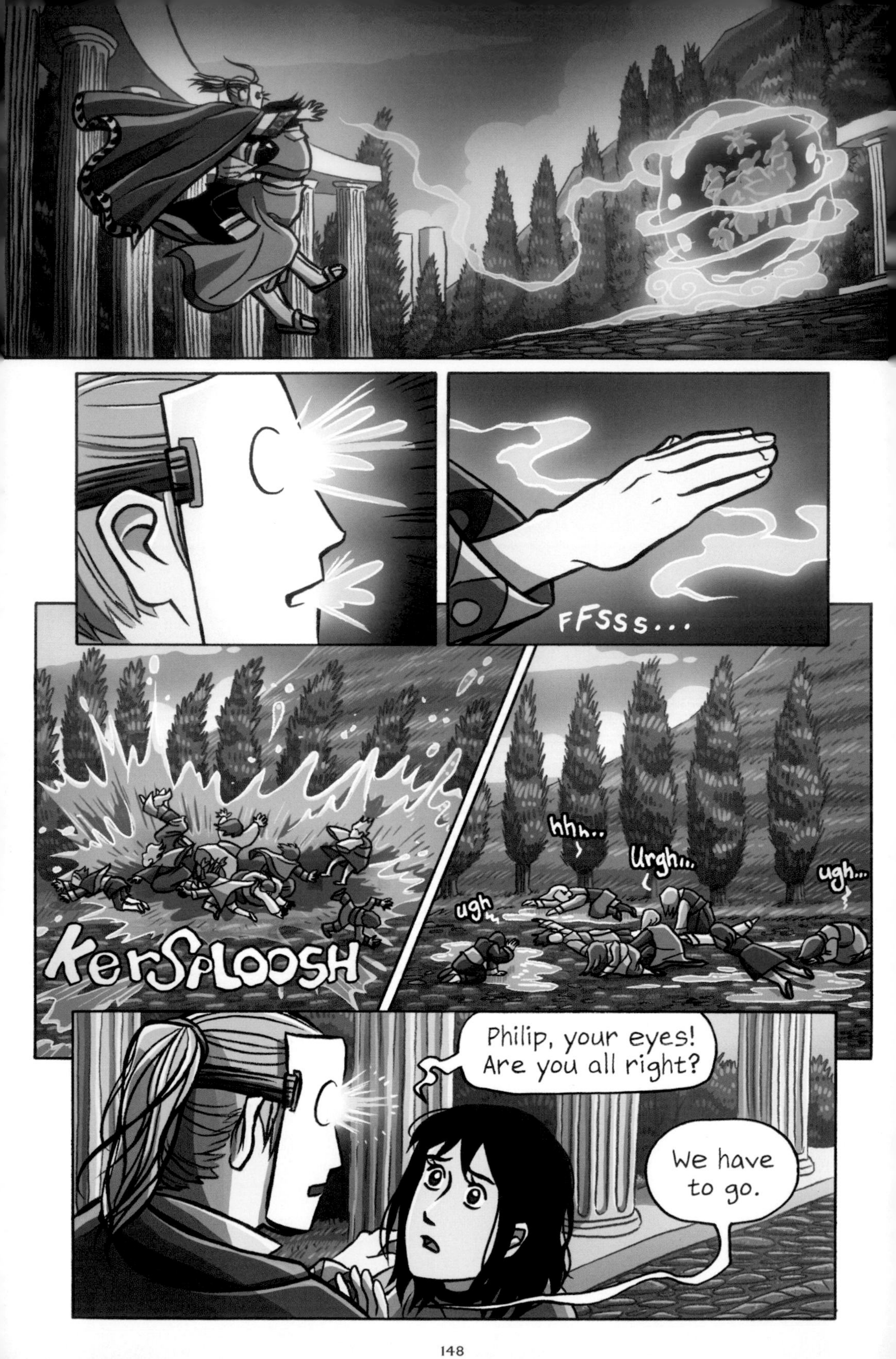
FFSSS...
KERSPLOOSH
hhh..
Urgh...
ugh...
ugh
Philip, your eyes! Are you all right?
We have to go.

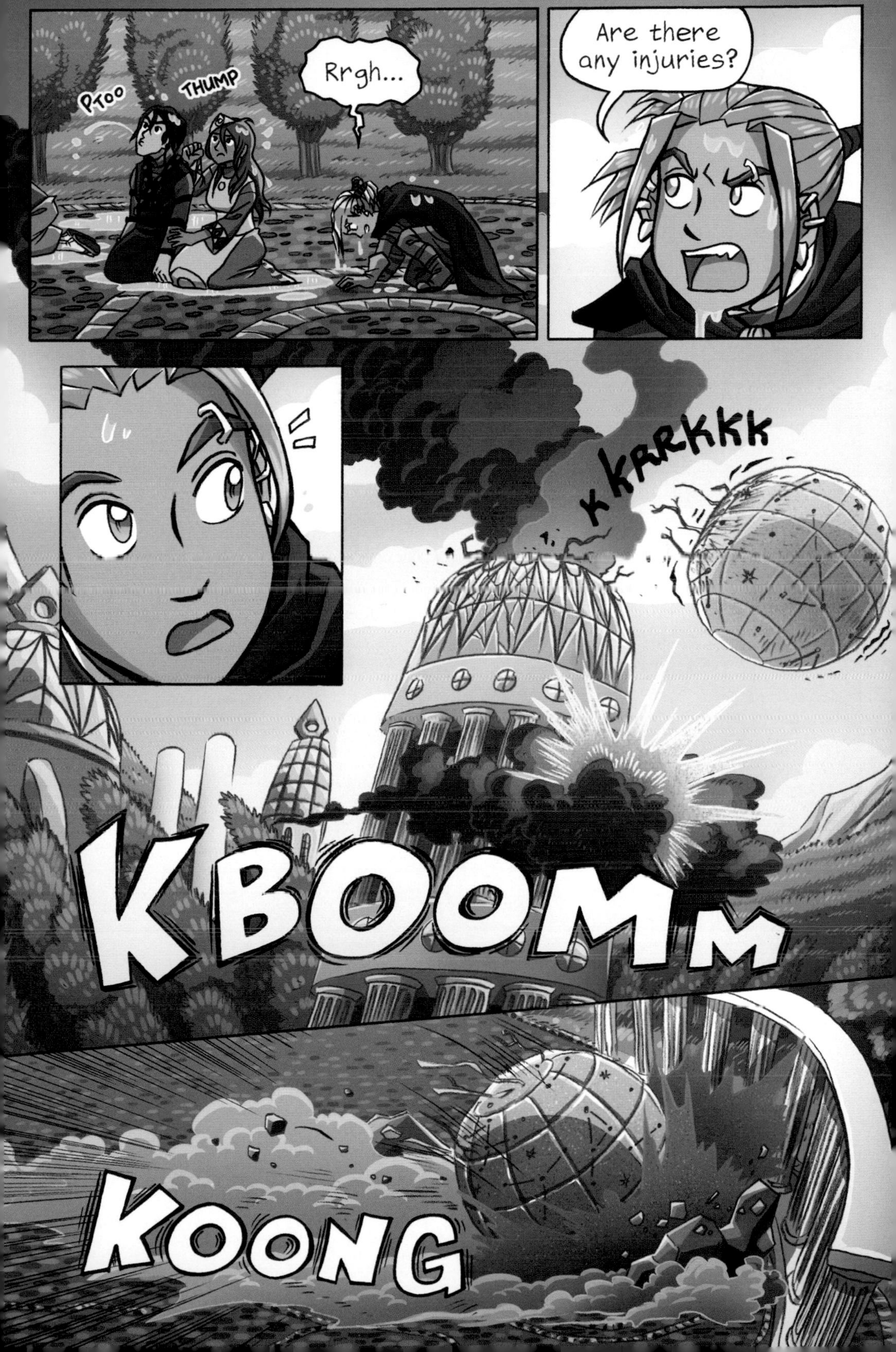
PTOO
THUMP
Rrgh...
Are there any injuries?
KKRRKKK
KBOOMM
KOONG

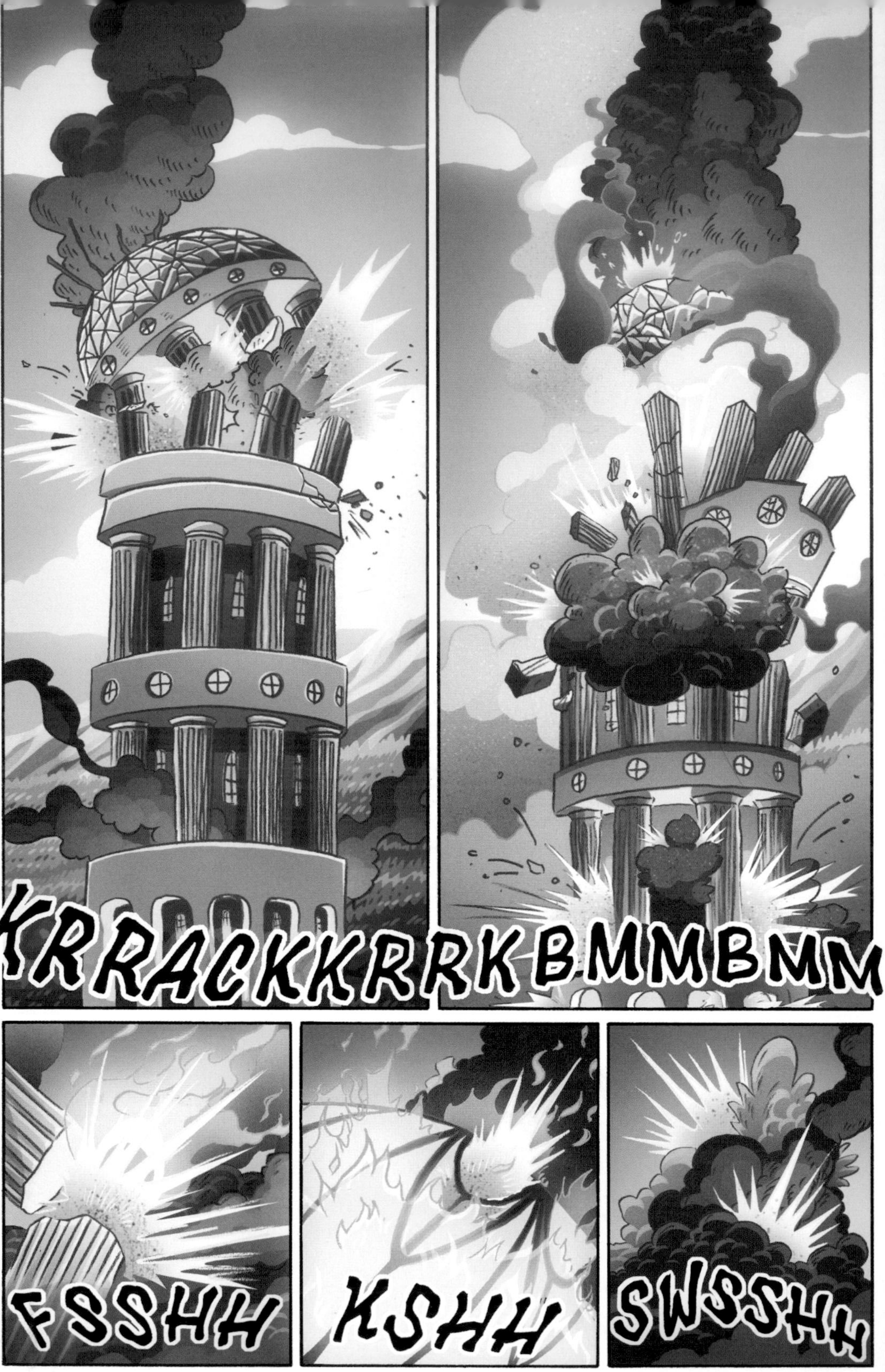
KRRACKKRRK
BMMBMM
FSSHH
KSHH
SWSSHH

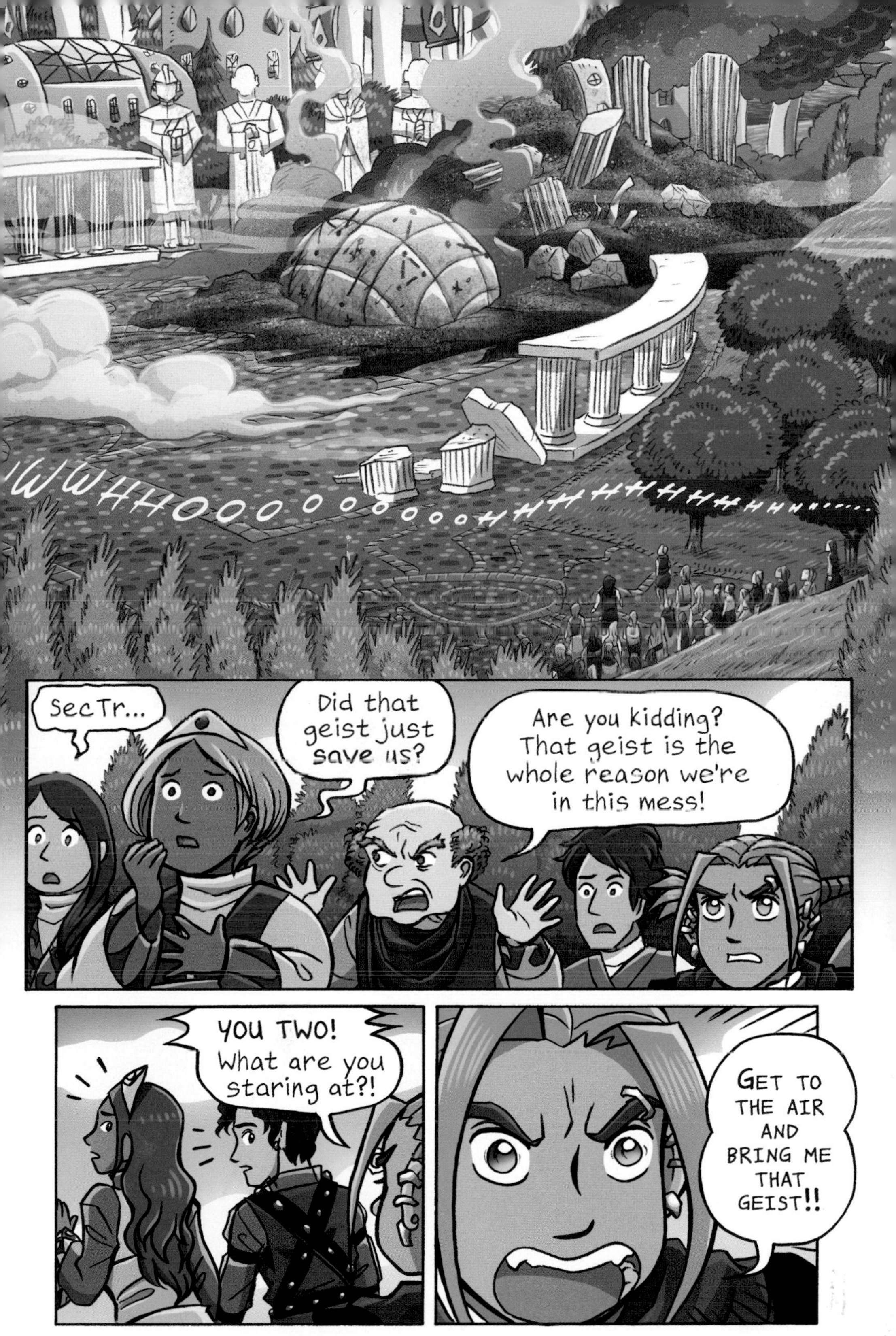
WWWHHOOOOOOOOOOOOHHHHHHHHHHHH.....
SecTr...
Did that geist just save us?
Are you kidding? That geist is the whole reason we're in this mess!
YOU TWO! What are you staring at?!
GET TO THE AIR AND BRING ME THAT GEIST!!

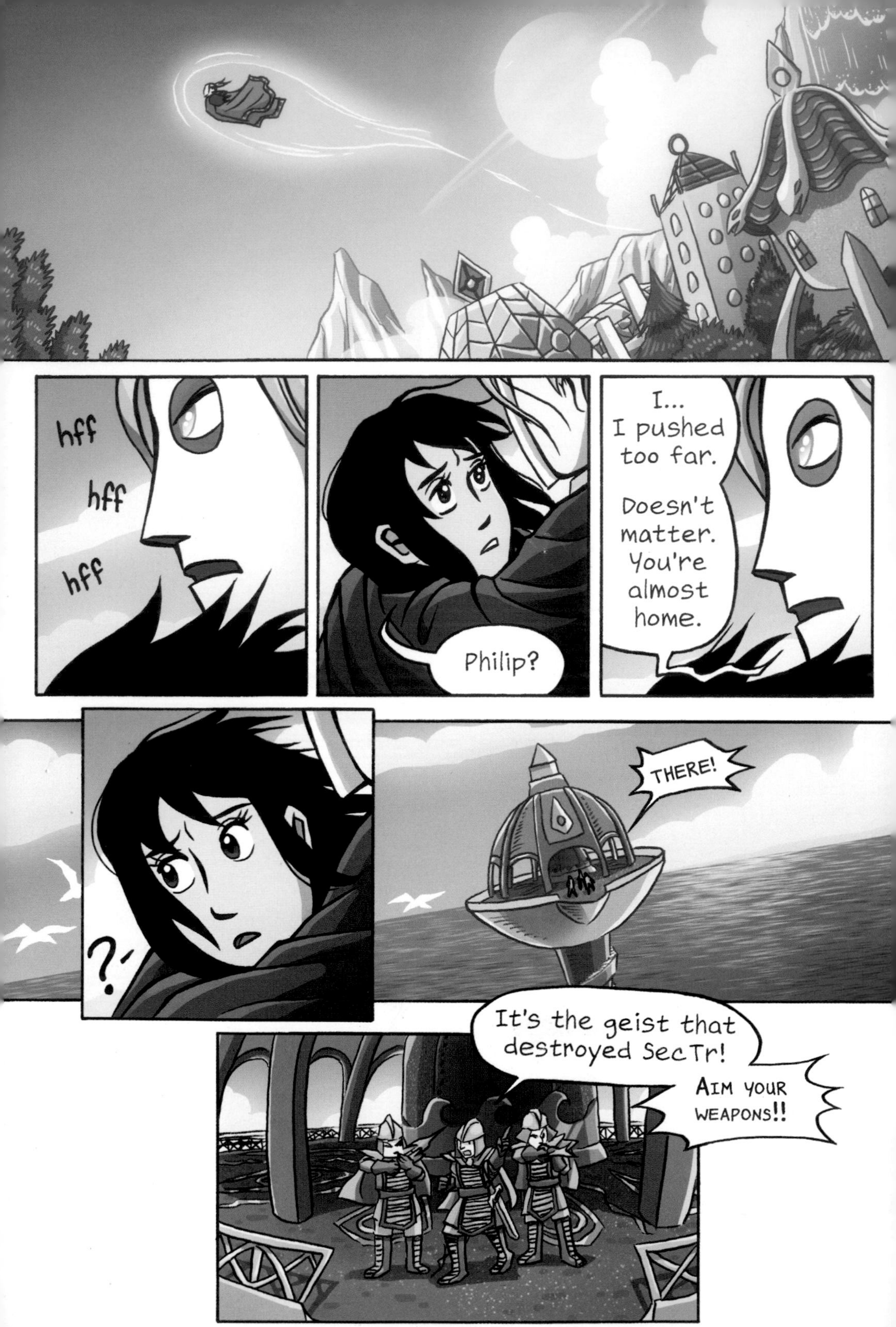
hff
hff
hff
Philip?
I...
I pushed too far.
Doesn't matter. You're almost home.
?
THERE!
It's the geist that destroyed SecTr!
AIM YOUR WEAPONS!!

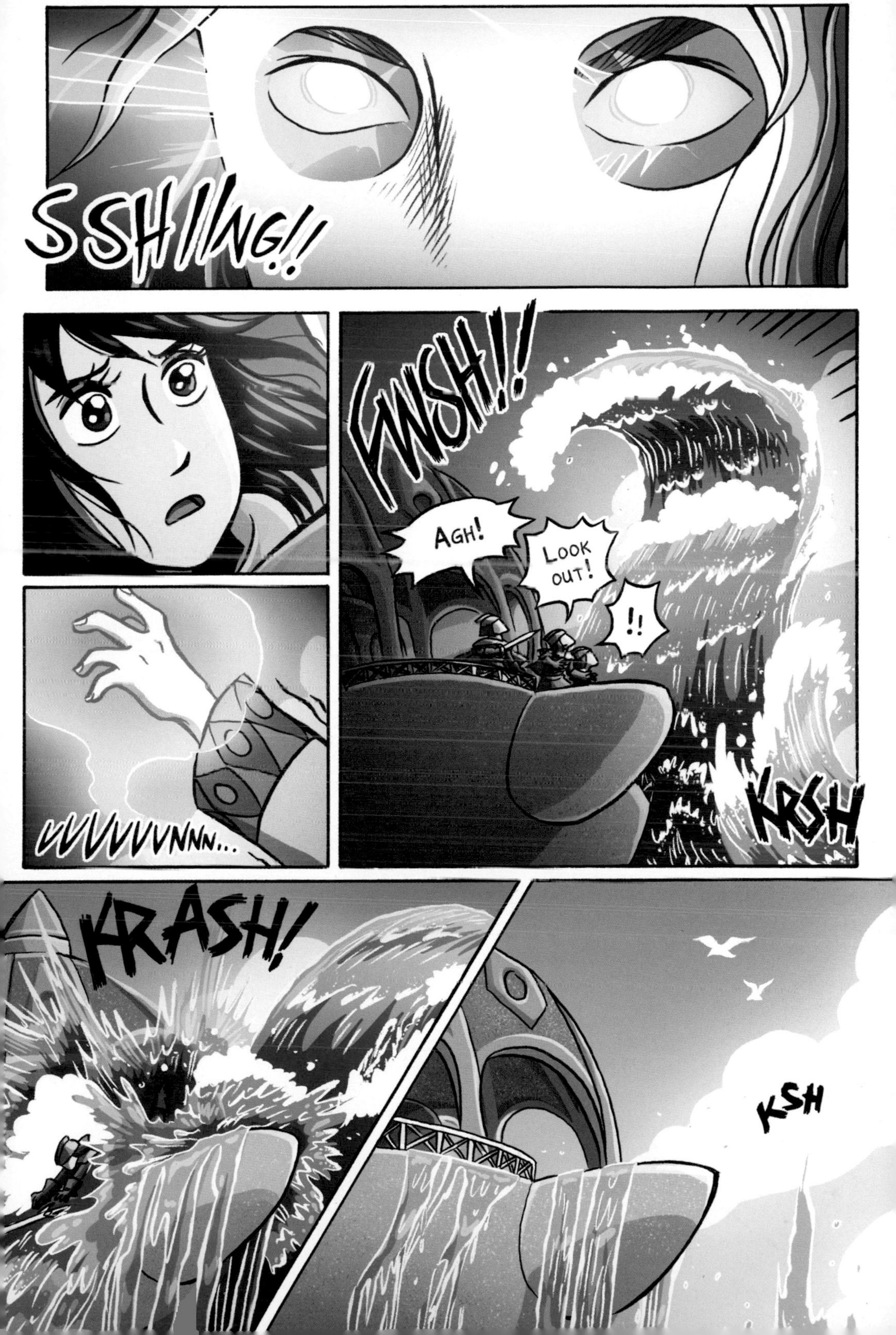
SSHIING!!
FWSH!!
AGH!
LOOK OUT!
!!
KRSH
VVVVVVVNNN...
KRASH!
KSH

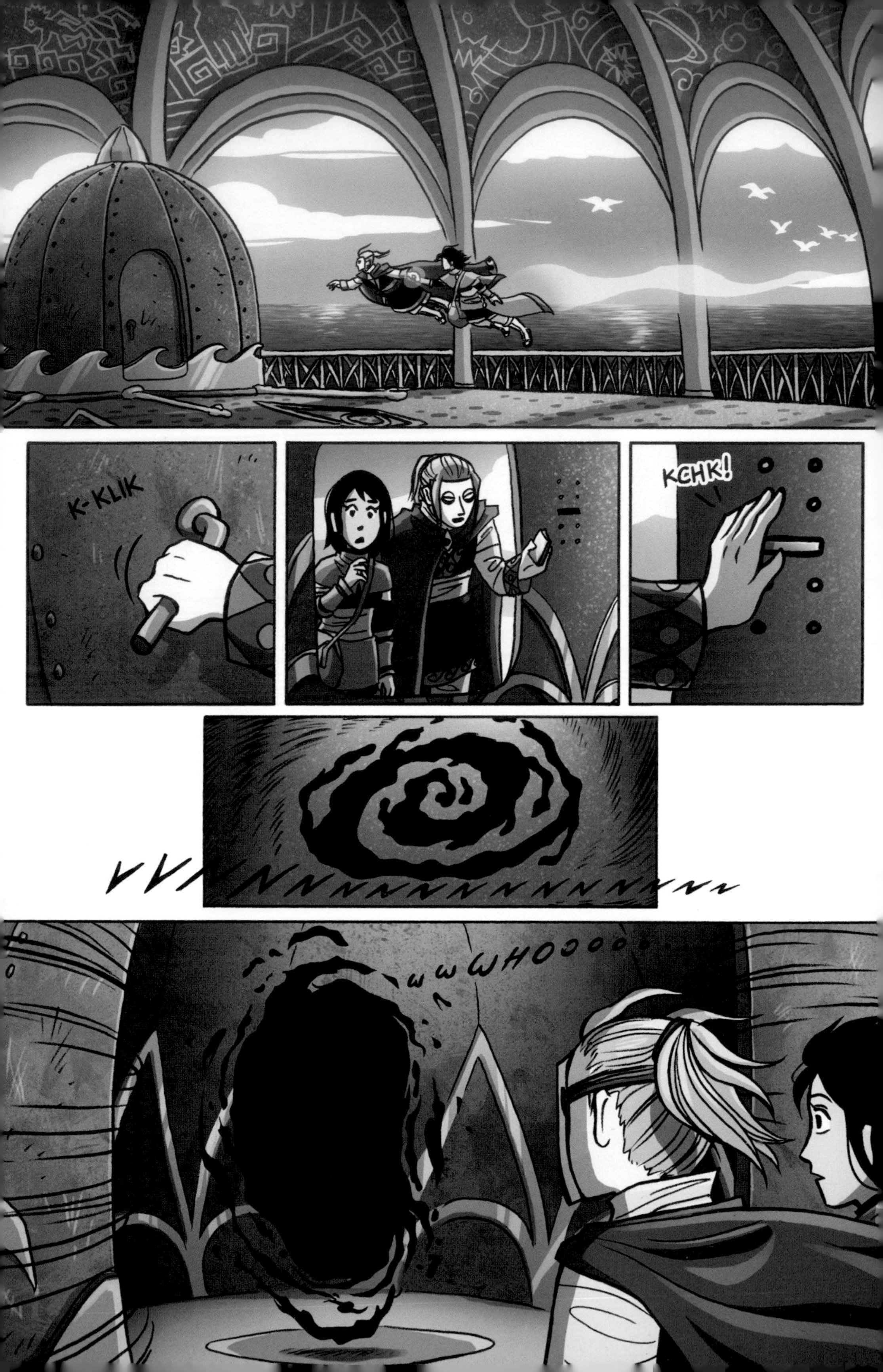
K-KLIK
KCHK!
VVNNNNNNNNNNNNNNNN
wwWHOOOOO...

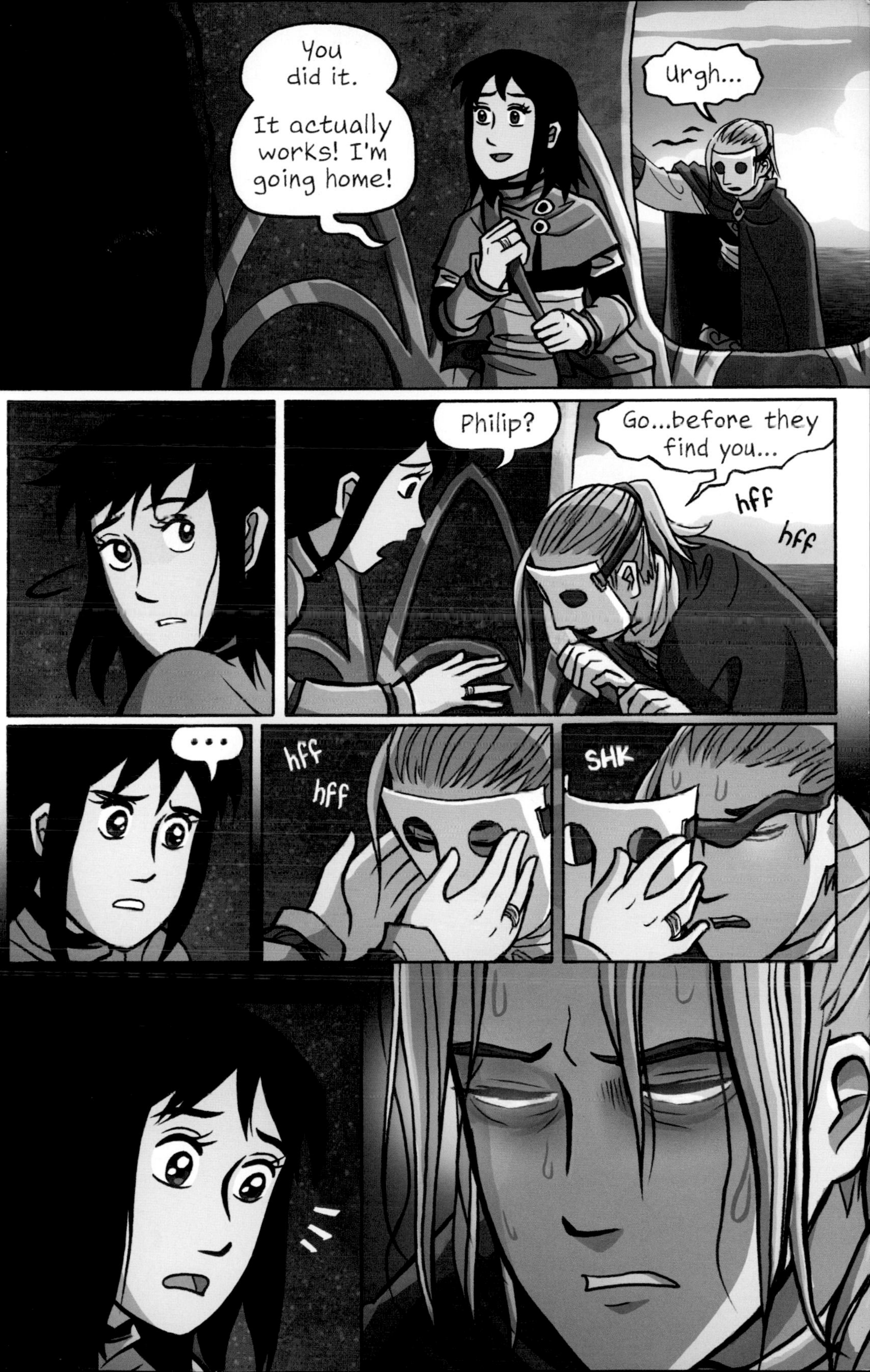
You did it.
It actually works! I'm going home!
Urgh...
Philip?
Go...before they find you...
hff
hff
...
hff
hff
SHK

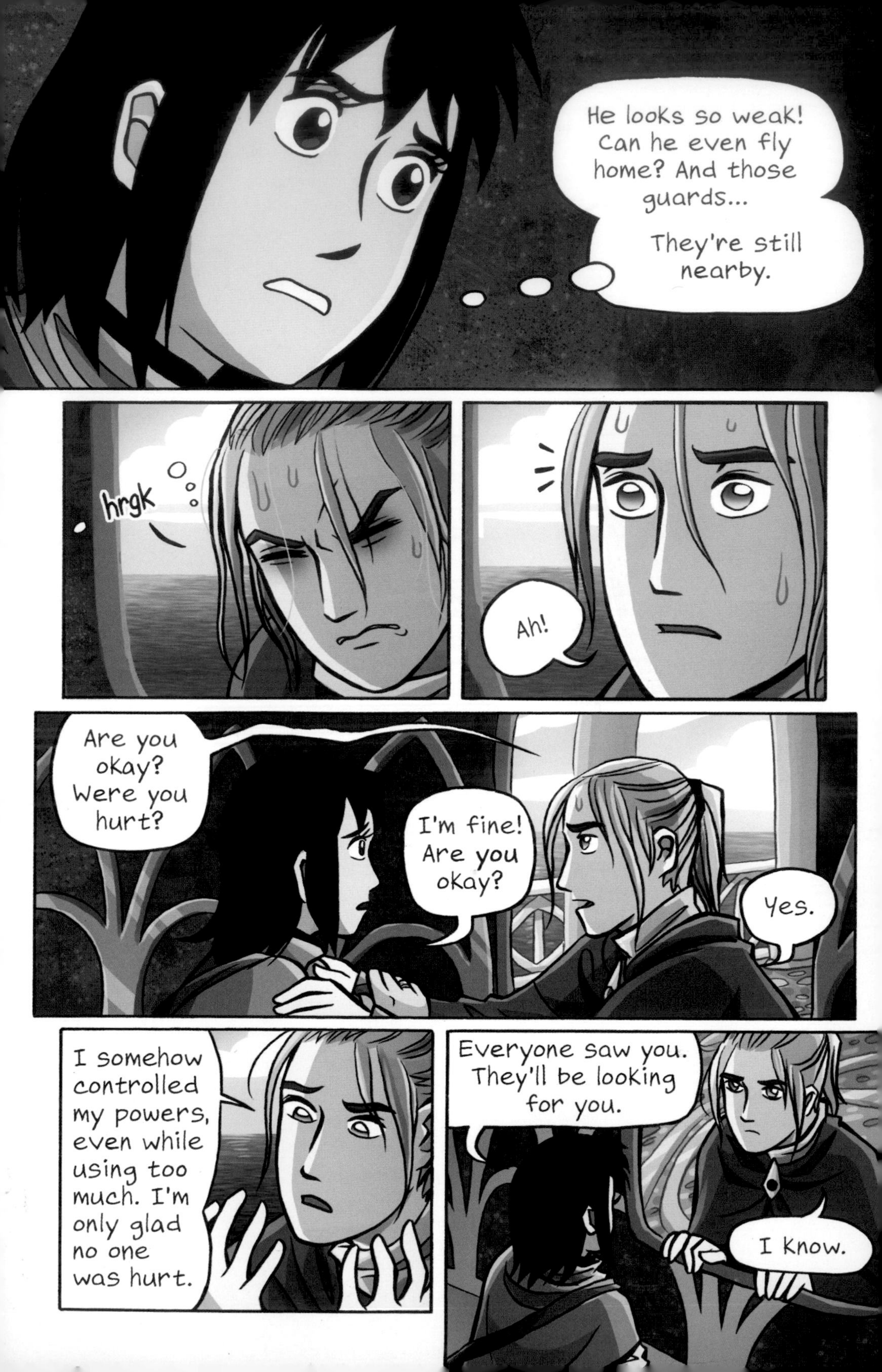
He looks so weak! Can he even fly home? And those guards...
They're still nearby.
hrgk
Ah!
Are you okay? Were you hurt?
I'm fine! Are you okay?
Yes.
I somehow controlled my powers, even while using too much. I'm only glad no one was hurt.
Everyone saw you. They'll be looking for you.
I know.

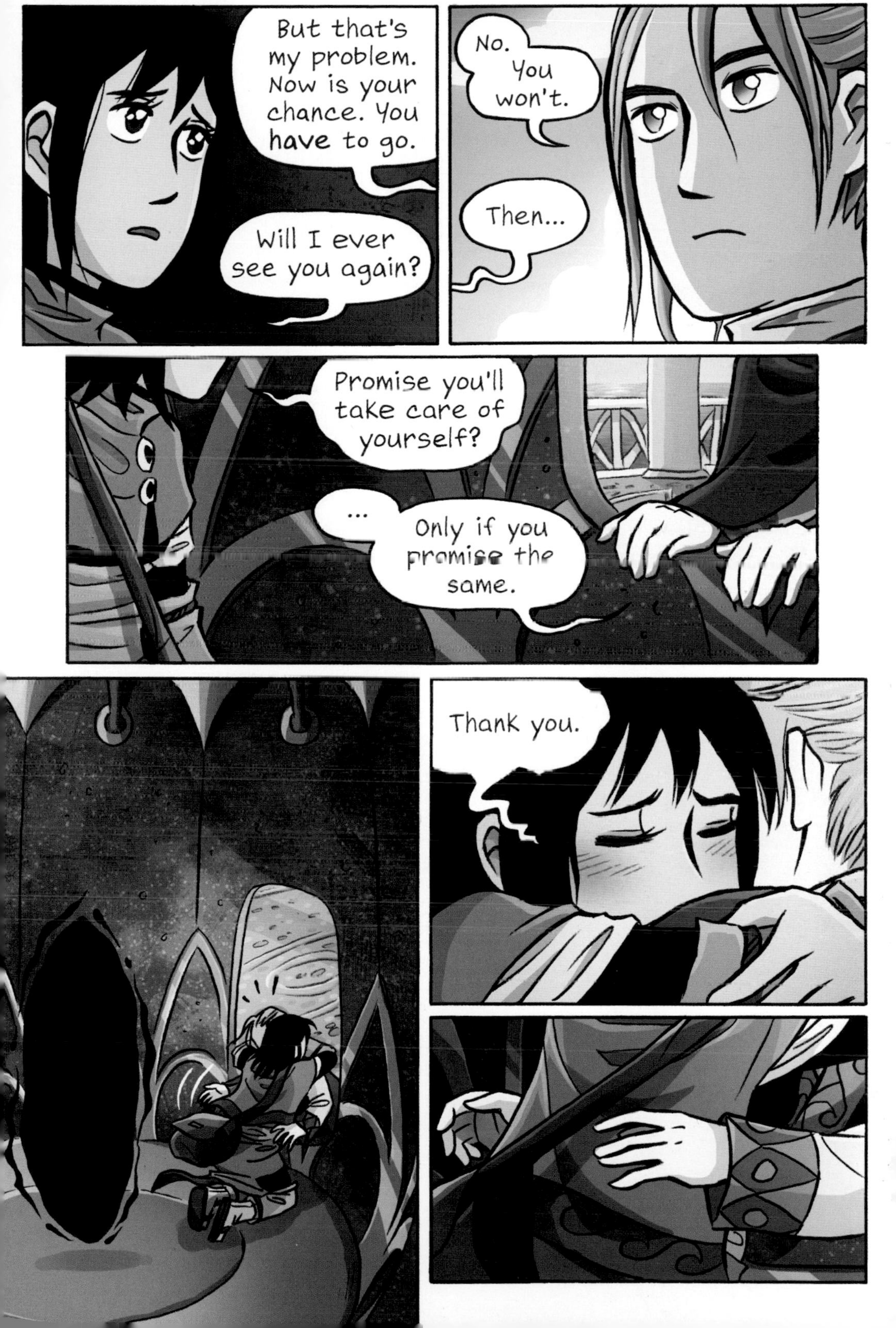
But that's my problem. Now is your chance. You have to go.
Will I ever see you again?
No. You won't.
Then...
Promise you'll take care of yourself?
...
Only if you promise the same.
Thank you.

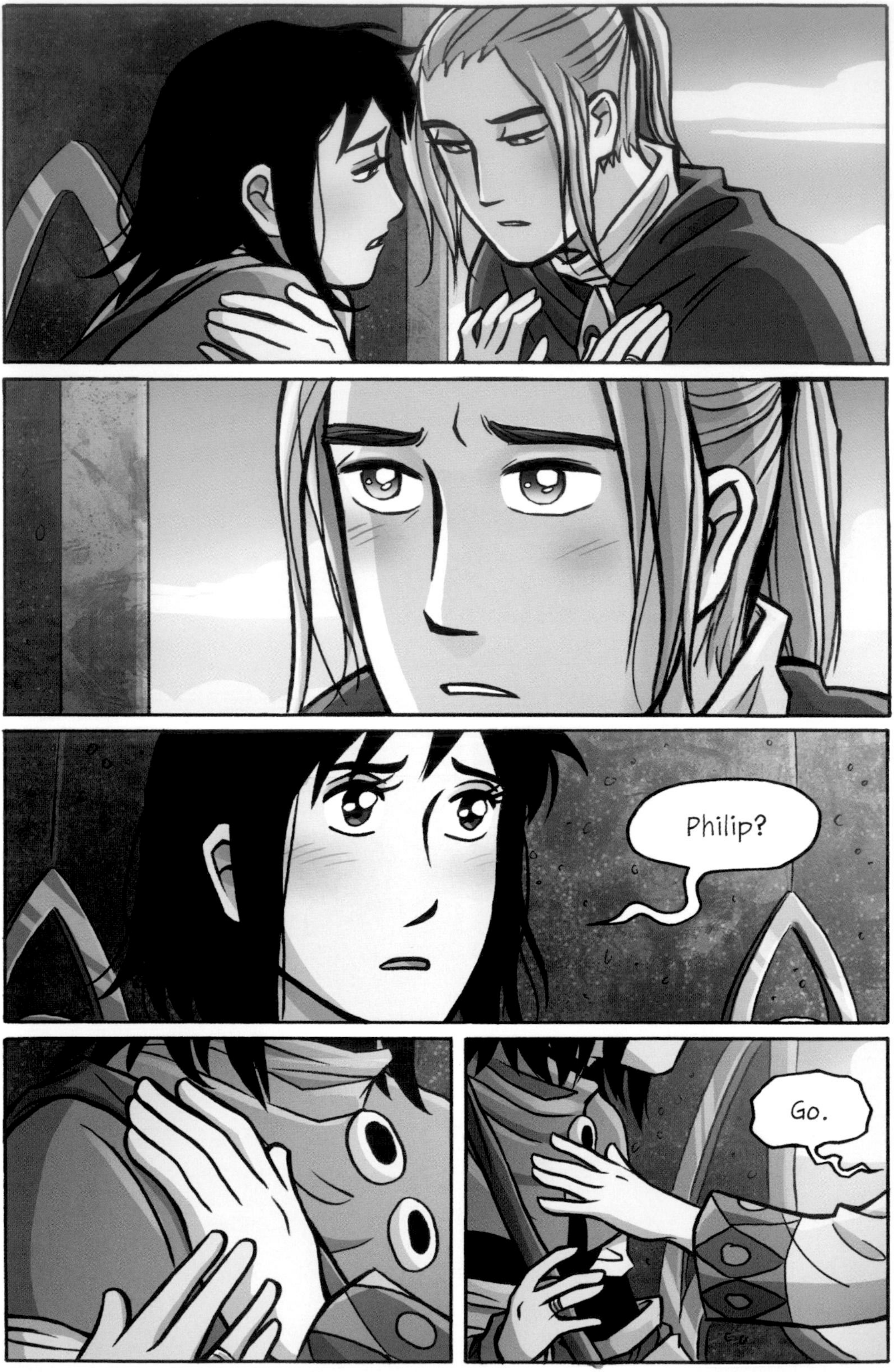
Philip?
Go.

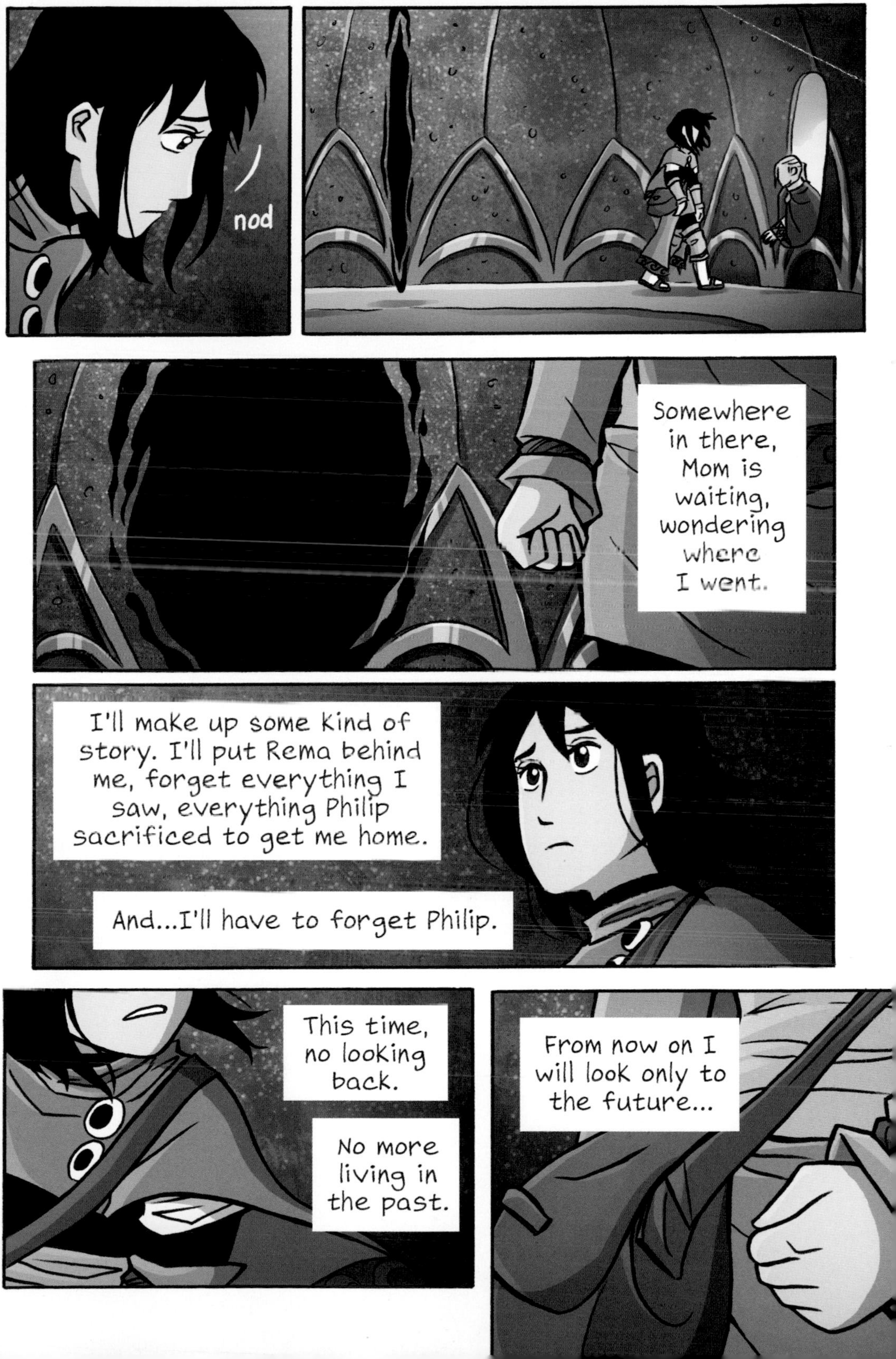
nod
Somewhere in there, Mom is waiting, wondering where I went.
I'll make up some kind of story. I'll put Rema behind me, forget everything I saw, everything Philip sacrificed to get me home.
And...I'll have to forget Philip.
This time, no looking back.
No more living in the past.
From now on I will look only to the future...

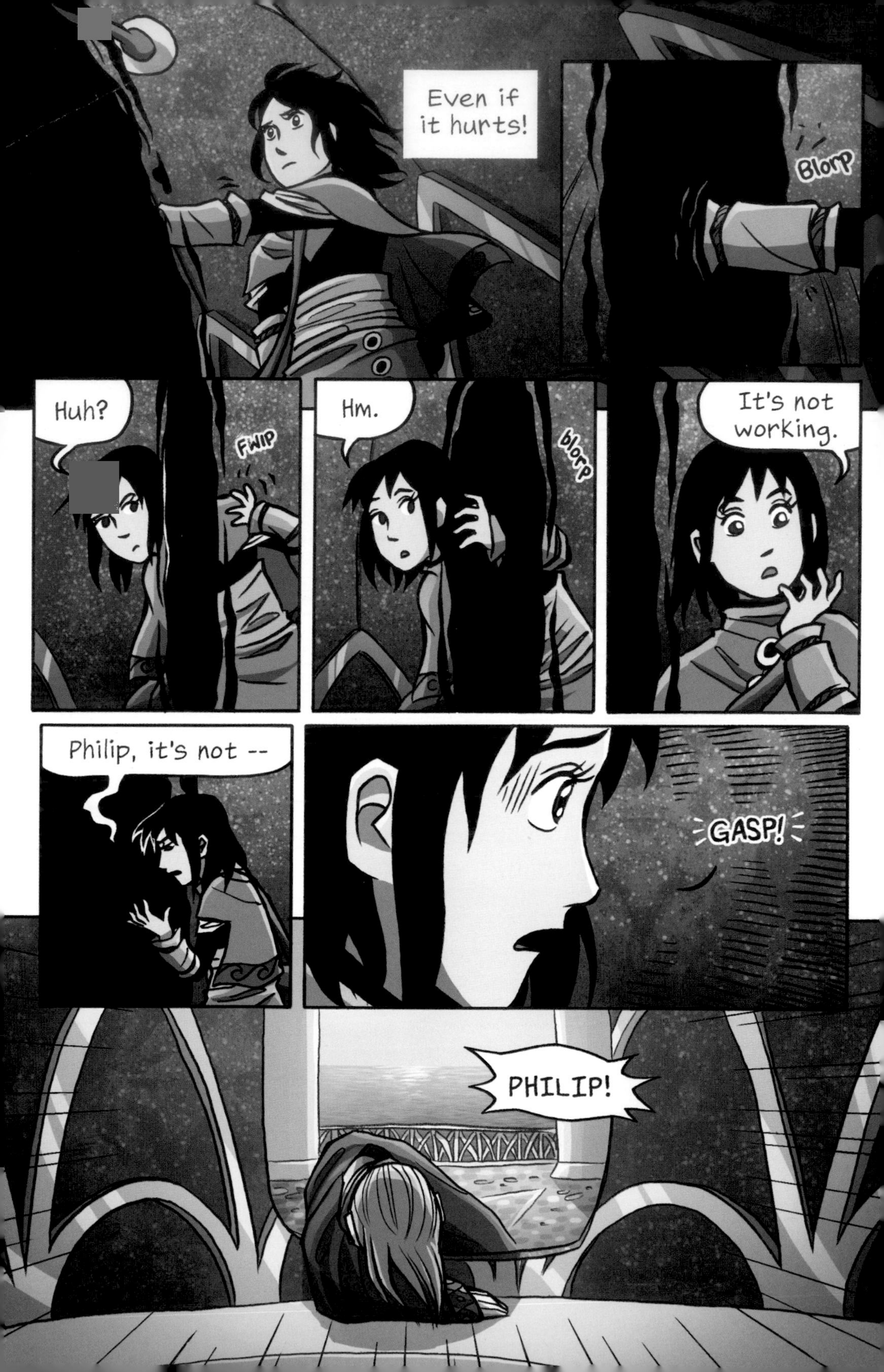
Even if it hurts!
Blorp
Huh?
FWIP
Hm.
blorp
It's not working.
Philip, it's not --
GASP!
PHILIP!

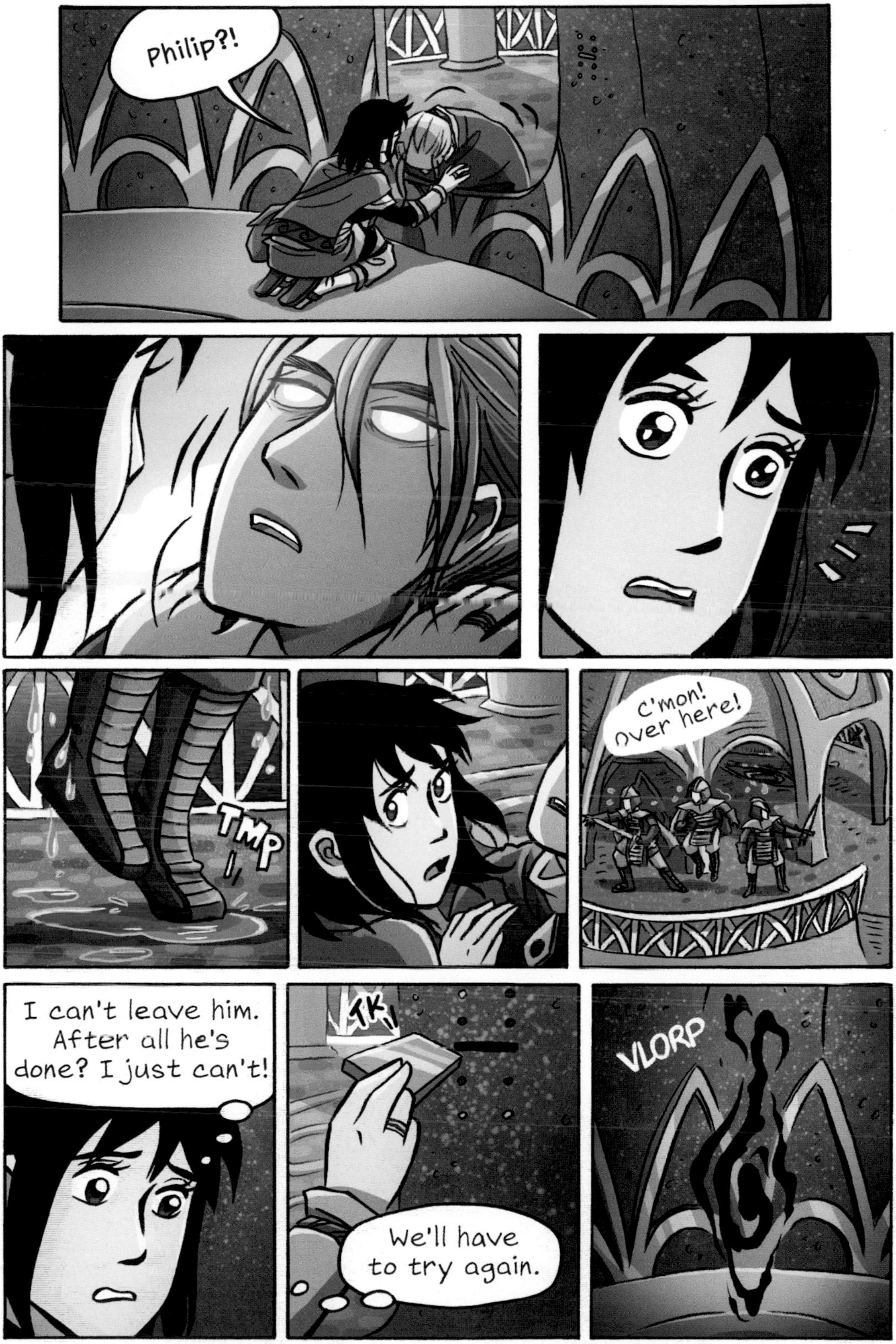
Philip?!
TMP
C'mon! Over here!
I can't leave him. After all he's done? I just can't!
TK
We'll have to try again.
VLORP

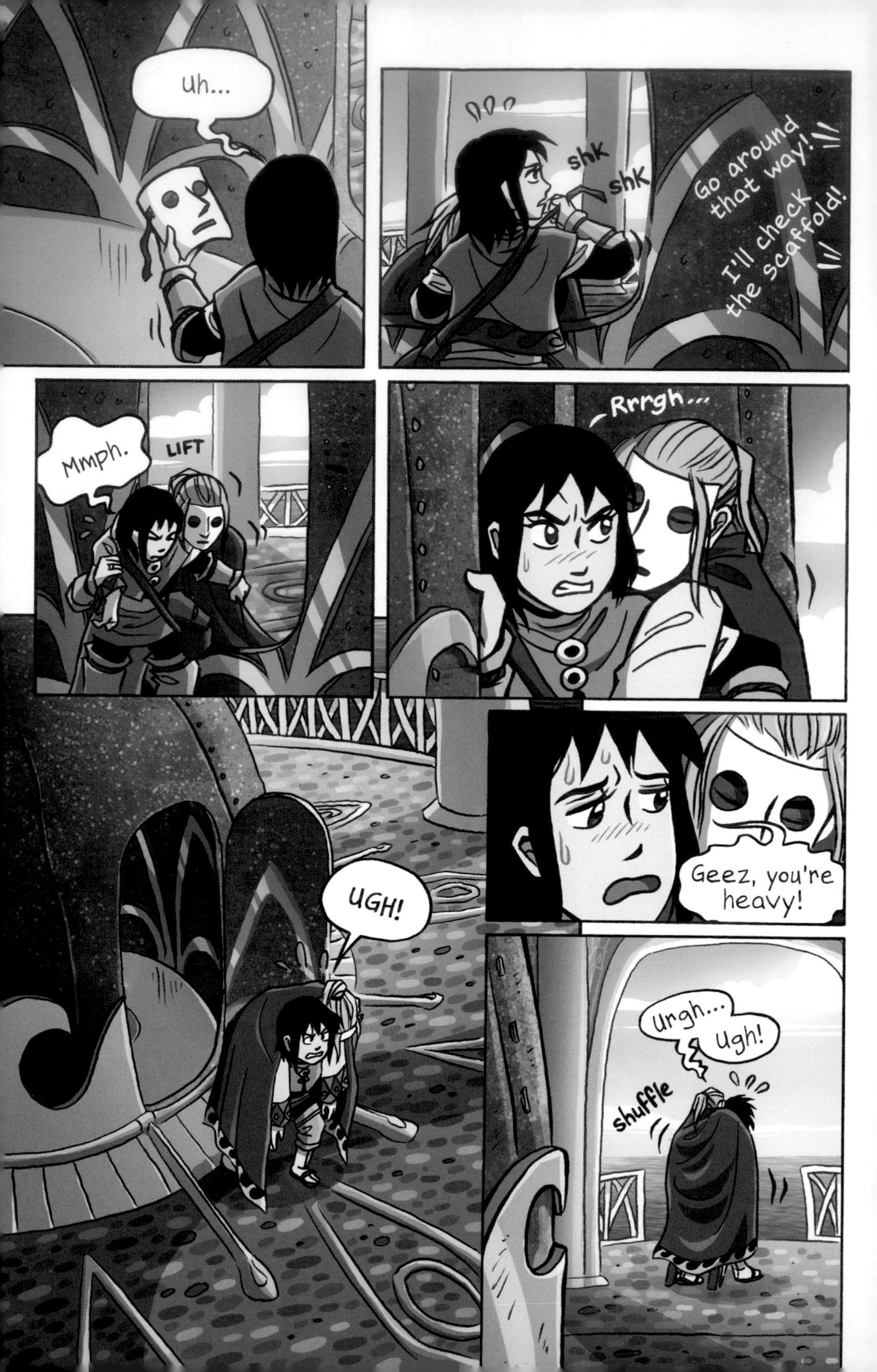
uh...
shk
shk
Go around that way!
I'll check the scaffold!
Mmph.
LIFT
Rrrgh...
Geez, you're heavy!
UGH!
Urgh...
Ugh!
shuffle

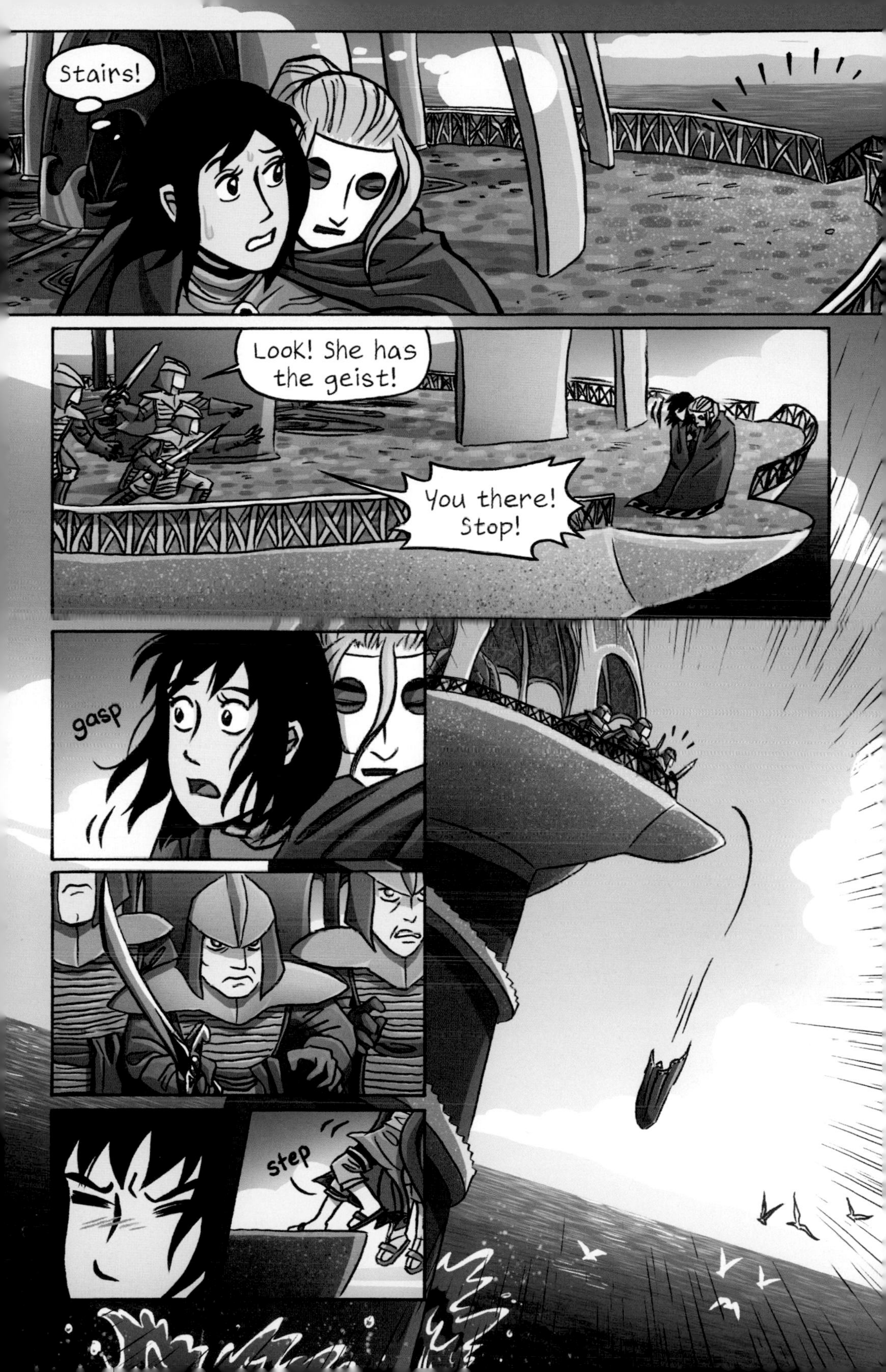
Stairs!
Look! She has the geist!
You there! Stop!
gasp
step

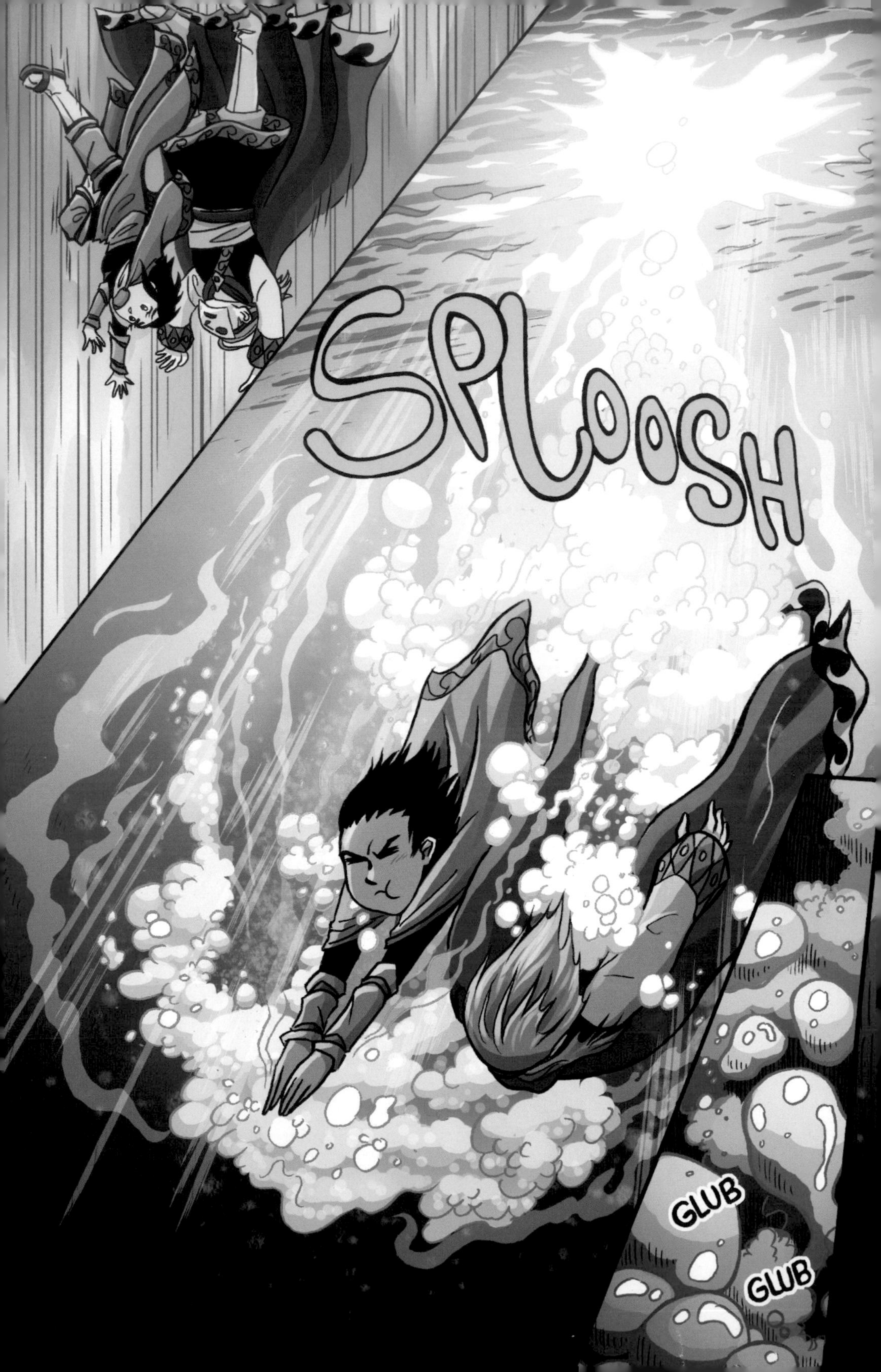
SPLOOSH
GLUB
GLUB

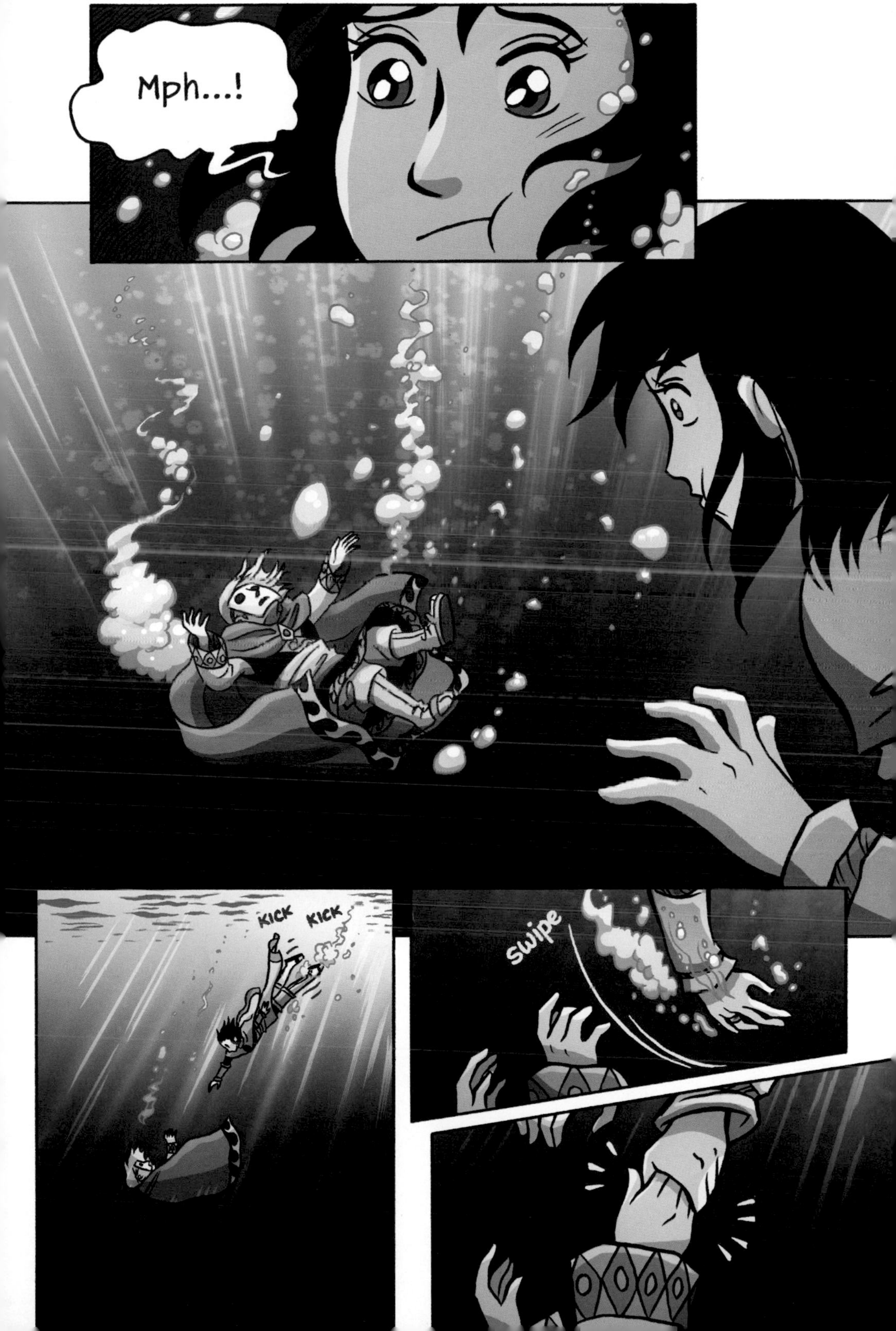
Mph...!
KICK
KICK
SWIPE

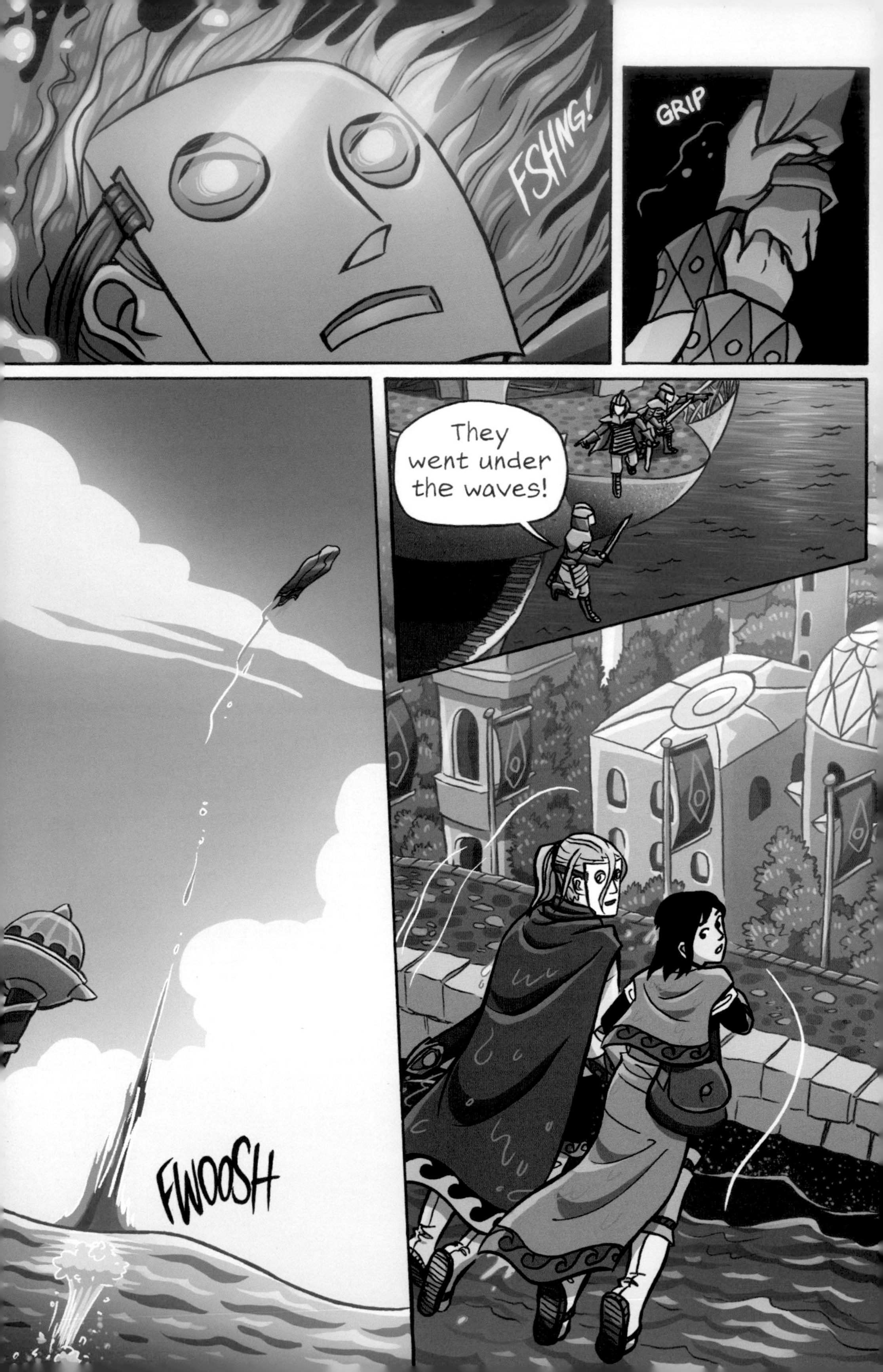
FSHNG!
GRIP
FWOOSH
They went under the waves!

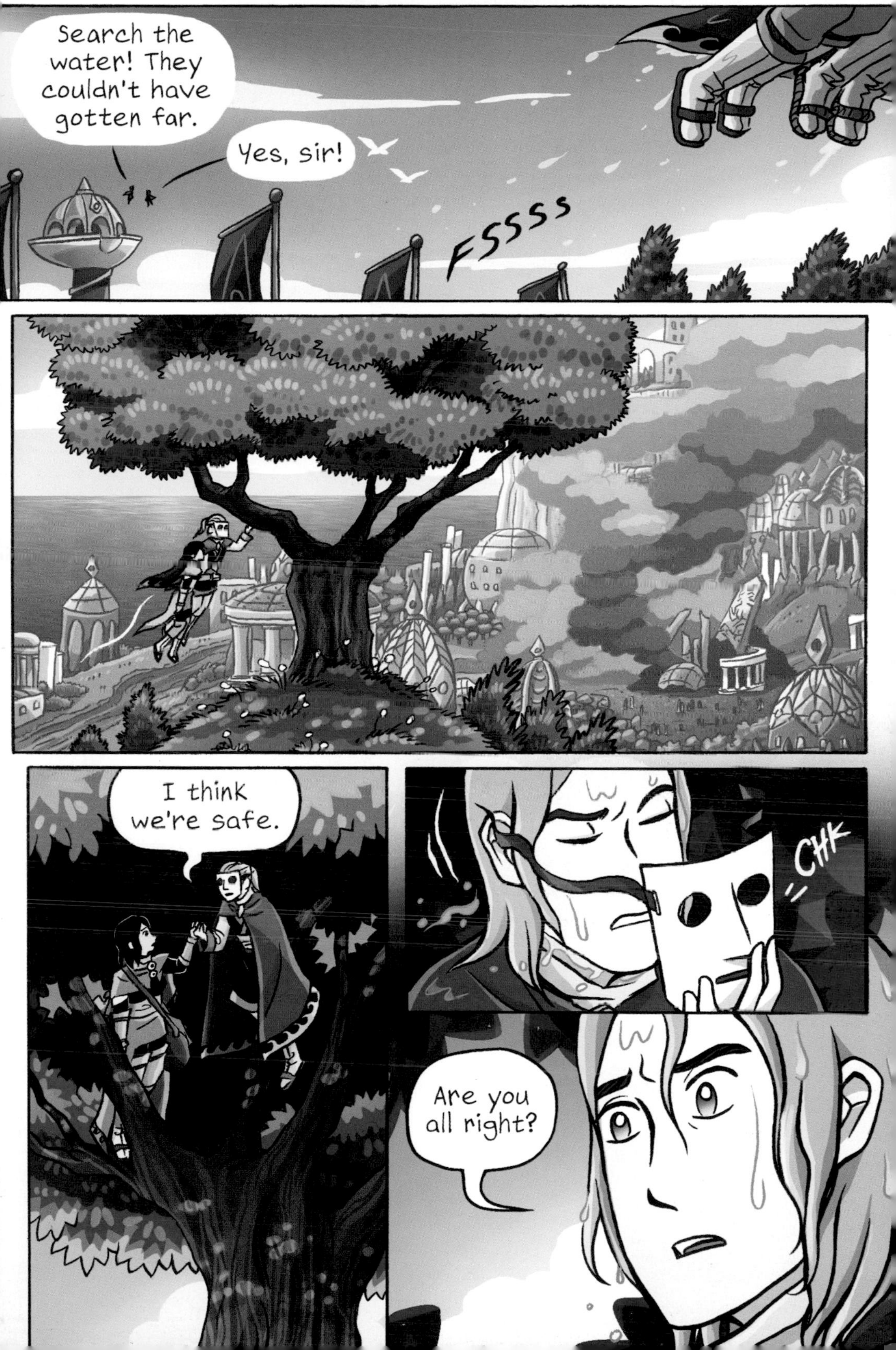
Search the water! They couldn't have gotten far.
Yes, sir!
FSSSS
I think we're safe.
CHK
Are you all right?

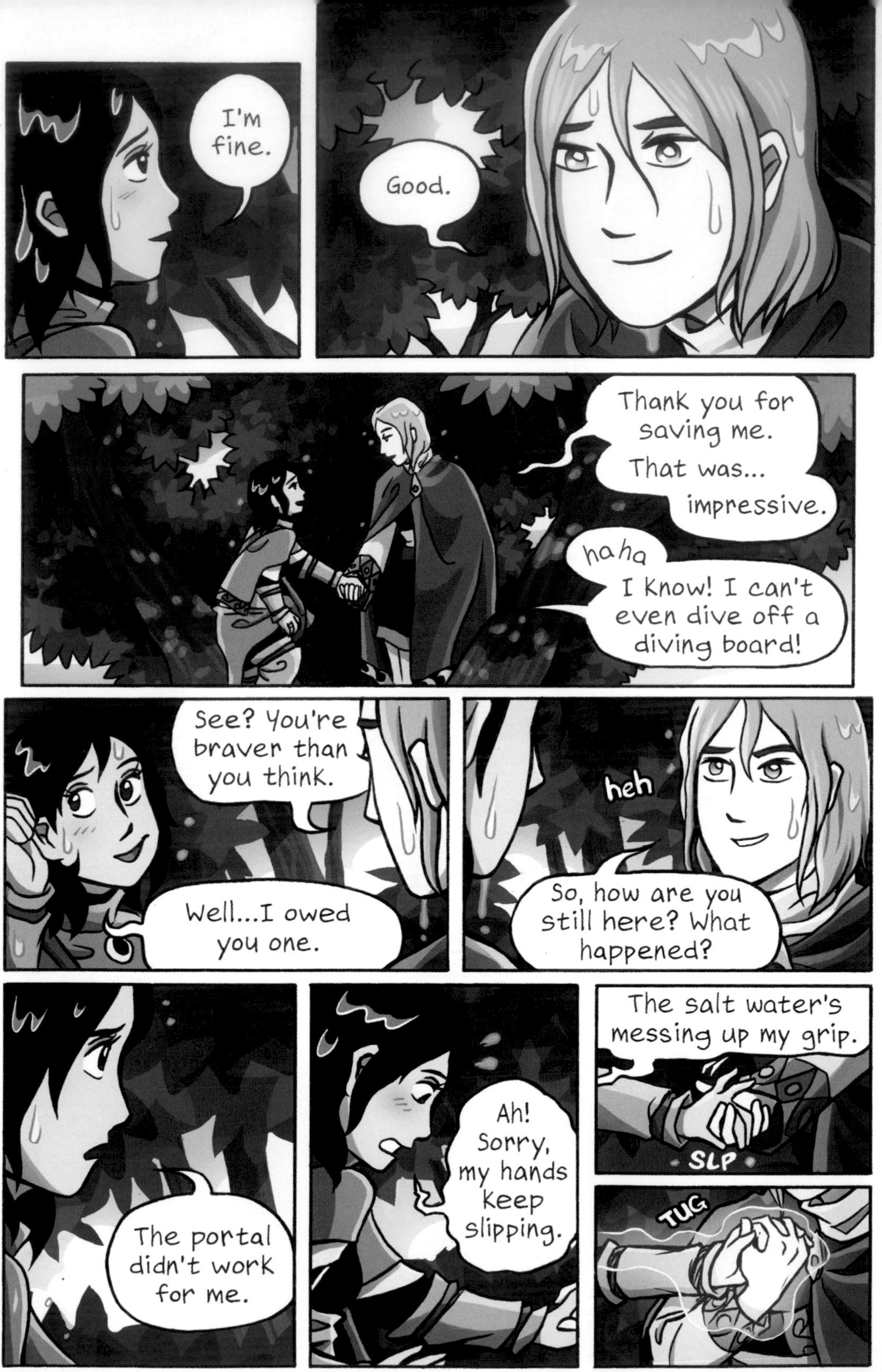
I'm fine.
Good.
Thank you for saving me.
That was... impressive.
haha
I know! I can't even dive off a diving board!
See? You're braver than you think.
Well...I owed you one.
heh
So, how are you still here? What happened?
The portal didn't work for me.
Ah! Sorry, my hands keep slipping.
The salt water's messing up my grip.
SLP
TUG

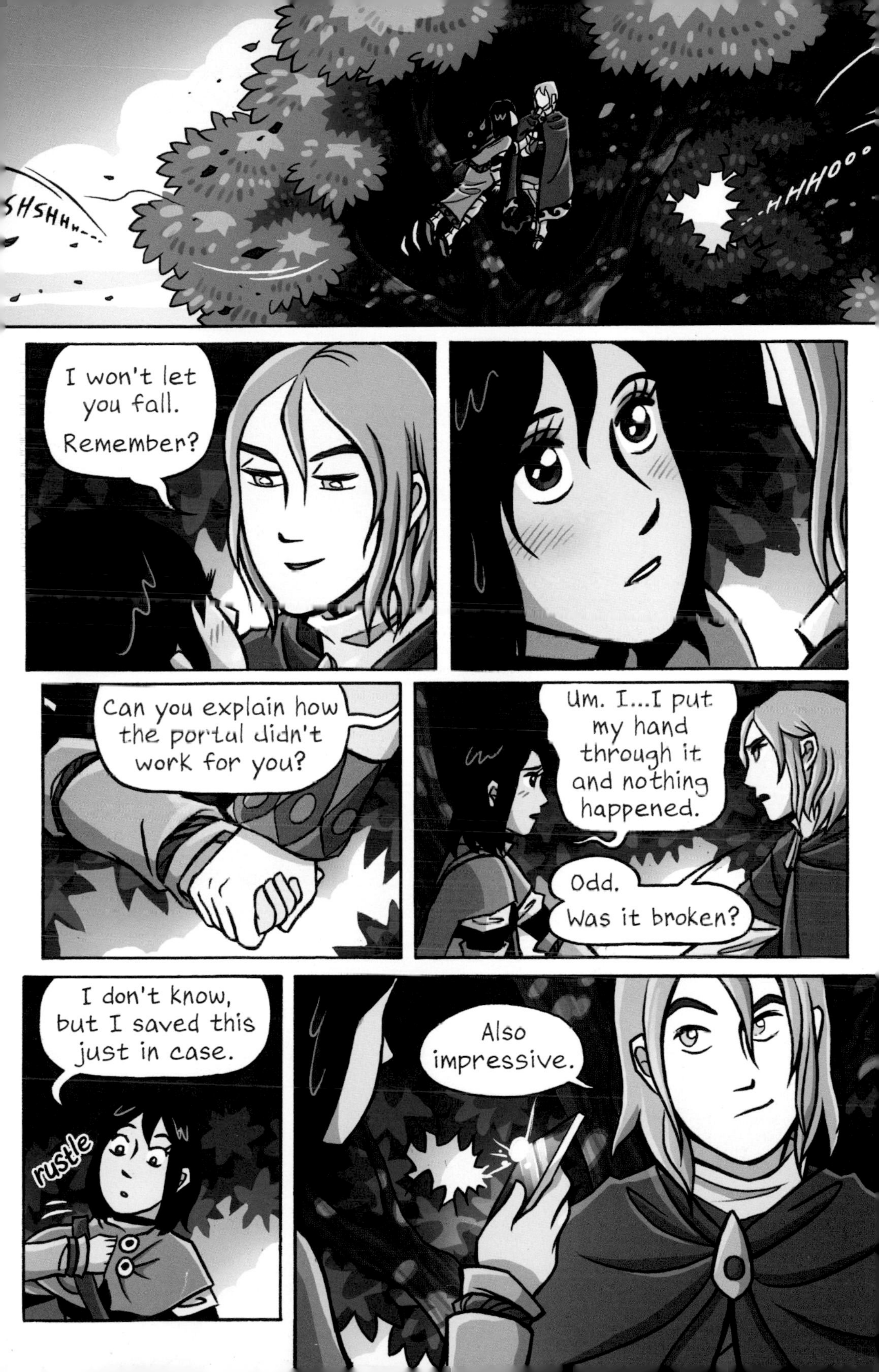
SHSHHw...
...HHHOoo
I won't let you fall.
Remember?
Can you explain how the portal didn't work for you?
Um. I...I put my hand through it and nothing happened.
Odd.
Was it broken?
I don't know, but I saved this just in case.
rustle
Also impressive.

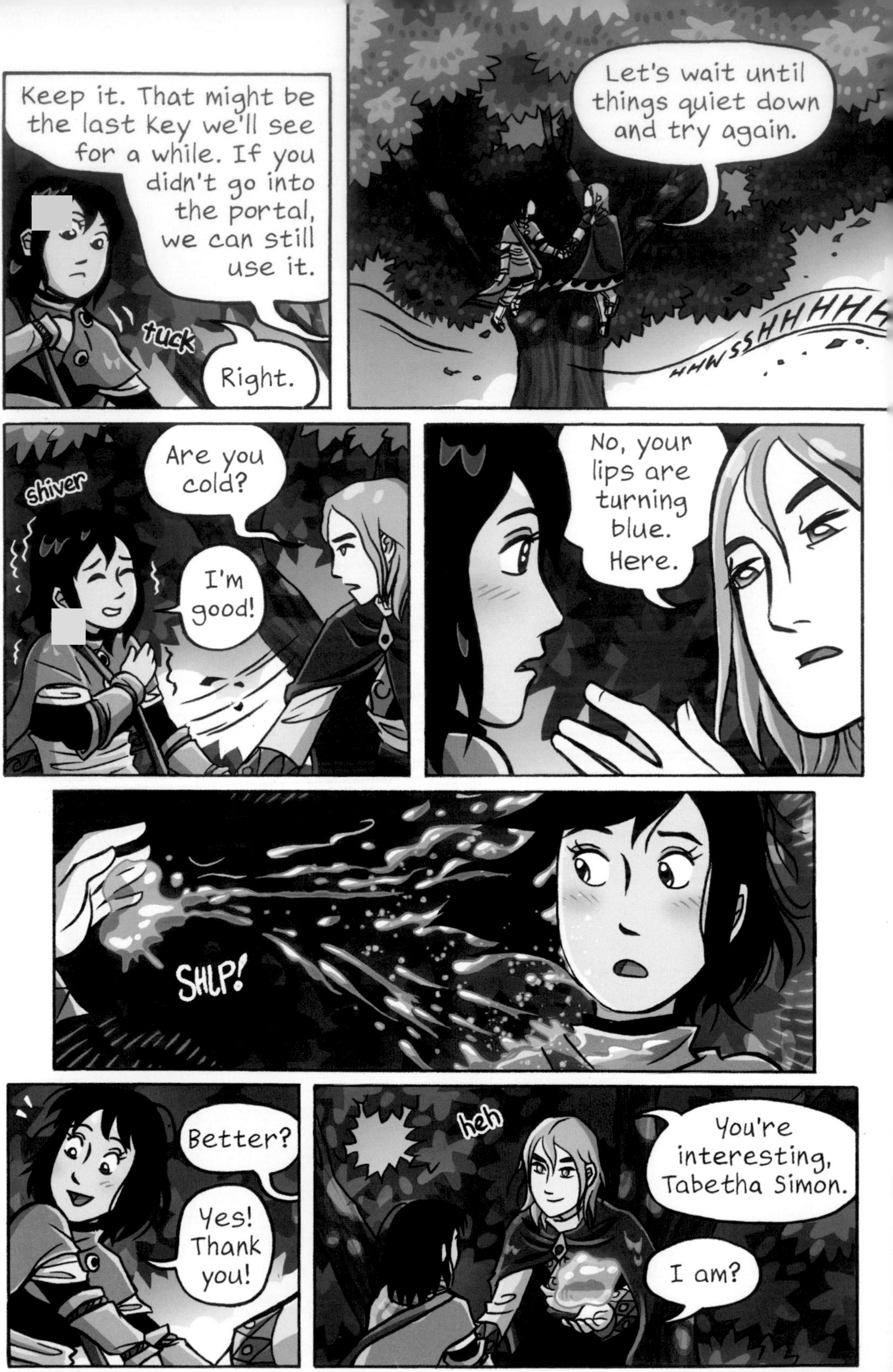
Keep it. That might be the last key we'll see for a while. If you didn't go into the portal, we can still use it.
tuck
Right.
Let's wait until things quiet down and try again.
HHWSSHHHHH
shiver
Are you cold?
I'm good!
No, your lips are turning blue. Here.
SHLP!
Better?
Yes! Thank you!
heh
You're interesting, Tabetha Simon.
I am?

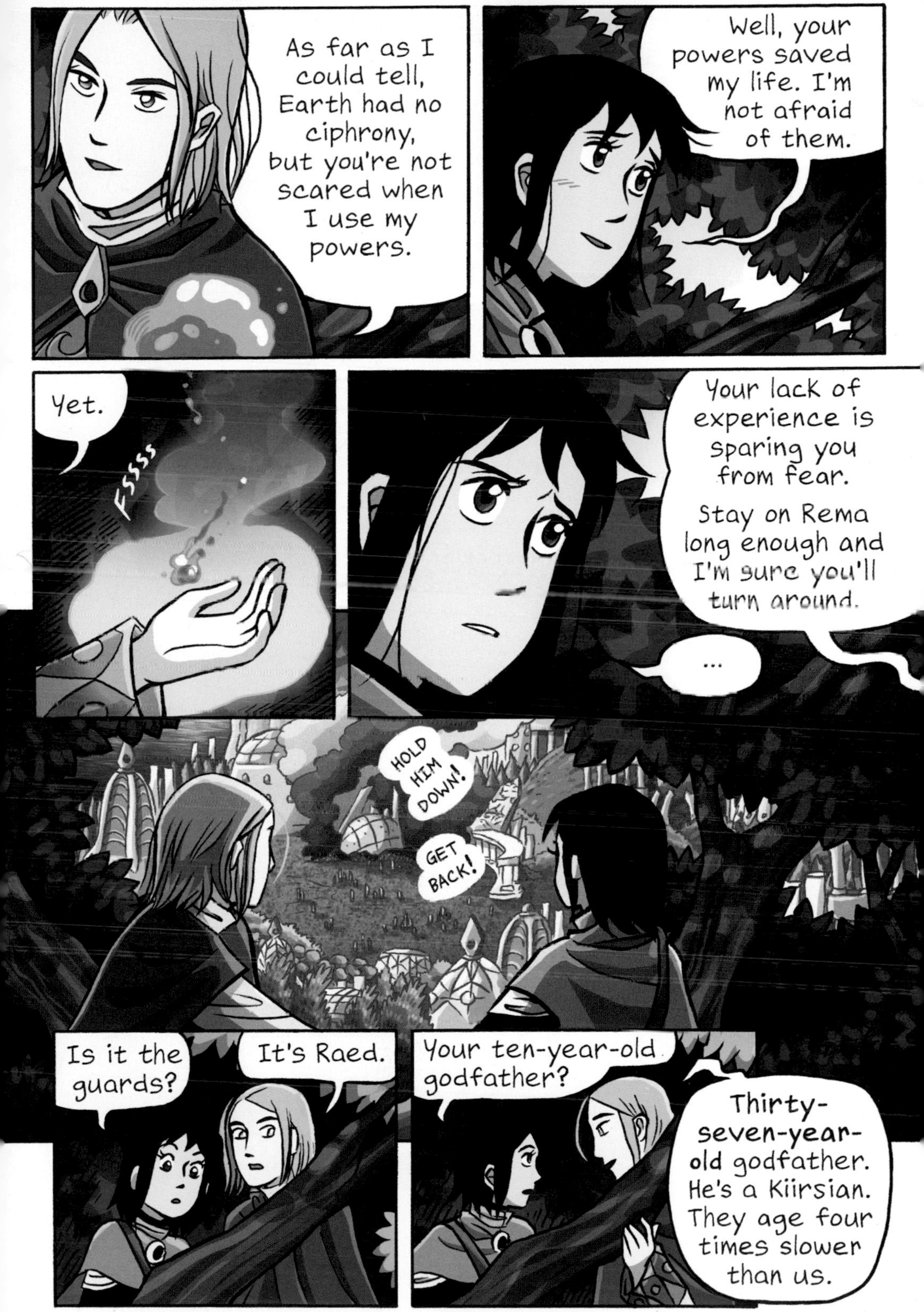
As far as I could tell, Earth had no ciphrony, but you're not scared when I use my powers.
Well, your powers saved my life. I'm not afraid of them.
Yet.
FSSSS
Your lack of experience is sparing you from fear.
Stay on Rema long enough and I'm sure you'll turn around.
...
HOLD HIM DOWN!
GET BACK!
Is it the guards?
It's Raed.
Your ten-year-old godfather?
Thirty-seven-year-old godfather. He's a Kiirsian. They age four times slower than us.

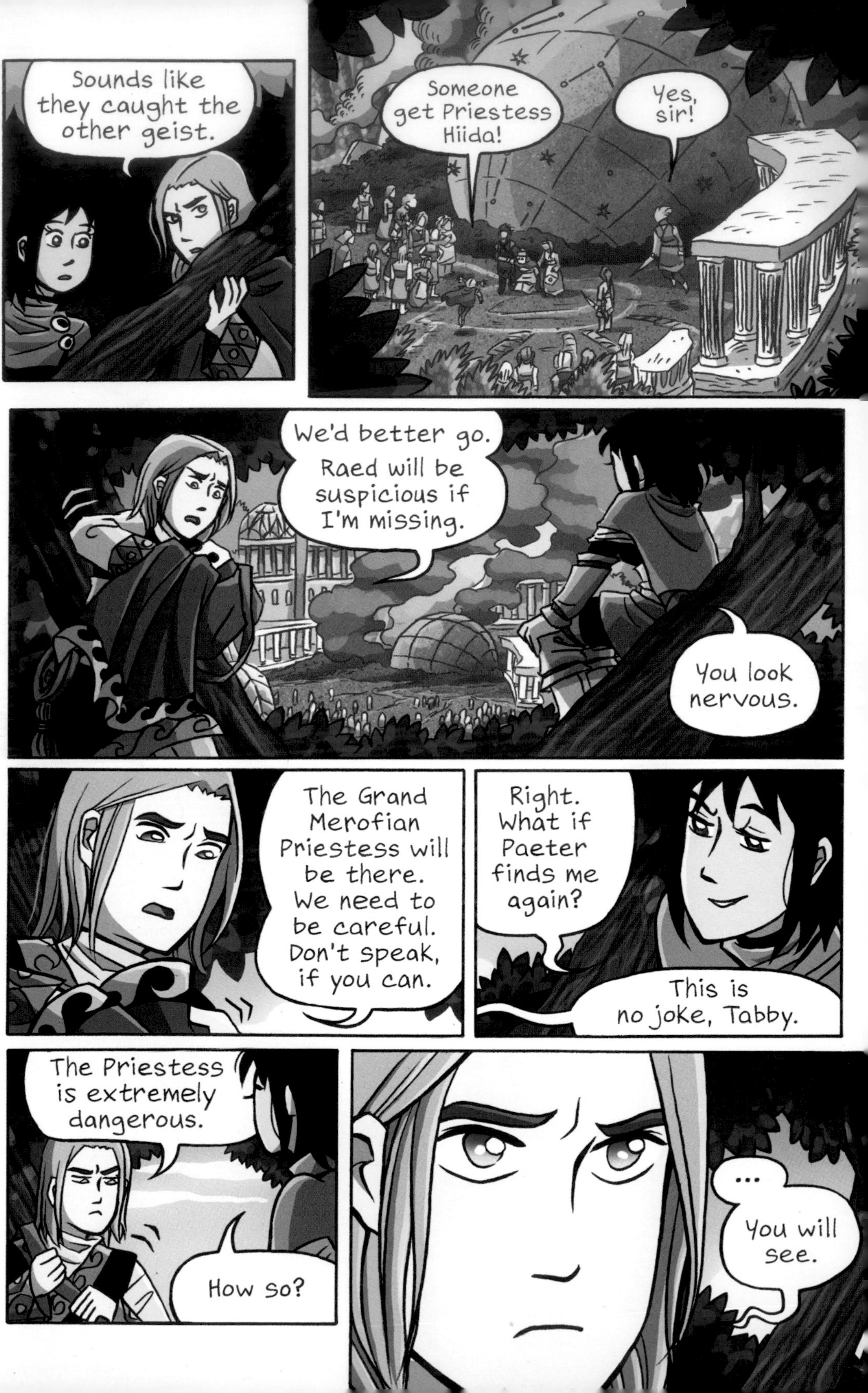
Sounds like they caught the other geist.
Someone get Priestess Hiida!
Yes, sir!
We'd better go.
Raed will be suspicious if I'm missing.
You look nervous.
The Grand Merofian Priestess will be there. We need to be careful. Don't speak, if you can.
Right. What if Paeter finds me again?
This is no joke, Tabby.
The Priestess is extremely dangerous.
How so?
...
You will see.

PART III
THE PRIESTESS

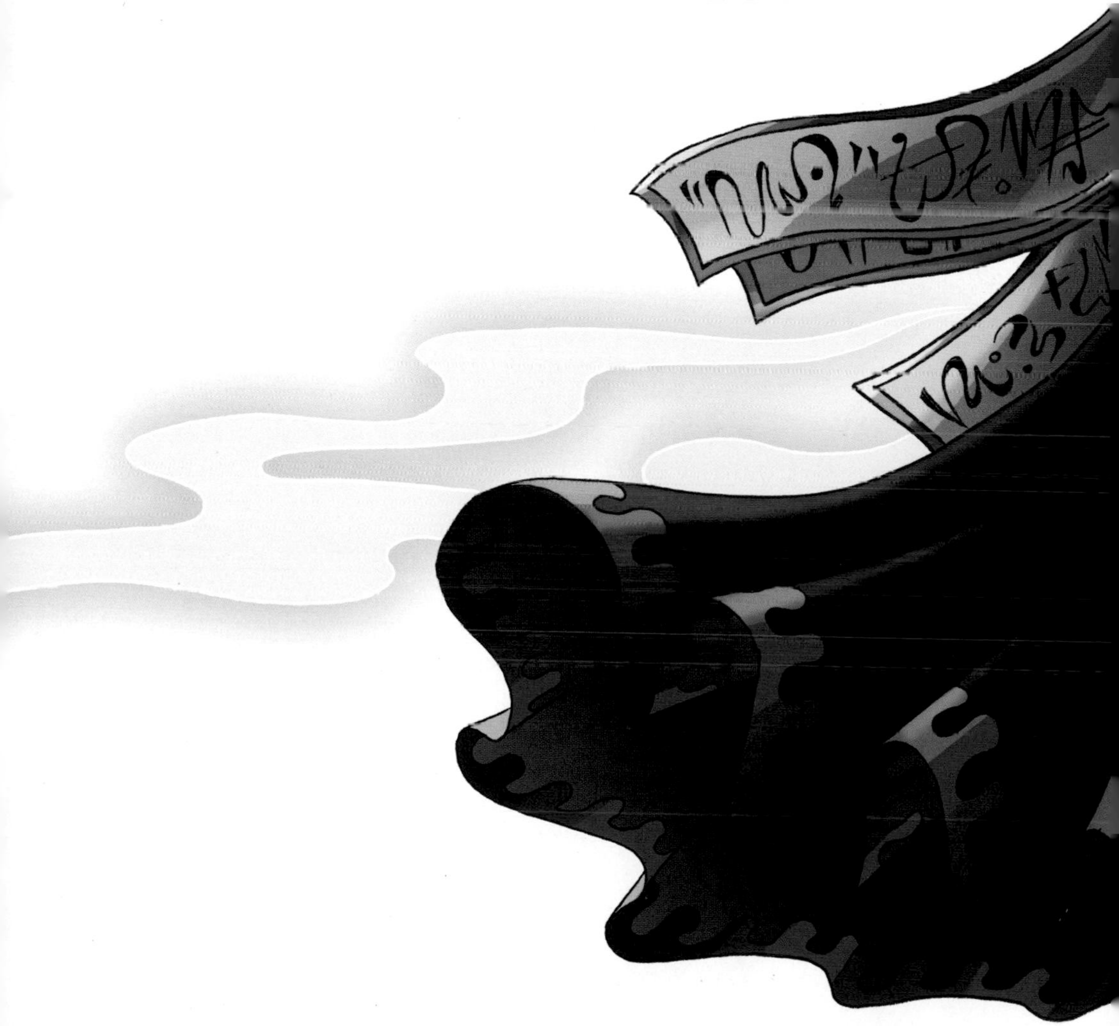

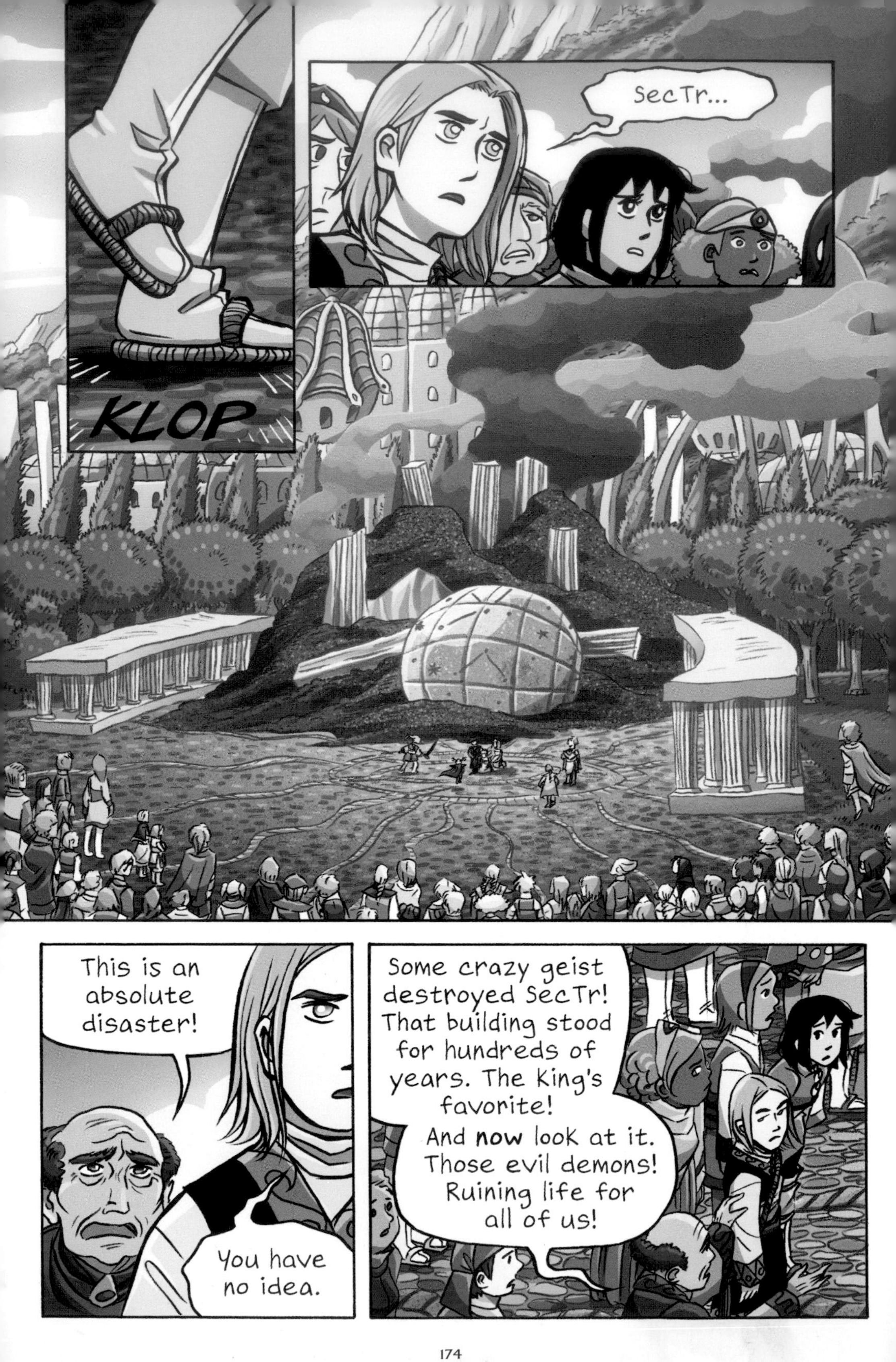
KLOP
SecTr...
This is an absolute disaster!
You have no idea.
Some crazy geist destroyed SecTr! That building stood for hundreds of years. The King's favorite!
And **now** look at it. Those evil demons! Ruining life for all of us!

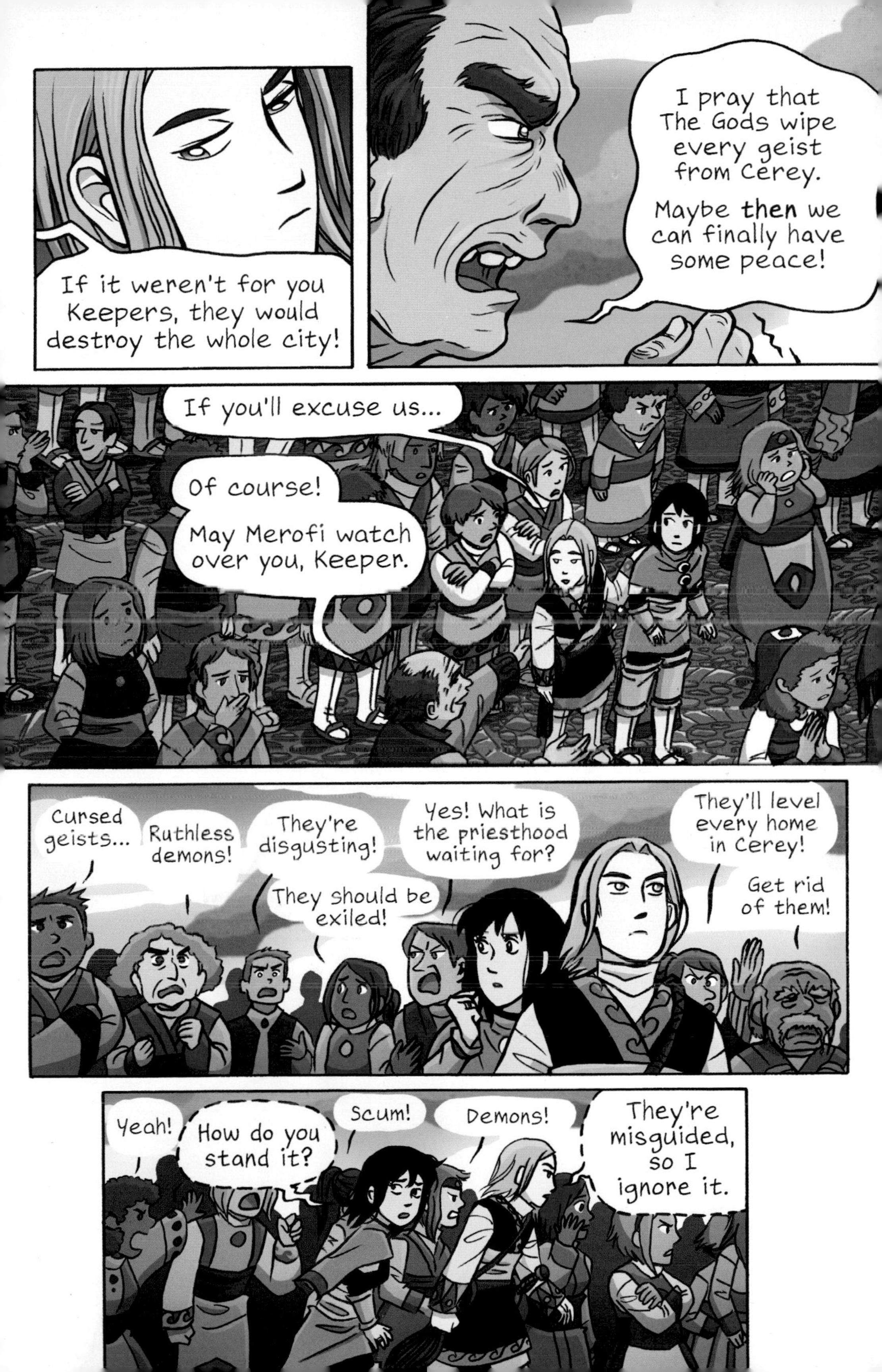
If it weren't for you Keepers, they would destroy the whole city!
I pray that The Gods wipe every geist from Cerey.
Maybe **then** we can finally have some peace!
If you'll excuse us...
Of course!
May Merofi watch over you, Keeper.
Cursed geists...
Ruthless demons!
They're disgusting!
They should be exiled!
Yes! What is the priesthood waiting for?
They'll level every home in Cerey!
Get rid of them!
Yeah!
How do you stand it?
Scum!
Demons!
They're misguided, so I ignore it.

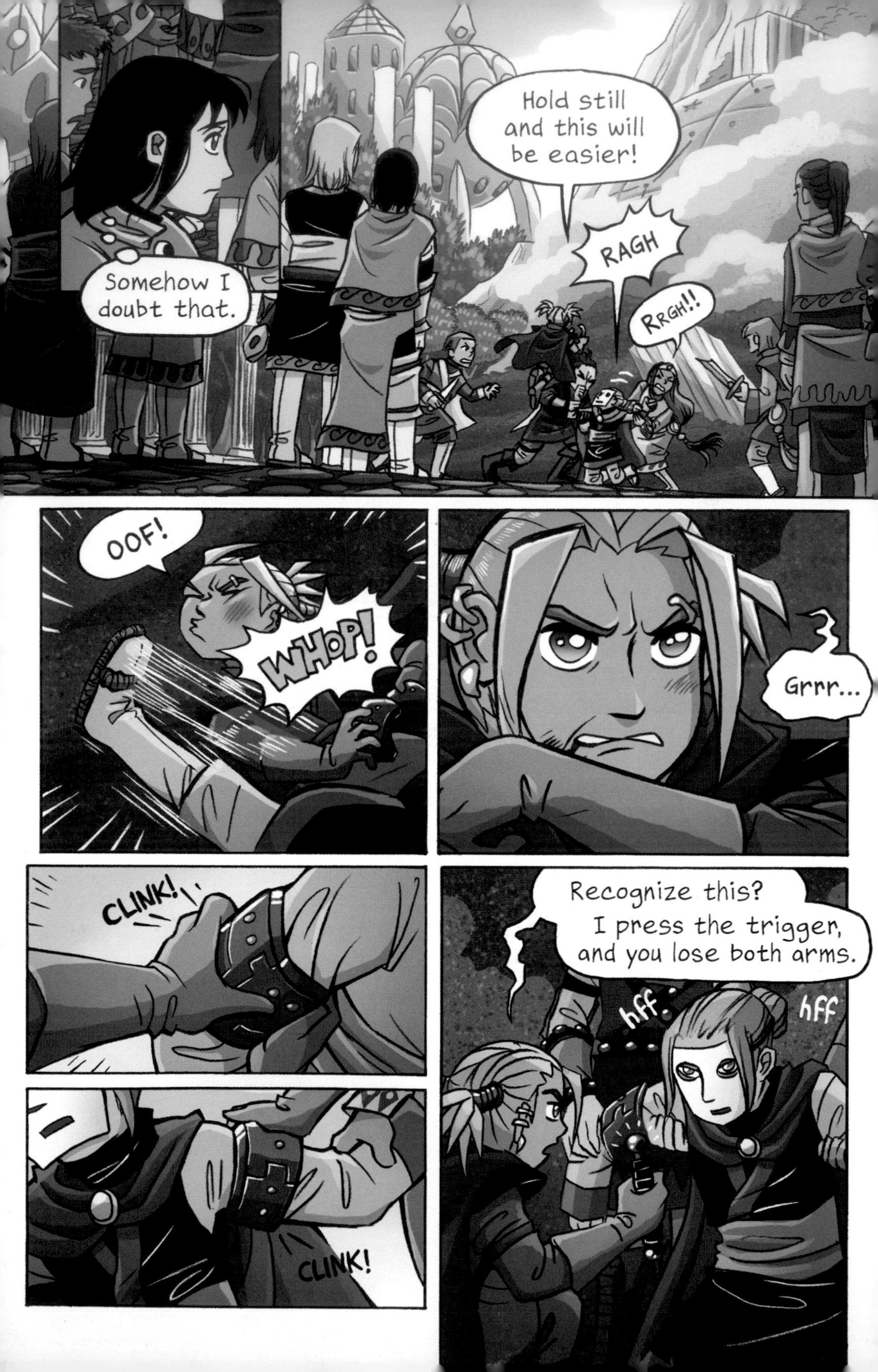
Somehow I doubt that.
Hold still and this will be easier!
RAGH
RRGH!!
OOF!
WHOP!
Grrr...
CLINK!
CLINK!
Recognize this? I press the trigger, and you lose both arms.
hff
hff

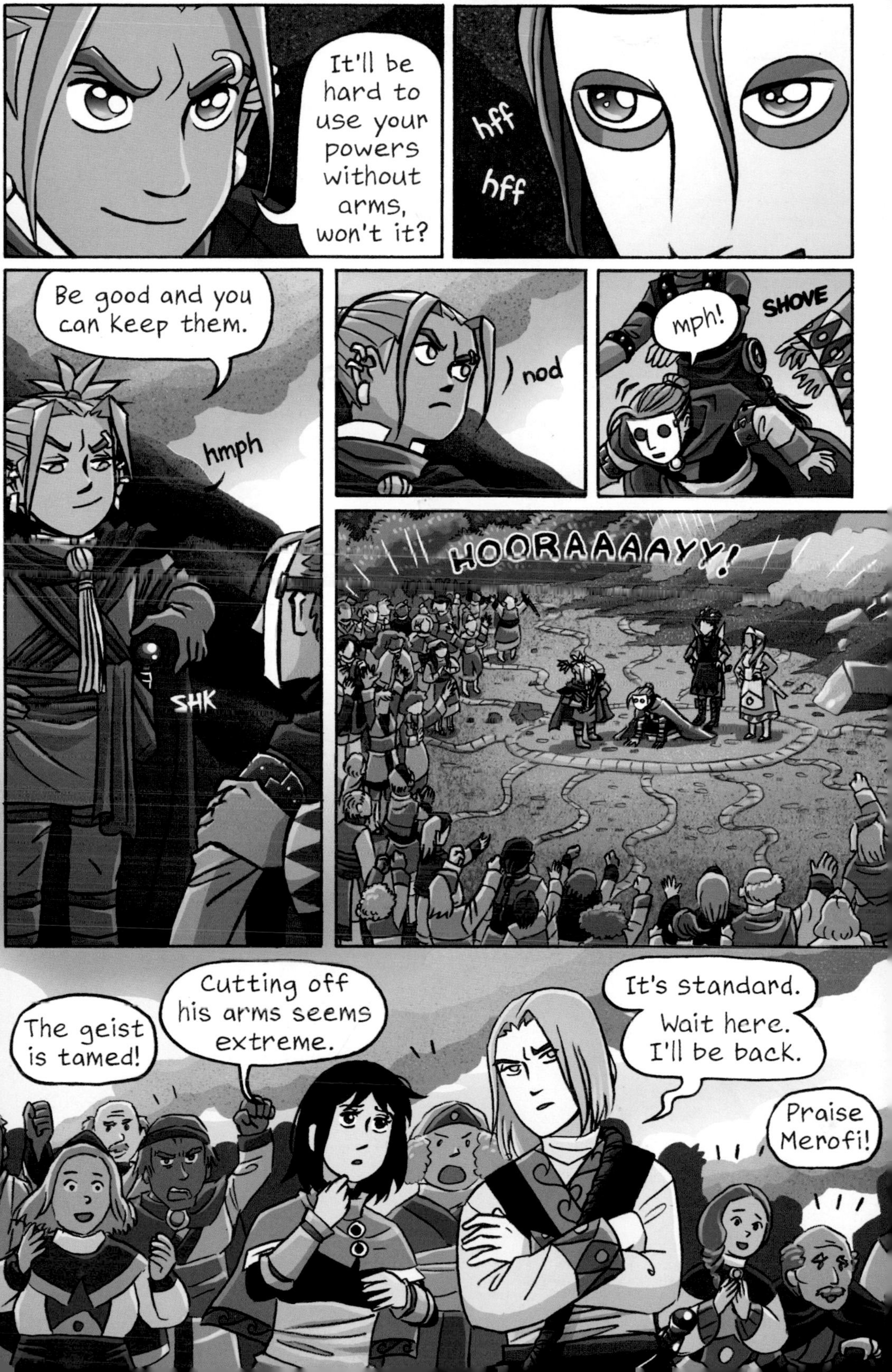
It'll be hard to use your powers without arms, won't it?
hff
hff
Be good and you can keep them.
hmph
SHK
nod
mph!
SHOVE
HOORAAAAAYY!
The geist is tamed!
Cutting off his arms seems extreme.
It's standard.
Wait here. I'll be back.
Praise Merofi!

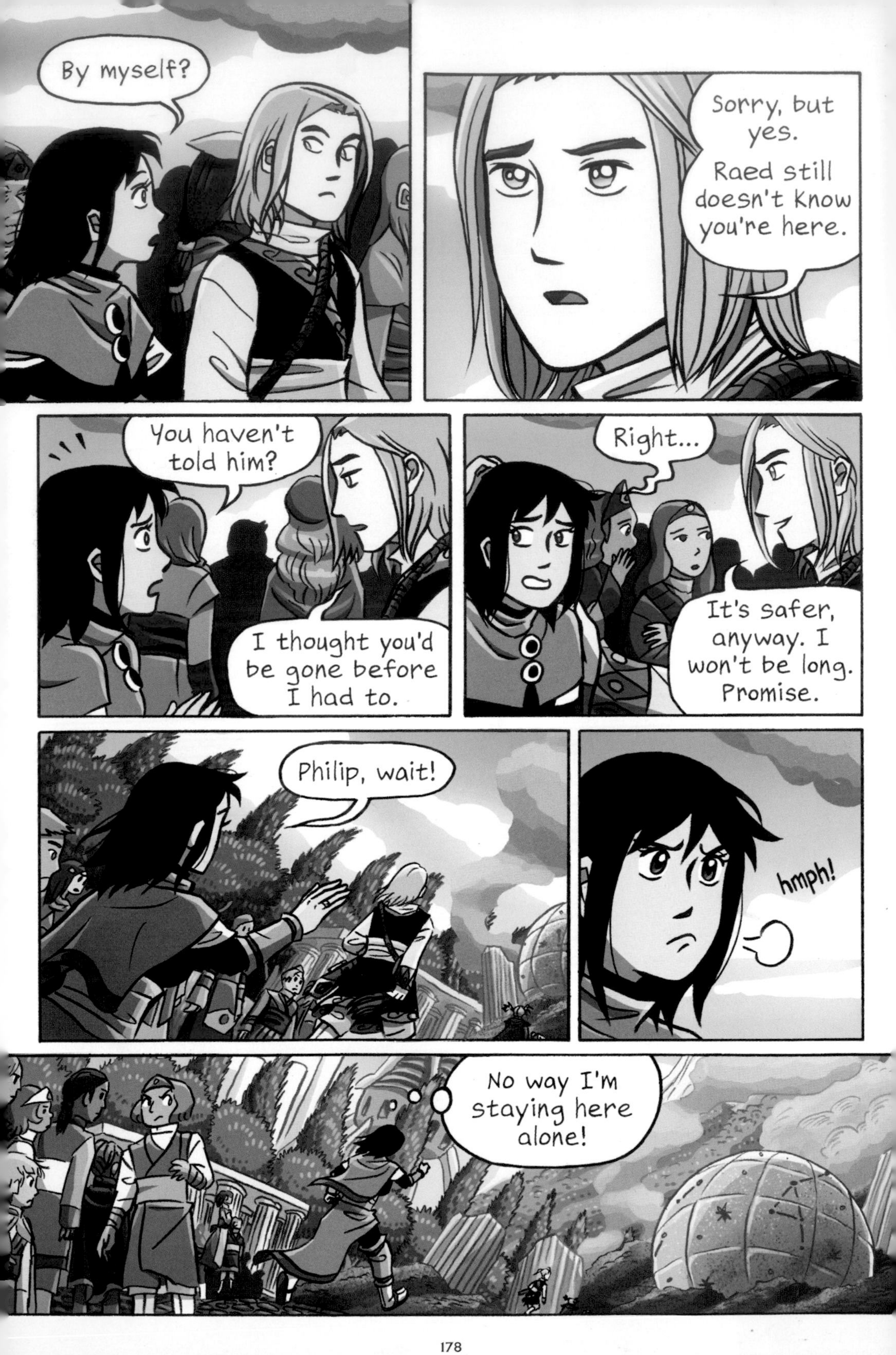
By myself?
Sorry, but yes.
Raed still doesn't know you're here.
You haven't told him?
I thought you'd be gone before I had to.
Right...
It's safer, anyway. I won't be long. Promise.
Philip, wait!
hmph!
No way I'm staying here alone!

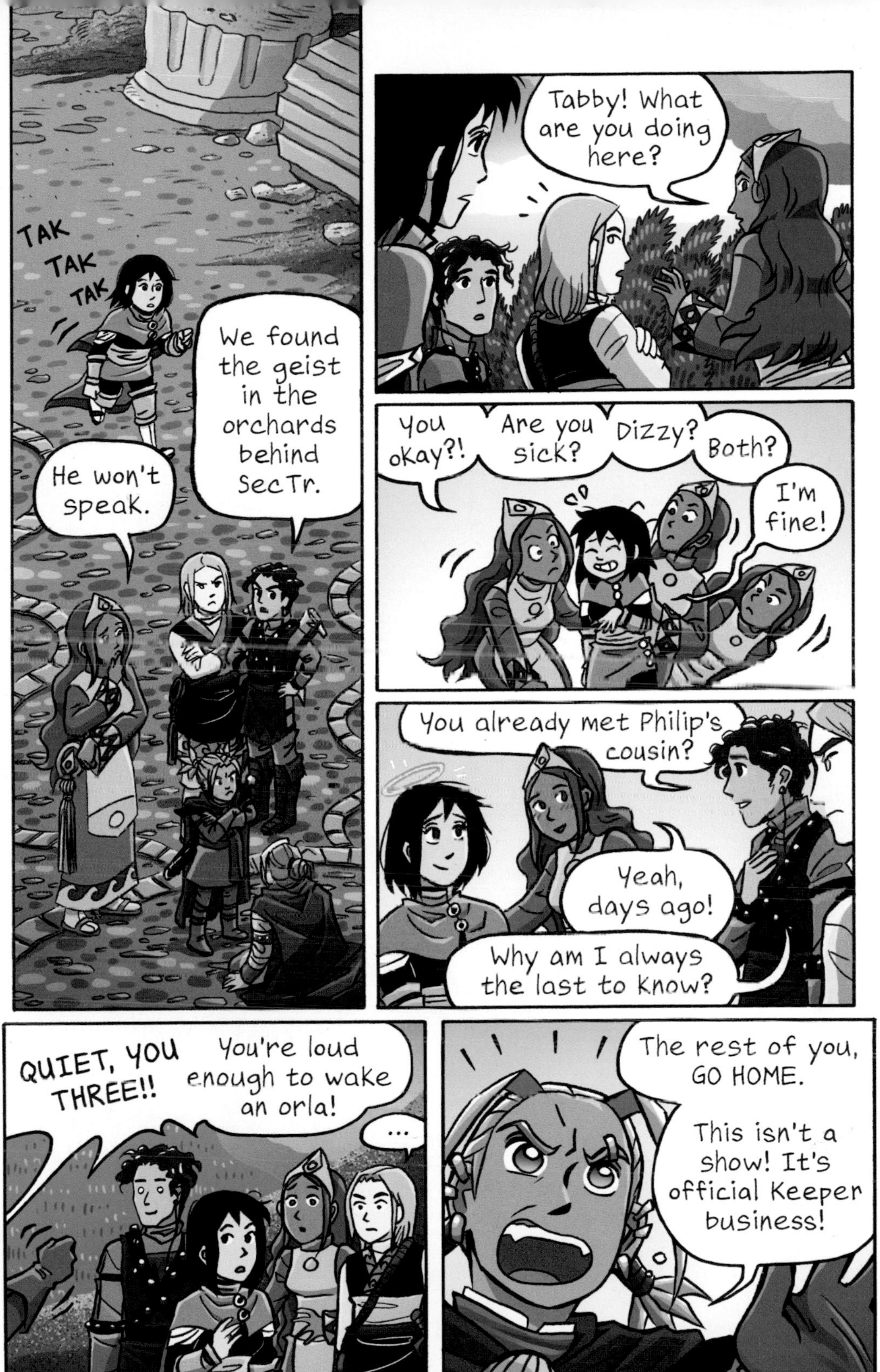
TAK
TAK
TAK
We found the geist in the orchards behind SecTr.
He won't speak.
Tabby! What are you doing here?
You okay?!
Are you sick?
Dizzy?
Both?
I'm fine!
You already met Philip's cousin?
Yeah, days ago!
Why am I always the last to know?
QUIET, YOU THREE!!
You're loud enough to wake an orla!
...
The rest of you, GO HOME.
This isn't a show! It's official Keeper business!

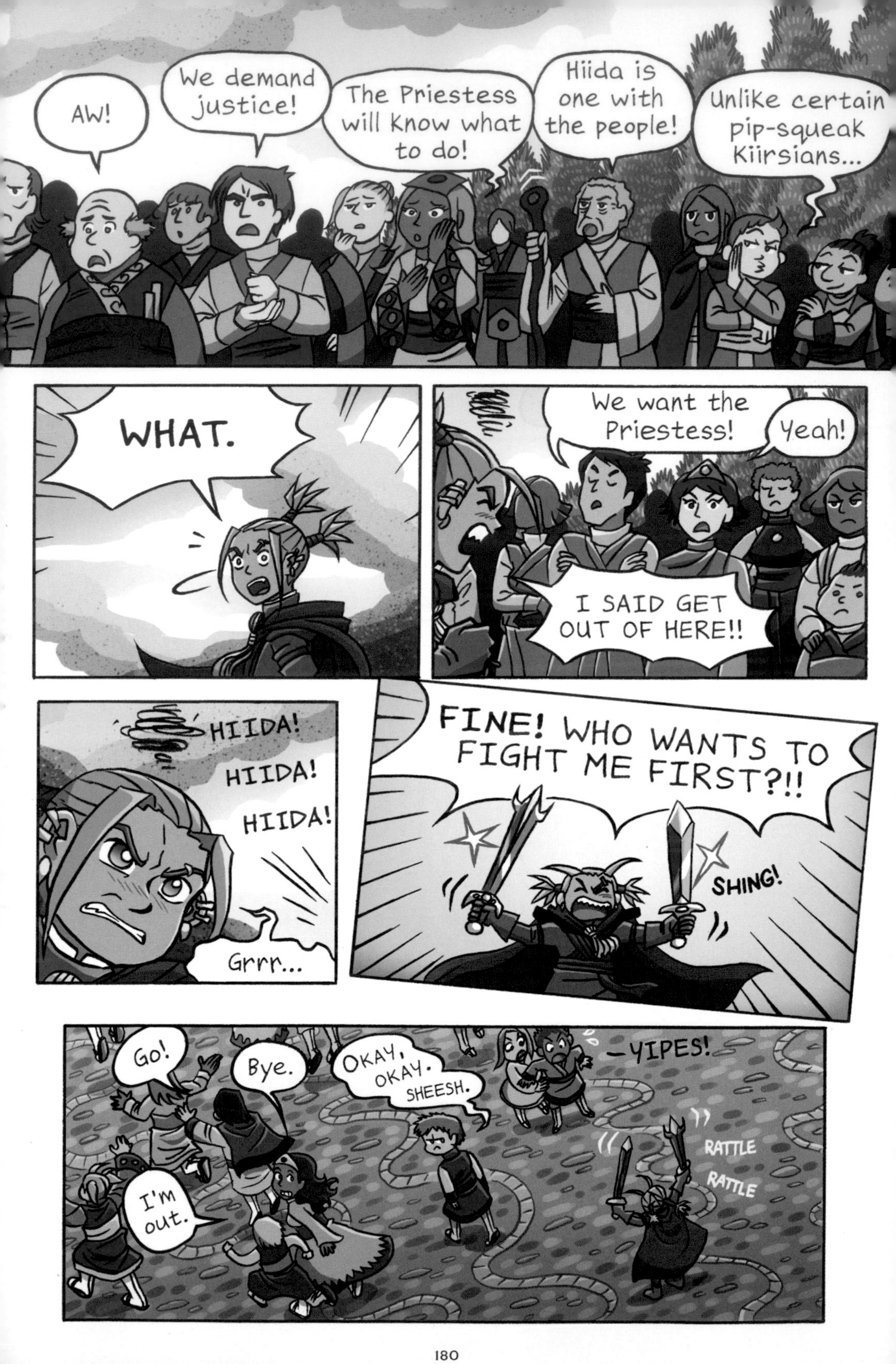
AW!
We demand justice!
The Priestess will know what to do!
Hiida is one with the people!
Unlike certain pip-squeak Kiirsians...
WHAT.
We want the Priestess!
Yeah!
I SAID GET OUT OF HERE!!
HIIDA!
HIIDA!
HIIDA!
Grrr...
FINE! WHO WANTS TO FIGHT ME FIRST?!!
SHING!
Go!
Bye.
OKAY, OKAY.
SHEESH.
—YIPES!
RATTLE
RATTLE
I'm out.

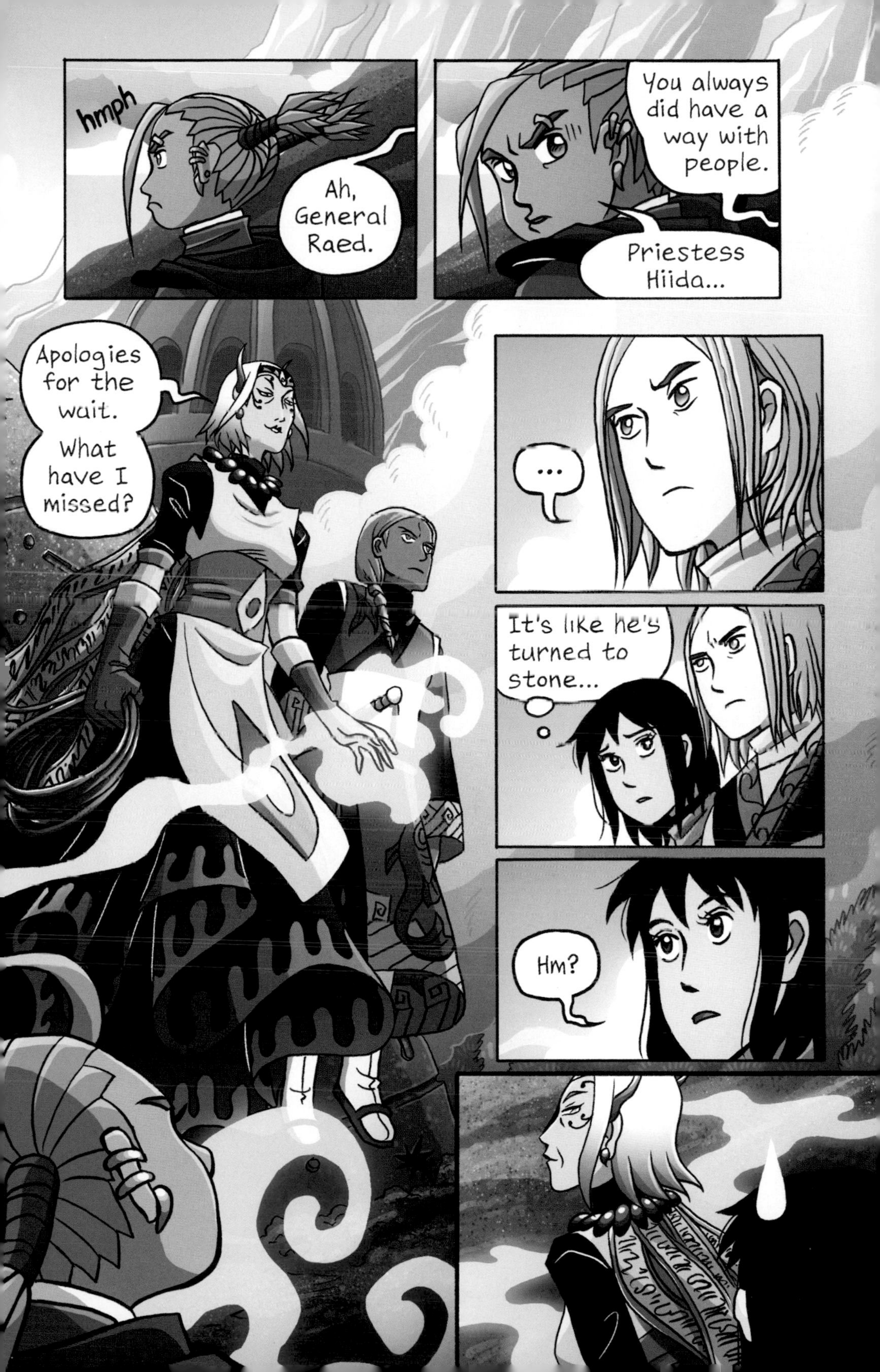
hmph
Ah, General Raed.
You always did have a way with people.
Priestess Hiida...
Apologies for the wait.
What have I missed?
...
It's like he's turned to stone...
Hm?

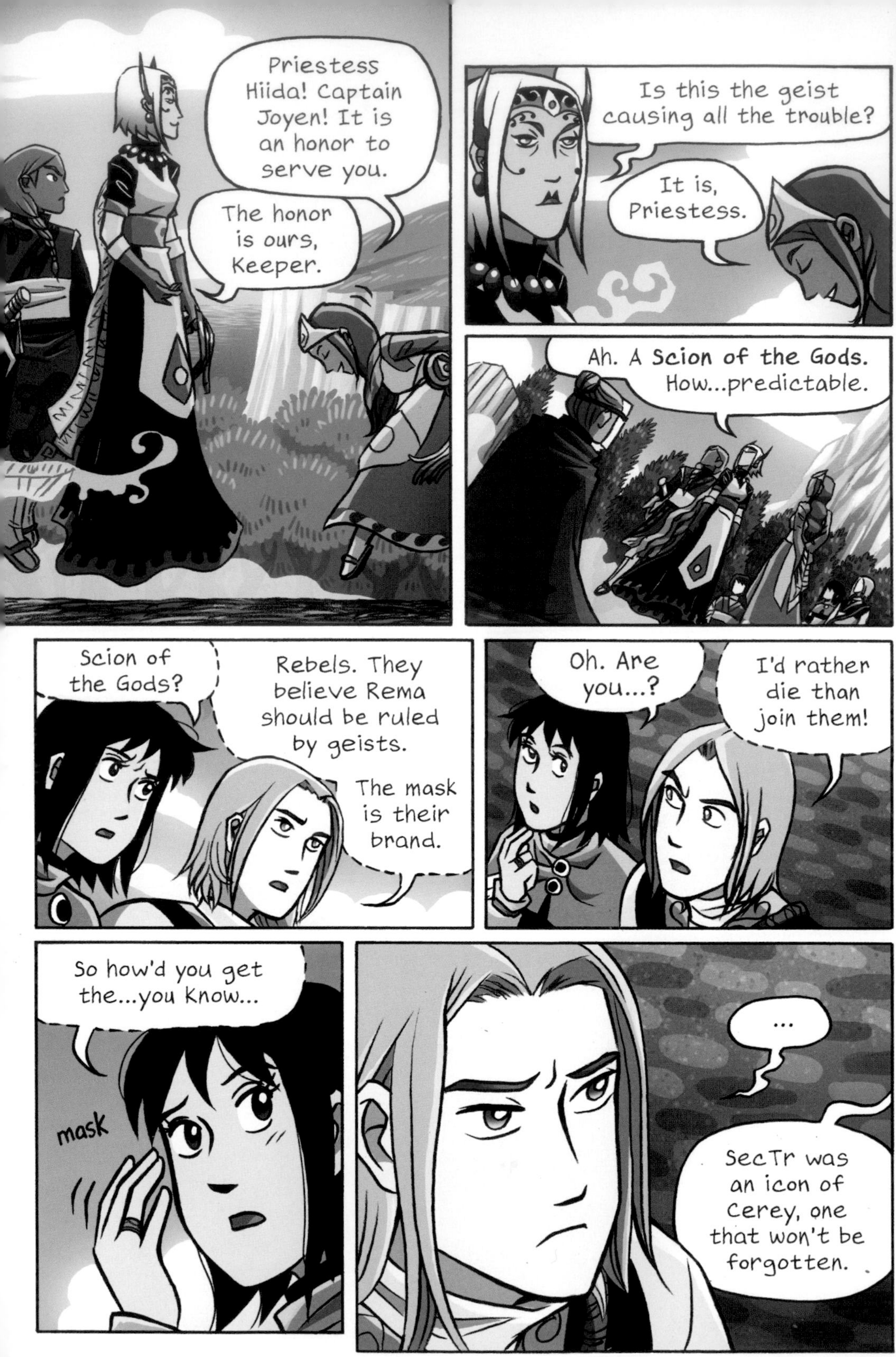
Priestess Hiida! Captain Joyen! It is an honor to serve you.
The honor is ours, Keeper.
Is this the geist causing all the trouble?
It is, Priestess.
Ah. A **Scion of the Gods.** How...predictable.
Scion of the Gods?
Rebels. They believe Rema should be ruled by geists.
The mask is their brand.
Oh. Are you...?
I'd rather die than join them!
So how'd you get the...you know...
mask
...
SecTr was an icon of Cerey, one that won't be forgotten.

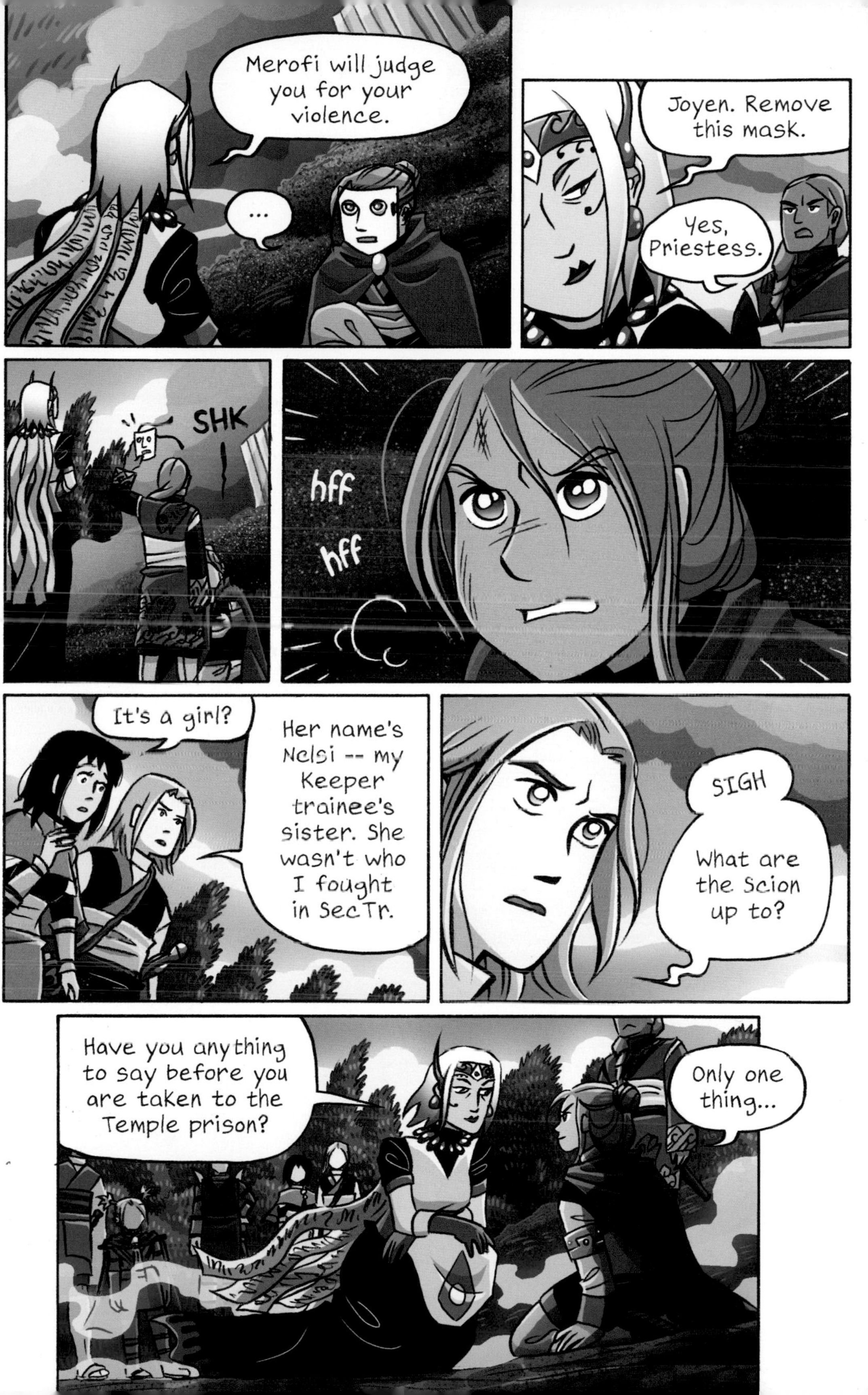
Merofi will judge you for your violence.
...
Joyen. Remove this mask.
Yes, Priestess.
SHK
hff
hff
It's a girl?
Her name's Nelsi -- my Keeper trainee's sister. She wasn't who I fought in SecTr.
SIGH
What are the Scion up to?
Have you anything to say before you are taken to the Temple prison?
Only one thing...

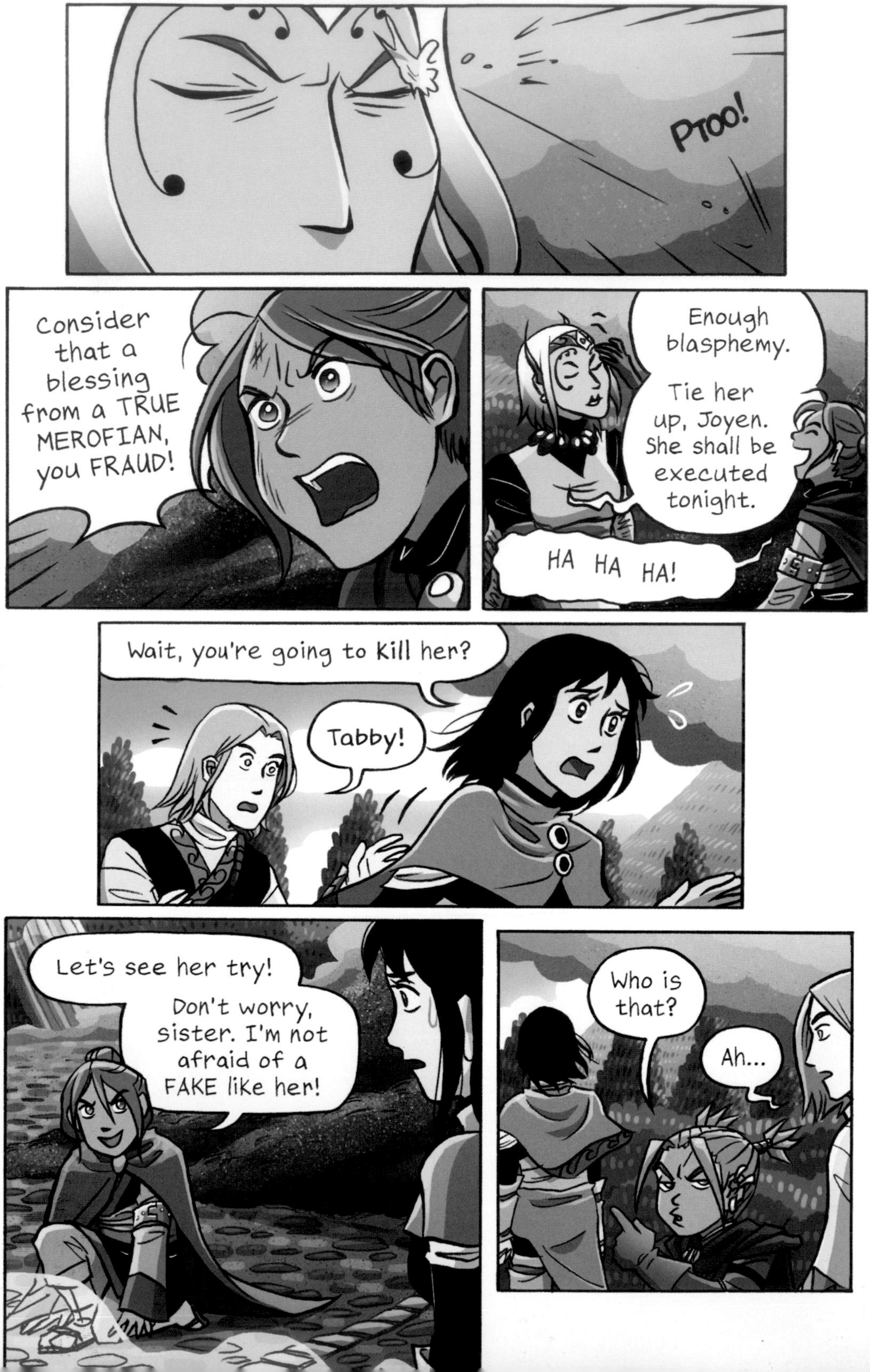
PTOO!
Consider that a blessing from a TRUE MEROFIAN, you FRAUD!
Enough blasphemy.
Tie her up, Joyen. She shall be executed tonight.
HA HA HA!
Wait, you're going to kill her?
Tabby!
Let's see her try!
Don't worry, sister. I'm not afraid of a FAKE like her!
Who is that?
Ah...

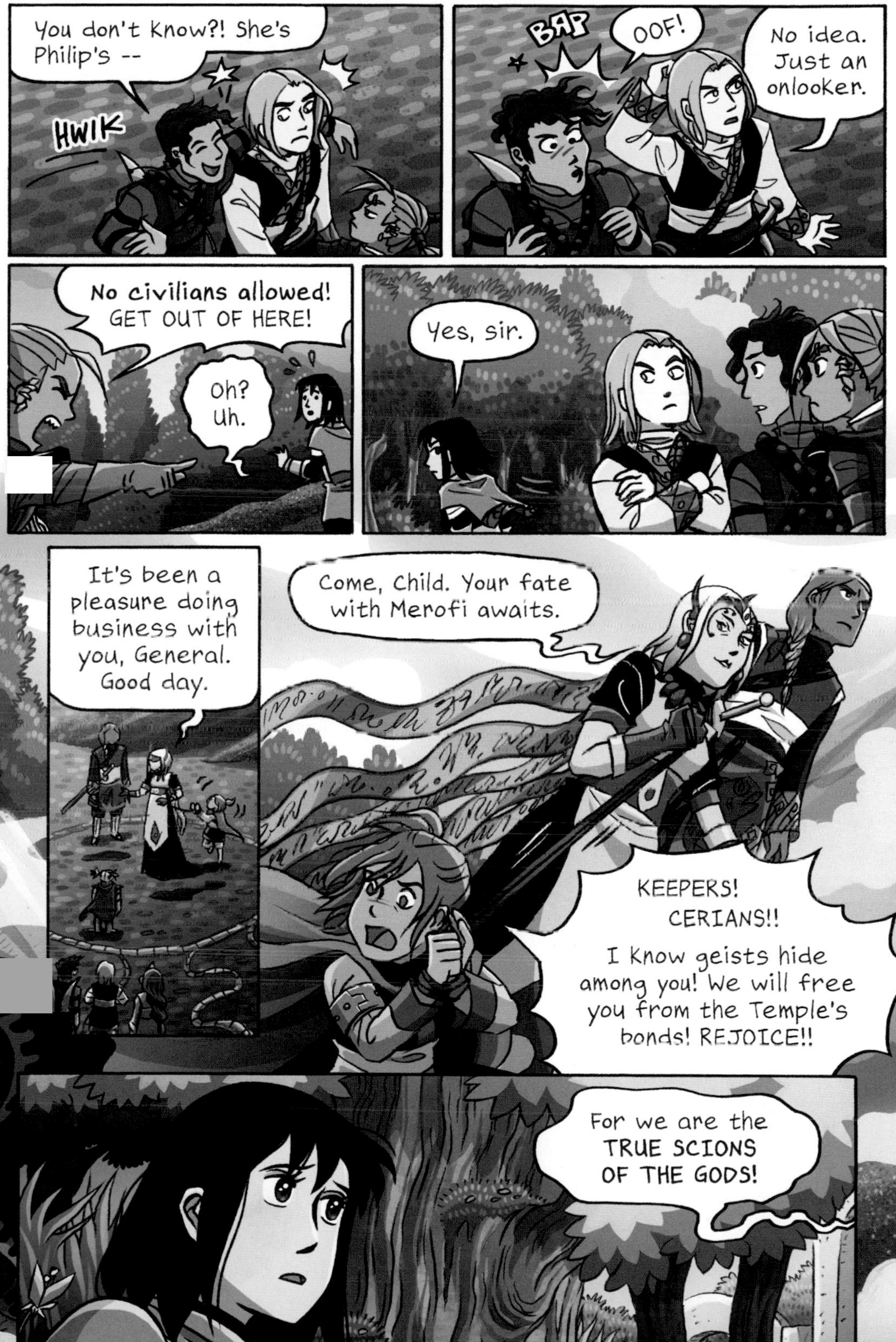
You don't Know?! She's Philip's --
HWIK
BAP
OOF!
No idea. Just an onlooker.
No civilians allowed! GET OUT OF HERE!
Oh? Uh.
Yes, sir.
It's been a pleasure doing business with you, General. Good day.
Come, Child. Your fate with Merofi awaits.
KEEPERS! CERIANS!!
I Know geists hide among you! We will free you from the Temple's bonds! REJOICE!!
For we are the TRUE SCIONS OF THE GODS!

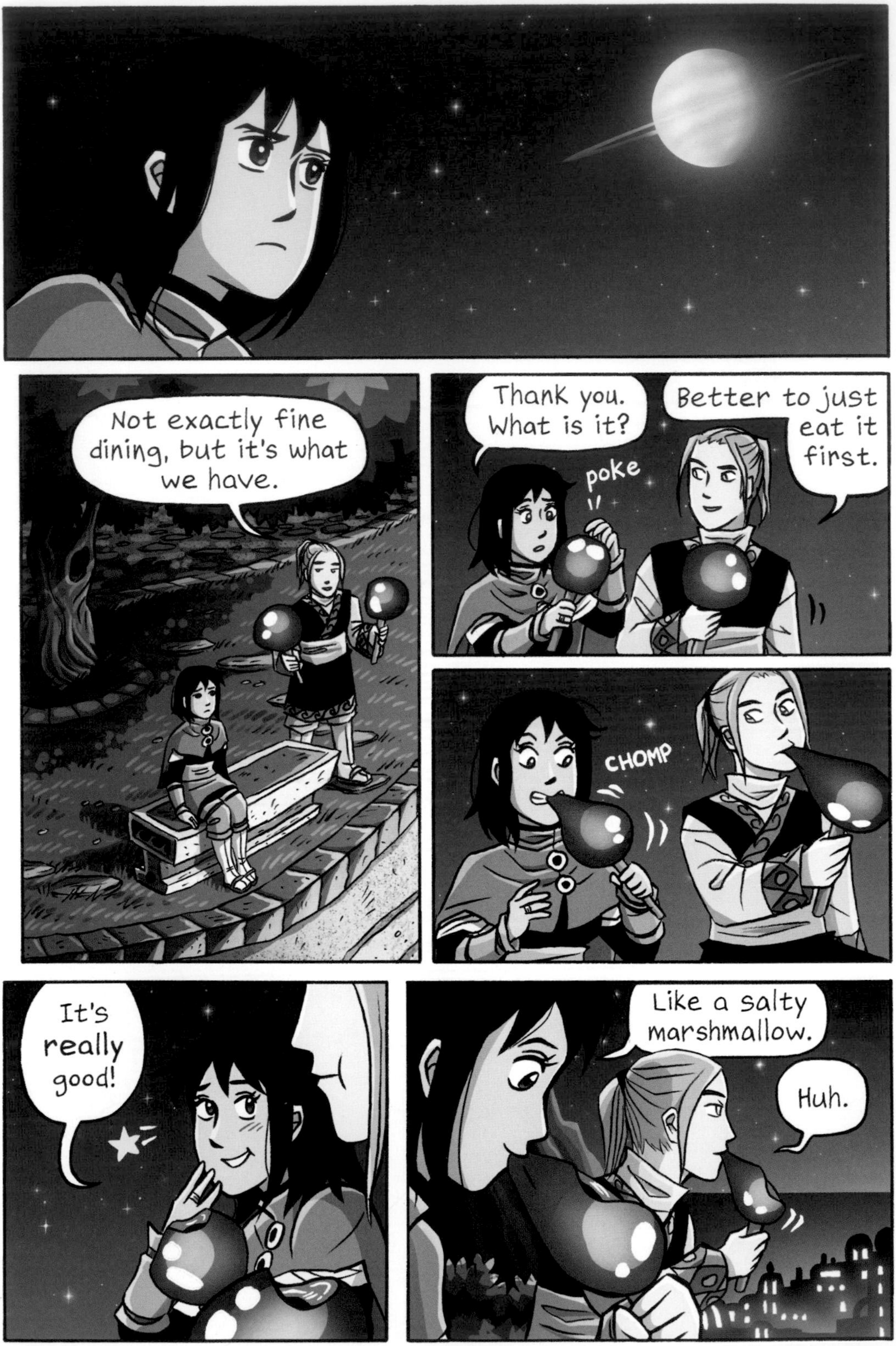
Not exactly fine dining, but it's what we have.
Thank you. What is it?
poke
Better to just eat it first.
CHOMP
It's really good!
Like a salty marshmallow.
Huh.

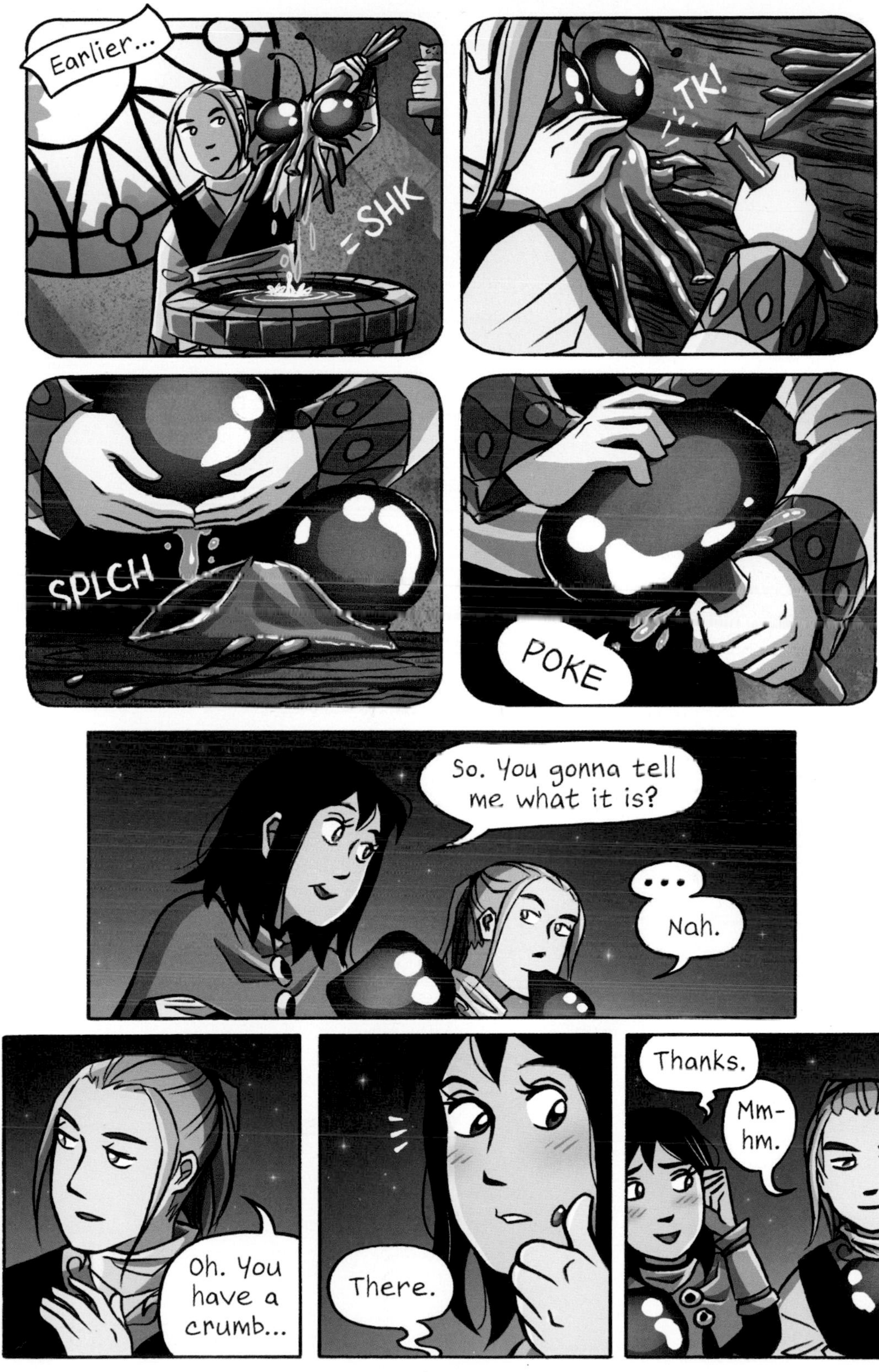
Earlier...
SHK
TK!
SPLCH
POKE
So. You gonna tell me what it is?
...
Nah.
Oh. You have a crumb...
There.
Thanks.
Mm-hm.

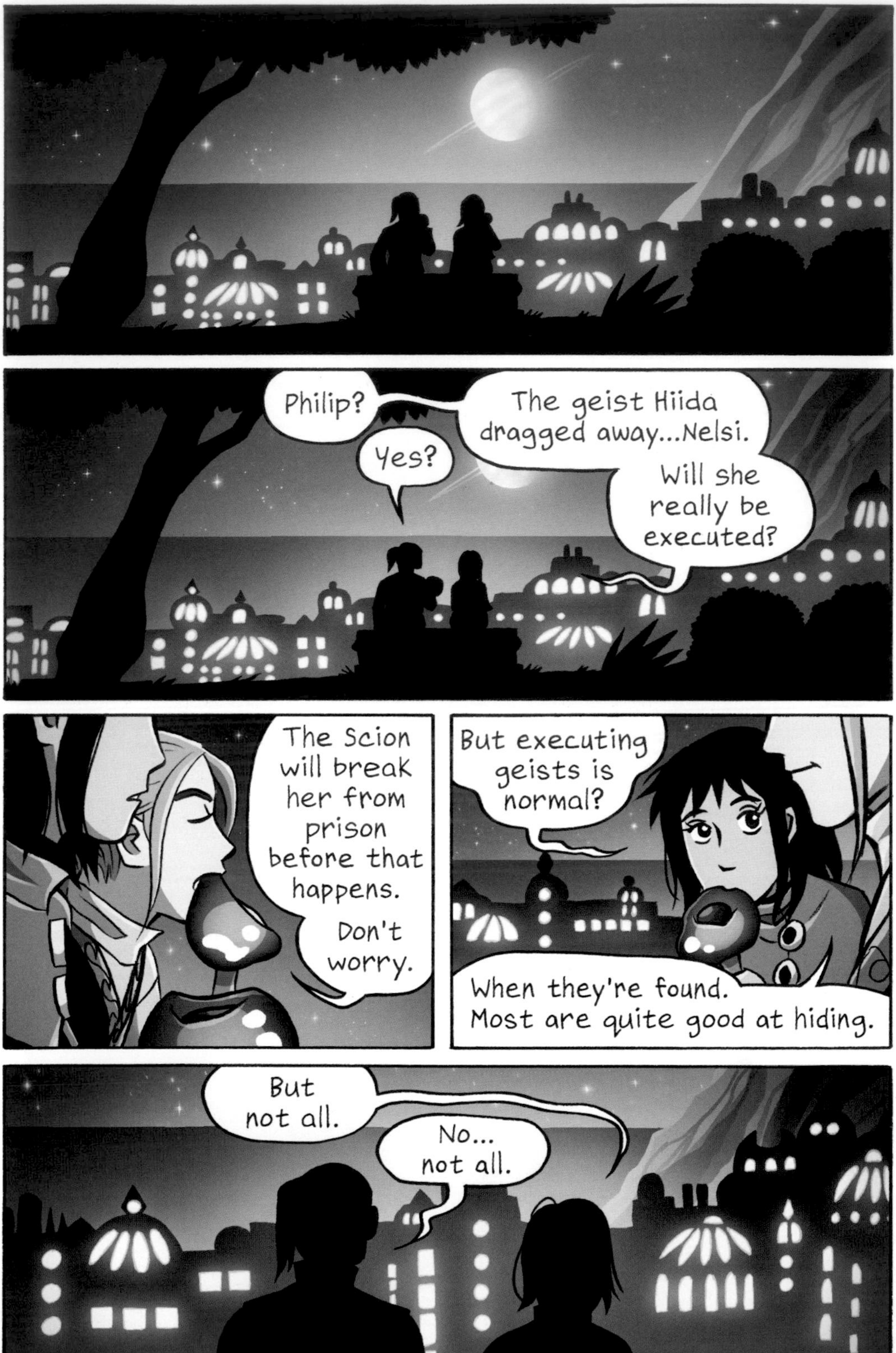
Philip?
Yes?
The geist Hiida dragged away...Nelsi.
Will she really be executed?
The Scion will break her from prison before that happens.
Don't worry.
But executing geists is normal?
When they're found. Most are quite good at hiding.
But not all.
No... not all.

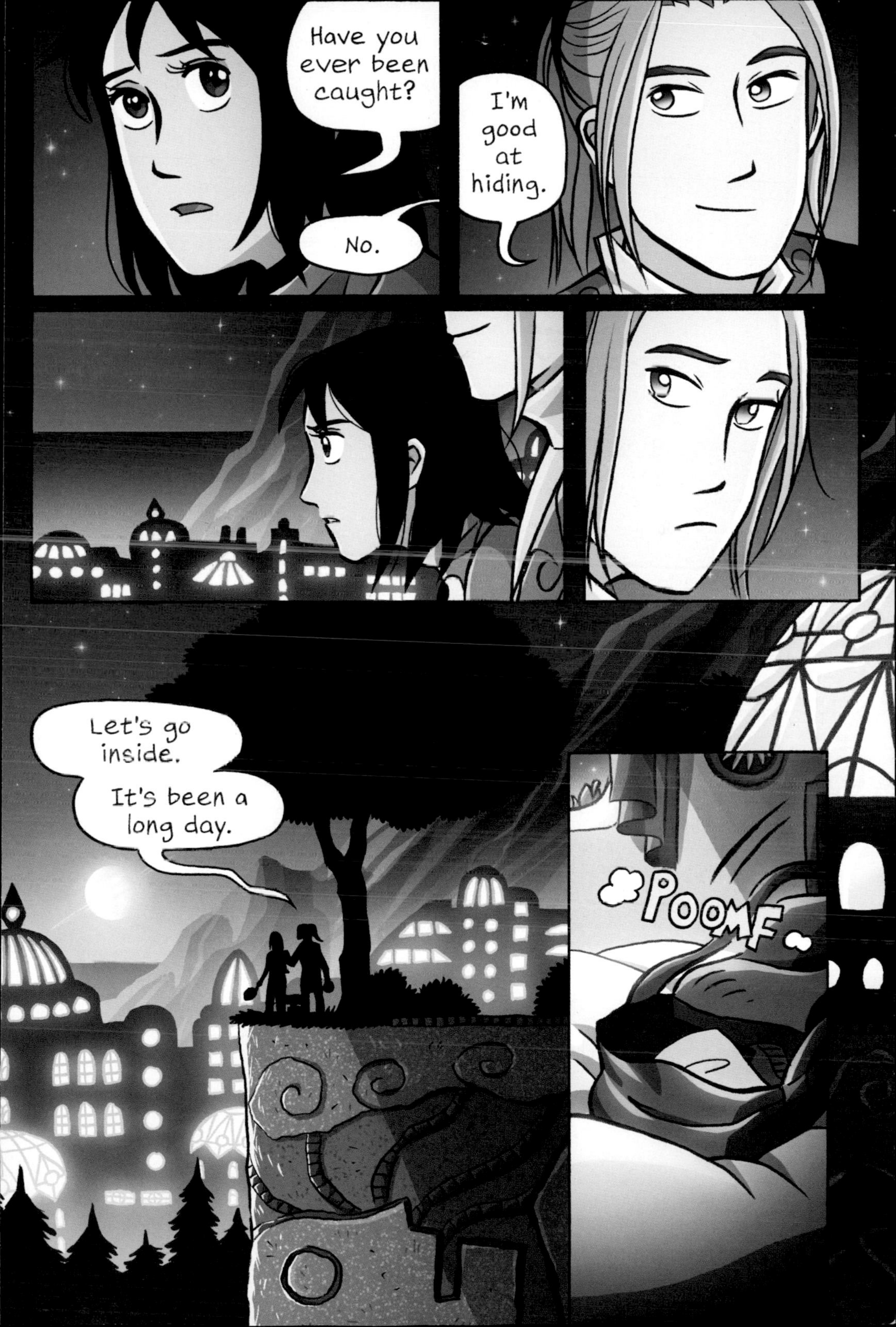
Have you ever been caught?
No.
I'm good at hiding.
Let's go inside.
It's been a long day.
POOMF

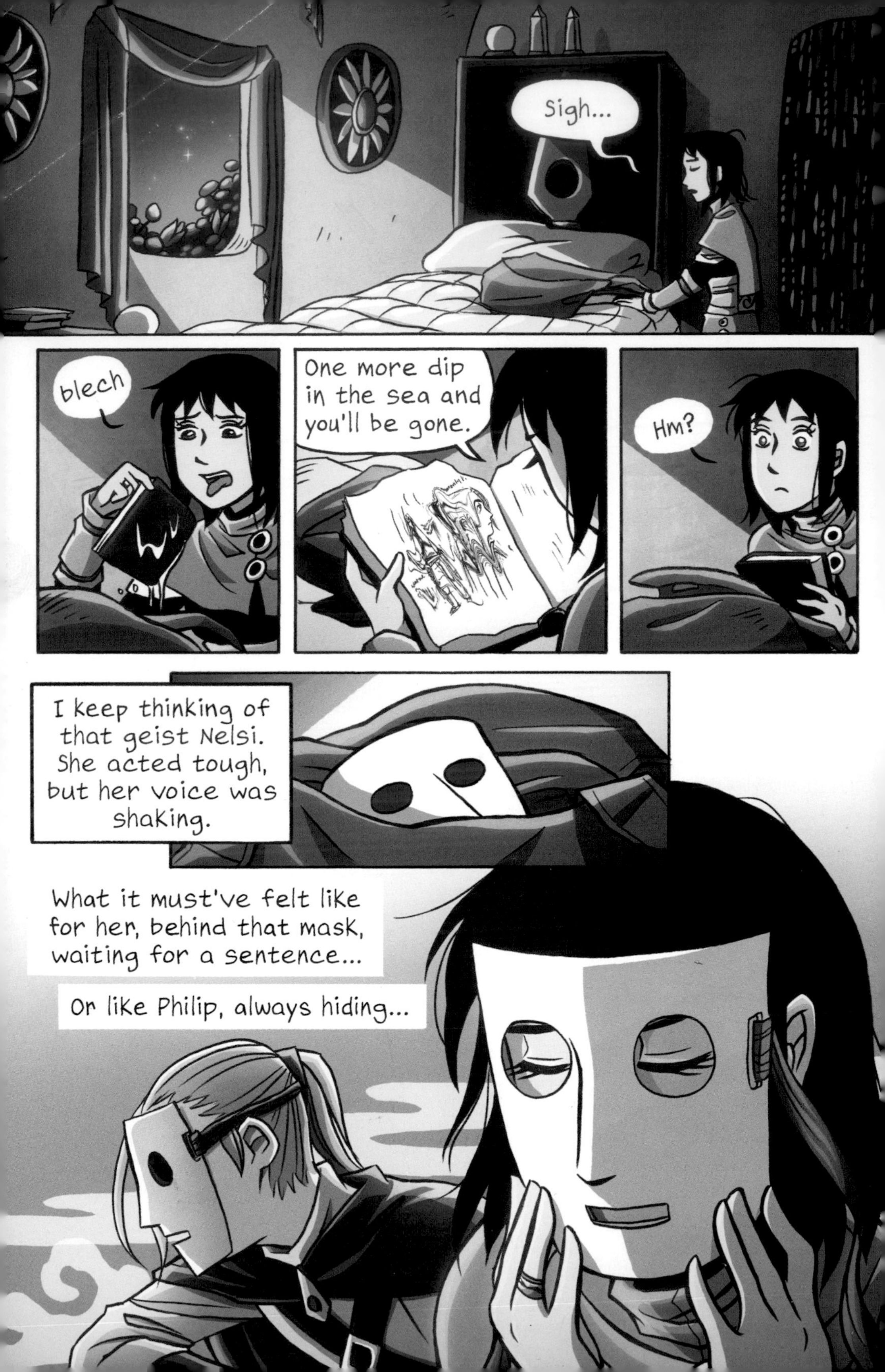
Sigh...
blech
One more dip
in the sea and
you'll be gone.
Hm?
I keep thinking of that geist Nelsi. She acted tough, but her voice was shaking.
What it must've felt like for her, behind that mask, waiting for a sentence...
Or like Philip, always hiding...

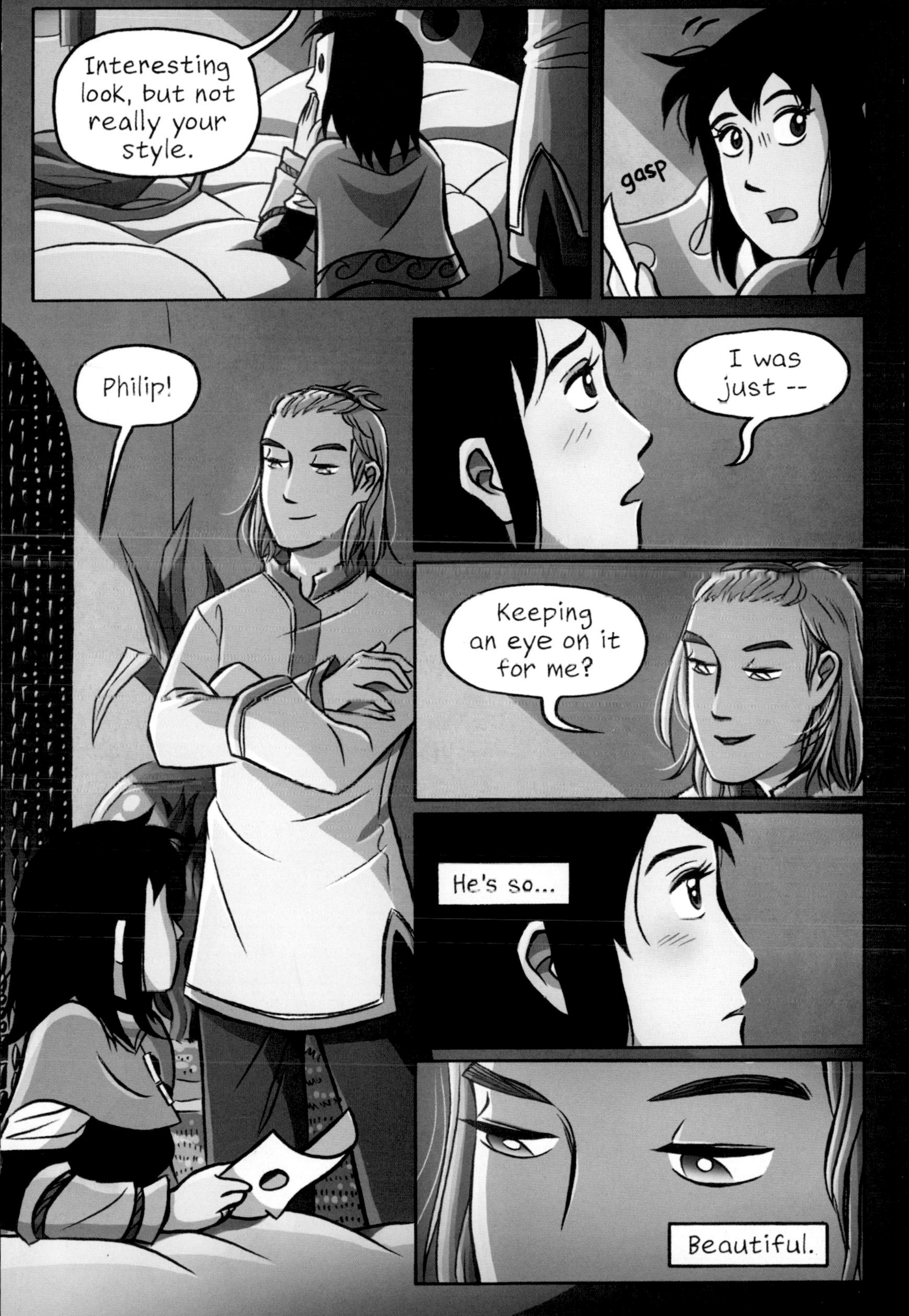

Interesting look, but not really your style.
gasp
Philip!
I was just --
Keeping an eye on it for me?
He's so...
Beautiful.

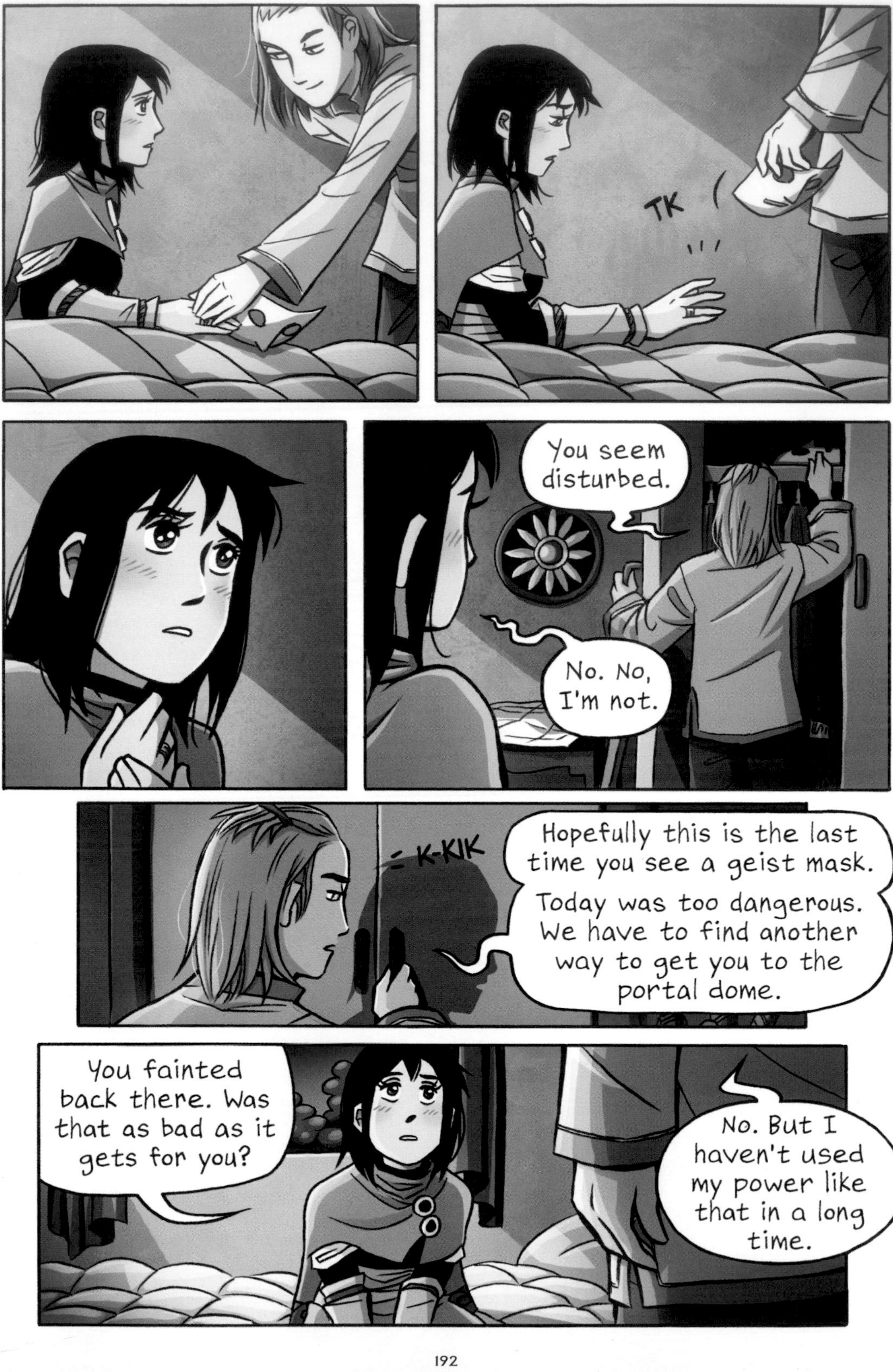
TK
You seem disturbed.
No. No, I'm not.
K-KIK
Hopefully this is the last time you see a geist mask.
Today was too dangerous. We have to find another way to get you to the portal dome.
You fainted back there. Was that as bad as it gets for you?
No. But I haven't used my power like that in a long time.

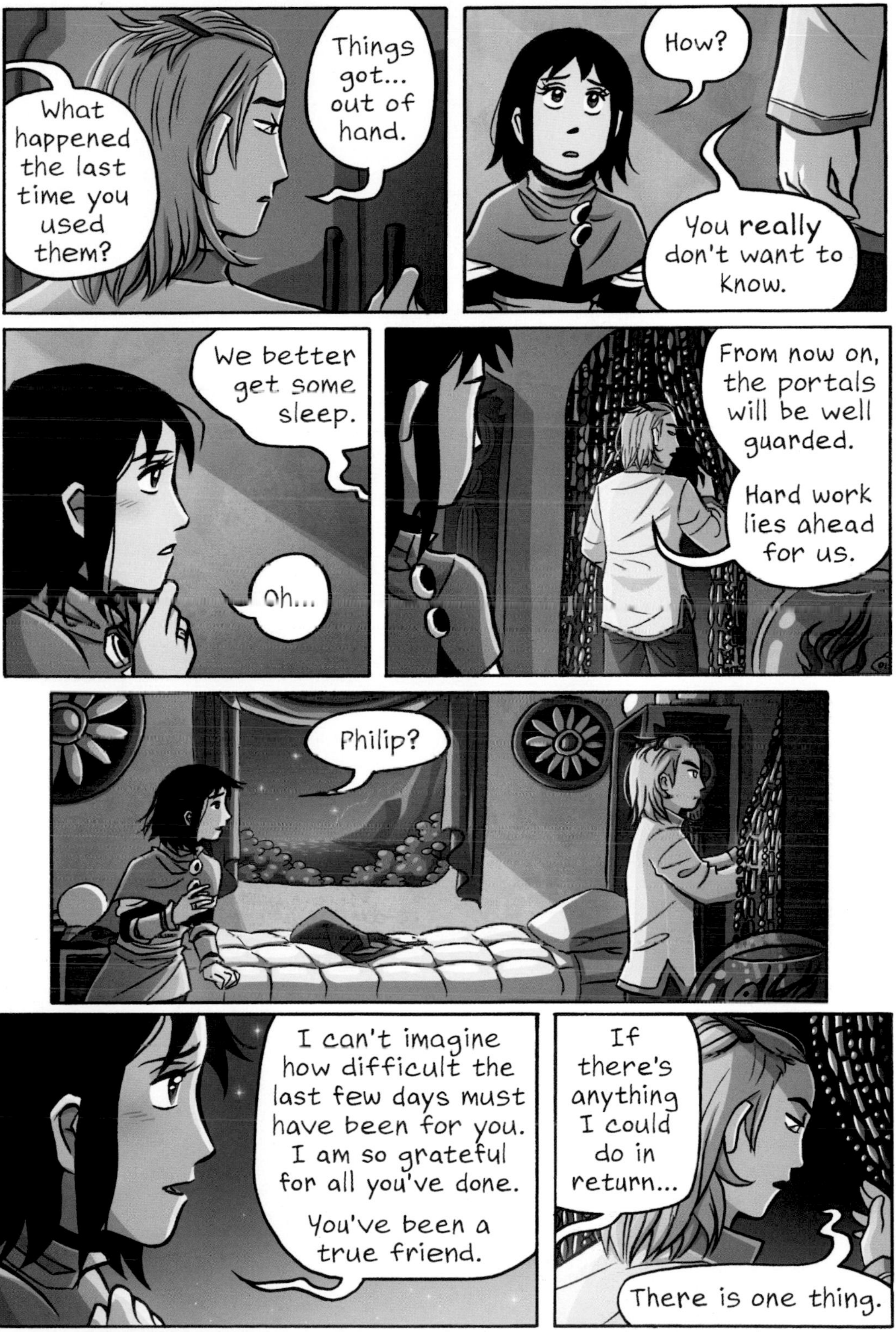
What happened the last time you used them?
Things got... out of hand.
How?
You **really** don't want to know.
We better get some sleep.
Oh...
From now on, the portals will be well guarded.
Hard work lies ahead for us.
Philip?
I can't imagine how difficult the last few days must have been for you. I am so grateful for all you've done.
You've been a true friend.
If there's anything I could do in return...
There is one thing.

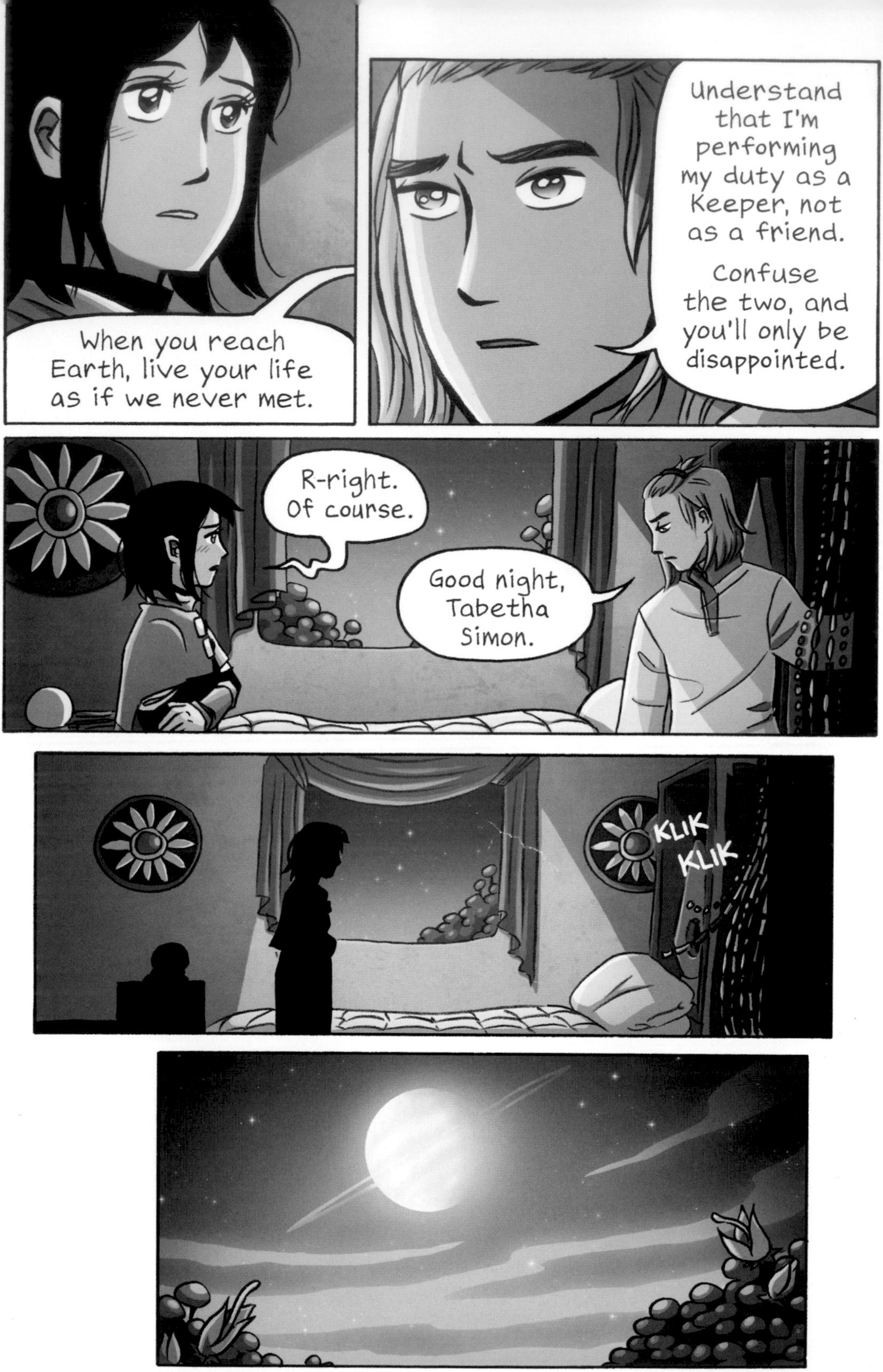
When you reach Earth, live your life as if we never met.
Understand that I'm performing my duty as a Keeper, not as a friend.
Confuse the two, and you'll only be disappointed.
R-right. Of course.
Good night, Tabetha Simon.
KLIK
KLIK

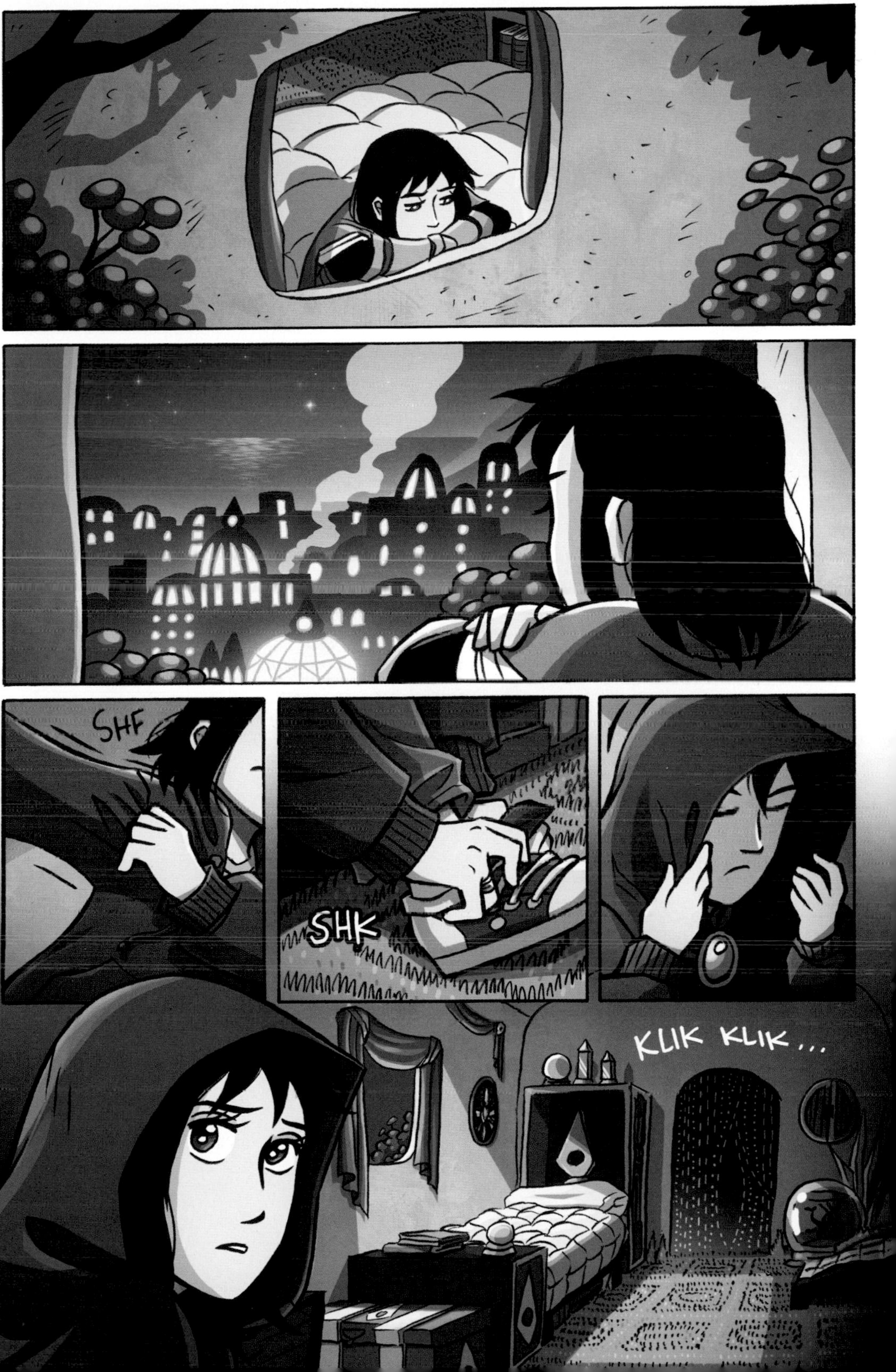
SHF
SHK
KLIK KLIK...

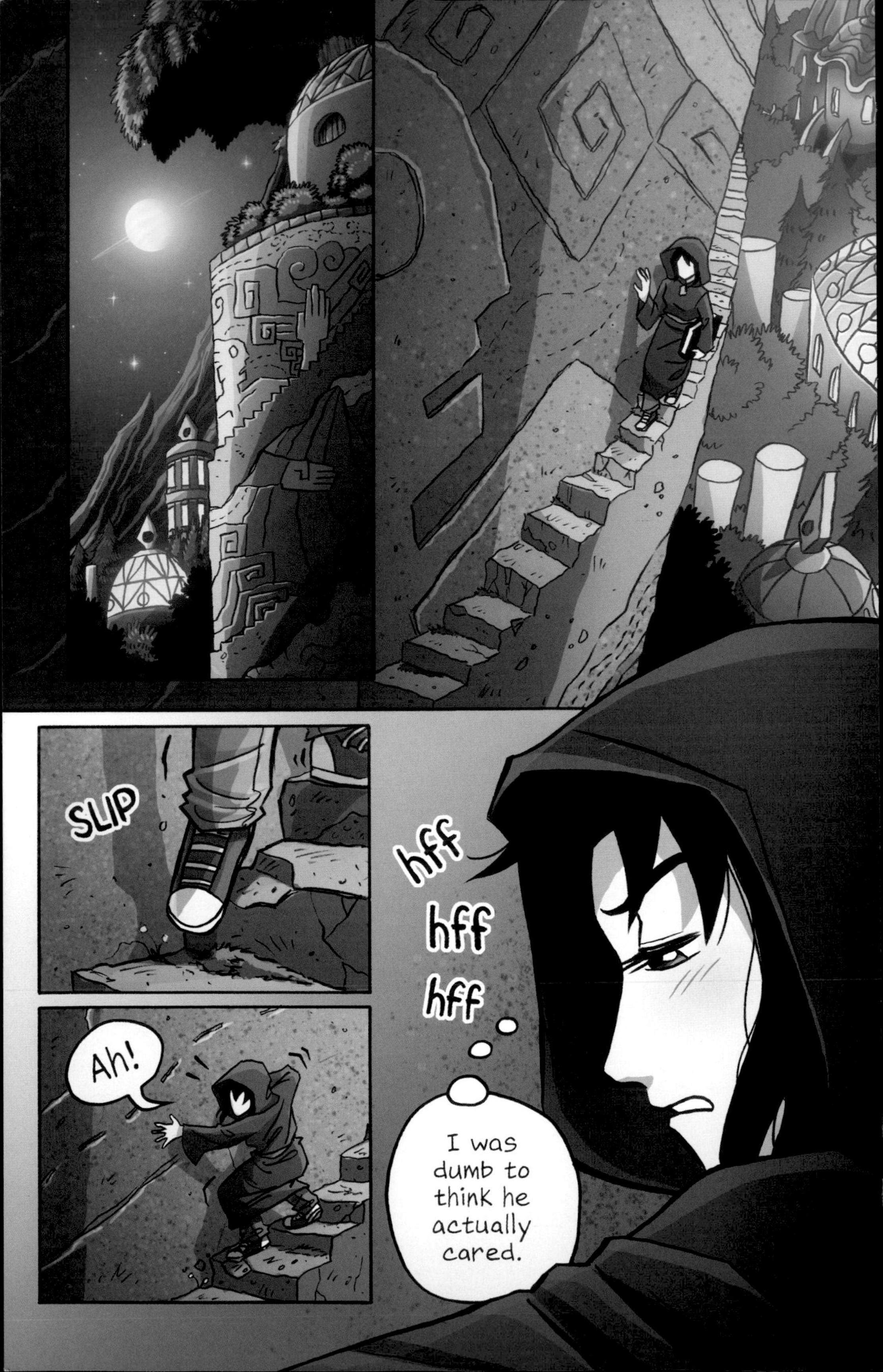
SLIP
Ah!
hff
hff
hff
I was dumb to think he actually cared.

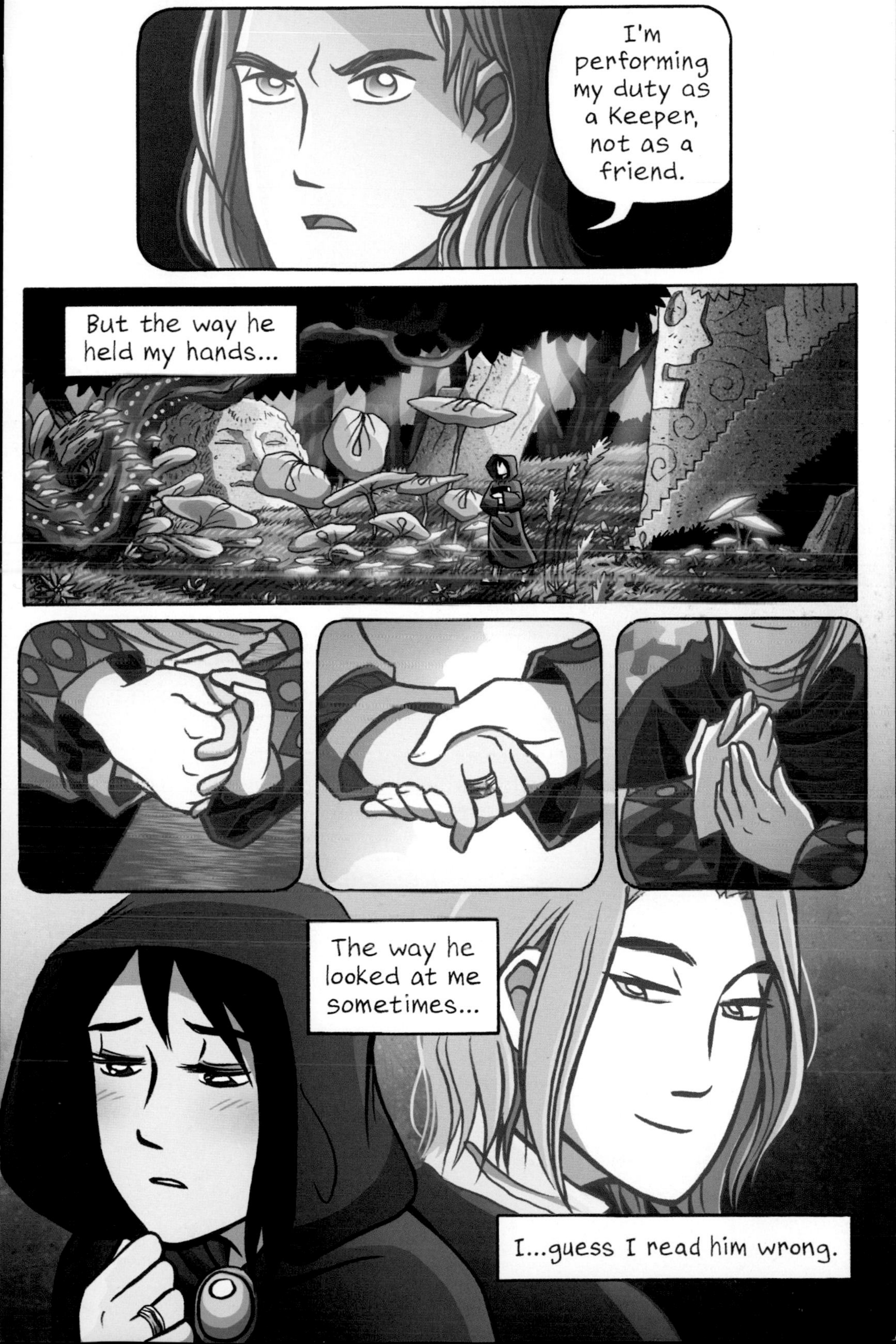
I'm performing my duty as a Keeper, not as a friend.
But the way he held my hands...
The way he looked at me sometimes...
I...guess I read him wrong.

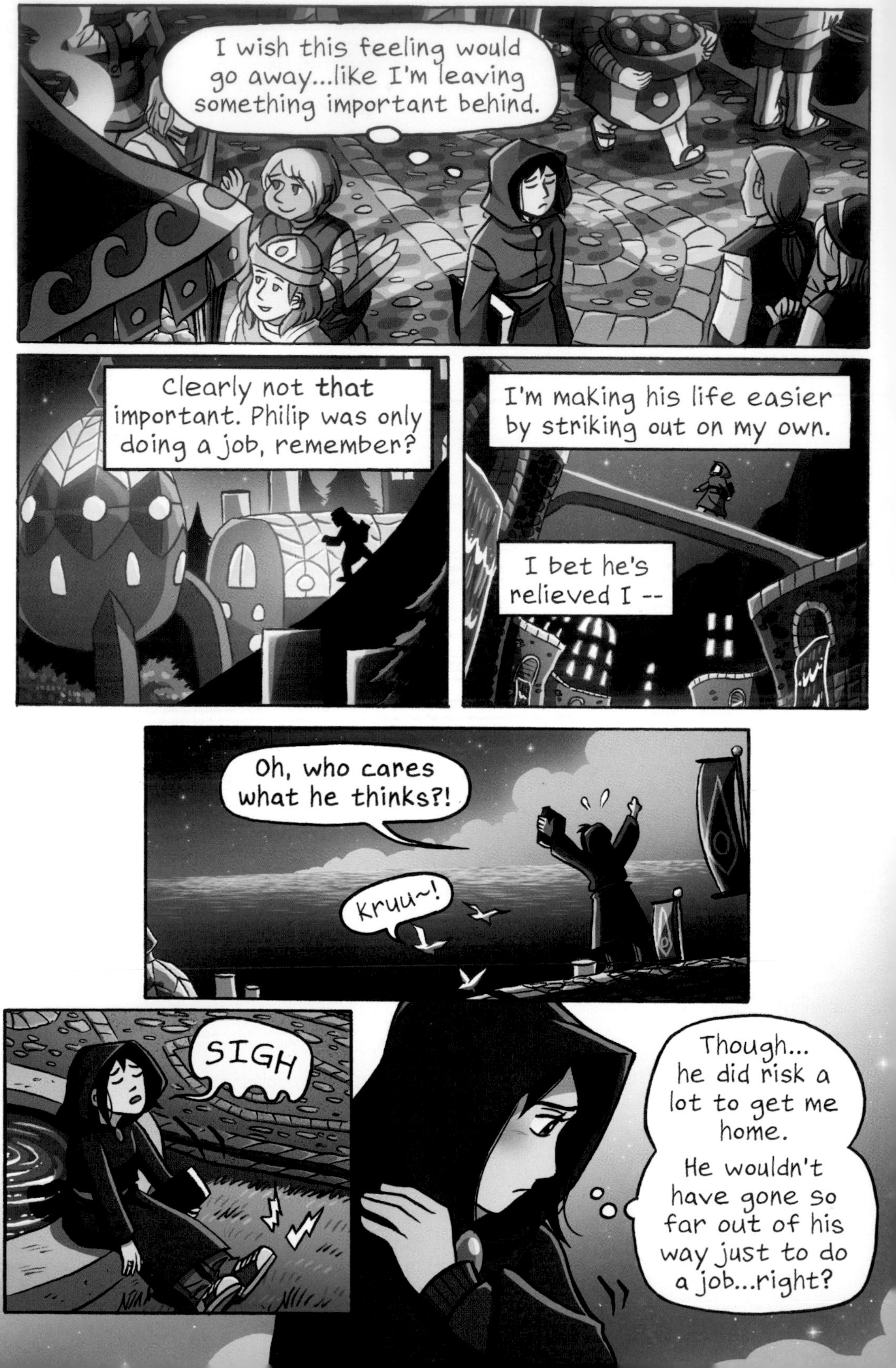
I wish this feeling would go away...like I'm leaving something important behind.
Clearly not that important. Philip was only doing a job, remember?
I'm making his life easier by striking out on my own.
I bet he's relieved I --
Oh, who cares what he thinks?!
Kruu~!
SIGH
Though... he did risk a lot to get me home.
He wouldn't have gone so far out of his way just to do a job...right?

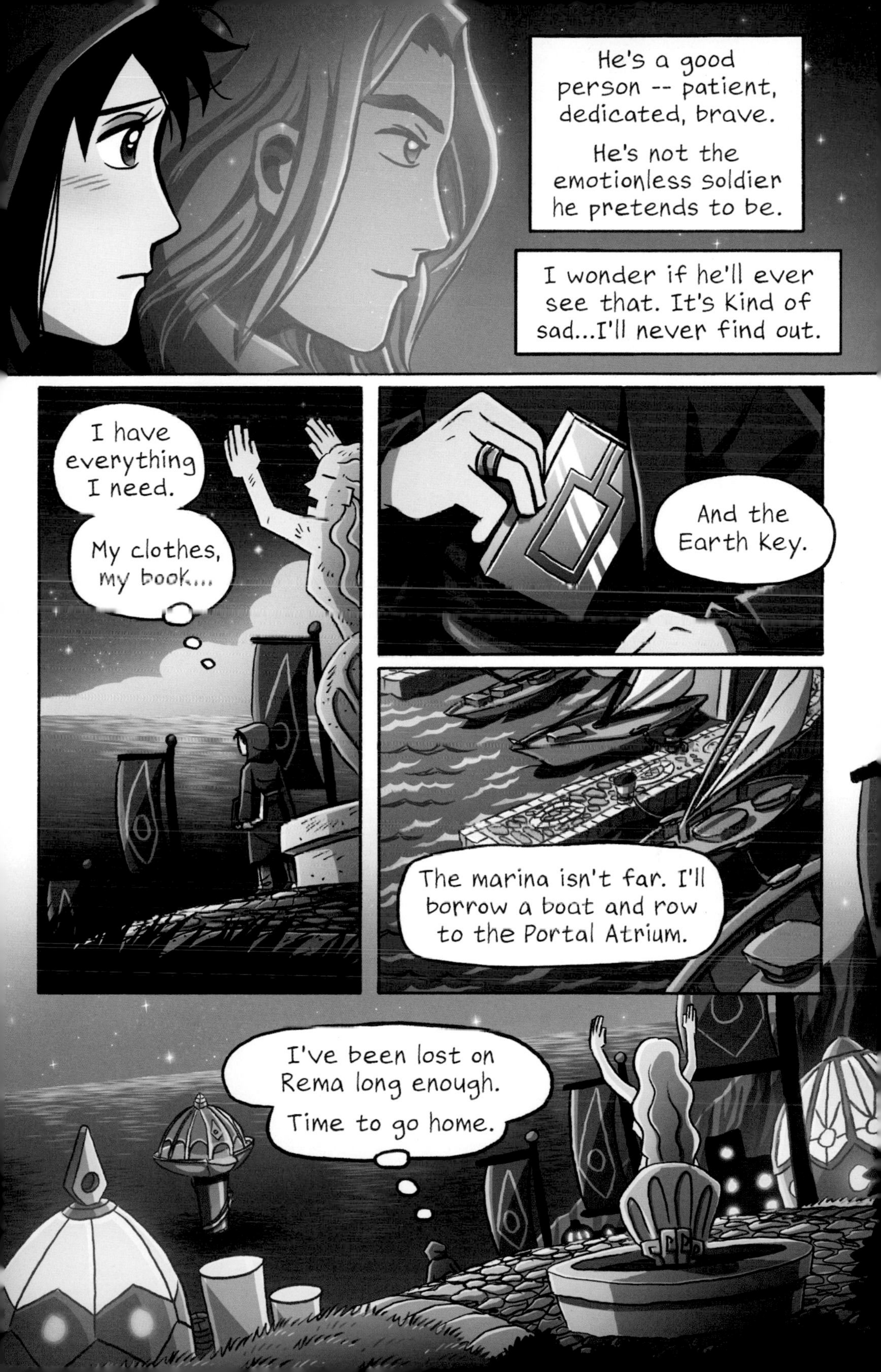
He's a good person -- patient, dedicated, brave.
He's not the emotionless soldier he pretends to be.
I wonder if he'll ever see that. It's kind of sad...I'll never find out.
I have everything I need.
My clothes, my book...
And the Earth Key.
The marina isn't far. I'll borrow a boat and row to the Portal Atrium.
I've been lost on Rema long enough.
Time to go home.

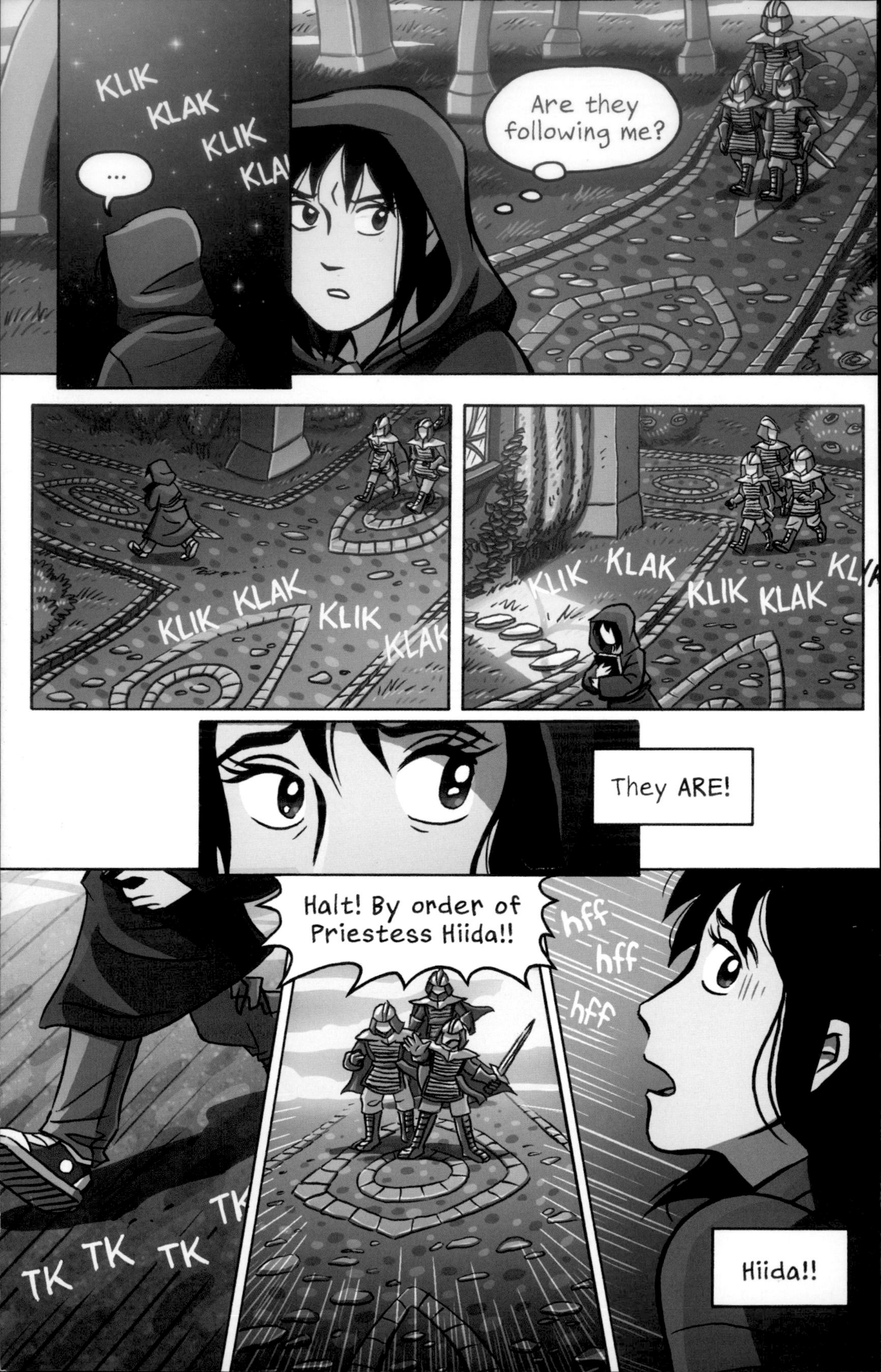
KLIK
KLAK
KLIK
KLAK
...
Are they following me?
KLIK KLAK KLIK KLAK
KLIK KLAK KLIK KLAK
They ARE!
Halt! By order of Priestess Hiida!!
hff
hff
hff
TK TK TK TK
Hiida!!

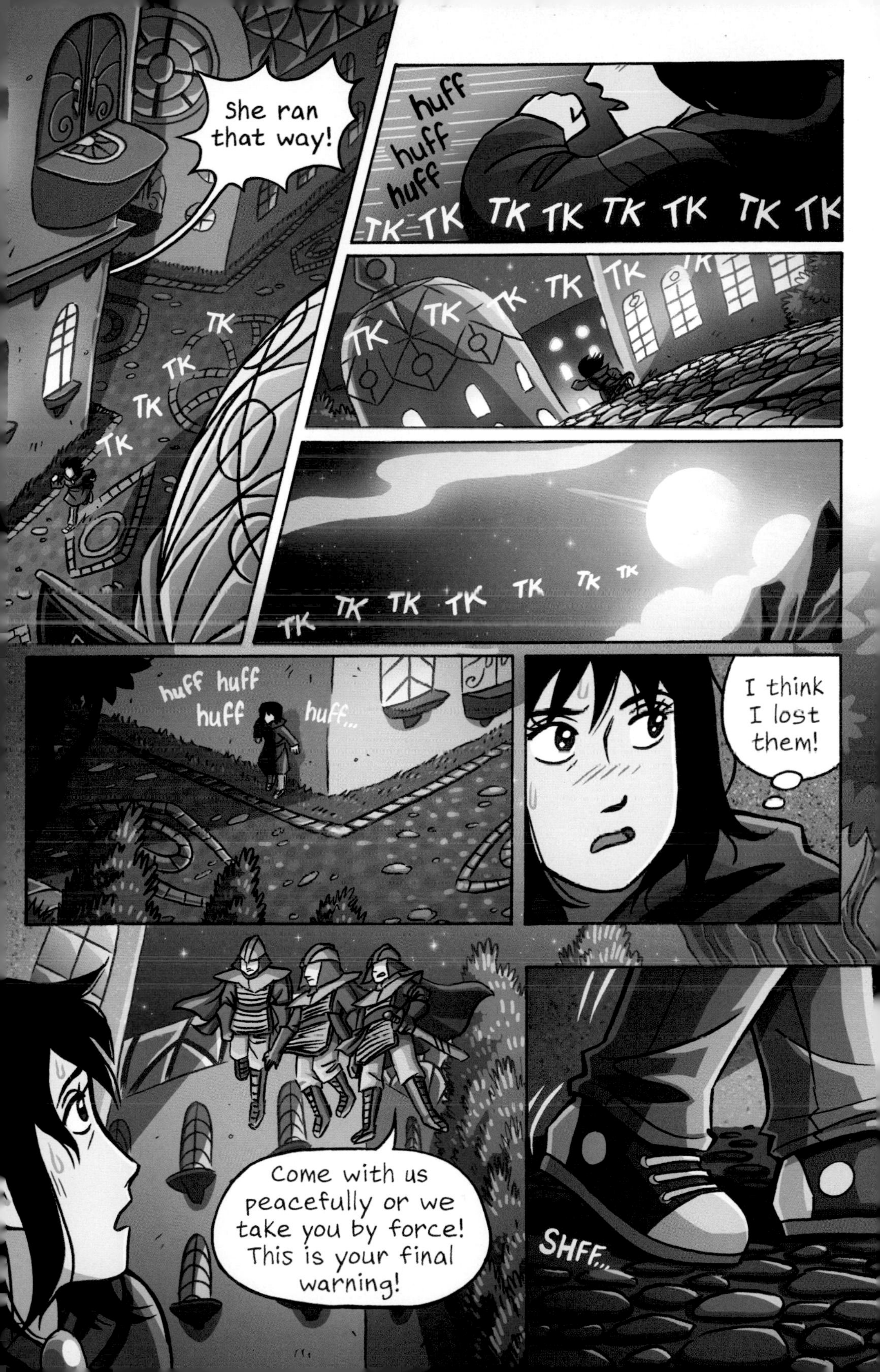
She ran that way!
huff huff huff
TK TK TK TK TK TK TK TK
TK TK TK TK
TK TK TK TK TK
TK TK TK TK TK TK TK
huff huff huff huff...
I think I lost them!
Come with us peacefully or we take you by force! This is your final warning!
SHFF...

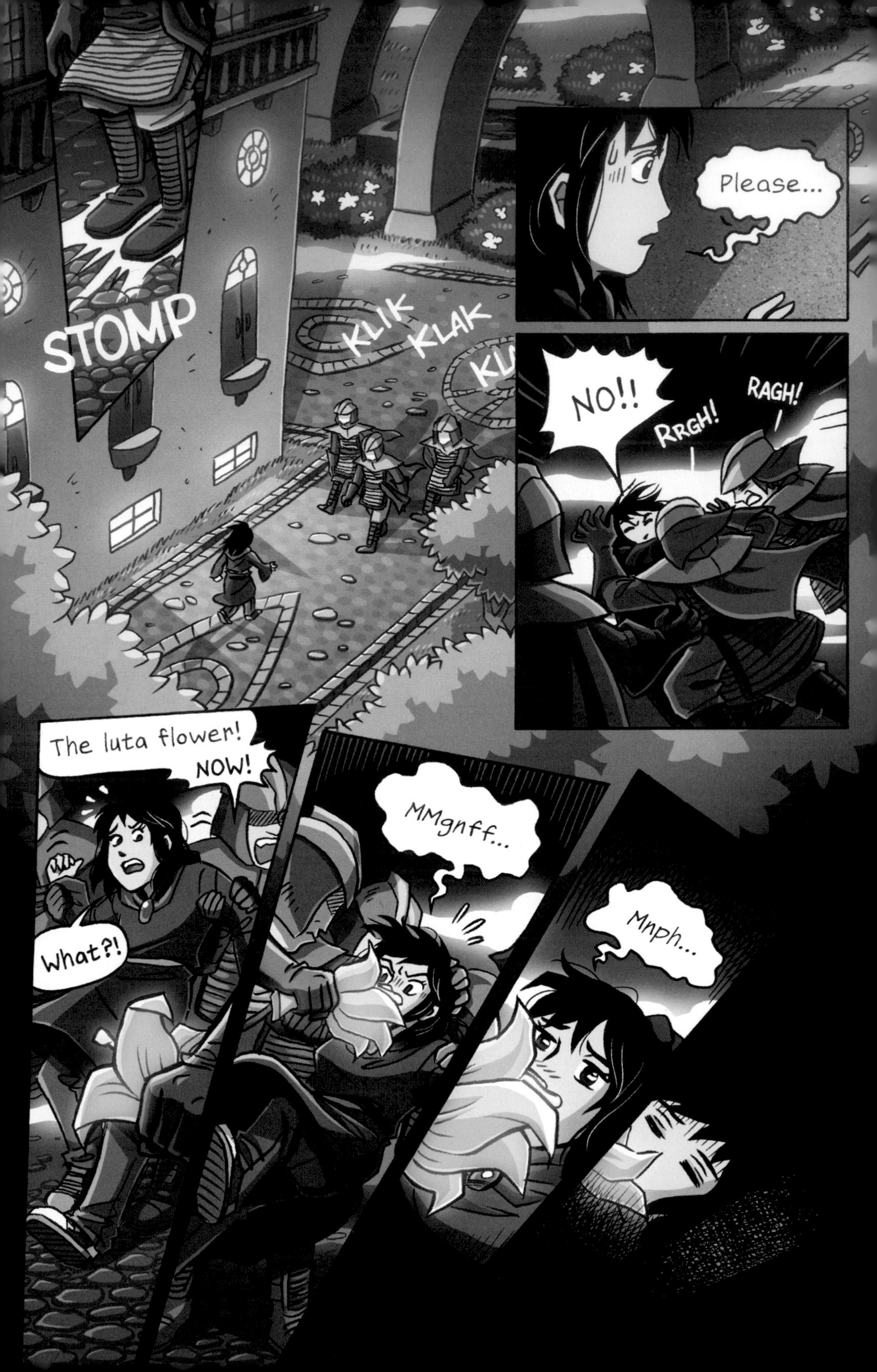
STOMP
KLIK
KLAK
KL
Please...
NO!!
RRGH!
RAGH!
The luta flower!
NOW!
What?!
MMgnff...
Mnph...

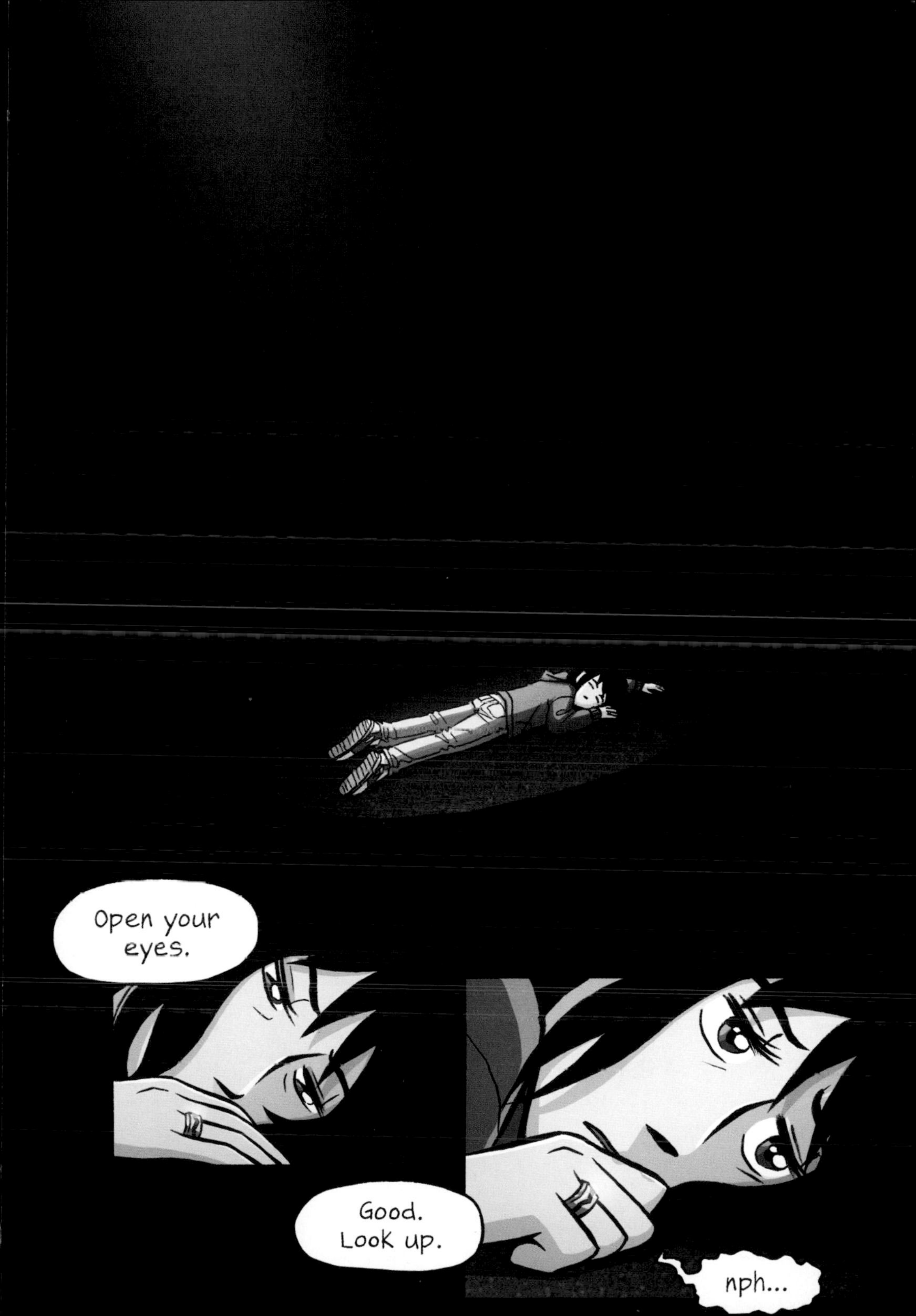
Open your eyes.
Good. Look up.
nph...

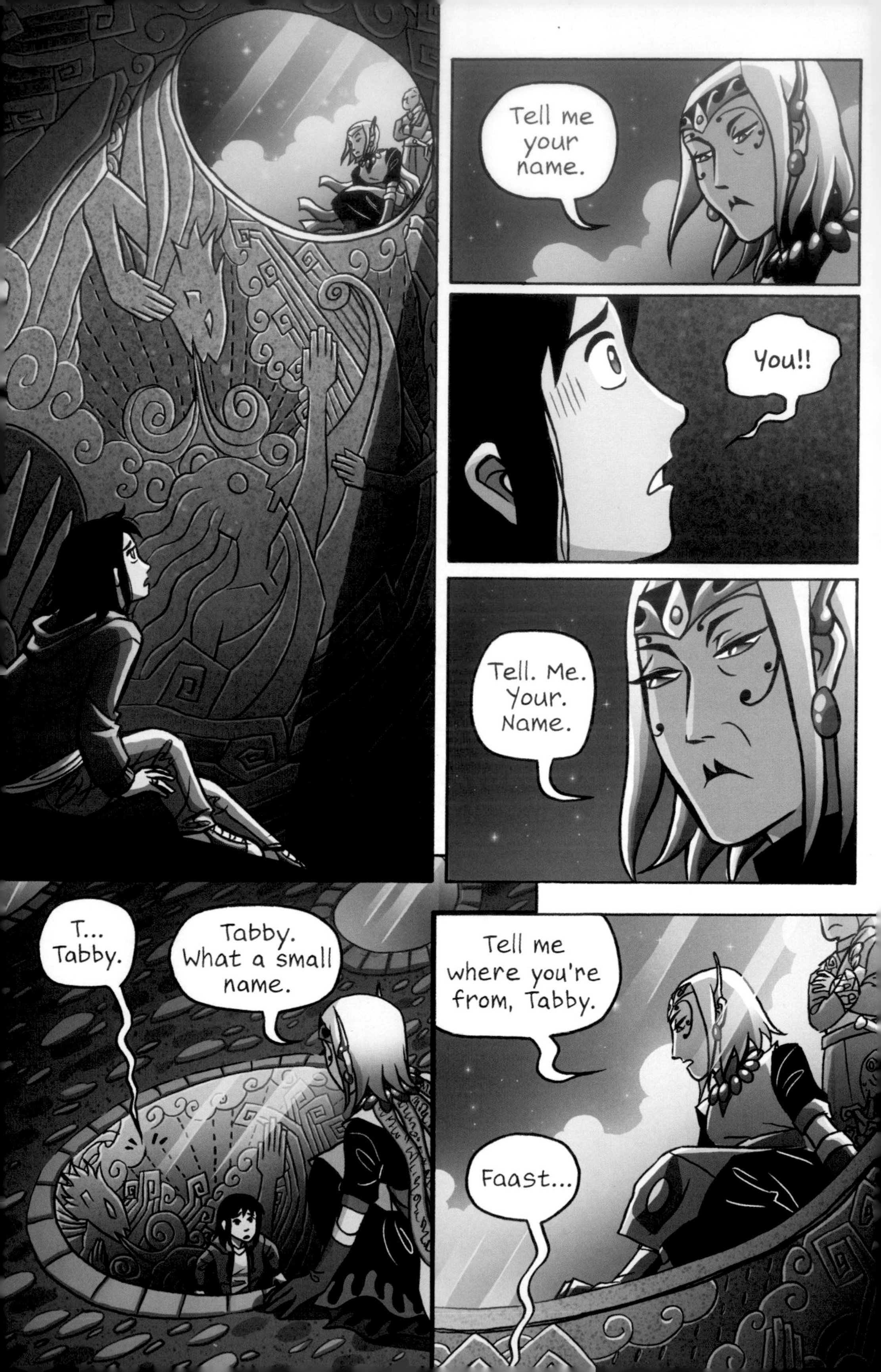
Tell me your name.
You!!
Tell. Me. Your. Name.
T... Tabby.
Tabby. What a small name.
Tell me where you're from, Tabby.
Faast...

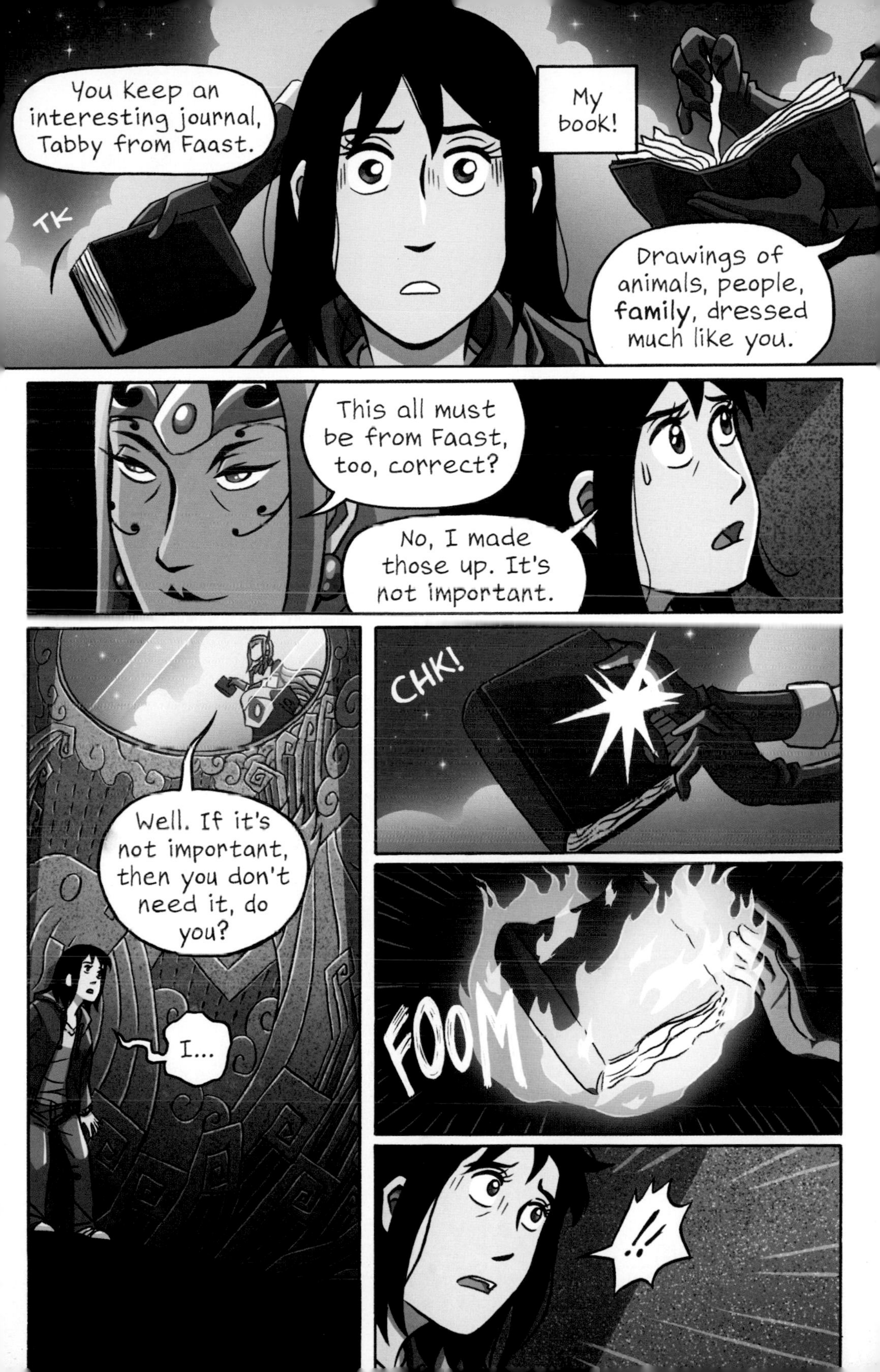
You keep an interesting journal, Tabby from Faast.
My book!
TK
Drawings of animals, people, family, dressed much like you.
This all must be from Faast, too, correct?
No, I made those up. It's not important.
Well. If it's not important, then you don't need it, do you?
I...
CHK!
FOOM
!!

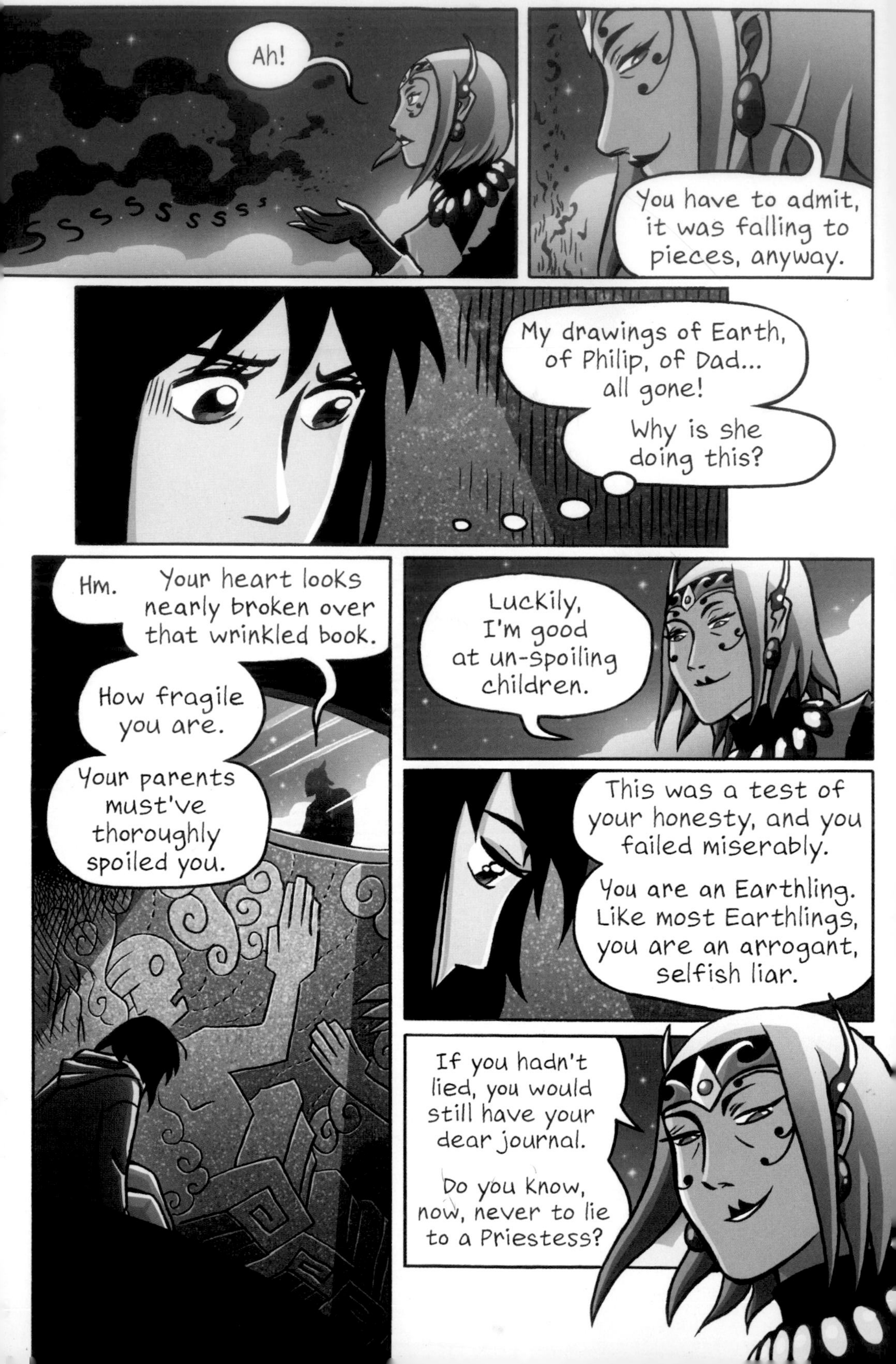
Ah!
SSSSSSSSS
You have to admit, it was falling to pieces, anyway.
My drawings of Earth, of Philip, of Dad... all gone!
Why is she doing this?
Hm.
Your heart looks nearly broken over that wrinkled book.
How fragile you are.
Your parents must've thoroughly spoiled you.
Luckily, I'm good at un-spoiling children.
This was a test of your honesty, and you failed miserably.
You are an Earthling. Like most Earthlings, you are an arrogant, selfish liar.
If you hadn't lied, you would still have your dear journal.
Do you know, now, never to lie to a Priestess?

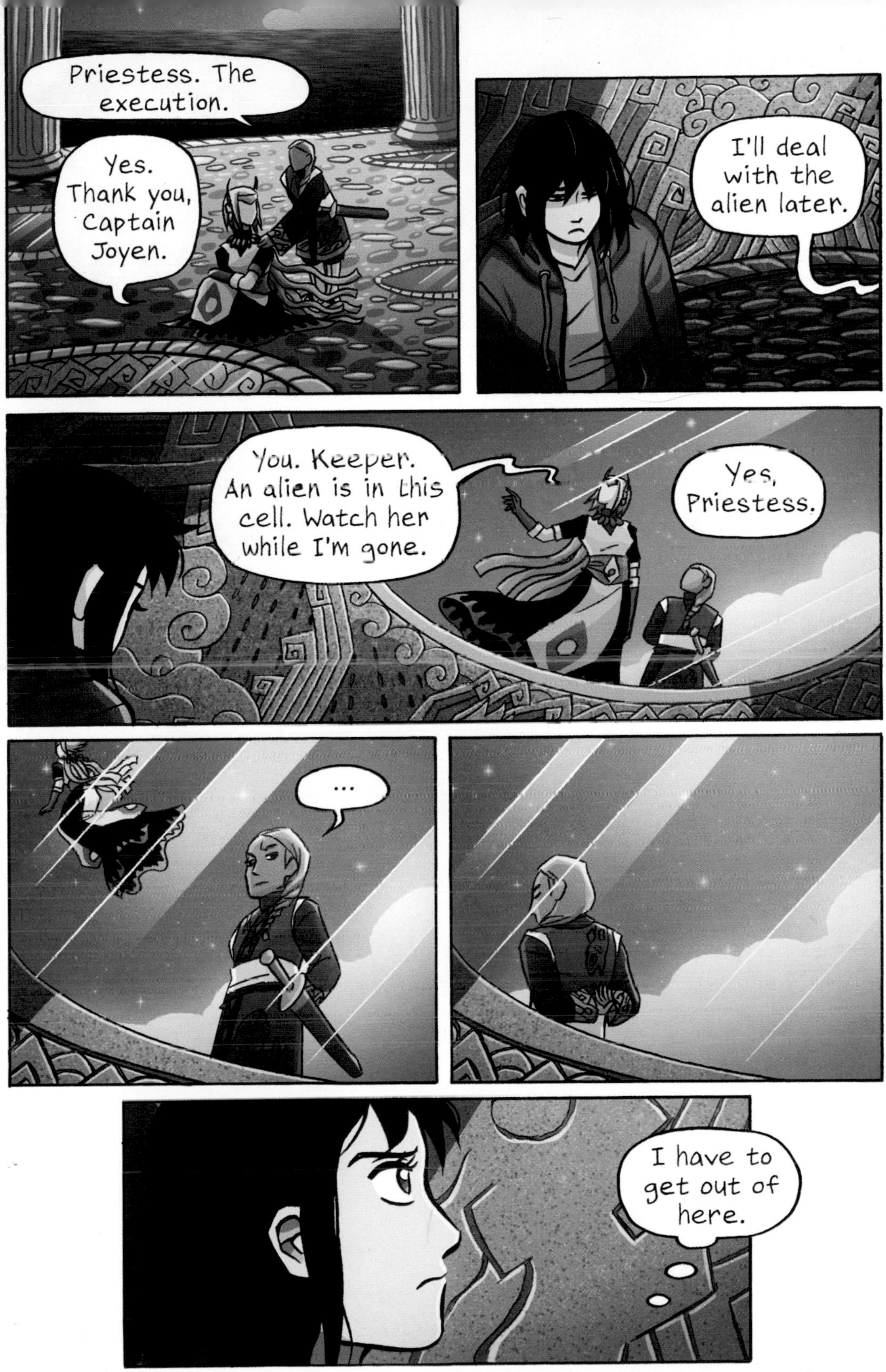

Priestess. The execution.
Yes. Thank you, Captain Joyen.
I'll deal with the alien later.
You. Keeper. An alien is in this cell. Watch her while I'm gone.
Yes, Priestess.
...
I have to get out of here.

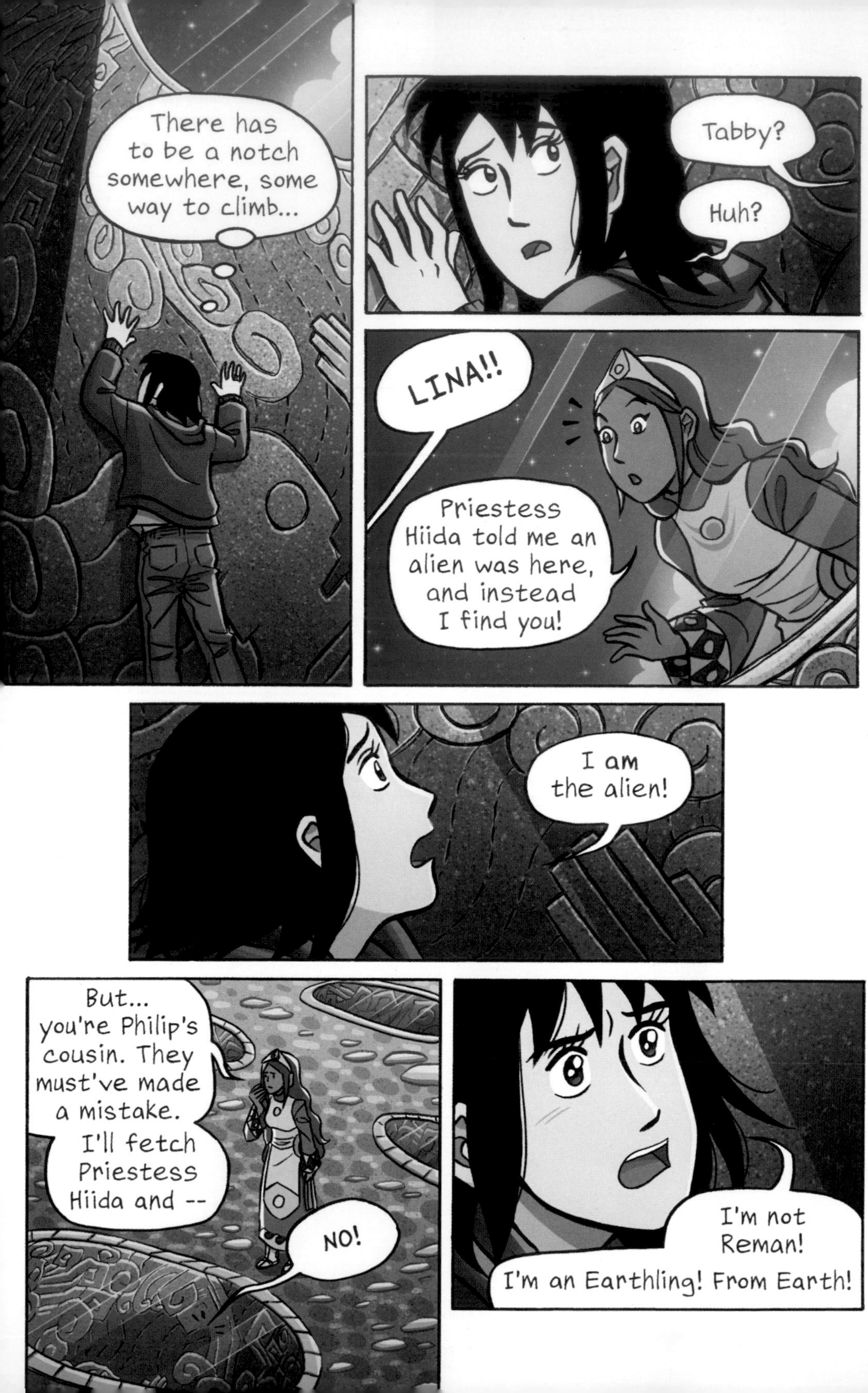
There has to be a notch somewhere, some way to climb...
Tabby?
Huh?
LINA!!
Priestess Hiida told me an alien was here, and instead I find you!
I am the alien!
But... you're Philip's cousin. They must've made a mistake.
I'll fetch Priestess Hiida and --
NO!
I'm not Reman!
I'm an Earthling! From Earth!

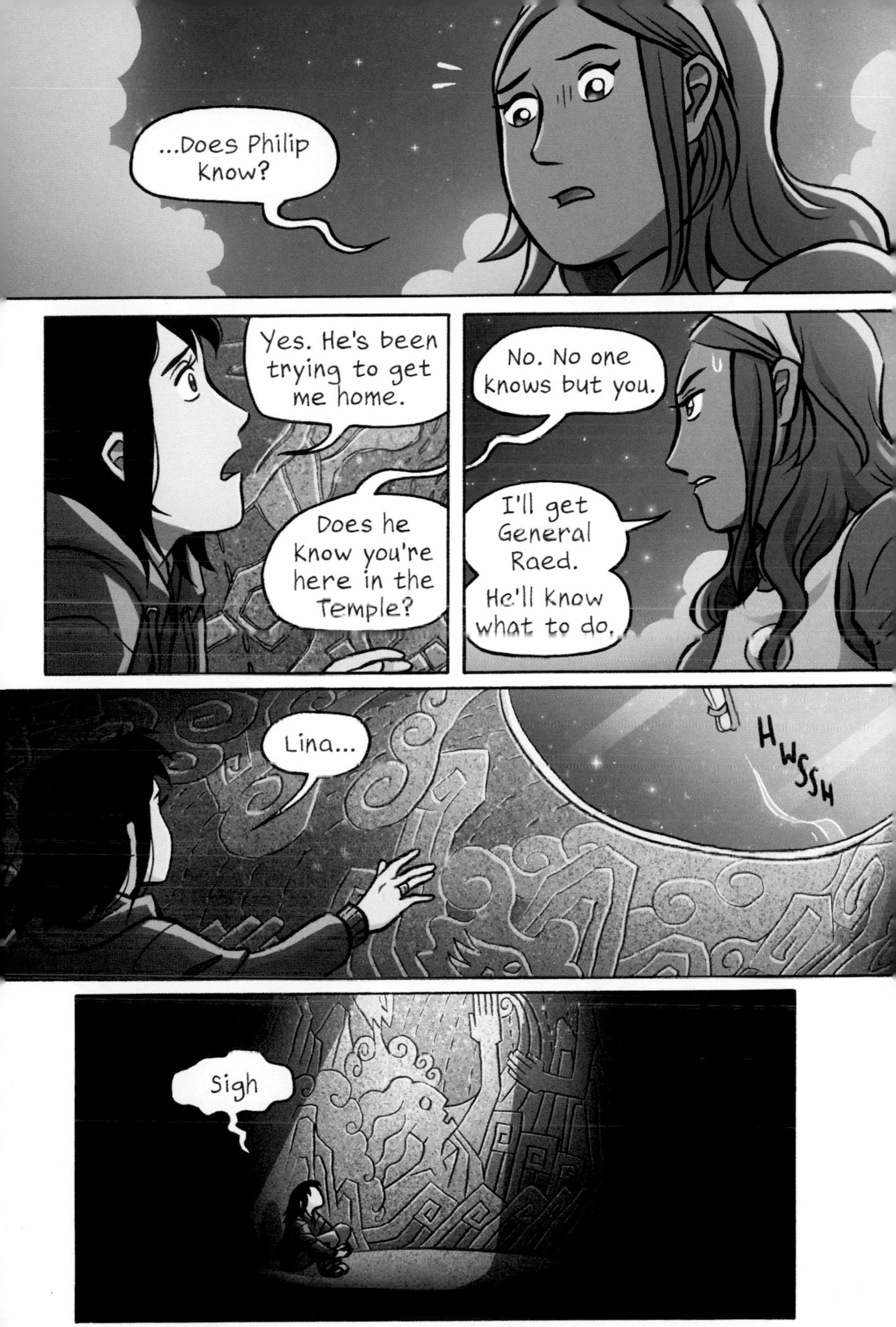
...Does Philip Know?
Yes. He's been trying to get me home.
No. No one knows but you.
Does he Know you're here in the Temple?
I'll get General Raed.
He'll Know what to do.
Lina...
HWSSH
Sigh

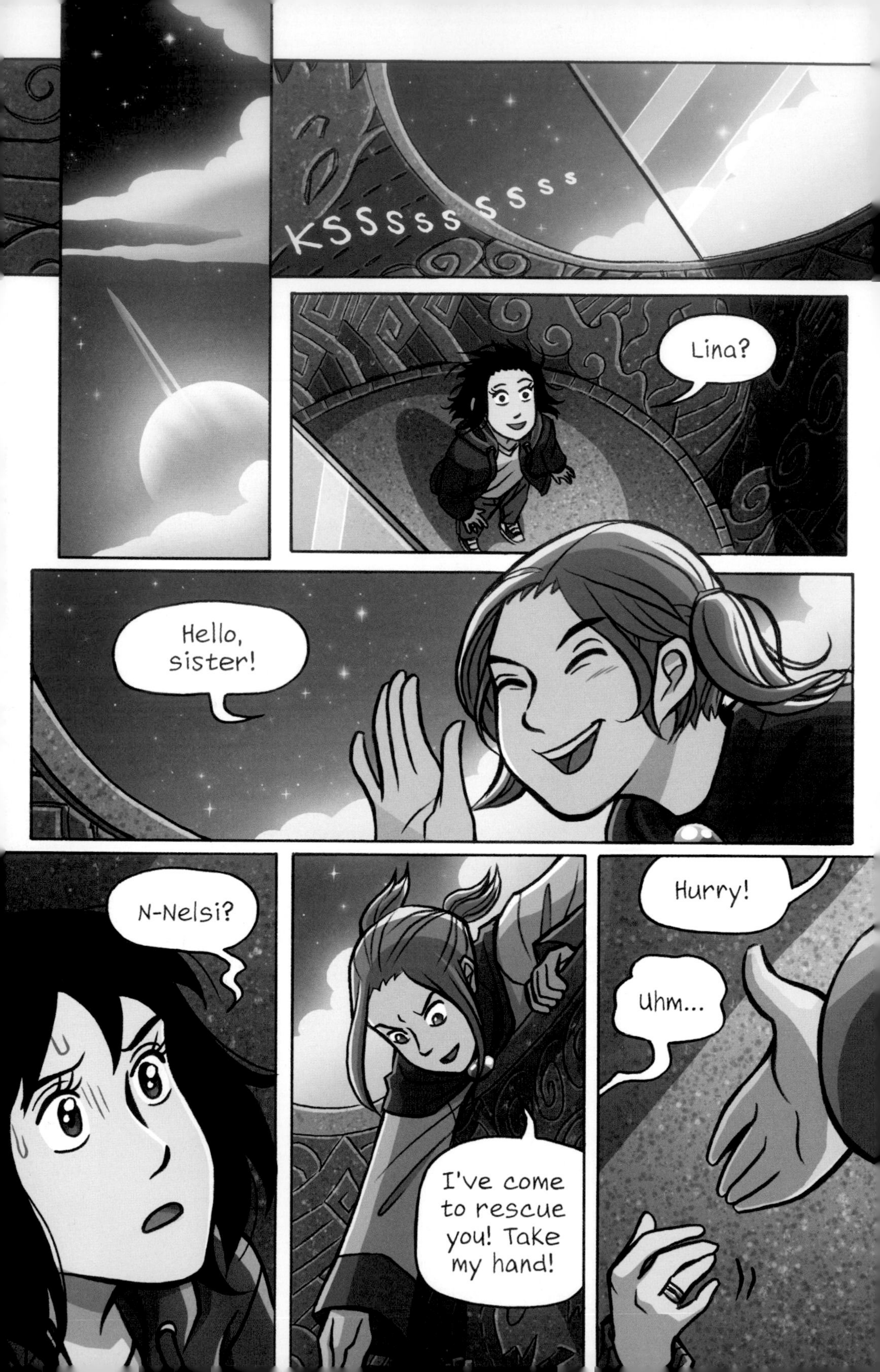
KSSSSSSSSSS
Lina?
Hello, sister!
N-Nelsi?
I've come to rescue you! Take my hand!
Hurry!
Uhm...

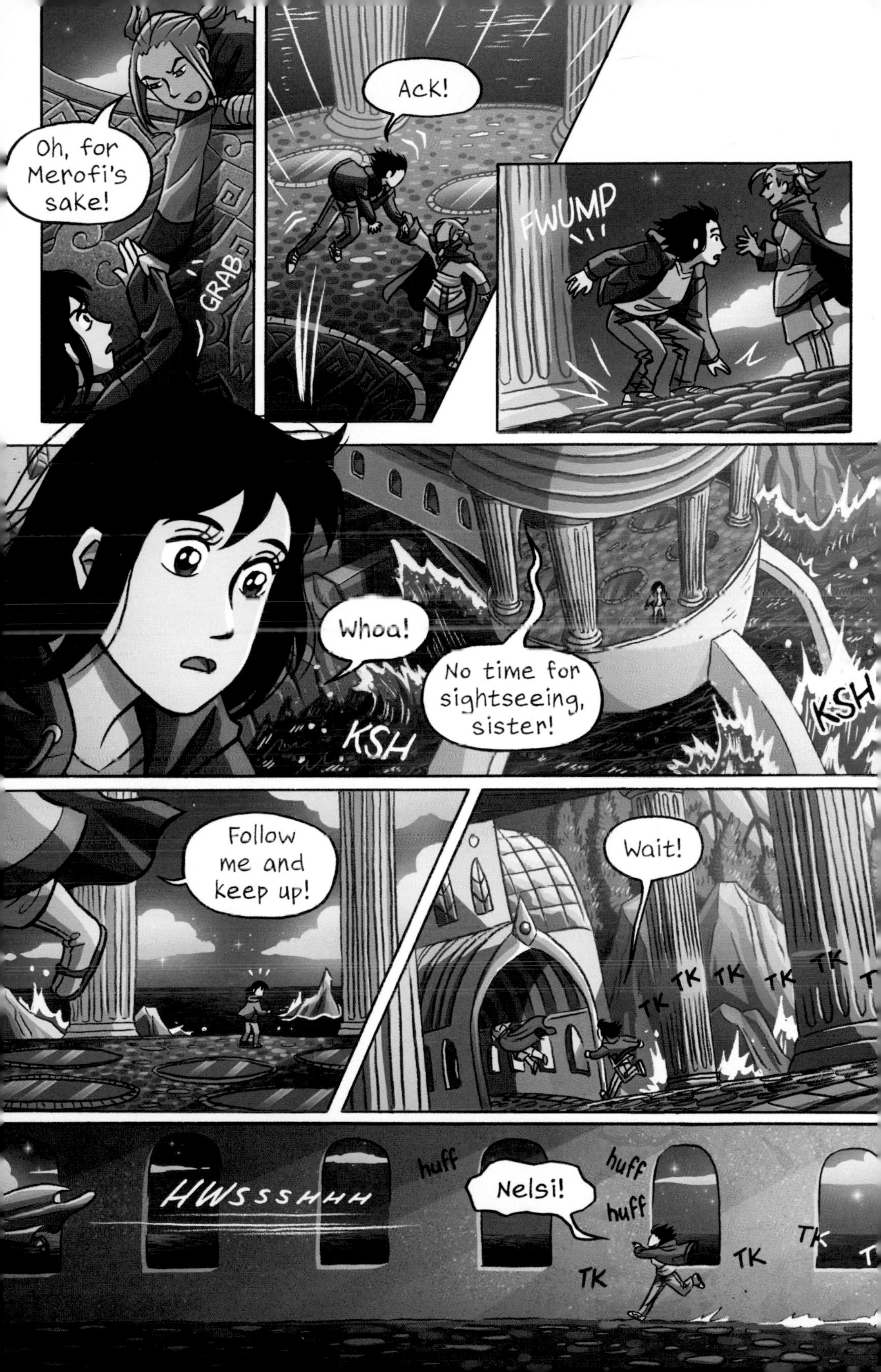
Oh, for Merofi's sake!
GRAB
Ack!
FWUMP
Whoa!
No time for sightseeing, sister!
KSH
KSH
Follow me and keep up!
Wait!
TK TK TK TK TK
HWSSSHHH
huff
Nelsi!
huff
huff
TK
TK
TK

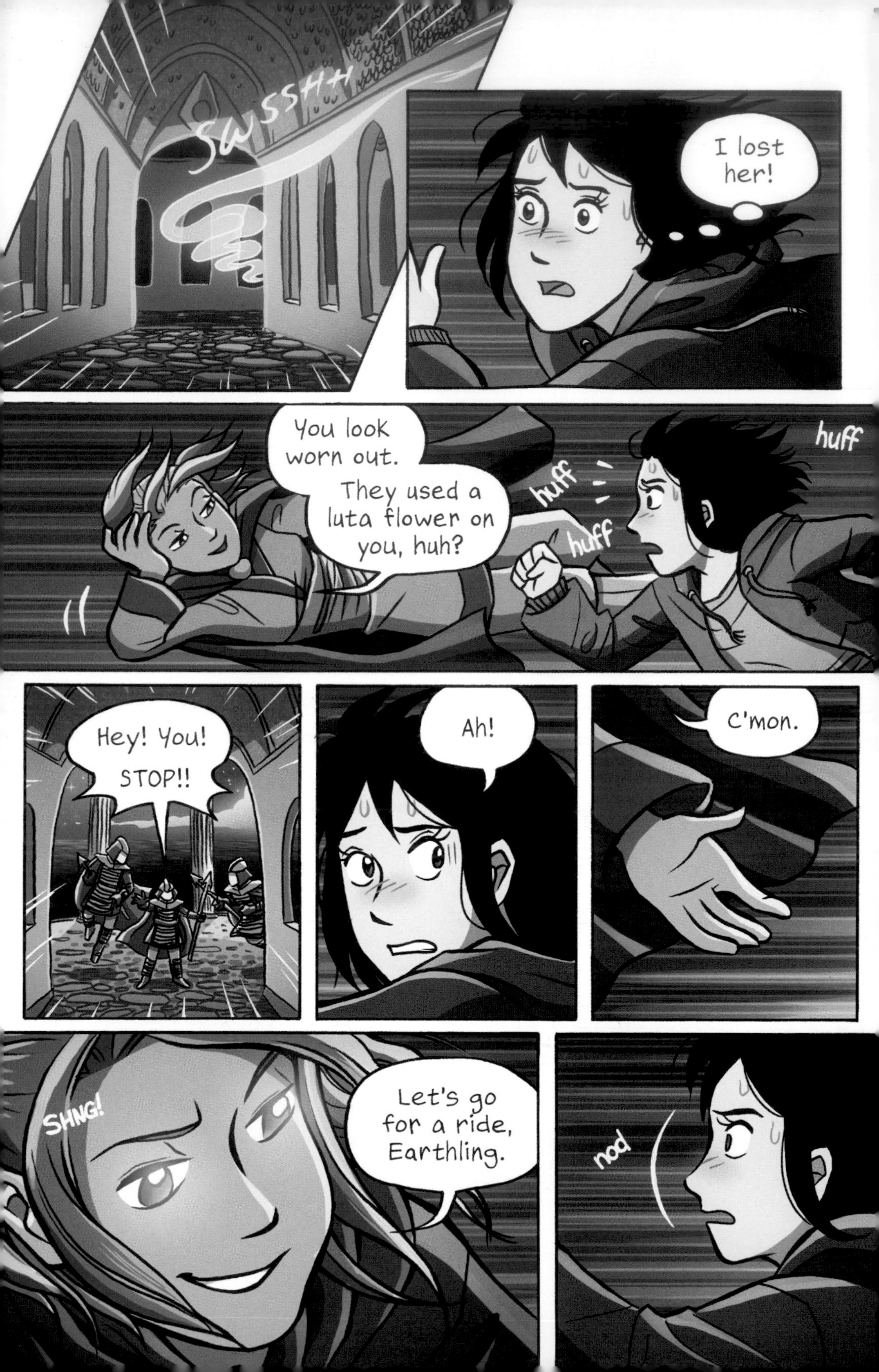
SWSSHH
I lost her!
You look worn out.
They used a luta flower on you, huh?
huff
huff
huff
Hey! You! STOP!!
Ah!
C'mon.
SHNG!
Let's go for a ride, Earthling.
nod

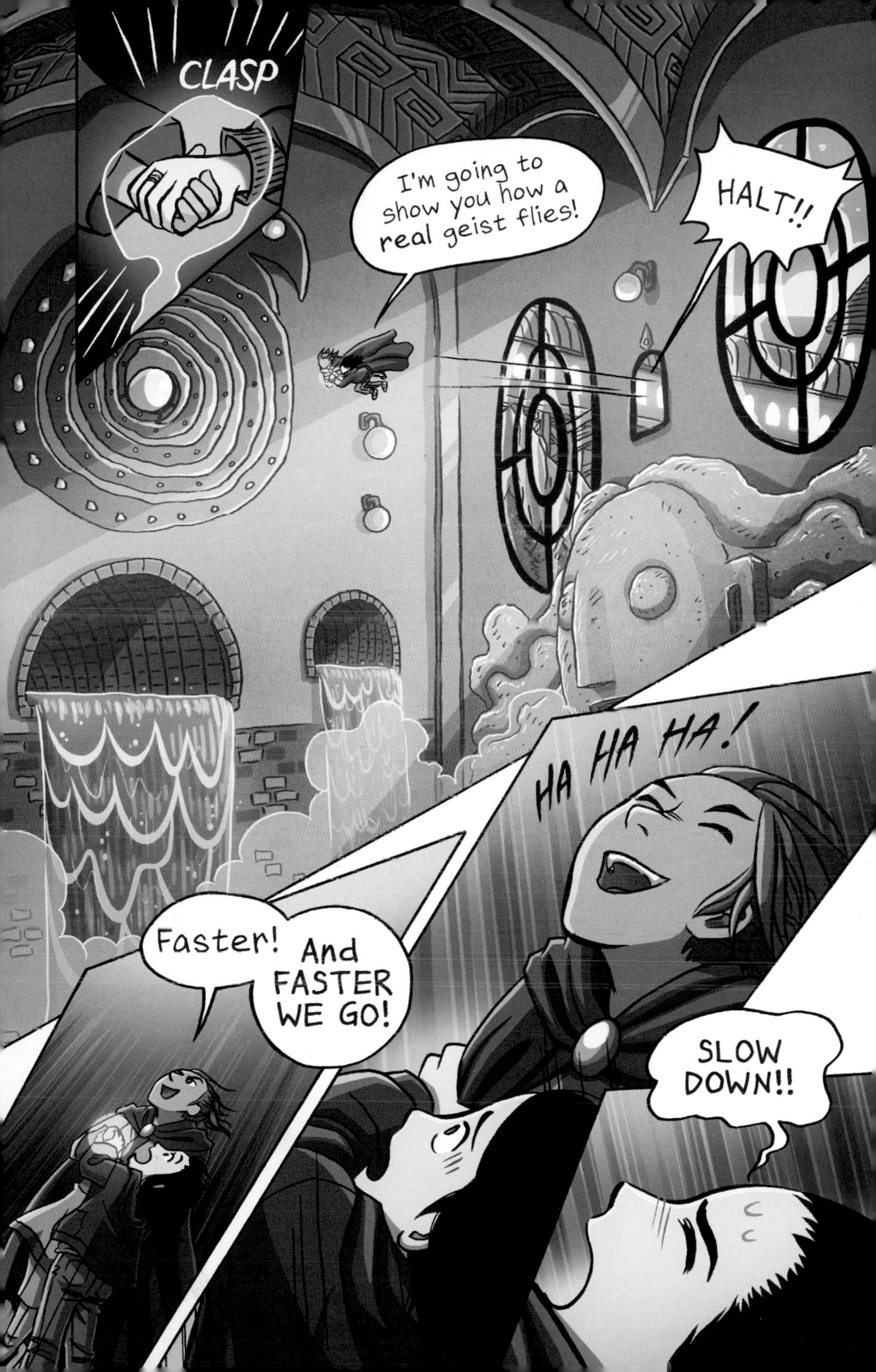
CLASP
I'm going to show you how a real geist flies!
HALT!!
HA HA HA!
Faster!
And FASTER WE GO!
SLOW DOWN!!

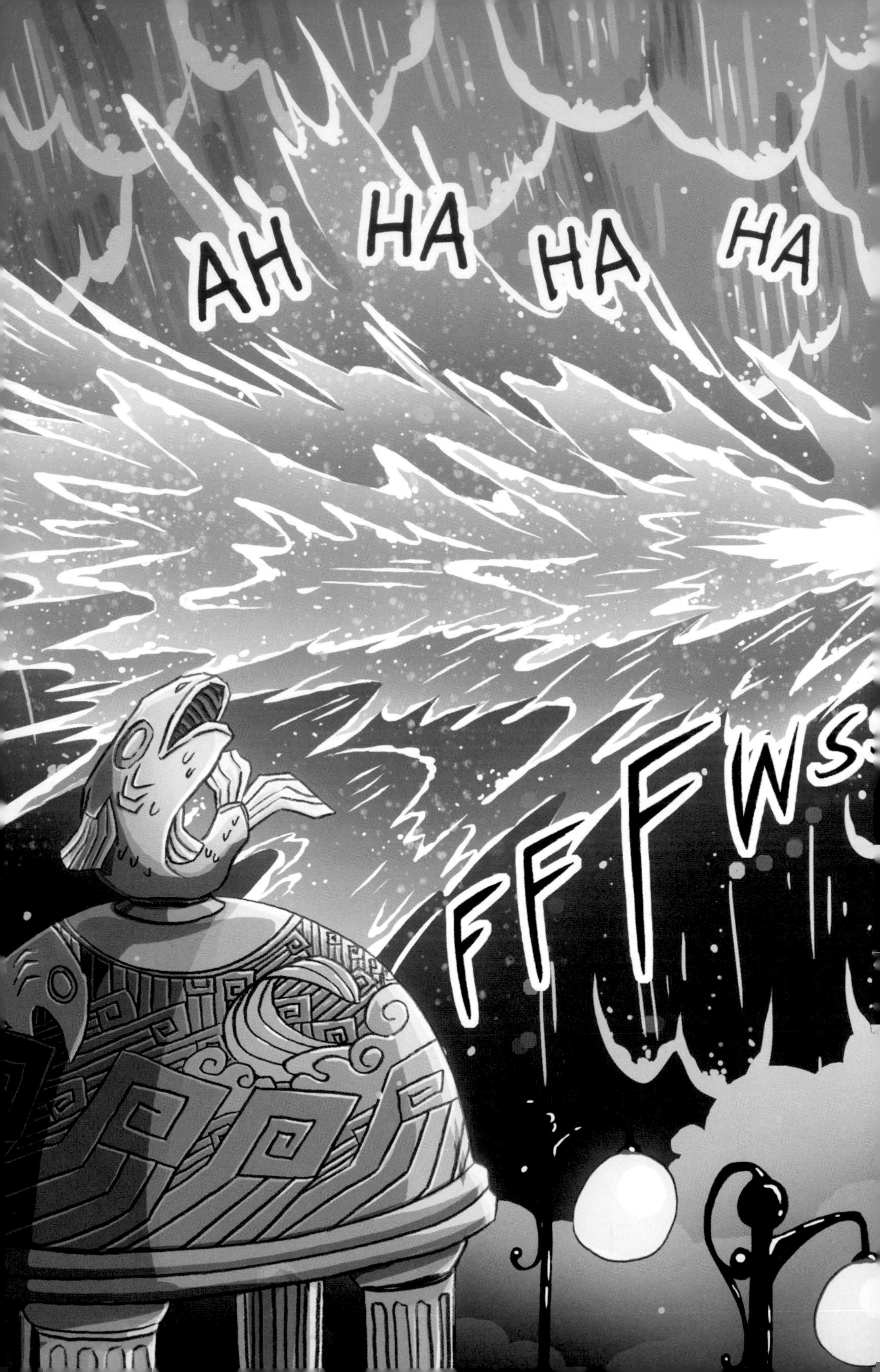
AH HA HA HA
FFFWS

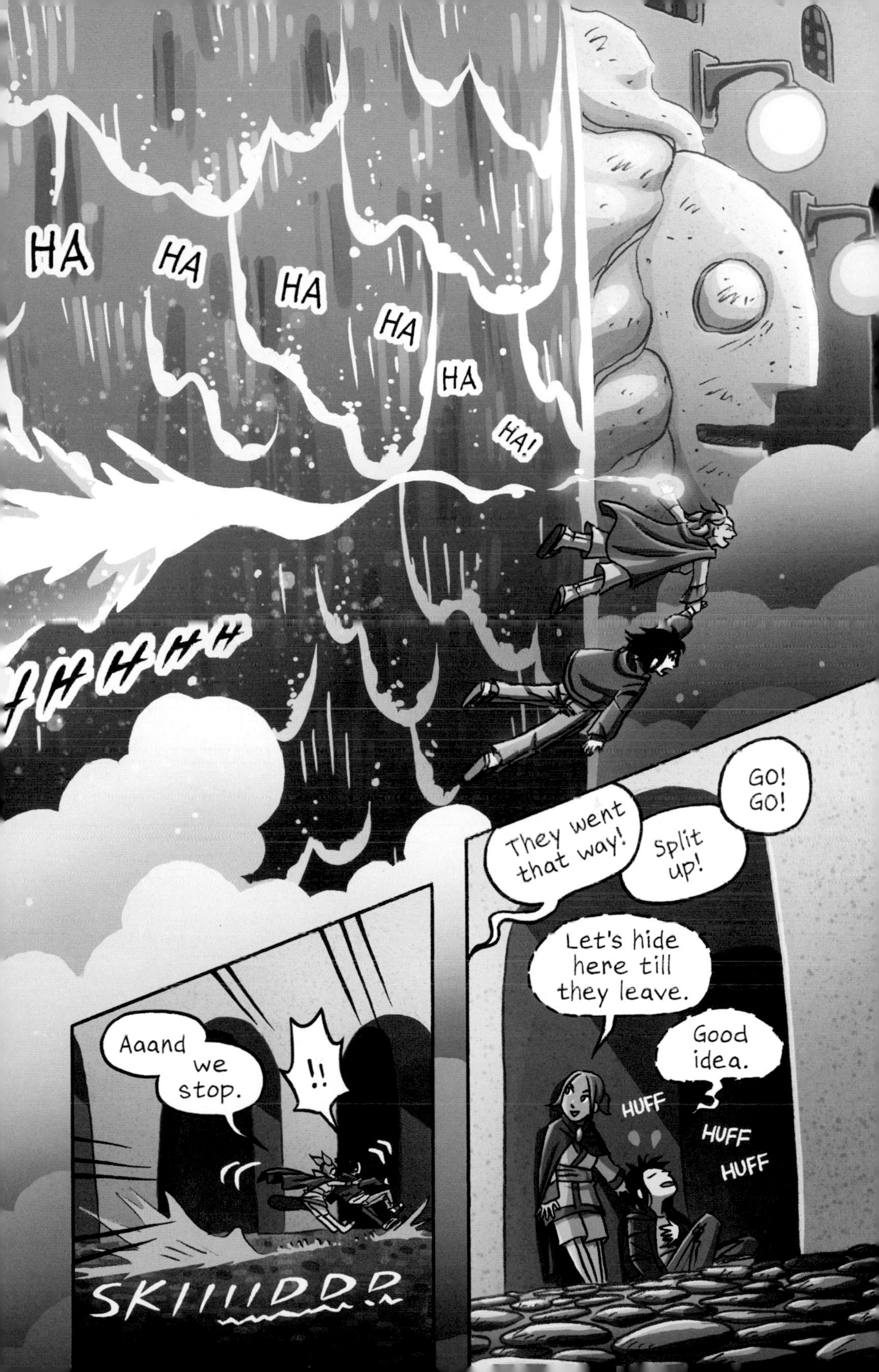
HA
HA
HA
HA
HA
HA!
They went that way!
Split up!
GO! GO!
Let's hide here till they leave.
Good idea.
HUFF
HUFF
HUFF
Aaand we stop.
!!
SKIIIDDD

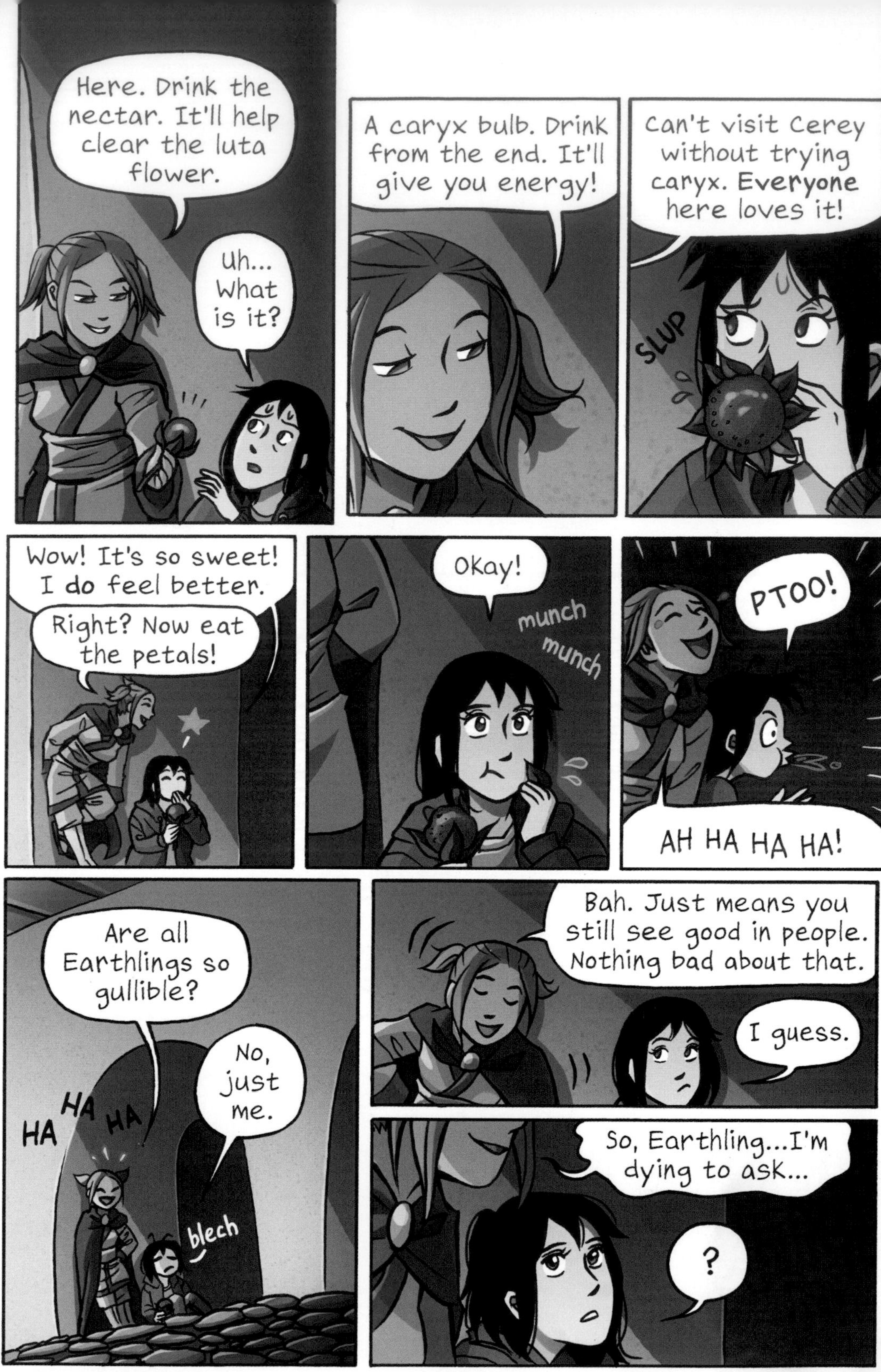
Here. Drink the nectar. It'll help clear the luta flower.
Uh... What is it?
A caryx bulb. Drink from the end. It'll give you energy!
Can't visit Cerey without trying caryx. **Everyone** here loves it!
SLUP
Wow! It's so sweet! I do feel better.
Right? Now eat the petals!
Okay!
munch
munch
PTOO!
AH HA HA HA!
Are all Earthlings so gullible?
No, just me.
HA
HA
HA
blech
Bah. Just means you still see good in people. Nothing bad about that.
I guess.
So, Earthling...I'm dying to ask...
?

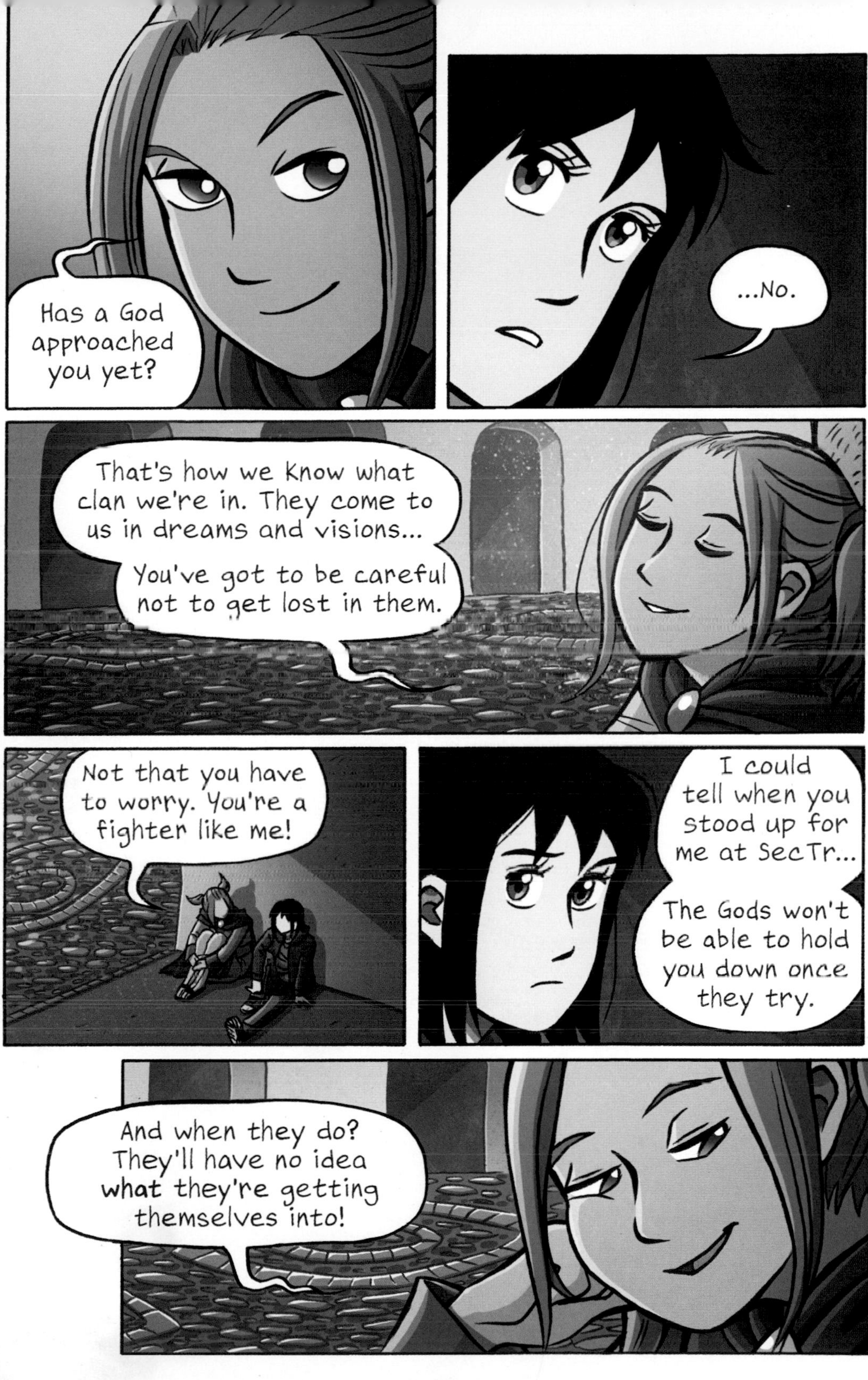
Has a God approached you yet?
...No.
That's how we know what clan we're in. They come to us in dreams and visions...
You've got to be careful not to get lost in them.
Not that you have to worry. You're a fighter like me!
I could tell when you stood up for me at SecTr...
The Gods won't be able to hold you down once they try.
And when they do? They'll have no idea **what** they're getting themselves into!

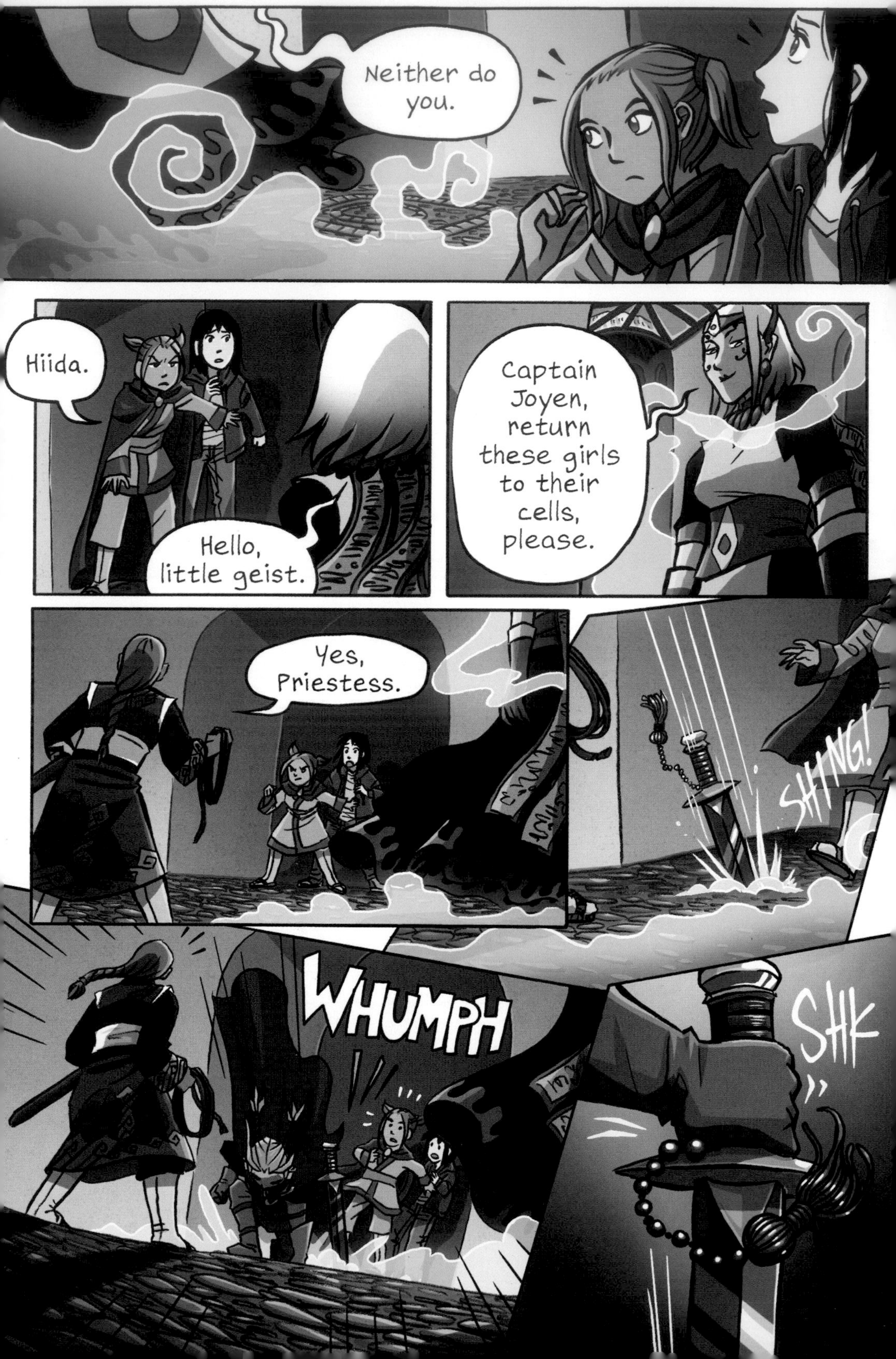
Neither do you.
Hiida.
Hello, little geist.
Captain Joyen, return these girls to their cells, please.
Yes, Priestess.
SHING!
WHUMPH
SHK

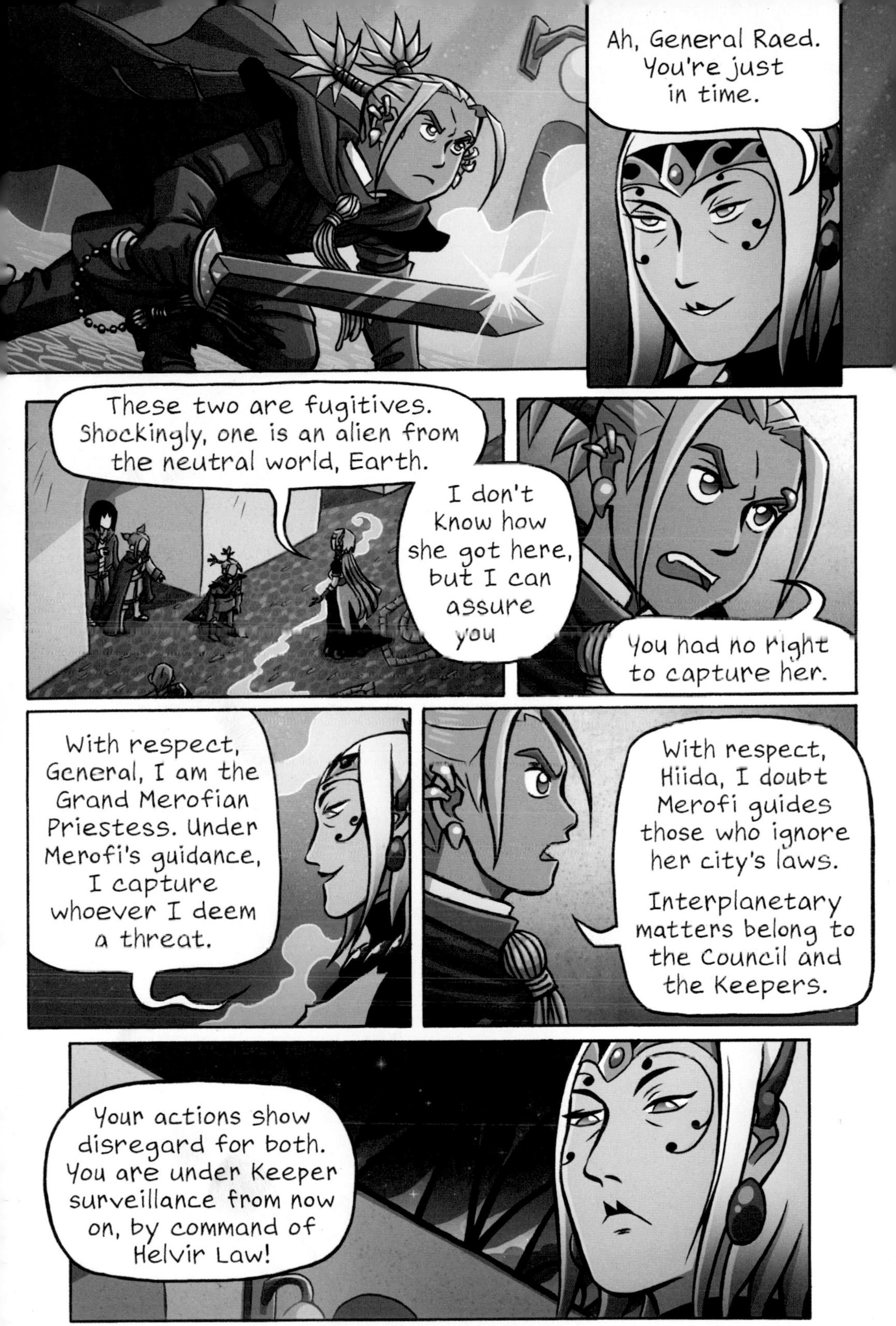

Ah, General Raed. You're just in time.
These two are fugitives. Shockingly, one is an alien from the neutral world, Earth.
I don't know how she got here, but I can assure you
You had no right to capture her.
With respect, General, I am the Grand Merofian Priestess. Under Merofi's guidance, I capture whoever I deem a threat.
With respect, Hiida, I doubt Merofi guides those who ignore her city's laws.
Interplanetary matters belong to the Council and the Keepers.
Your actions show disregard for both. You are under Keeper surveillance from now on, by command of Helvir Law!

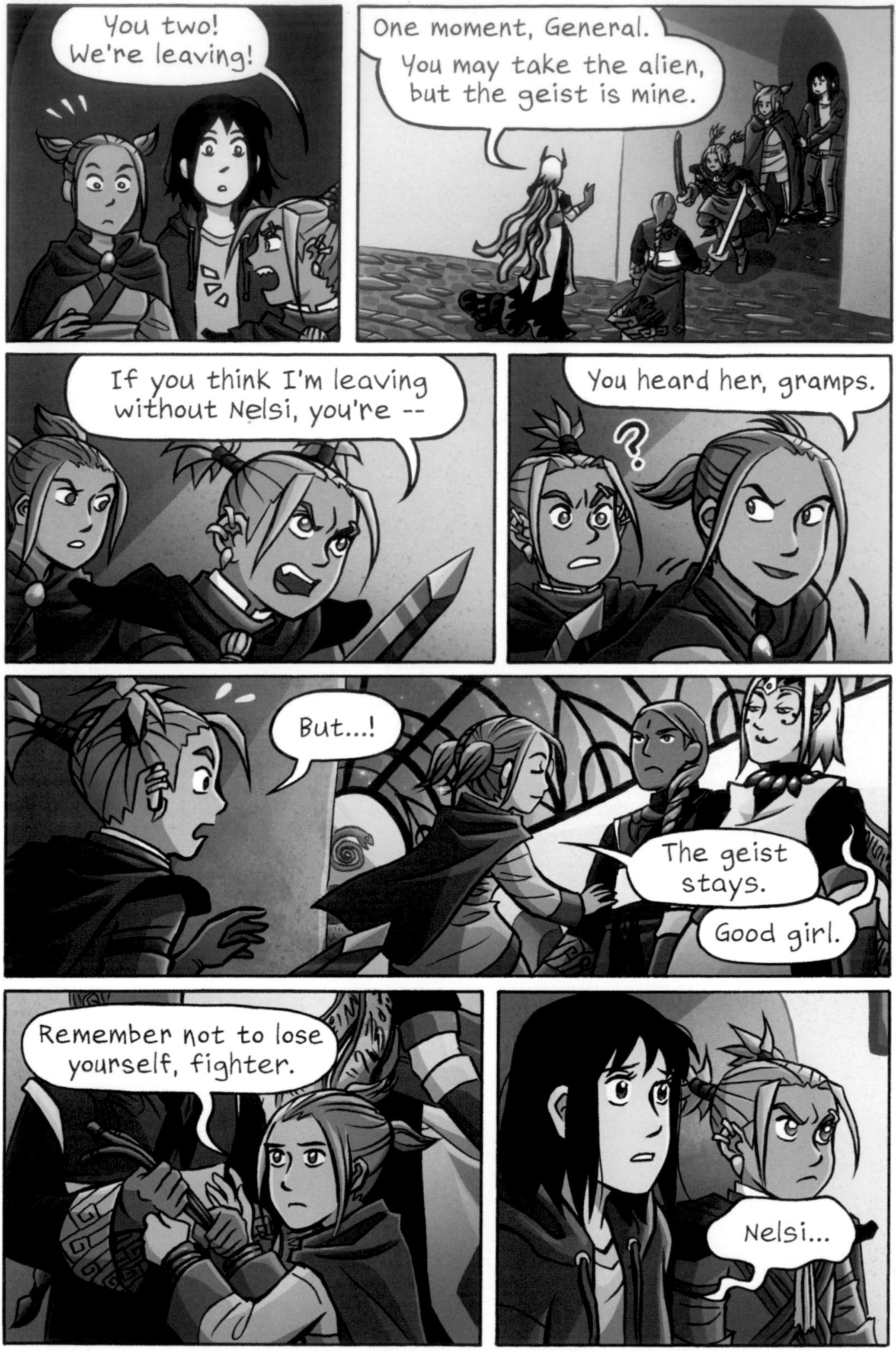
You two! We're leaving!
One moment, General.
You may take the alien, but the geist is mine.
If you think I'm leaving without Nelsi, you're --
You heard her, gramps.
?
But...!
The geist stays.
Good girl.
Remember not to lose yourself, fighter.
Nelsi...

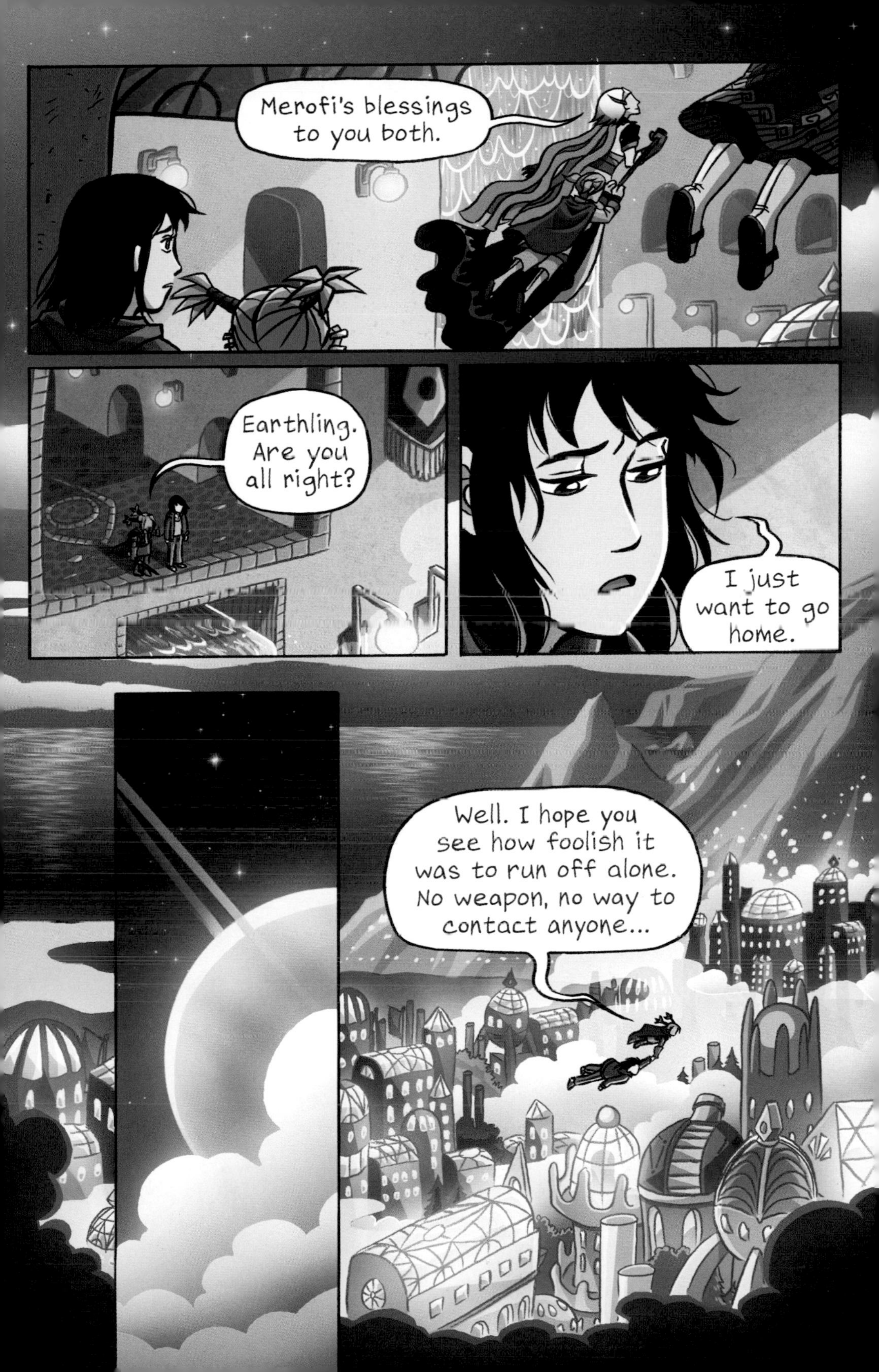
Merofi's blessings to you both.
Earthling. Are you all right?
I just want to go home.
Well. I hope you see how foolish it was to run off alone. No weapon, no way to contact anyone...

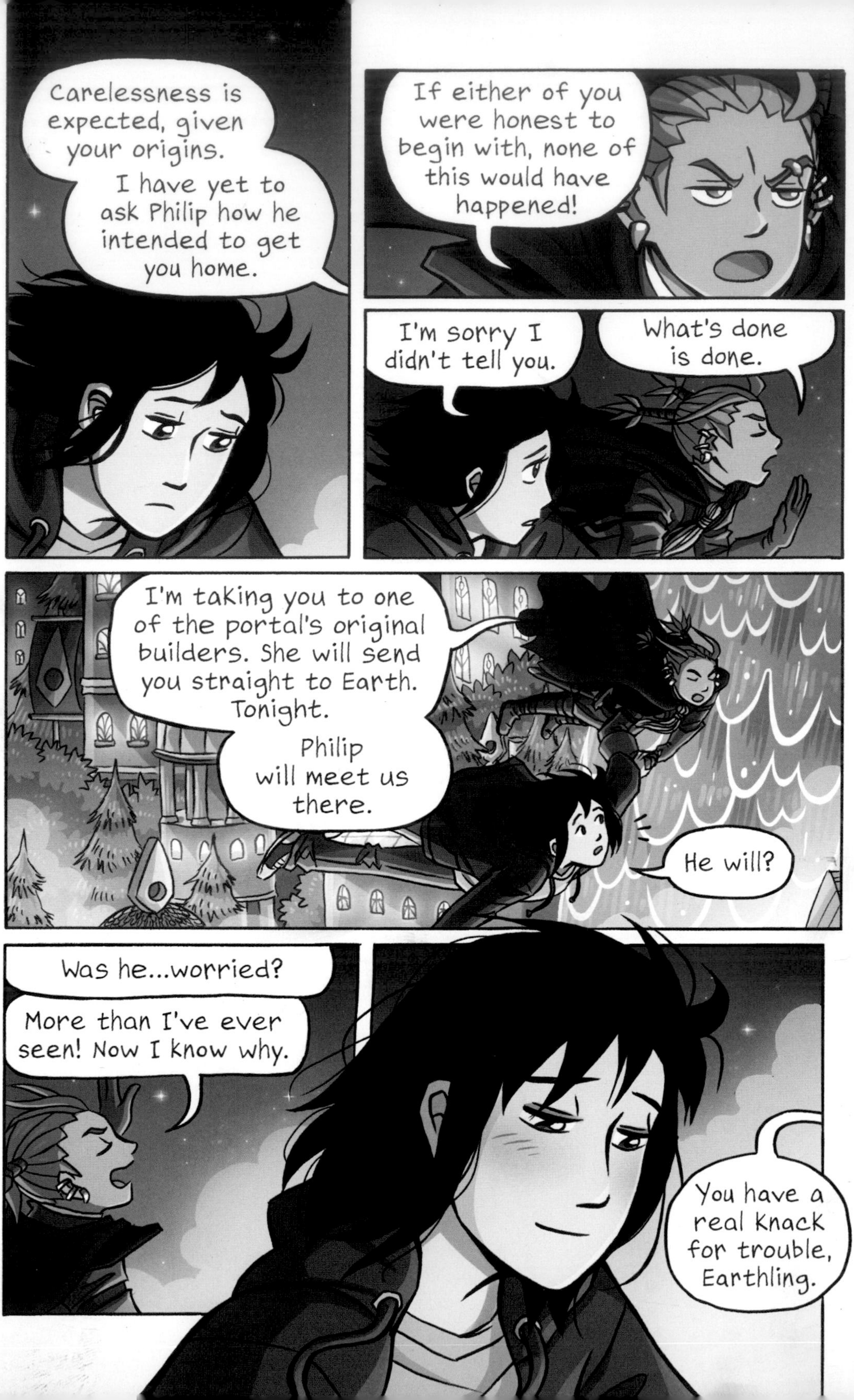

Carelessness is expected, given your origins.
I have yet to ask Philip how he intended to get you home.
If either of you were honest to begin with, none of this would have happened!
I'm sorry I didn't tell you.
What's done is done.
I'm taking you to one of the portal's original builders. She will send you straight to Earth. Tonight.
Philip will meet us there.
He will?
Was he...worried?
More than I've ever seen! Now I know why.
You have a real knack for trouble, Earthling.

PART IV
THE GHOST

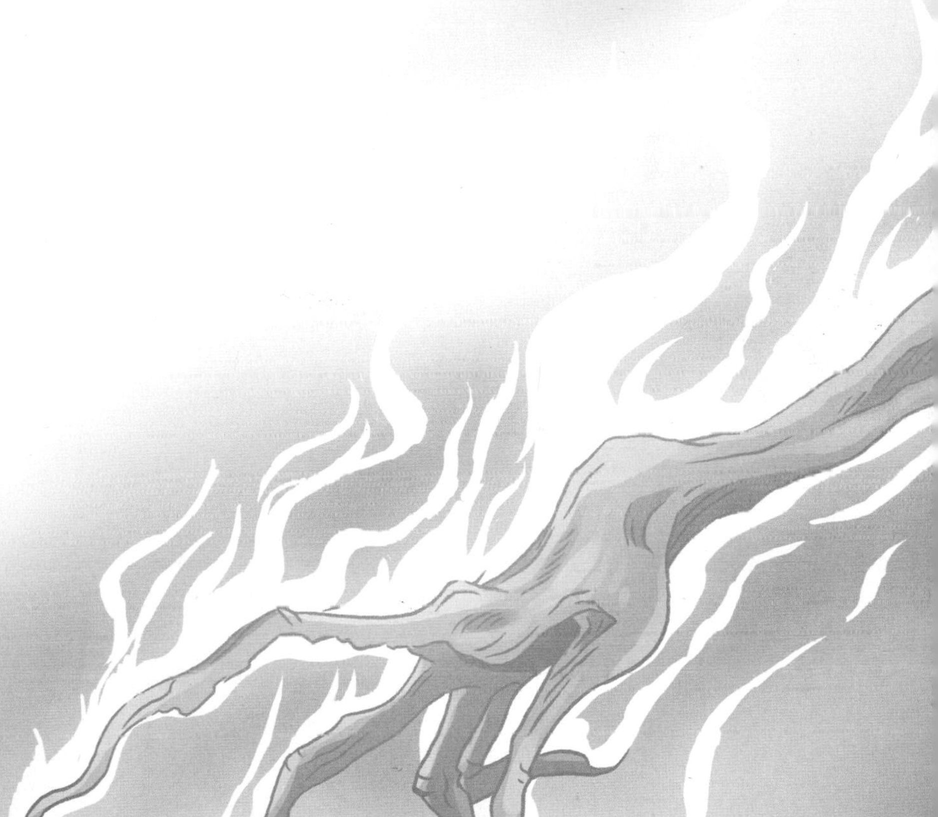

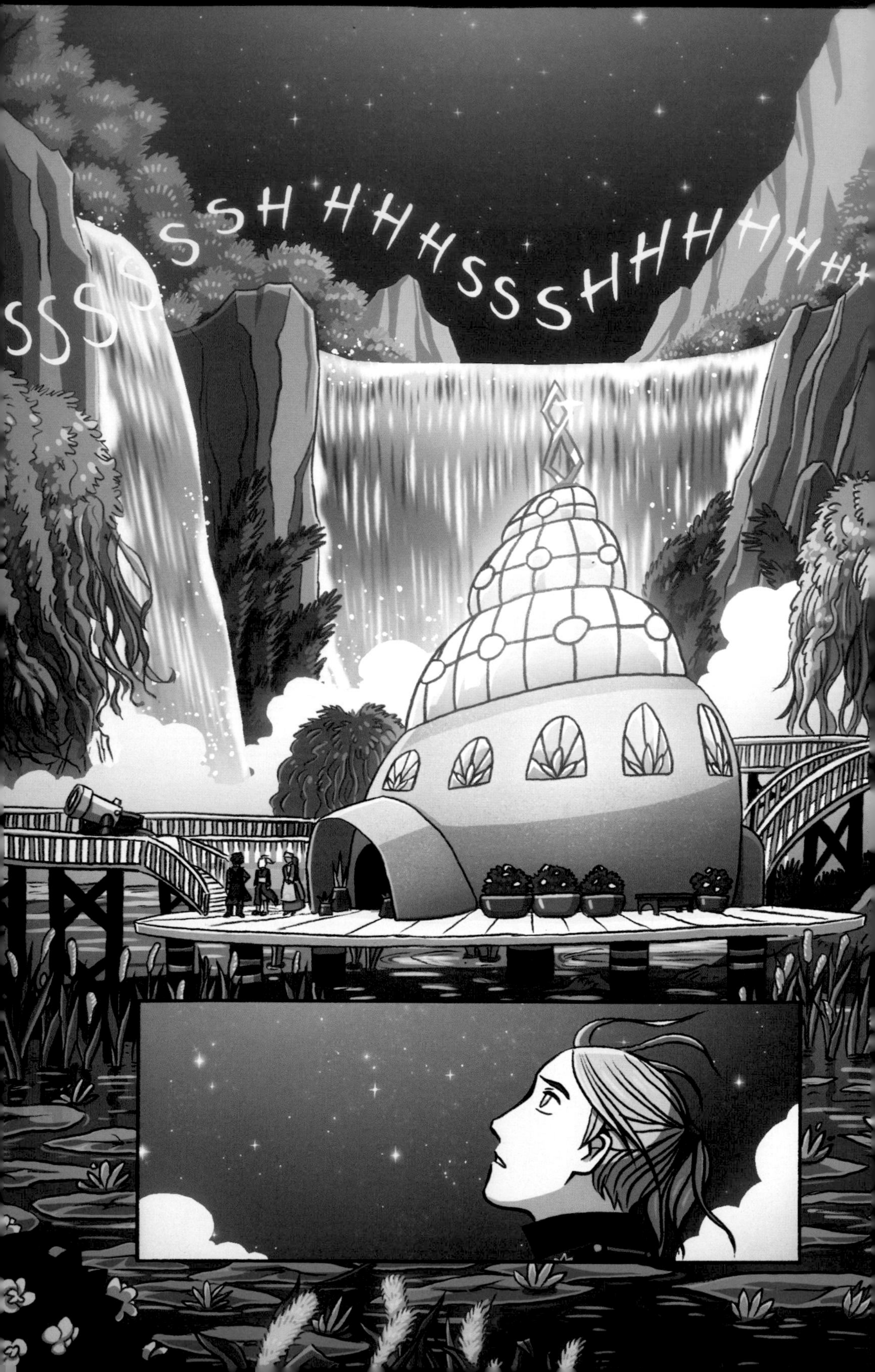
SSSSSHHHHHSSSSHHHHHHH

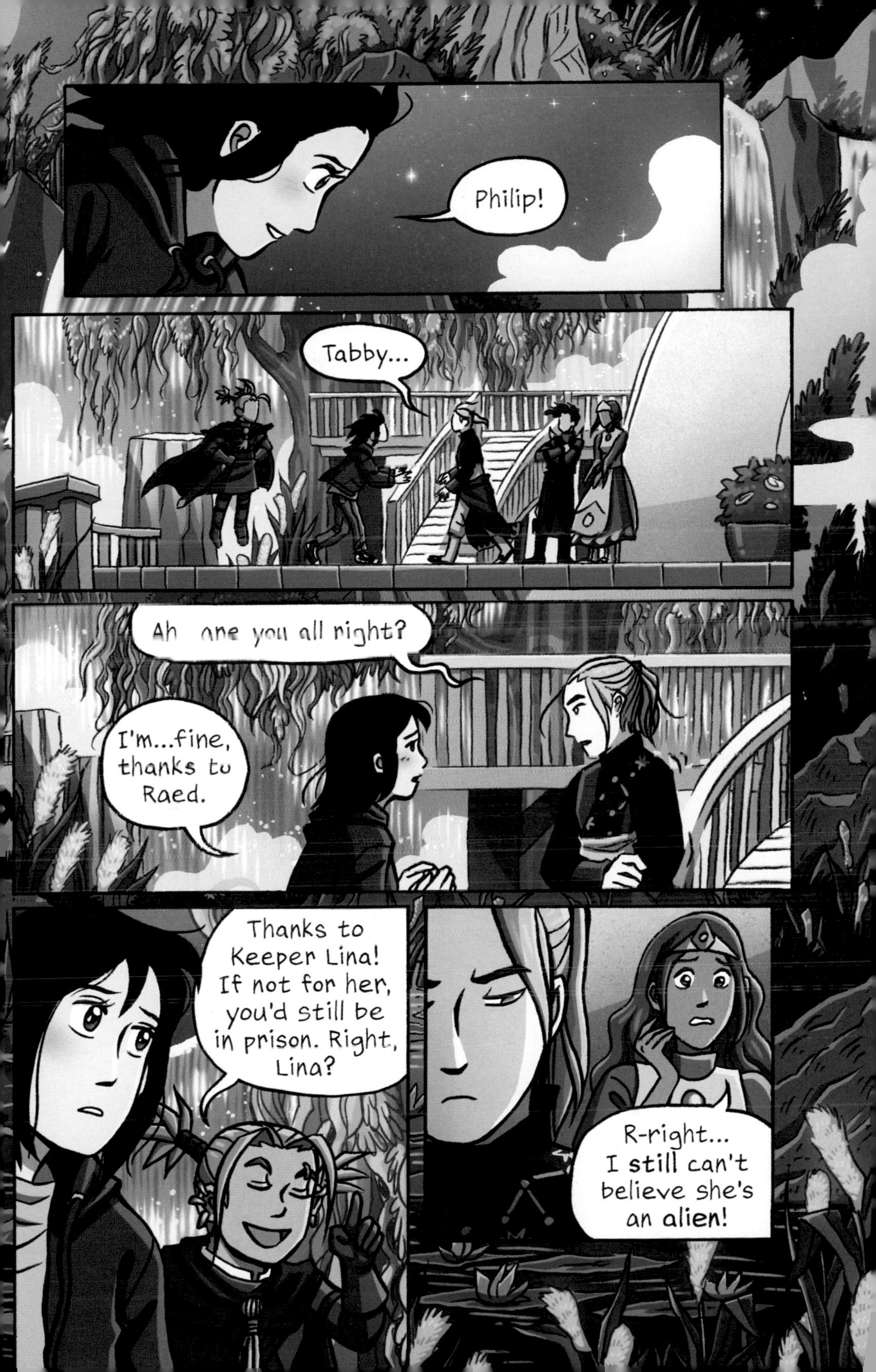
Philip!
Tabby...
Ah are you all right?
I'm...fine, thanks to Raed.
Thanks to Keeper Lina! If not for her, you'd still be in prison. Right, Lina?
R-right... I still can't believe she's an alien!

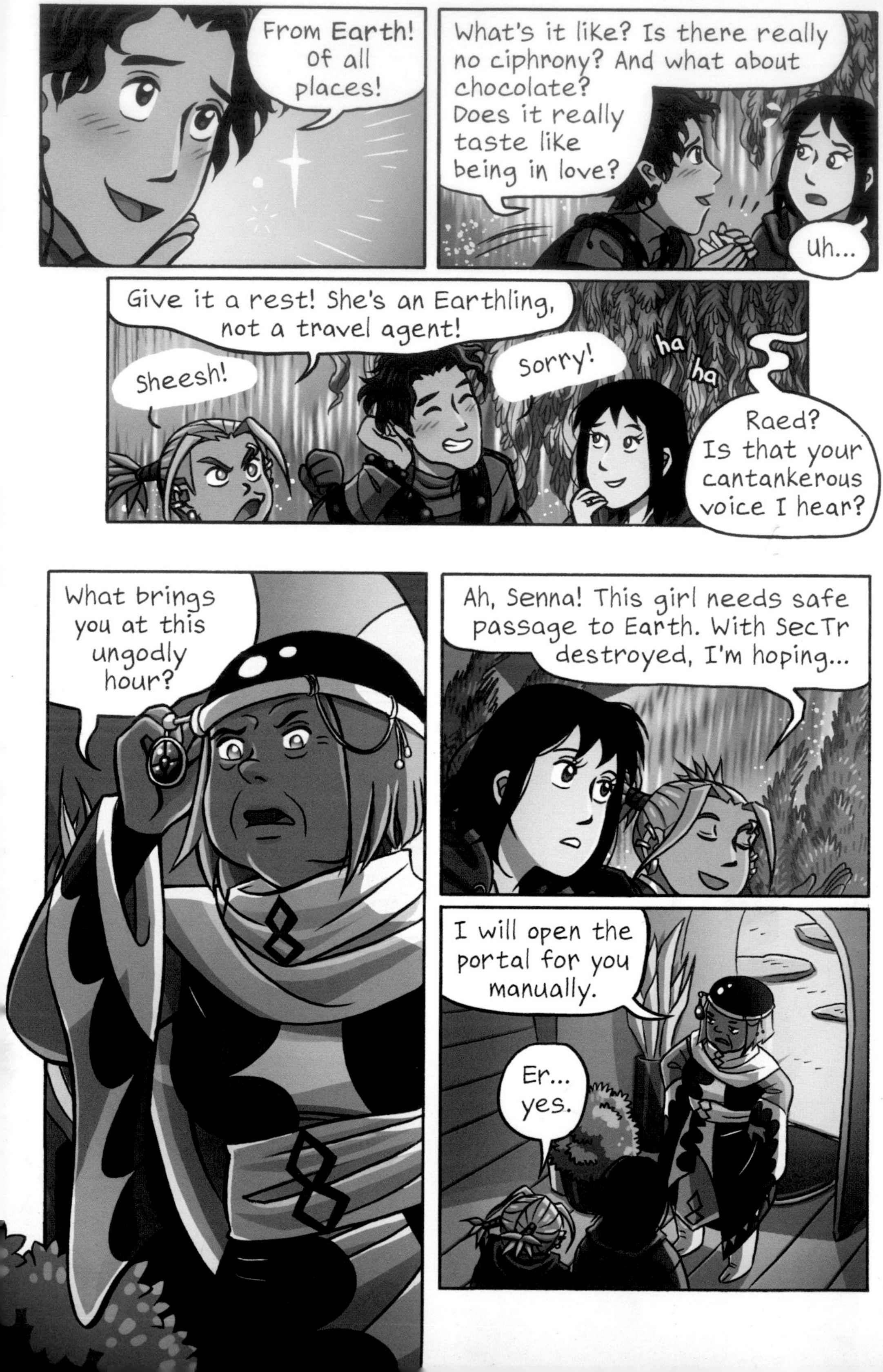

From Earth! Of all places!
What's it like? Is there really no ciphrony? And what about chocolate? Does it really taste like being in love?
Uh...
Give it a rest! She's an Earthling, not a travel agent!
Sheesh!
Sorry!
ha ha
Raed? Is that your cantankerous voice I hear?
What brings you at this ungodly hour?
Ah, Senna! This girl needs safe passage to Earth. With SecTr destroyed, I'm hoping...
I will open the portal for you manually.
Er... yes.

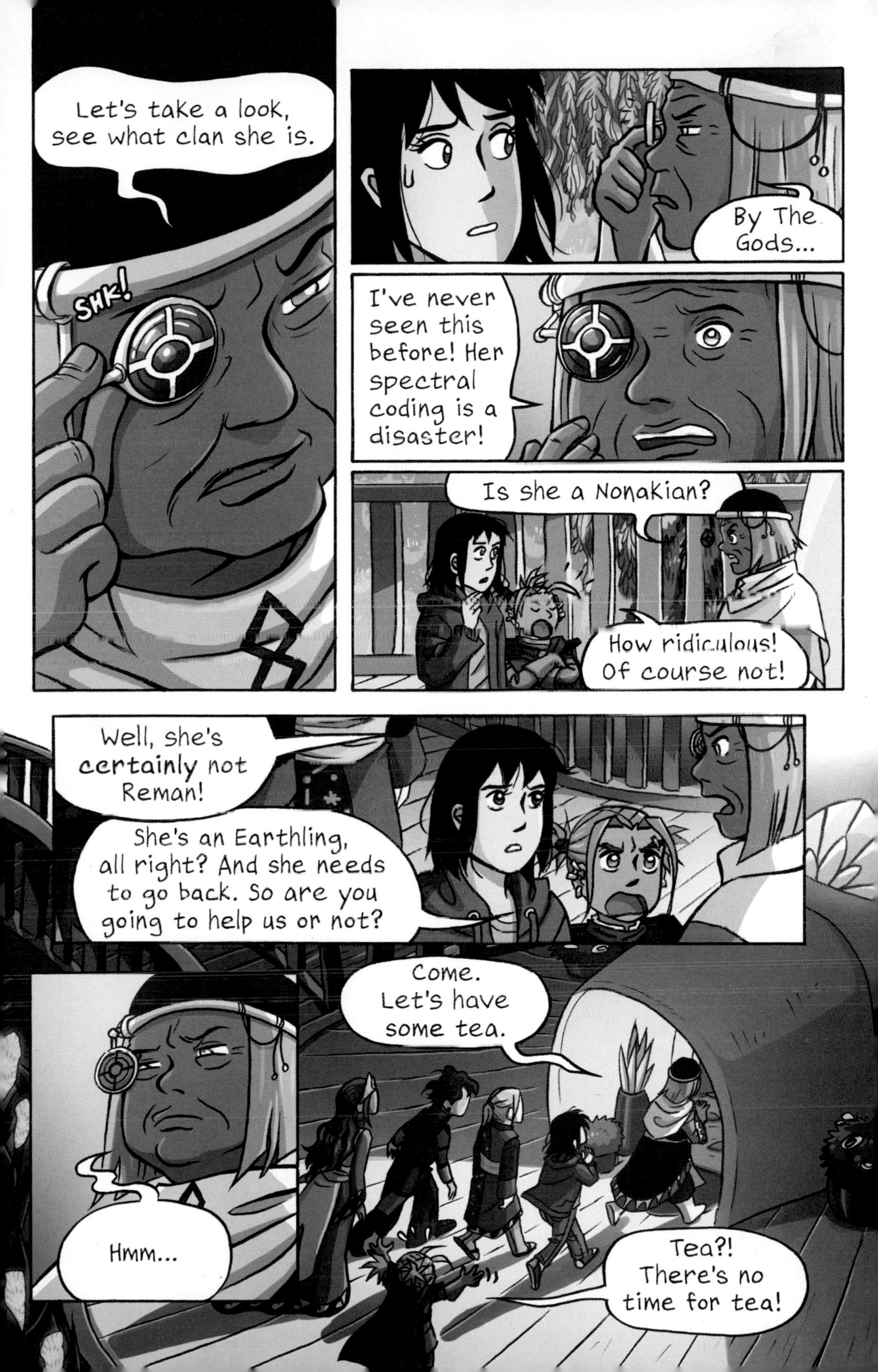

Let's take a look, see what clan she is.
SHK!
By The Gods...
I've never seen this before! Her spectral coding is a disaster!
Is she a Nonakian?
How ridiculous! Of course not!
Well, she's **certainly** not Reman!
She's an Earthling, all right? And she needs to go back. So are you going to help us or not?
Hmm...
Come. Let's have some tea.
Tea?! There's no time for tea!

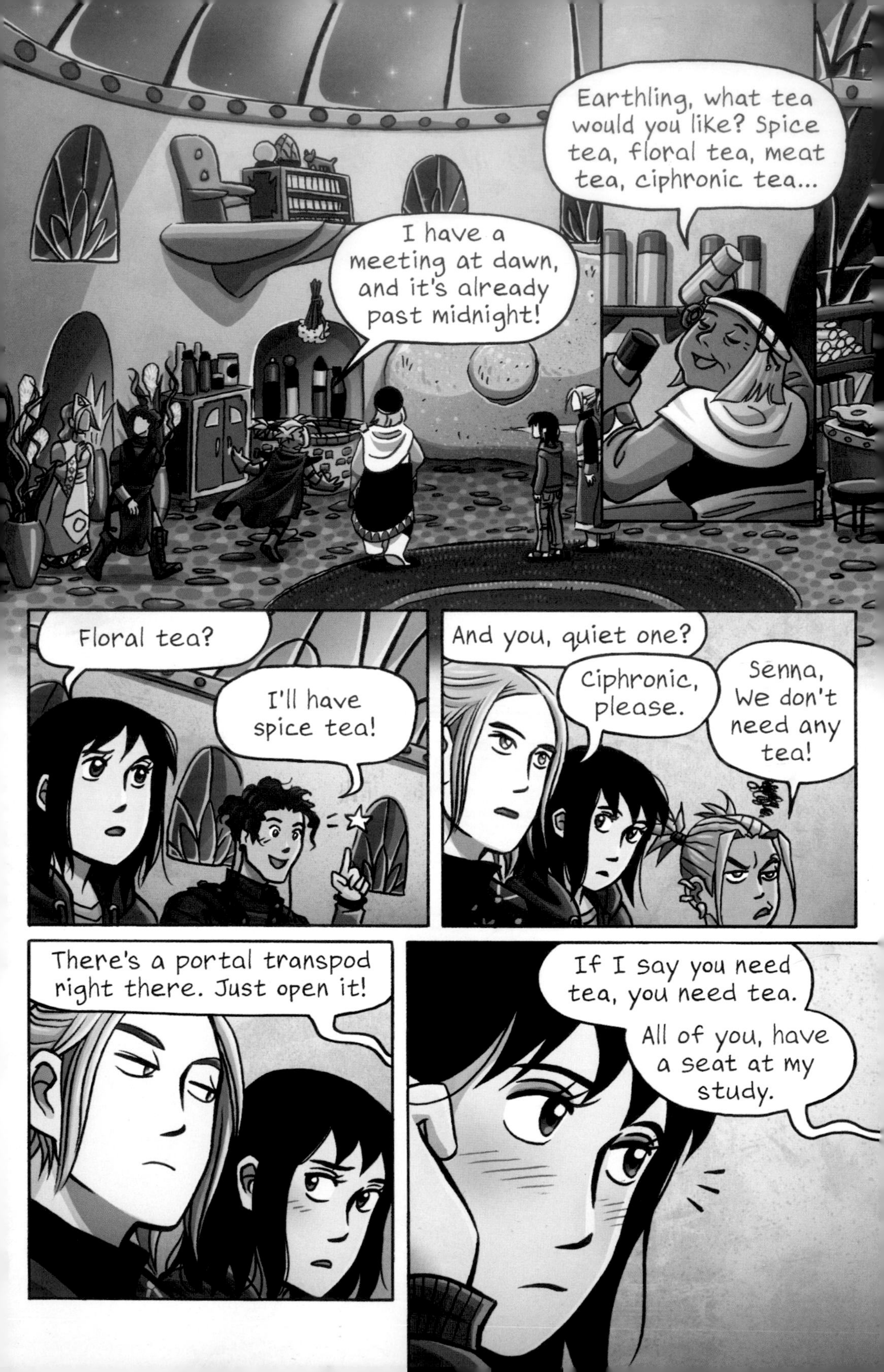
Earthling, what tea would you like? Spice tea, floral tea, meat tea, ciphronic tea...
I have a meeting at dawn, and it's already past midnight!
Floral tea?
I'll have spice tea!
And you, quiet one?
Ciphronic, please.
Senna, We don't need any tea!
There's a portal transpod right there. Just open it!
If I say you need tea, you need tea.
All of you, have a seat at my study.

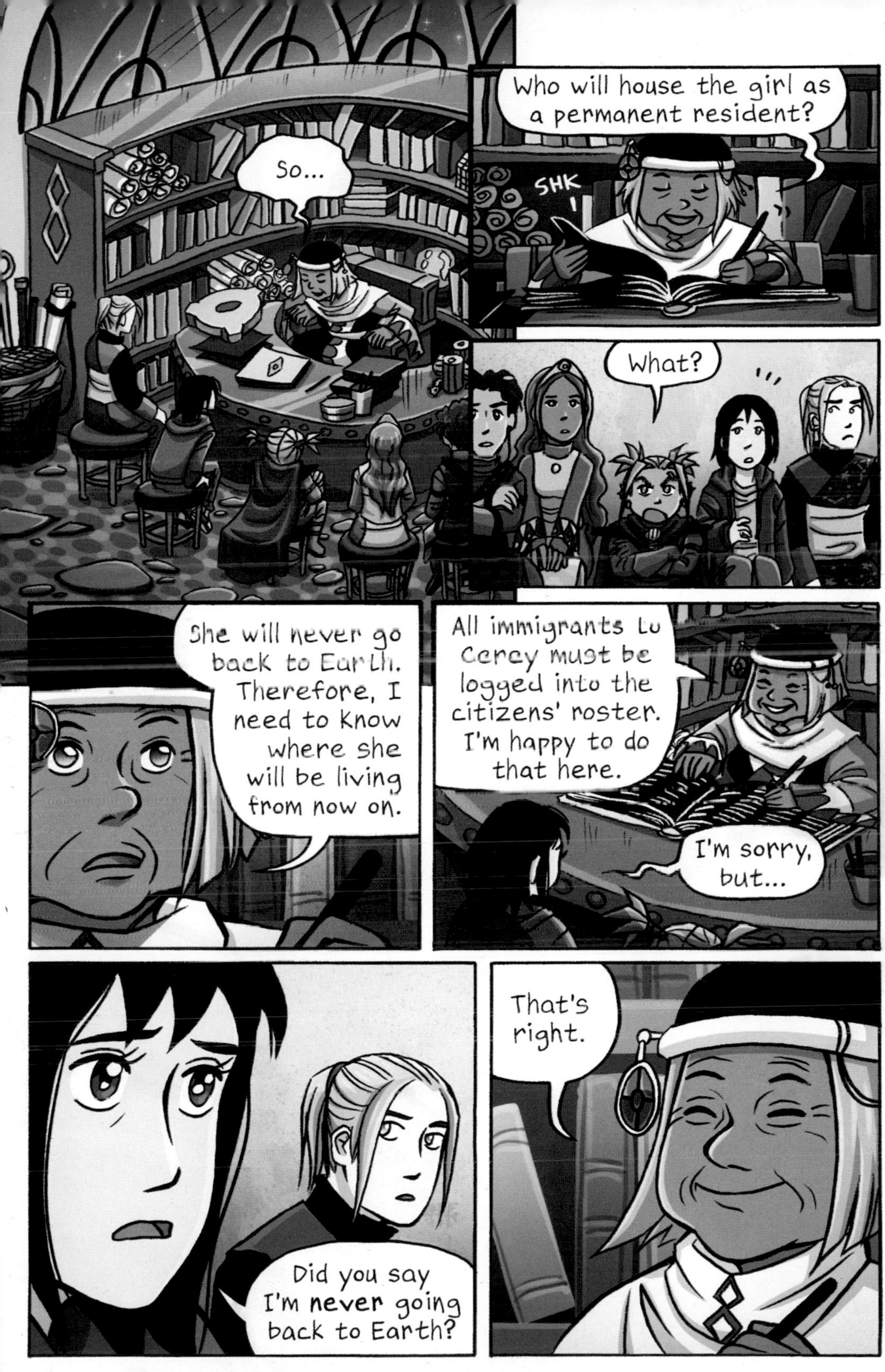
So...
Who will house the girl as a permanent resident?
SHK
What?
She will never go back to Earth. Therefore, I need to know where she will be living from now on.
All immigrants to Cerey must be logged into the citizens' roster. I'm happy to do that here.
I'm sorry, but...
Did you say I'm **never** going back to Earth?
That's right.

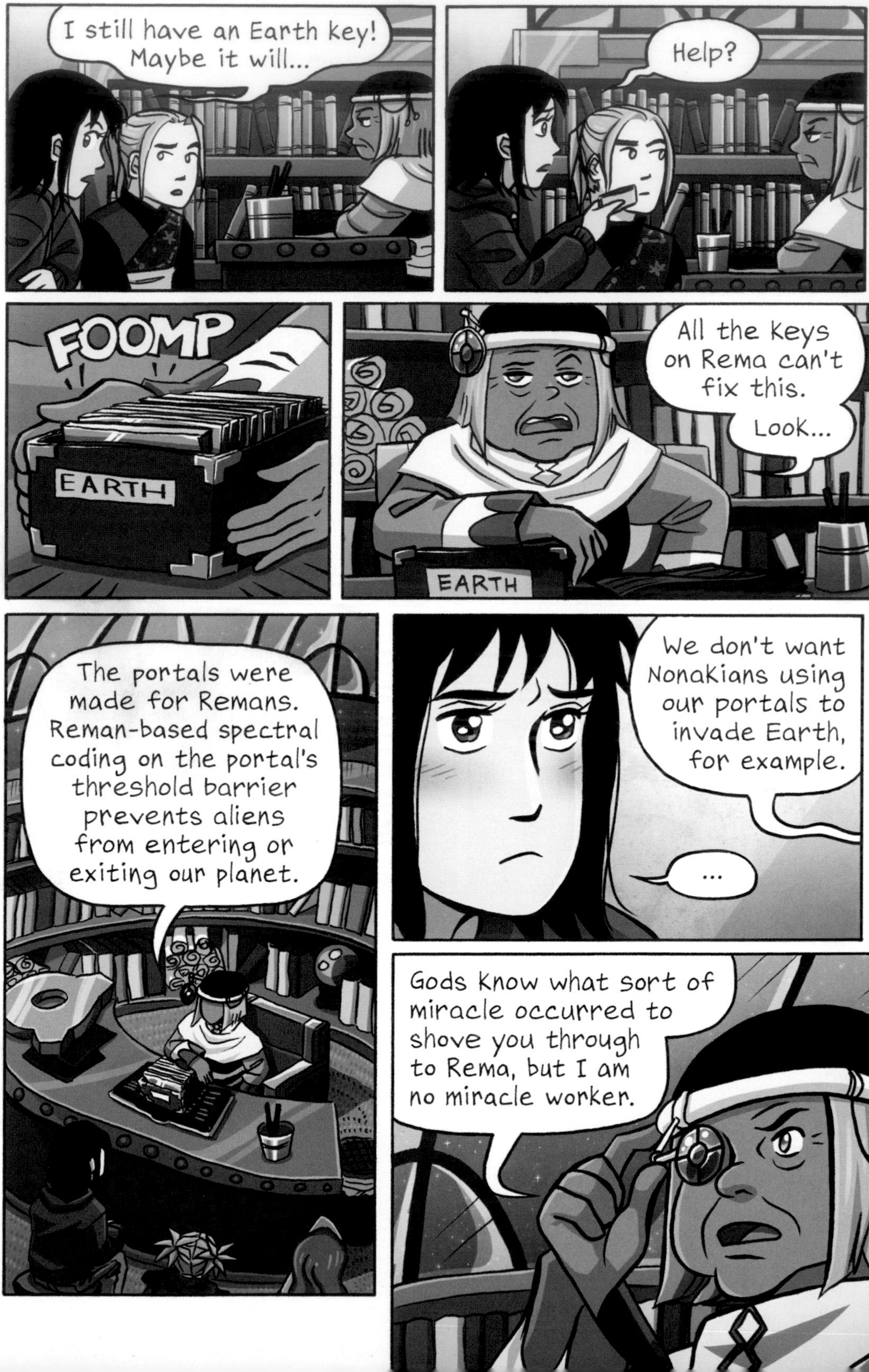
I still have an Earth key! Maybe it will...
Help?
FOOMP
EARTH
All the keys on Rema can't fix this.
Look...
EARTH
The portals were made for Remans. Reman-based spectral coding on the portal's threshold barrier prevents aliens from entering or exiting our planet.
We don't want Nonakians using our portals to invade Earth, for example.
...
Gods know what sort of miracle occurred to shove you through to Rema, but I am no miracle worker.

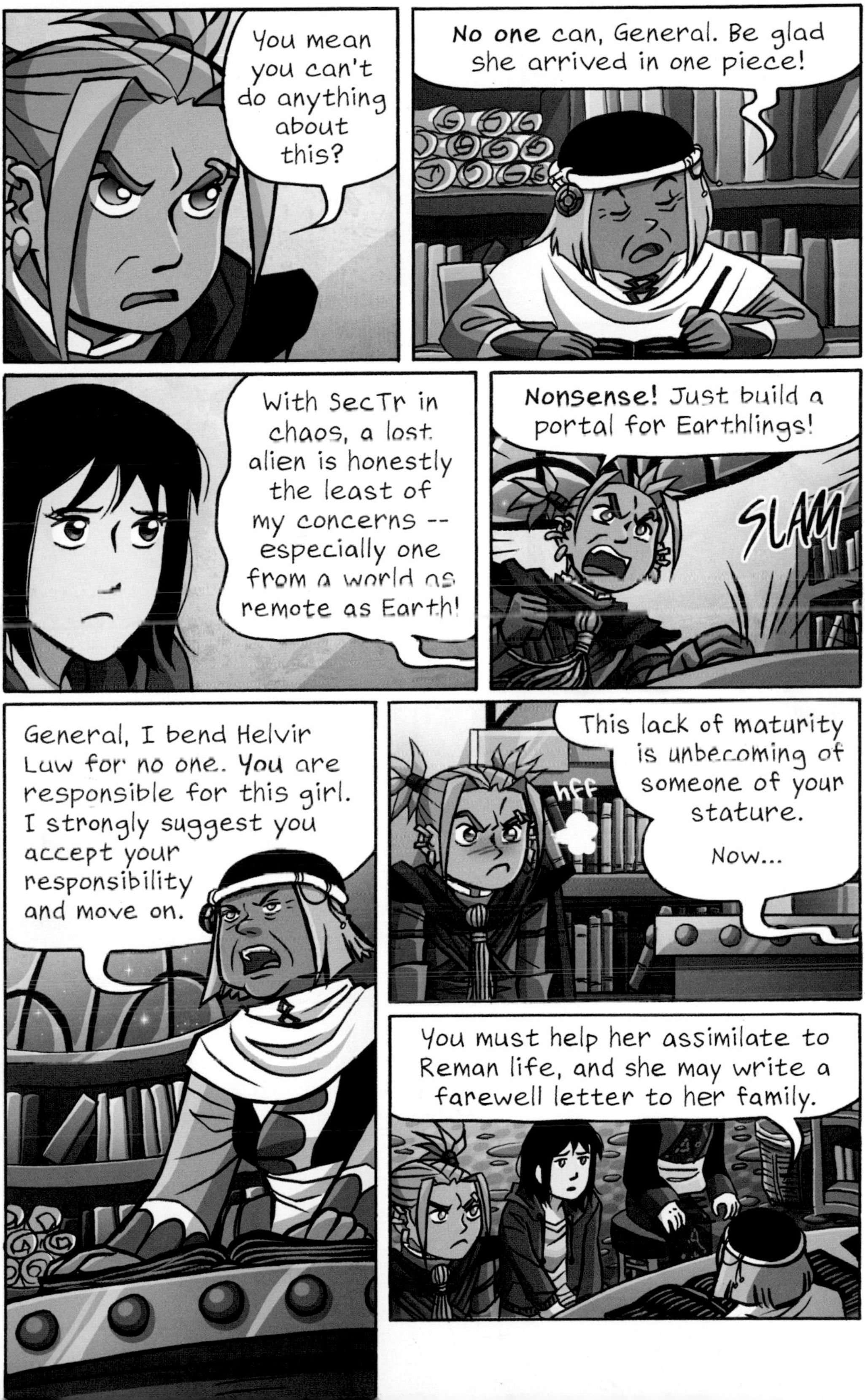

You mean you can't do anything about this?
No one can, General. Be glad she arrived in one piece!
With SecTr in chaos, a lost alien is honestly the least of my concerns -- especially one from a world as remote as Earth!
Nonsense! Just build a portal for Earthlings!
SLAM
General, I bend Helvir Law for no one. You are responsible for this girl. I strongly suggest you accept your responsibility and move on.
hff
This lack of maturity is unbecoming of someone of your stature.
Now...
You must help her assimilate to Reman life, and she may write a farewell letter to her family.

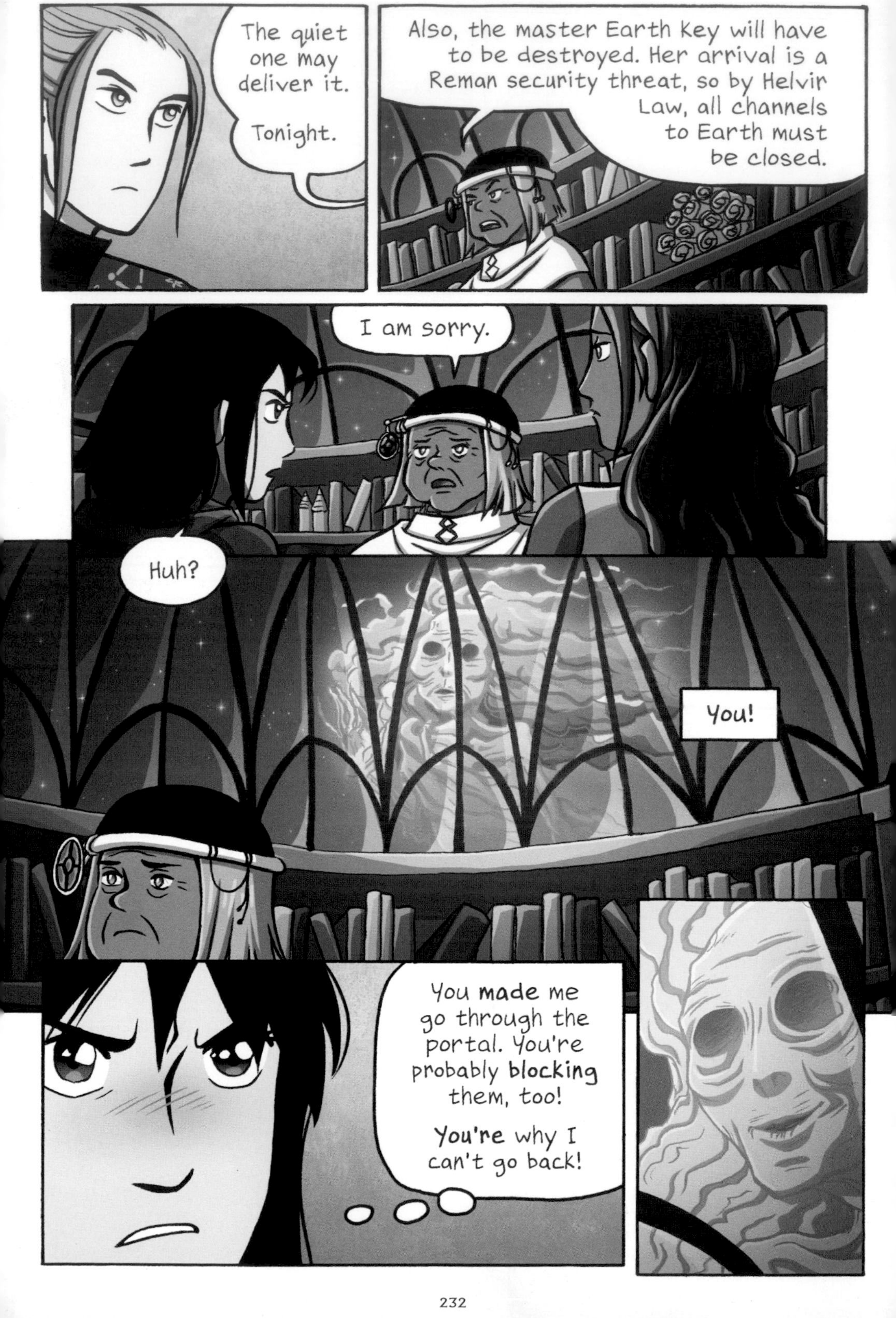

The quiet one may deliver it.
Tonight.
Also, the master Earth Key will have to be destroyed. Her arrival is a Reman security threat, so by Helvir Law, all channels to Earth must be closed.
I am sorry.
Huh?
You!
You **made** me go through the portal. You're probably **blocking** them, too!
You're why I can't go back!

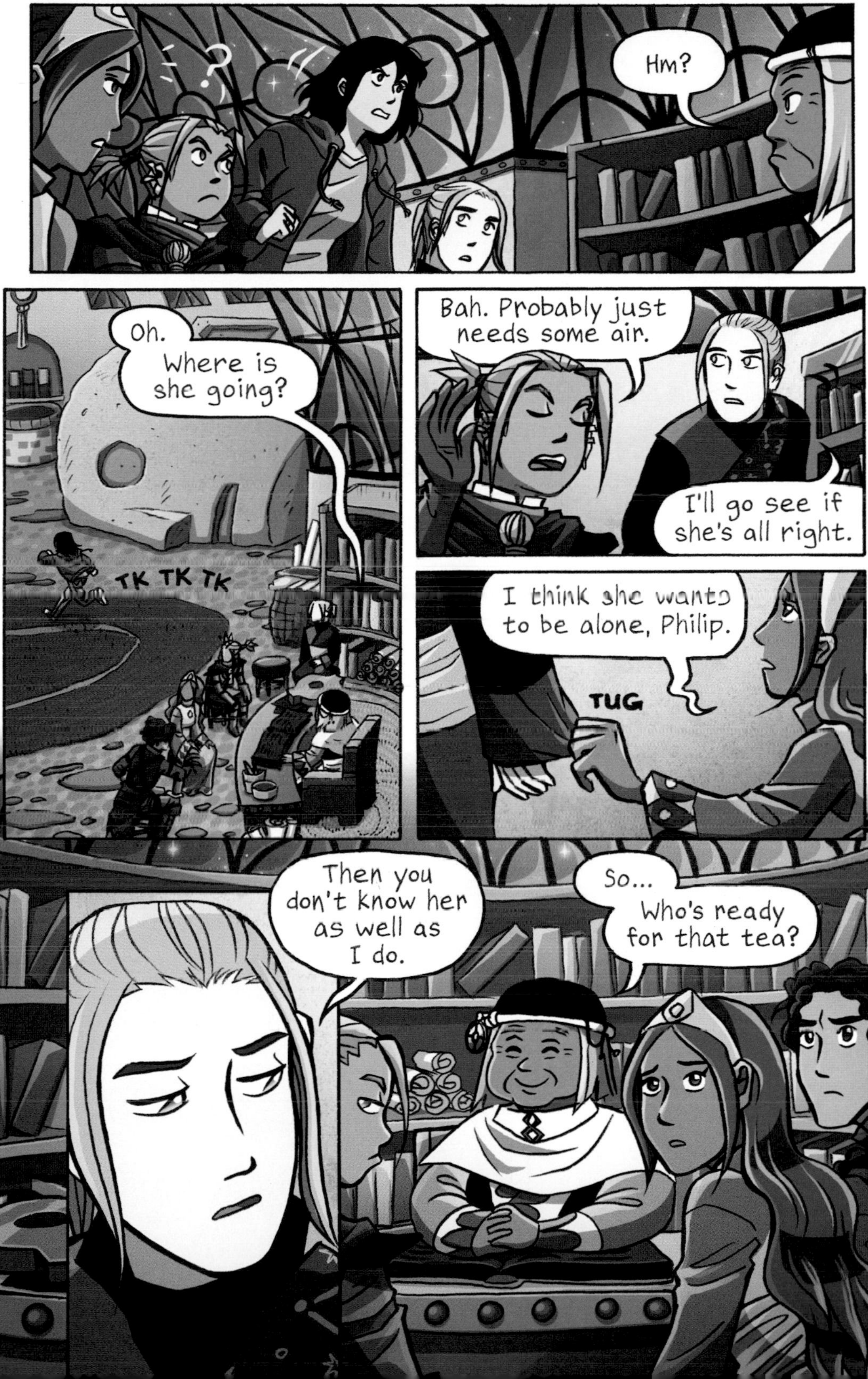
Hm?
Oh.
Where is she going?
TK TK TK
Bah. Probably just needs some air.
I'll go see if she's all right.
I think she wants to be alone, Philip.
TUG
Then you don't know her as well as I do.
So...
Who's ready for that tea?

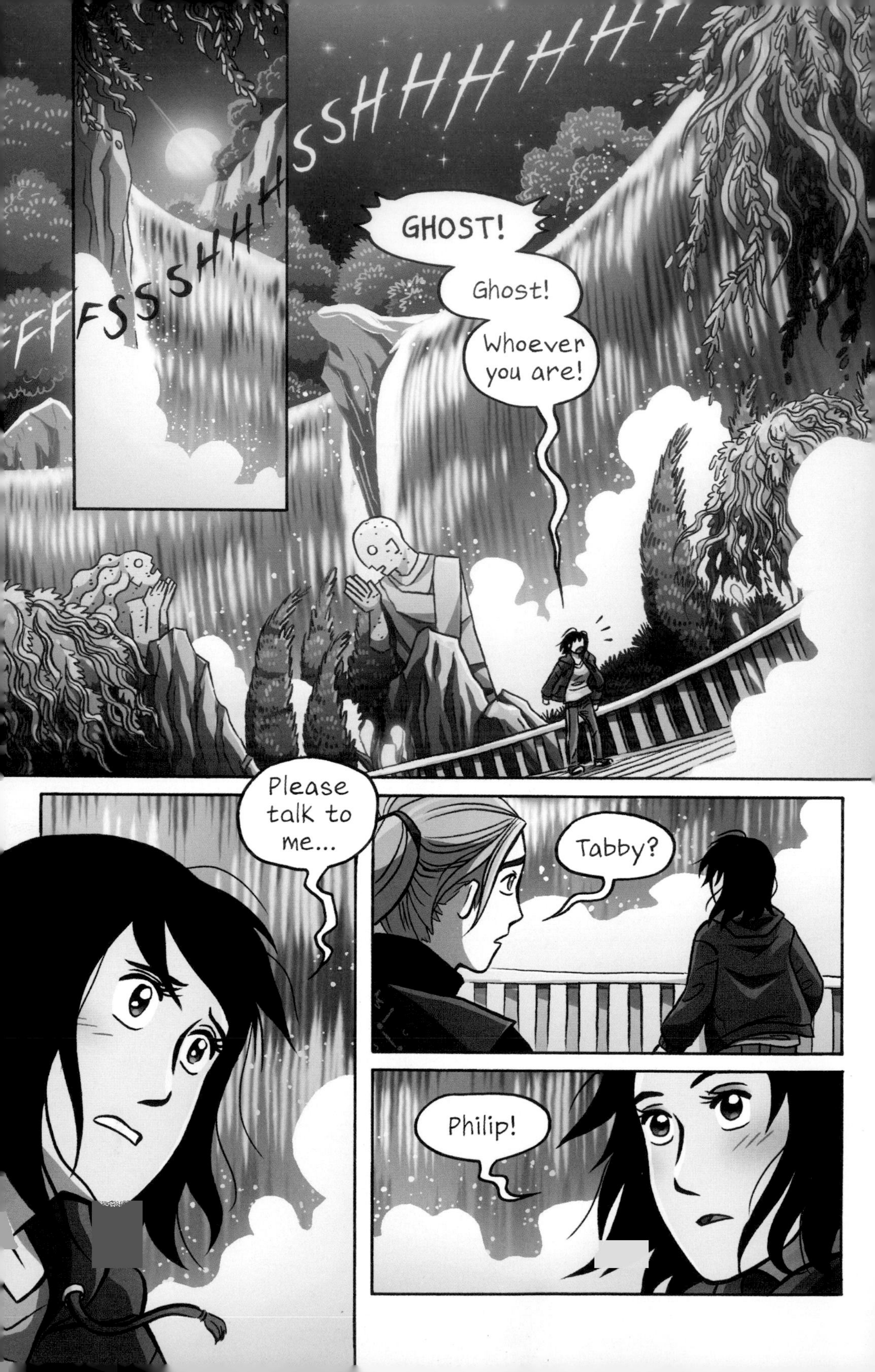
GHOST!
Ghost!
Whoever you are!
Please talk to me...
Tabby?
Philip!

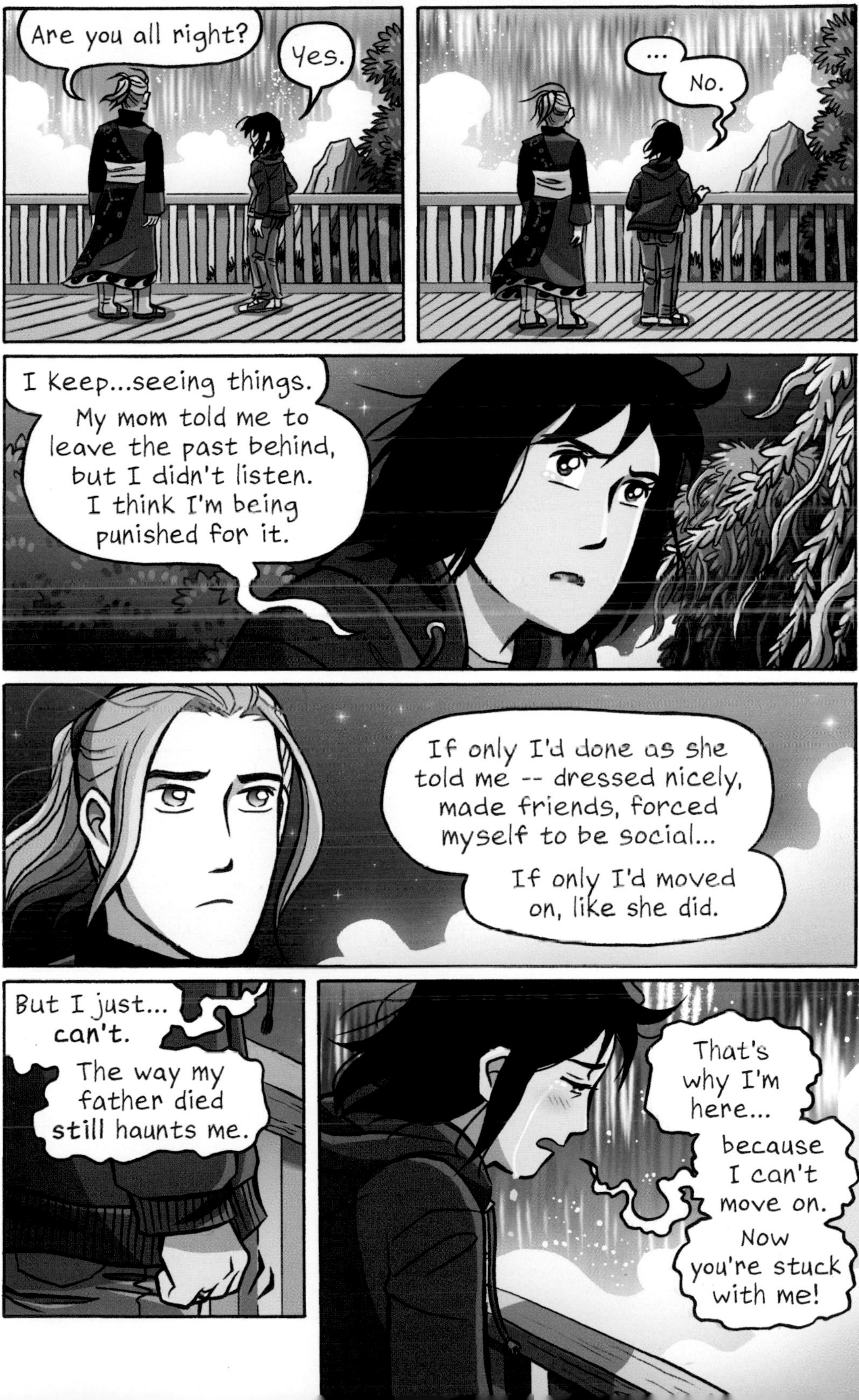
Are you all right?
Yes.
...
No.
I keep...seeing things.
My mom told me to leave the past behind, but I didn't listen. I think I'm being punished for it.
If only I'd done as she told me -- dressed nicely, made friends, forced myself to be social...
If only I'd moved on, like she did.
But I just... can't.
The way my father died still haunts me.
That's why I'm here...
because I can't move on.
Now you're stuck with me!

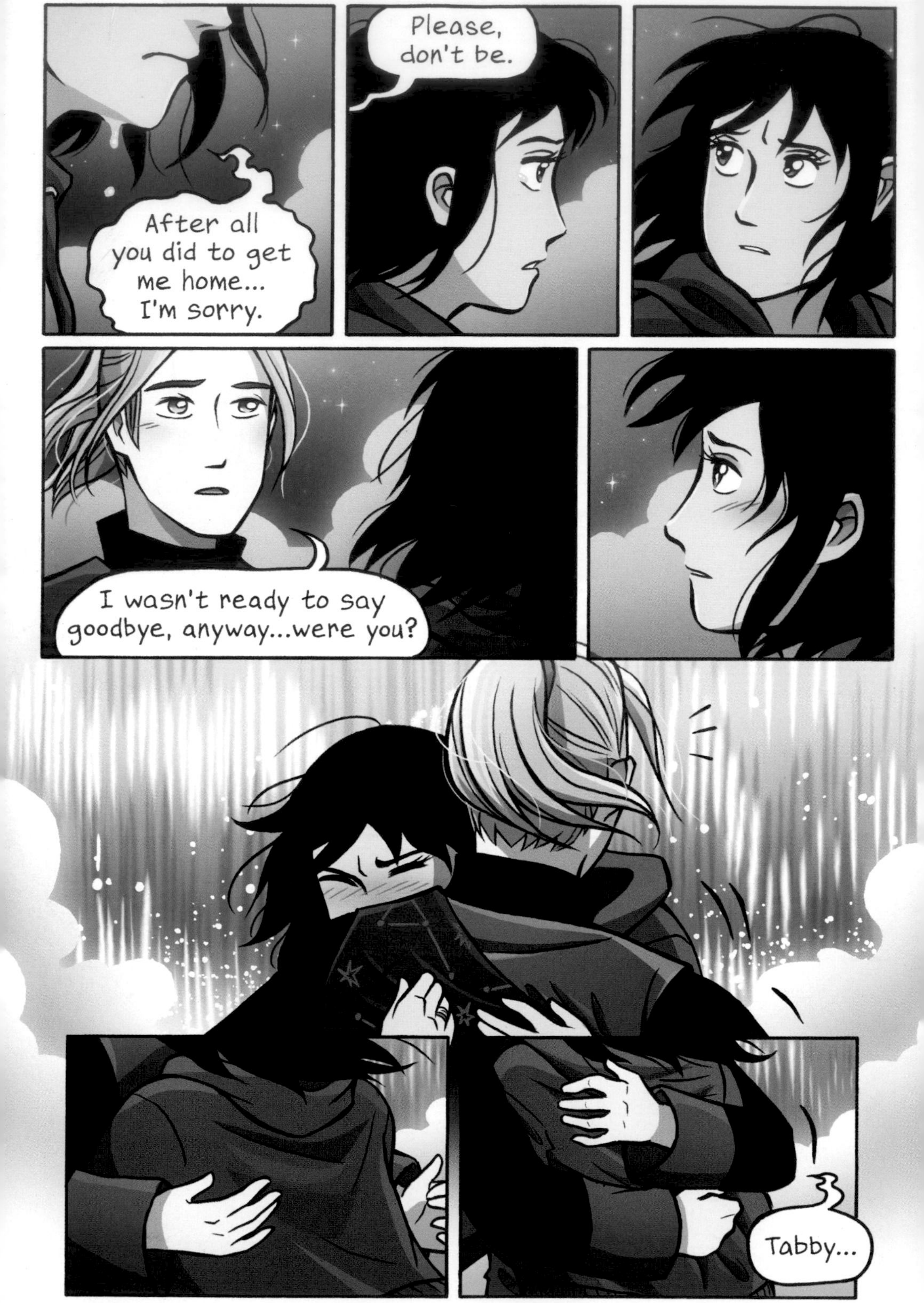
After all you did to get me home... I'm sorry.
Please, don't be.
I wasn't ready to say goodbye, anyway...were you?
Tabby...

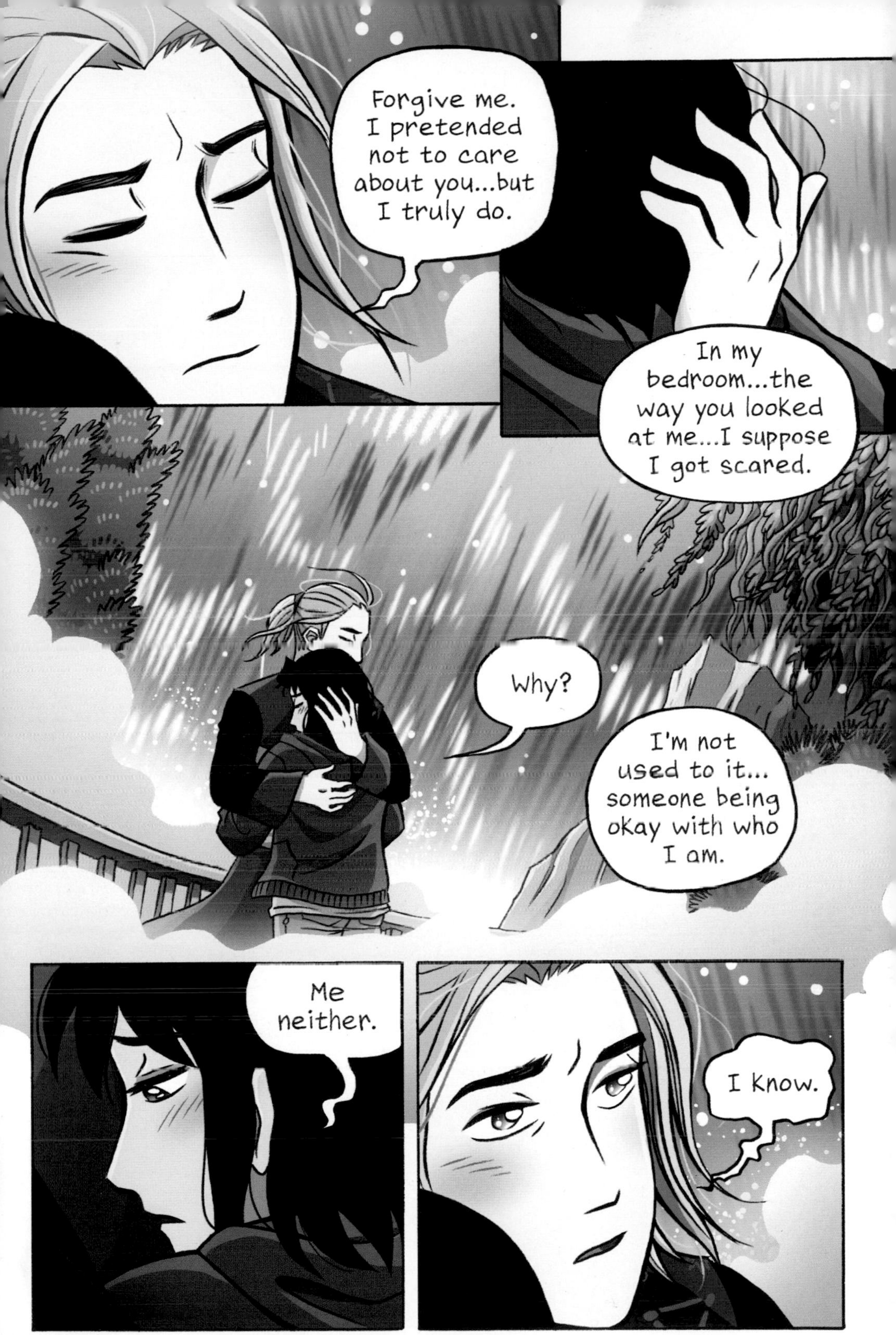
Forgive me. I pretended not to care about you...but I truly do.
In my bedroom...the way you looked at me...I suppose I got scared.
Why?
I'm not used to it... someone being okay with who I am.
Me neither.
I know.

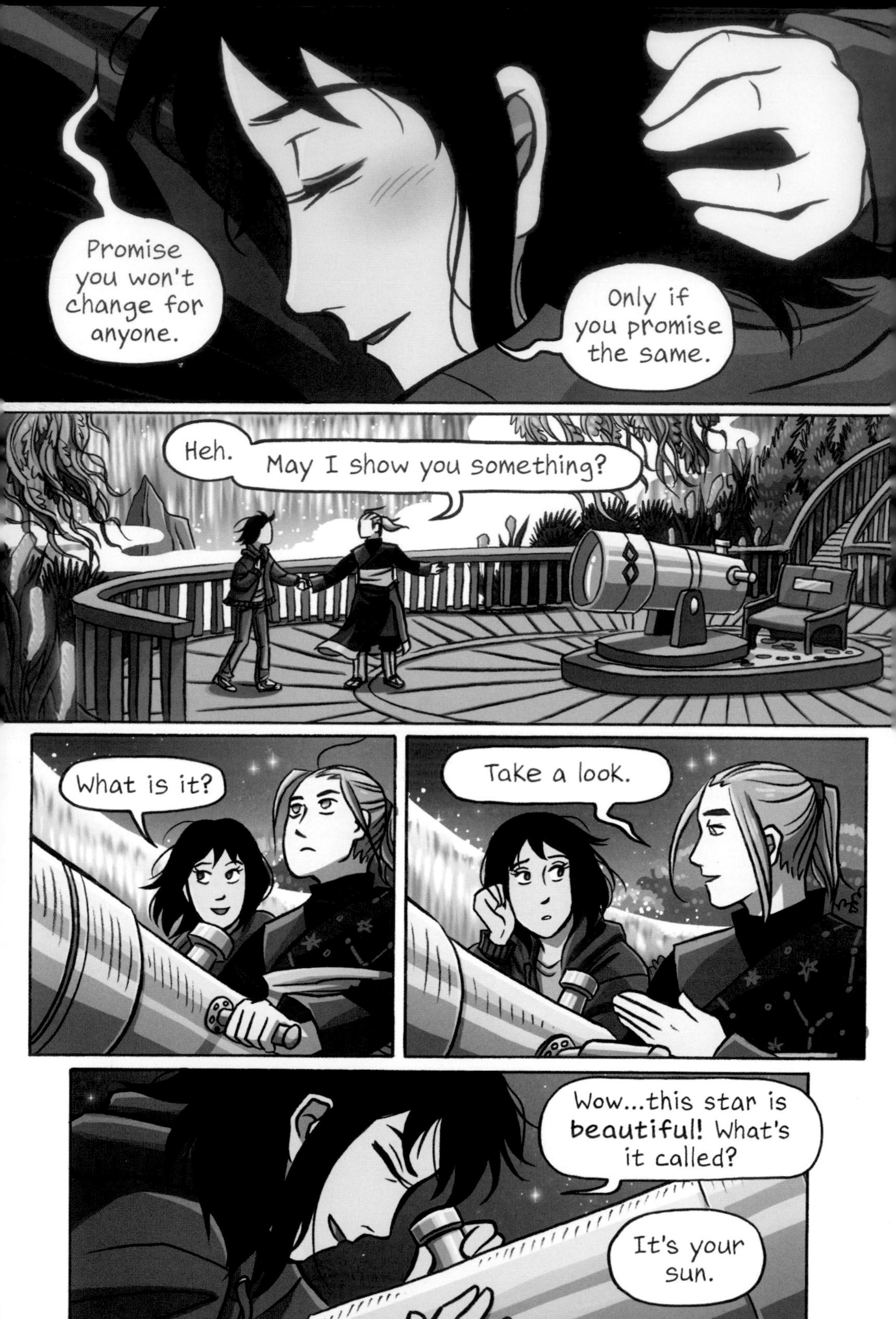
Promise you won't change for anyone.
Only if you promise the same.
Heh.
May I show you something?
What is it?
Take a look.
Wow...this star is beautiful! What's it called?
It's your sun.

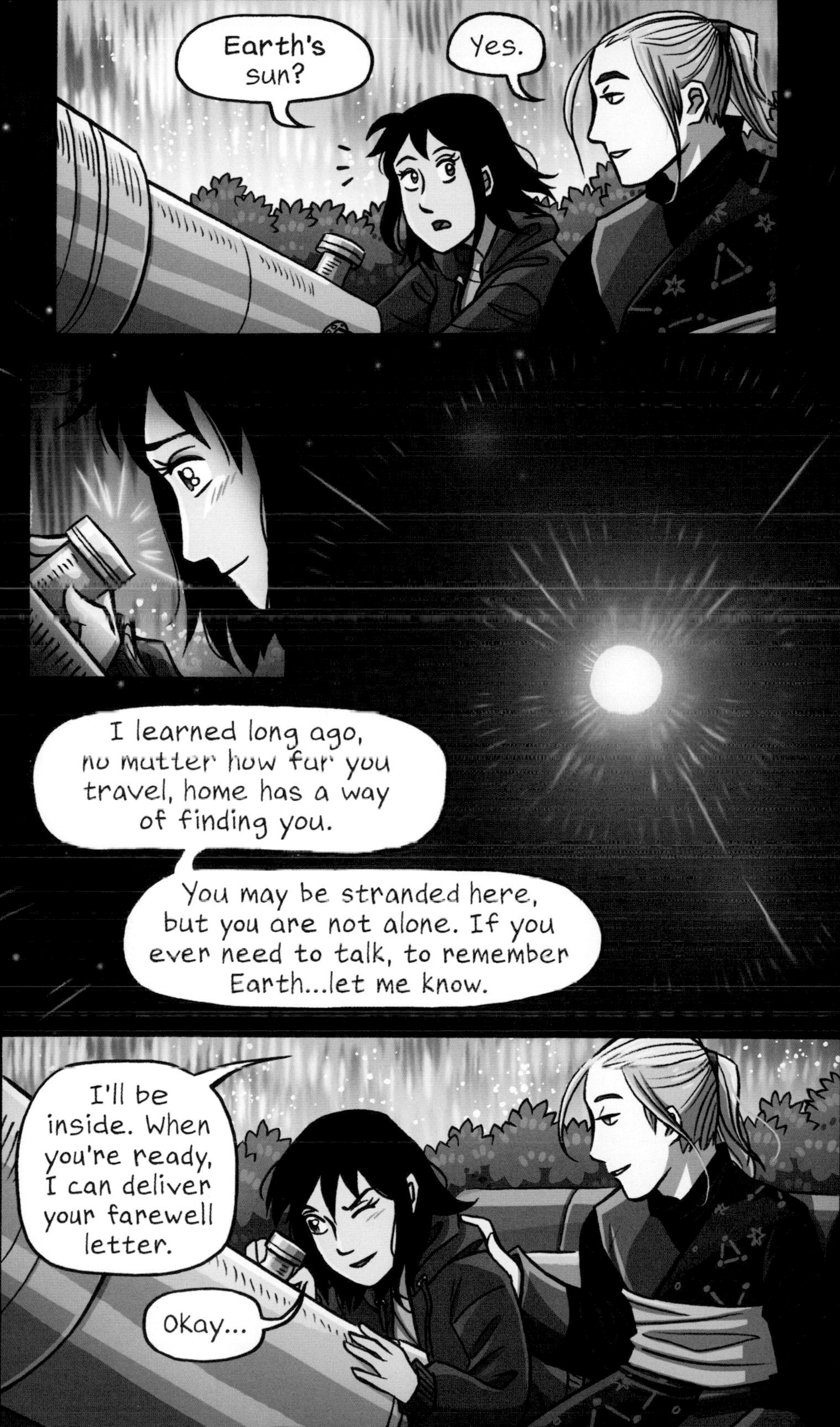
Earth's sun?
Yes.
I learned long ago, no matter how far you travel, home has a way of finding you.
You may be stranded here, but you are not alone. If you ever need to talk, to remember Earth...let me know.
I'll be inside. When you're ready, I can deliver your farewell letter.
Okay...

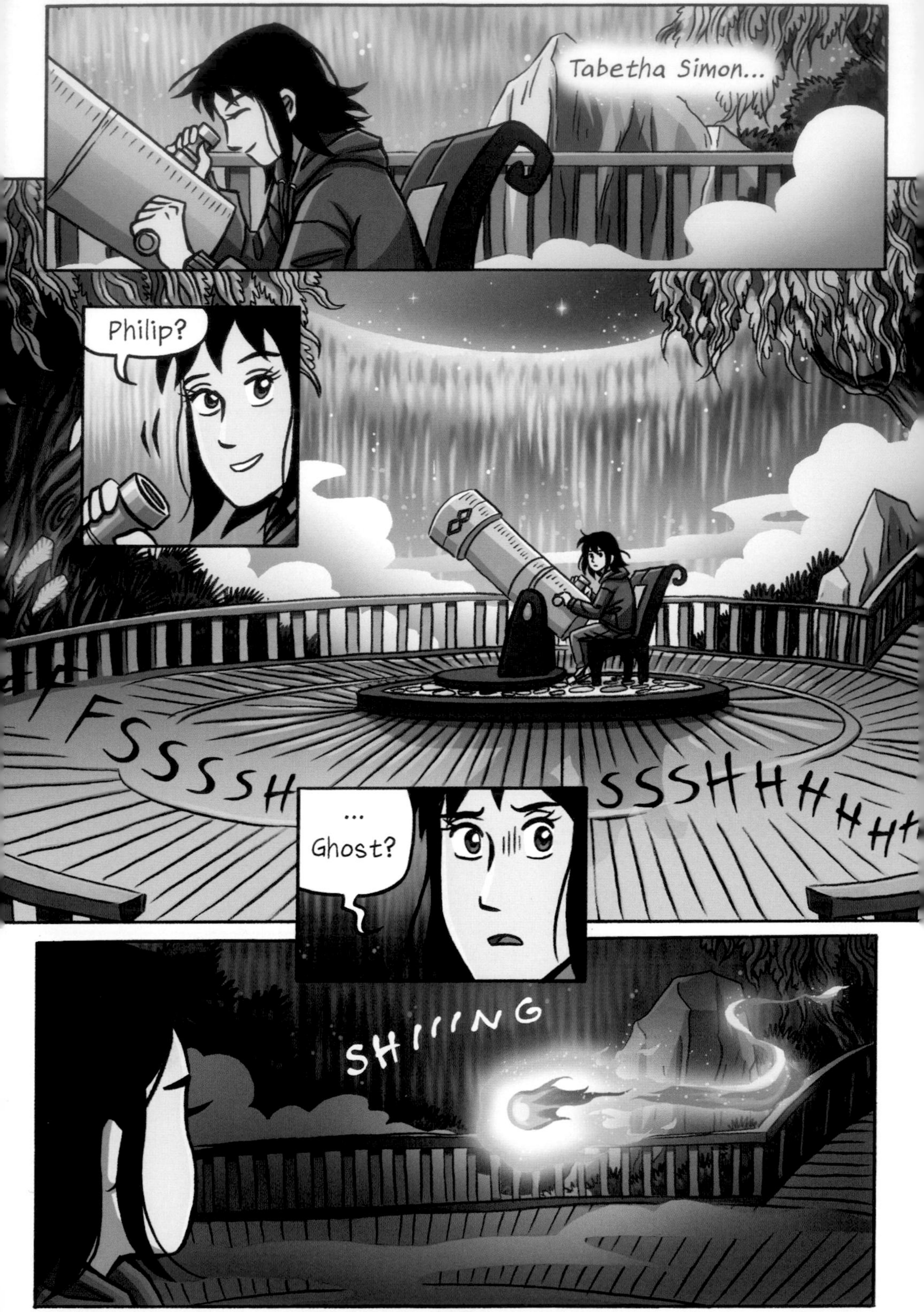

Tabetha Simon...
Philip?
FSSSSH
SSSHHHHH
...
Ghost?
SHIIING

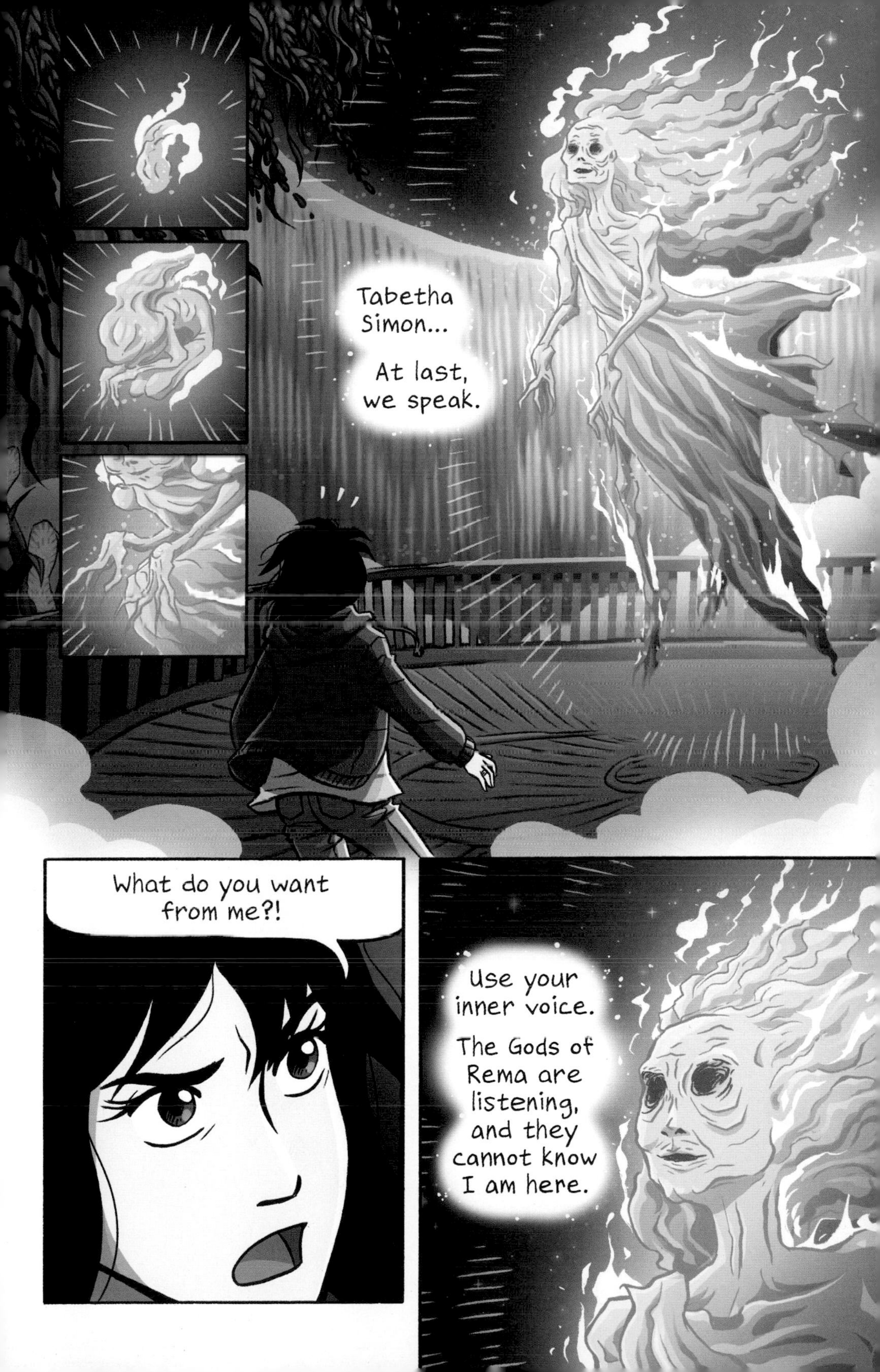
Tabetha Simon...
At last, we speak.
What do you want from me?!
Use your inner voice.
The Gods of Rema are listening, and they cannot know I am here.

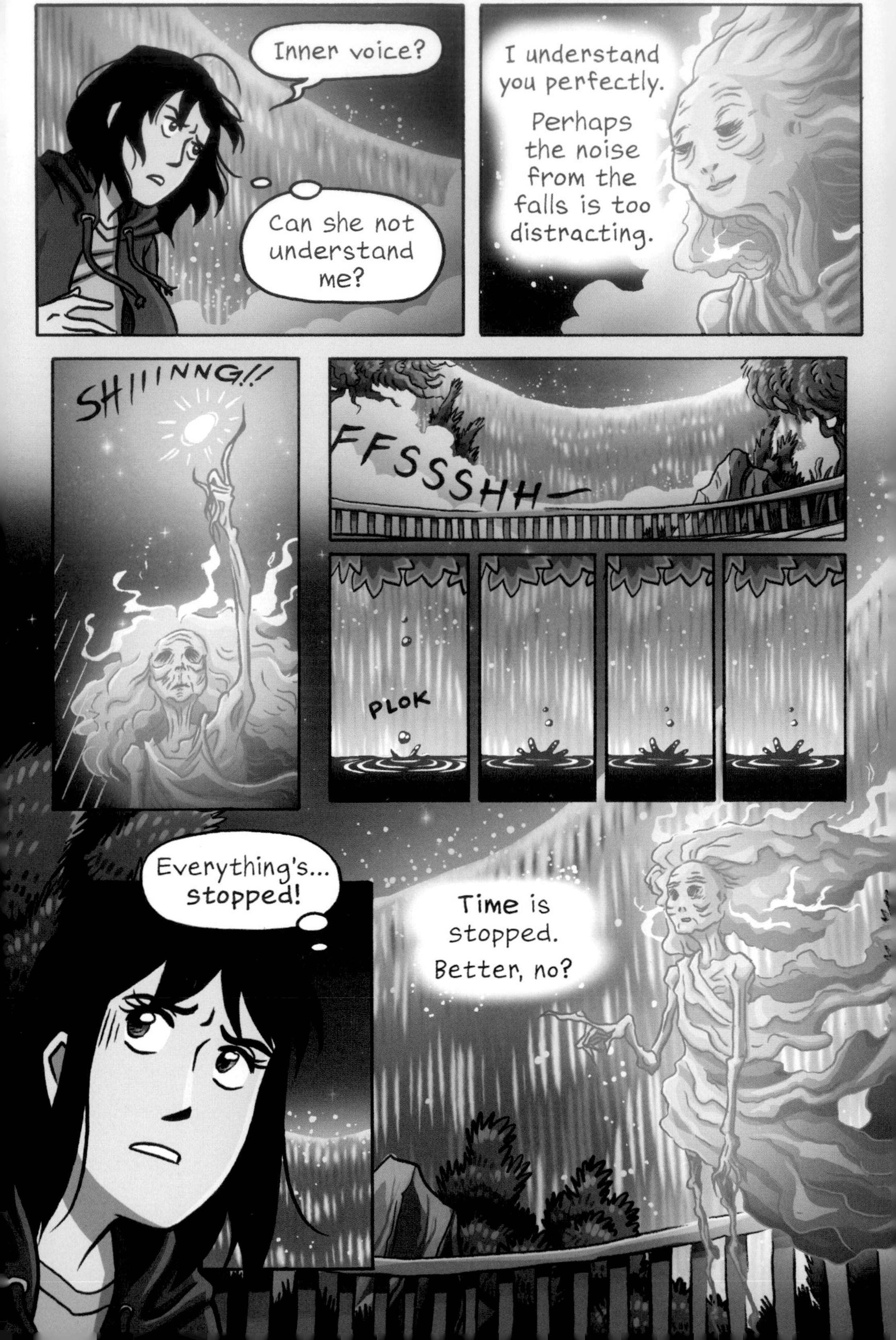
Inner voice?
Can she not understand me?
I understand you perfectly.
Perhaps the noise from the falls is too distracting.
SHIIINNG!!
FFSSSSHH—
PLOK
Everything's... stopped!
Time is stopped.
Better, no?

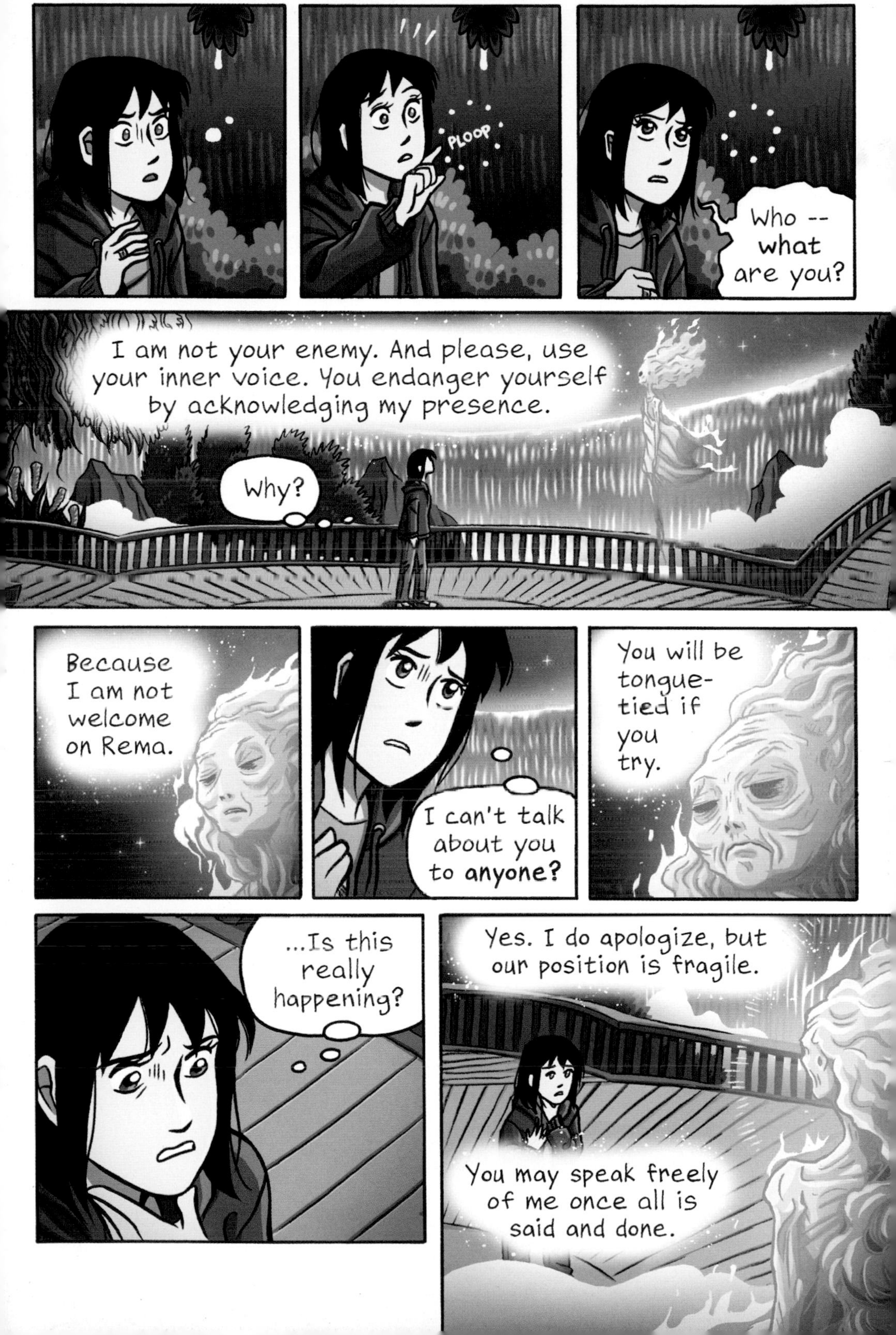
PLOOP
Who -- what are you?
I am not your enemy. And please, use your inner voice. You endanger yourself by acknowledging my presence.
Why?
Because I am not welcome on Rema.
I can't talk about you to anyone?
You will be tongue-tied if you try.
...Is this really happening?
Yes. I do apologize, but our position is fragile.
You may speak freely of me once all is said and done.

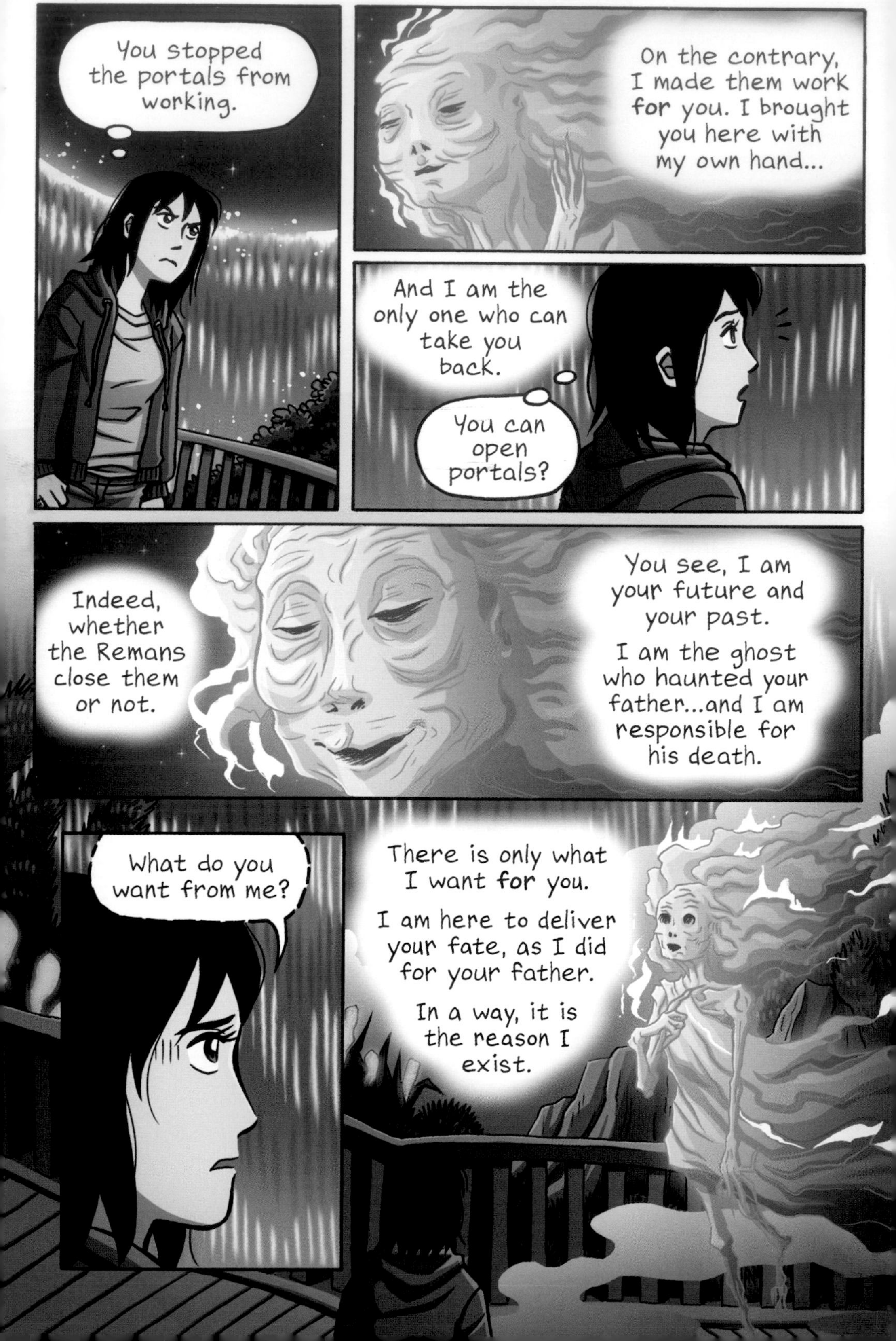
You stopped the portals from working.
On the contrary, I made them work for you. I brought you here with my own hand...
And I am the only one who can take you back.
You can open portals?
Indeed, whether the Remans close them or not.
You see, I am your future and your past.
I am the ghost who haunted your father...and I am responsible for his death.
What do you want from me?
There is only what I want for you.
I am here to deliver your fate, as I did for your father.
In a way, it is the reason I exist.

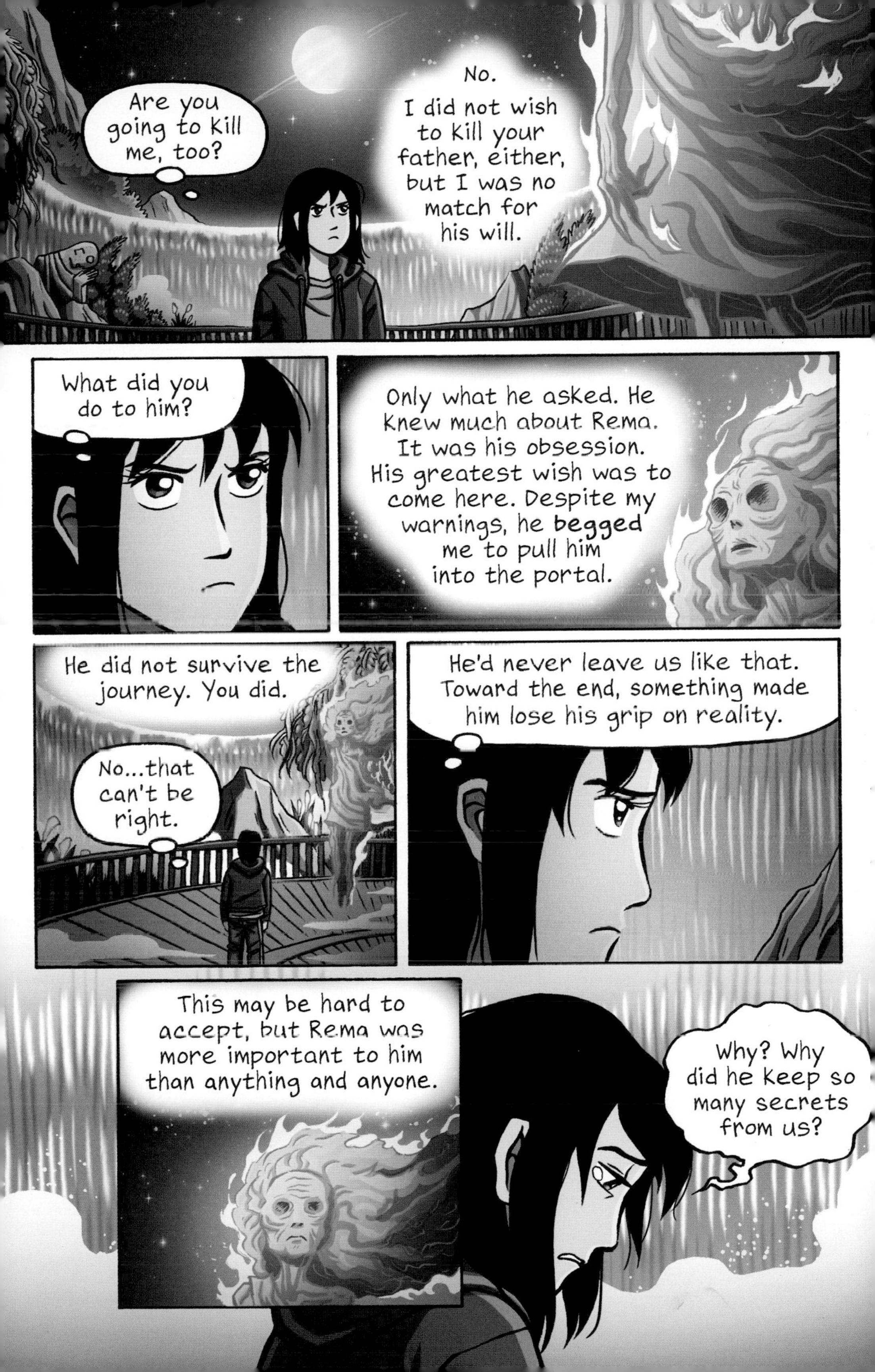
Are you going to kill me, too?
No.
I did not wish to kill your father, either, but I was no match for his will.
What did you do to him?
Only what he asked. He knew much about Rema. It was his obsession. His greatest wish was to come here. Despite my warnings, he begged me to pull him into the portal.
He did not survive the journey. You did.
No...that can't be right.
He'd never leave us like that. Toward the end, something made him lose his grip on reality.
This may be hard to accept, but Rema was more important to him than anything and anyone.
Why? Why did he keep so many secrets from us?

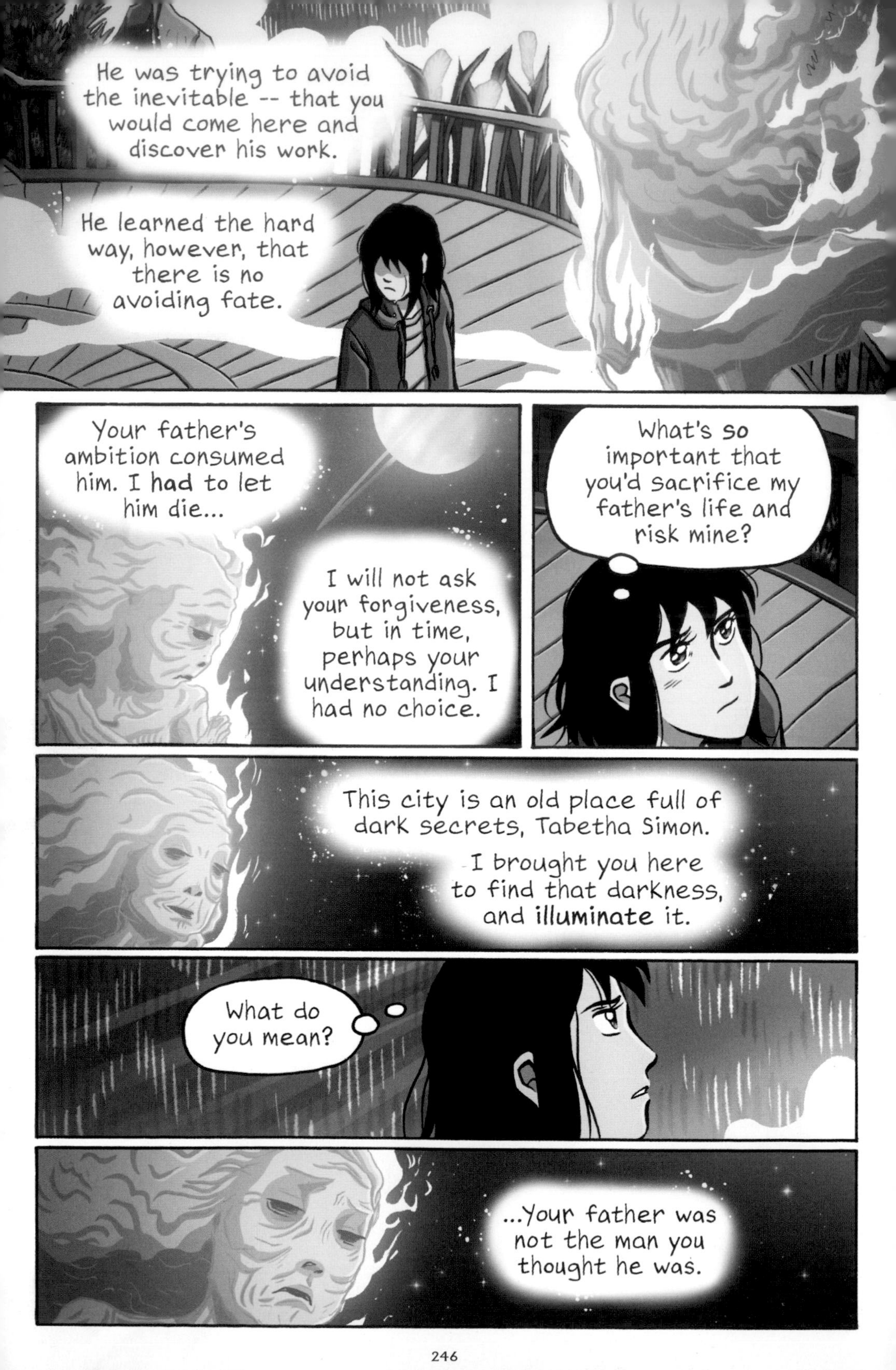
He was trying to avoid the inevitable -- that you would come here and discover his work.
He learned the hard way, however, that there is no avoiding fate.
Your father's ambition consumed him. I **had** to let him die...
I will not ask your forgiveness, but in time, perhaps your understanding. I had no choice.
What's **so** important that you'd sacrifice my father's life and risk mine?
This city is an old place full of dark secrets, Tabetha Simon.
I brought you here to find that darkness, and **illuminate** it.
What do you mean?
...Your father was not the man you thought he was.

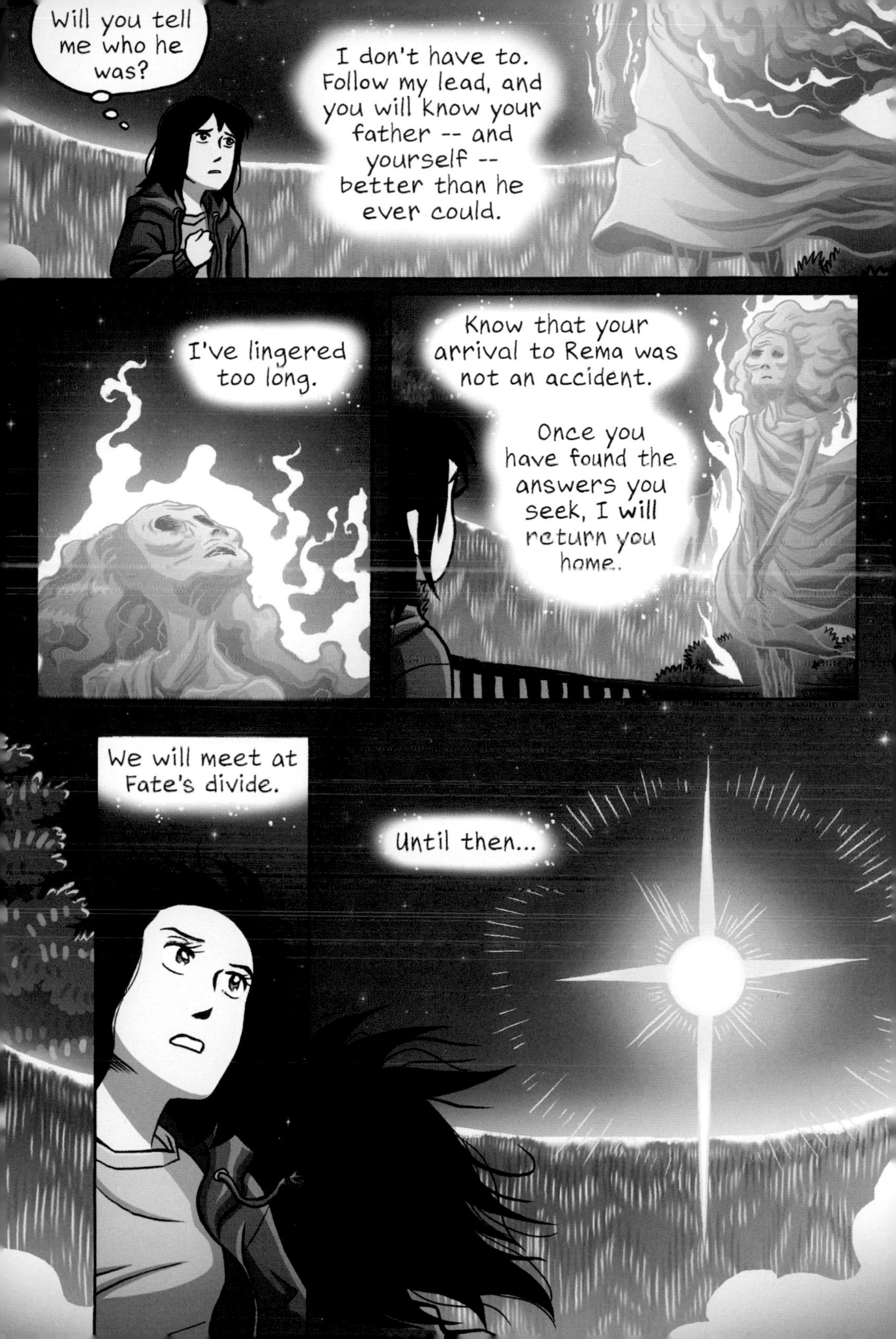

Will you tell me who he was?
I don't have to. Follow my lead, and you will know your father -- and yourself -- better than he ever could.
I've lingered too long.
Know that your arrival to Rema was not an accident.
Once you have found the answers you seek, I will return you home.
We will meet at Fate's divide.
Until then...

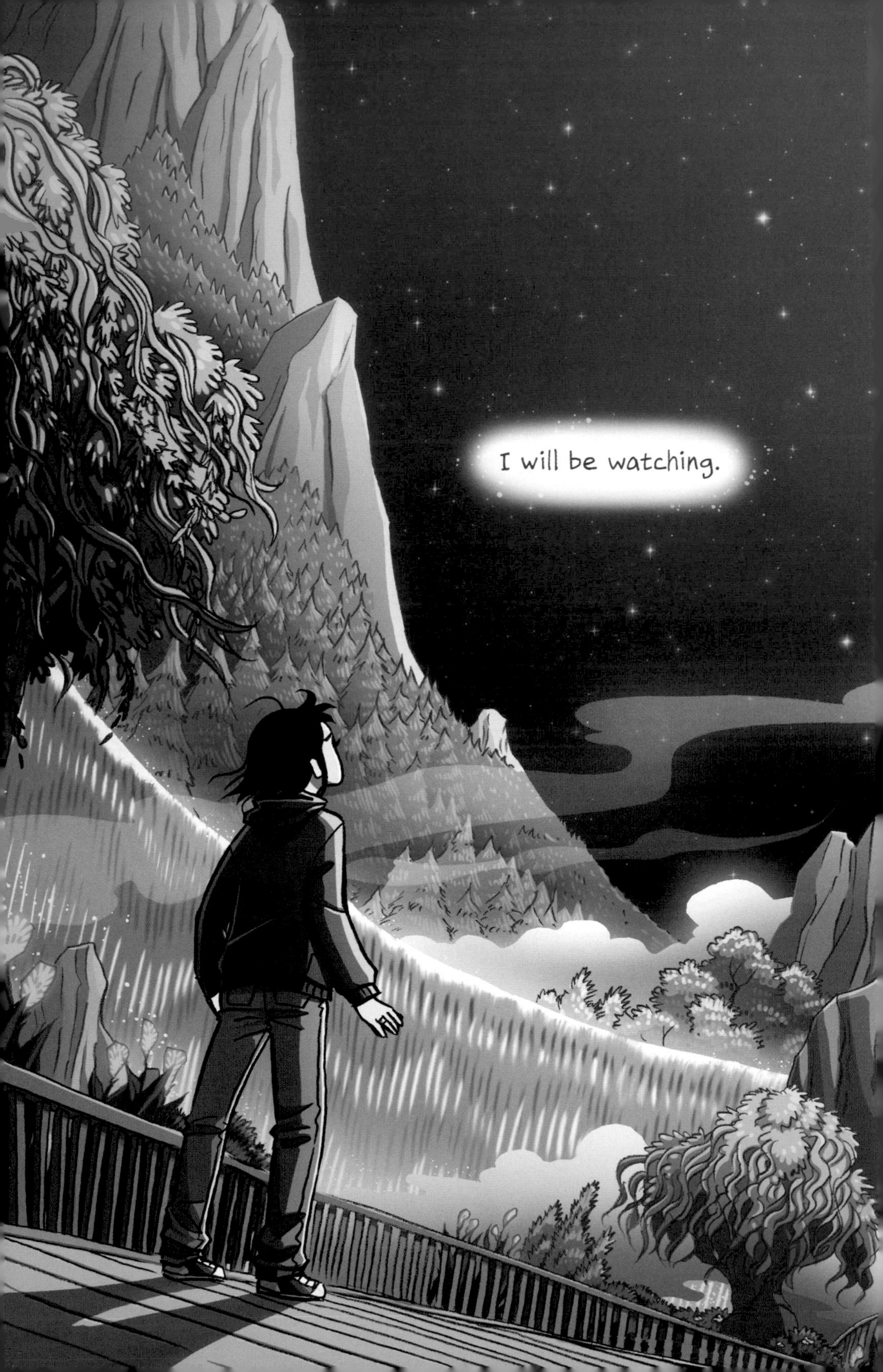
I will be watching.

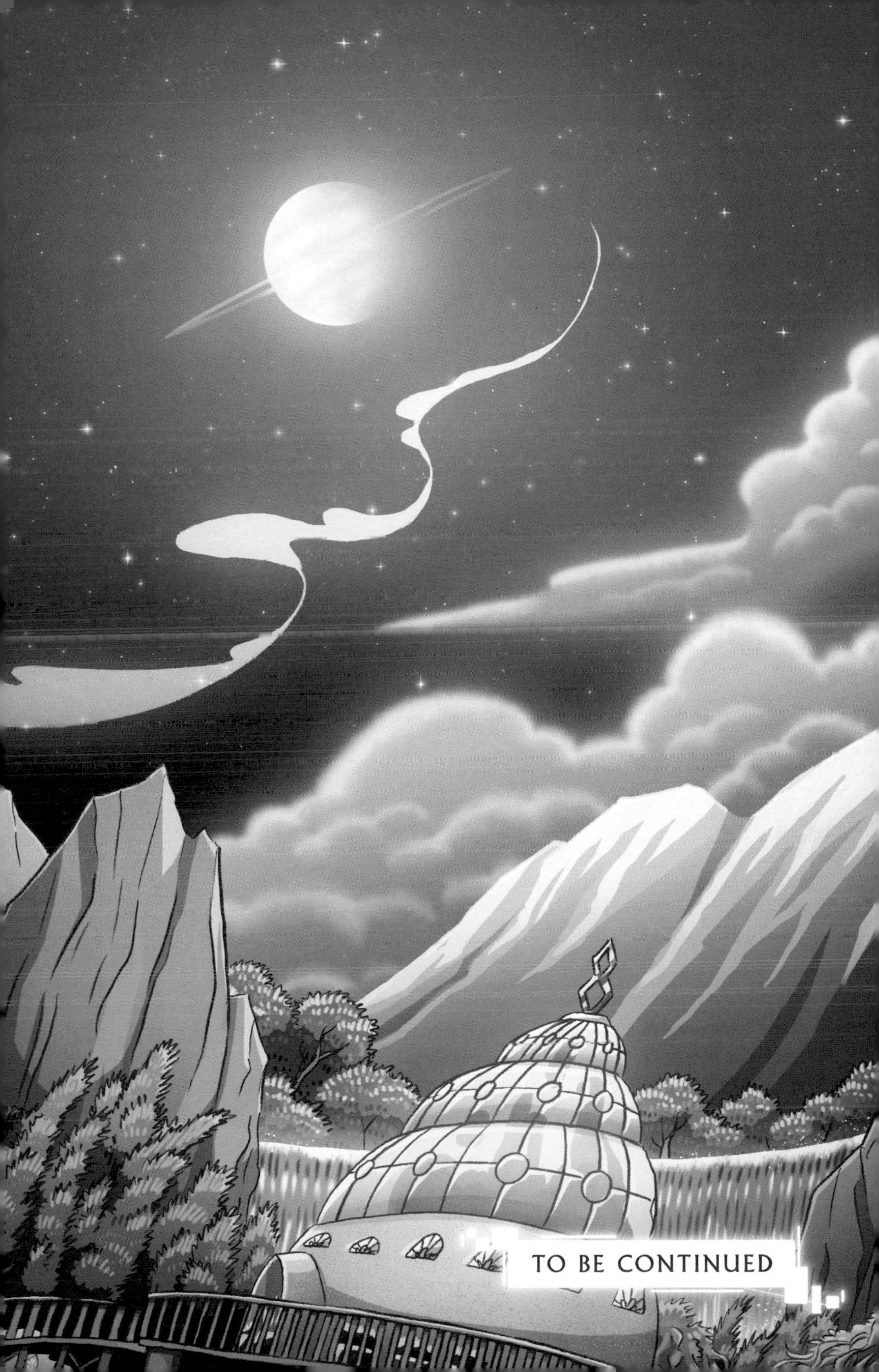
TO BE CONTINUED

Don't miss the next book in Tabby's adventure.
Here's a sneak peek . . .

THE REMA

CHRONICLES

BOOK TWO
KINGDOM OF WATER

PART I
THE LETTER

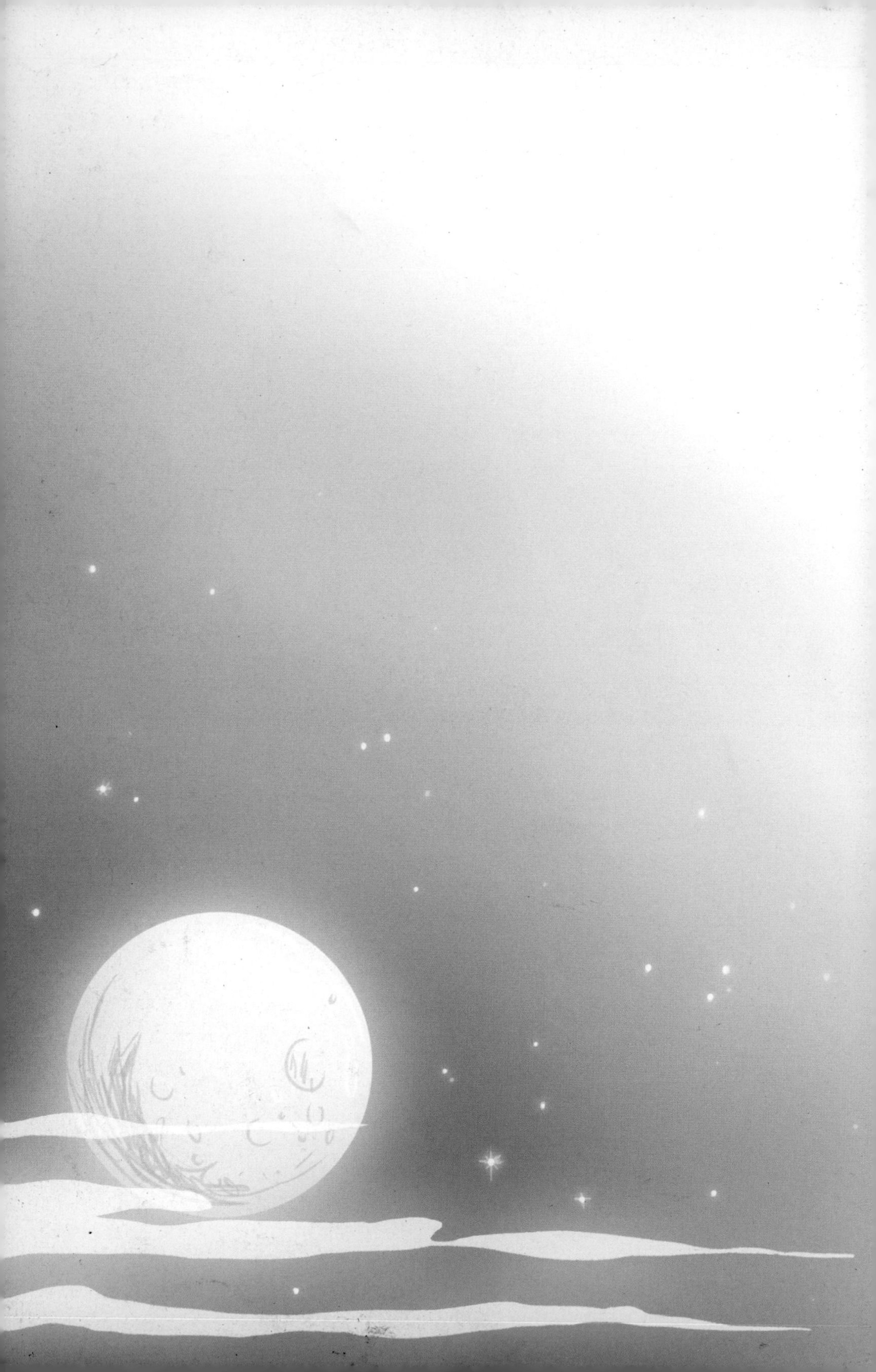

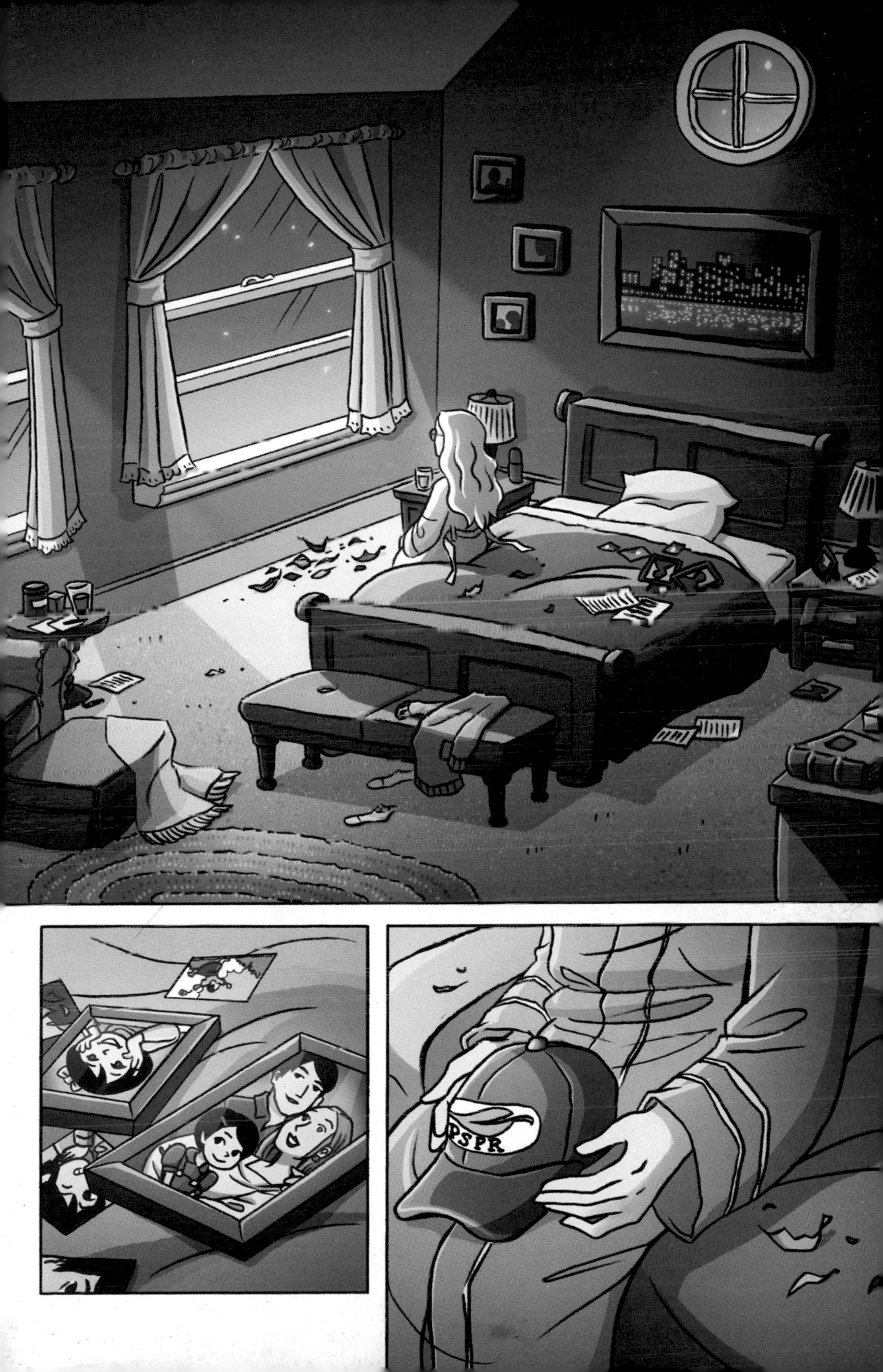
PSPR

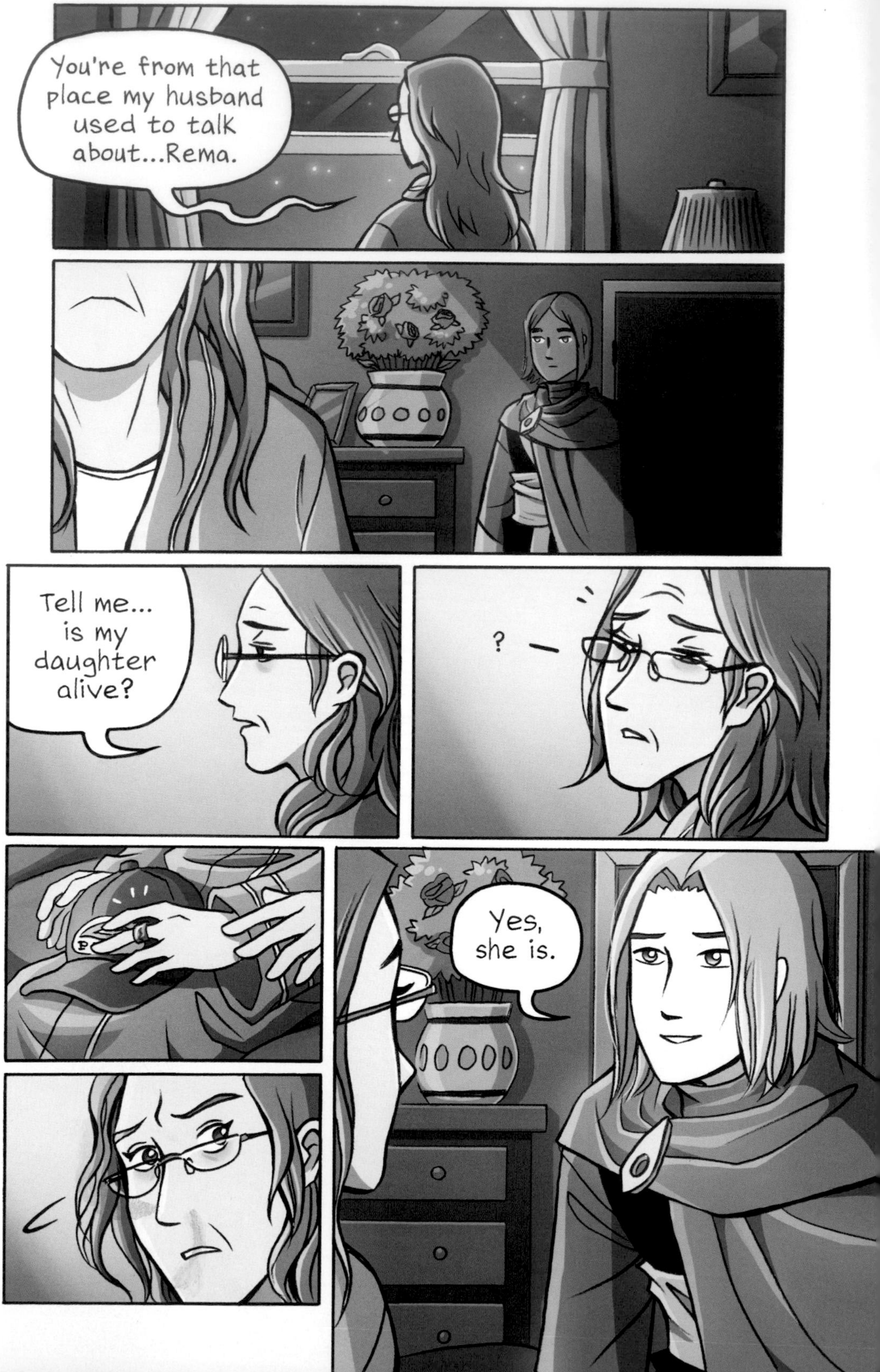
You're from that place my husband used to talk about...Rema.
Tell me... is my daughter alive?
?
Yes, she is.

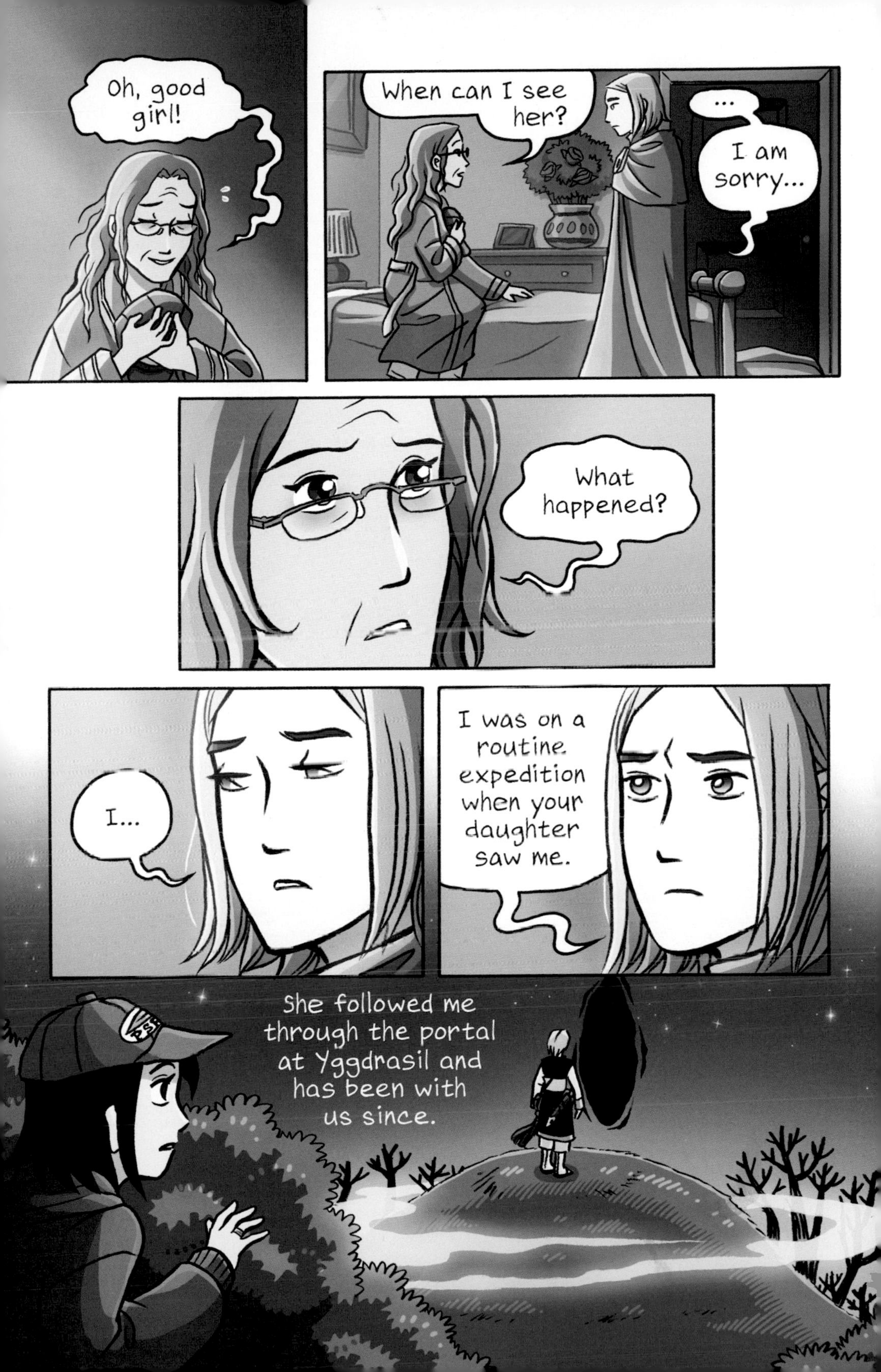
Oh, good girl!
When can I see her?
...
I am sorry...
What happened?
I...
I was on a routine expedition when your daughter saw me.
She followed me through the portal at Yggdrasil and has been with us since.

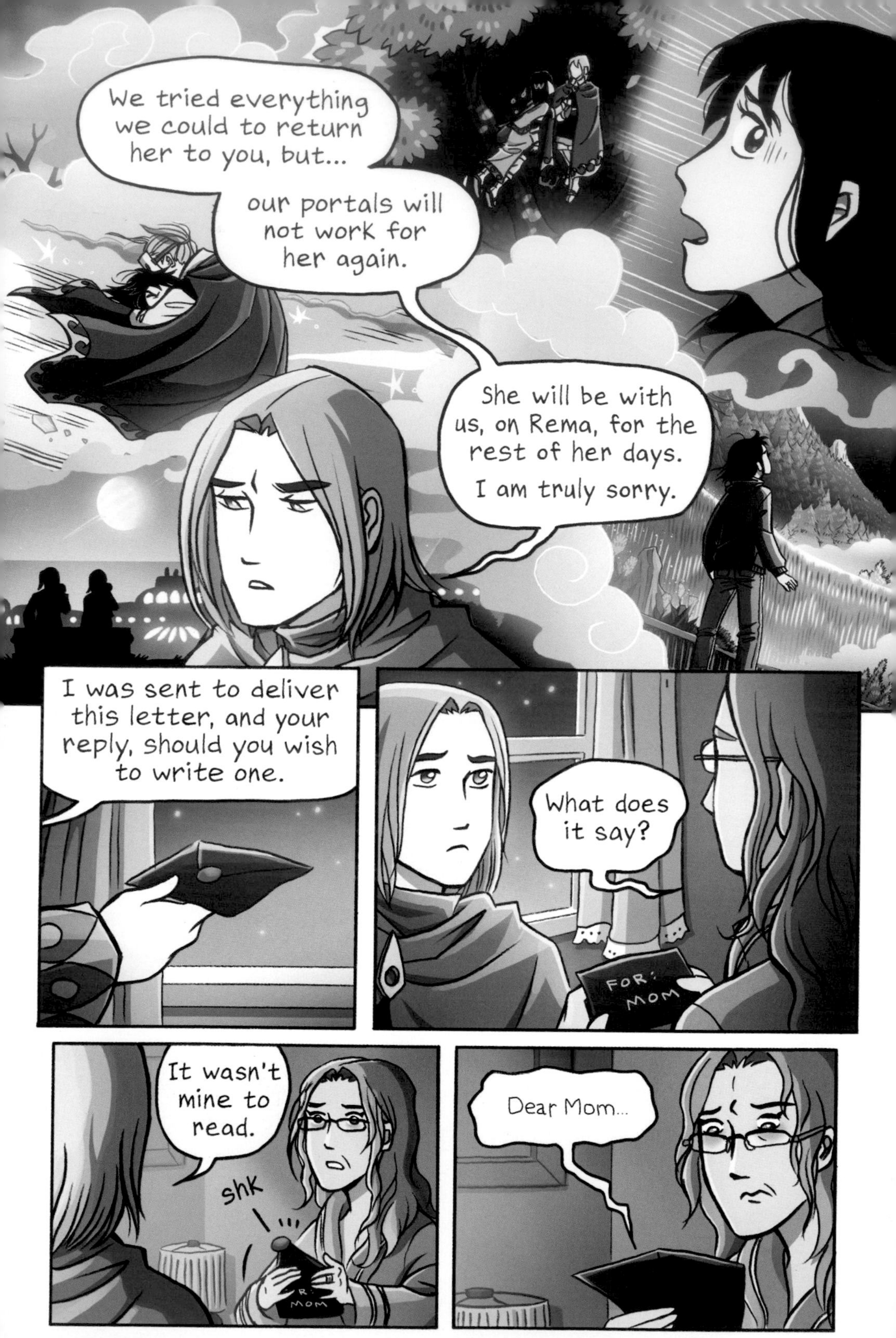
We tried everything we could to return her to you, but...
our portals will not work for her again.
She will be with us, on Rema, for the rest of her days.
I am truly sorry.
I was sent to deliver this letter, and your reply, should you wish to write one.
What does it say?
FOR: MOM
It wasn't mine to read.
shk
Dear Mom...

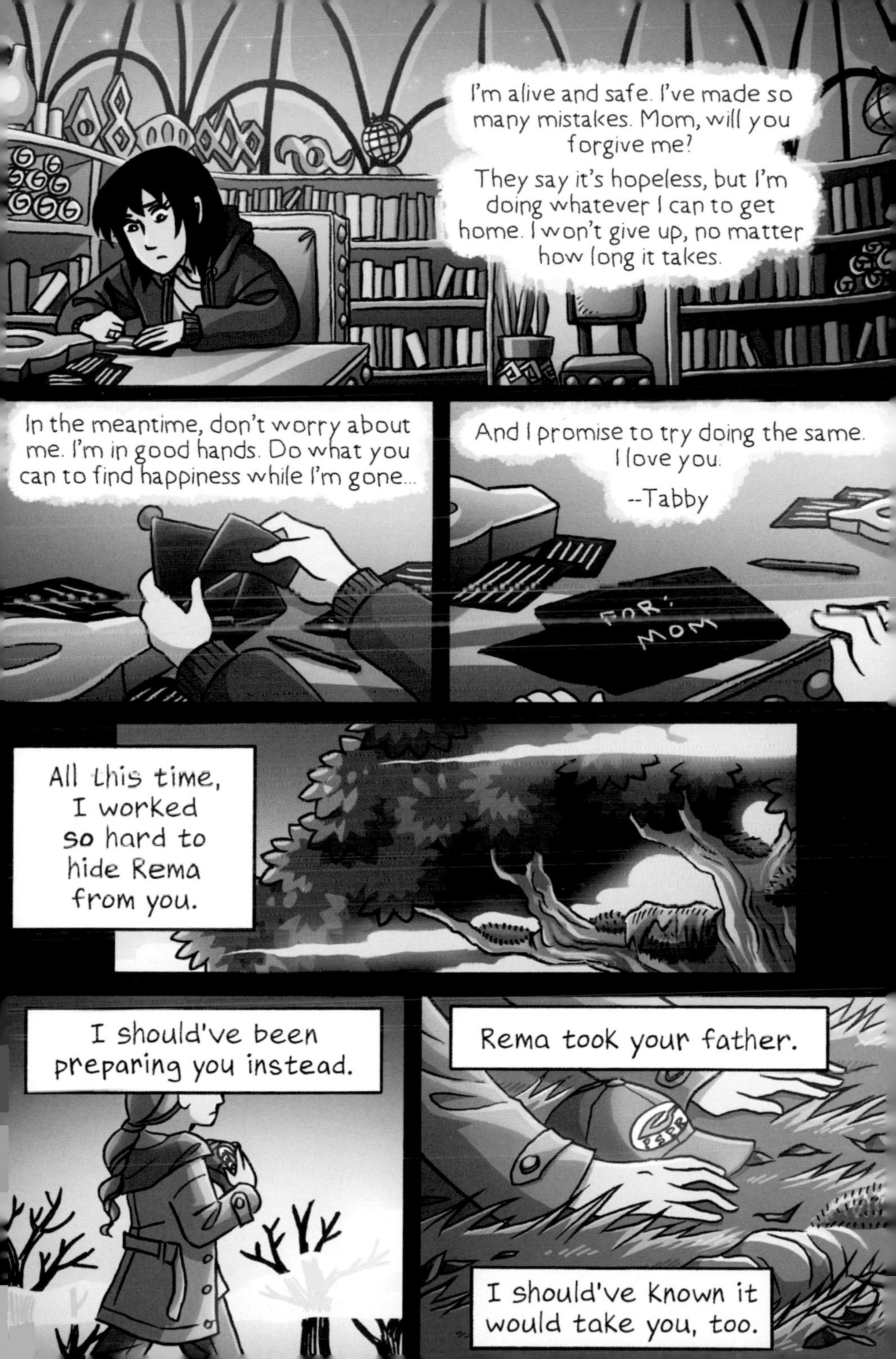
I'm alive and safe. I've made so many mistakes. Mom, will you forgive me?
They say it's hopeless, but I'm doing whatever I can to get home. I won't give up, no matter how long it takes.
In the meantime, don't worry about me. I'm in good hands. Do what you can to find happiness while I'm gone...
And I promise to try doing the same. I love you.
--Tabby
FOR: MOM
All this time, I worked so hard to hide Rema from you.
I should've been preparing you instead.
Rema took your father.
PSPR
I should've known it would take you, too.

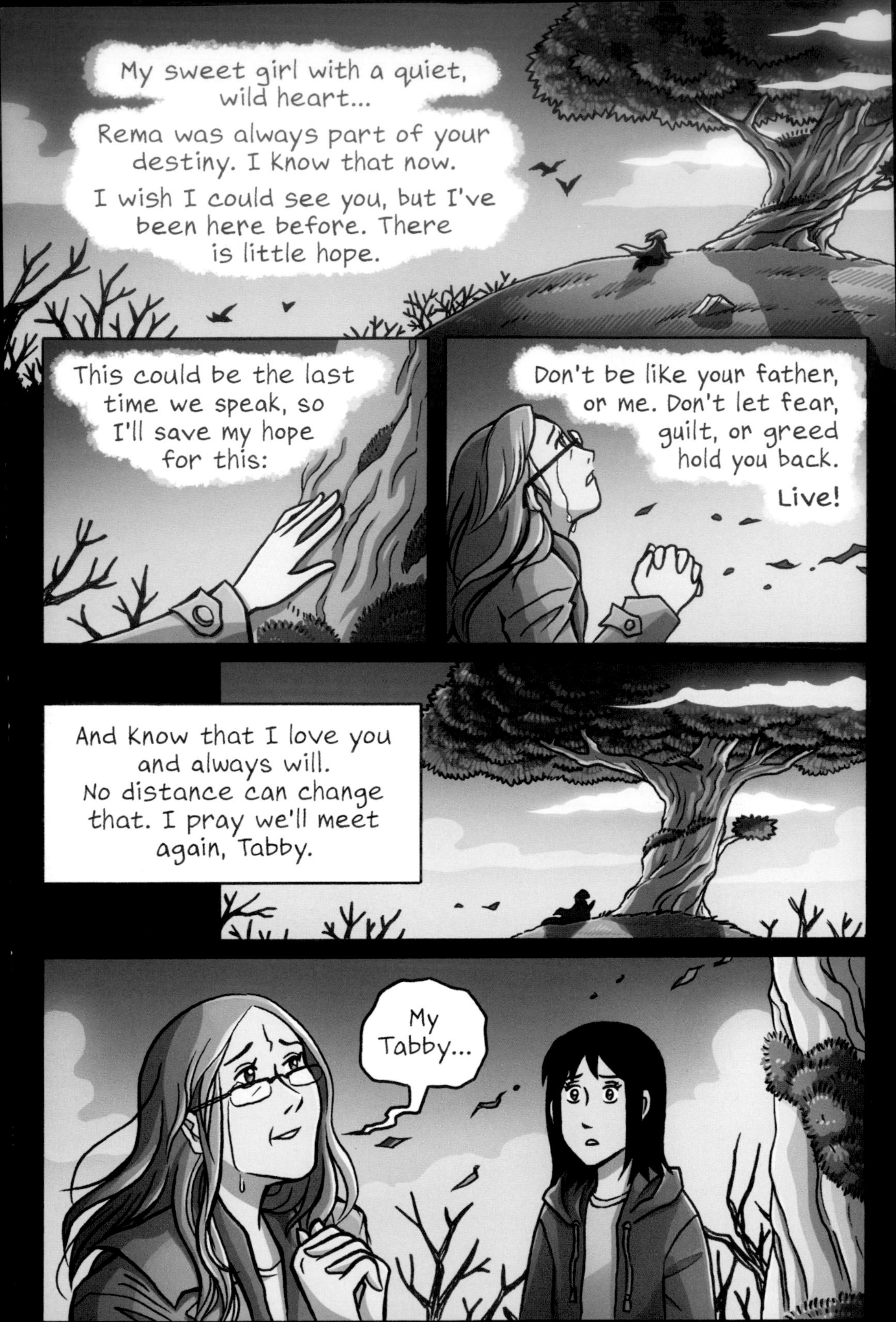
My sweet girl with a quiet, wild heart...
Rema was always part of your destiny. I know that now.
I wish I could see you, but I've been here before. There is little hope.
This could be the last time we speak, so I'll save my hope for this:
Don't be like your father, or me. Don't let fear, guilt, or greed hold you back.
Live!
And know that I love you and always will. No distance can change that. I pray we'll meet again, Tabby.
My Tabby...

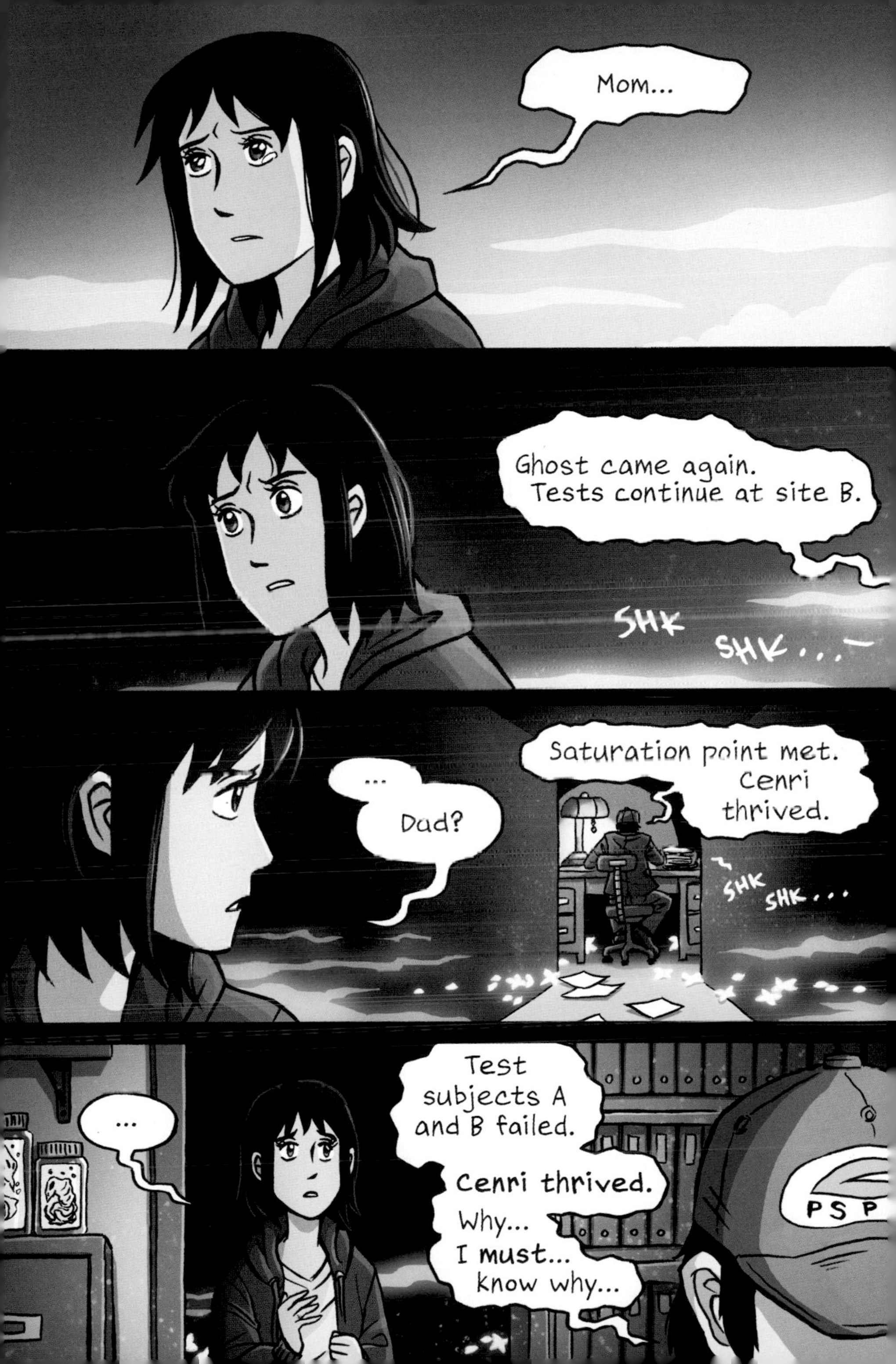
Mom...
Ghost came again. Tests continue at site B.
SHK
SHK...
Saturation point met. Cenri thrived.
...
Dad?
SHK
SHK...
...
Test subjects A and B failed.
Cenri thrived.
Why...
I must... know why...
PSP

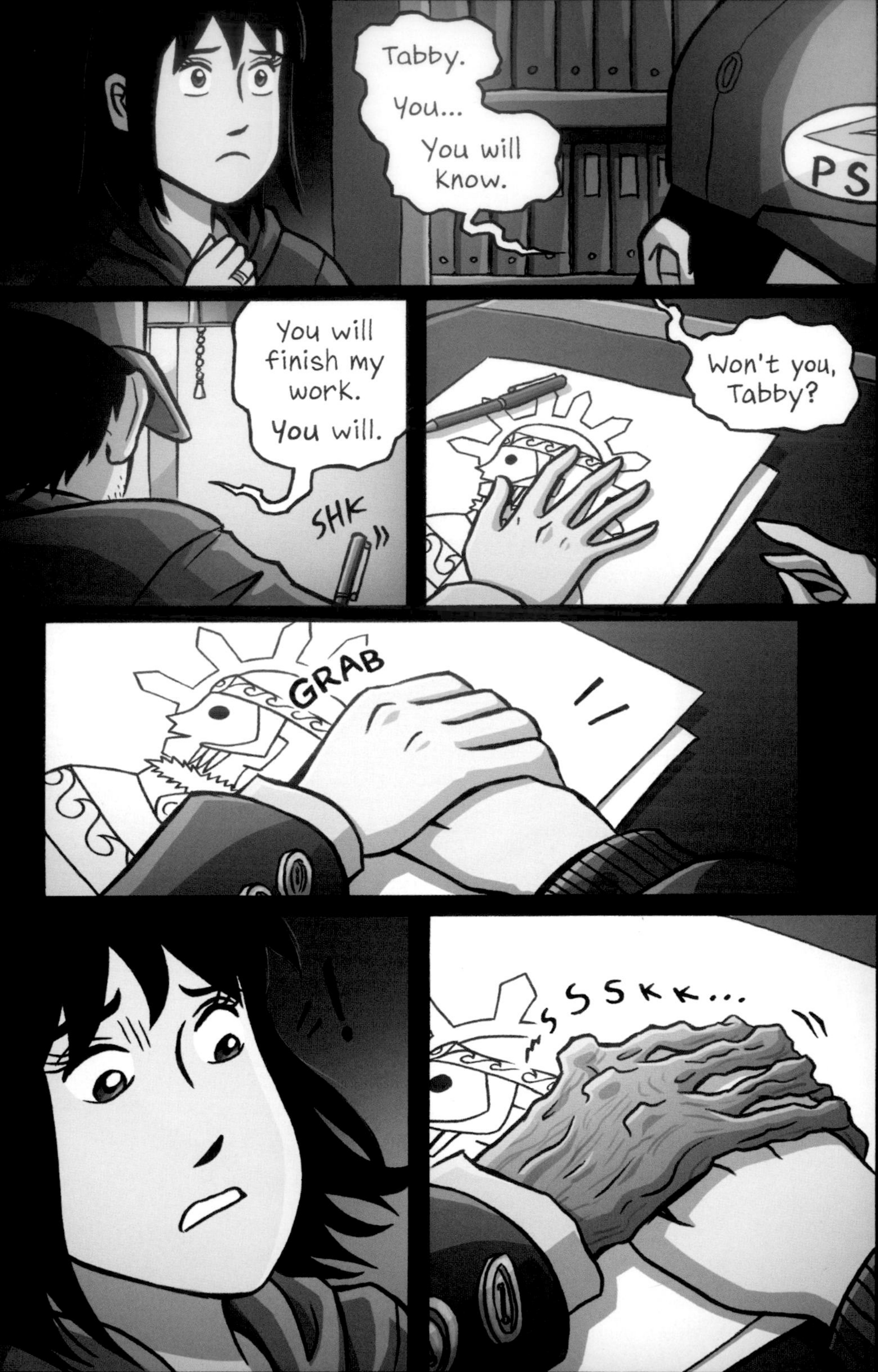
Tabby.
You...
You will know.
PS
You will finish my work.
You will.
SHK
Won't you, Tabby?
GRAB
SSSKK...

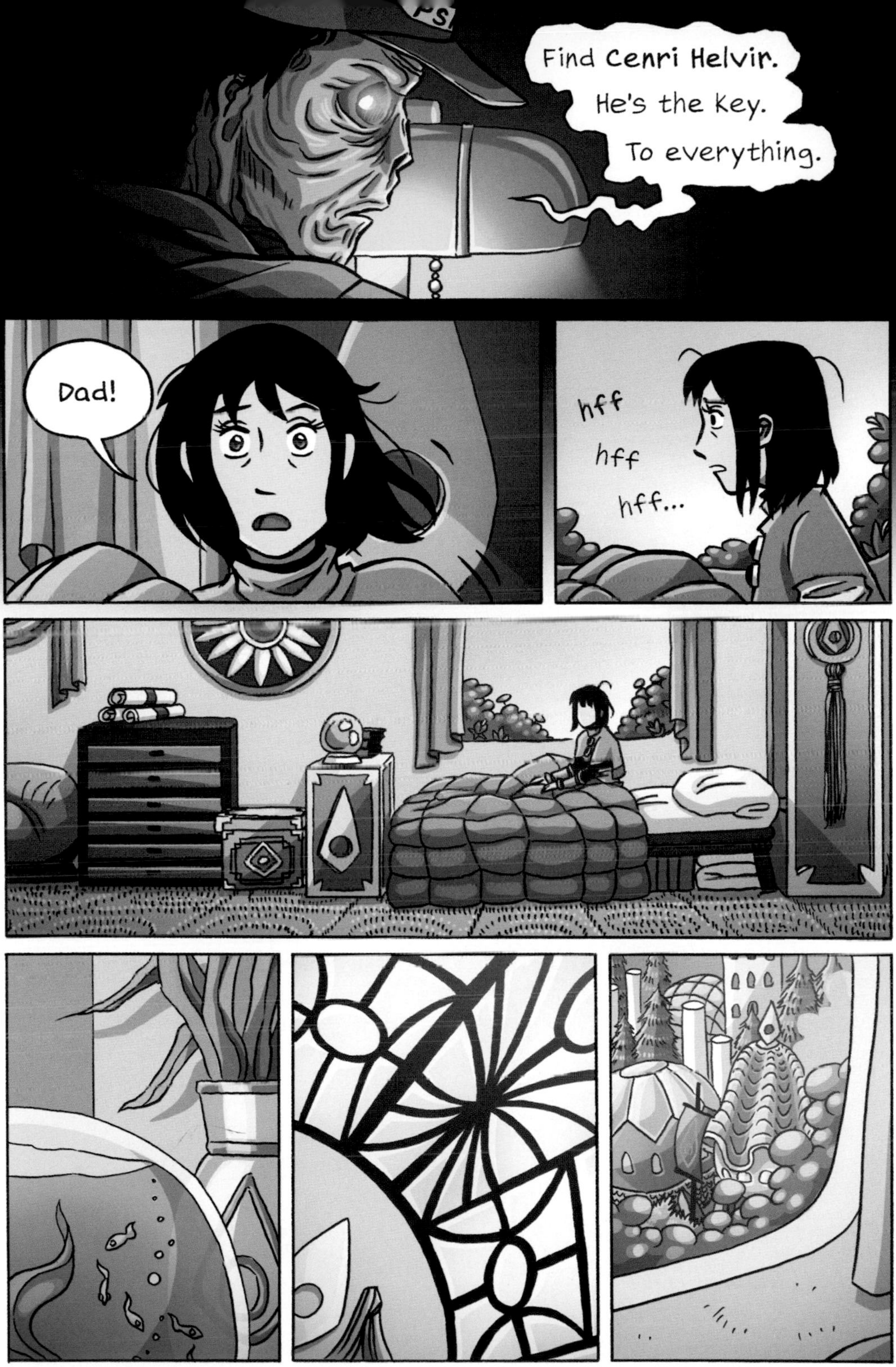
PSI
Find Cenri Helvir.
He's the key.
To everything.
Dad!
hff
hff
hff...

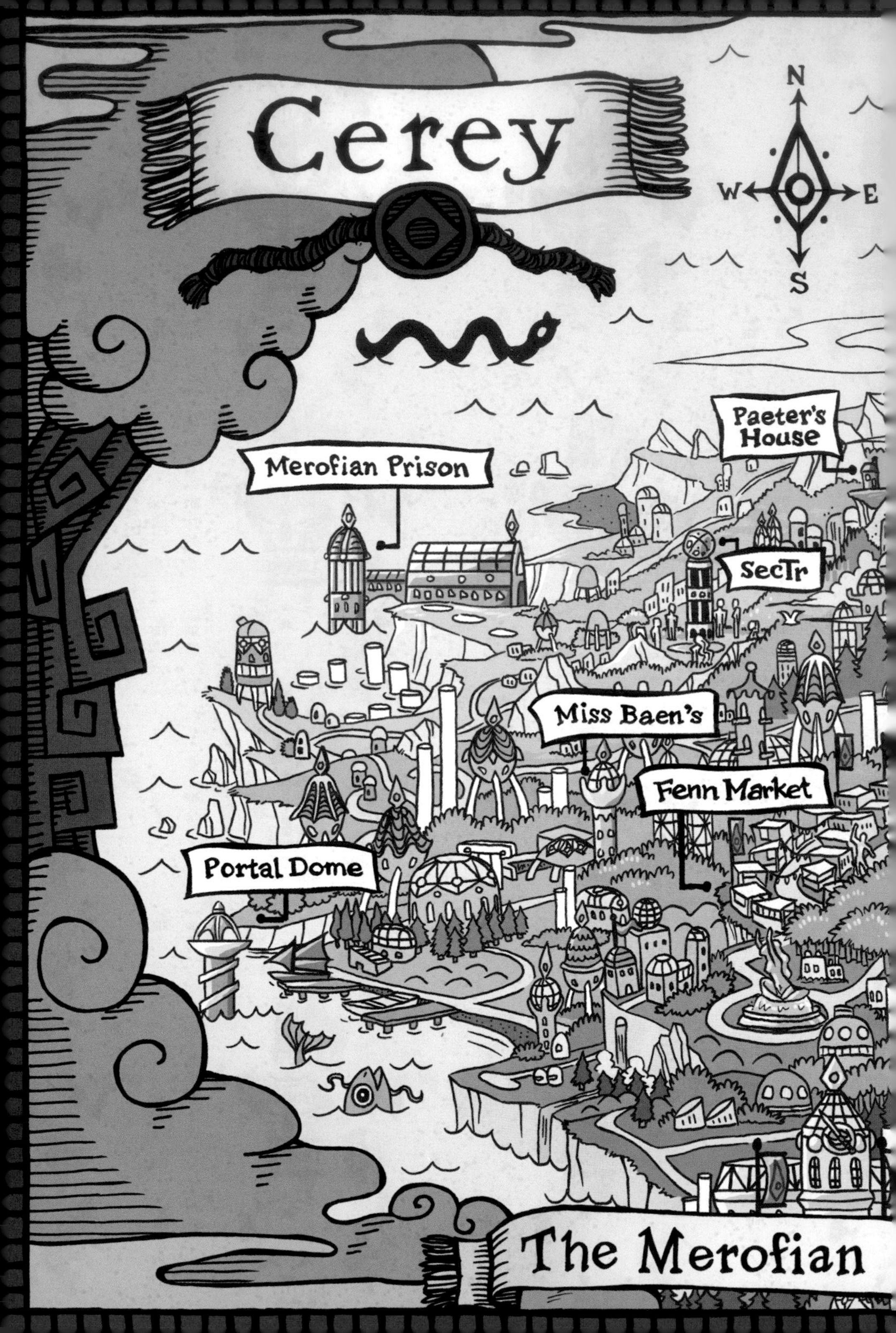
Cerey
N
W
E
S
Paeter's House
Merofian Prison
SecTr
Miss Baen's
Fenn Market
Portal Dome
The Merofian

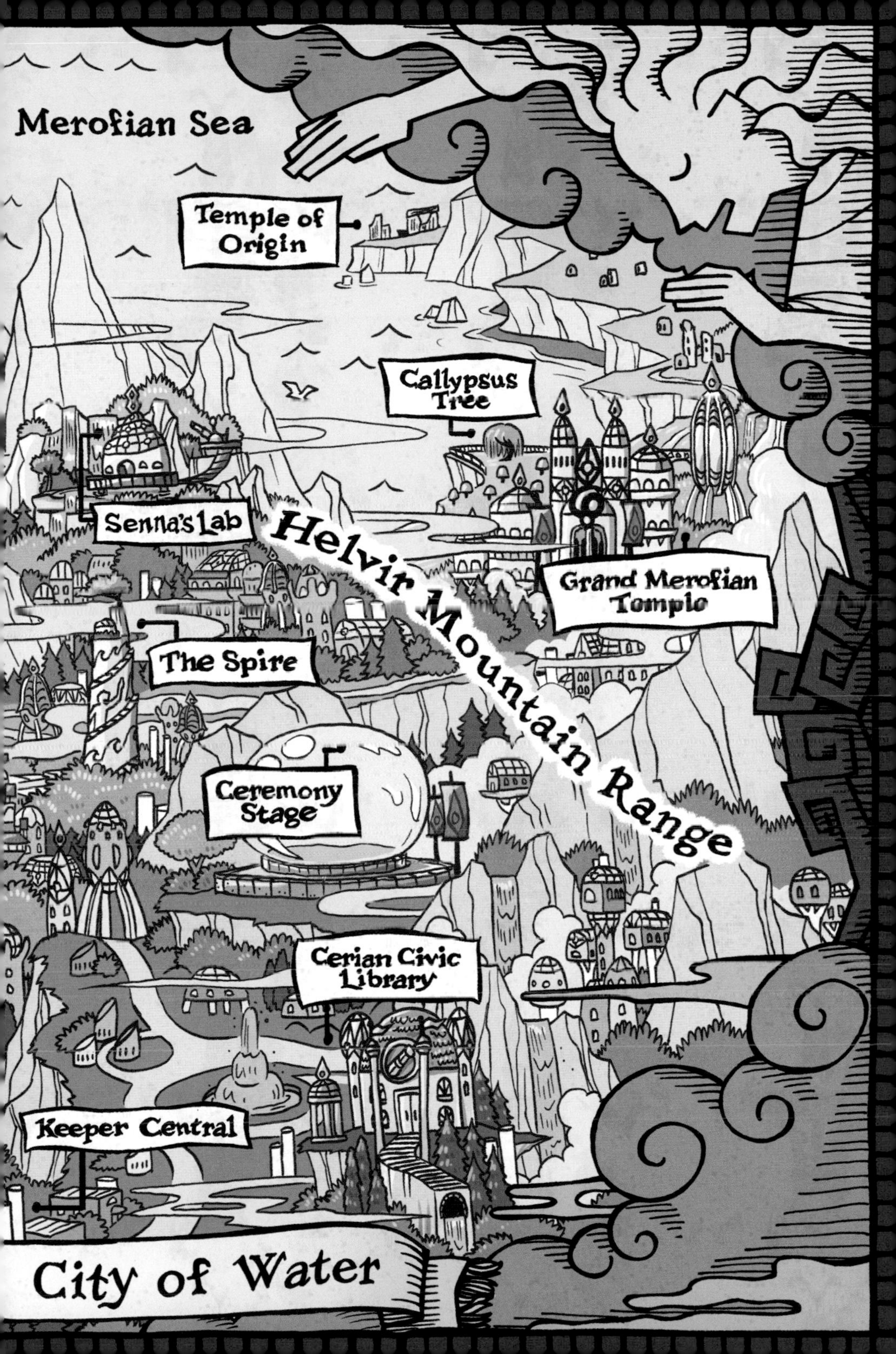
Merofian Sea
Temple of Origin
Callypsus Tree
Senna's Lab
Helvir Mountain Range
Grand Merofian Temple
The Spire
Ceremony Stage
Cerian Civic Library
Keeper Central
City of Water

ACKNOWLEDGMENTS

Rema has been a sanctuary through many phases of my life — as a teen struggling with family hardships, as a post-college graduate searching for my voice, and as a mother of young children finding peace in the chaos. So many friends, family, mentors, and online readers had an impact on this story. Thanking everyone would be impossible, so if you ever encountered The Rema Chronicles as a webcomic, zine, or online novel — you were the distant voices cheering this project on. My first thanks are to you.

Key people understood this story better than I did at times. One is Jen Lee Quick, who, when we met in college, recommended I turn my scattered drawings of Rema into a comic, and who always knew exactly what to say to inspire me to keep going. Another is Maurene Goo, who read my broken prose more times than I can count yet was still excited to see what happened next.

This book wouldn't be possible without my family: my beautiful mother and my hero, Sun Hui Kim, my brother, Tim Ganter, who always believed in Rema no matter what, and my two sweet children — thank you for keeping me grounded as I worked.

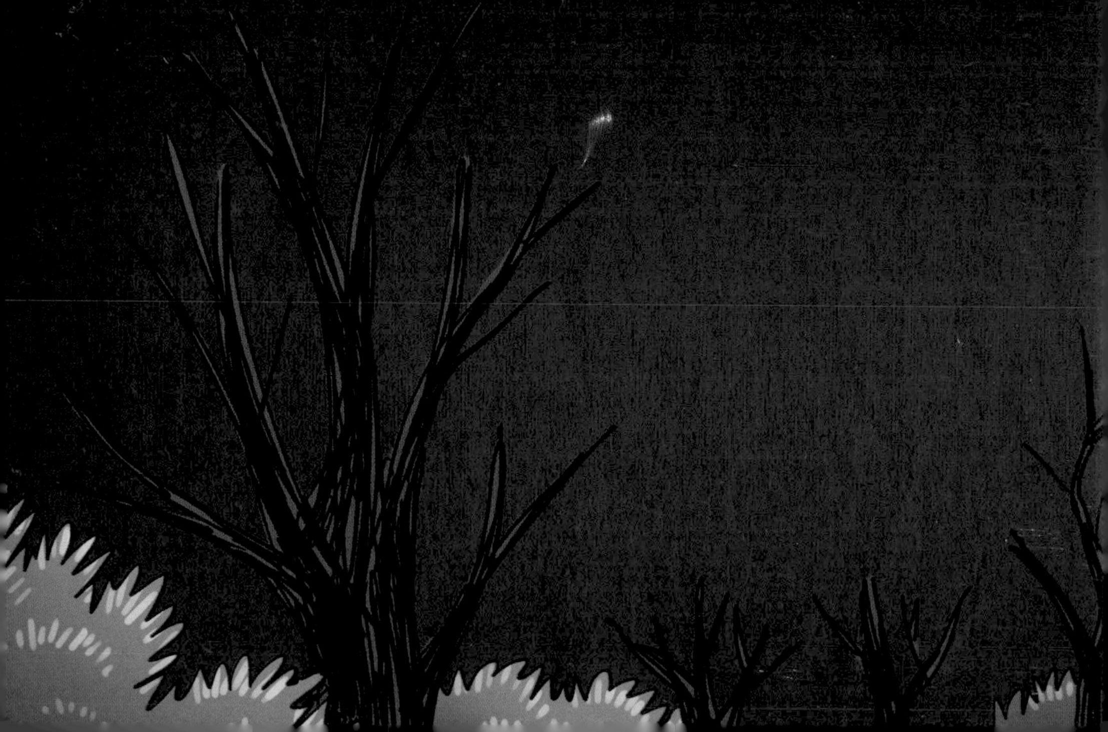

Thank you to my editor, Cassandra Pelham Fulton, who helped usher this project onto the public stage in a way I never thought possible, to David Saylor for his steadfast support, to Phil Falco for his keen eye, and to everyone at Scholastic who had a hand in finalizing the book. Rema couldn't have asked for a better home.

These pages wouldn't look nearly as good without the many hours of coloring assistance from Emmy Toyonaga and especially Audra Furuichi, who has repeatedly gone above and beyond for Rema. I couldn't have finished this book without either of your help and good company. To my incredible agent, Judy Hansen, you have been through so much with this project. I truly couldn't have done this without your wisdom, hard truths, and positive attitude.

My biggest, most heartfelt thanks are reserved for my dear husband, Kazu Kibuishi. My coach, my harshest critic, and my biggest cheerleader — your undying faith in me and this project, and your vision for what it could be, has never wavered. I love you with all my heart and soul. This book is for you.

ABOUT THE AUTHOR

Amy Kim Kibuishi has been drawing and writing in earnest since she was ten years old. She graduated from the School of Visual Arts with a degree in Cartooning and is the creator of Sorcerers & Secretaries, a graphic novel duology. The first volume was a YALSA Great Graphic Novels for Teens selection. She was also a contributor to the acclaimed Flight anthology series edited by Kazu Kibuishi, and adapted a story for *Goosebumps: Terror Trips* by R.L. Stine. Amy lives in Washington State with her husband, Kazu, and their two children.

CREATED AT

BOLT CITY
PRODUCTIONS

WITH COLOR ASSISTANCE BY
AUDRA FURUICHI
EMMY TOYONAGA

PAGE FLATTING BY
AUDRA FURUICHI

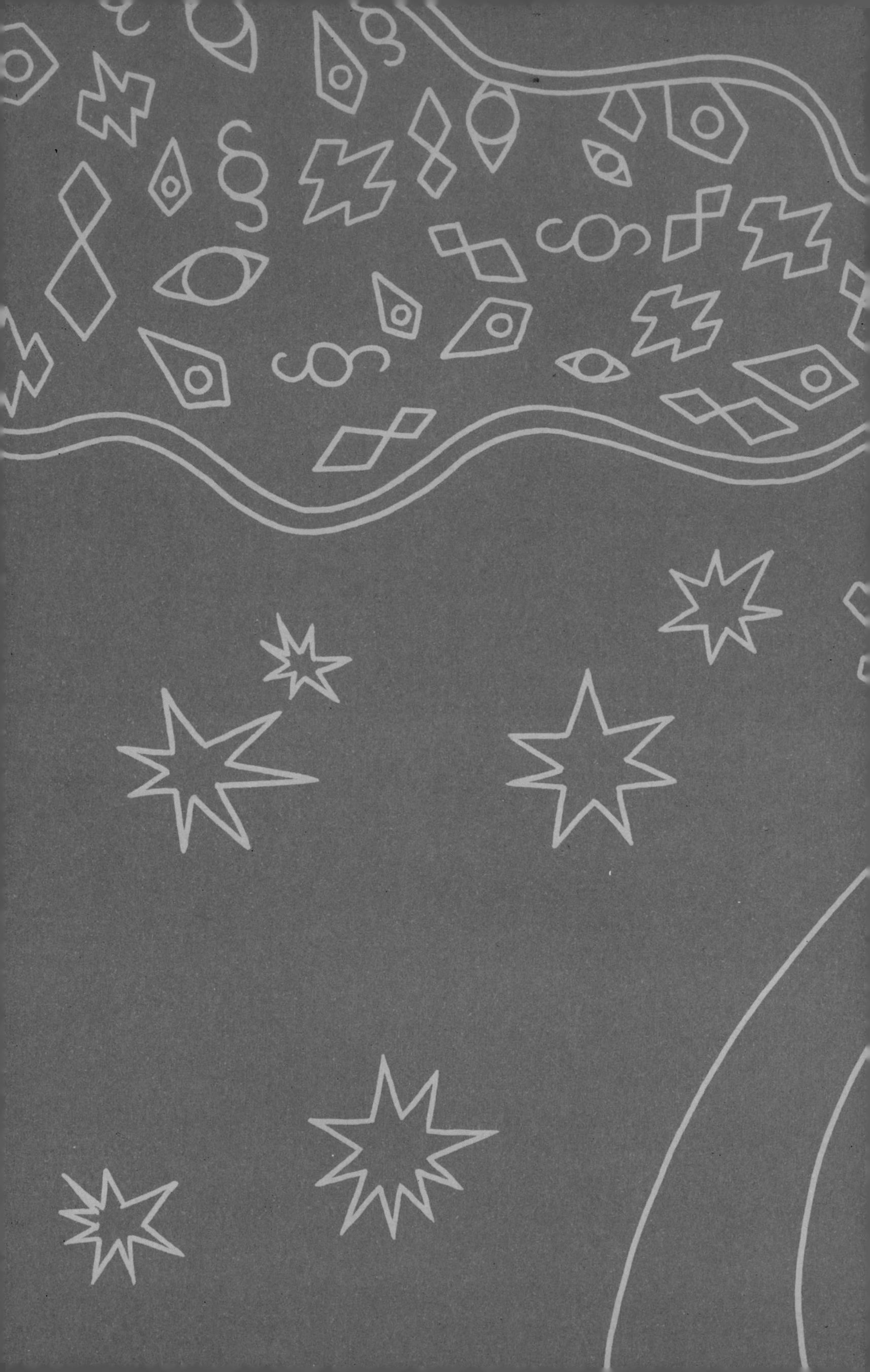